I0748370

HOW TO BE A MISERABLE FAILURE

HOW TO BE A MISERABLE FAILURE

The Complete Guide For Destroying Your Life

STEVEN D. SNYDER
&
THE MONTY

First Printing, 2020

Contents

This book is dedicated to all of the people in our lives who said we'd never amount to anything...You were right.

ACKNOWLEDGEMENTS

- Shotgun Vodka® (very cheap, will make you shit-faced quickly, only slightly tastes like rust with a hint of armpit musk).
- Corrections Officer Martinez (thanks for all the cigarettes and "forgetting" to lock our cell during our short stint in the joint).
- Black Jack Condoms® (LOL!!! JUST KIDDING! We don't use condoms).
- Terry and Pat Henderson from Pahrump, NV (the best Shepherd's pie and three-way we ever had).
- The "Low IQ Excuse" (because the "Diarrhea Excuse" DOES have its limits).
- The mile marker 84 gender-neutral truck stop bathroom (thanks for the memories, Fat Pete).
- Bacon (because cocaine and weight gain weren't quite enough to cause our first heart attacks).
- Paul Fleming, Jr. (for not suing us after what happened to his crippled father during that tragic hooker boat cruise in 2016).
- Buddy Bear All-Natural Stain Remover® (the only product that gets blood, vomit, and semen out of wedding dresses).
- Dale "Dilly" Dillon (sadly, you told us about your fear of clowns, but not about the pacemaker...).
- Personal Trainer #8, Larry "The Long" Dong (for making us

feel like shit about our excessive carb intake and continuous weight gain. Thanks for the eating disorders).

- Blue Grass Country Western Music (for being the soundtrack of all deep dark depression).
- Percy's Pure Grain Alcohol® (temporary blindness and/or paralysis equals terrible sex).
- The Soft Touch Carwash on 52nd Street (for never asking questions about the small woodland animals and passed-out hookers).
- Drunk Aunt Rhonda (the best "drug mule" any prisoner could hope for).
- Parole Officer Smith (thanks for "forgetting" to drug test us).
- Therapist #6, Dr. Anne Marie Richardson (our first four therapists did in fact commit suicide, so you win the prize of not being dead yet).
- AA Sponsors #13 and #14, Frank and George (thanks for taking our late-night drunken phone calls, and we're still very sorry about the whole *"sleeping with both of your wives"* thing).
- Sir William Edward Westchester III (the $10 you paid us to flash our junk is still good money, so thanks for funding our bad habits).

mis·er·a·ble
ˈmiz(ə)rəb(ə)l/
adjective

1. Wretchedly unhappy, unsatisfied or uncomfortable.
2. Habitually morose.
3. Pitiably small or inadequate.
4. Horrible pain and suffering.

fail·ure
ˈfālyər/
noun

1. Lack of success.
2. Nonfulfillment, defeat,
3. An unsuccessful person, enterprise, or thing.
4. The omission of expected or required action.
5. A lack or deficiency of a desirable quality.
6. The action or state of not functioning.

I

INTRODUCTION

Why Be a Miserable Failure?

Hey, asshole, you just spent your money on a book that can only make things in your life horribly WORSE! Reading this glorious book from cover to cover is a terrible life choice, but one we strongly encourage you make. Following the advice contained within is social suicide, or a one-way ticket to herpes, **at best**. If you hope to achieve anything positive in your pathetic excuse for a life, you're much better off putting this book down **(now)**, and sprinting (not running) into oncoming traffic. That's right! The sweet, seventy-mile an hour kiss of a tour bus filled with overweight country music fans will benefit you more than continuing to read this book. To be absolutely clear, this material's sole purpose is to hurt, not help you. If you're looking to improve your life, try reading anything else. We're absolutely serious when we suggest that you'd be better off reading the directions on a douche bottle than this book.

The material contained within these pages will reveal to you a great secret. No, not "The Secret" where you attract good things to your life through positive visualization, and uplifting thinking. Although that method of pretending life isn't real is very effective at producing unsuccessful people, our goal is to produce miserable failures. The secret unveiled in the following pages is the great truth that when you give up your ambitions for greatness, willingly make bad choices **OFTEN**, and start to hope for the worst **ALWAYS** (NOTE: try negative visualizations like seeing yourself slowly drowning in a tub of tears, or being eaten alive by a Bengal tiger), you truly become free. Free from the expectations, standards, and negative blood tests that have repeatedly plagued your existence with false hope. Free from the biased opinions of family members who say *"you still have a chance"* (HINT: you don't). Free from the hope that your big victory is just around the corner (HINT: it's not). There is a word to describe people like you and it's not "champion," or "non-sex offender." **It's "failure."**

Up until this point, you've probably gone through life trying to do the best you can. How's that been working out for you? Pretty horrible, right? That's what we thought. You are not alone. Most societies place emphasis on achieving greatness, but fail to recognize that most people just aren't that great. The common person fights so hard to "win" on a daily basis that the frequent barrage of failures they experience easily overshadows the tiny and infrequent victories afforded to them. The result is a constant feeling of **worthlessness and undeniable shame**. No more! It's time to feel good about being bad! Truly, the best course of action is to "give up" on getting ahead! Flip your script! It's time for you to do the worst you can, and celebrate the terrible consequences!

While on your personal journey to becoming a miserable failure, it's important to track your progress. Initially, we crafted a clever equation that calculated an individual's pursuit of failing miserably, using common benchmarks such as the number of active paternity cases, or days without showering. After quickly realizing that we lack even the most basic math skills, it was decided that the best method for gauging someone's status as a miserable failure was to develop an understanding how others perceive you, and react to your disgusting existence. These perceptions and reactions are even more significant when they're coming from those who know you best (family, friends, co-workers, spouses, parole officers, etc.).

If you follow the methodology outlined in this book precisely, all those who loyally love and care about you now will quickly begin to regret their decision to stick by your side. Within the first ninety days of your pursuit of becoming a miserable failure, you can, at a minimum, expect your grandparents, favorite drunk aunts and uncles, siblings, and both of your biological parents to begin referring to you as one or ALL of the following nicknames:

- Idiot (because of all your bad choices).
- Loser (because you'll make all of those bad choices, again).
- Douche Bag (because you suck at life, a lot).
- Doucher (the rare douchebag + loser combo).
- Waste of Life (you should just donate all your disease-ridden organs right now, or try selling them on the black market for straight cash).
- Waste of Space (and waste of breathable air).
- Creep Show (you've taken "creepy" to a whole new level).
- Perv (there's no denying this one).
- Cock Bite (your 97-year-old grandmother came up with this one).
- Bastard (despite several paternity tests, your mother will claim she never gave birth to you).
- Hopeless (so true).
- Useless (also true).
- Fat, Slow and Stupid (a combo to be proud of).
- Alcoholic or Druggie (neither of these terms fully describes the depths of your addictions).
- Piece of Shit (Mom started this one).

- Giant Piece of Shit (Dad started this one).
- Asshole (your kids do say the darndest things).

NOTE: If more than ninety days pass, and you haven't been referred to as one of the above-listed nicknames, and/or you still have people who consider themselves to be your family or friends, you're doing something wrong. First, punch yourself in the face as hard as you possibly can. Then, go back and start rereading this "work of art" from the beginning. This time, make sure you increase your alcohol intake, and cancel all future psychiatric appointments.

Success is temporary, but failure (if done correctly) can last **forever**. You've had more failures than successes throughout your life. Pause, and really think about it. Yes, you may have won the occasional participation trophy or perfect attendance award as a kid, but overall, you've NOT been a winner. You can expect this trend of losing to continue for the rest of your life. **Despite the best efforts of your counselors, teachers, AA sponsors, life coaches, therapists, personal trainers, and parole officers, --you will keep failing.** It's easy to see how this cycle of trying and failing can lead to terrible disappointment. However, this disappointment can only be present when you set high standards, or have optimistic expectations for the future. So, start expecting to fail (at least you'll finally be right about something)! Start hoping for the absolute worst! Consider each divorce another victory! Think of every bad credit report as reaching a new benchmark! Set your watch to collection calls! The freedom that you can only find through failure is just a few bad checks, empty whiskey bottles, and multiple broken condoms away! **This is your life to destroy!** This is **your** reputation to defame! So, let's get started! We wish you horribly bad luck, and many miserable failings to come!!!

Who Can Be a Miserable Failure?

Reaching the highest levels of miserable "failuredom" requires no special circumstances. Anyone, despite past or present situations, can become a miserable failure with the proper mindset. Becoming a miserable failure only requires that you let go of your hope for "the good life" and fully embrace "the shit life." In other words, if you are ready to lose BIG in life, **this is the book for you**. Becoming a miserable failure is truly possible for everyone, but it's not a quick or easy target to hit. It's going to be a long and sloppy road filled with parole hearings, nervous breakdowns, mystery stains, divorces, drinking, depression, financial disasters, STDs and lots of odd smells coming from your homemade meth lab. No matter how long your metamorphosis takes, don't be discouraged. You will get there! You must begin to see every missed bath or overdrawn checking account as **progress**. It's these little losses (NOTE: "wins" for you) along the way that will keep you motivated to continue your pursuit of "sucking donkey balls" at life. Some beginners to becoming a miserable failure may already have an extensive history of failing that gives them an advantage over the average person. Don't let the miserable progress of others motivate, or dissuade, you from attaining your goal! It would be unfair and inaccurate for you to gauge your progress in achieving the coveted, "miserable failure status" based on the results of others who may have significant head start advantages (gripping meth addictions, staph infections from not bathing, multiple bankruptcies, etc.). This is your own personal journey of failure. So, make it count, asshole!

When first hearing the term "miserable failure," the average person understandably assumes that it refers to society's "normal" losers such as federal prisoners, high school dropouts, drug addicts, psychopaths, homeless "crazies," sexually depraved stalkers, unemployed circus clowns, and creepy uncle Frank who slept on your couch as a kid (NOTE: he still loves tickle fights a little **too much**). Although these people might be "miserable" and certainly qualify as "failures", they lack the appropriate combination of undesirable traits required to truly be a legitimate, 100% certified "miserable failure." A thief, someone considered by most to be less than admirable, can steal a can of baked beans and still behave like a polite citizen. A miserable failure, however, would never just steal a can of baked beans. This would require too much effort, and is lacking in "flair." The miserable failure would instead use the rusty knife they always keep hidden in their underwear to open the can of beans in the grocery store. Then immediately eat them while standing in the middle of the isle. Hoping to add insult to injury, the miserable failure would then proceed to "slip and fall" on the bean mess that THEY created, threaten to call a lawyer to sue, and then attempt to return the empty can for a full "refund." In this scenario, the miserable failure was a thief as well as an inconsiderate asshole, and total douche bag (awesome!). It's this combination, or "multi-mastery," of shitty traits and behaviors that make the miserable failure so unique, original, and amazing! Again, becoming a miserable failure is not an easy task, but it is attainable for anyone who has the will to do so. Just believe that in time, your lack of effort, poor choices, and terrible hygiene will carry you over the shit- covered finish line! The "bad life" can, and should, be yours!

2

PERSONAL RELATIONSHIPS

Painful Relationships

There is an old saying that goes: *"It's better to have loved and lost than never to have loved at all."* Trust in the fact that if you follow the advice contained within this section, you will lose in love and friendship, **MANY TIMES**, during what's left of your pathetic excuse for a life. The following sections are NOT designed to prevent you from entering into a romantic relationship, or beginning a new friendship. In fact, it is essential that you hook a new "fish to fry" at some point. Although miserable failures are most often single, they do occasionally enjoy the temporary benefits of a relationship (when the proper deception is deployed). A large mane of unkempt pubic hair makes genital warts virtually invisible. Swallowing an entire pack of any cinnamon gum prior to a date means **TEMPORARILY** saying goodbye to your wallpaper-curling halitosis for at least twenty-five minutes. Criminal records, and forced mental health hospital commitments, can be easily concealed by simply giving a false name like "Rudolph," "Charlotte," "Tits McGee," or "Big Dick Master." No matter the circumstances, hiding your "flaws" from a new friend or lover is always a better choice than being open about "what" you really are (NOTE: if anyone knew "what" you really are, the police hostage rescue team and national guard would be called). Eventually, anyone with half a brain will catch onto your games, and abruptly part ways with you, potentially ripping your heart out in the process (#FingersCrossed).

A true miserable failure finds a great partner, falls deeply in love with them, sleeps with their best friend(s), videotapes it, posts said video on social media, and writes the following caption to their soon-to-be ex: *"Pay no attention to this video, ignore what your therapist is saying, and marry me."* Unless they're dating a dumb and blind person AGAIN, the answer is definitely "NO," and the three-week relationship is over. Then the miserable failure, despite clearly being the party responsible for the breakup, should very publicly deny any and all fault of wrongdoing for the relationship ending, while pondering such prolific questions as: *"Should I stop sleeping with their mom now?"* and/or *"Do I have to stop using their Social Security number on payday loan applications?"* The answer to both questions is **NO**.

Remember, it's not about having the one-time experience of completely destroying a potentially wonderful romance, or friendship. Rather, the goal is to repeat the process of self-induced heartbreak over and over again. At least until you have no self-esteem left, or are incarcerated for stalking again (more on how to pick the worst public defender in a later section). To ensure that maximum self-damage is done, the miserable failure is careful with whom they share their heart. Choosing a partner who is kind, understanding, and possesses good moral character is useful for a while, but ultimately will not get you to your goal of being completely miserable. These "good people" are generally very trusting, have strong credit scores, and will not fuck your roommate behind your back (no matter how much you encourage them). Put little to no effort into relationships with these "goodies."

Save your energy, attention, and love for the most morally bankrupt and vile partner you can attract (or get drunk enough to sleep with you). If your new potential partner is so coked-up, and drunk on the first date that they shit their pants, **ask them to move in with you.** If your partner's weekly child visitation has to be supervised by a police officer, **get matching neck tattoos**. If you come home to them having a foursome with your half-brother Phil, your quadriplegic neighbor Terry, and your high school principal Mrs. Jenkins, **immediately get down on one knee and propose marriage** (and then "join in" of course).

You should always strive to date, and/or marry other horrible people. Sure, it's fun to assist a "goodie" in becoming a "baddie," and having a "failure buddy" can sometimes be beneficial. However, the miserable failure should BE AWARE that although your intentions to aid in a goody's corruption may be pure, they may actually have hidden, more sinister motives. In an act known as the "goodie bait and switch," someone who typically does not use hard drugs, and have sex with prostitutes will do so temporarily in order to gain your trust. They perform this act of manipulation with the hopes of eventually convincing you to change your life for the better (no thanks). You need, and deserve, to find a **real** piece of shit for your partner. You should only be with someone who encourages you to drink entire handles of vodka in one sitting, smoke five packs of cigarettes daily, use hard drugs first thing in the morning, and have unprotected sex with lots of hookers. If you are currently in a relationship with someone who hasn't had an orgy with your prison parolee friends, won't steal from the elderly, and doesn't wear a court–ordered ankle-monitoring bracelet...**END IT NOW**. Be sure to give special to attention to all of the information contained in the forthcoming sections, for it is only through the experience of massive heartbreak (over and over again) that a "failure" becomes truly "miserable."

The "AIDS Excuse"

You should never strive to hurt others, but encourage them to destroy you. You can safely anticipate that there will always be "decent folks" out there who, despite you being unfaithful and attempting to sell their pets for cash, will give you second and even third chances. This annoying loyalty from anyone, especially a love interest, will quickly end if you use the full-blown "AIDS excuse." Even though you don't have AIDS, lying about it can get you out of jams (also provide you with horrible karma). This little lie simply involves telling your romantic partner that you went to the doctor ("free" health clinic), and now have *"full-blown, don't want me to sneeze on you, you better get tested too, going to die really soon, no hope, AIDS."* Be sure to specifically state that you have full-blown AIDS, and not just middle of the road, humdrum, HIV. HIV leaves room for hope, and at the minimum a few more decent years of normal life. A good person may also offer to support you during the tough times that HIV is sure to bring. However, nobody, no matter how kindhearted they are, will stick around for full-blown AIDS. (HOT TIP: the "full-blown AIDS excuse" also works great for debt collectors and avoiding ALL child support payments.).

The Miserable Friendship

It's important that you build destructive relationships with horrible friends on a regular basis. As a miserable failure, making bad choices must become one of your specialties (like shoplifting camping gear, capturing pigeons, and drunk driving on a snowmobile). It's crucial that you tune in your talent for making shitty decisions when picking your close friends. You should only choose individuals who understand (because they're pretty screwed up themselves), and support your pursuit of becoming a miserable failure. Friends of good nature and high moral standards (snore......) will only slow you down as you dive head first into the oblivion.

We will award bonus points if you befriend someone who is currently a true miserable failure, like you're hoping to be. **IF** you are lucky enough to have this happen, remain attentive and take careful notes during your, sure-to-be-short-lived friendship with a real-life miserable failure. Remember, **you are in the presence of true greatness at not being great!** Before they're arrested again, or experience their nightly blackout, follow them closely, and attempt to emulate their behavior exactly. Don't worry because you have nothing to fear from the often-experienced "downside" of being friends with a miserable failure (a new criminal record, neck tattoo and armpit rash). The more exposure you have to people who have mastered the art of losing, the faster you'll be catapulted into becoming the next BIG thing in the "miserable failure-verse" yourself.

Locating and befriending a real-life miserable failure can be so difficult, and time- consuming, that you may eventually give up on the notion of it altogether. We encourage you to not quit, and only focus on the benefits that this terrible friendship could bring to your pursuit of failing miserably. It's best to begin your search efforts at locations they've been known to frequent, and to also use the appropriate "bait" to lure them out. To quickly find a miserable failure to begin a new destructive friendship with, visit the following locations often with large quantities of alcohol, drugs, pornographic magazines, and scratch-off lottery tickets:

- Supermarkets after 2:00 a.m. (they'll be the quiet person wearing a cape & shoplifting lubricants).
- State Fair Portable Toilets (used for taking naps, or enjoying a semi-private "bathing experience").
- Crack Dens (a classy step above the "crack house").
- Weight Loss Surgery Waiting Rooms (a great way to find sex partners who will also be enablers).
- County Jail Parking Lots (it's like a high school reunion for miserable failures).
- Your creepy uncle Frank's apartment (are you surprised?).

- Cowboy-Themed Nightclubs (just go to one and you'll see why...).
- Gas Station Truck Stop Bathrooms (FYI: this where your parents first met, and how you were conceived).
- Curling Tournaments (you should also try bowling and video gaming tournaments).
- The Original "Rosie's Adult No, No Land Theater" on Beecher Street (this is an "Official Miserable Failure Safe Zone").
- Any Dark Alleyway (be sure to arm yourself first).
- Swap Meets (full of drunk, unemployed, degenerates like yourself).

The Benefits of Having a Lousy Marriage and Painful Divorce

Despite being overweight, with bad hygiene, a yet-to-be-identified venereal disease, and the credit score of a ten-year-old Cambodian immigrant, the miserable failure can still find someone willing to marry them (SUCKER!!!!). That's right! Some pathetically depraved loser, most likely in the depths of a dark, clinical depression, will actually agree to spend the rest of their life married to a complete failure like you. You should always be seeking to marry the most self-destructive, and morally bankrupt person you can find. Knowingly marrying someone who's already stolen your identity twice is an example of the perfect choice (they want to be with you, AND be you). Tying the knot at home because your new spouse is under house arrest is a real money saver (BTW: this leaves lots of extra cash for your "crack den honeymoon"). Saying, "*I do*" with someone who "isn't into the whole bathing thing," and/or doesn't "believe in wiping," shows the world how "progressive" you've become. One thing is absolutely clear: getting married to the right "wrong person" is the undisputed champion of quickly making your life completely miserable, so DO IT!

The Joy of Divorce

If you are currently experiencing the lack of sex and constant bickering that comes with a "normal" marriage, relax; **it'll all be over REAL soon!** Following the advice in this horrible section will quickly take the average bad marriage, from terrible to **NUCLEAR!** Failing miserably at marriage brings a unique opportunity to experience pain and suffering that can never come from destroying a simple dating relationship. It's only through the "loss" of a spouse that a miserable failure can simultaneously "gain" so much wonderful financial stress, and outstanding emotional trauma at the same time (SCORE!). In addition to the normal heartbreak that comes from "losing" a boyfriend or girlfriend, divorce also brings the added bonuses of expensive court battles, long child custody hearings, splitting the retirement account you worked a lifetime to build, and dishing out years of spousal support while your ex stays at home fucking your former best friend (#ThanksAgainPat). Are you excited yet? You should be! There is no other voluntary activity that will ever completely destroy your life as quickly, and effectively, as marriage (REMEMBER: matrimony is something you knowingly decided to do, like when you sold your kidney for beer money).

Understandably, after hearing about the wonders of divorce, someone seeking to become a miserable failure may rush to destroy their marriage with one grand act of debauchery. While it may seem perfectly logical to have a sexy "five-way" with both sets of your spouse's grandparents, this type of extreme (i.e., legendary) behavior will actually bring you to divorce court entirely too quickly. **DO NOT do anything "outlandish" that will cause your spouse to immediately file for divorce unless you've exceeded the three-year breakup deadline, or have found a dumber/wealthier mate.** Failing miserably at marriage is not a race to the finish line (you'd lose anyway), but should be a long, exhausting, sad, and painful process. It's only through this slow, and steady, decay of your marriage that you'll truly become most miserable.

If you're not yet married, you are still encouraged to study this information. Advanced knowledge of how to create a horrible marriage, and painful divorce, will only benefit you when it comes time for your own wedding. If you're a divorcee in between spouses, good for you! You're well on your way to becoming a completely miserable failure, and have many more bad things to look forward to. Keep in mind your previous marriage, and divorce experience while reading the following instructions about failing in matrimony. You are likely to identify areas where you can use these techniques to train-wreck your next marriage more effectively, and thus speeds up your descent into misery.

The Worst Wedding EVER

Whether you're already a miserable failure, or are well on your way to becoming one through marriage, it's important to start things off right with the "perfect wedding." This age-old ritual provides the perfect opportunity for public humiliation, desperate acts of self-sabotage, and complete financial destruction. It's rare in life that one single event gives you the chance to piss yourself in front of 300 people (NOTE: shitting your pants is optional and 100% ACCEPTABLE) while simultaneously maxing out all your credit cards on twenty-four midget servers, and an ice sculpture in the shape of a giant penis (it's a bold statement about things to come in your marriage).

If done correctly, your wedding(s) should serve as the first step toward a LONG and HARD divorce. Begin by scheduling the ceremony to take place on, or near a major holiday, and at a location that requires extensive travel (it's time for that Christmas wedding in South Korea you've been dreaming of!). This will frustrate your guests immensely, and thus put them in the right frame of mind prior to arrival (just wait until they see the "changes" you've made to the dollar dance).

The Miserable Decor

Upon arrival, your guest's eyes will immediately be drawn to the unique decorations you've chosen. A popular, and "normal" choice is to display large photos of the happy couple during their dating stage (kissing on a fun night out, snorkeling on vacation, etc.). Do this, but make "better" picture selections. Show your guests how "special" your relationship is, and use photos of your most impressive sex acts (BTW: the "Dirty Sanchez" is a real thing), screenshots of romantic text messages ("filthy whore" and "captain shrimp dick" are pet names), and recent "his and her" mug shots (the couple that shoplifts together, stays together). Your secret goal should be to have more guests go into therapy after this wedding than any of your previous ceremonies (nine may seem like a big number to best, but you can do it!).

Food for Failures

The food choice at your wedding is a great chance to bring some excitement, and adventure to your big day! Choose any cream-based soup, and then do your best to insult the catering staff (prior to food service, call them *"savages,"* and loudly refer to them as *"smelling like poverty"*). This should get you, and all your guests, some free "special sauce" in the crème brulee. To save money, you can also completely bypass the caterer, and go straight to the dumpster for food (it won't be your first time). Simply drive the alleys behind your favorite restaurants, soup kitchens, breadlines, or all-you-can-eat Chinese food buffets, and let the picking' begin! Be sure to bring a large storage container (a 50-gallon trashcan), and sturdy extraction tool (a snow shovel). Don't worry about separating the different types of food you find in each dumpster. You'll be cooking all the rotten chicken, rancid pork chops, and moldy dinner rolls in the same pot at the same time (NOTE: it's a dish you call, "I'll see you in hell").

Entertaining The Crowd

Your entertainment choice must also leave a lasting impression on your guests. Cancel the unprofessional DJ who constantly takes smoke breaks, and pass on the expensive band that doesn't know your favorite songs. When it comes to wedding entertainment, the miserable failure knows only four words: **"Live. Action. Stunt. Show."** Tables will be kicked over, glass will be broken, and shots will be fired. It may not be real, but to your unsuspecting guests and new spouse, it sure will feel legit! Imagine the look on everyone's face when great grandma gets a fake shotgun shoved in her face while the cowboy train robber screams, *"Suck my dick or die lady"* (BTW: this will be a moment to remember, so be sure your photographer is ready A.K.A. done doing blow in the parking lot).

DISCLAIMER

****Our asshole lawyer says we have to provide a disclaimer about the stunt show before we can continue... PLEASE MAKE SURE YOUR WEDDING IS A "GUN-FREE ZONE." It took us three weddings, and twelve dead actors to finally learn that lesson.****

Being The "Lowlife" of The Party

Finally, and most importantly, be sure to behave badly (grope the wedding party, pick fist fights with your new relatives, vomit in the punch bowl, give the pastor a "purple nurple," etc.). If you've been consuming your normal levels of drugs and alcohol, this type of behavior should come naturally to you. As your guests arrive at the reception, put that uncontrollable body odor to good use by hugging everyone tightly (like you're an animal marking your territory, but with an armpit). Make these cheek-to-cheek embraces awkwardly long while whispering sweet little nothings like *"It's too late now," "Can you feel my erection?"* (yes, women should say that one too), and *"If I don't fuck you soon, I might die"* (save that one for your new spouse's siblings, or parents).

When having conversations with your new spouse's extended family, always start by complimenting their bloodlines ability to grow such top-notch penises, or vaginas (NOTE: you should refer to them as *"peen-ees"* and *"vag-i-nees"*). When your new in-laws ask if you plan to have children just say, *"anything to get more welfare,"* and then abruptly walk away. If your new in-laws inquire about your job, simply choose an activity from your everyday life, and make up a position that sounds important. For example, you can say you're a "Hypodermic Supply Chain Supervisor" (you steal needles from the hospital), or you can explain to them that you're a "Waste Distribution Manager" (you piss and/or shit the bed most nights). Also, tell them the story of the first time you had sex with your new spouse (in graphic detail), and be sure to make it sound like borderline rape. For many of them, this will be their first introduction to your debauchery, and the beginning of their "hate affair" with you (great job!).

It's also crucial that your bad behavior includes multiple attempts to "borrow" (LOL), or collect money from your already disgusted guests. As people eat, visit their tables, and ask to borrow some cab money. If they offer to give you a ride, call them a *"fucking cheap skate,"* and throw your drink in their face. If you're a male miserable failure, when it's time for the "dollar dance" (this is when the bride dances with guests for a cash donation), make sure that you show off the famous "pimping skills" that scored you the marriage in the first place (that $600 "Pimping Made Easy" mail order course was worth it, wasn't it asshole?). Your new wife is now "open for business," and it's time for you to get paid. A good rule of thumb is $50 for "hand stuff," $75 for "mouth stuff," and $100 gets you in the "front, **OR** backdoor."

For a female miserable failure, during the bride's traditional flower toss, make sure that you form tackle the unlucky woman who catches your bouquet. Sit on her chest; repeatedly slap her face until she begins to cry, and then scream, *"Nobody steals from me."* While the tears are flowing, lean in and whisper, *"It's all just for show, save that pussy for me later."* Then seductively lick a tear from her cheek before going back to slapping the shit out of her. As your wedding guests are dragging you away be sure to flip-off the crowd, and tell everyone to *"fucking leave now, freeloaders."*

The Terrible Toast

Finally, all miserable failures, no matter if you're getting married or not, should have an awesome wedding speech ready to deliver at any time. You never know when you'll have the opportunity to grab the DJ's microphone at a wedding you were officially invited to, or a ceremony you drunkenly wonder into by accident. Here is a sample speech that can function as a guide for developing your own wedding toast:

"Hi, thank you for coming to our wedding! This is my ______ (insert number of times you've been married) *wedding. If you'd like to place a bet on how long our marriage will last, please see uncle Phil in the back near the keg. Put $20 down on 5 months for me, Phil. Wink, wink! I want to thank those of you who brought us gifts. We will be selling them in the parking later to fund my alcoholism, and heavy drug use later tonight. To those of you who did not bring us gifts, go to the ATM, or go fuck yourself. Also, if you're thinking of drinking and driving, I have just one thing to say to you.... Man, that shit is fun! Just be sure to blow if you get pulled over, and are asked to take a breathalyzer test. Yes, I mean blow on the cop's penis. Trust me, I've gotten out of well over eighteen DUIs by giving a hummer to prove how innocent I was. There's one more important announcement, if you still haven't had a turn with my spouse in the coat closet, you should act now. The suggested "donation" price will be going up as the evening progresses. Let's keep it classy, and I hope you enjoy the rest of the evening, you cheap motherfuckers.* ****DROPS MIC****

"Communication" is the Key to Disaster

Even the happiest married couples can experience communication problems. One could assume that a miserable failure's marriage would involve no communication, as it's a lack of communication that is commonly blamed for relationship breakdowns. However, this assessment couldn't be further from the truth for the miserable failure. A married miserable failure, or even one who is just dating, should make a "special" effort to engage in open and honest communication always. It's only through a regular "filter free" exchange of information, that a miserable failure can properly express how they feel about their spouse, and about being married in general. Communication with your spouse must be a constant, and should always be direct, but not verbally abusive. The title of this shitty book is "How To Be A Miserable Failure," not "How To Be A Verbally Abusive Asshole Who Deserves To Be Shot In The Kneecaps."

If someone asks their spouse how they look in a particular outfit, the spouse should NOT respond with *"Are you kidding me? Even if you were dressed in $100 bills, you'd still be fat. Burn some calories getting me a beer, and stop interrupting the fucking ballgame."* This form of verbal assault could quickly bring a halt to all communication, and it's crucially important for the miserable failure to, at a minimum, maintain a level of communication that allows for the covert use of "snide remarks." The most effective use of these remarks simply involves hiding multiple insults within one single compliment and/or expression of affection. The recipient (your soon-to-be ex-lover) is left feeling mildly depressed while also being confused about what your true intentions really are. When done consistently over time, this type of "verbal jujitsu" is a psychological "mind fuck," and is the single most effective form of slow relationship destruction in the miserable failure's arsenal. With proper practice, snide remarks can eventually bring someone to the point where the mere sound of your voice causes the immediate triggering of their gag reflex (NOTE: this is considered "unlocking" achievement #31 on the miserable failure "shit list"). Use the snide remarks listed below in your current relationship, and don't be afraid to develop new original insults that are more specific to your own marriage. Additionally, repeatedly practice using these remarks in front of a mirror to ensure you're regulating your facial expressions properly. Whenever delivering a snide remark, it's always best to do it with the biggest "shit-eating" grin possible, and end with a seductive wink or thumbs up (NOTE: you may have to put down one of your beers to accomplish the thumbs up). Some common snide remarks include:

- *"This shit is the worst food I've ever tasted. I stay on couch all day trying to find a job, only to have you come home from work and cook me garbage like this! Sometimes I wonder if I should stay married to you... And then I see your fat ass and instantly remember why I love you!"* (seductive wink).
- *" I don't need a large, or even average sized penis. Plus, you're big where it really matters, the heart."* (thumbs up).
- *"You're the smartest dumb person I've ever met."* (seductive wink).
- *"You are gorgeous, and if you lose 35lbs you'd be sexy enough for me to stop cheating on you."* (thumbs up)
- *"Your tits are so saggy that they look like ears on a basset hound, and I love dogs."* (seductive wink).

The Art of Arguing

Arguments are certainly to be expected in the miserable failure's marriage. The most epic arguments can last **hours**, be incredibly emotionally draining, and quickly do detrimental damage to your relationship (it's like a dream come true). There are far too many possibilities and variables that exist for an argument, so we can't cover them all in this section. Just be sure to follow these three basic principles:

1. **You're always right.**
2. **They're always wrong.**
3. **When in doubt, bring up the ex.**

There are many covert argument strategies that exist, but none are as effective as the "comparing them to your ex" technique (NOTE: we discuss you and your "exes" in the section immediately following this).

When used frequently, this technique can slowly grind away at your spouse's self-esteem, and leave them resenting you on a very deep emotional level. This deep resentment will inevitably lead to anger, and then your real arguments can finally begin! To properly engage the ex-comparison technique, simply **make it clear that your ex was superior to your current partner in all ways.** Their jokes were funnier, bank accounts more accessible to you, their body was in better shape with fewer infections, and sex with them was much more enjoyable (you didn't need to fake your orgasm). If you're able to survive the first few attempts at using this dangerous method without retribution, your current lover is basically giving you the "green light" to continue (FYI: you've now advanced to Round #2).

As advised in previous sections, if you're too overt with your rage-inducing statements, communication could completely breakdown. Bringing up the ex too often and too directly will significantly diminish the length of your relationship. Instead, use the same passive aggressive strategy employed for delivering snide remarks. For example, if your spouse buys you a new book as a birthday gift, remind them that your ex (who makes a lot more money than your current partner does) bought you a laptop computer, and paid off all your credit cards as a birthday gift. If your spouse cooks you a surprise romantic dinner at home, remind your partner that your ex (who was also a five-Star chef and yoga instructor) once cooked you crab cakes completely nude while doing "downward facing dog" on your face. The beauty of this technique is that it will likely take your spouse an extended amount of time to realize that you're actually arguing for your ex, and against them. Over time, with targeted repetition of the "comparing them to your ex" technique, your spouse will begin to develop a serious lack of self-confidence, a few eating disorders, and an intense feeling of inferiority (#MissionAccomplished). This is exactly how you want things to be in your marriage, while it lasts. When your spouse becomes a passive shell of their former self, they are far more likely to tolerate your continuous infidelity, chronic drug use, and lavish spending (FACT: "happy ending" massage packages and anal bleaches are not free).

Another communication technique that has been proven to be ultra-annoying, and induce violent rage is commonly called, "Jackass Method" of arguing. This method is both surprisingly simple to use, and extremely effective in completely disintegrating any final remnants of wanting to "talk about things" your spouse may still hold. Whenever your spouse starts an argument, respond to their complaint with a follow up statement that is completely unrelated to the subject they're upset about. For example, if your spouse says, *"I can't believe you punched my seventy-year-old grandfather and pushed him down a flight of stairs last night, you fucking drug addict,"* the miserable failure's jackass response could be, *"if you took my banana, I expect it back before sunset! Whoo!"* (RULE: always end every jackass statement with a short, but loud *"whoo"*). It will quickly become obvious to your spouse that in fact, you have NOT suffered from a mental breakdown, but have been intending to piss them off intentionally. So, **DO NOT** deploy this technique unless you're absolutely sure that your marriage will soon be ending, or if you've exceeded the three-year marriage time limit rule, and thus need to cause fast relationship destruction.

Chances are, that after many years of your spouse putting up with several affairs, trips to rehab, DUIs, and multiple personalities (your favorite personality is still "Big Chuck," the obese truck stop hooker with heart of gold), they will eventually reach their breaking point, and no longer have patience for a miserable failure like you. The likelihood that acting like a complete jackass, and refusing to communicate with your spouse will cause them to immediately end the marriage via your violent death, or (at the very least) painful beating, is very high. So, be ready to sleep alone tonight with one eye open. You should also be prepared to lose your easy access to your spouse's credit cards, and vehicle **(WARNING: this means drive-through-liquor-store marathon night MAY have to be cancelled this week)**.

Memorize the following statements commonly used when deploying the "Jackass Method" of arguing. They are very powerful, and should only be deployed when you are adequately prepared to suffer the terrible wrath associated with their use. (PRO TIP: be heavily intoxicated when using this method, and be prepared to dodge punches and/or bullets).

Spouse - *"I found someone's underwear in our bed. Are you cheating again?"*
You - *"Did someone say pancake?! You're crazy! I love you, but you're crazy! Whoo!"*

Spouse - *"The bank just called. They say we shouldn't write 'prostitute' in the memo sections on our checks, and that there isn't enough money in our account to cover your bill at 'Big Mama's Rub and Tug.'"*
You - *"Turn up the stereo, Jack! Got ants in my pants again! Whoo!"*

Spouse - *"My sister is coming over. Please don't make fun of her wheelchair again."*
You - *"An adult male elephant has a massive dick! Whoo!"*

Spouse - *"You drunk asshole! Thanks for taking a dump in the shower last night! Really made my morning!"*
You - *"Sled dogs were made for that! Cocaine on crackers you say? You got it! Whoo!"*

Spouse - *"The cat is dead! It got into the bag of crack you "hid" under its litter box, shithead!"*
You - *"Slutty Sally sells sea shells by the sea shore! That's right! Whoo!"*

Spouse - *"You need to start bathing and changing your clothes again. You're attracting rodents into our house. Your ass and armpits stink like a third-world hotel without air conditioning during an Indian food festival. The smell associated with your crotch could kill a small child!"*

You - *"I'm going to DJ school and you can't stop me! Free tacos after five, bitch! Whoo, whoo!"*

Spouse - *"You got fired from your job because you pissed on your bosses' desk?"*

You - *"I want to have a threesome with a you, and any ventriloquist. Is that weird? Yeah it is! Whoo!"*

Spouse - *"Another DUI? Great! Thanks for giving us all such a thoughtful early Christmas present! Happy holidays, fuck face."*

You - *"Let's go ride grizzly bears down a volcano! Their chicken tortilla soup is da bomb. Whoo!"*

Spouse - *"Your children joined a cult, and are currently in the basement using a Ouija board to conjure up evil warlock spirits from the eternal pits of hell. Maybe you should go say something?"*

You - *"Put a nipple in my mouth right now, or I'm out of here! I like Mr. Pickle face. Whoo!"*

All of the previous jackass statements are interchangeable, and can be used for any argument, no matter what the subject is. It's crucial that you deliver these bizarre statements, and eventually ones of your own creation, in response to a complaint from your soon to be ex-spouse immediately upon hearing it. Do so loudly (just below scream level), and with the most psychotic facial expression you can derive (HINT: think "mental patient" meets "constipated kitten"). If done correctly, and often enough, using the "Jackass Method" of arguing will turn your soon to be ex-spouse into a raging, psychotic person who can't wait to divorce you. The "pain train" is about to pull into the station, and you're the conductor. Drive that fucker off a cliff!

Exes

When they first reluctantly (at gunpoint) said *"yes"* to dating or marrying you, your ex never knew that they were actually saying **"yes"** to a lifetime of "missing" underwear, lighthearted stalking, and late-night booty calls. **No matter how many times your ex moves, changes their name, purchases a dozen more firearms for self-protection or files ANOTHER damn restraining order; you're not going anywhere!** Having multiple ex-lovers is an inevitable and welcomed result of being a seasoned and professional miserable failure. If you're just beginning your journey to becoming a miserable failure piece of shit, having painful interactions with multiple ex partners on a regular basis is essential to your complete and total downfall and breakdown into miserable failuredom. There is no greater injury than the wound inflicted by massive heartache brought upon by your ex-lovers. Being actively involved with your ex (viewing their social media posts, secretly squatting in their garage, popping up at their place of employment, secretly videotaping them, etc.) is the perfect way to tear that old love wound open, over and over again (NOTE: you should welcome this pain).

Miserable failures don't break up with anyone. In fact, the only way a relationship with a miserable failure comes to an end is through your imprisonment or your sudden disappearance. When **your** ex broke up with **you**, it was crushing. You were miserable and heartbroken (SCORE!!!). **You should LOVE the pain associated with being dumped, kicked out of the house, arrested for a domestic disturbance, or served with divorce papers.** These actions only further reinforce your extreme disdain and disapproval by others. Let's face it, you were dumped for **MANY reasons**. Some of which probably include but are not limited to:

- Your failure to lift the lid when you piss (for male miserable failures).
- Your excessive cheating **(NO SYMPATHY: anyone stupid**

enough to bang your stank ass deserves those STDs you gave them).

- Your relentless "surprise vacations" (the disgusting orgies and horrible gangbangs you arranged for your ex during your surprise trip to "Swinger's Night" on your vacation to Las Vegas).
- Your horrible drinking habits (waking up with a shot of straight moonshine is what separates **you** from the **crowd**).
- Your outrageous drug use (openly shooting heroin at the dinner table during Thanksgiving at your in-law's house was one of the last straws for your ex).
- Your multiple job firings (getting up early and being at work at 8:00 a.m. is for SUCKERS).
- Your unclean, unkempt and disgusting body (FYI: not showering for four months, while eating a diet consisting entirely of carbs and sugar, and avoiding going to the gym is yet another reason why you were booted out).
- Your disgusting "friends" you randomly bring by and allow to sleep on the couch (your pal, Lenny, from the homeless encampment in the park is quite a loud moaner on the couch while he masturbates himself to sleep on a nightly basis, isn't he?).
- Your multiple arrests (hey, a "free refill" means **limitless**, so stealing the entire soda fountain machine at the gas station should be considered legal).
- Your spending habits (being broke and unemployed means that you should use THEIR credit cards on MULTIPLE rolls of scratch off lottery tickets and SEVERAL cartons of cigarettes).
- Your numerous bankruptcies (HINT: filing chapter **seven** bankruptcy, **seven** times in as many states means that you're due for some BAD "miserable failure-style" luck).
- Your excessive verbal and psychological abuse (contrary to popular belief, screaming at the top of your lungs while insulting your partner for changing the TV channel **DOES have** a

profound negative impact on your relationship, believe it or not...).

- Your late nights out drinking (coming home at 4:00 in the morning smelling of booze, vomit and tacos **is not** a great way "to get the romance back" into the bedroom).
- Stealing and selling all of your ex's belongings in order to buy a nice, large crack rock (ADVICE: if it's in your house, you own part of it, technically).
- The multiple car repossessions, wage garnishments, lawsuits, unpaid parking tickets, the ankle monitoring bracelet, DUIs, and your low credit score (REMEMBER: miserable failures are horrible with money).

You should also strive to be reminded of the intense heartache associated with your failed relationships as frequently as humanly possible (NOTE: crying, depression and threats of self-harm are great tools to utilize). **A simple, yet effective way to wallow in your breakup misery is to always carry photos of your ex with you, and plaster them in heavily-trafficked areas of your home, trailer or studio bedroom housing project unit you live in.** Use old photos of you two before the breakup as well as recent pictures of them with their new lover (FYI: they look so much happier now, don't they?). Stare at these photos often, and repeat out loud the following affirmation:

"I've lost the only person who could ever love a miserable failure like me. There is no hope. I hate myself. I am a piece of shit."

Perform this exercise at least forty-four to fifty-nine times **daily** and attempt to end each session with a fit of uncontrollable sobbing (HINT: if you can't cry, pepper spray your eyes). Try to collect and store your tears in a glass jar labeled "YOU DID THIS, FUCKER" and ship them to your ex whenever the container is full (FYI: this should be an average of every four days or so). Also, feel free to send selfies of you crying while masturbating nude to your ex (NOTE: wearing an optional panda mask really shakes up their day and will scare the ever-loving shit out of them).

The Temple of the Ex

Another useful tool for continuously living in a painful past is "shrine building." An obscenely large shrine in your hoarder house dedicated to the extremely painful memories of your horribly failed relationship is the perfect daily reminder of how terrible your life will always be **without your ex** (NOTE: since your ex left you, they should be doing MUCH BETTER without **you** in their life). Build this shrine to your ex in your shit box bedroom so that it's the first thing you see when waking up every morning (BTW: this really sets the tone for the horrendous day you're about to experience). **Placing the shrine near your bed also serves as a deterrent to any new potential "sex partners" ("victims") that may (unfortunately for them) follow you home in a hazy drug-induced stumble after your AA meeting**.

Getting laid too soon post-breakup can bring unwanted emotional recovery, and possibly lead to unexpected new happiness (HAPPINESS? No thanks!). You need to wallow in your own misery and not improve your life at all. Besides, no one would want to bang your nasty ass anyway. Therefore, constructing a proper shrine to your ex is an artform in and of itself. Building a shrine also means that you have not fully "moved on" with your life since the breakup, the multiple restraining order(s) and when the police were called.

Your shrine to your ex must contain the appropriate balance of your painful past (CONTENTS: photos from your failed relationship, returned engagement rings, stolen underwear, birthday cards, love letters, pregnancy tests, used condoms, etc.), and your new "gifts" that remind you of your old relationship (CONTENTS: pictures of your ex with **their new partner**, your copy of the active restraining order, their new stolen underwear, etc.). The shrine you construct should be no less than

11.5ft tall (FYI: if your ceiling isn't high enough, **use a sledgehammer to open it up a bit, so you can get the entire shrine in there**) and contain a life-sized mural of your ex performing a sex act on any fictional television or movie character (use your imagination, you pervert). Before you say your pre-bedtime prayers to demons, warlocks and wizards, hold nightly vigils where you light hundreds of scented candles in exchange for your ex "getting back together with you." **(PLEASE NOTE: you can even do a blood offering to your shrine... just make sure you have a large bucket and a switchblade knife...).** Make a video of this nightly event, post it on social media, and tag your ex with the caption: *"we're still in love."* These acts may seem, sad, lonely, isolated, desperate and disgusting but, **SO ARE YOU!**

Getting "Involved"

You failed them once as a romantic partner (sexually, emotionally, physically), but you'll be damned if you're going fail them again as a secret best friend/desperate psychotic stalker! Despite taking little interest in your partner while in the actual relationship, **after the breakup, the miserable failure should be more involved with their ex than ever before**. Essentially, you should be an obsessed and crazed ex. Being an "involved ex" gives you the wonderful opportunity to do all the things you "should" have done before things got really bad in that awful relationship (NOTE: participating in an elderly swinger's orgy in a flea bag motel on your anniversary was probably **not** the best move towards achieving "better intimacy" with your ex when you were together). Your ex deserves special attention after all the broken promises **you made** and the trouble **you've caused** (REMEMBER: the time when you pawned all their shoes for money to buy crack cocaine?).

Being an "involved ex" does not require the consent of your former lover, and after the hellish shit storm that was your relationship, it's unlikely that they ever want to see your monster face again. The divorce or breakup may have been finalized months ago, but this time you'll remember to send a "thoughtful" gift to your ex's office on the first day of their new job (EXAMPLE: a clear plastic tub stuffed full of "heavily" used sexual bondage gear is a great option). When your ex finally moves into the dream house, new mobile home, or section-eight housing project, you'll be there (hiding in the closet) to share in the special and momentous occasion (HINT: surprise them wearing a ski mask, a hockey mask or a creepy clown mask and enjoy the baseball bat to your legs that will soon follow your brief appearance). When your ex decides to get married or in a relationship again, you'll finally give them the "shotgun wedding" you could never afford (BTW: the eleven-hour standoff with your former partner ended after your "genius" ex discovered the shotgun was plastic).

With all this new attention from you, your ex may attempt to relocate, obtain a firearm, change their name, or file yet, another restraining order. **DON'T LET THIS DETER YOU**. This is just their way of saying, *"you stole my identity to finance your porn addiction, and 'accidentally' punched my dog to death when you were high... I need space."* BE PERSISTENT, and eventually, your ex will accept the amazing friendship you're offering. Either way, you and your "support" are here to stay with or without their consent and with or without their knowledge...

Staying "In Touch"

It's only after breaking up that the miserable failure truly strives to communicate with their ex-partner. **Your years of horrible communication, lackadaisical miscommunication, violent bodily threats, extreme verbal abuse and horrific psychological exploitation are enough to break the strongest people—even your ex.** You should expect your former lover to be very "resistant" ("petrified") to opening up lines of communication with you once again (FYI: your previous "chats" via drunk text messages didn't go so well, did they?). Don't be discouraged by this and remember tremendous pain that awaits you, is worth the effort you're going to be putting in. Give your former partner a cooling off period of three to four weeks before extending the first *"I'm sorry I fucked your boss in the coat room at the Christmas Party"* verbal olive branch. This three to four-week period is enough time for them to calm down so they don't purchase that hand gun out of sheer fear and hatred for you. This amount of time with no attempted contact from you will give your ex the false sense of hope that you've moved on, and that they're finally "free" from you (LOL: try to hold your laughter). Start with sending some unexpected late night, drug-inspired, post failed suicide attempt texts and voicemails that emphasize the following attributes:

- *Creepiness* - Begin all your voicemails with heavy breathing or moaning and start texts with the phrase "I just drove by your house" or "I love your outfit you're wearing right now."
- *Insecurity* - Leave voicemails and send random texts that ask your ex how you compare to their new lover in bed. "Is his dick bigger?" and "Does she give you golden showers like I did?" are both perfect examples to utilize.
- *Anger* - Every third voicemail should only be the sounds of you screaming your ex's name, and breaking things in your shit hole apartment. Shout obscene vulgar phrases in between bouts of your uncontrollable weeping. Texts should be typed in all caps and all photos sent during this time should be pictures of horrific and gruesome car accidents that you found on the internet.
- *Loneliness* - The best voicemails SHOULD consist of you sobbing uncontrollably while begging your ex to take you back, or at least buy you another hooker (HINT: you're not picky). Frequently text your ex, self-written eulogies that state you died of a "broken heart," or that your "long battle with loneliness" has finally ended. Be sure to list the names and ages of surviving "pretend" children you would've had with your ex.
- *Desperation* - Around the hours of 2:00 a.m. to 5:00 a.m., send

your ex various texts begging and pleading for them to come back. Inform your ex that they have to take you back, because you "don't know what you're capable of doing."

- *Aggression* - Call any time on the weekend and leave them a two-minute voicemail of you growling and barking like a rabid dog (snorting super glue laced with crystal meth beforehand will add to the authenticity of the dog barks).

After getting a few late-night texts with attached photos of your genitals, nipples and some violent voicemails, your former partner will most likely block your phone number (they will probably make yet another phone call to the police as well). To overcome this situation, simply ask random people on the street if you can use their mobile phone to make an "emergency" call. This tactic is particularly effective because your ex has no idea it's you calling and may even answer their phone (HA HA sucker....). If your ex does answer, they'll hang up quickly, so be ready to use "scream statements" that pour your heart out in three seconds or less (as long as you last in bed before an orgasm). As soon as your ex answers the call, just scream, *"Relax, I just simply wanted to sleep with your cousin Terry,"* or *"Can you please just yell at me for not unloading the dishwasher while I touch myself?"* or *"It's not my gonorrhea, it's OUR gonorrhea!"* before they hang up. Be prepared for the random person whose phone you borrowed to be EXTREMELY upset when they realized the extent of your "emergency" for the need to borrow their phone. Eventually, in an attempt to end all phone contact with you, your ex will be forced to change their phone number, relocate cities or change their name. These actions should not deter you. You should find them online on social media for your next phase of stalking...

Being "Social"

Show your ex (as well as their friends, family, and coworkers) how much horrible pain this breakup has caused you by continuously posting about it on social media. Leave no stone unturned! **Truly express**

how you feel about your ex and your relationship openly and honestly. Your ex has probably stopped paying your phone and internet bills by now, so you'll have to use the public library to access social media (NOTE: assume a new identity when you apply for your library card and don't surf porn, or you'll get banned... **again**). Start by posting old photos from your failed relationship and add captions like, *"I fell asleep in a dumpster last night crying again just thinking about you,"* or *"Is getting super high, and having oral sex with a random carnival worker worth throwing this away?"* Create these pathetic posts late at night, heavily intoxicated and high on drugs, and be sure to tag your former partner's entire social circle to your posts (NOTE: for a really impactful effect, direct message said posts to your ex's parents, current lover, and boss...). **Quickly respond to any empathetic comments with propositions for sex, offers to sell them drugs, or simply ask to borrow money.**

You should also write a weekly fifteen to twenty paragraph essays (do not proofread or use spellcheck, you **dumb. illiterate. fuck.**) detailing what you miss most about your ex (favorite sexual position, them paying for everything, money they've given you, etc.), and how awful (or worse) your life has become **without them** (you now live under a bridge, crack and puddle water are your primary sources of nutrition, etc.). It's important to be in a terrible mood, and on multiple drugs when you type your suicidal masterpieces (IN OTHER WORDS: just be yourself). Post these writings to various social media platforms often, and always try to appear as pathetic/creepy as possible (again, just be yourself). Use the following sample paragraph as a guide for developing your own psychotic essays:

"Dear (insert your ex's name) *The Devastating Destroyer,*

When you locked me out of our apartment for the thirty-third time, I got mad, but that doesn't excuse my subsequent behaviors afterwards. I should have never put sugar in your gas tank or had sex with your best friend on our anniversary night. I apologize for the threats of violence against you and your family. In no way, shape or form do I want you and your relatives to "die be-

ing tortured in various slow and agonizing deaths that are broadcast live on a Russian TV station." That was just the beer talking... I am sorry for egging and toilet papering your house with my ex con prison parolee buddies on Christmas Eve. I also should never have pounded on your parent's door, drunk at 4:00 in the morning holding a toy handgun. That was rude of me. I also had no right to sell your dog on the street for cash to fund my champagne and ecstasy addictions, and no one deserves to lose their job over unfounded allegations of "international terrorism."

I also should have never sent your nudes to all of those online porn sites and I regret that I was not able to pay back the $13,000 I "borrowed" from you over the last few months of our horrible, train wreck relationship. You see, I am a miserable failure. Your life is probably ten times better WITHOUT ME in it. I'm so sorry, and I'm ready for you to take me back, or at least have sex with me again. I am a desperate fool and I have no integrity. I apologize for the verbal and psychological abuse I subjected you to. The "Dutch Ovens" and "Turkish Tucks" were completely childish of me. I also apologize for pawning off all of your personal possessions so I could have a nice, long weekend with a giant crack rock in Little Rock Arkansas. If you'll meet me under the dying oak tree in Washington Park, a nice Asian guy with a lisp, a large bag of crack cocaine, and my heart are waiting...

Love, (insert your name) *The Miserable Failure"*

The above "love letter" is a simple recommendation. Feel free to improvise, but the point is to show the entire social media world how fucked up and how low your self-esteem really is. Feel free to discuss all of your indiscretions openly and honestly on social media for all to read. Have no shame. Hold nothing back. If you truly desire to be a miserable failure, you need to focus on being a lunatic online. **Now is your chance to really make a mark on the world wide web by showing social media that you're a dangerous, delusional, disgusting and dysfunctional dickhead**.

Stalking Basics 101

Stalking is something that all miserable failures do. From the beginning stages of when you first got into a relationship, to all the way through the "post relationship experience," miserable failures need to know how to stalk their ex properly. The following is a basic overview consisting of the most common and effective stalking techniques as they relate to your current partner (your soon-to-be ex). **It's important to understand that a miserable failure does not stalk their ex with intentions of hurting them, but rather intends only to hurt themselves.** There is an old expression that goes, "the best revenge is living well." Secretly watching your ex thrive **without you** is an incredibly painful experience, and thus should be sought after by anyone hoping to become truly miserable (#goals). For a miserable failure, stalking is just a **natural** part of any "normal" relationship (like the occasional spousal screaming matches after the fifth of whiskey is gone, or the numerous red-headed step child beatings). Proper stalking includes a series of progressive phases in which the level of creepiness, depravity, and deviance will increase exponentially over long periods of time. Eventually, with persistence and a little luck, you'll either be under arrest (again), or enjoying the rekindling of your lost relationship (free money and semiannual sex is back!). Either way, you win! **You WIN at LOSING!**

Stalking Phase 1: "The Pre-Relationship Stalking Period"

Before you commit to exchanging bodily fluids and bank account info, you better know with whom you're really dealing with. This stalking phase typically takes place prior to the relationship becoming "exclusive" (FUN FACT: miserable failures are not "exclusive".... ever.) This phase typically also happens before experiencing penetration for the first time. Pre-relationship stalking can be done via closely investigating your new sex target's social media accounts (social media is a stalker's best friend). In years past, a stalker had to dig through trash, steal mail, and install hidden cameras (NOTE: which you have done in the past with **huge successes**) to gain the same information that today is listed for all to see on social media. Be sure to make note of all their major areas of interest (favorite music, movies, places to go, etc.). You can later use this info for the *"we must be soul mates because we like the same stuff"* classic manipulation tactic. Additionally, record all the names and contact info on their friends list. You'll find this data to be extremely valuable during the "turn all their loved ones against them" phase of your "relationship." Get to know everything you can before you start the ACTUAL stalking. Essentially, we want you to be a creeper online (or simply, just be yourself).

Stalking Phase 2: "The Lurking"

The lurking, or "creepy stare" stalking phase is engaged after becoming an official "item" with your new partner. Proper lurking is performed both covertly and overtly. This simply means that you should attempt to stay hidden while observing them, but if/when you're discovered, your only reaction should be to stare blankly back at them despite how much they scream in fright or ask for an explanation. Lurking needs to take place every time you see your partner. The best example for lurking is the classic "hotel creeper" situation. Let's say you and your partner are shacked up in a "classy" fleabag and cockroach-infested roadside motel room. Simply hide behind the drapes when they go to the bathroom for their post-sex piss. If while you're hiding behind the bedroom curtains watching your lover get dressed, and they notice your feet sticking out, just silently stare back at them, with a creepy and dull expression on your face. This is also an effective technique to use while your ex sleeps. While your ex is napping, sleeping ,or is passed out dead drunk, make it your habit to stand next to the bed and watch them (without blinking). Despite your understandably strong urge to do so, **PLEASE DO NOT MASTURBATE**. The sounds of you "talking matters into your own hands" may wake them.

Stalking Phase 3: "The Pop-In"

The pop-in stalking phase is similar to the behavior you'd expect from a jealous, or untrusting partner (BTW: the only "cheating" going on should between **you** and those **five sailors** you just met down at the local watering hole). Perform this pop-in stalking technique within the first ninety days of your new relationship (if it lasts that long). In this phase, you'll be "popping-in" uninvited, unannounced and unwarranted to all areas of your partner's daily life, and doing so in the most intrusive ways possible. For example, pop-in at their place of employment on the day of the big company board meeting and be completely shit-faced (BTW: start drinking the night before and refrain from sleeping). When the receptionist stops you at the front desk (because you puked in the lobby) start loudly yelling aggressive and vile statements or questions at her and the other the staff. Some common examples of phrases you could be shouting include but are not limited to:

- *"Where's the whore at?!"* (For male miserable failures.)
- *"If any of you sluts look at my man, I'll come back in here with a shotgun."* (For female miserable failures.)
- *"I just pissed blood and I need* (state partner's name*) to come and check out my wee wee."* (For male miserable failures.)
- *"I'm looking for the 'comes home from work late' motherfucker."* (For female miserable failures.)
- *"Do you know where I might find* (state partner's name)*? That son of a bitch forgot to leave me pizza and beer money!"* (For female miserable failures.)

These same principals can be applied to your lover's time with friends, gym visits, family reunions, weddings, birthdays, holidays, etc. **Just keep your pop-ins unexpected** and be sure to be heavily intoxicated/super high when you drop on by again (NOTE: the loudness and aggression will take care of itself).

Stalking Phase 4: "Following"

When the end of a miserable failure's relationship is near, it's natural for them to begin secretly following their soon-to-be ex (FYI: if your relationship has lasted more than nine days, your partner just might be marriage material for being able to put up with your bullshit shenanigans for that long). This "following" period allows for the recording of your partner's pre-breakup personal schedule (morning leave time, bathroom wiping habits, etc.), and for you to become aware of any new love interests they may have.

"Following" stalking involves no direct interactions with your partner (the "following" period of stalking should be sad, lonely, isolated and depressing...just like your sex life was with them the entire time), and is the most efficient way of easing into a long overdue, pain-filled, post breakup depression of crying, fake suicides and massive amounts of drinking (SCORE...). Your aim is to remain hidden and observe them from afar. A good rule for not being detected is to maintain at least a 500-foot distance between you and your soon-to-be ex (FYI: this should keep you out of their view and will be great practice for the coming restraining orders). It's preferable to dress in all black, paint your face like a mime, and have access to "low key" transportation at all times (the bicycle you stole from the middle school will do nicely). Carry a notebook with you at all times for record-keeping purposes and make special note of the times your "almost ex" is most vulnerable (it's your duty as their stalker to provide protection from would-be attackers no matter if you hired them or not).

Stalking Phase 5: "The Squatting"

After finally leaving your sorry ass, your now ex should have fully booted you out of their life and home. **Congratulations, you are now officially homeless!** As a miserable failure, you know there are a plethora of great places you can reside (dumpsters, under bridges, deserted nuclear testing sites, county jail, etc.). Despite all these wonderful options, you need to decide to make the loving choice, and continue to live with your ex (without their knowledge). **During the squatting phase, your**

goal is to remain undetected as you live alongside your ex, and continue to leach off them for all your basic needs. To do this effectively, you'll need to lessen your "environmental footprint" by beginning to consume less (NOT a reference to drugs, alcohol, or internet pornography). When your ex notices half their underwear missing, and a new empty jar of Spanish olives in the fridge, the jig is up! Play it small and only take what you need to survive. Limit your eating to only "nibbles" and set a stolen underwear goal of NO LESS than two undergarments per week. If your ex owns pets, you may have to become extra creative in where you sleep, and where you hide when they are home. Consider making home base in a cluttered corner in the garage, cobweb filled attic, or dusty and dangerous insect-ridden crawlspace. While your ex is at home, you'll need to remain hidden (FYI: passing out from drinking too much booze does the trick), but as soon as they leave, the place is all yours. Just do your best to keep things clean and don't damage or leave anything out of place.

You also must REMEMBER TO FLUSH! A forgotten "floater" can quickly end your squatting experience and provide law enforcement with all the DNA evidence they need for a conviction. Which is why we recommend that if you must go number two, you perform what is called, an "upper decker." **Simply remove the very top part of the toilet. Squat above the toilet and do your "business!"** This is a great way to avoid leaving skid marks in the toilet and also gives your ex a "nice little surprise" the next time they flush (INSERT: devilish smile here). Many miserable failures have taken their first (but certainly not last) trip to prison because of the easily avoidable fecal fiasco, so stick with the "upper decker."

Stalking Phase 6: "The Pop-Out"

Up until this point, you've enjoyed effortlessly stalking your ex through the distant view of a bedroom window, or from the comfort of a well-hidden backyard bush. You've even lovingly squatted in their home while successfully avoiding detection of any kind. Despite all your glorious efforts to remain in the shadows, you're eventually going to get caught (similar to the time you were caught stealing casino chips in Vegas... getting caught is going to "hurt"). It's better for you to take control of this situation now, rather than wait to be caught with your pants down (literally). It's finally time to make your presence known! Popping out is a risky move that ALWAYS pays off in your pursuit of becoming a complete and total, certified miserable failure. When you reveal to your ex that you've secretly been squatting in their laundry room for the last eighteen months, you can expect one of the following three reactions:

1. **The Movie Ending Response** - They immediately run into your arms. They beg and plead with you to take them back while on their knees. You then have incredible sex together streaming it on a live web cam (HINT: this is the **least likely result**).
2. **The Reality Ending Response** - They spray you with the bear mace, or shoot out your kneecap with a pistol they've been carrying since the breakup, call the police, and giggle while you lay in the fetal position before the fuzz arrives (NOTE: this result is more likely than the former).
3. **The Surprise Ending Response**- In a major twist, they reveal to you that they've known about the stalking/squatting the entire time, and that they've been waiting for you to reveal yourself on your own terms so that everything "looks legal" when the authorities find your dead and lifeless body. Your ex then empties an entire 9mm magazine into your crotch. As your ex watches you slowly bleed out on the floor, they will probably whisper into your cauliflower ear, "*Nice upper decker motherfucker*" (FYI: this will definitely happen).

It's important that you reveal your presence to your ex in a way that optimizes the element of surprise, increases fear, and stimulates the overall obsession/creepy romance level. Remember, your ultimate goals are to get them to take you back, have unprotected sex, get them to "loan" (LOL) you MORE money and then have them break your heart again and again. So, to ensure that neither of you become permanently injured during this process, refrain from "popping out" on rooftops, near sharp objects, or while your ex is cleaning their gun(s). No matter if you chose to pop-out from under their bed, hiding in the backseat of their car, or from their shower as they use the toilet, do it in the nude and make sure to be heavily intoxicated of course.

"Letting Go"

It's been three years, nine days, four failed relationships, one accidental pregnancy, and eleven restraining orders since you briefly dated your ex. They may have written you off immediately, but you never stopped thinking about them. Your actual relationship may have only lasted for one date, but during that magical period, you felt more real chemistry than you had ever before **(NOTE: you could have even had a "relationship" with a stranger in your own head, whom you never even met, and they still count as an actual "ex").** After multiple trips to the county lockup for violating your restraining orders and missing your scheduled parole meetings, you need to finally put person-to-person stalking behind you and decide to focus all your efforts on being the best "secret friend" and "sex partner in waiting" you can be.

You should never forget to send your ex yearly anonymous birthday gifts (remember last year when you drew a sketch of your genitals with a Christmas tree tattooed on it?). Their new lovers should also all go through your "security clearance" protocol (you "borrow" their identities and attempt to buy airline tickets), and you're always prepared to "share" a "make up sex" orgasm with your ex if they're desperate or drunk enough to do so (BTW: by "share" you mean "you have an orgasm and then take an immediate nap" without satisfying their sexual needs). Unfortunately, there are only 24 hours in a day, and the multiple ex partners you're already "involved" with will start to get less of your attention. If you've reached the saturation point of your heart, and something has to give. You're going to have to let go.

As time goes by, dealing with a break up will gradually become less painful (similar to the staph infection in your rectum), and in turn, less useful to you in your pursuit of becoming a miserable failure. Interacting with your ex may have once brought you tremendous heartache, but now only leaves you slightly irritated. This is not the best use of your time and will only serve to delay your journey down the path of becoming a total failure in life. It's time to cut ties with your former lover, and make room for a newer, more painful person. In true miserable failure fashion, you're going to make a statement on your way out and leave your ex with a lasting impression. Call them late one night, and as soon as they answer the phone scream out loud at the top of your lungs, "*I never stopped loving you,*" or "*This is your fault.*" Before they can respond, fire a pistol into the air, drop a sack full of potatoes on the ground, then remain silent (try not to giggle). This classic suicide prank is a memorable way to successfully end your time with a former partner. It should also be noted that your ex should be doing a round of applause and laughing hysterically when they think you killed yourself.

Cheating to Win

It's been widely said that, **"cheaters never win"**... That's PERFECT! Any activity that comes with the guarantee of horrendous and complete failure is a wonderful choice for all of you poor fuckers seeking to become miserable. **The miserable failure masters the art of avoiding victory at all costs and should have a deep seeded passion for "accomplishing" defeat.** Being a loser is more than simply losing to a five-year-old in a game of checkers (cheating little bastards), it's essentially your lifelong love. So, if a miserable failure loves to lose, why would they cheat to win? This answer is simple. **You should want and desperately**

desire to get caught cheating! It's been well documented throughout history that cheaters run the risk of losing everything if discovered. That's right, EVERYTHING! The act of cheating alone is so powerful that it can simultaneously end someone's social, and professional life forever (#SCORE). For instance, a professional athlete who gets caught bending the rules can instantly lose all their "loyal" fans, sponsors, and even their entire career. The only behavior that comes remotely close to having the life-destroying power of cheating is getting an incredibly offensive face tattoo (NOTE: a comprehensive list of approved face tattoo providers is available upon written request). While it's true that getting your infamous "Fuck You Dad" tattooed above your one remaining eyebrow is an effective way of becoming an unemployable societal outcast permanently, there are still circles of people that will accept your face tattoo, and even applaud your efforts to be "different", "unique", "special" and "one-of-a-kind." However, no one accepts or applauds a cheater and a loser, like you. No one wants to be associated or involved with a cheater, like you. People don't trust you and you should not even trust yourself. If done correctly, getting caught cheating in every single aspect and opportunity in life should rapidly lead to a clinical deep dark depression, poverty, homelessness, and being forced to work as a "can't say no" prostitute for drug money (fingers crossed). For a miserable failure, the benefits of cheating are almost too good to be true! So, get ready to start cheating.

Cheating is essentially the miserable failure's "win insurance." Being a "winner" means, among other "good" things, potentially becoming the recipient of positive praise and acknowledgment (NOTE: you don't need ANY positive bullshit whatsoever in your sad and pathetic excuse for a life). It should also be noted that **police lineups and STD tests are the only time you should hope for anything "positive."** Victory, in the "normal" sense, has no place in the life of any miserable failure (just like your failed sobriety). If you are unfortunate enough to score an accidental win, make sure you did so by cheating. With luck (NOTE: you should only have bad luck) you'll quickly be discovered to be a fraud and begin to endure a long, backbreaking, miserable fall from the top. **You, as a miserable failure, should be so driven to fail that you become an expert in turning anything, even victories, into MASSIVE defeats.** You may have "WON" the County Fair foot-long hot dog eating contest, but you LOST the "try not to fill your new gray sweat pants with 115 blood-soaked hotdogs" contest that happened later that evening (HINT: you should really see a doctor after that "experience" as well). Additionally, if you know that your victory came as a result of cheating, you will never be able to truly relish in its good feeling and are thus immune from any of its potentially positive attributes (BIG sigh of relief). In order to combat that feeling, we encourage you to inform all parties that you have won by cheating. Not only will you "lose" your winnings, you'll further alienate yourself from all positive social and personal relationships that was the result of your successful cheating.

Cheating "On"

The most common type of cheating occurs in "committed" relationships between lovers. While there are many reasons people cheat on their partner (alcohol, drugs, gangbangs, circle jerks, roofies, orgies, etc.), the most common is a lack of sexual satisfaction (NOTE: your level of sexual satisfaction for your partner should be slow, unexciting, uneventful and depressing). If you're unwilling to dress up like a Leprechaun, learn an erotic Irish step dance, and beat your partner into orgasm with a canoe paddle; someone ELSE is! As a miserable failure, your sexual needs are a labyrinth of dark, depraved, "semi-legal" desires that emphasize public exposure, hard drug use, roleplay, and forced groping. With your long desensitizing erotic history and extensive alcohol abuse, it's nearly impossible for you to achieve anything that remotely resembles arousal when attempting to have sex with a "familiar" partner (especially one that keeps CONSTANTLY asking for your half of the rent money). **Consistent variety is the miserable failure's only option for true sexual satisfaction** AND a sexual position called

"Scorched Earth." **(LEGAL NOTE: our legal team of lawyers say we're not allowed to discuss anything about this sexual situation in detail after what happened in Dallas two years ago...)** Even if your partner is willing to do anything to satisfy you sexually, they're still "your partner," and thus boring. So, a miserable failure does not cheat on their lover to hurt them emotionally, although this is often the case. **The miserable failure's motivation is always to satisfy an insatiable need for nastier, kinkier, more depraved, "shut the blinds," "spit in my mouth," drug-fueled sex...with someone else.**

A miserable failure doesn't cheat on all their partners, just the ones whose presence would impede their advancement toward failing miserably (those "nice and supporting people"). As mentioned previously, a miserable failure will occasionally meet their emotional and behavioral match. Normally, this is someone who is also on their way to becoming, or who has already become, a miserable failure themselves. Study these individuals closely in an earnest attempt to learn about them and from them. It's these scandalous, immoral, "love thieves" that the miserable failure should idolize and devote themselves to, fully and completely. Remain wholeheartedly faithful to these types of romantic partners despite them stealing your identity, wrecking your car multiple times, and openly cheating on you constantly (#BeStillMyHeart). However, a romantic partner who is NOT fucking your landlord, and adds to your life in "positive" ways should be cheated on... often... and **A LOT**. Understand that this behavior is **MANDATORY** if you wish to avoid the many pitfalls of a loving, warm, long-term, caring and intimate relationship. There is almost no greater danger to a miserable failure's mission than spending time with someone who cares more about them than the crack rock or bag of black tar heroin hidden between their butt cheeks (HAT TIP: thanks to Freddie from the Clark County jailhouse for that technique). Additionally, if you cheat on your partner with someone from their family (NOTE: step-siblings DO, in fact, count) you'll be awarded ultra, mega, bonus points. If you find someone **in your own family** to have an affair with (again, stepsiblings DO count) you'll be awarded **SUPER, MEGA, AWESOME, BONUS POINTS**! Remember, if your current partner is caring, loyal, loving, sweet, and honest, CHEAT ON THEM (that is of course someone wants to bang your stank ass). If your current partner is just as depraved, vile and as fucked up as you are, continue to insist (BEG) that they CHEAT ON YOU. Both scenarios and outcomes will add excruciating levels of uneasiness, unhappiness, and depression to your quest to become a miserable failure very fast.

Getting Caught... AGAIN

When you cheat, you're eventually going to get caught... AGAIN. Prior to being caught, a miserable failure never openly confesses to cheating, but rather leave a trail of "sexy breadcrumbs" leading their partner to the horrifying truth. "Accidentally" leaving scandalous emails to your "secret lover" open on a shared computer so that your partner will find them is a classic move for miserable failures. Making your booty calls at full volume while lying next to your "sleeping" spouse in bed is another unhealthy and wanted event. Film your extramarital affairs and upload them to the internet for all to see (again). Even if your partner is of extremely low intelligence (for a miserable failure this is highly probable), it won't be long until you're being confronted about your awful betrayal.

If, after multiple attempts to get caught, your partner still hasn't discovered your cheating, you'll simply have to be more direct. Give up sneaking away to random hotel rooms, abandoned parking lots, and back alley dumpsters for your torrid love affair(s) and escapades with sketchy, questionable, morally-deprived, and dangerous sickos. Instead, start having your affair at home in you and your partner's shared bed. You can even cheat in a common area where your significant other is likely to see you first thing upon arriving home from their third job **(NOTE: if you have a kind, caring lover, it is common for miserable failures to force their partner to take on three or four jobs, so they can**

fund your model rocket addiction). When your partner discovers that you've been fucking a gas station attendant, and not "looking for work," it should immediately send them into a spiral of hatred and physical violence directed solely at you (FUN FACT: they only got the third graveyard shift job in order to pay off your tattoo debts). We recommend getting caught in the kinkiest sexual position possible, either on your partner's birthday or your anniversary. You should be prepared for at least one or ALL of the following to occur after getting caught in the act:

- You will most likely be slapped, punched, kicked, stabbed, and/or shot repeatedly by your irate and soon-to-be former partner.
- If you survive, you will immediately be asked to leave, and thus will become homeless... again (#GOALS).
- Your most prized possessions (bongs, vintage dildo assortment, crack pipe collection, etc.) will quickly be thrown out, sold, or destroyed.
- Your soon-to-be ex will stop buying you illegal drugs and alcohol effective immediately (NOTE: hide your stash prior to getting caught, or it's going to be a very long night).

When normal people get caught cheating, it's embarrassing and sad. Average folks might even weep or try to get their partner to take them back. Regular people tend to feel guilty after cheating. Not you! So, it's time for you to confess to your indiscretions...

The Confession

Like cheating, lying is a tool used by the miserable failure to disrupt, or totally avoid establishing any trusting long-term relationships. No one, with the exception of another miserable failure, wants to be friends or lovers with a liar (this is PERFECT for you). **As a rule of thumb, lying is the miserable failure's default response for EVERYTHING in**

life. The exception to this rule is when you're being confronted with allegations of cheating, the miserable failure should be brutally honest. To forever hide or lie about your sexual cheating is to deny yourself the awesome consequences of being caught (EXAMPLES: painful divorces, loss of friends, financial collapse, job loss, excommunicated family, alcoholism, eating disorders, drug usage, etc.).

You should only confess to your sexy crime after there have been multiple failed attempts to PURPOSELY get caught while in the act of cheating. Your confession should NOT simply be you interrupting family dinner to blurt out, *"I've been sleeping with your dentist, now pass the mashed potatoes."* There is a particular method that should be used when confessing your infidelity in order to facilitate the maximum amount of damage, rage, and hatred that will subsequently be followed and directed solely at you. Follow the five-step process listed below when making your confession and get excited! This is the vomit-inducing moment you've been waiting for since your relationship began.

Step 1 - Deny, Deny, Deny...

Remember, it's never your goal to hurt others, but rather to have their pain directed back at you, multiplied and amplified 10,000 times. When caught cheating, the best way to "assist" your partner in developing the most intense rage possible towards you is to first deny committing the scandalous act altogether (even if you are caught physically having hardcore sex). Even if your spouse catches you in the middle of performing a "Jamaican Sunrise" on the pizza delivery person, **DENY, DENY, DENY.** This initial denial will either provide your partner with a temporary sense of hope that the cheating is all one big misunderstanding, or your lies, especially in combination with your infidelity, will only enrage them even further (NOTE: this might be the cause of your gruesome murder). In either way or scenario, **you lose, and that means that you win!**

Step 2 - Ask To "Borrow" MORE Money and Alcohol

This step is normally more successful with a partner who is still holding onto hope that you haven't actually cheated, and that the whole situation is a big "misunderstanding." Essentially, this is your last attempt at "milking" your soon-to-be ex-partner out of their hard-earned money ONCE AGAIN (and their entire alcohol and liquor collection). Whatever form of alcohol is offered to you by your soon-to-be-ex, you should rapidly drink it in an attempt to get more before the "well" dries up. Once you're good and liquored up, ask to "borrow" large amounts of money for essential things in life such as drugs, lottery tickets, action figures, and various psychic sessions. Assure your partner that you'll pay them back as soon as you get a job (relax, you're never getting another job). Be sure to perform these tasks immediately after your partner first questions you about the cheating, because in just a few minutes, your lover is never going to want to help you again (they're going to want your blood and not in a sexy vampire way either).

Step 3 - Cry

Essentially this step is just a second attempt at getting free money and booze. If your soon-to-be ex denied your initial request, it's most likely because you've already exhausted your ability to "borrow" anything else from them. Cry like a baby, moan about being depressed, and remember that as a miserable failure, you are never above begging and lowering your standards and pride (FYI: you're never above anything and you have no integrity). If you experience difficulty crying, just use your fingers to hold your eyes open until they sting and become saturated with tears. You can also try flicking your eyeballs, cutting an onion, and reliving your PAINFUL childhood memories (NOTE: your fucked-up childhood can make **anyone** cry). As a last resort, if you still can't get the water flowing, go into your meth bathroom lab, beat yourself in the head (with the Billy club you used for smashing baby seals during your "hunting" trip to Canada) and come out weeping like a schoolgirl.

Step 4 - Drop Da' Bomb

As a miserable failure, you're rarely honest about anything, but when you do confess it's through "dropping bombs." *"I'm gay, Dad," "The baby isn't yours,"* and *"They found the bodies"* are great examples of having a "bomb" dropped on you. These "truth bombs" bring with them a highly emotional impact, and are often "relationship enders." Once detonated, these bombs will not only destroy your relationship forever, but also cause your partner to immediately develop a violent rage directed solely at you (this is why you got them bear mace as a birthday gift, remember?). Your bomb drop should sound similar to the following:

> *"Baby. Please come sit down. I care about you deeply* (try to hold your laughter in) *and I think you're really awesome* (again, try to hold back laughing). *You are truly a wonderful person, a great partner, and are very sexy. Thinking about you makes me smile. It's because you make me so happy! I've been secretly fucking your boss and your cousin... At the same time."*

Setting yourself apart from normal people that cheat, is simple once you start dropping these truth bombs over and over again on your soon-to-be-ex partner.

Step 5 - Be Brutally Honest

Openly share the location ("Tom's Taco Hut" bathroom), the times and with whom your affair has been taking place (your partner's cousin and whoever else wanders into the bathroom and wants to insert things in certain places). Additionally, explain to your partner (in brutal, graphic detail) all of the sexual positions used, amount of orgasms you had, and the total number you faked. It's these minor details that will help your partner create a more vivid picture of you cheating in their mind, and thus make them more likely to attempt to completely destroy you with a golf club, gun, ice pick, hatchet, or crowbar (fingers crossed). Being honest might mean another stabbing. Shouting out truth bombs openly and honestly is also a great way to catch a baseball bat to both of your kneecaps.

You've been going to *"pick up milk"* and *"visit your grandmother in prison"* for too long. These excuses have run their course and your soon-to-be-ex partner is going to catch on. When this occurs, this is your opportunity to be honest about any bogus excuses you used to cover up your affair. Since you lied so often and did it for so long, it may be difficult to recall all your bullshit and fabricated excuses. **(IMPORTANT: besides having a goal to become hopeless, a miserable failure's life should be one, big, LIE.)** In the interest of having things quickly escalate to the level of "supreme hate" between you and your soon-to-be ex-lover, give special effort to remembering any bogus excuses that involved employment or income-related lies. As mentioned previously, your significant other should have paid all the bills (including financing your "rub and tug massage" addictions). So, learning that while they were working to pay off **your** credit cards, **you** were "working" to make their old college roommate have an orgasm. This fact alone should really piss them off royally. Follow the examples below for optimal success (and by optimal success, we mean them trying to run you over with a riding lawnmower while you lay in the grass):

Example #1 - *"Do you remember that big job interview I said I had last week? Well, I met actually met your old college roommate about a 'job,' but it was more of the 'suck,' 'lick,' and 'hand' type gig. Afterwards, I used the credit card I stole from you to purchase us some fast food."*

Example #2 - *"Thanks again for 'loaning' me the money to get resume paper, envelopes, and stamps. I used it to buy blindfolds, duct tape, and cherry-flavored lube for the skank I was banging."*

Example #3 - *"Every time you gave me a ride to the unemployment office, I gave someone at the unemployment office a ride on me."*

Example #4 - *"When you thought I was going to my AA meetings, I was secretly performing oral sex acts on various people downtown in the dark alleys."*

Example #5 - *"I never went and saw my therapist after they issued another restraining order on me. My 'therapist' is not someone who listens to me weekly. My 'therapist' is actually a bottle of scotch, a roofie, and five strangers in a fleabag motel room during the weekly circle jerk."*

Choosing Your Cheater- "Cheating Down"

When you cheat, make sure you cheat with someone who is MUCH **less attractive** than your current partner. Equally as important as your decision to cheat, is your choice of whom you'll cheat with. As previously mentioned, cheating on your partner with family (either yours or theirs) is a **great** choice. However, if your soon-to-be ex has no family that live nearby, and your family still has those pesky court-ordered restraining orders in place, you'll have to widen your aim when it comes to choosing a cheater. As a miserable failure, it's always your goal to "cheat down" (REMEMBER: you have ZERO standards, no moral compass, and lack all integrity). This means that **the person you cheat with should be less attractive in every way when compared to the person you're cheating on.** At times, this practice may become troublesome because you've already set the bar so low, but have faith that a miserable failure can always find the shit on the bottom of any shoe. Even if your current romantic partner is "slightly" overweight (still able to walk, but barely), missing their right eyebrow (it looks like they're winking), and smells like a dying armpit (it reminds you of mom's cooking before she went to federal prison), you can still do much worse. Stay focused on the big picture of complete and total personal self-destruction, and you'll soon find a "real fatty" (needs a motorized cart to "walk") with zero percent body hair and who's never held a toothbrush (BTW: their breath can kill a small dog). **Finding a real "gem" like this to bang is something only a real-life piece of shit would do.** Which is why it's perfect for a miserable failure to accomplish! Again, cheat down. Try to find a person who had any of the following physical characteristics:

- Someone that has a hair lip.
- Someone that has no teeth.
- Someone that has severe acne.
- Someone who has scars covering their body.
- Someone with a club foot.
- Someone with a lazy eye.
- Someone with a hook for a hand.
- Someone with no eyebrows.
- Someone with excessive boogers.
- Someone with boils, warts, freckles, and moles covering their face.
- Someone with cauliflower ear.

Also, if you can find that one, special "gem" that has all of these qualities, immediately ask them to marry you.

"Love" Thy Neighbor

You've been stealing their mail, and attempting to sell their pets since you moved in. Despite your best efforts to avoid "shitting where you eat," cheating within a 100ft radius of your home is just too easy and offers even more pain and misery upon being caught. As far as time and distance is concerned, the most convenient person to have "side sex" with is your neighbor (especially if you live in a fancy, section-8 housing project, or classy meth-filled trailer park). Banging your neighbor is not only a great way to save money on gasoline, but unlike sex partners that require travel, "neighbor banging" (with proper planning) should have no effect on your daytime TV viewing schedule (HINT: day time soap operas combined with handles of gin, provide the perfect blueprint for a miserable life).

Most importantly, banging your neighbor is the easiest way to "accidentally" get caught cheating when you need to quickly end a relationship in a terrible and awful way. It allows you to quickly maximize your own potential for negative personal impact by simultaneously pissing off your partner by banging someone that lives very near your home (NOTE: the chance of getting severely beaten and/or pistol-whipped in your own driveway goes up 200% when sleeping with your neighbor's spouse). Have purposely-loud sex with the windows open, and ALWAYS walk home naked. It won't be long until a nosey neighbor notices your scandalous behavior and alerts both of your spouses (send them a card hand-written in crayon thanking for their help and their "head's up" they provided). Things on the block should get really uncomfortable for everyone, real fast!

BFFF - "Best Fuck Friend Forever"

Your partner's best friend is the obvious first choice to cheat with. As a miserable failure, you should definitely try to "bed" all your partner's friends immediately after being introduced, but always give special attention to their "BFF" (best friend forever). The rage that will be directed at you after getting caught having an affair with someone on your partner's softball team is minuscule when compared to the wave of total destruction you'll experience when they walk-in on you performing the "Russian Squat," the "Doppelganger," the "New Jersey Turnpike," or the "Tyrannosaurus Simplex" on their best friend (SEE ALSO: "**A.S.P.R.V.**"... **A**dvanced **S**exual **P**ositions **R**equiring **V**odka).

Start with making passive sexual statements like *"You're their hottest friend," "I get so bored while they're at work,"* and *"They left to buy beer, let's fuck really quick."* After weeks of playing verbal "cat and mouse" (NOT a "role play" or "furry" reference), begin making overtly aggressive attempts to kiss with your partner's best friend **(DIRECTLY in front of your spouse)**. Maintain direct eye contact with your soon-to-be ex while you do this, and continuously announce that you are *"just playing around."* Gage both your partner and their BFF's reactions, if they appear to be into the possibility of a "threesome," YOU JUST WON THE MISERABLE FAILURE SEX LOTTERY! You can then enjoy the standard four-six weeks of raunchy group fluid exchange sex before the sexy house of cards you've built crashes down all around you in a big pile of "life shit." The inevitable jealousy explosion that will take place should destroy what's left of your relationship even faster than if you had simply been caught having a secret affair with the entire janitorial staff at the nuclear power plant (just like your STD outbreak, this should "burn baby burn").

If your partner and their BFF seem repulsed by the idea of sharing you, forge ahead anyway using the "wear down" method of seduction. This is simply the act of ignoring the words *"No thank you," "I'm not interested,"* and *"If you touch me again, I'll kick you in the crotch."* You'll eventually "wear them down" into having intercourse, or at a minimum, oral sex/hand stuff with you. At the very least, your partner's BFF will eventually start to avoid the situation altogether, and your soon-to-be ex will blame you (and rightfully so) for the loss of their best friend. In the end, the action of showing direct sexual interest in your lover's BFF serves two key purposes: 1.) increasing the total destruction of your relationship and 2.) creating a divide between best friends. In time, with proper focus and patience, your lover's BFF will become your new BFFF (best fuck friend forever).

The "High Five"

You've most likely heard of someone being caught in a torrid "love triangle." This is when one person (the ring leader) is simultaneously having a relationship with two different people. The two individuals who are in a "committed" (LOL) relationship with the "ring leader" are normally unaware that they're sharing their lover with someone else. Love triangles, and their inevitable nuclear destruction, commonly lead to intense physical pain, an emotional breakdown and personal loss for the ring leader. For a miserable failure, being the ring leader of a love triangle may seem like a logical tool to use in the pursuit of even greater misery and personal torment. However, your goal is NOT to become melancholy. It's to become miserable! Your aim isn't to "not do so well," but to completely fail. It's time to think big and go for the maximum amount of pain possible. It's time for the "high five!" The "high five" is not a clever name. You are literally going to "maintain" an ongoing cheating relationship with five different people simultaneously without them becoming aware of each other, or your soon-to-be ex finding out. You are also going to do this while being "high as fuck." Not "fucked up," "completely fucked," or "fucking trashed," but "HIGH AS FUCK." Being heavily intoxicated on illegal drugs while attempting to have MULTIPLE affairs with five people simultaneously will eventually be part of your downfall. The drugs will fog your mind, make your forgetful, and cloud your judgment. Mistakes will be made, and eventually, the entire situation is going to blow up in your face (YES!!!). If, after making many mistakes at concealing its secrecy, your five-person love pentagon is yet to be discovered, it's the perfect time for a "family meeting." Simply plan a romantic night out and invite all five of your lovers. Tell them all to meet you at a local park, or other public outdoor area. Being outdoors, and potentially away from crowds of people, will prolong the "hell storm" that is about to befall upon your worthless sack of shit life. There is also far less of a chance that a good Samaritan will attempt to physically intervene or contact the authorities once the screaming and shouting begins. It's best to stagger their arrival times in order to create maximum confusion and chaos. If all five of your lovers indicate that they're willing to share you in a sexy seven-way, don't get too excited, you passed out from the first punch and are definitely dreaming! The "high five" should end with 1.) a call to the police, 2.) a ride in an ambulance, 3.) a trip back to jail, 4.) a quick visit to the emergency room, and 5.) you being homeless, disfigured, and disabled.

Sex

For the miserable failure, sex provides a glorious opportunity for maximum psychological trauma for BOTH yourself and the horribly unlucky person who just had the unfortunate pleasure of making sweet love to you. **Even for the experienced lover, bad sex can happen, but in the case of the miserable failure, it's the only sex that happens.** When you have sex, it should be like your first time, every time (minus the bug bites and the troop scout leader's surprise "drop in's" inside of your tent). Laughable sex can be expected at age sixteen, but at thirty-five, it means that something is wrong (WINK, WINK: you're a miserable failure). Sex with you is a sloppy, awkward, and a truly sad thing to witness (similar to uncle Gary's wedding in Thailand), but you can still do worse—MUCH WORSE. Male miserable failures may orgasm too quickly. Female miserable failures might just lay their lifelessly ("the dead fish") adding more sadness to their partner's traumatic sexual experience. **However, a MISERABLE failure takes terrible sex to a level that only years of intense psychotherapy and electroshock therapy by a team of twenty-five shrinks, can fix.** The goal is to leave a lasting impact on your lover (NOTE: herpes works best) while furthering your feelings of inadequacy and climbing deeper into the dark chambers of clinical depression. Implement any of the following suggestions in your love-making life and start failing miserably at sex tonight (BTW: if no one will bang you, you're doing something right).

Lower your standards to get laid (HINT: you should have none). This practice greatly increases your chances of scoring. **If they have a pulse and they are warm, they're right for you!** No job is no problem (it just means they're more available). Their obesity makes them mostly bedridden (this is a great time and money saver). They have a hunch back (think of it as a handle.) The cheese smell still remains after showering (grab some crackers)! **Basically, if anyone is psychotic or delusional enough to have sex with you, just do it and do not think twice about it.**

Foodie Freak

Miserable failures can find amazing success in this first sexual maneuver we recommend. At the exact moment that the drugs and alcohol are kicking in on your sex partner, simply start to consume various foods as you have disgusting, unprotected sex. Eating food while having sex is such a fantastic move, many miserable failures over the years have done it so much, that when they eat food, they can have an orgasm (trips to the all-you-can-eat Mexican buffet will never be the same again...). Before pulling off this magnificent feat, you need to make sure that you go "shopping" ("shoplifting") for some foods that really get you in the mood. The following list is a sample guide for your sex shopping experience.

- **Clam Juice** - Nothing screams "romance" like the smell of concentrated clam juice as you two "bump uglies."
- **Anchovy Paste** - Squeeze the entire tube into your mouth before kissing begins.
- **Hot Sauce** - If you're ever in need of helping yourself get aroused, simply open the bottle, stick it in your rectum, and do a handstand.
- **Pearl Onions in a Can** - Pop one of these babies in your partner's belly button and try to springboard it into your disgusting, meth mouth.
- **Wasabi** - Rub this on your misshaped nipples and instruct your partner to lick it off.
- **Raw garlic** - Your partner might be a vampire, so just wear it like a necklace.
- **Canned Tuna** - Open this up as before oral sex commences.

- **Soy Sauce** - Drink this while you orgasm at the same time and try to say something in Japanese while doing so.
- **Vinegar** - Drinking this during sex will help your open sores in your mouth to stop bleeding so that you can temporarily enjoy sex.
- **Casu Marzu** - Maggots and cheese go VERY well with doggie style sex.

Eating these disgusting foods while you're trying to make love is going to cause your partner to vomit or leave the room screaming for the police. Either way, you win!

The Faker

Faking orgasms is fun! When done effectively, a good fake can end a sex session just in time for your favorite TV show or the weekly "surprise" visit from your new parole officer. Both male miserable failures and female miserable failure CAN utilize fake orgasms. **Female miserable failures have it fairly easy in this department, but with a little creativity, the guys can also master this.** The most effective fake for men is the infamous "snot rocket." At the point of "supposed" orgasm, pull out, then simply pinch one nostril and blow through your nose with maximum force. Do this while making the moaning and/or grunting noise normally associated with orgasms. This will keep her none the wiser while you send your "nostril particulates" onto her back (FYI: only do this while behind her.) Another great way for men to fake is to say they had an orgasm while they're wearing a condom. Again, we don't recommend condoms, but sometimes that is the only way you can have sex. Just start moaning and clinch your butt cheeks like you're trying to crack a hard walnut between them. She has no idea if you're telling the truth because you're wearing a condom. Simply, discard the "used" rubber by flushing it down the drain and thus destroying all evidence of your illusion and magical trickery. **Again, please remember that miserable failures SHOULD NOT wear condoms** (so don't make a habit out of this one). Why fake orgasms? It is simple. Sometimes you are bored with the sex and you just want to stop, roll over, take a hit of acid mixed with ecstasy, shotgun four beers and blackout. Essentially, faking orgasms gets you quicker to Valhalla (more drinking and drug usage), so make sure that you employ them often. For female miserable failures, faking orgasms is SUPER SIMPLE and easy. At any time during sex, simply moan and scream, *"I'm cumming"* as loud as you can, in order to end the sexual escapade so you can go huff some more glue in the parking lot. You can easily fake an orgasm whenever you want. Even if sex just started, feel free to fake it. He'll be none the wiser and soon enough, you'll be shooting heroin in the alley behind the bingo parlor with your friend, Ronda instead of having dirty sex with the local high school janitor.

The Crying Game

Simply put, crying after and especially DURING sex, really creeps people out and will make everyone in the room uncomfortable (especially the pizza delivery guys). Anyone wishing to become a miserable failure should make a habit of this behavior immediately (just like buying scratch-off lottery tickets with your welfare money). **Spontaneous sobbing during the actual lovemaking when "things are inserted" is the perfect chance to make your lover confused, grossed out, turned off, and most importantly, worried that you might be infected with something (#ROMANCE).** As you sob uncontrollably during sex, try moaning phrases like *"It still burns," "We should have used the condom,"* and *"Welcome to the club."* If they ask why you're crying or what you said, respond with, *"Shut up! I'm trying to cum"* (and then continue to cry.) Immediately after sex, again start sobbing and moaning loudly. This time when your lover asks you, *"What's wrong?"* Respond with, *"Do you have health insurance?"* and before they can answer, quickly move into the bathroom and lock the door behind you (NOTE: this is also a great opportunity to go through their medicine cabinet looking for prescriptions to steal and to continue your binge and purging eating disorder). When you come out of the bathroom, continue to cry as you shout vulgar obscenities about your parents and your red-headed stepchildren.

Laughter is the Best Medicine

You've cried at sex, but now it's time you started laughing your ass off. **Be a poker and a joker!** Sex and crying go together nicely (like crack and tin foil), however, laughing during sex is the ultimate mind bender. This works best for female miserable failures. When a man exposes his penis to a woman for the first time, it serves as a brief moment of 100% PURE judgment on her part. Men are keenly aware of this and will look to you for approval (they'll get none). Just begin to giggle slightly when he first reveals his manhood (BTW: even laugh if he has an 18" penis). Wait until he's inside you to begin laughing hysterically. Most men will ask why you are laughing. Again, your response should be, *"Are you even in yet little smoky?"* It's also very effective to continue to laugh post-sex. Sit on the edge of the bed and chuckle to yourself. When they ask why you're still laughing just say, *"I can't wait to tell my friends about the worst fuck I have ever gotten by the world's smallest cock,"* stand up, slap your own ass, and walk into the bathroom with your fist in the air. Besides being in a locked mental facility with paranoid psychotics, this will most likely be the strangest behavior your sexual partner ever witnessed. Miserable failures always know how to leave a lasting impression (SEE SECTION ON: "herpes and how to use it").

For male miserable failures, laughing at your partner's body is also a fantastic way to get them to develop an eating disorder that matches yours (NOTE: we must warn you that if you laugh before sex, you're probably not getting laid). When she takes off her clothes, start laughing. When she asks you why you're laughing, simply stare back at her for fifteen seconds and then say, *"You have flapjack titties!"* After this bizarre and rude exchange, those panties of hers will be coming up and put back on mighty fast! But if you want to give her the worst sex of her life, refrain from laughing until after you are well into your lovemaking. Right in the middle of your lovemaking, start laughing hysterically. When she asks you what is wrong, whisper into her ear, *"This is the worst lay I've ever had."* You know you're doing something right (wrong) when she whispers backs to you, *"Yes, I know..."* Relax, after this exchange, and the horrible sex, in no time she'll be fucking your fellow parolee ex-con buddies in the bathroom of a roadside tavern.

Living in the Past

Miserable failures live in the past, plan out a horrible future and royally fuck up the present. The best way to live in the past is to constantly talk about your ex. Do this on your date, and **also while making love**. Remember, the goal is to make this your first and last time with this person (unless they'll help you accomplish your goal of being a miserable failure faster because they're crazier than you). Winners have healthy long-term relationships and you're no winner (remember, you're a LOSER). Say things that will make your sexual partner extremely uncomfortable and potentially insulted. Be sure to do this spontaneously and with no reasoning. This behavior, in addition to the self-inflicted roofie cocktail you started your night with will add to your lover's overall sense of extreme confusion during the vomit-inducing hangover that the two of you will experience together. Great examples to follow are, *"My ex-boyfriend has a small dick too,"* and *"Wow! I guess my last girlfriend's vagina smelled weird, but yours takes the cake!"* Blurt out these statements loudly while never stopping the sex. If your sexual partner thinks you either have Tourette's or are mentally ill, you're doing it right.

Your Gas Leak

Miserable failures fart before, during, and after sex. You should really be a master of the art of passing gas. Proper gas passing should occur in three stages. Stage 1 is stealth mode. Many think they can accurately predict the sonic impact of their flatulence (the "Silent but Deadly," the "Sniper," or the "Thunder Dome"). This is a fool's game and a sure way to never reach Stage 3. What may begin as silent often erupts into "the machine gun." Take no chances and engage the "Panama Spread" when passing gas during sex (using your hands to spread your cheeks prior to release). Using the "Panama Spread" ensures no auditory detection will occur. You're in essence, becoming a fart sniper. Depending on your diet that day, the smell should come on faintly and build toward maximum impact as it fully surfaces from your scabies-infested bedspread **(NOTE: for our readers who live in the state of Utah, BE AWARE that if you've eaten a taco or any chili-based product in the last twenty-four hours, use of the "Panama Spread" is strictly prohibited).** Rest assured, after using the "Panama Spread" and as soon as you smell it, they will smell it. In this moment of horror and disgust, lock eyes with your lover and whisper to them, "*Was that you?*" This will cause temporary confusion and allow you easy access to the next gas passing stage. As the awkwardness and terrible odor begins to fade, act as if nothing happened and suggest you get on top. Once on top of your lover, give them a loving embrace and immediately begin Stage 2, the "Ass-A-Geddon." Hold nothing back and don't let the fear of unintentional and potential deification deter you. Let the bombs drop and laugh out loud as you do it (NOTE: pretend you're killing terrorists). The combination of their shock and the putrid smell emanating from your backside is sure to make them attempt an escape. Do not allow them to exit the bed. Quickly implement Stage 3: "The Dutch Oven." Pull the sheet or blanket over both of your bodies and clench onto the edges tightly. Like something out of a scary movie, this will effectively trap both of you and your unholy ass odor under the blanket. As they attempt not to breathe, continue releasing your deadly gas into the blanket atmosphere. Eventually, they'll give in and take a deep breath. This (if you're eating like a failure) should cause immediate loss of consciousness (and the perfect opportunity for a quick selfie #memories). When they eventually wake up, you'll be long gone, but the memory of that day will haunt their nostrils for years to come!

The Hail Mary

The "Hail Mary" is a classic technique. Again, unless their life is more pathetic than yours (in this case ask for advice), you should do all you can to prevent them from ever wanting to contact you again. If crying, laughing, talking about your ex, or passing gas during sex didn't make them run screaming into the hillside, you need to throw one final Hail Mary pass. A tried and true method of upsetting someone after sex is to hand them money and say, *"Thanks."* This will make them feel like a hooker (not a "sexy escort"... a "dirty hooker"). This should send them into an angry tirade where one of you leaves. If you don't have any money, (which you probably don't, you broke bastard) ask them if they take credit cards (even though yours are maxed out). If they do accept your money, and they don't run away screaming in fear, you just found yourself some marriage material.

Toilet Games

You can also try shitting with the bathroom door open. After the bad sex is over, walk to their bathroom to use it. Hold a conversation with them while you do this. Talk about what you had for lunch and the fact that you think it was rotten (NOTE: this happens when you dumpster dive for food, so more on this later). Also, while in the bathroom, use sink water and hand soap to wash your genitals. Make comments like, *"You really made it sloppy down there"* and *"I need to wash you off before going to dinner with my dead grandmother."* This is also a great opportunity to call your mother and say, *"I met someone and we're getting married"* (if mom is still in prison, just fake it). They'll think you're moving way too fast and most likely not want to see you again. A job well done, you miserable failure!

Other Sex Shenanigans

The techniques mentioned above are just some simple suggestions for having horrible sexual relations with your soon to be ex. Feel free to come up with your own! Be creative! Be a miserable failure at sex. Some final suggestions we recommend for sex, (but you need to search online for explicit details for yourself) include:

- "The Seattle Sewer"
- "Dave's Hopscotch"
- "The Gingerbread Man"
- "The Golden Rainbow"
- "Fast Friday"
- "The French Dolphin"
- "The Fog Machine"
- "The Dangerous Doug"
- "Leaping Lizards"
- "The Red-Hot Mamma"
- "Licking the Ice Post"
- "The Sparrow and the Oak Tree"

Some of these techniques mentioned above will take time for you to master. If you're having a difficult time knowing how to perform sexually in bed, just stick to the basics. If you're a male miserable failure, you should have a hard time getting an erection, a difficult time sustaining a hard-on and should have MANY premature ejaculations. If you're a female miserable failure, you should lay there like a dead fish during sex. You should also fake orgasms OFTEN and even fall asleep during sexual intercourse.

Birth Control

The title of this section can be misleading. Some readers may expect to learn about the best birth control methods to avoid pregnancy. This section will actually teach readers the best methods to **avoid birth control**. Remember, miserable failures don't use condoms or any type of birth control for that matter (BOOOORRRIIIINNNGGG). This is one of the reasons why you should have developed a plethora of sexually transmitted diseases over the years. To begin with, HPV ("genital warts") is a classic STD to begin your miserable failure "STD career" with. After obtaining this lifelong disease, we encourage you to develop and contact genital herpes, gonorrhea, chlamydia, and syphilis (in that particular order). The bottom line is this. It should burn when you pee and you should have several types of growths, sores, scabs, scars and various forms of puss permeating from your entire crotch area.

If you're a female miserable failure, unplanned or unwanted pregnancies bring about massive amounts of stress and worry (for normal people). However, for the miserable failure, an unexpected baby is the perfect way to temporarily trap their romantic partner in a REALLY bad relationship (remember, kids and constant suicidal threats keep a relationship strong). You should be extremely careful who you choose to trap by bringing in a "little monster" into this world (NOTE: all babies that come from your loins should be referred to as "little monsters," "demon babies," or "children of the underworld"). Any SOBER or rational person would run screaming from you in the first five minutes when you ask to have sexual relations with them. So, make sure that your pregnancy target is so unattractive they're unlikely to find another mate (fatties, deaf and blind mutes, and 90% burn victims are perfect matches), and most importantly, make sure they are wealthy (A.K.A. actually has a job or a career). These people have the means to provide you with eighteen years of child support payments and will stay in a relationship much longer than someone "without an eye patch." Once you've carefully chosen your pregnancy target (victim), use the following methods to "slip one past the goalie"**(NOTE: having unprotected sex with multiple partners is a great move for the miserable failure as it increases the monthly allotments you will receive from the welfare office).**

Birth Control (LOL) For Women

When it comes to attracting a sexual partner and intentionally causing a pregnancy, women have it the easiest. Men like to pretend they have standards where sex is concerned (HINT, HINT: they don't). As a female miserable failure, simply walk into any biker or trucker tavern, stand on top the bar and shout out, *"I'm ready to get fucked silly with no strings attached. It's flesh torpedo time, bitches! So, meet me outside in the alley and let's get this shit started!"* After said statement, you'll have a plethora of drunk slobs ready to bang you (#romance). The following is a simple list of "birth control" methods that should be employed by female miserable failures.

"The Lie"

Simply claim you're on birth control and then let his love sauce slamming begin! If your partner wants specifics, just say, *"I got my tubes tied."* Then, fake an orgasm (or two), light up a cigarette in the middle of sex, and tell him, *"Hurry up man, this isn't a rest home."*

"The Scorpion"

Despite it being "safe," your sexual partner may attempt to pull out. To stop this from happening, simply wrap your legs around him, thus preventing easy exit. This works best when used in conjunction with the "Portland Plumber" (punching your lover in the nose, and then pulling their ears at the moment of orgasm). The scorpion might be difficult to do if you're loosey-goosey down in your nether regions. So, try your best, you dirty slut.

"The Poke"

If, despite your best efforts to convince them otherwise, your lover still requires the use of a condom, always be sure they come from your personal supply that you stole from the health department during your last STD outbreak. This gives you the opportunity to leave some pre-poked holes in the latex, and you might be able to get him to put on the "French Tickler" condom (#HappyDaysAreHereAgain). Simply use a sewing needle to puncture the condom (or French Tickler) while it's still in the package and your pregnancy target will be none the wiser (ha, ha, ha, SUCKER). If your lover insists on bringing their own condoms, things can get a little tricky, but not impossible. Just like when you were in high school, put the condom on with your mouth (this makes women look talented, classy, and sophisticated). While using your lips to roll the rubber down Captain Winkie, make a small opening in the latex with your teeth.

"The Special Delivery"

If your lover does use an intact condom or somehow manages to pull out on time, all hope is not lost. A sperm filled condom can still contain a few surviving swimmers. After he finishes, offer to dispose of the soiled prophylactic yourself. As soon as you're out of sight, insert the open end of the condom into yourself. This same method can be used for facials and backsplashes as well as in conjunction with the "Fake Swallow," the "Dingle Daredevil," or the "Indian Giver."

Again, if you're a female miserable failure, it's important to get pregnant (as many times as possible and from as many DIFFERENT men as possible). Being a "mom" is great because you can utilize the "Human Excuse," the "Children Excuse," and get many months of FREE child support payments (CHA-CHING). Being a mother of ten bastard children also allows you the grand opportunity to be a really shitty parent while collecting massive amounts of welfare (that of course, you **will** waste on vibrators, dildos, and cigarettes).

Birth Control For Men

In the battle of the sexes, men are at a clear disadvantage when it comes to intentionally causing an unwanted pregnancy. **Any responsible woman, with a normal blood alcohol level, would never sleep with a deadbeat like YOU without a condom**, and she is probably at least on some passive form of birth control (the shot, IUD, the pill etc.). For this reason, make sure your pregnancy target is not a responsible woman. Good groups to scout are career fast food drive-thru employees, anyone who frequents the local free health clinic, and paroled moms without custody of their children (female miserable failures). If you are forced to use a condom or have a selfish partner that uses passive birth control, try the following techniques to overcome any of your personal borders to accomplish "male intentional unwanted impregnation" or MIUI (it's an art form). **Remember, a failure gets the wrong person pregnant at the worst time but does so over and over again over many consecutive years.**

"Stealthing"

She said you **had to wear a condom**, but she never mentioned for **how long!** "Stealthing" is the art of mid-sex covert condom removal and subsequent reinsertion. For most women, the average man's penis feels distinctly different when it's not wrapped in a condom. In most cases, if the condom is removed, she will immediately detect the difference and stop having sex with you (and the mailman). To limit your chances of detection and increase your odds of unwanted conception, focus on good timing and effective distraction techniques.

The best time to stealth is during the "missionary to doggy" position change because she will have her back turned to you. As soon as she is on all fours (barking like a dog), you're clear to free willy! Make sure you're also palming the condom post stealthing. Palming is the act of continuing to hold onto your condom once removed. Much like you'd palm a dollar bill to bribe a doorman to let you into an apartment building to steal shit, simply roll your rubber into a small ball and tuck it into your palm. This will keep the condom hidden while giving a miserable failure the opportunity to quickly slide it back on if detected (like a magician). **WARNING: Do not attempt stealthing while performing the "Honolulu Boomerang," the "Backdoor Bomber," or the "Coal Mine Slammer" (NOTE: you will get caught).**

To distract her during sex, use physical redirection techniques. The goal here is to get her to look in a different direction or momentarily think about something unrelated to the free-range meat rocket about to land in her love cushion. The best physical distractions are momentarily painful slaps or pinches that will be considered by her as another feeble attempt to increase her arousal (HINT, HINT: your butt acne—"butne"—arouses no one). The most effective slapping technique for distracting your pregnancy target is, "The Hitler." Start in the "Heil Hitler" hand position while behind her. Be sure to spread your fingers out as wide as possible while keeping your hand palm side down. Straighten your arm and do not bend your elbow. In a tomahawk motion, slam your palm down onto the small of her back. Do this with the same amount of force you would normally use to stop a child from asking stupid questions or when you knocked out your half-brother Fred at last year's Christmas. The key is to insert your latex-free manhood into her at the exact moment of impact (this may be difficult for the rhythmically challenged, so practice at home on your favorite blow-up doll first). Also, try pinching her in odd places like the armpit, eyebrow, back of neck, etc. in order to distract her. Again, do this in conjunction while inserting your flaccid, oddly shaped, poor excuse for a penis. If she reacts negatively to being pinched, say something romantic like, *"Slutty, naughty girls like you get it rough"* or *"I have Tourette's syndrome, you bitch"* (more on the "Tourette's Excuse" later in another section).

"The Camel"

This one takes true commitment to the intentional unwanted impregnation and requires a degree of security in one's own sexuality. Without going into graphic detail, camels are famous for spitting (figure out the rest on your own). When in doubt on this technique, shout in Arabic and tickle her ass for a bare minimum of fifteen consecutive minutes straight while attempting "The Camel."

"The Switch"

If she's using the birth control patch, you may still have a fighting chance at getting one in there! Birth control patches and nicotine patches look and feel similar enough, that a simple switch could give your waiting pocket rocket the access it needs to blast off into "Pregoland." Just wait until she's passed out from huffing gasoline and simply remove the birth control patch. Replace it with a nicotine patch. Unless they look closely, they'll never notice the difference. Plus, if she's not a regular smoker yet, don't worry! Her and the baby soon will be! When she regains consciousness and you've switched the patch, immediately start to get her in the mood again whispering softly into her ear, *"Are you ready for thirty more seconds in heaven baby?"*

"The Pill Ponder"

Honestly, when it comes to the pill, you don't really need to worry. Any lunatic willing to use birth control pills as their primary form of contraception is just counting the days until giving birth. Put trust in the fact that she will forget to take them after you get her addicted to crack, meth, and huffing spray paint. If you're still worried that you won't be able to get her pregnant, simply replace her pills with any type of aspirin.

"Gone Fishin'"

Any man who's had sex with a woman using the IUD knows you can feel it. For this technique, insert two fingers, find, and pull like a ripcord. Do this while performing oral sex on her. To provide a momentary distraction while you remove the implant, try a surprise nipple slap (just like your boy scout leader use to do to you at "summer camp" at Lake Minnetonka).

The "Vasectomy Excuse"

If someone is dumb enough to fall for this excuse in order for you to sleep with them, then they might be a keeper. Before intercourse, simply explain to the poor woman, that you've had a vasectomy and there is no need for you to use a condom. If she wants proof, show her your HPV and herpes scars on your crotch and inform her, "*That's where those fuckers cut me for my surgery.*" Once she buys your bullshit, feel free to have sweet forty-five seconds of lovemaking before your premature ejaculation occurs again.

Children

If you have children, once you become a miserable failure, they are going to hate you... With a PASSION. Children, they say, "make the world go 'round." However, for the miserable failure, children provide an opportunity to have PLENTY of free slave labor as well as an excuse for all of your DAILY and MULTIPLE fuck ups in life. **Be they biological, adopted, step, or bastard; children truly ARE the future for the miserable failure!** As a miserable failure, or someone who is striving to become a one, you really need the future to suck even more, and producing offspring that sprang from your disease-ridden and crab-infested loins is a great way to make the world even shittier than it already is. So, sit back, relax, and get ready to be the world's WORST parent!

Since today's kids are tomorrow's caregivers (and arresting officers),

it should be your goal to leave a lasting impression on every youngster you encounter. You didn't dedicate your entire life to being miserable only to have some "nice person" take "good" care of you after reaching old age. Yes, it's likely that you'll never grow old enough to ever be considered "elderly", and reside in a "retirement home" (NOTE: your weekend passion and horrible odds for playing games of Russian Rolette with your drugged-out homeless buddies WILL eventually catch up with you, unfortunately). However, if you do somehow outlive the odds, your retirement home will hopefully be staffed by the adult versions of the entitled, degenerate, unreliable, angry kids you're currently helping to mold in your own image. Enjoy not getting your insulin shots, never getting your adult diaper changed, and only bathing when your court-appointed guardian comes to "visit." (HINT: you earned it!) So, no matter what your current parental status is, read this section carefully, take meticulous notes (if you can write), and follow all instructions exactly as presented. Your shitty future may depend on it!

Why You Should "Make" Kids

If you haven't birthed any little "monsters" from your disgusting crotch, you're doing something wrong. After reading the steps outlined in previous sections, you know that "getting pregnant" is no challenge for the female miserable failure. Thanks to birth control methods like "pulling out," and "the condom poke," accidental pregnancies are easy to make happen. But, if you're a male miserable failure and you still haven't knocked some chick up yet, get busy getting naughty, you sick fuck... Eighteen years of child support payments and free labor are waiting for you! Any two-bit loser with a bag of candy, and a sad story about a missing puppy, can "borrow" a kid for a few years with a traditional, *"Get in the fucking van, now!"* kidnapping. However, in order to fully reap the long term "benefits" of terrible parenting, a miserable failure must "go all-in," and "make" children of their own. This is the fun part.

At this point in your metamorphosis, it's important to note

(#lawyerssuck) that the phrase "make kids" is NOT referring to you becoming a modern-day Dr. Frankenstein, and building a child from spare body parts in your basement (you already tried that with your pet kitten "Doloris" and failed miserably). To "make kids" is to, either through sex or adoption, produce legal children of your own. You should clearly understand that "making" a child is NOT the same as "having" a kid. To "have" a kid involves ACTUAL loving and nurturing "parenting" and "being there" for them (NOTE: you're not even "there" for yourself). From time to time you may provide your kids gentle nudges toward a life like you (a miserable and depressing existence of beer, unemployment, and facial tattoos). Thanks to your rock and roll lifestyle, you can only hope to "be there" for your kids in between jail sentences, tanning appointments, and trips to Mexico to purchase large quantities of black tar heroin. So, your kids are pretty much on their own from birth and are probably better off because of your inevitable absence. **Your job is never to raise children, but only to be a terrible role model who occasionally "borrows" money from their piggy bank to buy drugs. Period.**

With the exception of adoption and immaculate conception, making kids will require you to procreate naturally. Yes, there are other medical methods of getting pregnant that don't involve sex, but you can't afford them (while continuing to support your raging hooker and nachos habits and addictions). So, no matter if you're gay or straight; you must find a way for the sperm to meet the egg. For gay miserable failures, you're just going to have to suck it up (literally), and take one for the team (and literally "switch teams" for the night). A willing penis meeting a wanting vagina may not be "your thing," but it continues to be the most cost-effective way of making a baby (just close your eyes, put on the nipple clamps you stole from the sex shop and turn up the techno music to decibel 45). For straight, female miserable failures, since years of heavy drug use and untreated STDs have left your loins and crotch a barren wasteland, so you'll need to increase your odds of conception by "experiencing" multiple partners often and daily. Guess what? You now have a legitimate excuse for being a complete and total whore/skank/slut (BTW: it's all about the kids). If you're a male miserable failure, years of HEAVY drug use, various staph infections from STDs and HOURLY alcohol use has probably made your penis permanently broken and shrunken. To make sure you can still have sex to create kids, simply tape two plastic straws to each side of your tiny member in order to hold it up and make it "erect," then insert. Relax, the lovemaking won't last too long because you should be prematurely ejaculating within the first minute of "sex."

Paying it Forward

You weren't born with the wonderful behavioral problems, drug addictions, and mental illnesses you enjoy today. You had to "work hard" as an adult, to develop these undesirable traits, but the "shit seed" that grew into your awful and pathetic excuse for a life was probably first planted in childhood. If you were LUCKY enough to grow up with a mother in federal prison, both sets of grandparents in a drug rehab center, a sister who was a whore, and an absent crack-addicted "father" with an addiction to gender reassignment surgery, you have a distinct advantage over the average person when it comes to failing miserably on your quest (FYI: if you actually grew up in a loving and normal home, you're going to have to work much harder than your fellow other miserable failure trainees). If you grew up in a miserable failure lifestyle, thanks to all the extra "help" and "education" you received during adolescence (by age four you already knew how to roll a joint and tip a hooker CORRECTLY), your life should now be completely destroyed by now (EXCELLENT job). Your "day" is over, and now it's time to ensure that the next generation of sexually-confused, unhygienic deviants are born into this world!

Since you always wish for tomorrow to be worse than today (fingers and eyes crossed), **you must make it your personal duty to ensure that life's "river of shit" continues to flow into the minds of today's impressionable youth.** As an aging miserable failure, there will be no greater gift than to know that the "indiscretions" of your younger self have all been paid forward, to your extreme detriment! So, if you're slowly dying in a medical facility right now as you're reading this, you should smile as you lie helplessly in a urine and blood-stained hospital bed alone, with infected bed sores. The last thing you'll witness, before your painful death, will be the children you helped "mold" pawning your jewelry, draining your bank account, and selling your furniture (and both of your kidneys) for vacation money, laughing as you pass away. When the "leaders of tomorrow" learn to fail today, the future is fucked, and you wouldn't have it any other way!

The Golden Rule

Just like every sexual act you've ever been involved in (except the "Mexican Sex-Off"), **YOU should always come first.** Becoming a parent shouldn't change this behavior; it should accelerate it! When flying commercially (not your "special" flights across the border for "medicine"), the airlines advise you that in case of an emergency, first put on your own oxygen mask before assisting your children with theirs. A miserable failure simply applies this same principle to EVERY aspect of their life (especially parenting), and never attempts to help anyone (especially with oxygen masks). This is the "golden rule" for parenting like a miserable failure (AND being an asshole in general). **Always look out for numero uno.**

Due to your self-absorption, intentional lack of emotional and financial support, chances are, your children (IF they actually know you) really **hate** you. This is a great thing! **If your children detest, loathe, and downright hate you, they'll never stand in your way of becoming a truly miserable failure (IN FACT, they'll probably encourage it).** Your lack of providing good parenting, and any form of support at all may even produce intense feelings of personal guilt; which will only add to your dark, clinical depression, horrendous anxiety and your hourly panic attacks (BIG score). Just remember that no matter how much they cry, puke, or bleed, your kids never come first.

Mommy Loves You, Cock, and Crack Rock

The following section is solely directed toward "all natural" mommies because "surgically created" women cannot biologically make kids (or make the female Olympic team). So, you should pay close attention at this section if you have an actual disgusting and misshapen vagina between your hairy and flea-bitten legs. The ideas presented in this section can inspire any female miserable failure to formulate new terrible "parenting strategies", and in turn, produce even shittier kids. (DOUBLE Nice!!!)

Don't feel bad about being an awful mommy; feel great about it!!! As a female miserable failure and a mother, your ultimate goal is NOT to be a "good" parent, or anything remotely resembling a "decent" mom. Of course, you'd never physically hurt a kid, or knowingly allow anything illegal to happen to them. As a miserable failure mom, your mission is to create your own personal world of shit that only you are affected by. As a mother, your children should only add to the stinking pile of pain that is your life. Being neglected by your sex-crazed, street mime, bi-polar, cross-dressing father is one thing, but having "mom" forget every birthday, and your children's names is another. By adulthood, if you follow the rules outlined in this section, your children should be really screwed up, and hate you with a passion beyond words can describe. With luck (BTW: you only have bad luck), your estranged and now "thirsty for your destruction" children will one day soon seek revenge in the form of physical violence (a drunken knife fight caught on camera and posted online), or through the legal system (ANOTHER court order for you to "payback" overdue child support...LOL).

The most important rule to follow as a miserable failure mom is to never know, with 100% certainty, who your child's REAL father is. This means BANGING multiple guys, on the same day, on a regular basis, CONSTANTLY and with no birth control (BTW: it's just your "normal" Tuesday night at the truck stop parking lot). Screwing multiple partners at the same time, on the same night, is the most effective way to get knocked up quickly, and it will leave everyone involved guessing ("who is the father?"), especially your kids. If you can't find a guy to screw you one night, feel free to include other women, midgets, heroin amputees, various sex toys and small woodland animals in your "love-making orgies" just to "spice things up." However, we do strongly encourage you to seek out and arrange various gangbangs with groups of sketchy and strange fellas (BTW: this "sperm roulette" is more exciting than any trip to the casino your kids could ever take)! Spin the "magical wheel of paternity" on your kids eighteenth birthday to find out if their dad is:

1. Jake (A.K.A. Inmate #2445781).
2. Rick (a long-range truck driver with Type 2 Diabetes, PTSD, and a severe case of the gout).
3. An escaped mental patient named Dennis.
4. The old, chain-smoking, Italian guy who sells fruit at the local market.
5. Any member of the all-male cast of "Cocks on Ice."
6. "Mutton Chop" (A.K.A. Phil, the overweight "take no prisoners" leader of a local biker gang).
7. Richards (your ninth-grade math teacher who was fired for having sex with school desks, and stealing calculators).
8. Larry and Darryl, the conjoined twin's pizza delivery duo.
9. Sammy, the paralyzed dwarf from down the street.

Being "sexually available" (a super mega whore) doesn't necessarily mean you should loudly broadcast to everyone that your vagina is "open for business." Keep the fact that you've got a *"baby factory waiting for supplies"* to yourself. Knowing that you are purposely trying to get pregnant may turn some men off completely, and thus limit your sperm options.

If asked about your birth control "status" by a potential sex partner, just smile and grab his penis (BTW: men fall for that over and over and over and over again). Although you should be attempting to have sex with a large amount of men on a regular basis, DO NOT randomly hop on any willing meat rocket that presents itself (remember your senior year summer camp). You must be semi-selective when "choosing" a new sexual partner you intend to potentially impregnate you. Always be sure of that they have the ability to pay you child support, and/or score you booze/drugs (HEY, it's better than money). This means any new suitors should have a paying job. Give special attention to bartenders, pharmacists, medical doctors, and crack dealers (NOTE: pretty much anybody with easy access to drugs). So, hop on that cock honey, and become a pregnant slut as soon as humanly possible.

The Deadbeat Dad

Being a miserable failure father is actually quite simple, and SUPER fucking easy. Just think of all the TV sitcom fathers you watched growing up. They loved playing catch with their kids, helping them prepare for the big science fair, and were always emotionally available during those pesky, "tough times." These "gold star" dads always knew the right thing to say, never let their kids down, and always treated their children's mom like a proper gentleman. Basically, all you need to remember is to NOT do any of those things, **EVER**.

You are not a gold star dad. **You** are a fuck up, one-star, disgusting, rude, selfish, piece of shit, dad. The only time you've ever played actual catch with your kids was when you found the live hand grenade and played "hot potato" with it (the person missing the hand always loses). **If your twelve-year-old daughter needs help with her science fair project, you should probably quit assisting her when you realize it wouldn't get you closer access to an adequate supply of meth-making materials in the school science laboratory.** You will never "be there" for your kids during tough times because you'll be in prison (hopefully). You'll always let them down, and always say the wrong thing at the most inconvenient time (FOR EXAMPLE: *"The bad news is your puppy died, kid... the good news our new lawnmower is works like a charm"*). Without a doubt, you will not treat their mother like a "proper gentleman" unless "being a proper gentleman" includes "encouraging" regular orgies with seventeen men, weeklong drug binges, and committing check fraud (you'll need more cash to buy drugs and gas to drive to the next sex party).

The phrases "deadbeat dad" or "sperm donor" most often get used despite most people not truly understanding its meaning. When someone is referred to as a "deadbeat" parent, it is a reference to their bleak financial situation, and inability or unwillingness to pay their bills (NOTE: mainly child support). The male miserable failure should never, under any circumstances, **EVER** make a child support payment. Paying for your kids, shows signs of responsibility, maturity, and a wanting to benefit someone beside yourself. This is not the miserable failure way! **You must continue to be totally self-absorbed, and unwilling to provide support of any kind (emotional or financial).** The awesome benefits of not making your child support payments include, but are not limited to:

- More Jail Time (thanks for the free food and easy access to drugs, Judge Ronaldson).
- Garnished Wages (this is the first fun step toward bankruptcy and eventual homelessness).
- ANOTHER Suspended Driver's License (now, you can't pretend to "drive" to "work" every morning).
- A Pissed Off Ex (keep your fingers crossed for tire slashing and social media personal attacks).
- Children HELL Bent on Revenge (you miss payments, BUT they don't miss with their new bolt action rifle...).
- Ending Your Current Romantic Relationship (no women want to be next on your "seed and leave" list).

Feel free to use the "bankruptcy excuse," the "unemployment excuse," or the "identity theft excuse" when appearing before an angry Judge during any and all child support payment legal proceedings. Excuse-making will piss the judge off even more, and hopefully lead to a longer stay in jail for you (fingers crossed). If you have the unfortunate experience of dealing with a "reasonable" or "friendly" judge, there is a chance you'll be given an extension on your payments, and will serve no jail time at all (NOT COOL). Even worse, this "nice" judge may grant you visitation with your kids (what an asshole). In this situation, simply remind the *"prick"* judge that your children hate you because you're a terrible father, and that you live in a crack den (by "live" you mean "squat," and by "crack den" you mean "dumpster").

"Fighting" for Custody

During the divorce or breakup with your ex, you most likely "lost" custody of your kids (NOTE: with a police record like yours, you probably won't even have supervised visitation rights either). If, by some strange twist of fate, or a miracle, you are offered visitation, or even partial custody, just say *"no!"* However, do not voluntarily give up all your parental rights. In some family courts, by giving up your parental rights, you are also eliminating your requirement to pay child support. As stated previously, having court-ordered child support payments that you do not pay is a wonderful way to become more miserable, and an even bigger failure (SCORE).

Ultimately, your preference to not have custody of your children is based on many factors. The most obvious reason, is that kids cost money (FYI: you barely have enough cash for basic essentials like psychics, booze, cigarettes, and cocaine). Kids are also constantly needy, and expect you to show up for their stuff (HINT: you don't show up for anything, unless it involves money). Most importantly, kids cramp your style (REMINDER: you have zero style), and make it difficult to remain intoxicated most of the day. There is absolutely no room in your busy rock and roll lifestyle for diaper changing, soccer practice, help with their homework or "time outs." As you'll see below, being a miserable failure is a full-time job and is a good blueprint for how your life should be going right now.

Your Busy "Rock and Roll Lifestyle" Sample Schedule

2:00 p.m. – Wake up nude. Figure out whose bed you're in, and where the nearest exit is.

2:03 p.m. – Urinate (blood) in bed, due to laziness to get up from your drug and alcohol-induced sleep paralysis and your poor bladder control.

2:08 p.m. – Smoke your "required to function" morning cigarette and finally finish pissing yourself.

2:10 p.m. – Make yourself vomit in the trash can near the scabies-infested mattress to continue your eating disorder.

2:12 p.m. – Get out of bed quietly while being careful not to wake up the stranger(s) sleeping next to you, or disturb the possibly dead hooker lying on the floor.

2:13 p.m. – Attempt to find your clothing while accepting the fact that you most likely lost your shit-stained underwear AGAIN.

2:15 p.m. – Smoke another cigarette in the nude, and then get dressed in your customary robe and slippers (or your sweatpants and bloody t shirt).

2:19 p.m. – Check to see if the hooker is dead by softly kicking her in forehead a few (dozen) times.

2:20 p.m. –The hooker lives. Search their pockets for "clues" (and cash) before they regain consciousness.

2:25 p.m. – Your irritable bowel syndrome is acting up again. Make a run for the bathroom or nearest potted plant.

2:45 p.m. – Finally finished going #2. Either a.) do not wipe at all, or b.) wipe using the entire role of toilet paper.

2:49 p.m. – Search the room for drugs or booze before crawling out the fire escape.

2:51 p.m. – Immediately lick the table that looks like it has cocaine dust on it for a quick buzz.

2:51 p.m. – Fuck! It's salt. The bag of French fries, also on the table, should have been a dead giveaway, but you're a miserable failure.

2:52 p.m. – Attempt to snort the salt just to make sure it's really not cocaine.

2:53 p.m. – Fuck! It really **is** salt, and it burns. But you like the burning pain… so, do it again, just to punish yourself…

2:55 p.m. – The burning sensation caused by snorting salt finally starts to subside. A brief moment of pain induced mental clarity occurs.

2:57 p.m. – Undress and get back in bed with the unknown stranger(s).

3:00 p.m. – Drink an entire handle of vodka, mixed in with some barbiturates, cocaine, and heroin….

3:30 p.m. – Drunk dial former ex-lovers to harass.

4:00 p.m. – Pass the fuck out.

2:00 a.m. – Wake up to realize that your house has been robbed by the sleeping stranger(s), and that the passed-out hooker is now dead. Consider calling police, but decide to call for more hookers and cocaine instead.

Just remember, that not having custody of your children is the best situation for everybody! Hopefully, your absence opens the door for a caring stepparent to properly fill your parental role. **With you out of the picture, your children may actually have a normal life free of constant disappointment, near death experiences, and heavy drug use.** You will, in turn, get the awesome benefits of having estranged kids that hate you, and the corresponding court orders to prove it. Just never give up on giving up on your kids, it's the miserable failure way!

Showing Up at School

If you're trying to have sex with your kid's teacher(s) it may occasionally be necessary for you to attend a school event for appearance purposes ONLY. Remember to never attend your children's sporting or scholastic events unless you are drunk and/or high as fuck. Attending these events is the perfect excuse for being extremely **verbally abusive** to other parents, the teacher that rejected your sexual advances last semester, and the fat student selling candy at the concession stand (that little asshole wouldn't take an IOU hand-written in crayon from you).

The miserable failure also NEVER attends school events such as plays or musical performances alone. Bringing a person of the opposite sex is a great way to create jealousy among the teachers you're hoping to bang, and potentially piss off your ex's new step-parent fling (that's two birds with one shit-covered stone). Since you most likely don't have a stable relationship of any kind, you'll have to rent a friend or lover for the evening. Thanks to the power of the internet, both male and female "escorts" are only a few clicks away (NOTE: if you can't afford an escort, we recommend looting some loose change from several of the public wishing well fountains around the city to pay for your "friend"). Just remember to make sure your escort hasn't showered in the last forty-eight hours. When hookers go unwashed for a period of more than five hours, they quickly take on an odor similar to the combined fragrances of pot, semen, citrus air freshener, dry dog food, moth balls, and apple cider vinegar (strange, but 100% true). This "reverse aromatherapy" is an extremely effective way of making your presence known when arriving at a public event, and keeping others away from YOUR personal escort.

You should also randomly show up at your kid's school unannounced during regular class hours (in these situations the hooker is optional). Do this with the intention of lining up sex with one, or several of your child's teachers (yes... the janitor, bus driver, and cafeteria workers DO in fact count). After gaining "secret" entry (breaking the window) to the school building, quickly find the teacher's lounge, and wait for your "opportunity to flirt" (masturbate publicly). As an added bonus, there may even be free donuts and coffee available that you can bag up, and trade for drugs later. If you become impatient, or are unable to locate your new sex target in the lounge, head to the classrooms. When wandering the halls, be sure to wear your stained bathrobe, while chain smoke cigarettes, and loudly ask if anyone knows where your *"fucking kid is?"* Screaming your child's full given birth name is also an effective way of locating/embarrassing them, so remember to belt out their name as loud as possible while screaming vulgarities and profanities. **Remember, you're not just there to have sex with a teacher or janitor; you're also there to make your child hate you, EVEN MORE.**

When you've located your child's classroom, ask the teacher if you can sit in the back, and observe how your kid is doing. If you haven't been arrested, or asked to leave for openly smoking and drinking in a school; there is a strong chance your child's teacher(s) do want to bang you. Sit quietly in the back of the classroom, and immediately start passing love notes to your child's teacher. These should be hand written in magic marker, and include pictures you've drawn. Use the following love note example as inspiration:

Dear Miss/Mr. Love Machine.

Are you teaching social studies, or sex ed. right now? Because it's really HARD, and I might need some one-on-one tutoring (that means sex)... P.S. I hate condoms. How about you?

[INSERT ORANGE MAGIC MARKER DRAWING OF FULLY ERECT, VEINY PENIS HERE]

Love, (INSERT YOUR NAME), *The Miserable Failure*

If your child's classroom is empty because you've arrived during the lunch hour, make your way to the cafeteria. Upon arrival, crack open another beer, light up another cigarette, and scream your child's name loudly. Now that you have everyone's attention, the fun can begin! If you were a young miserable failure, you were probably treated very badly in the cafeteria. Bullies would probably flip your full lunch tray over onto your lap, gave you underwear "wedgies," and call you embarrassing names in front of the entire school (*"Needledick Nelson"* was your personal favorite). It's time for payback! No matter if your child is in first grade, or twelfth, you need to make it rain "emotional pain" on their classmates (for you and all the other miserable failures who got picked on in school). **To start, find the weakest looking male student and steal his lunch tray. Take a bite of his food, and quickly spit it back onto his tray. Then dump the remainder of the lunch tray on his lap** and say, *"Looks like the sissy boy had an accident in his pants"* (just like they used to do to you in high school before you dropped out). Then find the most overweight girl in the cafeteria, and loudly "fat shame" her. Use words and phrases like *"hippo" and "butterball."* Finally, locate your own child and deliver an "atomic wedgie" to whichever unfortunate soul is sitting nearest to them. Although this may be your child's best friend, at this moment they should represent all the bullies that picked on you for *"not having eyebrows"* and for *"not bathing regularly."* After completely shredding the "bully's" underwear, hand the torn pieces to your kid and say, *"Happy birthday, junior"* (this will make up for missing every birthday, EVER). Now that you've successfully embarrassed your kid, avenged your own school age bullying, and have an assault charge coming your way, it's time to try to get laid. Again, if no police have been called (YET), some parent, school worker or teacher at that school definitely wants to have sex with you. While you still have the attention of everyone in the cafeteria, announce loudly that *"I'll be under the bleachers waiting for you,"* but do not direct the message toward any specific adult. In only a few short minutes you should have one, or several DESPERATE school staff arrive for some unprotected, sweaty, drug-induced, "private tutoring".

Using Your Kids to Get Laid

(IMPORTANT NOTE ON SECTION: Due to your horrible hygiene, detestable physical appearance, rude attitude, and your foul

body odor, you'll probably never find someone dumb enough or sober enough to bang you). A miserable failure normally gets limited supervised visitation with their children, if they get any at all. If you are fortunate enough to have unsupervised time with your kids, it's a golden opportunity to use your children to score new sex partners. This is generally more effective with children who are yet to develop the ability to speak in compete sentences. When kids start to talk, they become less cute, more annoying, and can now tell people how shitty of a parent you actually are, while pointing out their deepest and darkest desires to stab you with a spork the next time you're passed out dead drunk (which should happen tonight).

The methodology behind this process is quite simple. Just send your youngest child (that is able to walk independently) out alone in a large public park during the daytime on a weekend. Drop them off near a popular sitting area, tell them to find a nice man/woman sitting alone, and then go hide behind a tree. Make sure they know that by "nice" you mean "clearly employed," able to "financially support your VARIOUS raging drug habits," and "not fat" (see section on bullying fat people). Once they've located a suitable nice person, they should approach them timidly, and appear to be frightened by the fact that they're alone. It's important to note that prior to this taking place, you should have conducted multiple manipulation-training sessions with your kids where you role-play these types of situations and scenarios out (practice makes perfect). If you have a really young one, since your child might be too little to speak in full sentences, they should use short phrases like *"me lost," "daddy gone,"* or *"where mommy?"* You should also teach them to "fake cry" while attempting to explain that they are lost, and looking for their parent (NOTE: this is the same method you used when you were **Dishonorably Discharged** from the armed services or when you were arrested for starting a violent riot, committing arson and looting stores). Continue to watch closely from your hidden location, and as soon as you are sure that the nice person is going to assist your child, swoop in and "save the day."

To save the day, just run up to your child, and give them a warm embrace. This may shock them since you are not normally the "hugging" type (BTW: you're more the, "won't acknowledge they're your biological child unless it involves free cash" type). Excitedly say, *"There you are," "You scared me,"* and *"I don't know what I'd do if I lost you"* (try to say this last one without laughing). Thank the nice person for helping your child, and tell them how tough it's been for you raising them alone after their other parent died suddenly (do this even if the other parent is still alive and feel free to use the "car accident excuse" here). As a reward for helping your child, offer to take them out for lunch (drinks and unprotected sex), or invite them over to your home for a nice dinner. If you've played your cards correctly (and you rarely do) you should be in line for a quick one-time "pity fuck" or maybe even a regular "charity fuck." Below we outline what these actually are...

"Pity Fuck" - Having one-time sex with someone out of extreme empathy for their dire situation.

"Charity Fuck" - Having occasional sex with a person because you recognize their total inability to get laid independently, due to circumstances beyond their control, or as a result of their direct actions.

The "My Kid Excuse"

One of the few attractive features of having children is your ability to use them as an excuse for EVERYTHING in your awful life. Almost all of your terrible behavior can be justified by, or blamed on your children. Furthermore, most people (including police, angry exes, parole officers, bookies, etc.) will actually forgive your past and future indiscretions when you use the "my kid" excuse properly. While having a lot of people pissed off at you is a helpful thing in your pursuit of becoming a miserable failure, it can limit your ability to "borrow" (LOL) money, and mooch other needed items. Invoking the "my kid" excuse does not provide permanent protection from people that are tired of helping you, but it does prolong the process (WINK, WINK: this means more FREE shit for you). Below are some common examples of how to effectively, and properly use the "my kid excuse." Keep in mind that this excuse can NEVER be overused, and should become your first line of defense when trying to explain away your terrible behavior (especially when dealing with landlords and employers).

Situation #1 - On your way to the Indian Casino for free pretzels and fire water, you get pulled over for drunk driving, and doing 105 MPH in a 55 MPH with your kid in the car:

"I'm so sorry officer! It's "shit-a-geddon" in here! My kid has the runs and he's about to open the floodgates again! Can we please borrow a towel, a camera and a plastic bag?"

Situation #2 - Your insatiable lust for DISGUSTING and DIRTY hookers, and stubborn tradition of finishing your last beer at dawn has made you three hours late for work, for the fourth time STRAIGHT this week:

"Sorry I'm late again, boss. I know I seem a little hungover again, but that's because my kid had me up all night worrying. She got into my stash, and I'm not exactly sure what was in there. Little bit of coke, probably some pot, definitely a shit ton of modeling glue. What are you gonna do, right? Kids, these days..."

Situation #3 - You're explaining to your current romantic partner why you've been divorced seven times, and have multiple untreated sexually transmitted diseases.

"I just couldn't let my kid bear witness to all of their bad behavior, especially the affairs. So, I had to get divorced, a lot. Oh yeah, by the way, I have a herpes outbreak right now."

The "Pregnancy Excuse"

Blaming everything on your kids doesn't have to wait until they're born! The "pregnancy excuse" is easy to implement anytime and anywhere, and can be used no matter if you're really pregnant or not. If you are a female miserable failure and you are pregnant, it's no surprise. If you're a female miserable failure and you're not pregnant, you'll simply fake it! Don't worry about being ousted as a faker. No one will question the validity of your pregnancy, and will naturally assume that you're just "not showing" yet. As your fake pregnancy progresses, simply stuff larger and larger pillows under your shirt to make it appear as though your baby is slowly growing. Be sure that the pillows are rounded, and at least somewhat resemble a pregnant stomach (A.K.A. couch cushions won't work, dumbass). **WARNING! Do not lose track of your fake pregnancy due date.** Many a miserable failure have fallen victim to bosses, and significant others doing the nine-month baby math. If it's been fourteen months, and you still haven't given birth, even the biggest morons will discover your horrible lie. We suggest investing (stealing) in a calendar, and marking the day of your fake due date for referencing later.

While pregnant (or faking being pregnant), you can blame all of your horrible behavior on the baby inside you. **Now, your constant mood swings (bipolar disorder), and increasingly violent outbursts (crystal meth addiction) can all be explained away as pregnancy hormones!** If you're caught in another six-way with the starting offensive line of the local college football team, it's not because you prefer your body being treated like a fondue pot, it's because *"the hormones are making you horny."* If you attempt to murder a coworker, it's not because they were going to tell the boss about your proclivity for stealing copy machines, it's because *"the hormones make it hard for you to control your emotions."* If you're arrested for public exposure, it's not because your clothing was stolen while you were passed out in a dumpster, it's because *"the hormones are giving you hot flashes."*

While pregnant (or fake pregnant) you can also make strange and extravagant demands that must be met immediately, or you're going to *"lose your shit"* again! **Usually, asking for buffalo flavored ice cream, a bottle of super glue, a case of beer and a bottle of breastmilk from a Turkish immigrant at 4:00 a.m. would be considered excessive (and fucking crazy), but it's perfectly normal for a pregnant person.** If you want a foot rub, manicure, and facial while you sit on the toilet and "read" porn magazines, you'll get it because you're *"pregnant."* When you need immediate cunnilingus performed on you by someone wearing a dolphin costume singing old show tunes, your significant other better get to the costume shop quick because you're *"pregnant!"*

Babysitters

So, if you're a single parent who, despite your best efforts, has retained some custody of your kids, then this section is for you. However, if you're still married, you can also implement the recommendations outlined below when you need to get a babysitter so you can go purchase another crack rock and another hit of Mexican black tar heroin. In order for you to keep up your rock and roll lifestyle, you'll need to hire the occasional babysitter. Do not call an agency, or find a sitter by asking others to recommend someone. Simply ask random people whom you meet at parties when they'd be free to watch your children. Ask the sketchiest and most questionable people first (basically anyone that rarely speaks and won't look you directly in the eye). Rest assured, this information will get back to your ex, which equals even more eventual pain for you (SCORE). **If you are yet to establish a regular back alley drug circle full of sketchy individuals who can babysit your kids, you're doing something wrong, and should punch yourself in the face ten times and start re-reading this book over from the beginning...** In any case, you'll need to expand the "hiring" search for your new babysitter. Listed below are some great babysitter options for any miserable failure looking to piss of their ex, and be the worst parent ever:

- Any single homeless person you meet who actively uses drugs, and is willing to have unprotected "dumpster sex" with you.
- Hookers (you know where to find them, how to avoid paying them and where the nearest hospital is from your beat down you just received from their pimp).
- Drug dealers who you owe money to (you won't tell them to sell the kids for cash, but if it happens... it happens).
- The creepy guy from your AA meetings who drives the van with the blacked out, spray-painted windows (he reminds you of your uncle Phil).
- Elderly strangers you meet in the mall (invite them over to watch your kids and then go rob their house).
- The obese crazy lady that lives in the basement apartment across the street (she might be 600 pounds, schizophrenic, and literally stuck to the couch, but at least your kids won't be going to bed hungry).

If all else fails, just stop at a random stranger's house in a "decent" neighborhood, and leave your children on their doorstep. DO NOT ring the doorbell, and try to escape before being detected. Just leave your kids there, and go. There's at least a 50% chance they'll be there when you get done at the horse track (and an 100% chance the police and/or child protective services will be called when you arrive drunk to pick them up). Your intention should never be to put your children in harm's way, but rather provide them with quality, "real world" experiences so they can grow and develop into miserable failures and massive pieces of shit (HINT, HINT: just like you). Choosing the perfect babysitter, or lack thereof, is a crucial step in that process. Just remember to let the drugs and alcohol guide you, and know that in the long run, your children are better off for it. If not, years of intense psychotherapy in the local asylum can fix anything (it worked for you... sort of... no... not at all).

Child Labor

As any good parent will tell you, teaching your kids about the value of "hard work" is important to their development. The miserable failure simply takes this premise to the ultra-extreme (because "you care"...LOL). **When you became a parent, in addition to an increased welfare payments, you also automatically received a faithful servant (SLAVE) for at least the next decade.** You can normally start requiring that your children perform manual labor tasks around age two (or as soon as they can walk). Unfortunately, due to bullshit child labor laws, you can no longer have your kids replace you at your place of employment, and then sit back and collect the paycheck (the good old GLORY days are gone forever, asshole). However, there is virtually no law in existence that prevents you from making them your personal maid, or butler (yes... you should make them wear the traditional house maid and English butler uniforms during these "slaving times" as well). The best part is that you will never pay them, and if they do a bad job you can punish them.

If you have been taking all the proper steps to become a miserable failure, your home is most likely a shitty studio apartment, cockroach-infested shithole in the projects, meth making trailer, or a certified crack house. No matter where you live, there is a 100% chance you haven't cleaned it—ever. So, besides making your kids shoplift scratch-off lottery tickets from the local gas station, you will primarily have them cleaning and doing your personal errands. It is IMPORTANT TO NOTE that we only recommend cleaning if **SOMEONE ELSE** is doing it for you for **FREE** (this includes YOUR own personal hygiene).

Do not use this free labor as an opportunity to be lazy, and not perform essential daily tasks. While being lazy certainly factors into your parenting choices, it is strongly recommended that you also use this time to teach your children about the harsh realities of the "daily grind." While your children are working, set the thermostat (if it still works) to ninety-five degrees or higher. Statistically speaking, the hotter it gets, the more irritated and violent people become. This models the modern day, *"I'm about to fucking snap"* working environment perfectly. To increase the tension in your shit box even more, play loud classical music by German composers continuously (NOTE: the Germans understand servitude and pain very well) while also screaming orders at your kids via a bullhorn. Give your kids a lunch break, but after those four to five "LONG" minutes, tell them their time is up, and they need to get their lazy asses back to work (of course, use the bullhorn to communicate this). You should also encourage your children, despite their age, to take regular smoke breaks. However, you should not provide their cigarettes for them, as this serves as another great opportunity to learn self-sufficiency, and how to shoplift properly **(NOTE: miserable failures encourage their children to take up smoking at any age possible, and encourage them to steal used cigarette butts from ashtrays outside of various office buildings downtown).**

Again, your goal is to create the atypical modern working environment for your children at home. So, you may want to consider canceling their "pensions" with no warning, doubling their workloads with no additional compensation, and only discussing their shortcomings (while completely ignoring any of their achievements). After a few years of this, they should be so browbeaten, and demoralized that they'll be perfectly prepared to go out into the world, and work a shitty job. In time, your children should be depressed enough to develop a steady drug habit, stressed out enough so they start to incorporate one of your eating disorders you taught them and angry enough to be a threat to everyone (good work, you miserable failure parent).

Are They Yours?

If you're a deadbeat dad, and you haven't gotten DNA testing to confirm your dickhead kids are actually yours, **DO IT NOW!** There is a possibility that you can reverse the court-ordered child support payments and wage garnishments. This means extra cash for booze, new face tattoos, and expanding your retro porn collection (sideburns and full bushes are sexy). If it turns out that your ex or current lover has produced children from an affair, you shouldn't be surprised. The "accidental" pregnancy (you encouraged the non-use of condoms) probably occurred the night those five large men ran a "sex train" on your wife (which you **arranged**, **orchestrated**, **planned out**, **FILMED**, **directed**, **cast**, and were **NOT allowed to participate in**). You'll also get the added benefit of being able to shame their mother publicly (again), and may even earn yourself a sympathy bang from your current sex target because you're "so sad" over the "loss" of your kids (NOTE: in reality you'll be doing back flips of joy).

Yes, having a few less legal children means that you'll have less angry kids who will one day attempt to kidnap, torture and slowly kill you. **However, this fact is of little consequence because there will still continue to be at least ten to fifteen other little bastards out there who you may have legally "seeded" that hardly know you, blame all their problems on you, and dream of one day making you suffer the consequences of absentee parenting.** Additionally, some of the children you thought were legally yours may continue to harbor resentment and intense hatred toward you, even after the DNA results come back confirming you're not their dad. This is to be expected, and should be encouraged. The more people who want you dead, and know your address, the better! If the DNA results come back confirming that you *do* have children (worst case scenario), remember that this means you still have FREE child slave labor, and a readily accepted excuse to blame all your terrible behaviors on (IMPORTANT: you can now take the gun out of your mouth, and go back to crying and drinking heavily right now).

The Shank-Making Experience

During your **BRIEF**, and closely supervised visitation time with your children (REMINDER: every other Wednesday from 3:00-3:30 p.m., under the watchful eye of Officer Reynolds with his gun drawn), you will undoubtedly get super bored. Watching movies and playing board games get old fast, and have no practical real-world application. It's your duty as a miserable failure parent to prepare your kids for an extremely shitty future. So, don't waste time with your kids on games, but instead use this as an opportunity to ready them for their inevitable prison stay. As anyone who's ever been in prison knows, shank making is an invaluable skill to have on the inside. Shanks, or homemade prison knifes as they're commonly called, are perfect for cutting food, carving pictures on the walls of your cell, and fatally stabbing the motherfucker that took your Ramen noodles.

For your unfortunate children, "shank making time" should feel similar to "arts and crafts time" at school. Keep the tone light hearted and fun, and be sure not to alert Officer Reynolds (and his hand cannon) that you're doing something dangerous, unethical and borderline illegal. Since you're always thoroughly searched before being allowed to visit with your kids (you only brought cocaine ONCE), you'll need to use items in your immediate surroundings to craft the perfect shank. Traditional "shankable" items like toothbrushes, broken shampoo bottles, and plastic forks work great, but are most likely not available in the small supervised room you visit your kids in. So, you'll need to encourage your kids to bring some shank making items with them to the next visit (this is in addition to the cash and cigarettes they bring you already). Good choices include anything made of papier mache (this can be made to be "pointy" easily), hard plastic frisbees (after adding a jagged edge, a frisbee easily becomes the ultimate prison ninja throwing star), and small metal screws (just glue them to your fists and let the fun begin).

This shank making activity teaches your children to be **resourceful**, creative, and provides them with MANY applicable life skills for their future role as a miserable failure. However, knowing how to build a shank is only half the battle. Your kids will need to learn how to effectively use, and dispose of their shank. It may be tempting to let your kids learn how to "shank fight" the same way you did, but encouraging them to fight each other, will probably get them arrested before they're ready. However, Officer Reynolds and his loaded gun make the perfect practice target. Officer Reynolds (or "Rey-Rey" as you call him) may be in possession of a firearm, but his diabetic neuropathy and love of fried food has kept him moving pretty slowly. **WARNING!!! DO NOT GIVE YOUR KIDS REAL SHANKS WHEN PRACTICING!** Instead, have your children simulate holding a small shank made of paper and cardboard, while performing a well-planned gang attack simulation on Rey-Rey. Be sure to have your kids work together, and scream phrases like *"Die, motherfucker, die"* and *"Those were my Ramen noodles, dead man."* This may startle or even upset Rey-Rey at first, but just smile and explain it away as kids being kids. Remember, you're just doing what any miserable failure parent should do: preparing you kids for prison (and to stab other inmates over commissary items if and when they get sent into the slammer).

How to Turn Your Kids into Cold, Hard Cash

No... The following sections will NOT teach you a mystical spell or put you in contact with ANOTHER "wizard." In order to turn your flesh and blood children into actual, physical money, you'll need to make sure you pay extra close attention to this section. Like your angry late-night calls to the psychic hotline, attempting such a feat is a complete waste of energy, and will only result in your being "reported" again. However, you can effectively use your children to make some extra side cash, and in turn, provide them with valuable real-world experiences on your quest to become a miserable failure. You didn't "decide" to "make" kids because you wanted pissed off little bastards running around your house breaking shit (you already have your friend "Gary

The Drunken Midget" for that job). A miserable failure "makes" kids because of the extraordinary potential for getting **free SHIT** (free slave labor, free kids' meals, free admission, free money, etc.). Follow the instructions listed in the below sections, and in no time, your kids can become YOUR golden ticket to free money. Easy street, here you come!!!

The "Parking Lot Routine"

As a way to "earn" extra income, the miserable failure parent should train their children to successfully "shake down" strangers for easy and quick cash by threatening frivolous lawsuits. If done correctly, this skill set can virtually serve as an endless ATM for your drug, paid sex, fireworks, action figure, adhesive, and alcohol habits. The best method for doing this is what miserable failures call the "parking lot routine." The parking lot routine basically works like this... Go to any busy parking lot in an affluent neighborhood, and wait for an expensive-looking car to back out of a spot. From a crouched position behind the car next to it, quickly move behind your "target car" as it's backing up. Be sure to have your child with you (babies work best), and make sure they are prepared to "fake cry" on demand. You may also want to apply some fake costume blood, and make-up bruising to your child in order to add to the realism of the scam and shakedown. Using the palm of your hand, smack the rear bumper with maximum force while your kid lies on ground behind the automobile. Tell your kid to start fake crying (NOTE: if you want them to shed real tears, simply inform them that they'll be staying in your shit box with you for the "foreseeable future"), then covertly scamper away out of sight. The combination of the loud thump, and sound of a child crying will cause the driver to get out of their car quickly, most likely in a total panic (this is PERFECT).

When the driver discovers that they've "accidentally" backed into a child, you should run up to the scene exclaiming, *"Oh! not by baby! You hurt my baby,"* or *"Why did you run over my kid, asshole?"* The driver will start to apologize, or may even become defensive. Interrupt them as they're speaking, and ask if they're drunk before telling them you're calling the cops (little do they know that you can't afford a cell phone and it is YOU that is in fact drunk). As you "search" for your phone, mumble words like *"racist," "intentional,"* and *"lawsuit."* This should really get the driver's heart rate up! As the driver is freaking out about running over "your baby" and possibly going to jail, wink at them before mentioning that a quick $500 in cash could make the whole situation simply "go away." Some drivers may laugh at you and choose to drive away. However, statically speaking, a LARGE portion of the drivers will willingly hand over FREE cash to you in an attempt to avoid the potential ramifications of "running" over a child. Repeat this process several times a day, and you can expect to make upwards of $2000 in a single parking lot (it's all a numbers game). Looks like your "fart porn" addiction has funding again!

"Oliver Twisting"

Thanks to your history of violent outbursts, and terrible body odor, panhandling normally doesn't go too well for you. That's why you became a parent! Asking strangers on the street for free money can be a low paying endeavor for ugly adults (REMINDER: there are not too many good-looking homeless), but when it comes to children panhandling, accept no substitute! Even the poorest individual will search their empty pockets for some change when a destitute child asks for help.

The method is called "Oliver Twisting" and its designed to tug at the heart strings of all who come in contact with your sad, sickly, and broken-looking kids. Dress your children in old, faded, stained, tattered and torn clothing (search dumpsters outside children's hospitals to find the best "used" kids' clothes). Lightly smear ash on their faces so they resemble a chimney sweep from the 1800s, and then show them how to make sad looking facial expressions (again just tell them they're going to live with you full-time and then watch the REAL tears start coming). **Next, require your children to use a British accent while begging for**

cash. You would be surprised at how much more money English kids begging for cash get when compared to the rest of the world! Finally, send your kids out each morning at 5:00 a.m. to beg on random street corners. DO NOT go with them! Your presence will kill the sad and lonely vibe that will bring them the most "free money." Instruct them not to return until the evening hours (11:00 p.m.), and make it clear that if they want to sleep inside tonight, they better have at least $150 with them. This may seem cruel, but after a few nights of trying to sleep while avoiding Terry "The Drifter," you'll get your $150 minimum from them (every night for now on).

MORE Welfare

Since it's been close to a decade since you had a real job (or an orgasm without being choked and spit on), getting a welfare check is pretty normal for you. **For years, the government has been unknowingly funding all of your bad habits via the welfare system.** The monthly handout from "Uncle Sam" should let you live a carefree life while also financially supporting your tireless crusade to "end condoms forever." You should become quite fond of not working, and getting paid for it. However, the current amount of welfare you receive each month may not be enough to fully cover your upcoming island vacation (you spend ten days in a sweat lodge doing cocaine and betting on Russian roulette matches with Vietnamese immigrants). After covering your basic expenses (karate class, monthly porn magazine subscriptions, emergency back-alley blood transfusions, etc.), the meager amount you "earn" each month in "government cheese" certainly won't pay for the ass implants you put on your vision board and Christmas list. It's time for you to get a promotion in the welfare system! It's time for you to FINALLY claim your kids, and as many other kids as you can!

The welfare system doesn't act in the same way as the family court system you've definitely become accustomed to by now (NOTE: you should be currently working on your eighth divorce/custody "battle").

In family court, the more children you claim to be yours, the more money in child support you're required to pay. The welfare system essentially operates in the exact opposite way. **The more kids you claim to be yours, the more money you get, for FREE.** Of course, this extra cash is for you to use toward the care of your children (LOL), and of course that's what you're going to do with it. You're going to put their happiness above all else. Just follow the series of equations below if you're confused:

Money for Drugs = Happy Parent

Happy Parent = Happy Kid

Even if you don't have children, or have never met your kids, you should apply for **MORE WELFARE** from the government. Additionally, you should attempt to claim any kids from your neighborhood who look like their parents are also miserable failures. The chance of these kids' parents being sober enough to sign the welfare application is highly unlikely. **This means their kids are "up for grabs" in "Welfare Land!"** After you finish your list of kids to claim as your own, skip on down to the local welfare office to cash-in, and finally get what is "owed" to you by the government for having unprotected sex that resulted in a pregnancy. You've been due for a raise for a long time and now is the time you got it.

Pickpocket Pupil

Teaching your children to pickpocket from others is the perfect thing to do before any family vacation! You may have had enough gas money to get your piece of shit van across the state line, but now you're stuck, unless you can score some quick cash. Since your kids are with you, you won't be able to do your infamous and normal "suck for a buck" routine. So, it's time to ONCE AGAIN put those ungrateful little bastards to work...

Busy shopping malls can be a treasure trove of endless possibility for a young, inconspicuous-looking pickpocket. Instruct your bastard child to target well-dressed men and women as they likely possess the most cash or credit cards on hand (new big screen TV, here you come!). If you have more than one kid, the best method for pick pocketing is to simply have one child "bump" into the target while the other little rascal takes their wallet, or puts a hand in their purse. This "bump" method temporarily distracts the target leaving a small window of opportunity to take their valuables undetected. If you only have one child, you'll have to bump into the target yourself while your "soon-to-be miserable failure" kid commits theft. Having only one child on "pickpocket day" is not preferable because it requires your involvement, and thus substantially limits your ability to "save" your kid (and their stolen "booty") from being arrested if they are caught. If your kids are caught in the act of pickpocketing, you'll need to quickly pose as a police officer, and tell the "victim" that you're taking the little hoodlum to jail **(NOTE: This may be a "hard sell" considering cops generally don't wear "fuck you" t-shirts, and have breath reeking of bourbon at 11:00 a.m. in a shopping mall).**

If you only have one child available to "work" on pickpocket day, your best bet is to target purses with the "swoop-in" or "hero" method. This method works extremely well for getting quick cash, doesn't involve you stealing anything, and could potentially get you laid. Find a wealthy-looking lady with a large purse, who is shopping alone. Instruct your delinquent bastard children to forcefully take her purse, and run away. As your child begins to run away with the stolen purse, you simply **"swoop in"** and be the hero. Snatch the purse from your child's hands, and allow them to "run away" to safety (NOTE: have them hide in the parking lot). Give the purse back, and ask the victim if they're okay. Say something like, *"Damn kids these days,"* or make a comment that *"The kid must have shitty parents who don't care"* (very true). Tell the victim that you're sorry you can't stay and chat because you have a "chemotherapy treatment" to get too (SEE ALSO: the "cancer excuse"). If you do this convincingly, they may decide to pay you for your heroic act because they know you're unemployed, sick, and broke (REMINDER: you can't buy drugs with charm). The victim of the potential purse snatching you thwarted may also offer to take you out for lunch, or dinner as a thank you. You should always view this as an offering for unprotected sex in the nearest "classy" restroom. Respond by saying, yes, wink seductively at them, and then just see where things go from there. If the victim only thanks you, but doesn't pay you, or make an offer of unprotected, disgusting mall bathroom sex, you'll need to get even. Follow them into the parking lot while loudly calling them a *"cheapskate"* and a *"tease."* Be sure that the volume of your voice is loud enough for your child (still hiding in the parking lot) to hear easily. This is their signal to pop-out from behind a parked car, and attempt to steal the same purse again (except this time you won't be the "hero").

3

FAMILY RELATIONS

Being a Miserable Failure Family Member

Life took you down some rough roads in the past. Along your quest to be a miserable failure, things will get pretty bad, very fast, and you will probably be very scared during your metamorphosis. During life's challenging moments, you will need unwavering support, caring advice, and strong shoulders to cry on. Friends and lovers, who often come into and then out of your life, can't be relied upon to "be there" for you when times get really tough. However, your family will be there for you in your darkest hour (at least, at the beginning stages of your "journey"). At the beginning stages of your transition, your family will be your "rocks" of never-ending support. It doesn't matter how bad things get; you can always count on your family to help (at the beginning...). **That's before you tried to have sex with your first cousin, got your nephew hooked on angel dust, stole your uncle's identity to buy a brown windowless panel van and opened up ANOTHER meth lab in your grandma's basement.** As far as your family is concerned, the person they knew and loved died a longtime ago (that's what happens when you try to sell the family dog for an eight ball of blow).

It is not enough to simply be the "typical" unemployed, unclean and unkempt, loser who crashes on family member's couches, and mooches their food (and money) for EXTREMELY LONG, extended periods of time. The true miserable failure blames all of their "completely fucked up" behavior on trauma stemming from a **fictional** and 100% fabricated "molestation" committed by a fictitious family member. Basically, you just need to be your normal, psychotic, masochistic, borderline personality disorder, back stabbing, double dealing, delusional, extremely odd, slightly dangerous, and sex and drug addicted **self**.

For a miserable failure, family is just another group of individuals invited to your personal "shit show" of broken dreams, poor decisions, fake excuses, DUIs, and awful life choices. If you've made it this far in life, and still have a good relationship with your family, don't worry; you'll soon have the complete and polar **OPPOSITE** of that. It takes time and focus to properly establish negative family relations. Remember, your family is programmed by society to "not give up on you," and "never stop loving you." In order to force your family to hate you, and "walk away" forever, you'll need to focus on being the biggest loser, EVER (THIS will NOT be difficult for you). Closely follow the instructions contained within these next sections, and it won't be long until your family completely writes you off. Soon you'll find yourself all alone, with nowhere to sleep, soaked in urine, eating peanuts out of a dirty casino ashtray...with a HUGE smile on your face.

A Quick Exercise to Skyrocket Your Family Destroying Power

You don't have to wait until you're done reading this book to "burn your bridges" with your family, **you can start right now!** Grab your cell phone (since you haven't paid the bill EVER, it might not work), or "ask" your neighbor (break into their trailer) if you can borrow theirs. Then, text message five family members, and request to borrow $5,000 in *"unmarked and non-consecutive $20 bills."* Clearly state in your text message that this money will **only** be used to pay off your sizeable gambling, payday loan, and prostitution debts. Then, just sit back and wait. You should begin to receive concerned texts from your family asking about your debt situation, especially the cash you owe to hookers. Tell them you're *"in a bad place"* personally, and need their money to *"turn things around"* for the better (NOTE: by "better," we mean "worse"). You'll most likely collect MUCH less than $5000 from each family member, but thank them and say, *"every little bit helps."* You should also encourage them to take out loans, or sell their personal items to help raise more money for you. After you've drained as much money from your family as possible, take ALL the cash you collected, and buy as much booze and hard drugs as possible. Invite multiple hookers to your home (that you never intend to pay) as well as a few of your recently paroled prison pals, and have a "$5000 sex, booze and drugs party." Be sure to document the event with high definition pictures that you can later send to your family in a thank you card. Add a hand-written note (in your own blood) that makes sure they know that their cash was put to good use paying for your addictions, and that you now owe even more money to even **more** prostitutes. This will probably end most, if not all, of your positive interactions with your family for some time (and it'll be fun!).

The Stepfamily Agenda

Sex, and then marriage. Marriage, and then sex with other people. It's the age-old tale of two people falling in love, starting a family, slowly growing to hate and resent each other, fucking MANY of each other's GOOD friends, getting arrested several times for domestic disturbances, going to rehab (multiple times), and eventually splitting up (oh, how sweet those marriages were....). Sadly (gladly), things didn't work out this time, but people who get divorced deserve to be happy again. Inevitably, they'll start to date, meet someone special, and eventually decide to give marriage another "try." However, this time they might not be starting from scratch. If both parents are carrying some serious **baggage** from their long list of FAILED relationships in form of shit head, privileged, whiny, douche bag, **offspring**; you're going to have a new family! Kids are a package deal. So, out of a need for lazy middle-aged sex, free child labor, and possibly becoming the recipient of child support payments for kids that **aren't** yours, the step-family is born!

The combining of two horribly broken homes to create an even more dysfunctional and destitute "hell hole" of a family is the perfect setting for a miserable failure to thrive in. Nothing will skyrocket you to the darkest roads of DEEP clinical depression, excessive drinking, gambling, and self-inflicted torture wounds faster than having a terrible step-family. There are only three types of stepfamilies:

1. The Young Stepfamily - The kids are all under ten years of age, and accept their new family.
2. The Old Stepfamily - The kids are all over ten years of age, and hate everything... ESPECIALLY **you**.
3. The Adult Stepfamily - You grew up in a step-family, and you, and all of your step-siblings are now adults.

The Young Stepfamily

Since there is no way you have custody of your own kids, being a stepparent might be your only shot at experiencing the many benefits of child rearing (free labor, an easy outlet for your anger, etc.). **If you were so fortunate enough to have kids yourself, by now they should REALLY hate you and you now have the opportunity to screw up someone else's children**. As a stepparent, it's important early on to lay the proper groundwork for developing certain attitudes and behaviors with your *"rotten and ungrateful"* step kids. Start by educating them on how to do the things in life that really matter; like opening a beer bottle with their armpit, how to properly detect fake angel dust, the art of shoplifting, tipping a hooker, building home tattoo machines, and how to pick pocket at Christmas charity events. This is valuable knowledge that any child in your life will need to know for basic survival purposes.

It's also important to teach your step kids the value of hard work. This will make them strong, experienced, and finally give you the forced labor camp you always wanted. Yes, some of the work they do should benefit your home, but it's also important to perform odd jobs for cash throughout the community. Of course, you're a miserable failure (or well on your way), and won't be sharing any of the profit with them (you're basically pimping out your stepchildren). Also, be sure to call them all, *"Cinderella"* as they work, and be quick to punish any break-taking (excluding smoke breaks of course). Here is a list of high-demand cash jobs that should be suitable for your stepchildren under ten years of age:

1.) Lawn Mowing - Children off all ages, but especially those under six, love the thrill of driving a dangerous riding lawnmower. It teaches them future drunk driving skills, and is much safer than using the push mower or weed whacker (NOTE: reserve these jobs for stepchildren over age six). Make sure the little rug rats mow your lawn, and half the neighborhood (whether or not your neighbors approve or consent). This should at least provide you with the daily funds needed to feed your malt liquor and nude playing card addictions (NOTE: if you don't actually own a riding lawnmower, encourage the children to *"take their time"* and mow your lawn with the pair of scissors that you previously tried to kill yourself with back in August).

2.) The "Charity" Carwash - Your step kids love it when you let them have a squirt gun fight, or play with water balloons (it's the only bath and/or drink they'll probably get during that day). Turn this fun into profit! Walking from house to house looking for dirty automobiles isn't nearly as effective as faking a charity carwash. Take your step kids to a busy intersection, and have them hold a cardboard homemade carwash sign. People are suckers when it comes to helping sick kids. Simply write on the signs, "Sick Kid Carwash" and watch the customers **ROLLLLLLLLL** in. Be sure to tell your step kids that talking to customers isn't allowed, and be sure to invoke "Protocol Four." Protocol Four basically states that upon your command, your step kids should fake rare and/or fictitious life-threatening diseases in order to get cash from strangers. They just simply act weak, sick, and pathetic (NOTE: they might be this way already thanks to the chemicals leaking through the vents of your downstairs bathroom meth lab) and watch the cold, hard cash flow directly into your pocket.

3.) **Maid Service** - We must preface this section by stating that you should **ONLY have a clean domicile if someone else cleans it for you**. Miserable failures don't do anything to improve their life, especially when it involves work of any kind. As any good stepparent should, you started teaching your new step kids to scrub toilets and wax floors the same day you married their biological parent (you were never going to pay the cleaning fee at the reception hall, and any step-child of yours should DEFINITELY be learning how to clean up vomit). Since your step kids moved in, your tub has never been cleaner (bleach **DOES** in fact work for blood), your carpets are actually white (except for the cigarette burns), and the source of the bad smell has FINALLY been located (playing "hide the poop" when you're drunk DOES have its drawbacks). Your step kids will certainly know how to make a house sparkle, and since you're going to need some extra cash for buying that orange and vintage pontoon boat you saw for sale online, putting them to work for money just makes sense (FYI: your new "boat" is just going to sit in the driveway rusting while slowly dragging down all home values in the entire neighborhood). Have your step kids make up some maid service flyers with crayons and markers. Once again, invoke "Protocol Four" and go hand out the flyers in front of local businesses (supermarkets, fast food restaurants, adult book stores, etc.).

IT'S IMPORTANT TO NOTE that prior to visiting any new customer's home, you are encouraged to have a long and stern talk with

your step kids about stealing. It is extremely important that they learn to target, and ONLY take items with a high resale value (TVs, stereos, oak furniture, exotic pets, etc.). For the miserable failure, the goal as the parent of a young step-family is not to damage, injure, or even upset your stepchildren. Yes, the dangerous and borderline illegal situations you put them in are not typical "good parent" behaviors, but you're only trying to prepare them for the shitty life that surely lies in front of them. Young stepchildren, because of their age and lack of experience, may even look up to you as a role model (try not to die laughing). They may even start to call you *"dad"* or *"mom."* This kind of behavior/thinking will only lead them to immense disappointment, and make the eventual breakup you have with their biological parent even more difficult and hard to swallow. So, make a habit of providing continuous verbal reminders to your young stepchildren that you are not their real parent. At random times, (wake them up in the middle of the night, etc.) sit down with your young step kids, hold their hand, look them straight in the eye, and say sternly, *"you are not my real kid, you little bastard."* You should also use this same verbiage anytime they need help with something, or ask for food. Again, these are young step kids who look up to you, and your goal as a miserable failure is never to intentionally hurt them. Reminding your step kids (HOURLY) that they did not come from your infested loins should give them hope for the future. The fact that they don't share your mutated, trashy, infected, trailer park DNA should be a HUGE positive aspect of their lives. Unfortunately, since they do share DNA with the same biological parent that made the moronic, drug-fueled, potentially mentally ill choice to marry you, they're probably screwed anyway.

The Old Stepfamily

Being a parent in an old step-family is highly recommended for anyone hoping to become a true miserable failure. The old step-family consists of kids over the age of ten. These are rebellious little bastards are old enough to see through all of your lies, and report your awful psychological abuse to their real parent. The raunchy sex and free rent you get from their biological parent may be great, but these little shits will make you question if it's worth all the trouble (HINT: it's not). The younger stepchildren might have looked up to you, willingly provided free child slave labor, and accepted you as a new parent. Older stepchildren , especially teenagers, will immediately resent you, never "volunteer" for your Vietnamese-style forced labor sweat shop "camp", and will repeatedly tell you that you're not their real parent. No matter how "nice" you are, teenage step kids will attempt to steal your poorly hidden stash of hard drugs, sell your vintage porn collection and "rat you out" for having an affair with the neighbor (YOUR ALIBI: you're just "friends" who wrestle naked). Above all else, the old step kid will seek to get you "removed" from their biological parent's life while also making your life a complete hell in the process (too late for that). These ungrateful little fuck faces deserve all the shit you can give them, so let them have it!

You need to make sure that YOU show them who is boss. While your step kids are sleeping, spray-paint all their hair bright red (paint is easier to apply than dye, and can easily be done while they're in bed). This will instantly make them the proverbial and dreaded, "redheaded stepchildren" and set the tone perfectly for everything to come their way. Since your teenage step kids will love to remind you that you're not their real parent, you should **require** that they call you *"Mommy"* or *"Daddy"* when they address you. This will really piss them off, especially when you make them do it in front of their friends. Whenever they refuse to follow your directions, and start to say disrespectful things like, *"my real parent would never make me shoplift liquor,"* remind them that their real mom or dad is "out of the picture," and that **YOU** are the "loser" that is in charge now. Sternly tell them the honest truth, that their "real parent" would still be married to their other parent if they knew how to please them in bed. Be sure to make this point very apparent by having your significant other loudly insult their ex during sex. Leave the bedroom door WIDE open, and make sure they speak loud enough for all your step kids to hear easily (NOTE: this is just one of the many reasons they'll be in therapy later in life). For male miserable failures, have your lover loudly exclaim something similar to, *"their dad's little dick never made me squeal like yours!"* For the female miserable failures, make your lover shout out loud during sex, *"my ex has a rotten crotch, and you taste like a rainbow!"* This will simultaneously gross your step kids out, make them hate you even more and also allow them time to start plotting how they intend on "injuring" you (score, score and **SCORE**).

Making Your Older Step Kids Feel Unwelcomed

Chances are, when you married their parent, you moved in with them (the trailer you were squatting in illegally just wasn't working out). Just because your step kids lived in the household first doesn't mean they should get any "special privileges" (access to food, pillows, running water, etc.), or feel like they have "dibs" on any of their personal items, or current living spaces (NOTE: you may soon need one of their bedrooms for your new "Anger Release Area" or your "Rage Room"). **All miserable failures can benefit from having an easily accessible "Anger Release Area" (A.R.A.) in their home.** The A.R.A. is a space where the miserable failure goes to safely "release" the frustration, anger, rage and lividness that inevitably builds from living the shittiest life possible (if your favorite crack dealer overdosed you'd be sad too... R.I.P. Carlos). For the miserable failure, "anger release" mainly includes loud cursing, throwing furniture, and the breaking of empty liquor bottles against the wall. Feel free to use various baseball bats, crowbars, metal pipes, hammers, shovels, sledgehammers, and even your fists in the A.R.A.

Make it very clear to your older step kids that they're NOT a welcomed addition to YOUR new family. The best way of doing this is by having obvious double standards. Begin by planning "family" photo shoots on the weekends your step kids are in the custody of their other REAL parent. Display these new family pictures, **that don't include them,** throughout your home (also consider gluing gigantic posters of said photos above your teenage step kid's beds). If, despite your best planning, it's unavoidable to have your teenage step kids present for a "family" photo shoot, simply have them stand in the back, or off to the side (they'll be easier to crop out later). Have your red spray paint on hand, and give their hair a good "touch up" before the pictures are taken, just in case cropping doesn't work. When guests (your drug dealer, parole officer, bookie, etc.) visit your home, proudly point out the family photos on the wall, and refer to your teenage step kids as the *"mistakes"* your spouse made before they met you. Do this in front of your step kids, as well as your spouse. You should also use the term *"mistakes"* when introducing your older step kids to people in public. For example, *"my name is Bob, this is my wife Rita, and her two red-headed mistakes"* is a classic phrase to use. If you're not comfortable using a "non-PC" term like *"mistakes,"* simply substitute it with *"fuck-tards," "shit kickers,"* or *"the reasons she tried to sue the condom company."*

The Old Stepfamily Vacation

The double standards directed toward your asshole step kids should also be extremely apparent when it comes to spending money, especially on vacations. Your well-meaning spouse may suggest planning a fun trip for the entire family to somewhere exotic. Yeah right! You're not going to be renting extra hotel rooms, or buying any plane tickets for those little shits. There's just not enough cash to bring them along, AND still afford to pay for your daily psychic readings, scratch off lottery tickets, and monstrous drug habits. So, in order to not piss off your spouse (REMEMBER: you still need access to their credit cards and vehicle), you'll need to plan something that involves the entire family, while also not ignoring your daily desire for drinking, buying fireworks, and gambling on sporting events. Additionally, since your step kids have a history of royally pissing you off, wherever you go on vacation should be semi-secluded (so no one will stop you from verbally berating them), and be prostitute-friendly (hookers fear large crowds, and no one expects you to only have sex with your spouse on vacation). **The perfect solution for everyone is camping!**

For a miserable failure, camping brings several "special benefits" that going to a "normal" vacation destination does not. As mentioned previously, choosing to camp allows you to visit remote locations where your terrible behavior isn't frowned upon. Most local campgrounds are heavily populated with judgmental jerks that won't tolerate your open drug use, unwillingness to wear pants on vacation, and affinity for taking "public" showers. You must locate an isolated area, away from prying eyes, where your hooker pals are free to graze, and (just like at home) you're safe to use the "toilet" wherever you'd like (mother nature and your step kids can handle the cleanup). Simply drive with your spouse, and "fuck head" step kids, to any secluded wooded area. Park your vehicle, grab your supplies (drugs, lubricant, cigarettes, homemade tattoo gun, etc.), and just start walking into the wilderness. If everyone is able to survive the grueling 25-mile hike, multiple wolf attacks, and refrain from eating the poison berries, you'll eventually find the perfect remote campsite to spend your "relaxing vacation" (and a good place for your stepchildren to hide your dead, lifeless body).

Any camping trip with your step kids should take place during the fiery hot days of late July, or early August. There are few things in life that suck worse than camping in warm weather. You can expect the sleepless nights, due to continuous sweating, to put everyone in a foul mood. Plus, you'll get the added bonus of poison ivy being in full bloom. Being overheated AND itchy, is a recipe for a MASSIVE step family vacation failure (and foul play). However, this doesn't mean you should suffer through it with everyone else. Prior to going camping, use your spouse's credit card to purchase a large tent, comfy king-sized air mattress, a mosquito net, and a solar powered air conditioner. These items will make your time in the woods much more comfortable, and will also give you something to lord over your step kids . If they want to get into the tent with you, simply tell them, *"finish making the Jell-O shots, rolling my joints, and then MAYBE you can spend two minutes in the tent.*" In reality, you're never going to let them in (to your tent, or your heart). Just drink your homemade tequila, and stare blankly at them through the mesh windows of your climate-controlled tent. Whenever a step-child stupidly gets within whispering (or grabbing) distance of the tent, verbally remind them that you, "*only put up with their shit*" in order to bang their real parent. Tell them you're "*starting to get bored with the whole thing,*" and that their "*time is coming*" soon. Do this with the intent of adding a "fear of no return" vibe to your step family vacation. Remember, this is all being done out of a sincere desire to prepare them for the shitty life ahead, AND because those little bastards deserve it (you basically want to personally camp comfortably while they suffer because it is going to bring you one step closer to them standing over you when you passed out ready with a baseball bat to "tend to you" with). Maybe after spending a sleepless weekend, swatting disease-carrying mosquitos, avoiding gang rape by a pack of grizzly bears, and drinking their own urine to survive, your step kids will finally realize you (and life) are not fucking around.

Since you purposely only brought enough food for the "adults," your step kids are really going to have to sharpen their survival skills if they want to eat. Begin by sending them into the deep woods on a "special mission" to find food. Make it clear that you're not going to feed them, and that this lack of support is actually for their own good. Explain that their "participation" in this "survival exercise" is essential to prepare them for the homelessness they don't know is waiting at home (you've secretly been spending the rent money on cocaine, and are currently being evicted). **DO NOT GIVE YOUR STEPKIDS WEAPONS**, and instruct your older stepchildren to hunt for food. If you do provide them with weapons, they will only end up using them on you (it took several step-families and multiple stab wounds to figure this one out). Instead, encourage your stepchildren to dig a series of large pits that will serve as animal traps. Explain that all they need to do is lure a wild animal near the pit, and then push it in. This "pit building" method will obviously NEVER work, but it will keep them occupied while you grill the juicy steaks and fresh lobsters you bought with their child support money. Any leftovers should be buried or burned, and under no circumstances be shared with your them. Eventually your step kids will tire of their pit building adventure, and return hungry, dehydrated and sunburned to your campsite. They will beg for food, and something to drink. JUST SAY NO! You're not doing them any favors by making THEIR life easy. It's your mission to prepare them for the shit storm waiting in their future (especially since you'll be mostly to blame for it). Just ignore their cries while you hangout in your air-conditioned tent, sipping red wine (your home-made prison wine), and having purposely-loud sex with their real parent.

If, thanks to your terrible case of gout, you were unable to travel to a remote campsite, hungry step kids can be quite useful. When they begin to complain about their hunger pains, just send them to other campsites on a food scavenger hunt (A.K.A. stealing other campers' grub). Tell your step kids that this is their only chance to eat today, and that you'll even let them sleep in the air-conditioned tent if they bring back any cash or jewelry (NOTE: no matter what they steal for you, they're still sleeping outside). If they are detected while on their food scavenger hunt, act surprised and encourage the victim to call the police. With any luck, they'll be hauled off to juvenile hall for the weekend, and you'll finally get the rest you deserve (FYI: the only thing you truly deserve is chlamydia).

Celebrating Your "Bastard" Step Kids

Once a year, on their birthdays, your teenage stepchildren may get the psychotic and delusional idea that you're actually going to give them attention and/or affection (LOL). Your alcohol consumption, and paint huffing may have given you multiple strokes, but your memory is just fine. These little devils give you shit all year round, and just because it's their "special day," you're not going to forget that. **Do NOT buy them a**

real present. They're most likely expecting you to show up to their party empty handed, so screw with their little demented brains, and bring a huge box wrapped in red wrapping paper (to match their hair). Hand it to them with a smile, and say something like, *"I know we have our problems, but please consider this a new start for us. I love you."* Although it will be extremely challenging, try to say it with a straight face. Laughing loudly, or calling them derogatory names will give your ruse away very quickly. If your step kids don't immediately have a seizure due to the shock of you bringing them a gift, and saying *"I love you,"* they will surely go into convulsions once they open the big red box.

Seven days prior to their birthday, you should start working on their "big gift." Begin by going through their room, and removing any items associated with your spouse's ex (A.K.A. their other real parent). Pictures, cards, and souvenirs from memorable family events with their other parent should all be collected. Place these priceless keepsakes into a fancy plastic shopping bag, and then use that bag as a portable toilet for the next week and a half. When the big birthday rolls around, just drop it into the biggest box you can find, wrap it up, and wait for the fun to begin. If they ask you why you shit all over their memories (literally), respond by saying, *"because your real dad/mom is a piece of shit."* **Your teenage step kids will get very upset, and may attempt to murder you AGAIN (eleventh time's the charm). This is to be expected, and should be taken as a sign of your success.** As an extra slap in the proverbial face, bake them a birthday cake with one of your own original flavors: "Toothpaste Paradise," "Dumpster Delight," or "Burnt Hair Bliss." These great cake recipes are all available in the "Miserable Failure's Cookbook" (available in the nearest heroin den wherever you live), and will really get everyone at your next dinner party vomiting.

Teenage Stepfamily Edict

When interacting with your teenage stepchildren, there are certain behaviors, attitudes, and actions, which you MUST observe in order to be **the best worst stepparent ever.** The ultimate goal is to make your teenage step kids NOT want to live with you anymore. For starters, you should NEVER close the bathroom door when using the toilet. Your step kids will really hate this, especially when you do it around their friends (shitting with the door wide open = weekly therapy appointments for your step kids). Thanks to your diet of mainly frozen pizzas, dog food, and pure grain alcohol, your bowel movements will need no announcing. Your fecal odor should be easily detectable from up to a quarter mile away, and will quickly fill your house with a semi-toxic gas that isn't safe for pets, or small children (HISTORY NOTE: your grotesque bowel movements have been listed as a Class A carcinogen with the federal government). While having a bowel movement, make loud descriptive comments about the size, shape, color and amount of effort required to produce said bowel movement. For example, grunt or moan loudly, before saying, *"kids, come check this out before I start trying to flush it!"* Take these massive, loud, open door shits when your teenage stepchildren have friends over. They'll hate you for it, and may even attempt to harm you again (mission accomplished "Stepparent of the Year"). With any luck, your semi-public shitting will make them chose to go live with their other parent, and finally give you the time and space you need to drain your spouse financially and emotionally (#RelationshipGoals).

If one of your step kids goes on a first date with a new love interest, make it mandatory that they bring the person by the house to meet **you** first. This is your opportunity to answer the door wearing only dirty and stained underwear, nipple tassels and a trucker hat. DEMAND that their date immediately states an intention for marriage, and pledge that their parents give you "thirty chickens and ten acres of farmland" as a dowry payment for your blessing. DO NOT allow the date to take place until you've got everything agreed upon in writing (in your own blood). Once, you have a written agreement, encourage your teenage step kid's new love interest to "try out the goods" on their date, and make it clear that you have zero expectations about what time they should return

(NEVER would be okay with you). In fact, toss them a carton of cigarettes and a six pack of beer you stole from the liquor store earlier in the day and encourage them to *"go get into trouble."*

If you are forced by your spouse to show up for a parent-teacher conference, immediately start drinking as soon as you find out that your attendance is required (NOTE: this should not change your current 24/7/365 schedule). It doesn't matter if it's the night before, or the week before, just start drinking immediately, and don't stop until the conference. This will ensure that you arrive completely HAMMERED, and thus fully ready to try to have sex with a teacher again (yes.... the janitor, bus drivers and cafeteria staff all **still** count). Just like when you were in school, show up early to huff paint and super glue in the parking lot before the meeting. Not only will this send you on a fun trip down memory lane, but it will help you further relax your bowels for shitting purposes later on.

The Adult Stepfamily

If you have decided to leave your normal life to pursue the "miserable failure life," then this section might be tricky for you to comprehend. If you grew up with a regular and non-divorced family, then this section is just for pure entertainment purposes. However, if you grew up in a broken home (#HappyDaysAreHereAgain), then you need to take note on how to properly behave with your current adult stepfamily. Now, if you have always been a piece of shit, chances are that you had miserable failures as parents. Since the rotten apple never falls far from the shit tree, if you were born a miserable failure, you probably have fully grown stepsiblings yourself. Your dad really loved your mom, but he really, **REALLY** loved truck stop bathroom hookers ("Gloria" from mile marker 5 on interstate 55 was his favorite). Your mom always spent too much money, especially when she hired that hit man to try to kill your father. Your parent's marriage ended quickly, only for them to attempt lifelong matrimony a second, third, and even fourth time. Each new "blessed union" brought with it, a more deranged step family situation (and more STDs). You somehow survived being a child of multiple broken homes, and turned out a miserable failure. Now, as an adult, you must learn to navigate the treacherous world of having grown stepsiblings, and aging stepparents.

Your biggest challenge will be "managing your relationships" with attractive stepsiblings. Don't blame yourself (or the massive pile of cocaine you did forty-five minutes ago) for this odd attraction, its only genetics at play. Your biological parent was attracted to their biological parent, and now you're biologically attracted to them. When you were younger, your attraction to your stepsibling was harmless, and even considered "cute" by both your parents. You'd do innocent stuff like write them love notes, kiss them on the cheek, and hide in the shower while they use the toilet. Now that you're both adults, your sexual attraction to your stepsibling isn't cute anymore; it's FUCKING AWESOME (by miserable failure standards). However, despite the fact that you don't share DNA (it's NOT a perfect world), having a relationship with your smoking hot stepsibling will never be accepted by society (no matter how far south you move). That does NOT mean you shouldn't attempt to sleep with them. Society's negative judgment of stepsibling sex only means that you should 100%, absolutely, without a doubt, DO IT!

Hooking up with your stepsibling means two important things. **You'll finally win the prize you've been drooling over since you were a kid, and sleeping with a family member technically makes you an even bigger failure.** If you're unlucky (you are), your entire family may completely disown you, and you'll essentially be eliminating a potentially troublesome barrier on your road to failing miserably. Initially, you may get some resistance from your attractive stepsibling. They may even say things like, *"you're a fucking weirdo," "start stealing my underwear again, and I'll call the police,"* and *"you're not invited to Christmas anymore."* Ignore these comments, as they are just a sign of their stubbornness or "shyness."

Take this opportunity to educate your sexy adult stepsibling on the value of winning at losing. Describe your own personal pursuit of PURE failure, and the freedom you've found in becoming miserable. Persuade them to join you on your "journey to hell," so that they too can become a miserable failure (and buy you as many drugs as possible). Remember, they spent part of their childhood with you, and are probably pretty screwed up as well. The idea of finally being good at something (even its sucking at life) should be very appealing to them, just like it was to you. In fact, there is no better way for your stepsibling to begin the process of becoming a miserable failure (like you) than by banging a family member. Be sure to fully capitalize on miserable failure-making power of this "special event" by sharing your new love affair with EVERYONE in the family. Post after sex selfies on social media, and tag BOTH of your parents in the pictures online. Come to family events holding hands and fondle each other under the table during Sunday feast (be sure to make it obvious). During holidays, sit near each other at the table during dinner and lick each other's tongues in front of your disgusted and completely grossed-out family. There's nothing to be ashamed about, you're both miserable failures now, and you just might start a new trend at your next stepfamily reunion!

Becoming A Beneficiary

If you were a teenage step kid, you probably hated your stepparent, and they more than likely definitely despised you. There was the time you "accidentally" ("purposely") wrecked their brand-new car when you entered it into the demolition derby at the state fair. It was quite the scene when they busted you behind the garage smoking meth with your shop teacher (again). No amount of niceness will ever negate the fact that you would urinate in their coffee mug each morning (it's the best part of waking up). You'll never forget the loving names they called you (*"douche bag"*, *"abortion poster child"*, etc.), and they'll always remember the time you tried to kill them (you would have succeeded if it wasn't for those pesky kids and their dog). No matter the reasons you two can't stand each other, it's time to let bygones be bygones. You're both adults now, and the past is behind you. Remember, your stepparent is getting old, and could die any day now (fingers crossed for inheritance purposes ONLY). When that "unfortunate" (LOL) time comes, you want to be sure you're part of the will, and have been listed as one of the life insurance beneficiaries. Getting free money, and property is one of the major staples of living life as a miserable failure. Working, or "earning your own way," does not leave enough time for drinking, drug abuse, and daily-unprotected sex with multiple partners.

How, after years of infighting, do you regain the affection, and trust of your aging stepparent? Just start being nice to them. Yes, it's that simple. You should obviously wait until your stepparent is nearing death. Your ability to put on this "loving and caring" charade will only last so long. A safe amount of time to become "lovingly involved" is within six months of your aging step-parent's "life time expectancy date" or immediately after a terminal diagnosis. You may also even be able to skyrocket their death rate by performing unexpected acts of affection. The shock of you actually doing something nice for them could potentially send them into cardiac arrest, and at the very least, put you in their good graces. Start out simple by calling your stepparent *"mom"* or *"dad."* Hearing this instead of the normal *"cock-sucker ass face"* or *"dick-head shit bag"* may actually stop their heart from shock completely. Do something completely "out of the norm" for you and show up to their birthday party (completely sober and without a prostitute). Send them a nice gift on Mother's or Father's Day that was NOT purchased with the credit card you stole from their wallet (you really needed a video gaming system). In other words, just stop being a dick for a short period of time (use the cash and the property you're going to inherit as motivation).

No matter how much you're able to convince your aging stepparent you've changed, and now love them, they're never going to add you to their will, or life insurance policy. It's just NOT going to happen. So, the reason for your new kind and caring behavior is not to change your step-parent's heart. Instead, your hope is to gain some new favors with them to the point where you can once again be a welcomed AND **trusted** guest in their home (you've been banned since the "that's not my dildo" incident a few years ago). With a little time, persistence, and alcohol (just add it to their coffee) you can gain access to their will, living trust, and their life insurance policies. When you locate said documents, secretly add your name to the list of beneficiaries/inheritors (write legibly and **DON'T use red crayon, or green magic marker this time**), and be sure to "will" yourself the following items:

- Any pornography collections (magazines, movies, selfies, etc.).
- All weapons including knifes and firearms (just in case the zombie apocalypse comes sooner than your psychic predicted).
- Leather Bondage Material (to ensure the "family ball gag" gets passed on from generation to generation).

Just try to act surprised at the reading of the will, as well as when your life insurance check arrives. Other members of your family may protest your inheritance, and try to legally derail your "rightful" claim to said monies. Fuck them! They didn't have to put up with the shit you did, and they don't understand what it's like being a miserable failure (and trying to maintain a drug habit while unemployed). In a way, these "surprise" inheritances represent your final victory over your aging stepparent, after a lifetime of fighting. They may have defeated you in many battles, but you won the war. They're dead. You only wish you were. The only GOOD drawback to you committing forgery is the fact that you are probably going to get caught and spend several years in a federal prison.

Family Secrets, Creepy Uncles, and Attraction to Cousins

All real families share several common denominators (NOTE: not your fantasies about inbreeding). Most families have DEEP and DARK secrets. It's YOUR job to share those secrets! Most families have a safe or a vault where they keep their valuables. It's **your job** to post the combination on social media along with the times that your parents are conveniently away from their house! In this section, we are going to cover your creepy uncles, disclosing family secrets and why you should try to bang your cousins.

If you don't have any uncles that fit the categories below, we encourage you to create and invent them (just like you did with your imaginary friends). Now, most miserable failures have that one, proverbial "creepy uncle" and you should ENCOURAGE them to molest you, so you are able to use the infamous, "molestation excuse" (even though you begged for it). If you have a cousin you've always wanted to bang (first cousins are the best), make sure you publicly announce it on social media. You should essentially strive to have sex with ALL of your first cousins as often as humanly possible. Accomplishing these important tasks and feats should completely alienate your family (fingers crossed), and in turn, remove a layer of crucial support that would only stand as a barrier to you failing miserably. The less people in your corner, the better! You are a sad and lone wolf and you should fly solo in life.

One of the ways in which you can royally piss off your family is to air all of your family's secrets on social media. Airing all your family's secrets on social media is easy. If you don't have any disturbing family issues to share with the world, just make something up. Again, the easy play is to STICK WITH THE MOLESTATION. Everyone is too afraid to ask questions, and eventually they'll call you a hero for coming forward. We suggest doing a "tell-all" video to accomplish this confession. Although a written post can be quite damaging, a video allows you to hold up a doll, and point to where you were "touched." You should of course blame this on your fictitious and fabricated "creepy uncle." Creating completely made up characters in your life is something that miserable failures do on a regular basis. Before you create and invent a fictitious uncle, make sure you really get the description right. **Your creepy uncle you invent and fabricate should have a thin mustache, abnormally pink lips, an obsession with people's hands, and fondness for "wrestling down in the basement."** In short, you need to make him an easily believable molester (more on this later).

Your Real & Fake Uncles

When attempting to maximize the miserable failure-making ability of a creepy uncle you invented, it's important to first understand which type of creep you can invent. Most creepy uncles fall into one of three categories:

1. **The Molester** - This version of a creepy uncle is, without a doubt, the most valuable to a miserable failure. Lying about being molested by a fictitious family member allows you to take on a lifelong "victim mentality role" with your entire family. You can now blame ALL your terrible behaviors on the "abuse" you suffered, and the fact that no one in your family did anything about it (NOTE: your family will begin to suspect you're completely full of shit when they realize no one has ever heard of "Uncle Ronny").
2. **The Drunk** - This type of creepy uncle serves as the perfect role model for a miserable failure! Drunk uncles have been getting shit faced for over 3000 years, and have a lot of alcoholic wisdom to share. Study their habits, and recognize areas in your own personal pursuit of alcoholism that need improvement. If you don't have an alcoholic uncle in your family, just remember to create one (like you do your imaginary friends).
3. **The Unemployable Couch Uncle** - He's been too prison (a

few times), and thanks to his tendency toward violent and physical "conflict resolution," he's definitely going back again pretty soon. With an arrest record going back three decades; this creepy uncle has no hope of ever being hired by any employer. To make money, he owns and operates his very own mobile meth lab. Yesterday, he punched a small child, and stole their bicycle, just because he could. There's a lot you can learn from this guy (and there's a good chance he may stab you), so pay close attention to him. Again, if you don't have the unemployed and violent creepy uncle who stays on families couches for several months on end, just create him and make him up.

Once you've invented these fraudulent uncles or discovered (you actually have these uncles), you need to establish which type of creepy uncle you're dealing with for each scenario you get yourself in to. As stated before, the molester uncle can be used as a "valid" excuse for why you're such a fuck up. He touched your "no-no" parts when you were twenty-five, and now you can't help but steal, do drugs, and bang prostitutes because of it. All your past, and future misgivings will be forgiven, allowing you to perform your present misgivings without the fear of retribution. Normally, your family's support would be a barrier to you becoming a more miserable failure. However, the new "family secret" that you, your drunk creepy uncle, your violent meth making creepy uncle, and your sexy cousin are about to make, should completely eliminate your family support FOREVER (you'll also be documenting the orgy for social media).

Kissin' Cousins

What's blood relation mean when you're an entire family apart? For your sexy FIRST cousin; **the answer is nothing!** It's important to note that we are completely condoning hooking up with your first cousins. After you do this, take note of how quickly it can totally erode any troublesome, nagging and pesky "family support." And if anybody is going to bang your hot cousin, it should be you (and two of your uncles... at the same time...). It's also extremely likely that, just like the adult step-sibling you currently sleep with on a regular basis, your cousin is also a miserable failure, or should be well on their way to becoming one (NOTE: if your first cousin is willing to bang you voluntarily, THEY ARE A MISERABLE FAILURE TOO). In this case, you'll only need to facilitate a "meet-up" between the four of you (you, your cousin and two uncles). Rent a skanky motel room right near the interstate truck stop, purchase a large bag of cocaine, open a bottle of tequila, send a group text, and let what happens, happen. Just have your cell phone camera ready, and be prepared for an "unforgettable" evening (NOTE: your therapist and your life couch aren't going to like this).

If by some freak of nature your hot cousin is actually normal, they're probably not interested in banging family members to get back at their dad. In fact, they're most likely already not speaking to you, and are already VERY leery of your CREEPY presence. In other words, you'll need to make the first move. Start by publicly declaring your hot and steamy love fantasies about your cousin, while attempting to fondle them at various family events. For example, let's say it's your family reunion, and your first cousin Rhonda is looking smoking hot in her cut off daisy duke jean shorts (this applies to both male and female failures). It's not enough to simply stare at her, and secretly masturbate from behind the living room curtains (BOOOORRRRIIINNNGGG: been there, done that...). Let your taboo attraction be known to all by loudly announcing how nice you think her ass looks. Do this at dinner, while extremely intoxicated on stolen wine coolers (thanks Aunt Debbie), and be sure to pair it with multiple attempts to fondle your cousin under the table with your foot. Just run your leg up their leg, and say something romantic like, *"I know you're my first cousin, we're going to make love."* Chances are, you may be physically assaulted by your cousin, or at the very least be screamed at by your family for making sexual advances toward your cousin. Just consider doing simple foreplay, and continue attempting to cop a feel while boldly decreeing your intense lust for her.

Rhonda will continue to resist you, but not because you haven't bathed in five weeks, and smell like mold, onions and rotten vinegar **(FYI: your body odor could also smell like "rotten asshole", "garbage dump" and "sewer plant").** Your rejection has nothing to do with the fact that both your creepy uncles (who you've asked to "join in") are technically unemployed, and both wear court-ordered electronic ankle bracelets. Truth be told, Rhonda (who's had a "rough" life) isn't really that concerned with you four being blood related either (she's done worse...). No, you're being given the STOP sign for one simple reason; she's not that drunk, **yet!** Just bring on the booze, and be persistent. When the time is right, just use some of the cocaine to sprinkle a trail of "almost incest breadcrumbs" leading to the garage, or any other romantic, semi-private area. Again, just be ready with the cell phone camera, and a taser (your violent creepy Uncle Dan can get a little "scary" sometimes).

Exploiting Your Family

Knowing your family member's "weaknesses" and how to exploit them is a critical factor in your development as a miserable failure. Booze, drugs, fireworks, psychics, lottery tickets, action figures and pornography cost money. Since you're chronically unemployed, most of your income has to be produced via stealing, getting married, or running scans and cons. **Fortunately, you have the ability to accomplish all of these "income-earning strategies" within your own family.** However, funding your harmful habits (without working) is not the primary reason for exploiting your family's weaknesses. As a miserable failure, you should have an end goal of being unlovable, rejected, preferably incarcerated (#FreeFood), and completely alone. As mentioned previously, family support can only hinder your progress at failing miserably. So, it's time to finally piss off your family so much that they leave you alone

(FOREVER). It's time to openly exploit ALL their weaknesses. Remember, their weakness is **YOUR STRENGTH**. Here are a few common examples of family members, and the areas of their life you can most easily exploit:

- **Grandpa** - Papa can't see anymore... Guess what? He can't "see you" (wink, wink) stealing his blank checks. If any of your other family members have poor vision, or are disabled in anyway WHATSOEVER, take full advantage of their crippling ailment by taking anything from their home that you can pawn off to fund your cough syrup and muscle relaxer addictions.
- **Sister** - Big sis is severely depressed... Guess what? You'll give her something to be really depressed about when you accidentally "spill the beans" (and "the pictures") about the orgy she had on Spring Break with those fifteen Turkish foreign exchange students.
- **Brother** - Your brother works VERY hard in his prestigious career and spends lots of times away from his family. Guess what? It's time that you played "family" and tried to coerce his wife into sleeping with you (HINT: good luck, asshole, she doesn't bang nasties like you).
- **Dad** - Your father is still sad about losing his job last month... Guess what? He's really going to have something to cry about when **you DEMAND $15,000** to NOT tell mom about his extramarital affair. Now you can finally make your last down payment on that new spider neck tattoo to Jimmy "The Inker."
- **Mom** - Mommy dearest can't put down the prescription pill bottle... Guess what? She just gave you the green light to loot her pill cabinet. Not only will you be potentially saving her from the dangers of prescription drug abuse, you'll be able to trade her pills for sex (FYI: hookers love "freebie" prescrip-

tions). The tough part is going to be when she realizes you accidentally took her heart medicine too.

If you've done everything mentioned above previously to piss off, and permanently alienate your family, and they're still staying by your side, you'll need to throw a few "Hail Mary" passes. Hopefully, they'll be so mortified by the combination of the following acts we are about to highlight, that'll they'll RUN away from you, and never look back. It's important to note, that in order for the following actions to be effective, you must perform them in the sequence listed below, and not deviate from their written descriptions. Follow this plan to completion, and in only ten days it'll all be over.

- **Day 1** - Send nude selfies to your sister (gender does not matter here). She will probably text back saying something like, *"gross!"* Simply respond to her by sending another photo (spread eagle this time), and text the word, *"hungry?"*.
- **Day 2** - At a random time, push your grandfather out of his rocking chair, and mock him for being so old and feeble (of course you should film it and post it on social media). Also, when he's down on the ground, lift his wallet and tickle the shit out of him.
- **Day 3** - Throw a loud, hooker-filled, late-night party in your parent's basement **without their consent.** Stock this event full of booze, and drugs (that you paid for with your mother's "misplaced" credit card). It's okay to invite all your "hungry" buddies from Skid Row over, and let them take a self-guided tour of the house. Just make it clear that you get to cherry pick and get to steal half of whatever the pawnshop gives them.
- **Day 4** - Steal all your grandmother's cigarettes, and replace the tobacco with marijuana. This is completely safe, and may even help her if she's suffering from cataracts. Just be sure to make the switch in secret, and do it right before her next bingo night

outing. Grandma's going to have a great time, and she might even loosen up enough to FINALLY sign that extra life insurance policy you have been working on (for which you are the sole beneficiary).

- **Day 5** - While your father sits peacefully on the toilet, burst into the bathroom, and begin pelting him with eggs while slapping him uncontrollably. There is no special reason for this act. It'll just piss him off, and be a whole lot of fun for you. Repeat this same act daily, or until you run out of eggs or your hands hurt from the slaps.
- **Day 6** - Burn ALL your parent's clothes while they're at work. Do it in their backyard, and don't forget the marshmallows. When asked why you did it, just tell them you were *"hungry."* Next, demand that **they** take **you** clothes shopping.
- **Day 7** - If you're a male miserable failure, get your cousin pregnant. It's bad enough that you're sleeping with her, but at least everyone could pretend like nothing was happening. When she gets knocked up, there will be no ignoring it. If you are a female miserable failure, you can still be an active participant in the "getting your cousin pregnant" part. Just take her out to the bar, get her drunk, and encourage unprotected sex with multiple shady-looking partners. Feel free to let the gang of drunk bar strangers in the alley have their way with you too (hey, you might as well enjoy yourself as well). With any luck she'll get a baby, and you'll get the blame.
- **Day 8** - Shit in your favorite uncle's car. This one is pretty self-explanatory. Uncle Frank has ALWAYS defended you against the rest of the family's criticisms. It's HIGH time to make him look really stupid for trusting you. Ask to borrow his car, pick a seat to use as your toilet, and then just let it rip. It's best to perform this act post "all-you-can-eat" chili cook-off.
- **Day 9** - Make a new sibling. Just replace your mother's birth control pills with candy, and keep your fingers crossed. If your

mother uses the birth control patch, gets the birth control shot, or has an implanted birth control device, you'll have to take extreme actions. Even small doses of antibiotics can temporary disrupt the pregnancy prevention power of almost any birth control method. You'll only need your mom to ingest a small amount of antibiotics to create a secret pregnancy window for the next few days. Just tap into your abnormally large personal stash of penicillin (#STDs), and then (in a crushed powder form) add it their next cocktail. Wait till your mom has another sexual encounter (if she's a slut who cheats on your dad, it will be soon), and then tell her about what you did with a nice homemade construction paper card (she'll treasure it forever).

- **Day 10** - Finally, use the "Nuclear Option." You've made the last nine days hell for anyone related to you. If you've come this far, chances are there are still a few family members that, despite EVERYTHING, are still standing by you. **You need to cut these anti-miserable failure making assholes out of your life immediately.** To do this, just tell them you have Ebola or Typhoid Fever. They won't want to stand by, or even breath by you anymore.

Mooching Food and Toiletries 101

Lying? Check. **Cheating?** Check. **Stealing?** Check. As you're reading this, you're probably wondering why we highlight how to mooch, steal and confiscate food, toiletries, money, alcohol and personal possessions (NOTE: all of which we strongly encourage you to pawn off for some fast cash). This is useful information when you need to start "crashing" on a family member's couch for extremely long and arduous extended periods of time, or when you officially move back into your mother's basement (FYI: moving back into your mother's basement will be your last chance before complete and total homelessness, so make sure you FAIL miserably at that as well). Stealing "free shit" from your unsuspecting family members is just part of the game for the miserable failure. It's not enough that you blew the $2000 loan your father gave you for food and bills, on e-cigarettes and river boat gambling trips. You need to mooch ("steal") as much "free shit" (their "stuff") from your family as humanly possible.

Mooching 101

Let's face it, it's more than likely that, you're going to be poor and unemployed when you start becoming a professional squatter in your family's domicile. The only rule of mooching food and toiletries from your family is simple: **THERE ARE NO RULES**. This is key and a true miserable failure needs to know this very important aspect and rule of the game. After all, you're the one who is unemployed, so **you should get special treatment** from **your family**. **You** are the **guest**, so **you** should get "first dibs" in the bathroom in the morning to take your thirty-minute blessing of the toilet after consuming an entire pot of coffee and two cups of chia seeds. **You** are the one who is broke, so **you** should have full access to your parents checking and savings accounts (more on finding a shitty lawyer for identity theft in a later section).

Take advantage of your family as much as possible. Your dad just ordered pizza for the family? Make sure to take the **last slice**. You see a $5 bill sitting on the counter after your sister went shopping? Finders keepers, losers' weepers... Your grandparent's liquor cabinet is left open and unlocked? **Drink up**! The point here is to "make yourself at home" wherever you are living. If at your home, you generally walk around nude, be sure to do it at your parent's house. If you like to play loud, heavy metal, eardrum-bursting rage music in the morning at 4:00 a.m. after you finish your eight ball of blow, do it proudly and loudly! Suppose you are ready to go to sleep at 7:00 p.m. and you're crashing on your brother's couch. Guess what? It's time for you to **DEMAND** (screaming and throwing temper tantrums are a professional move here) that he and his family *"turn the fucking TV off"* so you can *"pass out peacefully"* from the gallon of grain alcohol you've just consumed. Be aggressive. Be rude. Be demanding and high maintenance. After all, you're secretly trying to get kicked out of the FREE and desperate living situation that you find yourself in because you need the pain and you are a miserable failure.

Food Hoarding and Vomiting

Mooching food from your family while you're staying with them **rent-free**, is also a key and essential part of becoming a miserable failure. This can be accomplished from either stealing and hoarding food, or consuming certain foods at particular times. Make your family as uncomfortable by your presence as possible, especially when dealing with the subject of "food." To begin with, **the miserable failure takes pride by forcefully taking the biggest piece of chicken first, AND before anyone else is served.** To add to this technique, we recommend looking the other family members in their eyes as you do so (laughter and finger pointing as an intimidation tactic are strongly encouraged here). The miserable failure also eats the entire bag of potato chips in the cabinet right before the food is served during the Sunday family dinner. The true miserable failure takes all of the "good food" (non-moldy food) from the refrigerator and claims it as their own personal possessions by putting sticky notes with your name on them as well as the consequences for consuming "your" food (EXAMPLE: *"eat this string cheese and you're losing a finger"*). The most opportune time for doing this is right after your family member gets home with new groceries (which you didn't pay for or help carry in) adds insult to the injury. It is also a good idea for the miserable failure to forcefully make themselves vomit up food in the bathroom right in the middle of a family dinner (make sure to make as much vomiting noises as possible during your pukefest from the bathroom during THEIR dinner). To maximize the sound, simply leave the door to the bathroom WIDE OPEN (just like you do when you go in there to smoke crack).

Toiletries

Toiletries are a little trickier subject to deal with for a miserable failure. Let us preface the fact that **we want you to avoid all general hygiene, skin care, hair grooming and personal health maintenance as you go through the transformation to becoming a miserable failure.** Having mentioned that, we still encourage you to wastefully use as many toiletries from your family as possible. A new tube of toothpaste is in the medicine cabinet? Use it all at once! Mom brings home generic toilet paper? Make sure she knows you're disappointed in her broke ass purchase by pooping on her side of the bed like a dog. We also encourage the miserable failure to use and gather up all of the dental floss in the house in order to fashion a noose when you need attention from your ungrateful family for your soon to be fake suicide attempt (BTW: more on the importance and benefits of faking a suicide in a later section).

The point here on food and toiletries is simple. When, not if, but **WHEN** you do get kicked out of your family's home for your **shenanigans** we previously mentioned, you're going to need extra food and toiletries for black market trading with other miserable failures on the streets. A good rule of thumb is that a can of baked beans and a box of band aids generally trades for around 2 cigarettes on the black-market alleys which you'll soon be living in. A case of Ramen soup can sometimes get you a small crack rock (FYI: more on using and combining drugs and alcohol in a later chapter). Be sure to load up on as much of your family's toiletries as possible when you are being escorted out of their home by the local Sheriff deputy. As you're getting kicked out of their house, make sure you grab one of your bags (a trash bag) and load up from the medicine cabinet. The more prescription pills you take, the better chance you'll have at scoring that elusive black tar heroin on the streets that you so desperately covet.

How to Steal from your Grandparents

After your parents kick you out of their basement because you "forgot" to pay them their menial requested "$50 per month rent" for the past two and a half years, chances are, your grandparents might take you in like a lost puppy. Grandma and grandpa were always there for you. Now you need to convince them to take you in (NOTE: make sure to invite yourself in with threats of self-inflicted violence if needed only as a last resort backup plan). Make sure you inform them that you'll *"help them out around the house"* (try to not laugh while saying this), *"be clean"* (LOL!), *"be quiet" and be respectful"* (in other words... LIE YOUR ASS OFF). After all, **YOU** are their legacy. Your grandparents **OWE** this to you. Demand that they take you in by brute force as a last-ditch effort if they are still apprehensive in your unusual squatting request.

Making Yourself at Home

Now that you're in (suckers...), it's time for you to take over their entire home. From occupying the "big bedroom" down the hall, to making sure you keep the thermostat at a cool sixty-two degrees 24/7/365, living with your grandparents is going to bring much joy to the miserable failure's worthless existence. **First, you need to make sure that you only wear grandpa's robes and slippers. This is also the typical look for you (an unemployed, useless, worthless, psychopath, fuckface).** Also, grandparents generally will never require you to pay them rent or contribute to the groceries in any way, shape or form. So right off the bat, the miserable failure has free room and board, but it doesn't stop there! In fact, **Grandma is now your personal slave**. That old silver BAG is going to be cooking for you and waiting on you hand and foot (even if she is in a wheelchair). From frying you up moldy and expired frozen chicken strips from the bottom of the freezer that expired thirteen years ago, to cleaning the bathroom after you had a long night of boozing with your imaginary friends, you will now be on easy street (NOTE: we recommend calling your grandma *"Toby"* and your grandfather *"Isaac"* as you verbally spout your rude and insensitive demands). Having two personal slaves is fantastic news for the miserable failure as this will give you plenty of time to treat yourself to whatever you want in their house. Let's face it, after you downed a few bottles of cough syrup mixed with gin and peyote, you'll have control of the TV remote when grandma and grandpa go to bed at 7:00 p.m. After you put them to bed, it's your time to:

- Raid the liquor cabinet for your personal consumption.
- Find Grandpa's loose change collection and "help yourself" to it.
- Load up on their pharmaceuticals from their medicine cabinet (Xanax, opioids and valium are the three big winners).
- Find their Will and do some creative "re-writing" in the beneficiary section.
- Find grandpa's nudie girl magazine collection and "act accordingly" (this includes female miserable failures).
- Loot their antique collection for future pawning purposes.
- Rent a few "adult" movies on their pay-per-view.

The Milk Cows

Since your grandparents are financially well off, you should also DEMAND to "borrow" money from them (of course, follow the "miserable failure nonpayment protocol" and never pay them back). **Besides, you are going to need some fast cash in order to fund your online gambling addictions, and to pay for the ounce of Mexican black tar heroin that you have coming in from your drug mule buddies.** The miserable failure needs to basically use their grandparent's house like a giant shopping mall. You need to make sure that you're extra nice to your grandparents because they took you in when you were performing oral sex acts on the street corner and shitting in alleys (more advice on said activities later on in the book). The key to stealing from your grandparents is to make certain that the rest of your family sees how much your grandparents are "giving" and providing for you. You need to play the role of "favorite grandchild" by making your other cousins as well as your brother and sister **jealous** as HELL. Remember, you're not just stealing from your grandparents, you're allowing them to get one more shot in at raising a child (something most grandparents want). Make it count. They are going to be **THRILLED** to have you living with them at the beginning. However, we must strongly caution that the miserable failure will typically wear out their welcome by month seventeen or eighteen as long as you stay on the course previously mentioned. Generally, by then, one or more of the grandparents will start to catch on to your shenanigans, lies and disrespect. Perhaps you'll get caught with a hooker in the billiards room (this again, applies to female miserable failures as well). Maybe they'll realize how loose change mysteriously "disappears" DIRECTLY into your robe pockets. Or perhaps grandma and grandpa's checking account is a little **lighter** this month due to your excessive requests for food, alcohol, cigarettes and action figures. Essentially, they will eventually kick your sorry ass out of their house (even these old codgers have a limit). This is why the miserable failure needs to accomplish the activities mentioned above in the seventeenth or eighteenth month. If you really want to be a miserable failure, you're going to have to steal from your grandparents.

If you've followed our ENTIRE step by step guide to destroying ALL of your entire family relationships, then congratulations, dickhead! You made it! You're finally free! No longer will you have a pesky **family** standing in **your** way of becoming a truly miserable failure. Their respect, caring, and love for you should be gone forever (#goals). Unfortunately, you won't have access to their resources anymore, but you will now have a clear path to your own personal destruction and self-loathing.

4

FRIENDSHIPS

Poor Friendships

Good friends, just like loving family members, have many temporary uses for the miserable failure. However, any prolonged involvement with individuals who have your "best interest" at heart, can only slow your drug-fueled progression toward hitting rock bottom (NOTE: "hitting rock bottom" = selling your body for crack cocaine from a group of paralyzed midgets). So, essentially, you need to take full advantage of your friends (while you have them), but be prepared to quickly force them out of your life when the time is right. Getting rid of friends will inflict and bring upon massive pain and suffering for yourself. The following sections will explain in great detail the best ways of "getting the most" from your friendships, and then how to end them, badly. With study and practice, you too can quickly become the master of:

- Ruining Pizza Night (you're only one well-directed, snot-filled sneeze rocket away from the controversial "last slice").
- How to properly use the "Cancer Excuse" on your buddies to

gain sympathy, and undeserving forgiveness for MAJOR past discretion's (EXAMPLE: *"I didn't fuck your husband... It was just my pesky 'cancer' acting up again"*).

- Attending your friend's family gathering that you were never invited to (nudity and heavy drug use are 100% acceptable and strongly encouraged at said event).
- "Borrowing" items from your friends with no intent to return them *("Say... That's a nice wallet you got there, Pete")*.
- The "BFF Spousal Management System" (the art of "slightly" going too far with your BFF's spouse, repeatedly, until you score... and/or get physically assaulted from your BFF).

If, thanks to your pungent body odor, and tendency toward public masturbation, you currently do not have any friends, it's essential that you quickly make some. It may seem counterproductive to make new friends knowing that your primary goal is to eventually lose them. However, without friends, the miserable failure has no one to mooch off of, and no one to eventually become their new arch enemy. Failing at friendship is part of your mission towards your metamorphosis as a miserable failure. So, go get social, and make some friends to totally screw over!

HELPFUL HINT: Since you lack in nearly every area that matters when making new friends (personality, humor, not smelling like shit, etc.), use your heavy drug use as a way to attract new people into your circle of buddies. Promise anyone that hangs out with you 100% free drugs, and you'll have a long line of potential new BFFs in no time.

Losing Friends

Much like sculpting a beautiful statue (or masturbating while driving), losing your friends is a form of art. Lose them too quickly, and you'll miss many wonderful opportunities for mooching, and easy identify theft. Keep them around too long, and their caring attempts to "intervene" will quickly become an annoying hindrance to your daily advancement toward failing miserably. Even having friendships which a "normal" person would consider "bad" (being friends with druggies, felons, the crazies, etc.), are not suitable long-term for a miserable failure. Yes, having MULTIPLE crack heads, or another public indecent exposer around has its advantages, but these people will eventually "steal your thunder" when you are ready to go to prison. So, even your "worst friends" will have to go away and get out of your miserable life in the end. Getting rid of this "bad" element is easier than you may think. Just stop handing out free drugs, and require everyone to wear pants. Cutting out the crack and the nudity should eliminate well over half of your friendships, instantly. It's your "normal" or "good" friends that will require more coaxing and severe manipulation (as well as psychological and financial punishment) to lose.

There are many ways for a miserable failure to effectively lose good friends. So many in fact, that this section will not be able to list them all. The information provided to you here is more than sufficient to obliterate most friendships, but do not allow the few ideas presented in this book to block your shitty creativity. If you think of an original way to ruin and destroy a friendship, just give it a try! Worst case scenario, is you're stuck with the same old *"I won't loan you anymore money to buy cocaine"* friends you had before. Best case scenario is, you eliminate another nuisance in your pursuit of personal destruction, and inevitably end up in "The Official Miserable Failure Hall of Fame" (A.K.A. The FBI'S Most Wanted List).

Banging, Stealing, and Whining Your Way To Less Friends

When it comes to losing good friends, there is no substitute for the tried and true "banging of the spouse" method. This strategy of destroying friendships is not only effective, but it's also fun and extremely dangerous! It's just like your grandfather and scout leaders always use to tell you, *"If you're going to do something stupid, you might as well have an or-*

gasm." It's important to remember that a miserable failure doesn't simply have sex with their friend's spouse, but they also record it, post the video on social media, upload the video on multiple pornography sites and tag their friend's family in the social media post. This extra effort will almost certainly ensure that you'll lose a few more friends in the process (#bonus), and get the majority of your teeth knocked out via the lead pipe from your jealous ex-friend (thus helping you achieve "the missing teeth sexy look" you're going for).

Another great way to lose a good friend is by actually mimicking them and becoming them. Identity theft, for a miserable failure, is more than just using a stolen credit card to purchase lottery tickets, malt liquor, rubber cement glue and nude playing cards. A real miserable failure fully becomes their identity theft victim both financially, AND socially. Start by stealing, and then wearing your friend's clothing (including underwear) at all times. Come to their home during a family party (wearing their stolen clothing), and attempt to assume their role in the household. Discipline your friend's children, ask to borrow money from their grandparents, and make multiple attempts to have sex with their spouse (if the spouse resists, loudly accuse them of having ANOTHER affair). By this point, your friendship should be nearly over, and your friend will most likely be pointing a weapon at you (GOODIE, GOODIE). During this highly emotional moment, take the opportunity to let your friend know about their upcoming credit card bill that's going to be "a little higher than normal" (rub and tugs are NOT free unfortunately). This will certainly destroy whatever bond remains between you, and your friend. At the very least, anticipate being physically assaulted, and eventually arrested. No matter if you survive, or end up in jail again, you should be down at least one more friend by the end of this party (nice job!).

Another super effective, but less immediate way of eliminating friendships, is through proper use of the "Whinny Bitch" method. **This method simply involves you complaining, nonstop, about EVERY-**

THING in your own life that YOU are 100% responsible for. Do this in a high-pitched voice, at an excessive volume, and be sure to cry as much as possible. The goal is to wear your friends down over time by being a constant "downer". If one of your friends proudly announces they're going to be having a baby, it's the perfect opportunity to talk about the "abuse" you suffered as a child (NOTE: Uncle Danny's hands still haunt you to this day). If one of your friends gets a big promotion at work, it's YOUR chance to remind everyone that you've been unemployed for the last eleven years (and proud of it). It's especially important to complain about issues that you yourself are the primary cause of, and are in complete control of (much like your actions you've taken to become a miserable failure). Just be sure to NEVER accept personal responsibility of any kind, and make sure everyone knows you are the victim of your own choices. This whinny, victimhood mentality wears people down, really fast. For example, a miserable failure should constantly complain about being financially broke to their friends who have multiple jobs. You being unemployed is not because you can't find work (you've been holding out over a decade for that "management" position), but because **the "broken" welfare system doesn't cover your annual vacation costs to the Grand Cayman Islands.**

You should also make complaining/crying about your "terrible" romantic relationship a normal part of every conversation. No matter the topic, ALWAYS redirect it back to your shitty relationship. Saying things like, *"I'm sorry your grandma died. Hopefully she wasn't a huge bitch like my girlfriend"* is a classic line employed by many miserable failures over the years. As often as possible, you should uncontrollably sob at high-pitched volumes because you were "betrayed" when your partner cheated, despite you openly cheating on your partner since the beginning of your relationship (do this mainly at your friends' houses during parties, birthdays, graduations or other special events). Constantly talk about how you always argue with your partner (you like to start fights when you're high or drunk, so it's basically 100% of the time), and if your friends offer advice, immediately start to argue with them. Furthermore, make a habit of complaining to your friends that you don't have enough sex with your partner because they're always at work (they have three jobs because you're a worthless asshole), and that when you do have sex with your significant other, they refuse to "please" you (if they won't pee or poop on you, someone else will).

Overall, just remember to be a "Whinny Bitch" **all the time**, and it won't be long until no one (not even the nice folks at the suicide hotline) will want to talk to you. Dedicate yourself to mastering this method, and even **you** will hate being around **you**. Before too long, most of your potentially failure-delaying friendships will simply start to fade away off in the distance (just like your positive hopes and dreams did when you decided to become a miserable failure). They'll be no words exchanged, or confrontation of any kind. They'll all just be gone one day, and you'll finally be alone to pursue the worst life possible. Great job, you little "Whiny Bitch!"

Friends You Live With

Thanks to your easy access to hallucinogens, propensity for bringing home immigrant street prostitutes who don't speak your language, and ability to produce a multitude of culinary masterpieces (you learned to cook your third time in prison), you might have actually convinced some friends to let you move in with them. Their dreams of long, drug-fueled nights, filled with hookers and chocolate soufflés, will soon be shattered. When your asshole grandparents report their credit cards stolen (again), the drugs and hookers will quickly fade away. Also, the only "cooking" you'll do will be in the meth lab you built in their basement. Unfortunately, for those that live with you, it'll be too late to change their minds. You've nested, and it's going to take the complete destruction of your friendships to get you out (as well as the local SWAT team and the national guard).

Your "buddies" will soon learn that the only thing worse than being friends with you is living with you (there is a 100% chance of you attempting to sell the furniture for drug money). For the miserable failure, losing friends you live with is the perfect opportunity to give your pursuit of personal destruction the steroid injection it needs! Losing any friend can quickly lead to loneliness (AMAZING!), social boredom (playing Russian Roulette by yourself means you ALWAYS win), and the detonation of your character (your ex-friends told everyone about the infamous "Banana Incident"). Losing the friends, you live with, not only comes with all the regular benefits of a losing a good friend, but it also has the added bonus of immediate homelessness and desperation (it's like you won the "shit lottery"). So, carefully study the information in the following sections, and then do your best to manipulate your way into a living situation with your friends. Gain their trust, be their loyal best friend, and then let the "shit show" you call being a roommate begin.

Annoying Your Way To Homelessness

As a miserable failure who is currently living with friends, it should be your goal to eventually "annoy your way out" of said living situation. Although, simply annoying your roommates may never be enough to get you totally evicted, it can certainly serve as fuel to the "let's kick this perverted bastard out of our apartment" fire. Think of being "ridiculously annoying" as the equivalent to the paper cut that eventually makes you want to amputate the entire arm. Leaving soiled underwear in the microwave (it's how you sterilize them) will greatly annoy your roommates, but won't lead to them forcefully removing you. Using your fog horn to mark the passing of every hour on the hour, will royally piss off your sleeping roommates, but won't make them drag you out the front door kicking and screaming. Using the leaf blower to "clean up" INSIDE the house, drunk and at 2:00 in the morning will make them hate you, but you might still not get kicked out! However, the combination of soiled underwear in the microwave, your love of late-night fog horn use, your refusal to NOT display your human toe collection in the living room (it's a great conversation starter), AND the fact that you stole your roommate's identity to finance another facial bat tattoo and skull branding, should get you violently tossed out on your ass in no time.

When attempting to annoy your friendly roommates, being loud and messy may seem like low hanging fruit, but there is no better method for gradually inching yourself toward eviction. Remember, your goal is to only be evicted after you've had adequate time to take advantage of your roommates' kindness (you got lots of free stuff). So, starting out with being annoyingly loud, rather than trying to fuck their significant others, is the conservative choice. Your roommates, who are most likely employed full-time, so they need to get their rest in order to make it through another long workday. You, who haven't had a job in "a while," will often not sleep for days (thanks cocaine). So, when your roommates go to bed it's time for you to get loud!

Start by taking advantage of the extra floor space provides, and invite a few (dozen) "friends" over. Just place flyers around your neighborhood advertising "FREE BOOZE AND SING-ALONG," or go to a local bar around closing time and yell, *"After hours party at my place... FREE SEX."* Imagine the look on your roommate's faces when they awake to the sound of a large crowd of completely drunk STRANGERS in their living room singing show-tunes, and having a small orgy (only oral) at 3:00 in the morning. Just blame everything on your addiction to alcohol, sex, and Broadway musicals.

While your roommates' slumber, finally try out that "screaming rage yoga" technique the therapist in prison taught you. Screaming rage yoga is identical to regular yoga, but with the lots of screaming, cursing, spitting and threatening hand gestures. It really helps you blow off steam, and your roommates will definitely support that, right? Wrong. Scream at the top of your lungs while you're in the down dog position will really scare the ever-loving shit out of your roommates as they sleep.

You should also use this "alone time" to practice your drum solo, and learn to play the electric guitar (at full volume). If your roommates get pissed, remind them you're only one hit song away from paying rent. Basically, no matter what you do, do it loudly. This includes masturbating, shitting (with the bathroom door wide open of course), chewing food with your mouth open, talking on the phone, and watching TV (motor sports and war movies are best at absurdly high volumes).

The Miserable Failure's Top Three Rules for Being Really Fucking Messy

The next crucial step in your master plan to lose the friends you live with is to be MESSY AS FUCK. This is NOT "forgetting to vacuum" messy, or leaving "soiled clothing on the floor" messy. This is nasty, moldy, rotten, stank, MESSY AS FUCK! Just follow the rules below and it'll be easy...

Rule #1 "Always Forget To Flush" - With the obvious exception of hiding illegal drugs during a surprise police raid, never, ever, flush the toilet after you use it. Since your diet mainly consists of cheap vodka, expired beef jerky, and angel dust, the "deposits" you leave in the "porcelain bank" should be quite interesting for your roommates (and their dates) to discover (everyday). If they complain, remind them to be thankful that you now use the toilet (most of the time), rather than the floor (which is more convenient and NEVER has a line). Also, we should note that you should avoid wiping altogether, OR wipe multiple times as you use three entire rolls of toilet paper in one bathroom visit.

Rule #2 "Leave Trash and Dirty Dishes EVERYWHERE" - This is more than just leaving half-full pizza boxes, empty liquor bottles, and used condoms all over the apartment (LOL! You don't use condoms). You're also going to make every dish extremely filthy (including pots and pans), and then strategically place them throughout your home for your roommates to find, once the kitchen sink is full of dirty dishes from your gourmet "Mexican fiesta" dinner last night. This is the most efficient way for a miserable failure to "do" dishes, and "take out" the trash. For instance, if one of your friendly roommates opens the hall closet, they should find their coat plus your now moldy, half-eaten bucket of fried chicken (you found it in an alley yesterday), a bloody t-shirt (don't ask), and sixty-five empty beer bottles (you drank them this morning and still haven't peed).

Rule #3 "Make EVERYTHING Your Napkin" - Paper towels, toilet paper, tissues, cloth napkins, wet wipes, etc. These items all serve their purpose, but are not as readily available and easily accessible as your shirtsleeve, a throw pillow, or the shower curtain. As a miserable failure, the world is your napkin! In addition to being amazingly convenient, this "solution" is a big money saver (again, another reason your roommates should pay you to live there). In fact, if you and your friendly roommates live in a carpeted home, you can completely eliminate the need to purchase toilet paper altogether (just channel a dog or a cat).

The Art of Not Paying

As a miserable failure, or someone hoping to achieve such a "prestigious" status, it is your sworn duty to NEVER, EVER, pay for anything (NOTE: you should however max out all of your credit cards on useless and worthless shit, but you still should not pay your credit card bills). **While you certainly won't be repaying any of your debts in the near future**, forking out real money (not the check you stole from your blind neighbor) for drugs, prostitutes, and your psychic (Cosmic Louie is "da bomb") may be unavoidable. However, not paying the friends you live with, your share of the rent, utility bills, and even the occasional pizza delivery, is an art form. Your goal is to maximize the amount of time you can take advantage of your roommate's generosity before they throw you out on the streets (just like the assholes at rehab did). The delicate dance between friend and leach can only go on for so long until the friends you live with become the ex-roommates attempting to sue you in civil court over past due rent (#HopesAndDreams).

First, and foremost, **never pay rent**. Whenever the first of the month comes around just be sure to roll out! Spend a couple days sleeping at another friend's house, or "camp out" in a greasy dumpster until everything blows over. Fortunately, since you were probably NOT part of the original lease, the landlord won't be bugging you for cash. It's your friendly roommates who will probably be on the hook for coming up with your portion of the rent. This will piss your friends off really fast, and is the quickest way to get evicted from the couch you call home. To buy more time before being tossed out on your ass, make promises to pay in full next month, but ALWAYS tie those promises to "long-shot-if" statements (this will give you an easy way out of NOT paying next month as well). For example, say something like, *"I can definitely pay rent IF I get my record contract soon for my rap songs."* Since you lack musical ability of any kind, and came up with this idea the night you woke up naked on the subway, your chances of snagging a multimillion dollar recording contract don't look too good. You can also try the infamous, *"I just bought thirty lottery tickets, IF I win I'm buying all of you a new car, AND paying rent next month."* Throwing in the part about the FREE CAR is a great way to get your friend's immediate support (you're going to need it!). In reality, instead of thirty lottery tickets you purchased ("shoplifted") buy thirty beers, and plan to drink them in the bathtub the moment your roommates leave for work (this will cut down on trips to the toilet). In the eyes of your roommates you're making a solid declaration to pay them back (it's best to get them REALLY HIGH prior to starting this conversation), but you secretly know you're NEVER giving them anything (except fleas, bedbugs and scabies from your disgusting and unkempt body).

You should also freely consume all the food in the house without ever going grocery shopping yourself, offering to contribute financially (there's not enough in your budget for food AND video poker), or ever saying thank you (they should be thanking you for all the free entertainment your presence provides). Whenever possible you should strive to consume the last of something, and always be sure to leave its remains in an easily discoverable location. For example, eat the last slice of pizza (that you didn't pay for), and leave the empty box on the living room floor (next to the overdosed hooker and new mystery stain). This simply adds insult to injury, and will only further agitate a hungry roommate. We also encourage you to write your name on all of the groceries in black magic marker. Try adding friendly messages like, "Touch and you will die motherfucker," and "I spit in this." This tactic is most effective when used on the same day your roommates go shopping for new food. When they arrive home with brand new food, help unpack the groceries, and then start writing your name on things in front of them. Furthermore, when your roommates get home with THEIR groceries, forcibly snatch them from their hands and start eating the food in the sacks like the disgusting animal that you are. Then, go into the corner, curl up and growl like a dog when they come to reclaim their newly purchased food.

If you've been following the steps listed in the previous sections, your roommates should be nearly ready to remove you from their property in the most violent way possible (#FANTASTICNEWS). In an attempt to stretch your "welcome" a few more days, promise that when you *"hit the big time,"* you'll take all your friendly roommates out to an expensive restaurant for an extravagant meal. This gesture may buy you a few more weeks of free food and rent, but eventually your time will run out. When all your promises of payback no longer have any strength, you'll need to use the "nuclear option." The nuclear option is simple... **Actually, take your friends out somewhere nice, and let them order whatever they want**. Yes, this action may appear as though it is in direct violation of the NEVER, EVER pay for anything rule. However, when the check arrives you'll be halfway home (giving you just enough time to grab all your stuff and run before your irate and psychotic roommates get back). Just encourage everyone to order dessert at the end of your meal. While you're waiting to be served, excuse yourself to the bathroom to powder your nose (do cocaine), and then exit unseen out the side door (stealing as many dinner roles as possible in the process). When the large bill arrives at the table, your roommates will be left to pay for it. This will officially be your final meal with your friends, and the end of your living arrangement.

Borrowing Personal Items

No matter if you live with your friends, or not, there is one simple rule to remember when it comes to "borrowing" personal items; their shit is your shit! This does NOT go both ways (death will come to those who touch your stuff). To fully understand the miserable failure's philosophy on personal property you must first understand their definition of "borrowing." For the miserable failure to "borrow" something actually means one, or most likely ALL of the following:

1. You are going to immediately sell, or pawn it for tattoo/poker/glue/fortune teller/drug money.
2. You are going to destroy it, or make it unusable within hours, and have no intention of ever returning it in a recognizable condition.
3. You are going to trade it for sexual favors, steal it back from the prostitute, and return it (weeks later) covered in cherry lubricant.

The miserable failure borrows anything they want, from whomever they want, whenever they want. This includes gas stations, sex shops, and Asian grocery stores (the same places you "cruise" for hotties at). However, the *"I'm just borrowing it, officer"* excuse is seldom effective for keeping you out of handcuffs. You're better off just borrowing things from friends, and selling them for usable cash (strippers don't tip themselves). Of course, you could always ask your friends to borrow some cash, but this luxury will quickly fade away when your buddies realize YOU'RE NEVER GOING TO PAY THEM BACK (you're such a fucking failure).

A good example of a miserable failure's philosophy on taking personal items is the, "can I borrow your car" situation. After your seventh DUI, your driver's license will be permanently revoked (you've technically had fourteen DUIs, but only seven as a "legally licensed" driver). Due to your lack of a license, you began to constantly ask your friends for rides. This worked well for a while, but eventually your friends probably grew tired of driving you to see your parole officer, and to buy your daily ounce of Mexican black tar heroin. They didn't want to drive you anymore, and after multiple weeks of constant begging, pleading and crying on your part, they decide to "just let you borrow" their vehicle for a few hours (#BIGmistake). Little did they know that what you meant by "borrow" was to drive their vehicle directly to the junkyard, and sell it for the current price of scrap metal (about $300). Then, loose the entire $300 later that hour by gambling at the local casino (NOTE: just tell your friend it was stolen while you were volunteering at animal shelter, even though you're legally not supposed to get within 500ft of any caged animal). If you can't sell their car for some fast car, here is a checklist of places you need to go when you "borrow" their car:

- **Stop #1 - Your crack dealer's trailer (once you smoke crack, there's never going back).**
- **Stop #2 - Your ex-partner's house (see section on "stalking" for details).**
- **Stop #3 - Your psychic (maybe this time, the psychic will see a million dollars coming for you in her crystal ball and not another horrible bout of herpes).**
- **Stop #4 - The local casino (to lose the money you just got from selling your blood plasma).**

- **Stop #5 - To the local gas station (where you can attempt another robbery using the old "finger in the pocket" gun stick up).**

Borrowing Without Asking

Borrowing without first asking for permission is sometimes referred to (by judgmental assholes) as "stealing." However, in the mind of the miserable failure, it's not possible to steal from a friend because everything they possess is rightfully yours anyway. In fact, the miserable failure should never ask to borrow an item from a friend, but rather they should forcibly take it out of their friend's possession while being extremely verbally abusive at the same time. Although getting your ass "royally kicked" has its miserable failure making benefits, if your friend is larger, or stronger than you, forcibly taking something from them may not be possible. In this case, simply break into your friend's home, and "borrow" the item(s) at 2:00 a.m. while they're sleeping. Be sure to ONLY do this after a vicious day of binge drinking, and heavy cocaine use with your new biker gang friends **(PRO TIP: Inviting a few of them to tag-along in exchange for "more blow" will almost insure your success).**

Motorcycles, and constant gang sex can be quite noisy. So, be prepared for your friend(s) to wake up, and not be pleased with who they discover in their house. They may react in anger, and do something "silly" and "uncalled for" like brandish a weapon, or call the "authorities." This will NOT go well with the bikers, and the "vibe" of the whole "break-in thing" will probably change rapidly. This is the miserable failure's queue to begin heading to the restroom, and borrow (A.K.A. "stuff in pants") as many toiletries as possible before quietly crawling out of the nearby window. Try to get out before the shooting starts, or severe beatings begin **(PRO TIP: Consider leaving your new biker friends at the bar, keep the remaining blow for later that night when you get back to your section-8 apartment, housing complex or dumpster).**

The "Infamous Chip in Pizza Party" Night

Inevitably, during 99% of any prolonged friendship (this even includes your friendships with other drug abusers, former cellmates, orgy buddies, etc.) you will be invited to a pizza party night. If, for some unknown reason, you are not invited (you ruined the last social event by literally shitting in the microwave #thanksLSD), but somehow receive word that said pizza night is taking place, it's your sworn duty as a miserable failure to crash that party as drunk, stoned, and nude as possible (just like your 8th grade graduation). Just burst through the door unannounced, proclaim to everyone *"it's party time,"* and offer to chip-in toward the cost of the pizza (you of course have no plans of ever paying, but do plan to eat the vast majority of the pizza). Your friends will most likely be so embarrassed that they "forgot" to invite you, that they'll overlook the whip cream underwear you chose to wear, and invite you in with open arms (#HUGEmistake).

If you were actually invited to the pizza party, you've been doing something wrong. Go back and review the section on being the worst friend ever, then pummel yourself in the head with a frying pan for being a damn fool. That being said, even if you are on the invite list, you should still show up heavily intoxicated, nearly nude, and without any money whatsoever. **Remember that showing up bombed in your birthday suit is the best way to start any social gathering** (especially weddings, anniversary parties, graduations, funerals, and bar mitzvahs).

When it's time to order the pizzas, you must quickly assert your complete and total dominance over the entire group. Just be the first to loudly voice your choice of toppings and crust style. Simply yell-over anyone else trying to state their opinion on the type of pizza that should be purchased, and immediately follow your yelling with a vague threat directed at their personal property. A great line often employed by miserable failures during this time is to say, *"We're not getting a cheese pizza! It's a waste of a pizza, and your car might catch fire."* Obviously, there is no actual correlation between ordering a cheese pizza, and someone lighting a kerosene-soaked rag stuffed in their gas tank, but they'll get the hint. Make it immediately clear to everyone that when it comes to pizza (and pretty much everything else), there is no democracy. **You** are the dictator, and **you** will be the only one making decisions (and probably the only one reaching orgasm in the orgy later).

To further earn your new title of "Pizza Nazi," be sure to include strange topping combination requests that most people would consider to be absolutely disgusting. Not only will this further assert your control over the group, it should mean a lot of extra pizza for you to take home later (#MoreCashForCrack). We strongly encourage you to insist on the following proven toppings and crust combinations that will make most normal people vomit:

The Miserable Failure's Perfect Pizzas

- "The Seat Cushion" - Anchovies, ketchup and onions. It looks like shit and smells like the twenty-five-year-old seat cushion your grandmother uses to pad her wheelchair.
- "The Shit In-A-Box" - Chile, corn, sausage, and rice pudding with no crust. Have this one delivered, and you'll quickly realize how it got its name.
- "The Jim Crowe" - Black Olives with alfredo sauce and no cheese. This pizza is both controversial and completely awful.
- "The Sneaky Cousin" - Jalapeno, bologna and diced apples on a stale, cracker crust. This one causes surprise-explosive diarrhea that is perfect for any pool/pizza party.
- "The Date Night" - This pizza can be made with any meat, veggie, or crust combination, as long as you include the secret

ingredient... ROOFIES! Just call Mark's Pizza Palace, and ask Leroy for "the special."
- "The Dusty Pickle" - Onions, mustard, ranch dressing and dill pickle spears, and goat cheese on deep-dish crust. If you're already suicidal, watch out for this one!
- "The Coin Flip" - Just ask for your pizza sauce to be replaced with mayonnaise, and be extremely rude to the person taking your order over the phone. You'll have about a 50/50 chance of getting mayo, OR someone's "something else" in the sauce.

Inevitably, your friends will agree to order a few "regular" pizzas, and some of your "special" pizzas. Once all the pizzas have been ordered, everyone will be asked to "chip in" some money to cover the cost. Since, prior to ordering, you ensured everyone that you would be contributing financially, you'll need to use a good excuse for why you're not paying (no... the fact that you're saving for calve implants does not qualify as a "good" excuse). Here are a few good examples of excuses to try first:

- *"A drug-crazed bum beat me up, and robbed me on the way here"* (since you live in a dumpster they may believe this one and you should also punch yourself in the face a few times to make it look realistic).
- *"I got fired yesterday"* (you haven't worked in over a decade, so this excuse only works with new friends).
- *"All my money is tied up in investments"* (by "investments" you mean, "calling the fortune teller hotline daily").
- *"I'll pay you back"* (try not to laugh out loud in their face).

If, after your best efforts to lie, your friends are still not accepting any of your excuses, you can also attempt the *"I'll pay you back later"* play. Although, if you've been friends with these people for more than a few weeks, they already know that's complete bullshit.

Pre-Pizza Time

Knowing that delicious pizzas are on the way puts everyone in a great state of mind. While waiting for the pizzas to arrive, the miserable failure should take advantage of this uplift in mood, and begin to drink as much of your friends' alcohol as fast as humanly possible. Since everyone is anticipating eating some tasty pizza soon, they will pay you and your overindulgence no mind. Raid their liquor cabinet, refrigerator, and any beer-filled coolers (be sure to pocket any cash you discover along the way). Don't ask for permission- **JUST START DRINKING**. The more "shit-faced" you are before the pizzas arrive, the better! You're going to need your "drunk thinking" to outwit your fellow pizza eaters when the deliver finally arrives **(NOTE: by "outwit" the miserable failure actually means "yelling obscenities at pets and children until losing consciousness").**

The Pie Arrival

When the pizza arrives, immediately sprint towards it, and violently push everyone out of the way (including children, paralyzed midgets, the elderly, invalids, cripples, etc.) to ensure you are first in line to get the best slices. Go directly for the good stuff (pepperoni pizzas, cheese pizzas, Italian sausage pizzas, etc.), and be sure to secure at least three pieces of each. Your fellow pizza eaters may attempt to stop your total demolishment of the "normal" pizza. They will remind you of the type of pizza you begged for, and instead present you with the "dusty pickle," or the "coin-flip" to consume. In this case, just say something like, *"I'm not eating those! Who in their right fucking mind would order this SHIT?"* slam the pizza on the ground, and make more passive aggressive threats toward their personal property. A good line often used by miserable failures is to say, *"Be careful, eating all of that three-cheese pizza could cause a break-in."* Wink, wink.

After originally taking three slices of each of the most popular pizzas, make sure you again sprint to get a second helping. The miserable failure should do this while still having several slices remaining from the first round (this will really infuriate your pizza pals). When getting seconds, take all of whatever good pizza remains, and only leave the (still untouched) "seat cushion" and "sneaky cousin" for your friends to choke down. Again, if your buddies say anything about the pizza injustice that just occurred, make more vague threats toward their personal property. A good saying often used by miserable failures is, "*Watch out, all that bitching might break the windows in your house. Just saying...*" If you correctly followed the instructions outlined in this section, your friends should already be fantasizing about you getting hit by a car when you leave. Great job, you miserable failure!

The "Last Slice"

In most "normal" social situations, no one wants to be the person who lays claims to the last of anything. It can make you seem slothful (PERFECT!), and insensitive to other's needs (Yep!). As a miserable failure, you don't give "two shits" about any of that garbage! Screw everyone else, that bitch is yours! The best method of insuring that the final slice of "edible" pizza ends up in your stomach, is called "The Old Sneezy." Simply pretend to sneeze loudly, and cover your nose with your bare hands. Then immediately pick up the final slice, and offer it to everyone in the room. This allows you to appear kind and caring while also knowing full well that nobody wants to eat anything you've touched with snot covered hands. If one of your friends attempts to get the final slice prior to you deploying "The Old Sneezy" method, **forcefully** take it from them, and shove the entire slice into your mouth. Chew the pizza sloppily while also brandishing your middle finger, and making HIGHLY-SEXUALIZED pelvic thrusts toward the rest of the group. This move, will definitely ensure that you never get invited to another pizza party, and should ruin your friendships with everyone there. Mission accomplished, douche bag!

Destroying Your BFF's Relationship and Making Them Hate You Forever

Although you're rarely invited, and never welcome, you'll always "be there" for your friends—especially your BFF (best friend forever). You'll "be there" to ride the coattails, steal the glory, puke in the backseat, shit in the bathtub, mooch food and bang their partner or spouse (in that exact order)! As described previously, there are many ways to quickly lose the loyalty and compassion of a good friend, but all fail in comparison to how you treat your best friend's lover. The next section is designed to teach you how to destroy your BFF's intimate relationship, not because you wish to do harm, but because you wish to be harmed **(physically, emotionally, spiritually and publicly).**

You will be hard-pressed to find someone more determined to see you suffer than a close friend who holds you personally responsible for the loss of his or her lover. Once you get involved in their relationship, not only will they be feeling the pain of their broken heart, but also the anger of your ultimate betrayal. In the truest sense of the word, they will hate you, and immediately seek painful revenge (fingers crossed for hired hitman). Be prepared for your BFF's "hate missile" to come in many forms. Calling the cops during your "special time" in the basement ("special time" = "meth cooking"), cutting up your collection of stolen credit cards (this is sure to have a negative impact on our porn consumption), or maybe even an old fashion attempted murder could take place (if you're lucky). So, pay special attention to the methods outlined in the following sections, and do your best to apply them to your own friendship. **WARNING: This stuff is powerful, and can create a mortal enemy literally overnight.** So, be prepared for some powerful blowback.

For Male Miserable Failures

If anyone knows how to royally fuck up a relationship, it's you! More than likely, your current best friend's girlfriend already doesn't like you. Okay, if you're being honest, she really, really hates you (SCORE). Maybe she never fully got over the whole "you secretly filmed her having sex and posted it online" thing, or she might still feel weird about the gangbang (#ThankYouBeer). No matter the reason for her current disdain, it's definitely justified, and is going to get a whole lot worse as time goes on. Your presence in the life of her significant other (A.K.A. your BFF), represents a clear and present danger to her romantic relationship. She knows, and you know, that it's only a matter of time until your passion for paid sex, animal tattoos, and shoplifting children's toys "rubs off" on your best buddy. Your terrible influence, in combination with your deliberate and intentional sabotage, is going to be the relationship's downfall. She'll do her best to convince your BFF to "dump" you as a friend before that happens, but ultimately, he won't be able to resist the "bros before hoes" speech (and free cocaine) you always give him during tough times. However, when the end comes (and it will) there will be little doubt, in BOTH of their minds, that there is only one destitute, disgusting, smelly, unemployed, degenerate, illiterate, grease-ball reason for the breakup... **YOU!** Be on your guard because the aggressive retaliation will begin as soon as they both realize that you methodically ruined and destroyed their entire relationship. Remember, every miserable failure needs a few mortal enemies to keep things "real."

What Happens In Vegas

One of the best methods for "indirectly" (LOL) sabotaging your BFF's relationship is by telling "old stories" that plant shrewd and cunning seeds of doubt about your friend's character and integrity. There are no better stories to tell than those that come from past Vegas vacations (the hookers, the drugs, and the life-destroying gambling addictions). Las Vegas is a hot-bed of personal destruction (#ThankYouMafia), and is considered to be the "Miserable Failure Retirement Capital of The World" (third behind prison or the nut house). While an entire book can be written about how to properly utilize the nearly endless miserable failure-making possibilities presented by Las Vegas, for the purposes of sabotaging your BFF's relationship, simply recount some of your most "memorable" experiences there with your best friend. Just "inadvertently" (**PURPOSELY**), during a normal conversation involving your BFF's girlfriend, "slip-in" an amusing anecdote about:

- "Heather The Hooker With Herpes" (A.K.A. "the triple H") that you two got hummers from in in a casino parking lot, and never paid. High-five!
- Getting arrested for not wearing pants, and playing "swords" in the hotel lobby. Penis fencing WILL be an Olympic sport one day, and you WILL be kicked out for doping.
- Waking up in your hotel room "mostly nude," severely sun burned, still "tripping balls," locked inside of a wooden trunk filled with cotton candy, and with no memory of the past seventy-two hours whatsoever. Viva Las Vegas!
- His MULTIPLE pregnancy scare(s) with VARIOUS hookers.
- Your short-term marriage(s) with strippers he "may or may not have" got pregnant.

As always, the miserable failure should strive to make as many inappropriate, and unsettling comments as possible while in the presence of anyone, and especially when near his BFF's girlfriend. It's also important that statements that make it seem like you might not be totally serious follow your deliberate off-putting comments, and snide sexual advances. Creating this "verbal gray area" will slightly delay either your friend, or his lover from doing battle with you before you're properly prepared to receive the maximum miserable failure-making benefits of losing your BFF. Use phrases like *"just kidding,"* or *"I'm just playing"* and fake laughter to easily mask your true sinister intentions while waiting for things to "boil over" naturally (and boil over they will)! Here are a few great examples of how to talk to your BFF's girlfriend, and not get shot (right away at least):

- *"You have really nice legs. Come sit on my face... Just kidding! Whoo!!"*
- *"I like to shit with the bathroom door open. Wanna watch? You know I'm just playing."*
- *"Hey* [insert GF name]! *How did you get to be such a bitch? Ha ha* (use fake laugh), *just kidding!*
- Slap her on the ass and say, *"That dinner isn't going to cook itself, sweet cheeks. Just playing!"* (If "sweet cheeks" is too strong of a pet name to use, simply substitute it with "cupcake," "toots," "broad," "slut," "skank," "twat," "female," "woman," "cock gobbler," or "battle axe".
- *"Do the vacuuming. Do the laundry. Do the dishes, or I will make sure he fucks someone next time we go out. I am so serious! Absolutely not joking at all!... Just kidding!"*
- When she first arrives at you and your BFF's shitty apartment, shout out, *"Speaking of garbage, you need to take the trash out. NOW!"* (while throwing the bag of trash at her feet).
- *"I haven't seen some boobs in a while. Can you pop a titty out really quick? You know I'm playing..."*
- *"It's important that you would keep me apprised of your menstrual cycles. Ha ha* (fake laugh).

Any combination of these comments, when used consistently over time, will royally piss off your best friend, and/or create a fair amount of tension between him and his lover. At first, your BFF will probably defend you, or make excuses for your behavior (*"It's just the crack talking baby"*). As you progressively become brasher and harsher in your use of intrusive behavior, and terrible comments, there will be no defending you. And soon, you'll be losing your BFF (and possibly an ear lobe) after they beat the ever-loving shit out of you for ruining their life and destroying their relationship.

The Bedroom Intruder

The bedroom is a sacred "safe space" for couples that the miserable failure should strive to infiltrate, and control. Doing this should cause a lot of problems in your friend's intimate relationship, and will only speed up the process of destroying your friendship. It is STRONGLY encouraged that you randomly "pop in" to your buddy's bedroom during odd hours of the night, especially when he's having sex with his girlfriend (to ensure good timing, just check the hidden cameras you secretly installed over his bed and in the bathroom). When you enter, if they're sleeping, jump on the bed until they both wakeup, and then demand (in a loud voice) that they immediately come with you to build a pillow fort in the front room (and to do more cocaine). If they're in the middle of having sex, quickly charge the bed, slap your best friend on the ass (and his lover if possible), and demand that you be "cut in" on the action. Then just sit silently at the end of the bed, and watch (touching yourself at this point is purely optional). Repeat this act consistently over several weeks, and it will undoubtedly lead to some intense, miserable failure-making, long term friendship-destroying, conflict (or ANOTHER threesome).

Guys Night

An AWESOME and SUPER EFFECTIVE method of destroying your BFF's relationship is by keeping him up (not necessarily a penis reference), and keeping him out (not necessarily a penis reference). Just start inviting your buddy out for an all-night "guys night" every night (of course you're going to "forget" your wallet and make him pay for everything). These fun-filled nights should ALWAYS include drinking alcohol in excess, using hard drugs, paying for sex, and not returning home until the sun rises (if at all). Some of the more "uptight" girlfriends out there may not approve of their boyfriends drinking heavily, doing cocaine off midget stripper's asses (it's a "bucket list" thing), and occasionally sleeping in alleys behind adult bookstores with a banana hanging out of their ass. His girlfriend already hates you, and will despise you all the more for "forcing" her, otherwise well behaved, man, to do all those terrible things. She will do her absolute best to remove you from their lives, and cause you as much pain as possible in the process (dreams do come true).

His Choice

"*Mega Bitch*" (as you affectionately call her) will undoubtedly attempt to turn your BFF against you by requiring that he make a choice between you, or her. Since your goal is to destroy your friend's relationship (and ultimately your friendship), you also want to pressure your BFF to choose between having fun with you, and keeping his girlfriend happy. This will create a massive amount of depression-inducing tension in your buddy's life, and can only lead to disaster. If he chooses his girlfriend, he'll lose his best friend. If he chooses his best friend, he'll lose his lover. When in reality, any scenario that involves you staying in his life is a horrible outcome for him (NOTE: you still plan on stealing his identity and eventually his car). When things have progressed to the point where your BFF must finally make a choice between love, and friendship, you should propose a "Contest of Champions." This is a simple, head-to-head, competition in which the intelligence, physical prowess, mental fortitude, and sheer will of each competitor is tested in a serious of simulated death camp scenarios. The winner gets your BFF/meal ticket/ride/free shelter provider/enabler/favorite person to blame everything on. You will of course cheat your way to victory via the use of performance enhancing drugs (mainly crack cocaine, meth, and ecstasy), or (if you're most likely NOT going to be the winner) you'll suggest a quick round of Russian Roulette to settle things (even if you lose, you still win!).

For Female Miserable Failures

So, you screwed things up with your family (you were disowned for having consensual sex with your first cousin last Halloween, but it was "*hot*"), and most of your friends have already given up on you (who can blame them?). In fact, anyone that spends more than a few moments with you generally ends up suffering in some way (mainly by tolerating your intense body odor and accidentally contracting one your **many** STDs). Despite all your awful behavior, and the inevitable repercussions of even being near you, your fellow female BFF has stood by your side through it all (#GirlPower). Now it's time to finally pay her back for being such a loyal friend, by completely destroying her romantic relationship (#BitchPower)!

It's important to remember that you're not just a selfish cunt who finds joy in hurting others. You do what you do because you have an important goal in mind, and that's losing your best friend fast. Yes, there was a time when the free shelter, cosigning loans, and food they provided was important to your survival. That time has passed, and you are now finally ready to evolve. Having a loyal BFF will only slow your progress toward ANOTHER unplanned pregnancy, and bad credit. There is absolutely no room in the life of a miserable failure for anyone that encourages positive choices, or serves as a safety net against total personal destruction.

Dress To Impress

No matter if your goal is to piss him off, or have him piss on you (let the "golden shower" games begin), your pursuit of your friend's boyfriend should begin immediately. Again, you're not doing this to be mean-spirited, but because you know the only assured way to lose a female BFF forever is to screw with her man (and screw him you will!). To begin, you must always remember to observe the proper dress code. No matter if you live with your BFF, or not, when your best friend's boyfriend is around it's **MANDATORY** (if you are still **somewhat** hot, slutty, sexy, attractive and trashy) that you wear one of the following outfit combinations listed below:

NOTE ON PERSONAL APPEARANCE: If you look like a fat, disgusting, dirty, old, homeless, drunk, drugged-out, hippie with no teeth and underarm hair so long you can braid it, do not attempt to dress "sexy" and instead just simply take a massive shit in the middle of their dinner table during those romantic nights that they cook and eat together. However, if you are still somewhat sexy, attractive, good-looking, or have a great body, you need to dress like a complete and total slut/skank/whore around your BFF's significant other...

- "The Whiskey Chick" - Cut off jean shorts that ride up your ass (since you haven't shaved "down there" for months, it should look "interesting" to others), a white tank top with no bra (you don't own one anyway), and red high heels (that were purchased with the credit card you "borrowed" from your BFF's purse while she was sleeping). Whenever possible you should also use a whiskey bottle as a "prop" (just use your imagination).
- "Your Pajamas" - Fishnet stockings, black leather "fuck me boots," a garter belt, a red lace thong, a see-through black push up bra, nipple tassels and four grams of bomb ass cocaine on a small mirror near your vagina. On your way to bed, say something like, *"I'm hitting the sack now. I don't how I'm going to fall asleep being this horny. Maybe some cocaine will help?"* (NOTE: This phrase will cause even the most LOYAL men to become sex and drug-crazed perverts.)
- "The Oops Outfit" - Tight black yoga pants, and that's it! Just pretend you weren't expecting him to walk into the living room during your morning stretch routine (FYI: make sure those nipples are hard and perky as well).
- "The Borrowed Outfit" - One of her boyfriend's button-down

dress shirts and a string thong. Wear this outfit while sharing an early morning cup of coffee with your BFF's boyfriend, and say, *"I hope it was okay that I borrowed your shirt. I like the way it smells."*

- "The Body Suit" - A black, skin tight, spandex bodysuit with fully erect nipples (just use ice cubes), and easily visible camel toe (a moose knuckle is acceptable). Wear this when performing everyday household tasks like vacuuming, and scraping your (binge and purge eating disorder) vomit out of the carpet.

Wearing the above-mentioned outfits will inevitably cause your BFF's boyfriend to fuck your brains out- EVENTUALLY. When this happens, be sure to record the video, post it on various online porn sites (and social media sites) and text it to your BFF.

The Contest

A shared dinner is the perfect opportunity to get into a heated debate about which one of you girls gives the best oral sex. Ultimately, a stalemate will occur in this argument with the only solution being a "blowjob contest" judged by her boyfriend. Initially, your BFF may resist doing this because she is almost 100% assured to lose (NOTE: you're a pro at the "Clocky, Clocky 10000"). Your oral sex skills have been sharpened from decades of paid back-alley blowjobs, and "licky quickies" during gym class (you really miss your high school gym teacher, the janitor, and the bus driver). You are also a fellatio legend among the sex worker community, and once made a man orgasm using only the suction from your left nostril (you also famously snorted a line of coke at the same time with your right nostril...#LEGENDARYSTATUS).

To put your BFF at ease, assure her that she's not going to be embarrassed in front of her boyfriend because you're going to let her win. Convince her that you're only participating for her benefit, to make her look good. Promise to purposely give the worst blowjob ever (just the tip, with lots of teeth). Truly, your goal is not to be the winner, but to simply "break the ice" by getting his cock in your mouth ASAP. Once the "genitals in the mouth" barrier has been broken, full vaginal penetration is next on the list (woohoo!!!). It will only be a matter of time until your threesomes become twosomes, and you eventually steal his affection from her entirely (#SlutPower).

Planting The Seed (not a pregnancy reference)

Although your vagina has a strong track record of "insertion success" when it comes to stealing men's affection (and smuggling drugs through the airport), over the years your "Va Jay Jay" has taken a pounding/beating (by 2,364 men, women, objects, and animals) and may now be lacking some of its former glory (swing low sweet chariot). Thus, as a female miserable failure hoping to permanently sever ties with their BFF, it's important to not solely rely upon the lure of your "pink purse" to adequately disrupt your best friend's romantic relationship. So, in addition to making constant sexual advances toward your BFF's lover, you'll also need to begin planting mental seeds of "relationship doubt" in her mind. These mental seeds are easily planted with "off handed" suggestions related to the potential causes of her significant other's behavior, and the overall security of her relationship (you are such a bitch).

If done subtly and timed correctly, these tiny seeds will grow, and eventually blossom into BIG issues for your BFF's romantic relationship (the growth and blossoming motioned in this sentence is the exact opposite reaction you get from most penises). Just exercise the same mental control over your best friend that you used to help her develop those eating disorders, and body image issues (*"Are you REALLY going to eat that, fatty"*). Good timing is crucial, so be sure to only plant your poison seeds when your best friend is already questioning, or feeling insecure about her relationship (NOTE: the average woman does this 40-600 times per day, so you'll have lots of opportunities). Below you will find a short list of mental seeds to plant in the mind of your easily influenced BFF...

The "Gay" Seed: *"Yeah, he's a nice guy, but isn't he a little too nice sometimes? He dresses well, and has good hygiene too. Don't worry, he's probably NOT gay."*

The "He's Seeing Someone Else" Seed: *"Don't you think it's strange that your boyfriend always answers his phone in private, and disappears for days at a time? The pile of used condoms I saw in the backseat of his car were probably left there by a "friend." It's cool! There's no way he's seeing someone else. He loves you too much to do that, and we BOTH know he never uses condoms."*

The "That's Not His Real Name" Seed: *"Your boyfriend looks just like the guy on the news the cops are looking for. You know, the guy who been going around raping pets and farm animals. But it can't be him though, they've got different names."*

The "I Blew Him Last Night While You Were At Work" Seed: *"Damn! My jaw is sore. I don't know how you do it, girl. He's a big boy! Oops! I mean I'm late for a job interview* (LOL), *and have to go."*

If all goes as planned (none of your plans ever go as planned), in a relatively short period of time your BFF's relationship will start to crumble, and ultimately your influence (and vagina) will be the obvious things to blame! If your best friend is kind of stupid (since they chose a failure like you to be their BFF it's HIGHLY likely they're VERY stupid) they may need assistance "connecting the dots" before they can begin directing their immense anger toward you (#MortalEnemy). In this situation, you'll need to literally spell things out for your BFF. So, do exactly that, and write her a letter. Here is an easy to use template for your confession:

"Dear Best Friend Forever. I'm sorry to see that your relationship with [in-

sert boyfriend name], *or "President Long Dong McHutchinson" (as he forces me to call him) is coming to an end. I know you blame yourself, and think you totally blew it with a great guy. That's not true! I'm the only one who blew it. Mostly while you were at work, and once in the coat room during your birthday party. What did you expect? I'm a miserable failure slut."*

If all the methods listed above are deployed with the proper timing and resolve, it will only be a short period of time until you begin to suffer the unimaginable wrath of an ex-best friend (#CatFight). The type of gruesome payback normally inflicted by a former BFF is extremely painful mainly due to its personal, well-informed nature (the remainder of your greasy, lice-infested hair will probably be ripped out during the cat fight). When your friend finally discovers that you've been the primary source of their stress all along, all of your known weaknesses and shortcomings will begin to be used powerfully against you (FINALLY!). You may easily foresee that your ex-BFF has hired several homeless people to assault you, and that they are waiting in the shadows near your favorite paint huffing dumpster. Intellectually you know that walking down that dark alley will only lead to getting your ass kicked (or worse), but you do it anyway because of your drug problem (you are a hopeless addict...GREAT JOB!). This is a perfect example of how your unmanaged addictions, and proclivity towards public dumpsters make you a predictable and easy target for an angry BFF. You'll basically be under constant attack by someone with first-hand knowledge of your daily routine, purchase habits, and emotional triggers. Essentially, you're fucked (emotionally, spiritually, socially, and physically), and that's right where you want to be!

Un-Friendly Social Media

Today, more than any other time in history, our lives are on public display thanks to social media. For the miserable failure, this presents a **plethora of opportunity** for deliberate personal "electronic sabotage" (posting videos of yourself on the toilet, performing a tutorial on how to make yourself vomit, etc.), and obliterating close friendships. Again, your goal isn't to hurt anyone, but rather to have him or her **hurt you.** Pain ALWAYS equals gain for the miserable failure! Good friends, and their caring nature, will only delay your descent into desolation, and serve as a barrier to you achieving your ultimate goal of being a complete miserable failure. So, get rid of them, and their love for you ASAP!

It goes without saying that during your ongoing attempts to steal your friends' identities, you've been collecting their user names and passwords. We recommend that after you verify the legitimacy of your stolen login information that you immediately change it. Be sure to change ALL of your friends' stolen login information to the miserable failure's default username and password (Username: FUCKFACE, Password: FUCKFACE). This way, no matter how high, and/or drunk you find yourself; you'll be able to remember the needed login info (HINT: if you can't remember your new login info, remember what your family calls you when they rant about you at Christmas dinner... "FUCKFACE").

Begin sabotaging your friends' social media status by posting fake updates about the many daily challenges you face, but massive joy you feel from sticking random things up your ass (this can include penises, but NOT exclusively). If the fake "sticking things up your ass" tactic seems extremely juvenile, not very creative, and overall a little below standard to you, **STOP READING THIS SECTION IMMEDIATELY,** and start this entire book over AGAIN from page one. You've apparently missed some BIG points along the way (FURTHERMORE: punch yourself in the face three times...).

When you are on their social media pages, simply start posting pictures of random items (large zucchinis, small woodland animals, collectable action figures, etc.) that you intend to, or have just finished sticking up your ass. Be sure to include suitable captions as well. For instance:

When you're posting a photo of something you're planning on sticking up your rectum...

"Just stopped bleeding and then I see this BIG thing at the store! Challenge accepted! It's time for some new gauze...#NoQuitTilYaHearDatRip."

When you're posting a photo of something you've just finished sticking up your rectum...

"It fit! And it felt great! Still can't believe that just happened. Sorry about the mess. I'm going to go sit in an empty the bath tub loaded with ice right now."

Since you have full access to your friends' social media accounts, be sure to post across multiple platforms, and ALWAYS tag their family. Having to explain to their coworkers, and grandparents that they didn't really stick an electric turkey carver up their butt should piss your friends off ROYALLY (great job!).

Finally, just to keep everyone on their toes (and because you're an asshole), release a barrage of "creepy" middle of the night posts that include weird pictures (naked clowns, homeless excrement, people masturbating in public phone booths, etc.) with vaguely suicidal captions. For example, post a photo of two African rhinos mating, and write, *"And I'm alone? None of you will miss me, goodbye cruel world."* If you receive concerned messages through your friends' social media accounts just message back and say, *"I've been a little off lately, but the gender reassignment surgery I plan on doing to myself should fix that."* Then just stop responding, and let the momentum build. These methods will easily destroy your friends' social media lives. Just be sure they know who to thank, and where to find you (#HereComesThePainTrain).

The Art of Destroying Online Friendships

We all have "friends" on social media, or another type of online forum, that we've never actually met in "real life" or even talked to on the phone. Despite not remembering how they became our online friend in the first place (there is a 100% chance you were attempting to catfish, and/or have sex with them), we leave them on our "friends list" so that we can appear to be more popular. Most of the time, these people have little impact on your life, but there is still potential for them to slow your downward spiral toward total personal destruction. For instance, if you post another video of one of your many failed suicide attempts (the pellet gun was unable to penetrate your skull) they could potentially attempt to intervene by positioning themselves as a positive influence in your life (you don't need that bullshit nonsense). So, in order to avoid the uplifting messages, they might send you, the interventions they might plan for you, and the surprise home visit they might make to "save" you, you'll need to remove them from your life ASAP. Follow the simple steps below, and you'll be totally alone in no time!

1. **Set Your Profile Picture to a Photo of a Creepy Clown** - It's creepy, weird and sets the tone perfectly for anyone reading your profile.
2. **Post Daily Suicidal Threats Related To Strange Medical Issues** - People will soon get sick of your *"I'm going to throw myself in front of a speeding bus because of this jock itch"*
3. **Be An Asshole** - If your online friend Debbie just had a baby, comment on how ugly the baby is, and how her husband should get a paternity test.
4. **Constantly Ask To Borrow Money** - If your chat room buddy Doug just posted about a raise he got at work, immediately message him and ask to borrow $500.
5. **Only Make Inappropriate Comments** - A wildfire is destroy-

ing the California wilderness? Make a comment about firefighters being overpaid. Your friend Tom's mother just got diagnosed with terminal cancer? Make a few jokes about life insurance, and then tell him not worry because *"she's probably faking."*

6. **Post "After Digestion" Food Photos** - People love to post pictures of delicious food they've prepared, or eaten at a restaurant. You should simply do that in reverse. Post the "after" photos of your bowel movements in the toilet (or whatever drain gutter you're using as a toilet for that particular day). Be sure to create similar captions to those used in food photos. Post something like, *"I don't know what the hell that is. I don't remember eating that."*
7. **Make Unnecessary Sexual Comments** - Your online buddy Dan posts a picture of him playing High School football, make a comment about him needing a "big jock strap" to keep his "manaconda" under control. Jessica, your friend from the sex addicts chat group, just posted a rant about her boss being a "pain in the ass" (this one is just too easy). It's time to publicly let her know about all the other reasons she could be experiencing that pain in her ass, mainly the multiple things you/her "slipped" into it last weekend.

In general, just be overly negative, constantly weird, incredibly repulsive, and get into as many online arguments as possible. You'll either lose all your online friends (hell yeah!), or get banned by the site administrators over your shenanigans (commie bastards). In the end, you'll end up alone, and/or hated by most of the Internet (just like you are when you're put into solitary confinement in the prison by the angry jail guards). So, pat yourself on the back (avoid patting the rash), and take a moment to recognize your great accomplishment in sucking. You can only truly become a miserable failure when you **DO NOT HAVE FRIENDS**.

Redesigning Friendships

For years, your friends have been providing you free food, rent, and liquor (SUCKERS....). They've put up with your constant stealing, intense body odor, and attempts to "bed" their spouses. As a reward for them not killing you, it's time to finally say, "thank you" the miserable failure way (that does NOT mean mailing them another jar of your urine). It's time for you to perform a "surprise" home renovation!

Remodeling their Domicile

Be sure to do this while your friends are at work so they don't "spoil the surprise" (A.K.A. "call the police"). Be prepared for extreme blowback and only deploy this method when you are absolutely ready to end a friendship (because they're going to fucking hate you afterward). Additionally, before beginning your surprise renovation, get really, really, really high (OUR "GO TO" SUGGESTION: crystal meth). Chances are that you'll be doing a surprise renovation at more than just one of your friend's homes. Using drugs will increase your creativity, and help you bring a "unique" flare to each individual project (and you really like being high).

To begin with, their couch (A.K.A. your sometimes bed) can easily be made into three separate chairs. Just use the chainsaw your friend keeps in the garage to chop their couch into thirds. This will be loud, and quite messy (like your normal Friday night). The best part is that after you're done with the couch, you can immediately pawn the chainsaw for your action figure collection money, and your buddy is sure to "appreciate" having three new chairs (NOTE: If you find any loose change in the couch, during your cutting, it's yours by right).

Next, you'll be "installing" some new windows (A.K.A. making large holes in the wall with a sledgehammer). Let the drugs lead you, and place them in random locations throughout your friend's ENTIRE house. It's important that you punch all the way through the wall in order to create a true window. So, swing that sledgehammer like you mean it! We suggest using a more "aggressive" drug like crack for this portion of the renovation (it's science). As a way to put the finishing touches on your work, give your friend's home a new paint job. Of course, you won't be painting any surface in its entirety, but rather splattering random paint colors wherever you see fit. Use bright colors, and don't hold back (this is your chance to express yourself). You should also take the time to paint "detailed" murals on the ceiling above your friend's bed, and on a living room wall. Remember, even those who possess zero art skills can at least manage to paint stick figures, and you'll be super high (which helps any art project). Focus on depicting large orgy scenes, and/or heinous acts of gruesome, grotesque violence (preferable together). For example, you can paint ten male stick figures, and one female stick figure playing "let's make it fit" while they beat each other with canoe paddles covered in razor blades and cobra snakes (HINT: just like summer camp when you were a kid).

The Friendly Unemployment

So, your pathetic, sorry ass has been sleeping rent free on your friend's couch for months (and thanks to your alcoholism you "shit" that couch most nights). Despite the fact that you've never gone grocery shopping, the house (and your stomach) is always filled with food. When you're low on cash (which is always) you just steal your buddy's credit card, or attempt to sell some of their property again (you got $50 for the dishwasher AND microwave). All of this is possible because your buddy has a paying job, but that's all going to change after today. Just like every relationship you've ever had; the free ride is about to end (YES PLEASE). You're going to grace your BFF with a surprise visit at their place of employment, and you can bet on it being their last day at work! You're the worst friend/roommate EVER, and now it's time to truly bite the hand that feeds you (NOT a reference to cannibalism... at least not yet.).

Begin "prepping" for your visit by staying up all night doing cocaine, and drinking heavily (A.K.A. your typical Sunday night after you spray-painted the church with graffiti). Along with your terrible personal hygiene, this should give you the perfect "look", and smell for interacting with your buddy's coworkers. Additionally, the combination of sleep deprivation, illegal stimulants, and alcohol has not served you well in the past (punching yourself until you blackout, masturbating in taxi-cabs, etc.). Wait until your friend has been at work for several hours before making your "grand entrance" at their place of employment (this will give you more time to do drugs, drink, and get angry). Ignore any security protocol, and simply walk right in. Besides being incredibly intoxicated, you should also NOT wear pants. This will make it easier to urinate at will, and should keep anyone from attempting to physically remove you from the premise (those exposed gangrene sores on your inner thighs will help too).

Loudly yell your BFF's name as you wander the halls knocking over potted plants, and taking "swings" at threats that are not there (pretend you're boxing your imaginary friends at the company Christmas party again). In between dry heaves, start screaming that you're *"looking for the boss"* because *"you've got a package for him"* (remember to gesture toward your crotch when saying *"package"*). When you finally locate the boss' office, introduce yourself as "The Enforcer," and make ALL of the following statements:

- *"You're much uglier than I was told by* _______ (state best friend's full name)."
- *"Wanna know who takes extra-long lunch breaks because they masturbate in their car?* _______ (state best friend's full name)."
- *"I was told that you're a total loser and a real big douchebag by* _______ (state best friend's full name)."

- *"I know someone who comes back to work high after lunch AND steals copy paper. His name is ______* (state best friend's name)."

Before you leave the boss' office, be sure to urinate on all the chairs (no matter who's sitting in them), and break any windows with the metal flask you've been carrying around. Just to ensure that the entire workplace knows the purpose of your disruptive visit, as the police are escorting you out, yell your former best friend's name a few more times. As you're slurring your words (thanks again pure grain alcohol) be sure to make strange sexual requests along with your screams for your friend (this will definitely cause your friend's coworkers to view him in a different light). For example, *"Larry! Lare Bear! I need someone to punch me so I can cum. Anyone? Lare Bear?!"* This will really "stir the pot" for your best buddy at work, and should lead to their immediate termination. Remember that, although they may never realize it, you kind of did your "BFF no-more" an unintentional favor. They hated that job, and its financial support was holding you both back from a much more unsatisfying life and even more miserable failings. Furthermore, since you clearly know how to get yourself fired, you should be happy as you now have experience in getting OTHERS fired.

Now you'll have to find a new place to sleep, and your former friend will most likely seek to exact revenge (let's hope so). If you get released from jail that same day, quickly head to your friend's house to collect your personal items from the front lawn (your buddy has most likely "left" them there for you with the added feature of being on fire). Sit on the curb near their house with all your charred personal items stacked around you (mostly porn mags and soiled clothing), crying, screaming and begging for forgiveness like a deranged and unhinged lunatic. This behavior will not help you gain any favor with your ex-friend, but it, and the three peyote buttons you just ate, will give you something to do for the next few days. Eventually (after the peyote wears off), you'll need to relocate, and find someone new to leach off of. We encourage the miserable failure to ask their parole officer, AA sponsor, suicidal life coach, or court-appointed therapist if they can crash on one of their couches for a *"few days"* (LOL). If any of them are dumb enough to take you in, simply repeat all the steps mentioned above until you once again find yourself on a curb crying, alone, cuddling with burnt pornography and old underwear (#HopesAndDreams).

How to Ruin Parties and Events

Sometimes by mistake, or by people who haven't known you long enough to hate you (RELAX.... just give them time), the miserable failure will actually still get invited to parties, or social gatherings **(PLEASE NOTE: these do NOT include your own drug and alcohol interventions)**. For NORMAL PEOPLE (not you), parties are a great chance to come together with those they love, and celebrate something important. For the miserable failure, a social gathering presents a plethora of opportunities to look like an asshole in front of people, lose fistfights, get drunk for free, and attempt to "borrow" money from EVERYONE (including the children). The best social gatherings to attend include the following:

- High School Graduation Parties - LOTS of "legal" eighteen-year old's and free booze (PERVERT).
- Nursing Home Holiday Parties - Years of sexual experience in one location. Enough said.
- Your Ex's Birthday Party- There is a 100% chance you will lose multiple fistfights, and be arrested for public exposure (it's a birthday party, so wear your birthday suit).
- Retirement Parties - The #1 choice for "borrowing" money (most guests will have a job, and/or pension).
- Divorce parties - They're FINALLY single and VERY vulnerable.

The First and Final Invite

If, by some miracle freak of nature, you've invited to a party, it's your duty to leave a long-lasting impression in the mind of every guest (you will haunt their dreams for months) by not leaving until you've accomplished ALL of the following:

1. The police show up (it doesn't count if they were already their waiting for you).
2. All toilets are clogged (just use the "entire roll per wipe" method).
3. You pissed in the pool (from the diving board).
4. Someone had their hands around your throat (for aggressive and/or sexual reasons).
5. Something, or someone caught on fire (do both at once and YOU ARE LEGEND).

The Early Bird

Unlike all the jobs you've been fired from (that's every job you've had), when you're invited to a party, ALWAYS show up REALLY early. The last thing that a host is expecting is for a "guest" to randomly show up at their home five hours before the party starts. It's weird, RUDE, awkward, and really inconvenient (which is precisely why you should do it). In this scenario, you must temporarily keep your awful behavior to a minimum to ensure that you're not kicked out before the party even begins (so no stealing and DO NOT expose your genitals.... YET). When first arriving, your initial conversation should go something like this:

Host - *"Hey* [YOUR NAME]. *What's up?"*

Miserable Failure - *"I'm here for the party, buddy!"*

Host - *"The party doesn't start until 7:00. It's only 2:00 now. You're a little early. Did I invite you?"*

Miserable Failure - *"It's no big deal. I'll just chillax on the couch until everyone gets here"* (say this as you physically force yourself through the door very aggressively).

Host - *"Okay. That's fine... I could use some help setting up. Can I get you something to drink first?"*

Miserable Failure - *"Don't worry about it! You're busy getting everything ready. Where is your liquor cabinet? I'll just help myself."*

Normally, this would be the perfect time for you to offer the host some assistance in finishing getting everything ready for the party. However, exclusive and unsupervised access to the liquor and food supply is only available for a limited time. So, act now! Tell the host that you *"threw out your back at the cock fighting match last night,"* and due to your injury, you're unable to assist them in setting up for the party. This serves two purposes; it gets you out of doing any work, and makes you appear dangerous (being contagious is the only thing dangerous about you). Knowledge of your fake "fighting ability" at the party will make any guest think twice before they "turn you in" for doing cocaine off their children's dressers (if there was enough to share you'd do it in the living room).

Begin your party destruction by waiting until the host is totally preoccupied with party preparations, and then seek out any hor d'oeuvres, or desserts. Taste every item on all trays (by licking each one), and then line your pockets (and heavily soiled underwear) with your favorites. Next, find the booze, and immediately begin massive consumption. You should do this act very fast, and figure that even the most seasoned, smelly, "I think I fucked my dog last night," sloppy drunk, alcoholic would be in awe based on how quick you guzzle booze. Just use the "miserable failure speed drinking method," and you'll be totally shit-faced in no time. This involves opening every bottle and/or can, taking a large gulp, and then leaving the mostly full open container where you found it. This will really piss off your fellow party guests, especially when they realize it was you (the person with the open herpes sore on their lip) who put their mouth on every bottle.

After you've secured the best food for yourself (via stuffing it down your pants), and have done the appropriate amount of speed drinking, it's time to relax. Find a couch, or comfy chair in front of the television, remove your shoes (if you're wearing any), unbutton your pants (if you're wearing any), and just chill out. It's important to remember that even if your host does not currently subscribe to any adult, or XXX movie channels, with only a click of a button, they can be (wink wink). So, find a good "dirty" movie (preferably something with amputees and/or barn yard animals), and crank the volume up to its maximum decibel level. Blaring pornography throughout the home should easily get your host's attention (as well as their neighbors). If they ask you to turn down the volume, or shut the porno off completely, just ignore them. If they persist (like the anti-porn asshole they are), just shout, *"Get me a fucking beer already!"* and *"Lame party, dickhead!"* When they return with your beer, be a "good friend" and encourage them to get back to work prepping for the party. This will give you the opportunity to not "waste" the free porn, and masturbate uninterrupted and unimpeded (in the unlikely event that you're able to become aroused). After climax, button your pants (optional), and drift off to sleep for a nice two-hour, black out, drunken nap. You're going to need your strength (and more cocaine), and since the other guests will be arriving soon, this means lots of people to ask for money, potentially have drunken sex with, and score free drugs from (NICE!).

Gift Giving at Birthday Parties

When you show up uninvited and unwelcomed at a birthday party, make sure that you always come empty-handed. **DO NOT BRING A GIFT**. However, if your therapist, life coach or parole officer really insist on you bringing a gift, and you know FOR A FACT that they'll be opening it up in front of the other guests LIVE at the party, we recommend one of the following gifts:

- An old, and clearly "used" porn magazine (sticky pages are optional).
- A graphed and mapped out local county police checkpoint breathalyzer map.
- Your used crack pipe (just say it's a Christmas ornament).
- A birthday card that's hand written in crayon on a sticky note.
- Your self-published picture book, *Gory Auto Accident Deaths Illustrated- Volume 33* (this one is a real crowd pleaser...).
- A fake gift certificate, and map to your crack dealer's house (Leroy does NOT take gift certificates, OR take kindly to strangers).
- Your used spring break t-shirt with brown stains, and an oddly placed hole in it (it's a mystery).
- A used condom in a box with a note that reads, "Surprise!" (you don't use condoms... just think about it).

Your "unique" gifts should really **add some life to the party**, and remember, YOU'RE doing everyone a favor! They're going to be telling the story of your present for years to come. If the birthday party doesn't have a gift exchange, you should create one. Take up a collection for the birthday person, and after you give them the money, ask to borrow $100. It's uncomfortable, inappropriate, and really awkward (just like your sex life with your robot doll). Do it anyway. Who knows? You might get a FREE $100 (and thus the chance to finish your pit bull neck tattoo before you start the next season of the dog fighting ring you created) by simply asking.

The Grub

If you weren't able to arrive three hours before everyone else, unfortunately, you'll have to "share" the best party food with all the guests. This doesn't mean you should do it willingly, or make anyone feel comfortable near "your food." Begin by locating the food line, and then removing your grease-covered, slightly torn, "pit-stained" tank top. As long as you've been sticking to the "Miserable Failure Diet Plan" (mostly grain alcohol and expired gas station hotdogs), the sight of your grotesque physical appearance should cause many partiers to gag, vomit, or run for the exits. This will immediately curb their appetites, and thus leave more free food for you (SCORE!). You should also use the "sneeze method" to protect "your food" as previously outlined in the "chip-in pizza party section." ONLY as a final resort, should you cut in the food line, intentionally knock over the table, and wildly begin stuffing appetizers down your pants (try to save this one for the end of the party, or if you're **100% SURE** the police have already been called).

If the freshly cooked food is being served via outdoor grilling, ask if they have any *"vegan chicken breasts from Iceland," "fresh caught Maine lobsters,"* or *"organic, non-GMO, 100% grass fed, aged Kobe beef hamburgers from Japan."* When the host responds with a no, violently slam your paper plate on the ground, and begin to curse loudly (especially if children are present). Then, proceed to **DEMAND** that they make up for this *"terrible atrocity"* by serving you *"whatever crap"* they're cooking before anyone else gets to eat. If the host isn't willing to meet your demands IMMEDIATELY, you should proceed to use what little physical force you still possess to push your way to the front of the food line (just be prepared to lose your first fist fight of the evening). Stack at least two plates with the biggest pieces of meat, and make your way back toward the alcohol. Just grab **another** fifth of whiskey from their liquor cabinet as your dinner beverage (no need for a cup or ice), and head to the pool (if they don't have a swimming pool just relax in their bathtub). Remember.....water + drinking alcohol + eating + a really high miserable failure = **DISASTER**.

Lounge by the pool (or tub) shirtless, and be sure to only take one bite from each piece of meat before throwing it into the water. In between large chugs of whiskey, shout profane comments such as, "*Who cooked this shit?*" and "*I've had better meals in a dumpster*" (100% true). Finally, if you feel the need to "relieve" yourself (bowel or bladder), don't waste time making the long trip to the restroom. The pool can easily serve as a toilet. Just remember, you can't swim, and right now (thanks to your gout and heavy drug use) you can barely walk. So, don't fall in. The idea behind this book is to help you be miserable, NOT dead. If you've just been hanging out in their bathtub because they don't have a swimming pool, there is no need to move at all. Simply lay back, and let it ALL go!!!

The Uninvited

By this point in your reading, you should have accomplished the important goal of losing nearly all of your close friendships. This means that party invites are going to be few and far between. So, if you are "accidentally" stalking one of your recent ex-friends, and become aware of a party they're hosting, you should immediately seize this amazing opportunity to be publicly shamed and humiliated (which will hopefully lead to a shitty self-image, thus making you more miserable...FINGERS CROSSED). Make sure to show up in the middle of the party when more people will be intoxicated. You need to remain unannounced for as long as possible in order to score the most free stuff, and everyone being a little buzzed should help keep your presence a secret (at least until they recognize your outfit).

Wear your customary party clothes; dirty robe, slippers, nipple tassels and stained boxers (you call this look the "Excellence in Failuredom"). Remember, your days of trying to impress these people are over, and most of them already hate you (MISSION COMPLETE). It's time to finally "let yourself go" and that means showing up **D.H.H.S. (drunk,**

high, horny and smelly). Use these descriptions as a checklist to follow before arriving at any social event:

DRUNK: You started drinking yesterday on the floor of a nightclub bathroom, and haven't stopped. The phrase "shit-faced" applied to you eleven hours ago. Now, you've reached the next level of drunkenness called "shit everything." You're going to be lots of fun tonight (alcohol poisoning here we come!).

HIGH: The drug cocktail you consume on a daily basis would put most people in a coma. Be sure to "protect your buzz" at the party by making regular trips to the bathroom to "freshen up." If there is any white remaining in your eyes, you're not doing it right.

HORNY: Outside of paid sex, and the occasional back-alley "dumpster roll," you have no sex life. In order to be at maximum horniness, refrain from your normal masturbation schedule (every hour on the hour, no matter where you are), and instead "work out" all that energy at the party in the form of ass-grabs, gropes, and extremely inappropriate sexual comments (EXAMPLES: *"I can see your wee wee in those pants," "Give me some sugar, candy crotch,"* etc.).

SMELLY: As a miserable failure, or someone hoping to become a miserable failure, bathing and hygiene just isn't your "thing." Your body odor should be so bad that people with asthma cannot legally be around you or they might die. For the party, take special care to really "pump up" the potency of your unholy musk. Prior to arrival, put on your favorite full-body leather bondage gear, slightly shit yourself (if you haven't already), and proceed to do heavy cardio exercise in a well-heated area for a few hours. The results will be instantaneous, and long lasting.

Once someone recognizes you, and the party's host is alerted to your presence, it's only a short matter of time until you'll be asked to leave, or severely beaten for your crimes against EVERYONE. When the inevitable occurs, and a party guest detects you, try to play it off like you were actually invited. This may delay them telling the host you are crashing the party. No matter your gender, shout out, *"What's up fuckers? Glad you made it! Where's the pussy?"* Say this while grabbing your crotch, and while pumping your fist in the air. This will confuse them, and allow you to retreat from the scene. While being as stealth as possible (you should have worn your stalking outfit), begin maximizing the FREE consumption of (1) alcohol, (2) drugs, (3) money, (4) food, and (5) sex. Remaining mindful that the "kick your ass out" clock is ticking, immediately make your way to the food and liquor. Since there is no time for utensils, use your bare hands to eat directly from all the serving dishes (especially if spaghetti is being served), and begin pouring full bottles of alcohol directly down your throat. During this process of maximum free consumption, you will most likely encounter many party guests. Ask EVERYONE of them if you can borrow some cash, if they have any drugs to share, and if they'd like to have unprotected sex with you in the garage. You have nothing to lose, and it never hurts to ask (well sometimes it hurts in the form of pepper spray and a brass knuckle punch to the sternum).

Getting Busted!

When the "jig" is finally up, and everyone knows you've crashed the party, be prepared for anything. Consider how severe your infraction against the host was, as this may allow you to plan for a certain level of retribution. Also, if you had sex with their spouse, be ready to "fight" (A.K.A. "curl up into a ball on the ground and cry"). If you got them fired from their job (you "accidentally" downloaded fart porn on their work computer and stole a copy machine), be ready to get arrested AGAIN. If you got them hopelessly addicted to angel dust, be ready for their "sponsor" to forcefully remove you from the premises (FUN FACT: your sponsors all seem to commit suicide). Overall, just become fully aware that no matter what the reason you weren't "officially" invited, NO ONE wants you there (like your family reunions). Even people at the party that don't know you will follow the mob when everyone starts to physically assault and accost you (also like your family reunions). Little do they know that having this massive degree of hatred and hostility directed at you is where you feel most at home, and where you can fully thrive as a miserable failure. In other words, IT'S ON! And let the pounding commence!

The Party Pooper

Yes, you may have already been exiled by your friend group, and possibly beaten for your terrible behavior (#DreamsCanComeTrue). However, in many instances, you may be excommunicated solely for being annoying, smelling terribly, or being completely smashed 24/7. In this situation, your presence at the party won't provoke hostility, and will only make the host uncomfortable, or maybe even a little embarrassed that you now know you weren't invited. This could cause the host to hesitate before asking you to leave because you really haven't done anything "that bad" to them yet. In this scenario, it's your duty to give them a few good reasons for sending you flying out the front door, face first! It's time for you to become "The Party Pooper."

As "The Party Pooper," it's your job to loudly express negative views about EVERYTHING, encourage the discussion of incredibly uncomfortable and morbid topics, and make insulting personal comments about EVERYONE. If one of your ex-friends at the party is pregnant, make jokes about them not knowing who the real father is, and how the *"slut apple"* probably won't fall far from the *"slut tree."* If one of your ex-friends has gained some weight, be sure to point that fact out in great detail by "highlighting" (A.K.A. pointing and laughing at) the parts of their body that have become larger. Then proceed into a diatribe about how you hate fat people and how you're prejudiced against their *"fat asses."* If one of your "old buddies" brings a new love interest to the party, it's your responsibility to tell the "prostitute, methamphetamine, and beef jerky" story that happened at their birthday party six years ago (you should also "accidentally" mention that herpes is incurable). You also better make DAMN SURE you talk about the following subjects as much as possible:

- Politics (you're for a national "battle royale" kill fest where it's broadcast live on national TV).
- Racism (you only hate yourself).
- Religion (you want to bring back human sacrifice, if you can be first in line).
- Things Found in Your Stool This Morning (CONTENTS CHECK: wrist watch, bottle cap, heroin balloon, blood, etc.).
- Abortion (you AND your parents wish you had been aborted).
- Sex (talk about your "fecal fantasy" and "golden shower dreams" over dessert).
- Money (ask everyone what their yearly salary is and for a personal loan).
- Body Image (ask everyone their weight and age).

Eventually, the host and the rest of guests are going to have enough of your shenanigans. Maybe it was asking ALL the women their bra size, or ALL the men how big their penises are (it was probably the "measuring contest" you suggested). Despite which crude comment, or awful behavior officially wore out your welcome (well, since you weren't invited you were never really welcome), it's definitely time to "leave" (A.K.A. "be forcibly removed and tasered"). On your way out the door, make sure to "ask" for souvenirs. While you're being dragged out, randomly grab a vase, framed photos on the wall, or whatever other home décor you can manage to stuff down your pants. Remember, like your ability to become sexually aroused without drugs, you're not coming back. So, you'll need to take something to remember the occasion, and immediately pawn for cash (scratch-off lottery tickets aren't free).

The "Friend Zone"

Although you have absolutely **no standards** when it comes to sex, your friends likely have them, and you are (without a doubt) far-far-far-far below any reasonable person's "standard." In fact, not only do your friends have ZERO sexual interest in you WHATSOEVER, they should be physically repulsed by your body (it's probably the rash), and the mere mention of your name and sex in the same sentence might possibly cause them to become violently ill. This is great news for the miserable failure because, inevitably, you are going to develop a sexual attraction to a soon to be ex-friend, and they are NOT going to share the same feelings. Rejection, especially sexual rejection by a friend, can be an emotionally painful experience, and lead to a severe lack of self-confidence (#BeStillMyHeart). However, the pain of rejection fails in comparison to the prolonged torture of being placed in the "friend zone" by a love interest. To be "placed in the friend zone" means that, not only have you been rejected, but you've also been asked to stick around and watch as your "sex target" actively dates, marries or fucks other people. This situation has been known to drive sane people crazy, and make peaceful folks "lust for blood" (you were neither sane nor peaceful to begin with...).

Start this painful process by expressing your undying love, and intense sexual attraction to your friend publicly (invite both your families and stream it live on social media). Plan a grandiose first show of your affection with a surprise marching band, dancing flash mob, or a traveling circus. As soon as your "buddy" (A.K.A. your "crush") realizes something out of the normal is taking place, drop down to one knee, and ask for their hand in marriage. Going from being friends to proposing marriage, with absolutely nothing in between, will instantly lead to your total rejection. Thanks to you expressing your love in public, you'll also have the added benefit of looking like a complete buffoon in front of EVERYONE (that's like winning the "asshole lottery"). Your friend will be embarrassed, and maybe a little angry with you (this is EXACTLY what you want). Just fake cry, and pretend to be suicidal (LOL! **Pretend**...). It's then that you'll first hear your buddy say something like, *"I just don't feel that way about you. You're like a brother, (or sister) to me."* Yes, completely ignore the fact that being related to someone never stopped you before, and say something back like, *"Okay. Let's just be friends."* This will start the clock ticking on the "time bomb" that is your friendship, and in a short period of time, you'll go from the friend zone to the "danger zone" (that's what a miserable failure calls progress!).

In the days following first being placed in the friend zone, start showing up randomly at your friend's home at rather inconvenient times. Do this in the hopes of "catching" them with someone their actually romantically interested in (NOTE: if you do catch them in the act of sex with another person, sit in the corner, cry, video tape it and touch yourself). If this occurs, DO NOT react negatively (this will only get you thrown out). Instead, shake the person's hand, and let them know they've found a *"great vagina"* or *"awesome cock"* with your friend. Tell them that a friend of your friend is a friend of yours too, and ask for their contact information (it goes without saying that you'll use this info to stalk them later). Then, just linger until it starts to feel very uncomfortable for everyone. If you're asked to leave so they can have privacy, tell your friend you'll just hangout alone in a different room, and that you'll be so quiet they won't even know you're there (OF COURSE you're going to scream sexual profanities as loud as possible as soon as you're left alone). When your buddy insists you leave, get a really depressed look on your face, and tell them you'll be back later (and by later you mean every day until the cops are called).

If you show up at your friend's place, and they are not home, be sure to leave an anonymous "love note" taped to their front door. It should read, *"From your secret admirer, because I like watching you as I pinch my nipples."* Your friend will probably know it's you leaving the notes (your awful handwriting is very "distinctive" and by the fact that you always use a red crayon), but this shouldn't worry you. You're not in this for the long haul, just immediate pain. The best-case scenario is that your friend invites you to stay the night because they are afraid to be alone if the person who wrote the note comes back.

(IMPORTANT POINT: Every opportunity to stay the night with your pal equals another chance to be sexually rejected and thus feel more like shit... Everyone knows you're NEVER getting laid.)

You should also leave a nice bouquet of flowers (or colorful weeds) that you "found" in the cemetery, or picked from the ditch you woke up in this morning (thanks again, LSD). For extra effect, leave the flowers/weeds on their bedroom windowsill with a condom and bottle of cheap liquor (whatever you can manage to shoplift). Smear the numbers 9-1-1 on the window with some of the infection from that "thing" in your armpit, and the leave the rest up to their imagination.

It's also very important that your friend-crush has no other close friendships, and extremely limited interactions with their own family members while you're up to your friend zone "tricks." Forcing your buddy to watch a video of you having sex with an elderly couple on spring break may seem "normal" to them, but outside influences may recognize this behavior as odd, and encourage them to discontinue your friendship. You need to "nip this in the bud" right away! Is a grandparent spending too much time over at their house? Maybe grandpa needs to be given a "special visit" at the retirement home for a good old' fashion "Indian burn" on both his arms. After you're done, just whisper in his ear, *"Back off, or the next time, I'll break your hip."* Has your friend been taking their ANNOYING special needs brother out for ice cream too often? Maybe you should go along next time, and while your buddy is in the bathroom, replace the brother's rocky road with your "secret recipe" ice cream (INGREDIENTS: mayonnaise, ranch, sour cream, sugar and peyote). It'll be the last time they take out their brother for a long while! Did their parents invite them over on Christmas for *"family bullshit,"* and leave you off the invite list? No problem! On Christmas Eve, just pay their home a little visit, miserable failure style. Get completely high sniffing rubbing alcohol, wear the vomit-stained Santa outfit you keep with you year-round, and drop down your "future in-laws" chimney for some fun. "Borrow" all the presents under the tree (A.K.A. pawn them for video poker and firework money), defecate on the sofa (in the rare event that you're able to get your bowels to move), and tear all the family photos off the wall (you should put the pictures in the bathtub and urinate on them). Do this, and nobody will be invited over this Christmas! Remember, your friend can ONLY have one person in their life, and that manipulative, infected, hopelessly-addicted, smelly, sexually deviant person is NOT going to be you.

Next, on your social media accounts, post that you and your friend are now officially in a relationship. Write long, boring diatribes about your endless love for your friend, and be sure to state that you hope the baby is a boy/girl. Obviously, since you haven't had sex with them (and all drug abuse has made it nearly impossible for you to reproduce) this pregnancy post is bogus, but it sure will get their family excited! Edit both your faces into multiple pornographic photos, caption them with *"this is how we made our baby,"* and post them frequently (this is sad, desperate and creepy act, but SO ARE YOU). This act will likely prompt your friend to de-friend you on social media, and cut you out of their life completely (fingers crossed). This is when the "fun" can finally begin!

You've now been fully excommunicated from the life of the friend you want to fuck. It's time to put on your stalker clothes, and get to work (RELAX! It's "get" to work, not "go" to work). Begin sending your ex-friend text messages at odd hours expressing (in graphic detail) your deepest sexual fantasies, and their role in each of them. Don't hold anything back! If in describing your crazy sexual fantasies you don't use the phrases, *"And you hold the bucket," "We can watch while it bleeds out,"* and *"Don't worry we'll make it fit,"* you need to start doing more hard drugs and hanging out in even darker alleys to become a better and more creative writer.

Finally, it's your duty to make it apparent that if you can't have your friend sexually, nobody can. The contact information you were able to get from your ex-friend's current love interest can now come in handy. Put your stalker skills and irritable bowel syndrome to good use, and start playing "Ding-Dong-Dump" at their home. After a long night of drinking, and eating out of trashcans, come to their new love interest's door about 4:00 a.m. Drop your pants (in the unlikely event that your wearing any), and then drop a load on their doorstep. Thanks to your terrible diet (eating out of trashcans and dumpsters isn't that nutritious), and multiple stomach parasites, any fecal matter that comes out of you is definitely NOT solid. Besides potentially containing an infectious disease, your excrement can cause damage in the form of a tripping hazard for anyone that answers the door (or just something really gross and stinky to step in). Lastly, ring the doorbell, and run like hell!

(IMPORTANT POINT: If you are wearing pants, remember to pull them up before you start running. If not, you'll end up falling over and smashing your face into the sidewalk. You need your few remaining teeth to chew through the restraints if you're kidnapped in Mexico AGAIN.)

If you are discovered by the love interest during your "shit show", the only recourse you have is to act "fucking crazy." Please refer to the "Miserable Failure Crazy Scale" below for a list of appropriate actions to take:

- **Nuts** - Hanging out in public bathrooms and encouraging people not to flush so you can collect their urine.
- **Crazy** - Slowly, over the course of several weeks, filling your bathtub full of stranger's urine.

- **Fucking Nuts** - Having a bathtub full of stranger's urine, and inviting all your "friends" to the "pee pool party."
- **Fucking Crazy** - Swimming in a bathtub full of stranger's urine, and wondering why you have no friends.

Your first step in order to effectively act "fucking crazy" is to begin screaming nonsensical gibberish at your love interest. Don't actually speak any real words. Just be loud, and use lots of threatening hand gestures (EXAMPLE: *"ka basha coo loo pay habba dabba"*). Stare directly into the eyes of the love interest, and start to literally pull your own hair out (if you're bald, simply begin to rapidly punch yourself in the right ear). When you've removed a significant amount of air, or (for our bald miserable failures) lost the ability to hear from one ear, stop and break your left index finger. As your finger snaps yell, *"This is what you're doing to my heart!"* This will really freak them out, and earn you another restraining order (that makes a baker's dozen...this month alone). Most importantly, your "crazy as fuck" actions will keep your crush single. They definitely still won't have sex with you (your raging herpes outbreaks aren't "hot"), but they won't be having sex with anyone else either (ruining both of your lives sexually? CHECK).

Free Shitty Advice

Like your "mystery toenail" collection, a miserable failure also takes PRIDE in giving really terrible advice to their friend. We encourage you to offer EVERYONE you come in contact with, especially your close friends and buddy, love interests advice that only a moron like yourself would ever consider following. Remember, the goal here is not to intentionally hurt your friend (although it's going to happen A LOT), but rather to endure the pain of systematically losing ALL of them. If you attempt to lead them up the same "shit hill" you rolled down, nobody will ever want to become, or stay your BFF (unless they're mentally ill, in that case, ask them to move in with you). In essence, you should observe any problematic situation faced by your friends, consider what any REASONABLE human would do, and then tell them to do the exact opposite (this process can and should include hard drugs for both of you). This way, when your friend's entire life goes to "shit town" (like yours did when you started reading this book), the obvious choice for whom to blame will invariably be **you**. You'll then successfully be able to eliminate one more potentially failure-blocking friend from your life (total loneliness and despair, here you come). Below, you will find several examples of common scenarios, and the free shitty advice that you could potentially give a friend:

Scenario #1

Your old cellmate George just got a divorced from his wife of nineteen years, and needs advice on how to start his life over.

Miserable Failure Advice - Start drinking every day before noon (only stopping to sob uncontrollably). Watch copious amounts of violent pornography online, and get a facial tattoo of a warthog. Prior to bed, consume enough hallucinogenic drugs to induce a coma (every night). Buy a box of razor blades.

Scenario #2

Your friendly neighbor Tammy just lost her job and is afraid of losing her home.

Miserable Failure Advice - Inform Tammy that losing her job is actually GREAT because now she'll have more time to have unprotected sex with multiple partners (including you) at the same time in a sketchy motel room. To save cash, encourage her to max out her credit cards, stop paying her utility bills, and not worry about making that "pesky mortgage payment." It's time to drink five bottles of merlot, and do some online shopping!

Scenario #3

Your BFF Bobby found out that he has cancer, and will need extensive treatment if he hopes to survive.

Miserable Failure Advice - Deadly cancer ALWAYS means one thing for the miserable failure... It's hooker and blow time! Advise Bobby to forgo any treatment, and instead take out a large personal loan. They should then go spend all the cash on prostitutes and drugs. They'll be dead soon anyway, so tell them to not worry about paying the loan back, or using condoms with the street hookers (which is like playing Russian roulette with your genitals). You should also let Bobby know about the awesome power of the "cancer excuse."

Scenario #4

Your best girlfriend Sylvia found out her husband is having an affair, and is considering divorce.

Miserable Failure Advice - Before filing for divorce, encourage her to first visit the local "glory hole" (OF COURSE you'll accompany her for "emotional support"), and perform oral sex on the same number of men as years they've been married (OF COURSE there's a minimum of four). Then tell her to go home, wake up her cheating husband with a deep French kiss, and whisper in his hear, *"I'm pregnant."* If he doesn't react negatively, tell her to simply do what any "reasonable" woman would do, and pay three to five homeless dudes (who clearly have mental health issues) to make a "dumpster sex tape" with her (OF COURSE you should make sure she uploads it to the internet).

Scenario #5

After years of horrible meth addiction, your friend William must have his teeth replaced, and worries about using a high-interest credit card to pay for the procedure.

Miserable Failure Advice - Encourage Billy Boy to max out all of his credit cards, but not for the procedure. Tell him to cash advance his credit line until he's reached his limit, and then to use the cash for more meth. Tell him that *"quitters never win"* and that he needs to *"chill the fuck out"* because you'll *"handle"* his dental issue. When he is completely "methed-out" hand him a pair of pliers, tell him that his teeth are demons from the fiery pits of hell, and then command him to *"start pulling"* the evil out of his mouth before they *"destroy his brain."*

Scenario #6

Your best girlfriend Mary wants to know how she can lose weight and needs advice.

Miserable Failure Advice - To motivate Mary, tell her she looks like a cow, and make *"moo"* sounds whenever she enters the room. When her self-esteem has reached its lowest, introduce her to the various eating disorder options she has. A new cocaine addiction and chain cigarette smoking are also viable options, just be sure to include yourself in that fun.

Scenario #7

Your friend Tony from the drug rehab center caught his eleven-year-old son smoking cigarettes and needs to know what to do.

Miserable Failure Advice - Tell Tony to celebrate this "rite of passage" in his young son's life. Encourage Tony to buy his son a few cartons of cigarettes, and several cases of cheap beer in order to "keep the momentum going." Then, purchase (steal) a keg of beer and proceed to throw a party for his son and his entire group of friends.

Scenario #8

Your former roommate Juan has become hopelessly addicted to prescription pills, and knows that you've "overcome" this same issue. He asks you how to change his life for the better.

Miserable Failure Advice - Begin by giving Juan a good "verbal tongue lashing" for not sharing the pills with you. Tell him that you quitting was just an illusion for the benefit of your parole officer, and court appointed drug counselor. Start to teach Juan how to stay high, AND undetected moving forward. Finally, ask to borrow a few pills so the two of you can *"go get all messed up together."*

Scenario #9

Rhonda, a girl you're trying to bang, says she gets into too many arguments with her husband, but is afraid to leave him because of the kids.

Miserable Failure- Encourage her to leave her husband, sell her children on the black market for straight cash, and then go on a Mexican vacation (that she pays for) with you.

You get the point! Wherever there is shitty advice, you'll find a miserable failure (this also applies to wherever there is bad hygiene, low credit scores, hopeless addictions, or genitals that leak fluids). Remember, miserable failures never try to injure anyone. All the shitty advice you give, you've first taken and tried yourself (it's got you to HERE). If any of your "regular" friends are dumb enough to actually follow your advice, you may soon have a new "miserable failure friend" to share needles with! Just live by the following simple equation, and you can't go wrong...

Miserable Failure + Shitty Advice = Lives Altered, Ruined and Destroyed Forever

Your Imaginary Friends

Be it the magical elf that sleeps in the dumpster you call home, or the sex-addicted dolphin that lives in your toilet, the only "friends" a miserable failure has (besides cocaine and beer), that won't block your treacherous path down "shit hill," are **imaginary friends**. Yes, miserable failures do hallucinate often, but that's thanks to years of sniffing spray paint, snorting over-the-counter cough syrup, and the multiple concussions you "achieved" during bar brawls. Imaginary friends are not involuntary hallucinations brought on by drug abuse, but rather chosen invisible companions that can serve whatever purpose you deem necessary. For example, if you're feeling lonely, and need a little excitement, just hang out with your imaginary friend, Pete "The Ass Grabbler" Marshal. Mr. Marshal is always good for a laugh, and "makes" you grab random strangers' asses while on the subway (#BrokenHand). Pete is not only fun and interesting, but he also makes the perfect excuse to tell the Judge when you get arrested for groping.

All of your imaginary friends (if you're doing it right) will only serve as negative influences, and should be your immediate "fall back" excuse whenever confronted about your terrible behaviors (got caught banging the baby sitter? Blame it on your buddy, "Phil the Drunk Pickle"). Be aware that using imaginary friends as an excuse may not "fly" with most ordinary people, but will more than suffice as an explanation during your court-appointed psychiatric evaluation and subsequent electroshock therapy treatments. Some of the more infamous imaginary friends a miserable failure should have include, but are not limited to:

Tommy "The Fecal Freak" Maddox - Tommy is a homeless man who lost all of his money on the infamous "Nigerian Prince" email scam. Tommy is a bitter over his misfortune, and follows you around asking to watch you go #2 in the toilet. Bring him "out" during times of intense constipation due to prolonged meth, or cocaine use.

Denise "The Nugget" Livingston - Denise is a stripper who works hard for the money dancing at "Frank's Topless Bar, Grill & Driving Range." Denise does not have any legs or arms, and thus lives as a "nugget" with her perv daddy, Titus. Use her when you're bored with "regular" masturbation.

Willard "Fiddlestick" Filmore - Willard is a successful wheelchair salesman from Queens with a passion for cheese, and a nose for blow. He is a part-man, part-bird and part-rat hybrid who loves to knock over furniture, and break windows with his twenty-inch steel penis. Let Willard "visit" when you have trouble explaining the "mystery" damage in the apartment to your soon-to-be ex-roommate.

Yolanda "The Couch Bound" Sloth - Yolanda weights just over 600-pounds, has lost seven toes to diabetes, and is working on her third heart attack. She hasn't been physically able to leave her home in over two years, is addicted to pizza delivery, and goes to the bathroom in a bucket behind the couch. She's best used on your "lazy days" when the "long" walk to the bathroom is just too much, and you don't want to miss any of the pirated pornography currently available through your stolen cable connection (your neighbor should've used the deadbolt too).

Danny "The Game" Dingleberry (A.K.A. Mr. Dingleberry The Great) - Danny is a troubled youth who ran away from home at seventeen, joined a motorcycle gang, and rose to the top ranks in record time. On a routine "let's find somebody to assault" ride, Danny was leading the pack when his entire gang is side swiped by a semi-truck. The accident results in the death of everyone, except Danny, who suffers brain damage resulting in mild mental retardation. Later, it's discovered that despite his lack of basic skills (like being able to wipe properly), Danny actually developed super powers as a result of the accident, and can now read other people's minds. He now spends his days going by "Mr. Dingleberry The Great" playing poker in Las Vegas with the help of his handler/representative payee, Todd. Save this guy for peyote weekends, acid flashbacks, and dry/sober wedding invites.

Ray "The Trucker" Smith - Ray is your best imaginary friend. After parking his big rig for the night, he hangs out at random truck stop parking lots in hopes of find true love/paid sex. He listens to country music, gets into bar fights, and never judges you. It's appropriate to let Ray "out" at any family event, including funerals and children's birthday parties.

Eddie "Lactate" Nielson - Eddie is a crippled midget who will only have sex with pregnant women. As Eddie always says, "*you can't get pregnant while you're pregnant, but you can get herpes.*" He normally likes to hang around hospitals, birthing centers, and baby stores in hopes of picking up knocked up women. Feel free to live vicariously through Eddie the next time you see a woman publicly breastfeeding, and decide "*it's your damn turn now.*"

Francine "Burns" Grover - Francine is a terribly burned, and scarred crack addict who regularly waits outside local grade schools to steal children's lunch money. All of this cash goes to fund her intelligently diversified investment portfolio, and life destroying crack addiction. Play with Francine when you're ready for sound investment advice, tough love, and lots of crack.

Doug "The Bug" Nelson - On some days, Doug self-identifies as a bug, sleeps under a bloody blanket outside a shopping mall and drives an ice cream truck during the summer. He chooses to walk on all four limbs, but states he'd rather it be eight. Doug is most effective as an imaginary friend when you are also currently sleeping outside a shopping mall under a bloody blanket pretending to be a cricket.

Lisa "Boner" Johnson - Lisa is part woman, and part dog. She enjoys "squatting" on friend's couches for weeks at a time without consent, and marking her territory via urinating on furniture. She also habitually sniffs people's asses, has terrible gas, and smells like a dill pickle/mothball/rotting tuna fish combination. Hang out with Lisa during your mandatory "rage therapy yoga" sessions, as well as child custody hearings.

Randy "The Hands" Kilroy - Randy is your alcoholic uncle, twice removed. He taught you how to kill a man before you were seven, and enjoys using the basement for recreating memories from his time in the war. Let Randy "assist" you in winning the "kidnap for cash" game, and hiding a "heart attack hooker" body (NOTE: "heart attack hooker" is a prostitute who, thanks to their prolonged drug addiction and lack of exercise, goes into cardiac arrest and dies while in your "service").

It should also be noted that even your imaginary friends should let you down, and eventually turn on you (like everyone else). If by some freak occurrence, you accidentally develop a positive imaginary friend who attempts to uplift you, and derail the "shit train" that is your life, immediately begin to consume MASSIVE amounts of opiates (while huffing diesel fuel) until they disappear forever into your subconscious. If, by another freak occurrence, they once again manifest, and attempt to "change your life for the better," simply kick them out of your mind by pouring tequila in your ear, and shaving all your body hair with a rusty, used and dirty razor you found in the dumpster behind the nut house.

The Asshole Checklist

You've been given a lot of life destroying information in the previous sections. Being that remembering things (and being sober) are NOT your strengths, let's recap...

- Ruined all your family relationships and tried to have sex with a first cousin... **CHECK**.
- Have no job, no plan to find one, and no one left to leach off of... **CHECK**.

- Zero loyal friends remaining (not counting your imaginary ones)... **CHECK**.
- Made your ex into a mortal enemy who seeks your total destruction... **CHECK**.
- If you have children, they fucking hate you... **CHECK**.
- Filled bankruptcy, again... **CHECK**.
- The thing-leaking puss under your armpit has doubled in size... **CHECK**.

Although you've "accomplished" many of pivotal tasks required to be a miserable failure, there is still work to be done. There are lots more restraining orders to **earn**, STDs to **contract**, and child support payments to **avoid**. So, huff some glue, scratch open a scab, and "buckle up." It's going to get A LOT WORSE....

5

STRANGERS

Other People

If you have been following the steps closely, **your worthless life should be in the shit box right about now**. Isolated and alone, you should have distanced yourself from virtually everyone in your life. Your family has probably kicked you out of the will and your inheritance (SCORE!!!). Your other family members have HOPEFULLY disowned you (EXCELLENT NEWS!!!). Your children SHOULD want nothing to do with you (FANTASTIC!!!). All fifteen of your ex-spouses should be in therapy due to the traumatic experience of being in a relationship with you (GOAL, COMPLETED!!!). Your friends have hopefully all filed restraining orders against you and your drinking and drug usage should be **continuing to climb**. So, who else is left for the miserable failure to annoy? Complete strangers...

Perfect Strangers

Strangers are a part of all of our lives. From going to the grocery store drunk and stoned while trying to steal a steak, to interacting with a clerk at a gas station by pretending to rob them with the old' "finger gun in the pocket" routine, you're going to have to know how to handle strangers and the best ways to interact with them. There are a number of fun scenarios for the miserable failure where you can lie, cheat, steal and frighten random people in society. Let's say that a single mother and her baby are in the mall watching you steal loose change from the fountain in your whitey tighties (this applies to you women as well.) This would be a good opportunity to start to twitch and scream bloody murder as you limp like a zombie over to the young mother, thus scaring the ever-living shit out of her which causes the baby to cry uncontrollably. **The miserable failure has just won in two ways. First, you have scared a woman. Second, you have made a baby cry.** See how simple it is? Another good example of how a miserable failure can showcase them self to the public as a worthless FUCKER is through subtle elder abuse. An old man might be trying to cross the street at a busy intersection. It's the job of the miserable failure to offer to "help" walk him across the street while stealing the old codger's wallet. Feel free to smack his ass and whisper to him, *"when you think of people beating and hurting their grandfather, I want you to think of me, you old, crusty bag."* Nothing on earth defines someone as a miserable failure, more than stealing and mentally assaulting a poor, helpless and defenseless, old man.

Your parole officer might not like the next piece of advice, but **making sure you hurl verbal insults toward police officers in public is also a great way to showcase your worthlessness as a horrible member of society.** If you see a cop ordering a doughnut at a morning coffee shop, say something like, *"eat another one, you fat ass, pig."* Police officers do not like comments like that and if you're lucky, you'll get a **free** night of "rest and relaxation" in the local county jail (again). The best part of hurling insults toward cops, is the fact that you have a very good chance of getting a good police brutality beating with several nightsticks as you continue to run your mouth off. This type of beatdown should be strongly desired for the miserable failure. This beatdown gives you an opportunity to file another police brutality lawsuit for $34.5 million (which you'll of course lose).

We also encourage the **miserable** failure to pick fistfights with the biggest guy in the bar (if you're a dude) and the biggest biker woman at the concert (if you're a chick). Getting your ass beat (and you will because you're a miserable failure who does not know how to fight) is a great way to showcase your external ugliness. **A broken nose, a smashed lip, two black eyes, several missing teeth, a fractured jaw, and cauliflower ear are all physical facial qualities that many current miserable failures should possess on a regular basis.** In this section, we will also focus on random miscellaneous people that the miserable failure will encounter. From angry loan officers, the repo man, schizophrenic homeless people, prostitutes, pimps and delivery folks; the miserable failure will have their work cut out for them as they go through their daily "to do" tasks. Run across a homeless man? Make sure that you steal his entire bag of cans. "Forgot" to pay the hooker? Threaten her 6'6" 250-pound, steroid-infested pimp with bodily injury when he shows up to collect his money. **Is your neighbor getting packages and boxes delivered on the doorstep around Christmas? Guess what? Now he's not. Those are YOUR PACKAGES.** The repo man is trying to reposes your car? Make sure to cut the gas line so he can't drive the car very far (FYI: if you need a good defense lawyer, call 1-800-EatMyAss). You took out another 300% interest quick payday cash loan from a shady bookie? Make sure that you refuse to pay and spit on his shoes when he comes to collect a payment from you (NOTE: please read the hygiene section on the importance of obtaining a compound bone fracture).

As the miserable failure continues down the life to become a hopeless, worthless, degenerate, drunken, cocksucking fuckface, you are going to have to remember that you must continue to ruin all of the relationships that are currently around you. From your brief "yelling and stealing" interaction with the fast food worker in the drive through, to the relationship that you have with your parole officer, you're going to have to make damn certain that the rest of world knows just how much of a fuckup, dipshit and lowlife you really are.

Senior Citizens

Most normal and fully-functioning members of adult society respect the elderly... **However, miserable failures DO NOT LIKE OLD PEOPLE** (FYI: you should also be prejudicial against all fat people too). You should know how to behave by now in front of senior citizens (asking to borrow money and telling funeral jokes are a couple of suggestions). As a miserable failure, we do want you to focus on things you should be doing to various old people you run across in your life. Fun activities involving the elderly might include:

- Asking an old lady her age and angrily demanding that she tell you while lifting her purse.
- Taking out million-dollar life insurance policies on your old, codger grandparents.
- Parking in handicapped spots outside of the bingo parlor before going in drunk and playing all night.
- Discussing your internal hatred of daytime TV game shows with them at the retirement home "volunteer hour" (by "volunteer hour," we mean "free meals and squatting hour").
- Being a little too aggressive with your handshakes when you meet them (#FrailBones #Crack).
- Tickling them while they are in their wheelchairs.
- Pointing to them at funerals and screaming out as loud as you can, "*you're next, motherfucker.*"

"Being There" for the Codgers

Chances are, you are out of money, out of work, have a family that hates you, have literally zero friends and potentially no place to live (SCORE!). You probably smell like a pile of dog shit mixed with body odor and bleach. **Your mangled, ugly face should match your personality- grotesque and disturbing.** These are just some quick reasons **why you can't find a job**, obtain legal housing or move forward and become useful and productive member in society. So, in order to combat your new life traits, you the miserable FUCK failure, need to get busy very fast in order to find a senior citizen to hang out with. **We not only encourage the miserable failure to search for senior citizens in retirement homes and hospitals, but also look for them at bingo parlors, all-you-can-eat buffets, dollar stores, yard sales and gambling riverboats.** These places are going to give you the best opportunity to find an old person to pal around with.

When you find an old person to be your friend, try to find one with dementia. This is the golden unicorn. If you are lucky enough to find one of these mythical creatures, cling to them like grim death. (NOTE: **Finding an old person with dementia to hang out with is like finding a $100 bill on the ground... every single day**). When you do find a new BFF with dementia in the local retirement home, feel free to move into their little one-bedroom apartment and make yourself at home. If you can pull this off, you'll live in a retirement home RENT FREE while dominating the chess, checkers, puzzles and board games during "play time." Finding an old person with dementia to crash with is fun and also provides you with a golden opportunity to help yourself to their prescription medicines. Here's how you pull this off. First, pretend to be their long-lost grandchild when visiting the retirement home. After you become acquainted with your new "old friend," grab your trash bags full of your possessions and move on into their apartment! Now, every single day, you'll need to remind them several times why you're living there, and who you are **(REMEMBER: you're their long-lost grandchild, and your age and race does not matter).** Finding an old person to crash with is also a fantastic way to consistently get **free cash**! Simply ask your "grandma" (or "grandpa") if you can have $20 every hour. Old people are rich, so you'll probably be able to pull this off **MULTIPLE** times throughout the day! If the retirement home staff begins to question you living with your new "old friend," simply call them an *"Elderphobe,"* threaten to call the police on them for senior citizen abuse and continue on your merry way (BTW: more on the importance of how to get out of a choke hold by an orderly in a retirement home in a later section). If the retirement home tries kicking you out, simply self-identify as a one-hundred-year-old person and call a civil liberties lawyer so you can threaten lawsuits. Sooner or later, if or when your "old friend" passes away, loot their apartment for items you can sell on the streets, go to the next retirement home and repeat.

Marrying and Having Sex with the Elderly

You're going to need some money. You're going to need food. You're going to need a place to live. This is why we **HIGHLY** encourage the miserable failure to find and marry an old person. Don't shoot for someone who is seventy-years old. Try to find someone who is over ninety-years-old. **If you are a female miserable failure, marry an old man who is as frail and fragile as a wet piece of toilet paper blowing in hurricane force winds.** His family might call you a "gold digger" (which you are). If you are a man, make sure you marry a woman who is not able to walk or who has severe dementia. Her family might call you a "gigolo" (HINT: you are **not**). Not only does marrying a senior citizen stranger give you a place to live, it also puts you in prime position to be cut into their will **($$$CHA-CHING$$$)**. Senior citizens are less likely to be able to see how disgusting you are visually and they are also less likely to be able to smell your paint-curling body and mouth odors.

Perhaps, the best way to find an old codger to marry you is to find one in a wheelchair or one who is senile, and constantly make love to them. Sometimes the miserable failure gets lucky and finds one with a combo package of **crippled** and **senile**. Romance them. Talk sweet nothings into their ears. Be around them. Be there for them. Take care of them. Feel free to also sleep on their couch in their retirement home, play bingo with them at night and eat pro bono at the cafeteria in their rest home. However, if you **have** to bang them, make sure you are hopped up on whatever pills you can find in their medicine cabinet because it's not going to be a fun experience for you (NOTE: remember, miserable failures have no standards regarding sex). We should also mention two mantras regarding the sex with your new husband of wife. You should try to live by these during your sexcapades with them.

For Male Miserable Failures

~You shouldn't be happy during sex until you hear her hip break~

For Female Miserable Failures

~Dose him up on massive amounts of erectile dysfunction pills and hop on top for a sloppy ride~

If the senior citizen has a family and they start to suspect that you're trying to cut in on their family fortune, call them, *"conspiracy theorists"* and tell them that they're all greedy dirt bags. Sometimes while you're drunk and passed out on the sofa of your new senior citizen companion's couch at 10:00 in the morning, their family might come over to try and convince your new spouse that you are a gold digger and you can't be trusted. **This will be your only weak spot. To combat this, the best thing to do is to start your drinking at 3:00 PM during their dinner. This gives you time after they go to bed at 6:00, to get as sloshed as much as you want, thus preventing you from passing out during visiting hours the following day.** Making sure that you stay very close to your new "lover" while you steal their loose change collection from their closet is a great step in getting yourself in position to be cut into their will.

BFFs

We also encourage the miserable failure to become BEST friends with as many old and decrepit fucks as possible. The best way to do this is to again, start sneaking your way into VARIOUS retirement homes to play board games with your new buddies during visiting hours (FYI: feel free to cheat at those board games as well). Make sure you hang out with them during arts and crafts time as much as possible as well (as this provides ample opportunity for glue huffing). We want you to be present as much as humanly possible in their lives. Even the Alzheimer's and senile people will forget who you are. If one of the retirement home staff members asks you to leave, tell them that you are a volunteer with the Federal Government's new "Elderly Society Companion Program" (the "ESCP"). **It's completely made up and 100% bullshit, but it sounds official and it will get them off of your ass.** The more you are around, the more likely you will be able to pawn off their old antiques that you "found" in their room.

When one of your elderly buddy's die, relax! Another one is coming soon... That's what's great about the elderly—there are plenty of them ready to go around! Trying to get cut into their will because you're their new friend is plausible if not likely. Play the odds. If you can hang out and become friends with as many elderly people as possible, when they start to drop off the planet earth one by one, you increase your odds of getting a random check delivered to you!

Playing the "Grim Reaper Game"

WARNING: playing this game will get you another, FREE, one-way ticket into the fiery pits of eternal hell when you die from your soon-to-be coming speed balling overdose.

Hanging around retirement homes all day is going to get boring, REAL FAST. To combat this boredom, we encourage that you play a game called the "Grim Reaper Game." This game is very simple and it will scare the shit out of the old bastards at the various retirement homes you frequent. Simply, dress in a black and hooded gown while carrying a scythe (if you can't find a scythe, feel free to steal one from any gardener). Dressing up like the Grim Reaper (A.K.A. "DEATH") while walking from room to room is a fantastic prank to pull on these frail senior citizens. During the "Grim Reaper Game," walk from room to room, telling each one you encounter that they *"need to come with you"* because *"now is the time."* Try to avoid letting two or more elderly cripples see you in your Grim Reaper outfit, or they probably won't believe that you are real. This is why you need to pick off these blue-haired snowbirds one at a time. Also, it is important that you don't give these elderly people any heart attacks. You need them around as your meal ticket. But the point of the "Grim Reaper Game" is to have some fun with these old cripples. Only a real lowlife, loser would do such a horrible prank, but hey... YOU'RE a miserable failure, so this is the game you should be playing weekly with your BFFs.

Police Officers

"Cops" and "miserable failures" go together like "pepperoni" and "pizza." If you are on your way to becoming a miserable failure, by now you should have run across a few cops (several hundred in fact) in your pathetic excuse for a life. If you've been following this book, the authorities probably have a LONG arrest sheet on you already. From the DUI you just got driving a golf cart during the charity golf outing, to the restraining order you received when your first crush moved away without informing you, you should have a long history with many different police departments and law enforcement agencies. If you are becoming a miserable failure, you probably have had many of the following run-ins and subsequent arrests with the cops:

- Arrested for the removal of your ankle monitor (followed by a classic chokehold from the officer).

- Arrested for public intoxication at your sister's wedding (followed by vomiting and crying in the back seat of the police cruiser).
- Arrested for trying to sell kids basil and pass it off as marijuana (which officially banned you from coming within 500 feet of **any** school).
- Arrested and detained at the airport after screaming, *"we're all going to die!"* (Which officially put you on the "Do Not Fly List.")
- Arrested for failing to disclose the drunk, passed out hooker in your trunk (which resulted in the infamous "nightstick beating" a few years ago).
- Arrested for smacking the police horse's ass in the park (and your name being on the sex offender registry that followed).
- Arrested and tasered for trying to steal the badge off the uniform of a female police officer (and the sexual assault lawsuit that followed).

You, the miserable failure should have a history in getting into mischief with the cops. Now, we want you to step it up a notch. **You should be constantly getting arrested as well as being the poster child for youngsters worldwide in the "How to Not Fuck Up Your Lives, Kids" campaign.**

Getting Pulled Over

Most people are nervous when they get pulled over. This is not the case for the miserable failure. Chances are, you should not be driving anyway, so the best thing you can do is to humor yourself. **Cops "LOVE" jokes and appreciate people with a sick sense of humor at 3:00 in the morning as they are stopped along the interstate.** Some of the activities that a miserable failure must do upon getting pulled over include:

- Get out of the car as soon as you stop and quickly run towards the cop to "explain" your innocence.
- Offer a random baseball card as your "driver's license" and your grocery receipt for the fifth of vodka you just consumed as your "proof of insurance."
- Tell the cop that you were speeding because, "*the demons in your head told you to go fast and to hit a pedestrian.*"
- Cry like a baby and take your shirt off while trying to grab the officer's firearm.
- Call the cop a *"fat pig"* and tell him, *"miserable failures' lives matter, bitch!"*
- Ask the cop if you get to go to the "just visiting" space instead of going "directly to jail."
- Force yourself to vomit on the cop and then demand that he give you $50 for your troubles.
- Don't pull over and instead, lead them on a high-speed chase (HELLLOOOOO 10:00 news!).

We want you to really stir some shit up when you get pulled over by the fuzz. How DARE that **this** cop interferes with **your** night of drinking, drug usage, stalking, stealing and public urination!?!? When you get pulled over by the cops, make sure to mock the cop and ridicule them as much as possible. When they get mad, inform them that you're joking and you know your rights (feel free to recite your Miranda Rights). Make sure to avoid eye contact and make DAMN certain that you use expletives and obscenities as frequently as possible during your conversation with the cop. If you follow the steps mentioned above, you will be ahead of the game in your quest to become a total and complete miserable failure.

Behaving in Public

When most normal people see a cop on a horse, they generally are thrilled to see such a magnificent and beautiful creature with an officer of the community gracefully sitting on top of the animal. A miserable failure informs the cop that he is a *"pig"* that is sitting on top of soon to be *"Mexican hamburger."* Making comments like that towards a cop on horseback is a great way to keep having a fun time in the park during your first week out of the nuthouse. **It's also a great way to go back to the county jail to visit some of your "old friends."** If a cop drives by in their patrol car, make sure you give him the middle finger salute. The cops will also enjoy this gesture followed by a crotch grab as you hurl obscenities simultaneously.

Sometimes, the miserable failure has an opportunity to speak with a cop on a bike, or directing traffic. **If you see a cop on a bike, make sure you laugh and mock them**. Then try to take their wallet and explain to them that you feel they are wasting your hard-earned tax dollars by riding a bike instead of a car. All of these actions combined will probably result in you visiting Judge Nelson again in court. Dealing with a cop directing traffic can also be a fun time for the miserable failure. If you are watching a cop direct traffic in a busy intersection, walk up to them and dance while trying to mimic his arm gestures. If you have access to grab the traffic cop's whistle to use it, make sure you confiscate it, blow it and yell *"rape"* as loud as you can while the cop chases you around in the intersection. If you see a cop parked alongside of the road outside of a high school, make sure you approach them and ask, *"where do these high school sluts hang out after school?"* You can also ask the cop, *"where would be a great place to buy some coke?"* **Chances are, your day will be cut short and you'll be in the back of the patrol car (again) with Officer Duke.** You, the miserable failure must keep these cops on their toes. Be resourceful and be creative. If you see a cop randomly in a restaurant eating, be sure to tell them that you witnessed the cook *"yank one out in their food."* You can also approach cops in public by saying random shit such as, *"I am in the CIA."* The bottom line is this, whenever you have a chance to interact with an officer, make sure you leave a long-lasting impression on that cop.

Going on Ride Alongs

Honest and upstanding members of the community that pay taxes (HINT, HINT: **not you**) are allowed to go on as many ride alongs as they want with their local law enforcement officials (city, county and state cops). However, YOU ARE NOT an upstanding member of society or even a taxpayer (BTW: paying taxes means that you have ACTUAL legal employment). When you want to book a time, make sure that you schedule your ride alongs on Friday or Saturday nights. Also, pick the graveyard shift (11:00 p.m.-7:00 a.m.) to roll along with the cops. These days and times are going to give you the best "bang for your buck" for seeing random, bizarre and crazy shit. **Friday nights and Saturday nights will no doubt give you a great opportunity run across some of your old buddies around town (thieves, drug dealers, hookers, home invaders, drunks, druggies, lunatics, crackheads, bullies and homicidal maniacs)** while also giving you some much needed entertainment. First, make sure you show up for your ride along, drunk as a skunk (you can also bring that "bottle of water" that is really filled with vodka, with you during your ride along). Having a semi-homeless, degenerate, ugly and stupid drunk miserable failure showing up for a ride along is a great story that you will be providing the cop for many years to come. When the ride along starts, ask if you can run the sirens and lights a few times. After the cop agrees for you to do this ONCE, then ask if you can hold the shotgun. When the cop refuses, try to grab the shotgun anyway. **After you regain consciousness from the thunder punch you sustained to your throat from the cop, ask if they have any day-old doughnuts laying around the car.** Cops don't like stereotypes and they might ask you to sit in the back seat (your usual place in a cop car).

When the cop pulls someone over for speeding, make sure that YOU get involved in ALL of the action as well. We recommend the miserable failure get out of the car and walk up to the vehicle, just to stir some shit up (the sight of a sketchy, drunk person wearing a dirty robe, shorts and slippers walking up to their car with a cop is a horrifying sight for the driver). After the officer tells you to get back into the car, you have two options. First, you can get back in the car, but this time in the driver's seat. Then, proceed to lock the doors while doing your stand-up comedy routine material on the megaphone intercom. Or, you can ignore the cop's request for you to get back in the car, and instead hop in the automobile of the person he just pulled over.

If the cop has to pursue a suspect on a foot chase, make sure **you** get in on the action as well. Run after the cop as they chase the suspect. First, try to help the cop by throwing random rocks at the suspect. If the cop can't catch the suspect, announce to the cop that you'll bring the car around to try and cut off the perpetrator, and then act accordingly by running back to the car. This is a great way to get the cop to decide to A.) go after the suspect, or B.) stop you from briefly stealing their patrol car. If the cop makes an arrest and the person is in the back seat, make sure you make small talk with the arrested individual. Making comments about *"prison sexual assault"* is a great icebreaker for the caught criminal on the ride downtown.

If you have to stop to go to the bathroom on your ride along, make sure that you tell him that you're in the process of *"transgendering"* and you need to find an officially certified and authorized "tranny bathroom" ASAP or you're suing the police department. Also, ORDER that the cop take you out for dinner on your ride along. When they reject your rather unusual request, make sure that you tell them that you are paying their salary through your (make-believe) taxes and demand to be taken to a fast food joint for a quick bite. Make the argument that your taxes have already paid for the meal that you are DEMANDING to eat. If you're ever in doubt what to do on a ride along with a cop, you can always resort to asking them if you can shoot their gun while simultaneously trying to grab it from their holster. This is a sure-fire way (no pun intended) to receive an elbow across the bridge of your nose and to get a nice tomahawk chop to your skull within a few seconds of your grabbing motion.

In the end, dealing with cops is like dealing with anyone else. Keep these fuckers on their toes while providing them with much-needed entertainment. Make them work and earn their salary and benefits. You are doing a service for them. You're keeping them prepared and steadfast. Saying sketchy and borderline illegal shit is a great start. Trying to use some of the officer's gear is also a fantastic way to follow up your verbal joking insults towards them. In the end, cops will be in your life as long as you are a miserable failure. It's just that plain and simple. You might be visited by a cop for missing child support payments or for failing to appear in court. You might be arrested by a cop for impersonating them on Halloween. Get accustomed to being around cops, public defenders, judges, parole officers, and court-ordered psychologists. YOU are a miserable failure and YOU are a complete fuckup. So, make sure you act accordingly around cops and all law enforcement officers.

College Students

A miserable failure CAN HAVE a college degree. In fact, a miserable failure can have MULTIPLE college degrees. There are MILLIONS of miserable failures right now with basically worthless and useless college degrees (a B.A. in "gender studies," a B.A. in "communications," a B.S. in "psychology," a B.A. in "social justice," etc.) who are living in mom's basement (NOTE: which we encourage) and who have thousands of dollars in student loan debt which will never be paid back. For these unfortunate youngsters, being a miserable failure can be expensive. Now, although many current miserable failures live at home while paying no rent (with no job), and owe massive amounts of money in loans, they still might possess a college degree. On the other hand, there are also MILLIONS of miserable failures who have never even opened up a book in their entire existence on planet Earth. **It doesn't matter if you're a miserable failure who has a college degree, or a miserable failure who never went to college, this section is for you.**

Chances are, miserable failures are older than most college students. This is good news. Being older than most college students is a great way to become "the creepy old guy" (or the "crazy old gal" if you're a female miserable failure) when your hanging around various college campuses drunk and stumbling around in the middle of the night during finals week in the quad while vomiting. Furthermore, people should refer to you as "scary" as you lurk around campus. How to properly behave and interact with college students for the miserable failure is paramount in your journey down your road to isolation, humiliation and destitution.

Crashing Parties

In addition to becoming the creepy, old, weirdo that lurches around outside of the female dorms at 2:00 in the morning (or around the freshman male dorms if you're a female miserable failure), the miserable failure needs to master the art of crashing parties on college campuses. **Now chances are, college security will have your photo plastered all over the campus as a warning to the students and faculty.** You might even be officially "trespassing" when you attend parties on college campuses. Showing up to parties, uninvited, unwelcomed and unwarranted is something that a miserable failure does on a weekly basis. From crashing the Sigma Pi "Thirsty Thursday" mixer, to showing up to the "Bead Bash" at Phi Alpha, the miserable failure needs to make crashing parties an art form. We encourage the miserable failure to keep their customary robe, underwear and slippers on when they crash the toga party, but **for regular parties, the miserable failure is ALLOWED to wear their sweatpants and a t-shirt** (NOTE: this is a chance to put a little "class" in your wardrobe for these parties).

When you FIRST get to a party, make sure you know where "the coke room" is. You can generally find this out from the kid talking a million miles a second, or the anorexic, skinny female (who is ironically on suicide watch from her sorority sisters). **If you play your cards right, you might end up doing FREE blow off of a dirty and pissed-stained toilet lid in the back bathroom of a party hall on campus** (#GOALS). We also MANDATE that the miserable failure steal and drink as much alcohol from the college kids as possible when crashing multiple parties. You also want to "work the room" and become everyone's best friend during these college drunk fests. This will be difficult because of your odor, your disgusting hygiene, your missing teeth, and your mangled face. However, you'll still need alcohol if you want to party hard. You will want to make friends with as many college students as possible so you can swindle them out of their liquor. You might get "free" cigarettes as well as pot from your new "college buddies." At the party, feel free to dance when music is playing while simultaneously slamming two beers "shotgun style." College kids don't mind massive amounts of beer, saliva, and vomit on them on the dance floor, so please act accordingly (WINK, WINK: dance "the sprinkler" as you vomit). If you get challenged to a fight over this practice, make sure you take the younger, bigger, soberer, and more athletic challenger outside. Your actions by going outside to fight a college linebacker at a party you just crashed will result in two things:

1.) You'll probably be knocked out cold from a thunder punch to your jaw.
2.) You might get sympathy sex out of your defeat in the fight.

Some desperate drunk people might even feel sorry enough for you and give you some cash for a cab ride home (of which you'd pocket the money and use it to purchase crystal meth from Lenny the homeless mute later on in the evening). Or, you might make new friends by getting your ass kicked and find a place to sleep at night out of pure sympathy (instead of crashing on the bench in the quad like normal). So, let's recap your actions at college parties:

- Steal beer and alcohol from your new college "friends." - CHECK
- Dance erotically with college kids while making sure to spill alcohol over as many as possible. - CHECK
- Make yourself vomit on the dance floor. - CHECK
- Get into a fight and get your ass ROYALLY kicked. - CHECK
- Attempt to swindle sympathy sex. - CHECK
- Get kicked out of the party. - CHECK
- Do drugs or get free drugs if possible. - CHECK
- Steal cigarettes. - CHECK
- Find a place to crash for the night. - CHECK

The Myth... The Legend

Miserable failures constantly need a place to stay. Evictions, bankruptcies and insurance fraud generally set the miserable failure apart from most normal people when dealing with their housing and living situations. Going back to college illegally involves living free on college campus. **Thus, the miserable failure, in addition to crashing parties, must find a way to squat illegally on a college campus.** This squatting might come in the form of being the typical "guy on the couch" for a group of rowdy Freshmen, or living in the cellar of the cafeteria building by making friends with the alcoholic and sketchy janitor. The best way to squat is to try to make new friends by being the "creepy old weirdo" on campus who is a wild and crazy party man (or party girl). You need to make yourself into legendary status. And here is how...

College kids love a crazy and rambunctious person who will do **anything** they are told in order to be "the life of the party." **This includes possibly receiving bodily injury from your stupid actions, potentially getting arrested from your poor life choices and being chased off cam-**

pus by college security. You need to try to be the life of the party whenever you can and impress some Freshman, so they give you a place to stay. We need you to make some temporary friends, just so you can find a place to crash. We encourage the miserable failure to allow Freshmen to throw darts at their bare ass during social gatherings as a party trick. We also recommend that the miserable failure do flaming shots of 100% pure grain alcohol with the freshman (NOTE: the resulting facial burns will make you an instant legend at the college). You must make sure to help your new little Freshman buddies purchase alcohol as well since many of them will be under the age of twenty-one. Since you are over twenty-one, a great way to make and to keep friends in college is to always be the "beer run person." This benefits you on three levels.

1.) You get to drive a car again (even though your driver's license is suspended).
2.) You're probably going to get free booze out of the deal.
3.) You are going to keep those little bastards happy.

You can also keep your new Freshman buddies happy by doing the following stunts, thus proclaiming your instant legendary status and allowing you the opportunity to crash on one of their dorm room couches—**indefinitely**.

- Drinking ten free extra spicy, quarts of salsa at the Mexican restaurant to showcase your "badassery" on Cinco de Mayo.
- Doing various on demand requests for your projectile vomiting skills at parties.
- Allowing your new friends to drunkenly urinate on you and post said video on social media.
- Going streaking through the quad on a dare in the middle of the day.
- Taking an "upper decker" shit in the President's house on graduation day.

- Playing "Afcanistan" batting practice with beer cans and a baseball bat outside of the science building during finals week.

You can also do various other party tricks and basically do anything that you are told. You want to become a legend; not the drunken, lush miserable failure legend that you're accustomed to being. We want you to become a legend on the college campus by being the fall person and by being the butt end of all of the jokes.

Your "Being Honest" Farewell Speech

In addition to pledging a fraternity or sorority as well as crashing classes drunk and high, the miserable failure needs to master the art of being brutally and completely honest with college kids. This is extremely important. **You are LITERALLY a walking example of how hard life can be and how unfortunate some people in life have it** (even though you're doing it to yourself on a path of self-destruction and self-deprivation). You need to tell your story to these youngsters. We encourage the miserable failure to stand in the middle of the quad up on a bench and speak the truth about life after college. Make sure to get on your soapbox drunk as a skunk (this will showcase your mangled face) as you stand in your customary night robe, underwear and slippers. Looking like a dangerous, mental asylum escapee is a great way to get people's attention. Chances are good that campus security is going to have you arrested, so you need to make this final speech count... You need to channel your "innermost miserable failure" in order to deliver the powerful message and wakeup call that these spoiled, rotten, entitled, little shits deserve.

Make sure to start off your speech by prefacing the fact that many of the graduating seniors will eventually become YOU over the years. **Next, after the screams and crying subsides, feel free to laugh like a maniac and then proceed to piss yourself.** This act really scares the living shit out of most college students. Make sure that these college kids know some of them will become miserable failures, and there is no disputing this fact. Explain to the college students that the economy sucks and getting a job that pays a decent wage is nearly impossible to get. **Inform these little fuckers that NO ONE CARES ABOUT THEIR FEELINGS and that safe spaces do not exist in the real hard knock life of the corporate America adult world.** After you've set the tone and a few hundred students have gathered around you videotaping it as a livestream on social media, take the time to point out the stereotypes and mock each of them by being brutally honest.

First, find the hot sorority sisters. **Be sure to point out that lonely, loser, creepy, weirdo, guys like yourself generally masturbate to their slutty Halloween pictures on social media multiple times per day in the months of October and November.** Tell them that they should be flattered by these acts. Next, let the nerds know that even though they will be making the most money after college, they'll still never get laid. Explain to the creepy goth kids who dress in black and worship Edgar Allan Poe that they will probably end up in federal prison for their crimes when they join an occult in their late twenties. Inform the athletes that hardly any of them are going to "go pro" in their sport that they currently play. In fact, let them know that their back, knees, hips, and shoulders will all require surgery later on in life due to the rigorous pounding the sport had on their bodies over the years. A little dose of reality can go a long way.

Make sure to inform the fraternity guys that 50% of them will probably end up just like you—**an alcoholic and druggie**—due to their EXTREME usage of these substances in their college days. Let the valedictorian know that employers "don't give a shit" about the fact they graduated #1 in their class, or their high GPA. All employers care about is how hot women who just graduated college look when they bring their boss coffee, or how submissive the men who just graduated college are as they are forced to work in the mail room in the cellar of the building. **Make damn certain that you let these college kids know how**

fucked they are on their student loans. Inform them that they'll never make a job that pays them enough money to be able to actually pay back their student loans. Laugh and point at them as you discuss these financial matters. Tell these kids that their parents' generation are responsible for the ten-fold increase in college tuition over the past thirty years. Recommend that they steal money from their parents as a form of payment and payback.

At this point during the shock of your speech, you'll probably be spotted by campus security (you've probably been avoiding and hiding from these guys all semester long). Inform them that their professors are brainwashing them and remind them that the only real reason to go to college is to party, get laid, drink and do drugs. As you are escorted off campus, while being tasered by the campus police department and while the crowd is cheering in the background, be sure to turn around and scream, *"remember me!"* at the top of your lungs. Becoming a legend on college campuses by being a miserable failure should take you as many years as possible. If you play your cards right, you might end up with a **free** college degree after your decade-plus living on and around the college campus.

The Homeless

If you have been following the advice given in this book thus far, **you might be homeless**. You might be sleeping in a sewer runoff ditch, drinking puddle water, shooting heroin with used needles and blowing wealthy businessmen for $5 a suck in dark alleys around the city. If this describes you and your current state of affairs right now, CONGRATULATIONS! You are really starting to become a miserable failure. But, you're not all the way there yet, asshole...

It should be noted that this particular chapter is not a knock on the homeless, nor are we disparaging them in any way. This section is rather an invitation for the miserable failure to **intentionally** become homeless, if you are not already. Chances are, if you have pissed off and isolated yourself from your only family and royally fucked over your friends, you might be homeless. These facts, combined with your current financial situation (no money) as well as your current employment status, (unemployed) basically means that you're "S.O.L." (shit out of luck). The miserable failure celebrates their homelessness first by stealing the bag of cans from their alley-dwelling neighbor. As you run away with the cans, mock him as he chases you. Scream something like, *"I am stealing your money, you damn bum!"* Don't be afraid to let the angry, schizophrenic, lunatic, psycho, homeless man to catch up to you and allow him to get a few good licks into your sorry ass. **His training from the military wars he fought in, will kick in and you'll find yourself getting a royal beat down from a crazy old man along the side of the road.** When you get your ass kicked by a homeless maniac, the resulting beat down will add to your mangled face, fractured cheekbone, busted lip, missing teeth, swollen eyes and cauliflower ears. Essentially, **you can't really get any lower than stealing a homeless man's cans, and then allowing him to kick the ever-loving shit out of you.** Those are very low points in the life of any miserable failure. We strongly encourage you to complete that task the first day you get onto Skid Row.

Free Grub and Food Fights

Living among the homeless for the first time can be quite challenging and intimidating for the miserable failure. To combat these feelings of depression and hunger, we encourage the miserable failure to stake out the best soup kitchens and breadlines in the city. We recommend the miserable failure use these places for food, rest and relaxation. **Eating in these locations can also aid in your eating disorder as well as your food fighting abilities with the other homeless on holiday feasts.** If it's Christmas and you go to the local soup kitchen, you should dress in your customary "Drunk Santa" outfit. Simply go into any store selling Santa outfits, snatch one and head for the doors! Dressing up like a drunk Santa is a great way to say *"Merry Christmas"* to all of your new homeless buddies. Then, proceed to start a vicious food fight with the others in the soup kitchen or breadline. Remember, there is no need to use the food on your plate to start the food fight. Go into the back pantry and grab some food that is still in the cans and boxes. Unopened cans of baked beans and corn niblets make great items to hurl during a food fight. Just be sure that you don't seriously injure other homeless. In fact, ENCOURAGE the other homeless to peg you with the full cans of green beans and soup that you got (stole) from the back pantry.

Begging for Money

We also strongly recommend that the miserable failure beg for money along the side of the road with the other homeless. Some great slogans you should have written on your brown cardboard sign could include:

- "Hey, you cheap asshole. I need some fast cash to fund my crack addiction. At least I'm honest!"
- "I'll let you enter me with whatever object you want, and video tape it for only $3."
- "Will clean your ENTIRE toilet with my tongue for $4."
- "Will allow your children to beat me with a baseball bat like a piñata for $2."
- "I'm hungry. I am about to start eating myself."
- "I need $100 for steak and lobster at the store."
- "I need a place to stay. Can I sleep in your bed?"
- "I'll be honest... I need $100 to purchase cigarettes, visit the local fortune teller, and buy scratch of lottery tickets."
- "Rest assured, I will use the money you give me on booze."
- "Free shitty advice, $1."
- "I need a date to the prom."

- "I need a free ride to my crack dealer's apartment."
- "I have thirty-seven illegitimate children at home going hungry and scraping asbestos off the ceiling. Help a bitch out."

If you're lucky enough to have a motorist give you some cash, make sure to blow the money on cigarettes, booze, crack head prostitutes, slot machine gambling, lottery tickets, VARIOUS narcotics, and alcohol (NOTE: never use the money for food). Make sure that you brag about your money acquisition to your homeless friends in style. If you have enough money to purchase some steak and lobster at the grocery store, make sure that you cook it over the open fire in the drum barrel in front of everyone at the homeless encampment. Make unnecessary comments and insulting remarks at your new BFF's as you don't share any of your fancy meal.

The Adopt-a-Cat Program

If you can't get any money from motorists along the side the road, we have two options for you. The first option is what we call, "Adopt-a-Cat Program." This is a great program to show your homeless buddies. In fact, you can get them to work for you on this program as well. There are plenty of feral, wild cats running around the city. **We encourage the miserable failure to collect as many of these wild and rabies-riddled felines as possible.** Put them in a crate or cage and try to sell them along the side the road. You'll probably be bleeding from their tooth and claw marks, but don't let this deter you. These little fur balls need a good home. You're also doing them a favor! **If you can't sell any of these wild cats to the motorists, we encourage the miserable failure to GENEROUSLY "donate" them to each family. This is a great way to "give back" to the community. If you spot a window unrolled, make sure this needy family gets a "free cat." Place the cat inside their car at the four-way stop.** Sometimes the people will not want the cat and you'll hear screams and cries coming from the car as it swerves down the road in a panic. This is just the cat getting "accustomed" to its new owners. Furthermore, you should be proud of yourself! You've provided a new home for an angry, feral wild cat. You've also given a loving family a pet that they can cherish for many years. Hooray for you!

The Tuck and Roll Program

The final way in which the miserable failure can interact with the homeless is through what we call, "The Tuck and Roll." We encourage you to teach your other homeless friends the importance of getting struck by a high-end luxury car. This event is called, "The Tuck and Roll." The Tuck and Roll basically involves waiting until a VERY EXPENSIVE CAR comes rolling down the road. Hide in the bushes and jump out in front of the car allowing it to strike you. **This may cause you to get some broken bones, shattered eye sockets and collapsed lungs. However, the lawsuit threat that you'll have is priceless**. If the car hasn't driven away, more than likely, the driver is going to be so shocked and scared that they will give you any amount of money that they have on them in order for you to **not** call the police. As you lay on the ground broken and dazed, threaten the driver with a lawsuit, and then watch their wallets open up. Even if you only get $50 out of them, make sure that they drive you to the hospital where you'll receive free painkillers, food and a nice warm bed to sleep in. "The Tuck and Roll" is a classic, fail-safe plan that you can do for yourself and one you can teach to the ENTIRE homeless community. Being a miserable failure involves being homeless at some point and having many unhealthy and unnecessary interactions with them.

Pimps, Prostitutes and Drug Dealers

In addition to homeless people, ex-con parolee criminals, and various law enforcement agencies, you're also going to run across some other real nasty people in your life as a miserable failure. If you are a miserable failure or you want to become one, sooner or later, you're going to have to deal with some very sketchy, scary and questionable "characters" in your life. There are three main groups of people that we will allude to in this next section—pimps, prostitutes and drug dealers. Now, it does not matter if you are male or female, all of the steps outlined below pertain to all miserable failures. Knowing how to handle an angry drug dealer, a crazed pimp, or a coked-out hooker is key when dealing with your life as a miserable failure.

Prostitutes

No one is going to bang you or even want to touch you sexually, which is why you're going to need to pay for prostitutes (NOTE: the high-end escorts, "middle class" hookers and crack head streetwalkers all count). Ordering sex from a nasty male or female prostitute is a key attribute of many miserable failures throughout the years. When you order a prostitute, make sure you ask for the, *"fattest, ugliest and most grotesque"* person that the pimp has on call that night. You are a miserable failure, so why should a hot prostitute bang you? When the horrific wildebeest hooker shows up to have sex with you, make sure that you have some fake and counterfeit money ready to give them that is wrapped in a $1 bill that you received panhandling earlier in the day.

If you are a female miserable failure, chances are, the male prostitute isn't going to be able to "get it up" due to your grotesque physical appearance as well as the foul odor that permeates from your entire body. **If you are a male miserable failure, you might have to get the hooker drunk off of your home-made prison wine before she will even attempt to touch your vile, nasty, stank ass.** If you're a female miserable failure, you better hope that your male prostitute has a sizable quantity of erectile dysfunction pills he can pop in order to get hard, otherwise, he might be just performing oral sex on you (NOTE: BAAAAADDDD NEWS for him...).

We also encourage the miserable failure to ask for (demand) various weird sexual requests from the prostitutes. Ask the hookers to *"piss on you"* (a "golden shower"). Ask that they address you as *"Big Dick Mamba"* (for you male miserable failures) and *"Cunt Face Punter"* (for you female miserable failures). Feel free to ask them to roleplay various sexual acts with you as well. Some classic examples of recommended sexual role-play include:

- "Angry Cops and Paraplegic Robbers"
- "Drunk Cowboys and High-as-Fuck Indians"
- "Quarterback and Tight End"
- "Preacher and Alter Boy"
- "Private and Drill Sergeant"

If you need to know what to do during sex with a prostitute, please refer to the section on sex. Follow those steps highlighted and outlined to a "T." If you do, the prostitute will proclaim for the entire alley of homeless bums to hear, that you were the *"worst lay they have ever had."* Take pride in your extremely poor sexual practices before the pimp makes his "grand entrance."

Sometimes a miserable failure will run across "prostitutes" while they are getting a massage. If you have miraculously gotten yourself on a massage table in either an upscale massage parlor, or a nice spa, making sure you ask for sex is paramount. The classier the massage parlor, the more likely you are to NOT be able to get extra "crotch stuff." For male miserable failures, most of the time, this involves you getting an "old fashion" (a "hand job," a "yank and tank," a "tug job," a "handy many," a "sandy handy," a "long beach hug," a "hand jibber," a "tugger," a "beef strokemeoff" or a "zip job"). When the massage comes to an end, grab the masseuse' hand and say, *"it's not going to get itself off, honey."* Now, if you are in a classier massage parlor and high-end spa, one of two things are bound to happen: 1.) you will be punched in your balls and you'll be arrested when you regain consciousness or 2.) you will get a happy ending, but it will "cost" you a few hundred dollars (don't worry, you're skipping out on the bill). If you are in a really run-down and sketchy massage parlor that stinks of cigarettes, mold, soy sauce and perfume, the sexual services at the end of your massage will happen whether you want it or not. Just sit back and enjoy whatever sex stuff that they perform on you. Whatever happens after your massage, make a break for the emergency door exit after you have "gotten your rocks off" and run like the dickens away; thus, skipping out on the massage bill and the tips you owe.

If you're a female miserable failure and you want to be finished off after getting a massage from the nice resort and spa, simply ask the masseuse, *"well, there it is, what are you waiting for?"* (while lifting up your robe). After you make this unusual request, one of two things are bound to happen: 1.) the masseuse will run from the room screaming asking for the police to be called, or 2.) the masseuse will give you one hell of a "sex job" and ask for a large tip. If you're in a skanky and sketchy massage parlor in the bad part of town, the "sex job" will be coming whether you are aware or not. In either case, you should be receiving a "female old fashion" (a "cucumbering," a "Minnesota light switch," a "grammar hammer," a "diddling bean," a "man in the canoe," a "hand puppet," or a "second fiddle"). When the "sex stuff" is over, locate the bathroom, crawl on top of the toilet and break through the ceiling to escape the massage payment and the sex tip.

Pimps

After the drunken, vomit-inducing, nasty, alley sex that just took place between you and the "high class" prostitute, make sure to tell them that you want your money back and you demand that they take you to a gas station *"on the bad side of town"* to buy you a large fountain soda. After phone calls to the angry pimp have been made, you need to start planning your escape route. The last thing you want is to get shot by a pimp, before you can complete your metamorphosis into a miserable failure. When the pimp arrives and gets out of the car in a methamphetamine-filled rage, make sure you tell the pimp how disappointed you were for the "services" you just received. **Tell the pimp that you're filing a complaint with the police, the better business bureau and also inform him that you'll be leaving a negative review online for his prostitution business.** Feel free to give him a good slap across the face as the cherry on top. After the pimp has hammered you in your face (shattering your jaw) and kicked you in the stomach with their steel toe work boots (lacerating your liver), make sure to run like hell to get away from the situation. Remember, the goal is to not die as you continue your quest to become a miserable failure. When you run, make sure to yell "*rape*" as loud as you can as you charge out into oncoming traffic from the dark alley (FYI: refer to the earlier section on using the "Tuck and Roll"). The pimp will probably leave the scene of the crime due to the fact that police and emergency services are on their way. The last thing a pimp wants to do is explain themselves to a cop as to why they were beating the ever-loving shit out of a drunken, nasty person wearing a dirty robe, slippers and underwear in the middle of the road. Knowing what to do and how to handle a pimp is a critical and crucial step for the miserable failure. So, let's recap...Step one, don't pay the hooker. Step two, allow the pimp to beat your sorry ass. Step three, avoid getting shot by doing the "Tuck and Roll" into oncoming traffic.

Drug Dealers

When you started out in your quest and journey to become a miserable failure, you might have drank a beer or two on the weekends. You might have even smoked pot a time or two in college. Let's face it, those were baby steps and gateways in your quest to become a drugged-out, lunatic, maniac. **For all miserable failures, their drug dealer is one of their BFFs.** In fact, your drug dealer should be listed in your "favorites" section in your phone. You need to be in constant communication with drug dealers in general, but specifically your "go-to main guy."

It's probably fair to say that you'll owe your drug dealer money from time to time (for which, you'll probably be **blessed** with a couple of broken legs as a form of "payment"). So, when you do need to purchase drugs, you're probably going to be on their "do not answer list." Or, if you call, they'll put you straight to voicemail on their burner phone. No need to worry here. We encourage the miserable failure to show up unexpected in the middle of the night to your drug dealer's house in order to get a quick fix. Most miserable failures do this multiple times, to SEVERAL drug dealers- a few times each week.

When you do get some fast cash for selling your hair, blood plasma and sperm (or eggs for females), make sure you call up your drug dealer, and tell them that you have money to pay them back and to purchase **MORE** drugs. When the deal is being made, we encourage the miserable failure to take the drugs without paying and run away as fast as you can during the transaction. When the drug dealer catches you and begins to nail you with blows on your legs with a hockey stick, make sure that you don't lose your drugs or money, so simply stick them up your ass (NOTE: there are places drug dealers WON'T go looking, and that includes your backside).

A really fun prank to pull on your drug dealer is the old' "undercover cops prank." Before you meet a drug dealer in an alley to purchase heavy narcotics, make sure the local cops and law enforcement are aware of your future transaction. Call the cops and let them know that a *"big drug deal is going down tonight"* and give them the precise time and the exact location of said transaction. When the cops show up and try to bust you, now is a good time to use your fake, plastic police badge that you stole out of a cereal box and show it to the cops. Scream something like, *"I'm undercover, you fuckers"* when they show up. At this point, you're looking at a felony and an arrest for impersonating a cop. You also just ruined another drug connection by doing this (SCORE!!!).

The "Usual's"

A miserable failure must take note that one of the ways that they are worthless is due to the crowd that they hang around with. From pimps, prostitutes, drug dealers, homeless psychopaths and politicians, your plate is going to be full of other fuckups that you can interact with. In fact, here is a comprehensive and complete list of certain types of people whom you should be hanging around with, or at least be seeing and interacting with on a daily basis:

- Petty thieves
- Degenerate gamblers
- Drug addicts
- Mentally disturbed individuals
- Hitchhikers
- Drunks
- Homeless maniacs
- Homicidal lunatics
- Angry current spouses
- Irate ex-spouses and partners
- Coked-out tow truck drivers
- Armed Robbers
- Ex-con parolees
- Meth head hookers
- Department of child and family services employees
- Road ragers
- Peeping Toms
- Pissed off repo men
- IRS investigators
- Dirty cops
- Bill collectors
- Habitual liars
- Welfare case workers
- Disowned children

Babies and Children

For the miserable failure, interacting and dealing with strange babies, kids and children can be an extremely valuable, educational and fun experience for all parties involved. If you have been following the steps by now, you are probably not legally able to be within 500 feet of anyone under the age of eighteen. This might have occurred a few months ago when you got hammered drunk and decided to take a piss in the middle of a high school parking lot right as school was getting out at 3:00. You must know that inevitably, you will be encountering strange children in your day-to-day life as you become a miserable failure, **so it's best to make sure small children learn valuable life lessons from what THEY SHOULDN'T DO** (HINT: your horrible life choices and bad decisions).

The Role Model

You should be asked at some point to be a "recovering addict" role model speaker during your miserable failure metamorphosis. This means that you're going to be invited to speak to the children at the local middle school (with a supervised police escort from the local county Sheriff's Department), as part of one of your parole plea bargain stipulations. **You are going to have to speak to a classroom full of children about being a miserable failure, while encouraging them to NOT BEHAVE LIKE YOU when they grow up.** This will be ordered by a judge, so make sure you show up to your arranged assembly (although being arrested and thrown in the country prison where you'll be physically, emotionally and verbally assaulted isn't a bad option either). When you show up for your speech to these little bastards, make sure that you're drunk and on some upper drug (methamphetamine, crack, cocaine or angel dust are recommended). This deadly combination will get you very agitated and get you sputtering nonsensical bullshit extremely fast during your speech. Start off by telling the children that you are a miserable failure and then walk them through this very step-by-step guide on how you came to be one. If kids don't want to be miserable failures, then they should be paying extra close and special attention to you and your terrible life story. **The fact that your face hasn't fully healed from the intense beatings you have been taking in life, as well as your missing teeth, will definitely scare the living shit out of these kids.** Also, make sure you're wearing your customary dirty robe, underwear (no bra for the female miserable failure) and house slippers when you deliver your soon-to-be infamous speech.

Inform the kids about each illegal drug and instruct them how you use them in GREAT detail. Speak about the pros and the cons of doing lines of cocaine off of your grandfather's casket at his funeral. Talk to the kids about your drinking and driving career. Speak a little about the drugs that you've taken in your past as well as the pills that you're currently on. **Explain to the kids where to get the good drugs and which drug dealers to avoid** (NOTE: a few tasers from the sheriff deputy at this point will be coming your way). Also tell the kids how to get alcohol and offer your services as a guy who will purchase them booze, in exchange for a pack of cigarettes and a 40 oz beer. At this point in your speech, you're probably going to be asked to leave. Don't leave. Stay engaged. Talk to these little bastards about:

- Where to find the "Good Hookers."
- The joys of being stabbed by a homeless man with a homemade shank.
- How to properly put a cigar out on your own arm.
- Stealing the free candy at the receptionist's desk.
- How to make yourself vomit if you have alcohol poisoning.
- Knowing which foods to avoid in county lockup.

- How to write a suicide note intended for your ungrateful and grieving mother.
- At what point in their lives they should avoid the meth and go for the crack rock.
- Knowing how to properly and successfully siphon gas from a state trooper's car.
- How to get out of restraining orders and non-disclosure agreements.

As you're talking to the kids about these subjects, you're probably also be physically escorted out of the room from the deputy. As this happens, make sure to yell at the kids, *"become me!!!"* **They probably won't be able to hear you through their screams and cries of fear.** When the cop takes you outside and tells you to leave, pull your pants down and moon him (this applies to both male and female miserable failures) before asking to borrow $5 from him. The bottom line is this... Your little outburst at the school in front of the children will not make the judge too happy. So, expect to go back to jail for a few days following your miserable failure appearance in front of the kids at the school.

Being Honest

Another important aspect of the miserable failure is to have 100% complete honesty when dealing with and speaking with kids and children (NOTE: this ALSO includes discussing your morning bowel movements in GREAT detail with strange and random neighborhood kids walking on their way to school). Normally, we encourage a miserable failure to lie, but on some occasions, being honest is simply the best policy. Similar to your honesty speech in in front of the middle schoolers mentioned above, as well as your psychotic, incoherent rant in front of college students outlined earlier, the miserable failure MUST BE HONEST sometimes in their fucked-up life. For example, if you see a little kid in public walking with their mom and dad and you don't think the kid looks ANYTHING like the father, make sure YOU speak up. **Tell that little bastard the man walking with him is probably not his real dad.** Mention to the kid that his real dad is probably the family gardener, the pizza delivery guy or the mail man. As the kid starts to cry and turn towards his mom, the father at this point is going to be your next threat. You can more than likely expect a variety of actions from the father. These include:

- A roundhouse kick to your face.
- A rabbit punch to your kidneys (resulting in pissing yourself).
- A chokehold followed by a body slam.
- A thunder punch to your wind pipe.

Another way you need to be honest with kids is when you're dealing with holidays. The best holiday to do this is at Christmas, or during the entire month of December. We encourage the miserable failure to show up on a busy Saturday afternoon to a local mall in December. Make sure that you're drunk as well as high from sniffing modeling glue in the parking garage. The reason for this is simple: **You need to tell the kids waiting in line to see Santa that he doesn't really exist and that their parents are lying to them.** Start off by walking up to the line while making comments about how great all of these "mommy asses" look (if you're a female miserable failure, PLEASE make the same comments). Then, when you reach the front of the line, shout as loud as you can, *"Santa Claus does not exist!"* Repeat this several **dozen** times. It really will add to the overall excitement of the mall Santa as well as the numerous parents, if you're actually wearing your broke ass, dirty, Santa outfit while you do this spectacle. Tell the children that Santa Claus is fake and that the *"fat fuck"* they're going to go see up there is just a retired postal worker looking to make a few extra bucks for the holidays. Also inform the kids that the mall Santa is more than likely a pervert or a creeper. Be HONEST! **Feel free to steal some candy canes and knock over the Santa village as mall security escorts you off of the premises and out in the back alley for an ass whooping.**

Giving Back...

The miserable failure needs to do something really special now. It's time for YOU to volunteer at a local kids' charity. If you can't pass the background check (which you probably will fail very badly), we encourage the miserable failure to simply donate some time down at the local foster home. Foster youth's need people to play with them, take them to go get ice cream and to be a support system for them. **Unfortunately for them, you will be providing none of those services or activities.** It's also time for you to cheat at board games, break shit when you lose at charades, and steal checkers as you play with the foster kids.

You need to show up at the foster home ready to have some fun! **If a kid is in a wheelchair, guess what? He is the first to get pummeled in the face with a rubber ball during the dodge ball game.** If you're asked to play a board game with several kids, make sure that you cheat as often as humanly possible. When it comes time to take the kids to the movies, make sure you choose an R or NC-17 rated movie. On the way to the theatre, feel free to give these little foster kids the "birds and the bees" talk. Also, if there is a red-head kid in the foster youth group, make sure that they get picked last for everything. Feel free to give them the old' *"red-headed stepchild"* routine and bust their balls a few times about their *"devil child"* ginger looks.

This is one of the few times in this book that we will ask that you do some volunteer work (SEE ALSO: section on volunteering at the suicide hotline). Trust us, as it will pay off for you. If you hang around long enough at the foster house, you have a better chance at confiscating more money from their piggy banks and you might even be able to be the "guy on the couch" if you play your cards right (#FREERENT). You're also going to get free food, a van to drive the kids around, and "free" prescription drugs from the nurse's medicine closet at the foster care center. Volunteering and giving back at a local foster home is a great step in becoming a miserable failure... But, only if you follow our shitty steps and horrible recommendations.

Baby Interactions

For the miserable failure, being around a stranger's babies and children can be quite an experience. If you have children and you have to visit them with a court-ordered supervisor present, chances are, you do not know how to properly behave in front of children altogether. Knowing how to properly be a miserable failure around babies and their parents is something that you need to be aware of. For example, if you see a woman breastfeeding in public, make sure to stare awkwardly at her with a slight, creepy smile on your face. Then, walk up to her and ask if you can, "*get a pull on that too*" (this also applies to female miserable failures as well). The sight of a half-dressed pathetic loser in a bathrobe and slippers holding a six-pack of beer is enough to send any mother into fight or flight mode (HELLLOOOO crotch kick). If you can avoid her pepper spray as she screams and yells at you, make sure that you make inappropriate and weird comments about the joys and "benefits" of breastfeeding strangers in public as she runs away in terror.

If you see a family pushing a stroller in public, we encourage the miserable failure to walk up to the family and ask the parents if you can hold their baby (still reach for the baby even if they say "*no*"). If they're stupid enough to let a piece of shit like you cuddle their baby, hold the baby like a football and yell, "*touchdown!*" **As you start to come to your senses from being knocked out cold, as you're lying on the ground in a pool of your own piss and blood in the middle of the mall, make sure that you yell "*rape*" as loud as you can as the family walks away dialing the police.** The sight of a drunk nut job lying down in the middle of a busy shopping mall in a dirty bathrobe and slippers is enough for the average person to pull out their cell phones and live-stream your pathetic ass on social media (#FAME).

Finally, we encourage the miserable failure to take some time to go visit the newborns in the new baby care unit at the local hospital. Walk up to the window where you can see the babies. Start to make the following comments to the parents and family members that are gathered around:

- *"I bet I know who the real father for that one is."*
- *"Did you know that you can get $35,000 for a black hair, green eyed baby on the black market?"*
- *"Where is the mommy breastfeeding public viewing room?"*
- *"Just think, over half of these little bastards are going to get divorced later on in life."*
- *"Do you think they'll let me in there to do some selfies with these little monsters?"*
- *"That one looks like a rotten dill pickle."*
- *"Whatever you do, make sure that you write on your baby with a black magic marker. They steal and switch babies at this hospital."*
- *"Where's my son?!!! The hospital lost my son!!!"*

After about ten minutes, you're probably going to have to deal with the hospital security guards. You also might be subdued and taken to the ground by a few angry fathers after your outburst comments above. Try to get away from these people. You need to get out of there fast so you can find the pill medicine cabinet area and stock up on your personal supply of Hydrocodone, Vicodin and Xanax before you leave the hospital. Finally, and most importantly, you're providing everyone at the hospital stories that they can tell forever. **The sight of a half-naked man (or woman) wearing boxers, slippers, and a formerly white bath robe running through the halls of the hospital at full speed while pooping is a great image that people will never forget.** You need to make it out of the hospital because you look like an escaping mental patient due to your wardrobe choice, and you don't want to be locked up in the psych ward (again).

Circus Clowns

Like a snake to a mongoose, the miserable failure has no truer rival than the infamous circus clown. These cheerful, smiling, happy, red nose-wearing, freak show, assholes represent the **opposite** of how you feel, or hope to feel (sad and desperate). A miserable failure doesn't fear circus clowns (like most normal people), but rather despises them because of their affinity for happiness and fun. As someone who is striving to be miserable, you don't need some big shoe-wearing, small car-driving, pervert spraying you with seltzer water from a fake flower. This may momentarily make you frown a little less, or at least allow you to temporarily forget about your awful excuse for a life. Knowing how to behave and interact with circus clowns is an essential step in becoming a complete miserable failure.

You hoped that your interactions with clowns would be limited since circuses and children's birthday parties are on your court mandated "do not attend list." Sometimes clowns will even perform for free at a local park or charity event in front of families and small children. So, despite your best efforts, you're going to have the occasional run-in with one of these floppy-footed fuckers. Even if you see them first and attempt to avoid them, they'll sense your need for their services and head straight in your direction (just like you're drawn to your frequent tarot card readings). The miserable failure's best defense against clowns is a great offense. **DO NOT BECOME VIOLENT** when battling with a circus clown. Yes, it's very tempting to punch them in their big fake red nose, but this will only attract more clowns **(NOTE: these bastards fight in teams of at least three, just like those damn gypsies do)**. Fighting with more than two people is in their "clown code." You may be able to taser two or three of them, but eventually you'll be overrun by a hoard of these confetti bucket-throwing assholes. You should also hate circus clowns because they have something going for them that you DO NOT- **an actual job**. Say what you want to about someone who chooses a career of dressing in bright colored clothing and creepy makeup in order to entertain others; **at least it's still a job.** That fact in and of itself is proof that a circus clown has ten times more going on for them than your sorry excuse for a life has **(NOTE: by now in your metamorphosis, you should be focused on getting sicker from the gangrene staph infection making its way up your left leg).**

Fighting Clowns

You must attack a clown in a way that won't alarm other clowns. You have to fight "stupid annoying fire" with "crazy as fuck randomness." Obviously, since you are well on your way to becoming, or already are a full-blown miserable failure, you SHOULD have a trunk full of water pistols, whipped cream, and aluminum pie pans (plus enough DNA evidence to put you away for life). When you see a clown or are approached by one, fill the water pistols with lemon juice and aim for the clown's eyes (BTW: what a clown can't see, they can't royally annoy the shit out of). Squirt the whipped cream you've been keeping for several months under your spare tire in the trunk of your car into the pie pans, and then throw them at the clown's ugly makeup-covered face. At this point, the whipped cream will have turned sour and should be producing quite a pungent odor (thus, aim for the mouth of the clown). From a distance, everything will appear normal to any passing clowns, and they will not come to the aide of their comrade. Little do they know that their wig-wearing, ball-juggling, circus friend is crying and gagging over his lemon juice-soaked eyes and mouth full of rotten whipped cream. The alternative to going on offense and "attacking" a circus clown is to allow them to royally beat the shit out of you. Here's how it works... Find a circus clown in public and immediately go up to them and kick them square in their ass—HARD. Then get down on your knees, put your hands behind your back and scream, *"what are you gonna do about it, motherfucker?!"* Once you're down on your knees in a defenseless position, the circus clown is going to unleash total and complete hell upon you. They'll use their big red shoes to curb stomp you.

They'll piss in their balloons and hurl them at you. The circus clowns might even run you over in their miniature car. Either way, you win!

The Clown Car Joyride

If you went on the offense and attacked the clown, by this point, the clown's eyes should be bleeding from the lemon juice (making it hard for them to track you), and their rotten whipped cream-induced gagging will have transitioned to vomiting (NOTE: this makes it hard for them to call to other clowns for help). Logic would dictate that now is the time to go in for the kill shot. **DO NOT KILL THE CLOWN!** This will surely land you on the "clown most wanted list," and those red nosed shit heads will never let you rest safely at night (FYI: the notion of "resting" and not putting in effort is paramount to being a miserable failure). If you went on offense, now is a great time and opportunity to steal their clown car (as your car might be getting repossessed by the repo man during your interactions and engagement with the clown). Clown cars are small vehicles that appear to only have enough room for four or five clowns, but in reality, can actually fit dozens of these seltzer-spraying assholes inside. This is not a parlor trick. This is dark clown black voodoo magic. STEAL the clown car and drive away fast (NOTE: you should be high on huffing spray paint before you help yourself into their car). Just be sure to check the glove box and trunk first to ensure there are no sleeping clowns waiting to pounce when you least expect it. Your new clown car's unlimited storage space is going to come in handy when you become homeless. If nothing else, park the clown car in a remote alley, and let homeless people use it as a toilet for a couple weeks. Drop it off at the circus before you run out of gas, and take solace in the fact that they won't be smiling when they see how the inside has been "redecorated." Those giggling, suspender-wearing, dumbass clowns deserve it for being so happy and nice all of the time.

The "Clown Excuse"

If you did not go on the offense and instead, allowed the clown to beat the ever-loving shit out of you, you need to know how to use, the "clown excuse." The "clown excuse" is a the most rarely used excuse in the horrible life of a miserable failure, but if you use it wisely, it can come in handy for MANY obstacles that you've created in your life. The "clown excuse" basically works like this... After you allow the clown to fuck you up, you can use this excuse to get you by in life. Think about it, how many people ACTUALLY get beat up by clowns on a daily basis? Hint, NOT MANY. This is specifically why the "clown excuse" is pure GOLD. Late for the big meeting in the conference room? Explain to your boss that a clown just kicked your ass. Got pulled over for driving without your headlights on at night? Inform the cop that a circus clown has given you a concussion and you need immediate medical care and an escort to the ER. Wife caught you sleeping with her sister (again)? Explain to her (even as she has the pistol pointed toward you) how you were just assaulted by a clown and your, *"judgment isn't what it used to be due to the brain aneurysm."* It should also be noted that how you treat circus clowns can be applied to the following other types of performance artists:

- Mimes
- Magicians
- Witches
- Comedians
- Acrobats
- Dancers
- Illusionists
- Ballerinas
- Singers
- Puppeteers
- Shakespearean Theater Actors
- Musicians
- Sword Swallowers

- Midgets (NOTE: beware of their magical spells)
- Daredevils
- Trapeze Artists
- Contortionists

The Cancer Excuse

Let's face it, only a real lowlife piece of shit would lie about having a life-threatening disease like cancer. This is precisely why you need to do it... Not all diseases are as recognizable, and thus as easily faked as having the life-altering disease of cancer. Millions of people have been affected and afflicted by it, and even those who have managed to avoid cancer still have a soft spot in their hearts for people who suffer from this horrible, debilitating disease. For the miserable failure, the "cancer excuse" provides the perfect opportunity to gain control over nearly any situation you weasel yourself into. The premise is very basic and should involve minimal effort. There is no need for theatrics, shaved heads, or even a basic knowledge of cancer and its symptoms. **It's truly simple. Just tell everyone you have cancer. Period. That's it...** When you want something and they won't give it (sex, manual labor, free condiments at restaurants, a loaded hand gun, etc.), just tell them you have cancer. When you get caught doing something you shouldn't (banging your spouse's cousin... **again**), just blame it on "the cancer." Missed another child support payment, tell the irate judge that you have cancer. No matter how insurmountable your life circumstances may seem, trust in the "cancer excuse" and use it as a powerful tool as much as humanly possible. This is the miserable failure's greatest asset when confronted with the consequences of their own awful and debilitating behavior and horrendous life-altering decisions. It's also the most effective method of acquiring free products or services (NOTE: most prostitutes will at least give you at least a 5% discount once they find out that you're "sick"). Finally, it should also be noted that miserable failures, ARE IN FACT, technically "sick"—you're extremely sick in the head.

There are a few pitfalls with the "cancer excuse" to avoid. **First and foremost, never box yourself in by claiming you have one particular type of cancer. Just say you have "cancer"** (keep it plain and generic) and never offer any more information than you have to. If you look downtrodden and upset when saying it (hopefully you always look this way) most folks won't ask for any more information. It's only when you say you have a certain type of cancer that people start asking questions, so keep your meth mouth shut about specifics. *"What treatment are you on?" "When did you first get diagnosed?" "What's your prognosis?" "Who's your doctor?"* Answering any or all of these questions will immediately expose you as the huge phony, fraud, and liar you really are **(FYI: again, take note that using the "cancer excuse" basically means you have a non-stop, one-way ticket into the fiery pits of hell when you die during your next speed balling binge).** You don't have the first clue what treatment is used for any type of cancer, and have no idea what the word "prognosis" really means (BTW: it's NOT a country in Africa, you dumb, degenerate asshole). You'll also be in real trouble if someone who actually knows about cancer hears you. If someone does press you to name your particular cancer, just say you have *"armpit cancer," "belly button cancer,"* or *"taint cancer."* It's not clear if these three pungent body locations can even develop cancer, but this fact actually makes them even better areas to use in your "cancer excuse" declaration. No one wants to talk about these body areas, and you can bring about an abrupt end to any inquiry by offering to show the person asking you. "Ass cancer" was previously to be the gold standard for faking cancer, but it's now too widely recognized and will easily expose you as the fraud and fake that you are.

It is also important how you present the "cancer excuse." You'll be tempted to lead off any conversation with it, almost like a substitute for a simple *"hello."* Here is a good example for how you could use the "cancer excuse" during your first encounter with someone...

Regular Normal Person - *"Hi! I'm Frank and what's your name?"*
Miserable Failure - *"I have cancer."*

This behavior is too abnormal (even for you), and will again expose you as a faker. It is addicting to immediately get sympathy (and maybe a LARGE cash donation) from everyone you speak to, but refrain from using the "cancer excuse" too early in the conversation with your new friends. Wait until you get caught royally screwing up **again** (HINT: you will...), or until someone has become so fed up with your behavior that they're going to cut all ties with you (a romantic partner breaking up with you, landlord evicting you, stripper no longer willing to provide "free" lap dances, a FURIOUS drug dealer, etc.). It's in these moments that the "cancer excuse" is most effective. Even if they think you may be making the whole thing up, they'll be slow to continue evacuating you from their life. Nobody (except a miserable failure) can ignore the "fact" that someone is actually suffering from cancer.

Not only is cancer a great way for the miserable failure to excuse current behavior, but it also works great for explaining away your awful and horrible past behaviors and decisions. This may give you a new "in" where you were previously shut out. Start by contacting previous romantic partners (this includes the sex workers you paid for intercourse with). Most of your former lovers (including those both STILL in prison and psychiatric hospitals) despise you, have tried to sue you in court, and have taken out death contracts on your life (hip, hip, HOORAY!!!). You ruined them emotionally and financially so you deserve any shit you do get. Don't go see them in person (NOTE: you'll probably get shanked **again**). Instead, contact them all via payphone (they won't recognize the phone number and will be more likely to pick up), and start your conversation off with, *"I had cancer the whole time."* Assure them that if they see you again, everything will be "different" this time (LOL) because the cancer no longer effects your brain since it has moved to your armpit or taint. Expect about 10% of your former romantic partners (the really dumb ones) to fall for this trick and agree to let you back into their lives. Move quickly on this because it's only a matter of time until they come to their senses and contact another lawyer or their old hit man as soon as you come back into their life. Your goal should be to "borrow" (LOL!!!) money, live rent free, and get easy, free sex from your ex (just like before). They will probably be very cautious about you moving back in with them so move quickly because they may not allow it (NOTE: your crack pipe fire that killed their cat, Betty is still a fresh memory). However, getting money and sex from them should be no challenge. Nobody can deny sex to someone dying from cancer (it could be their last orgasm), and everyone will donate money to a cancer patient to fund their "experimental treatments" (BTW: the "cocaine and heroin treatment" costs a lot of money).

You can also take advantage of everyone's giving attitude by leaving collection buckets at businesses, and holding a benefit concert for yourself. **DO NOT DO THIS IN THE CITY YOU LIVE IN**. Too many legal issues can arise very quickly. Instead, plan on doing this in another town at least fifty miles away (just hitchhike to get there, you pathetic moron). You will need a bucket in order to accomplish this particular feat. Keep your eyes open for any kind of bucket you can find and snatch them up. During the summer months, there should be a plethora of buckets available in children's sandboxes. Being careful not to violate another restraining order by going onto any grade school playground, so just walk through random people's backyards, and you'll score lots of these tiny treasures. Tape a photo of yourself on each bucket (BTW: your grotesque appearance may scare small children), and write the caption, *"I have cancer and need money."* It's short, simple, and it works! Then, think of a catchy title for a benefit concert like "Rock to Cure a Cock" (people will think it's for penis cancer), "Jamming Away Taint Cancer," or anything else that will grab people's attention. Create flyers that showcase the awesome talent that will be there to perform. No bands are really coming, so just make up names such as:

- "Harry and the Frankfurters"
- "The Attorneys at Law"
- "Dog Pillow"
- "La La Lu Lu & the Humpty Dumpty's"
- "The Purple Wind"
- "Ceri and the Plastics"
- "Curious and the Hallow Gang"
- "One-Armed Larry & The Snake Men"
- "The Dingleberries"
- "Fart Baby"
- "Shark Snopoly"
- "The Foofy Kitties"
- "Death Mushroom"
- "Hellfire Burning"
- "Zippermouth"
- "The Skidmarks"
- "The Marcus Thomas Lawrence Nelson Group"

Sell "tickets" for this event **well, WELL** in advance, and collect all the money yourself (NOTE: you should only take cash). On the day of the big event, everyone will be sad to the hear that the show is "cancelled." Unfortunately, you "died" last night. The armpit cancer "got the best of you", and they won't be getting a refund (#summerbummer). All the while, you'll be at least fifty miles away spending that stolen cash on another snake neck tattoo and the pet vulture you always wanted! You're on easy street! Well, at least until someone recognizes you from all the concert posters after you supposedly died. When one of these assholes approaches you and demands a refund, or threatens to call the police, just say *"I have cancer."* The cancer excuse is always worth another try (just like your "sobriety").

It's also important to use the "cancer excuse" in almost any situation. You should never be afraid to use it (NOTE: this is similar to the "molestation excuse" and the "bankruptcy excuse," which will be discussed later). Some of the following situations NEED the "cancer excuse" applied, utilized and used...

- When you get caught shoplifting a twelve-inch, steel, strap on dildos at the local mom and pop sex shop... use the "cancer excuse."
- During your divorce proceedings when the child support and alimony testimony is read by the judge... use the "cancer excuse."
- While you're getting dragged out in zip tie handcuffs by the Sheriff for your fifth eviction from your apartment or house... use the "cancer excuse."
- When you show up four hours late (again) to work smelling like cigarettes, strippers and alcohol... use the "cancer excuse."
- When you get caught banging your husband's father and brother on Christmas, in the hall closet, during the family gathering... use the "cancer excuse."
- During your next unscheduled and surprise "drop in" at your therapist's house... use the "cancer excuse."

Miserable Failure's Entourage

Most miserable failures don't have any **REAL** friends (unless you count Garry the schizophrenic homeless mute, as well as your various imaginary buddies as "friends"). Few miserable failures actually have a loving and supportive family, let alone any friends to lean on when the times get tough (NOTE: your life should be "tough" and in the shit box right about now, asshole). The only actual "support system" that you should have are your homeless buddies, druggie friends, and prison pals. This horrible "support system" needs to be put in place so they can keep you on the right track as you become a miserable failure. However, as much as you might be imitating these people's lives, and taking their advice, and following their orders, they really don't qualify as a true "support system." **A miserable failure's REAL support system basically consists of their parole officer, life coach, therapist, public defender, and AA sponsor.** As the miserable failure continues down their journey into becoming a sad and pathetic piece of shit, they will definitely encounter some or all of these individuals and use them as temporary lifelines for support as times get tougher. These next few people will be in your entourage...

Your Parole Officer

If you look down and you see an ankle-monitoring device strapped to your flea-infested, bitten up, staph-infected, bloody ankle, GOOD! You re on the right path to becoming a complete miserable failure! You see, through your various interactions with strange children, random people, your family and your ex-friends; you probably had a few drunken and violent nights of having your head slammed into the blacktop of a parking lot by a police officer as you were being arrested (NOTE: you deserved the police brutality and the pain, so there is no need for a lawsuit.... this time at least). You also probably have an arrest sheet longer than your STD medical history. If this is you, then you probably have what is called a "parole officer" in your horrendous life.

Parole officers are court-appointed, pseudo cops that monitor your activity to make sure that you're not bathing in mall fountains or exposing yourself to bank tellers (again). You basically can't do SHIT without your parole officer (your PO) knowing or finding out about it. Want to travel and sneak into a four-day concert to get completely fucked up on drugs and alcohol all weekend? Nope. PO Wilson says that you can't leave the county (FYI: if you're caught, you get thrown back into county lockup for a few more "drop the soap" nights). Want to go down to "buy" (steal) a six pack of beer and a frozen pizza from the grocery store? Nope. PO Rodriguez says that you're on home arrest this week (again). The bottom line is this, we ENCOURAGE, no, we... DEMAND that a miserable failure try to make nice with their parole officer, but only at first during the early stages of your relationship. If you can become BFFs with your PO, chances are you might have found a new "buddy" or even a "future roommate." If being overly nice to your parole officer isn't working for you, then we suggest trying the complete opposite in order to get them to leave you the fuck alone (just be yourself).

Your parole officer is essentially your legal guardian and protector. This is due to the fact that you can't stop yourself from stealing from street-performing mimes, exposing yourself in public and physically bullying fat people and the handicapped. We suggest that a miserable failure show up on a Saturday night at 3:00 in the morning (drunk, of course) to your parole officer's house. Make sure to bring illegally obtained, codeine-based prescription cough syrup, and lemon lime soda with you. When he comes to the door with his gun drawn and pointed at you in a complete and utter panic, ask him if he wants to smoke a joint with you, watch some midget porn and make some homemade "syzzurp." Another recommendation we have as a means to get your parole officer to become your buddy is or called "The Superhero." Call your parole officer up (crying uncontrollably) and ask him to come over to your shit box house because you're about to kill yourself and that you blame him for your misery. More than likely, he's going to be on his way over. When he gets there (before the police and medical units arrive) make sure to pretend that nothing is wrong with you. Act perfectly normal (PLEASE NOTE: you are allowed to remove your robe, slippers, and boxers for this occasion as you walk around completely nude.) Ask him if he'd like to watch a superhero movie with you and partake in some bootlegged, moonshine while you both practice killing the cockroaches covering your walls. If both of these attempts by you to get your parole officer to be your friend have failed, then it's time you go negative with this situation. Scream at your PO that you are an undercover superhero and that you need to *"borrow"* $50. When your parole officer declines your unusual request, simply steal their wallet and jump out of the window (like a superhero).

Losing an angry parole officer and replacing him with a newer one is as easy and as simple as getting divorced from your spouse **(FYI: except you won't need to fuck your parole officer's best friend in this particular situation).** Start off by never answering your phone when your PO calls. In fact, when they call, we encourage you to call the judge who is presiding over your legal case(s) and inform him about your sexual feelings towards your current parole officer. Explicitly explain to the judge that he has *"drinking and hooker problems"* (NOTE: use **your** real-life problems, but blame them on your PO). After a month or so of this, you're probably going to be assigned another parole officer. This is of course after your face heals from the several pistol whips you received from your first PO. When you do get another parole officer, please repeat the first steps in this section so you can attempt to become "friends" with them (again and again).

Your Life Coach

They are there to listen to you and all of your problems in order to give you sound and quality advice (which you WON'T take). They are there to guide your pathetic life in a positive light (yeah, right!) Life coaches will tell you that they ARE NOT YOUR THERAPISTS and they won't provide counseling to you, but you should still spill out all of your most inner, deepest and darkest desires as well as all of your twisted and psychotic thoughts and fantasies to them (DAILY). **So, unfortunately for your current life coach, they are going to be inundated with late night phone call crying sessions from you and surprise visits to their house at random times during the day.** Basically, the miserable failure's life coach is the guy who gets to bear the brunt of your social, financial and mental life problems. Life coaches are supposed to be friendly people to help guide you in your life. For the miserable failure, this will NEVER happen because your life is completely fucked up beyond any repair (FUBAR) or any type of moral salvaging. Make sure that you get a life coach that accepts cash only (BTW: you can use the cash that you stole at Christmas from the red bell ringer charity box to pay him). When you first get a life coach, tell him that you have the following life goals and that he needs to help you accomplish each goal:

- To become President of the United States.
- To stop using dirty and used heroin needles and only fresh ones.
- To win a Super Bowl as the starting quarterback.
- To win an Oscar for Best Actor.
- To do a line of cocaine off of the desk in the Oval Office.
- To prove once and for all that dinosaurs didn't exist.
- To get your credit score from 300 up to 850.
- To find Jimmy Hoffa's body.
- To find D.B. Cooper's money.
- To discover the truth about who killed JFK.
- To stop shitting in your hands and throwing it at strangers in various parking lots.

Jokingly inform your new life coach that if they can't help you accomplish ALL of your life goals, that you'll strangle them in from of their family at Christmas and then sexually assault their corpse with a bottle of Iron Wolf Whiskey (NOTE: this **WILL** MOTIVATE them from the start of your relationship). If they get scared, make sure you tell them that you were, *"just joking."* Once you begin working with your life coach, ask that they meet you for dinner so you can go over your life goal list mentioned above. When you meet for dinner, they are going to be expecting you to pay. Make sure that you only order the steak, lobster and the vintage 1945 bottle of French caberat from the Loire Valley (REMEMBER: you WON'T be paying). During dinner, discuss unconventional and controversial topics (such as politics, abortion, the death penalty, the history of torture, euthanasia, 9/11 and the holocaust) with your new "friend" and life coach in order to "lighten the mood." You should also chew your food with your mouth open and make sure to kick your feet up on the dinner table when you two chow down. Finally, at the end of dinner, when the bill comes, DEMAND that they pay. **This dinner will get you and your life coach off on the right track and prepare them for the shitstorm whirlwind in which they are about to embark on.**

You should also be making MULTIPLE drunk and crying psychotic and rambling phone calls as well as pop-in's DAILY when you first start the tumultuous relationship with your life coach. Feel free to stop by their house (drunk) during their birthday party (that you weren't invited over for). Feel free to monopolize their time with excessive demands, suicide threats and violent outbursts during your weekly sessions with your new life coach. When your weekly meeting sessions are scheduled, always show up 45 minutes late stinking of booze and marijuana. As you continue your **unpaid** sessions with your new life coach, chances are, they are going to block your number. This does not stop the miserable failure. Simply, find out where they live, go over to their house at 6:00 in the morning and bang on their door demanding that they come to help you fulfill your lifelong goals and dreams (mentioned above). It should also be noted that miserable failures lose life coaches as fast as they lose friends and heroin needles. **You should also be aware that MANY of your former life coaches will commit suicide after dealing with you.** You should not take pride in this, but use this for motivation when you threaten to kill yourself to your new life coach.

Your Therapist

Let's face it... **You are really mentally FUCKED UP.** This much is perfectly clear. Who else besides a true miserable failure would want to purposely destroy their own life? This is why you will probably have several therapists in your miserable excuse for a life. There is nothing wrong with a NORMAL PERSON seeing a mental health professional to relieve pain and suffering. However, **you are not normal.** In fact, you are extremely "special." It is important to remember that the miserable failure **WANTS** and **CRAVES** the mental pain and suffering associated with your metamorphosis. Now, you may have either been court-ordered into psychotherapy, were committed against your will into an insane asylum, or you chose therapy yourself purely for entertainment purposes. It doesn't matter how you actually got into therapy, the miserable failure must stay on the course prescribed below.

Similar to the ways you interacted with your life coach, we want you to use some of the same techniques on your therapist(s). If you have been a miserable failure for long periods of time, you have probably had more than one therapist. In fact, many of your former therapists have probably committed suicide (just like your life coaches) as they were actively counseling you. Let's begin with the fact that a registered psychologist or any mental health professional legally HAS TO DO NO HARM and they must assist and help you in some way if you ask for it (FYI: so, it doesn't matter that you have not and are actively refusing paying any of your very late and overdue bills and invoices that you get from them). Your therapist also has to report to the police if you're planning on hurting others or hurting yourself, so be careful that they not see your, "people to put in wheelchairs for the rest of their pathetic existence" list or your "ways to kill myself with various toy guns" list.

Let's start at the beginning of your relationship with your therapist. **When you go into your first therapy session, we encourage the miserable failure to bring their box of childhood action figure toys, a fifth of whiskey, a loaded handgun and a box of tissues.** Bringing said items will allow you the resources that you need to reenact, explain in detail and recreate your life thus far. Therapy sessions generally only last fifty minutes to an hour. Not for YOU! The miserable failure ALWAYS shows up **late** and stays **past their allotted time**, thus occupying the most and maximum amount of the therapist's time as possible. If you have an appointment from 9:00 a.m.-10:00 a.m., show up stoned at 9:27 a.m. crying at their office door (BTW: having your genitals exposed from your robe being wide open is a classic move). This action will keep your therapist on their toes with you. When you do have your first therapy session, make sure you **LET IT ALL OUT**. Talk about your **deepest desires, most embarrassing moments in your life** and **everything that you think you're capable of doing with your bare hands** (be creative). Talk about your disgusting hygiene, terrible eating habits, and your horrible financial and legal problems. Ramble on and on about your sad sex life (include the nasty details about your dirty hooker/golden shower obsessions), also talk about your attraction to your first cousin. Discuss your hatred for small woodland animals and inform your therapist that you expect to be allowed to tickle them a few times a year. If the therapist has not fled the room screaming in a mad panic as they call the police, feel free to cry like a baby, take a few more gulps of that whiskey and ask if you can talk about your hidden sexual fantasies next. Feel free at this time to even include your therapist in on your S&M (sadism and masochism) sexual fantasies. Next, crawl into a fetal position and suck your thumb as you explain to them WHY you became a miserable failure. Towards the end of your therapy session, grab the blanket on the back of their couch and build a fort with it. Next, grab your action figures and spend the next thirty minutes having a "war" in your new fort with your toys. When your therapist tells you that time is up and that you need to *"grow up and be an adult,"* peek your head out of one side of your blanket fort and yell, *"I am Jooku, wizard, warlord and King of Trinity. Now back! As I cast an ooga booga spell on you!"*

As your counseling sessions continue on with your therapist, you need to start developing a strange, unwarranted, unwelcomed and unprofessional sexual attraction to your therapist. The best way to do this is to tell them (your or their gender does not matter) that you are in love with them and that you want to "have sex with them across their desk" (again, gender does not matter here). At this point, they will probably tell you that you need to go see another therapist. They are then going to offer to refer you to see another one, and they are going to ask you to leave their office immediately (sometimes they might call the police or break out their own handgun for personal defense). This SHOULD NOT stop the miserable failure from becoming friends with their therapist and further developing the close bond and ties. The miserable failure drives past all of their ex-therapist's homes and their offices a few times each day (REMEMBER: your stalking techniques we taught you in the earlier chapters regarding your exes and former spouses). The miserable failure also calls the therapist and leaves them detailed recordings about their morning bowel movements on a daily basis. On the weekends, showing up randomly at their house in front of their family is also a classic move and will scare the ever-loving shit out of your petrified therapist. We recommend that the miserable failure do this act while wearing a mime or a clown costume. We encourage you to stop by their house at 3:00 in the morning on a weekend, with your prison parolee pals, after a night of HEAVY drinking and drug usage. **There is nothing more terrifying in the world than a former mental patient with a restraining order, showing up at their ex-therapist's house at night dressed as a mime and drunk surrounded by ex-cons.**

Still can't get your new BFF/former therapist's attention? **Wait outside their office for a patient of theirs to leave. After their patient leaves, barge into their office unwelcomed and just start rambling about how depressed, sad, anxious, angry, horny and drunk you are.** Then, proceed to disrobe and ask them if they'd like to *"make love now or later?"* Doing a variety of these activities mentioned above is crucial for the miserable failure when dealing with therapists. If you're going to be a miserable failure, you're going to have current and former therapists that are intimidated by the mere mention of your name. **Remember YOU'RE doing THEM a favor! They now have stories that they can tell for the rest of their lives at parties and psychotherapy conferences.** They should be thanking you for your entertainment and your uncanny honesty.

Your AA Sponsor

You have been drinking heavily (this includes several stints in the ER from alcohol poisoning) and doing massive amounts of illegal narcotics and black-market pharmaceutical drugs for quite some time now. You're going to eventually go through the twelve-step program at some point (relax, you won't actually complete each real step). It is probably going to be court-mandated that you go in for treatment after you get your seventeenth DUI (more on the role of your incompetent public defender later on). The twelve steps for the normal person are much different than the twelve steps for the miserable failure. Before we cover each one of your personal steps, we need you to find a sponsor. You need to find a sponsor that is someone who you can rely on as a parent figure and guardian to help keep you "clean and sober." Generally, AA sponsors can be found at AA meetings. So naturally, what you need to do is show up at a meeting. Now, most people introduce themselves like this at a meeting, *"my name is Terry and I am an alcoholic."* This is not the case for the miserable failure. The miserable failure stands up at the meeting when it's NOT their turn and screams, *"my name is______ and I am looking for a handle of vodka and some crack cocaine, so where can I score some?"* Next, hang around after the meeting and ask every single person if they will be your sponsor. This is a game of the law of numbers. The more people you ask, the better your chances are of finding a new friend and an AA sponsor. Once you get your AA sponsor, you need to start working on **your** personal twelve steps:

1. Accept no responsibility for ANY of your POOR actions. Blame everyone and everything for your MULTIPLE shortcomings in life.
2. Live in the past. No forward thinking unless it involved negative thoughts, horrible affirmations and self-hatred incantations.
3. Make a pledge to drink more alcohol and do massive amounts of drugs.
4. Look inward and admit that you are a miserable and worthless failure.
5. Admit that you're angry and severely mentally ill.

6. Inform your ex-lovers that you're not done *"fucking up their lives."*
7. Attend church and demand that that patrons fund your drinking, gambling and drug habits.
8. Sell your right kidney on the black market for a quick $35,000 to fund ALL of your drug and alcohol addictions.
9. Make a list of people who have fucked you over. Begin your threatening and harassing phone calls, disturbing texts and creepy "drive-byes."
10. Take inventory of your personal possessions. Decide that you're going to steal to get "more stuff."
11. Start actively practicing witchcraft, devil worship, black magic, and voodoo.
12. Accept the fact that you are worthless and there is no cure for being a miserable failure.

After you have completed **YOUR MISERABLE FAILURE twelve-step program**, you need to become a burden (a royal and colossal "pain in the ass") for your AA sponsor. Call late at night when you're wasted and inform your sponsor that you just let a bum insert himself into you for a hit of a crack rock (again their or your gender does not matter here). It's also a great idea to show up at your sponsor's house on their "AA sober birthday" with a case of beer and an eight ball of blow asking your sponsor if they're *"ready to party and quit this sober pussy bullshit"* in front of their recovering friends and family members (as you inconspicuously spike the punch bowl). After your AA sponsor has either fell off of the wagon, ended their own life because of your shenanigans, or stopped being your sponsor because of your bullshit, we STRONGLY ENCOURAGE the miserable failure find another AA sponsor. Then repeat the process mentioned above.

Your Public Defender

For the miserable failure, getting arrested and in legal trouble is so common that the DA, the judges and the bailiffs down at the county courthouse all address you by your common nickname, *"Fucky McFuckface"* every time you enter the premises. Now, you have attempted to defend yourself in the courtroom trials and hearings in the past. However, the judges at the courthouse have forbidden you from representing yourself in all future court cases due to your previous courtroom behavior and history that more than likely consisted of:

- Five years ago, when you screamed, *"you can't handle the truth"* at the top of your lungs in a mad panic at the traffic cop who took the stand to discuss your 6.8 blood alcohol level at the time of your 111th arrest and 12th
- Two years ago, when you did "the gallon challenge" by drinking your entire pitcher of water as well as the prosecution's pitcher, then vomited on the court recorder lady at your third jury trial for tax evasion.
- A year ago, when you launched yourself at the Judge to give him a "purple nurple" because he didn't grant your request to let your pet cat take the stand as a material witness in your arrest for stealing a cash register from a convenience store.

The miserable failure has no money. This is why you will be given a public defender. Public defender's get paid through taxes and sit around the courthouse all day waiting for their next "gig" ("gig" refers to another miserable failure that needs someone to represent them legally after an arrest). Public defenders are the **WORST LAWYERS EVER**, but this is fitting because you are the **WORST PERSON EVER**. There is an expression that says, "birds of the same feather flock together." This is true of your relationship with your public defender. However, YOU don't have a job and they do, so they are still 10000% better than you are. However, public defenders are still the "miserable failure of the legal system" (except that they don't shit and then wipe their ass with their own bare hand and then proceed to shake other's hands when they enter the court room like YOU do). **Public defenders finished LAST in law**

school and are forced to be shitty litigators who make a lousy $200 per day defending worthless, guilty assholes just like you. These guys are no match for the high-powered prosecutor from the DA's office. Most of the time, a public defender knows you're guilty and will offer little to no help to get you off and defend you. In fact, some of these assholes don't even know basic legal courtroom jargon or proper trial and hearing proceedings or etiquette. They'll basically work on plea deals for you and that is it.

Your public defender is going to be on your speed dial on your phone. Whatever legal trouble you get into, you need to call your public defender first. In fact, you need to call them on a daily basis, just to "check in." Feel free to call them when you're watching any legal TV show and ask to pick their brain on the cases that you just watched. Also ask to borrow money. Even though they are living in a shit box apartment like YOU, still ask for $50 whenever you can. Tell them, *"hey Mr. Fancy pants, I need some cash and you own me this for not getting me acquitted for my nude streaking case at half time during the local high school football game last week!"* Also make sure that when your public defender is defending you in court, that you make inappropriate sexual gestures with your hands and funny faces behind their back as they plead for the judge to go easy on you for your theft of the infamous "prescription free-for-all drug raid" at the nurses' station during your last emergency room visit. Your public defender is a crucial part of your entourage. Make sure you clear room on your schedule to incorporate these people as a part of your "crew." **This is how you roll- guilty as hell, with a sack of shit public defender at your side.**

6

LIFESTYLE

Failing at Life

The following sections are arguably the most important parts in this poor excuse for a book, so make sure you pay extra close and special attention below, asshole. Contained within this section, is a step-by-step guide for your horrible daily living. Read (if you can... you illiterate bastard) these sections out loud daily with furious anger in your voice (do this in public places if possible). Repeating and hearing these ideas over and over again everyday will imprint them in your severely damaged brain (NOTE: since you have multiple personalities there should be room). Commit these words to the drug abuse-filled nightmare you call a "memory." **Make the terrible behaviors you're about to learn, a habitual part of your daily life (just like your model paint and model glue sniffing addictions).** This is the daily blueprint for your welcomed demise.

Everywhere you turn, there will always be some asshole that tried to knock you off your chosen path of failure by offering to "help you turn your life around." Little do they know that the only thing you're turning around is the Titanic, so you can purposely hit the iceberg **again, and again, and again...** It's understandably easy to succumb to people's unsolicited assistance (NOTE: the only thing you solicit are hookers), and actually believe that things can get better for you (HINT: they can't and they won't...). These smiling positive idiots promise true happiness, peace in your heart, and a taste of the good life (try not to laugh). The road to happiness will inevitably lead you back to disappointment alley, as your heart has been too damaged by years of cocaine abuse to handle peace, and the "good life" tastes an awful lot like horseshit (BTW: it looked like a brownie when you were drunk on Bourbon Street during Mardi Gras).

Remember, the only thing you've ever truly won at, is **losing** (and beating senior citizens in potato sack races). Stop trying to make your inner tiger change its stripes (your inner tiger died weeks ago and is starting to stink). **You are not a winner, so start living like a complete and total LOSER.** The only way to become and stay a miserable failure is with full and total commitment to your daily routine. Learning how to consistently fail, and hate your own existence is only part of the equation. You have to make a lifestyle change (like some people do when they begin cross dressing or joining a gym). The habitual things you do every day have to scream: *"I'm a failure, I hate my life, and I don't care about anything"* (you should actually scream this sentence first thing when you wake up in order for the negative reinforcements to start taking over immediately). From the things you eat, to the bathing you **DON'T** do, all your actions must reflect someone who's given up on the "good life." If you smell normal, are well groomed, and still have all your teeth, you're not doing this whole "miserable failure thing" correctly. Don't try to reinvent the wheel (NOTE: the only thing you should be inventing are alibis), and simply follow these instructions exactly as written. Your lifestyle should match your soul: **dark, sad, lonely, pathetic, incapacitated, and disgusting.**

Thinking Negatively

Thinking negatively is a quality and trait that is buried deep inside of the miserable failure's DNA. Most normal people try to think positive and do their very best to look at poor situations as an opportunity to improve their lives and learn from their mistakes. **Miserable failures think negatively 100% of the time and have a poor outlook on life in nearly every single situation they go through.** Whatever happens to you, you should think negatively and always assume the **ABSOLUTE** worst is going to happen (BTW: it should always happen as you bring on most of your own personal, self-inflicting misery). You should also be going around doing all of your day-to-day activities with a negative disposition and have an unpleasant attitude towards anything and everything. Below are some situations that you might find yourself in, and they are paired with negative thinking from the miserable failure.

Situation: You stub your pinky toe.
Your Thinking: Go to the doctors at the hospital and inform them that you might have cancer, lupus, gangrene, or a broken pinky toe and they need to amputate in order to *"stop the spread of the zombie infection."*

Situation: You are getting your wages garnished for not making student loan payments (again).
Your Thinking: Begin to believe that you're going to be forced by the federal government to work in a slave pit in order to pay off your college student loans (NOTE: you STILL might get sent to jail if the IRS has to get involved).

Situation: You just received a jaywalking ticket.
Your Thinking: Assume that you're going to get arrested and beaten with a night stick (NOTE: you probably will be getting a good licking from an eager rookie police officer).

Situation: You're getting a divorce.

Your Thinking: Hypothesize that you will never have visitation rights to your children and also fantasize about having to pay your ex, spousal maintenance, alimony and punitive damages through various ongoing and costly legal battles (thinking about this as you masturbate while crying and drinking reinforces the negativity).

Situation: You bounced your rent check.
Your Thinking: Prepare yourself for your eviction by trashing your apartment (FYI: arson is not recommended for this) and expect a lawsuit for your MULTIPLE missed and late rent payments.

Situation: You're about to get into a bar fight.
Your Thinking: Fully and completely expect to get your ass royally handed to you and to spend a few days in the ER (FYI: make sure you get yourself an oxycontin prescription during your brief stay in the hospital).

Situation: You start a hoarding collection in your house.
Your Thinking: Theorize that the authorities will find your decayed corpse being eaten by your fourteen dogs and thirty-six cats in your shit hole of an apartment when you die.

Situation: Just got fired, again.
Your Thinking: Expect for your boss to withhold your final paycheck to cover the damages from the unsolicited and impromptu office party you threw over the weekend.

Winners expect to win. Losers expect to lose. Guess which one you are?... You should expect the worst and LITERALLY pray to Lucifer that horrible things are going to happen to you. Based on your previous life experiences, you should always have horrible things happen to you as much as humanly possible. **You bring on your own misery** and being a miserable failure involves negativity, pessimism, gloom, doom, and a disturbing cynical thought process. Being a miserable failure through negative thinking is going to be due in large part to your poor outlook on life as well as your deliberate actions following each negative life experience.

The Miserable Failure's Daily Checklist

You as a miserable failure need to get to work! The following is a "to do" list for the miserable failure on a DAILY basis. The more of these tasks you complete daily, the closer you'll be to becoming a full-blown miserable failure. Life will always get WORSE for the miserable failure, so make sure you practice the techniques listed below as often as possible in order to sustain the maximum damage to your own worthless life.

- Sleep in until at least noon every day.
- Prank call ALL of your ex-spouses (multiple times during the day).
- Masturbate excessively to various forms of pornographic material (minimum of five times per day).
- Drink a fifth of alcohol and inform your AA sponsor about how *"good it tasted"* (FYI: it's best to start drinking as soon as you wake up).
- Smoke at least one pack of cigarettes each day (professional miserable failures generally smoke seven packs of cigarettes each day).
- Steal prescription pills from your uncle's medicine cabinet for private consumption, or to sell on the streets
- Shoplift at a gun shop (NOTE: tampons work for plugging your bullet wounds).
- Text photos of yourself crying uncontrollably, dressed as a tiger to your therapist at 4:00 in the morning.

- Write an expletive-riddled, non-apology, and bullying letter to your children (if you don't have any kids, make sure that the local grade school gets your "thoughtful" letter).
- Make yourself vomit in the condiment aisle at the grocery store.
- "Borrow" your father's car for a quick joyride to the liquor store to re-fill up on your booze for the week.
- Sell your personal possessions at a very low discount and use said money to purchase illegal drugs, spray paint, and pay people who will urinate on you.
- Practice your racy, offensive and disgusting stand-up "comedy routine" in front of your life coach when you two meet for coffee in public.
- Go to your drug dealer's house to egg it and toilet paper it.
- Hang outside of a high school parking lot looking for kids who need someone to buy them beer (HINT: YOU are that someone who charges a nice, little commission).
- Check in with your parole officer via a phone call with fart noises.
- Cash advance money from your credit cards and go gambling at the local casino.
- File a bogus and anonymous police report on YOURSELF...
- Get another facial tattoo (snake, bat, wolf, scorpion, dragon, and spider tattoos are strongly encouraged).
- Load up with food supplies from your neighbor's refrigerator in their garage.
- Dial 911 at least five times, giggling like a schoolgirl at the operator each time.
- Eat at the buffet inside of the local strip club (NOTE: asking for "to-go" containers is a classic move).
- Go nude streaking throughout your neighborhood.
- Smoke crack (FYI: this goes without saying).

- Make threatening social media posts online towards your "friends."
- Attend an AA meeting drunk and or high while screaming at the top of your lungs, *"you're all quitters!"*

This is not a complete and exhaustive list. You can add many more things to this daily to do list. This is just a rough outline for you to follow. However, the more of these situations you complete, the better you'll feel as you become more of a miserable failure. As a miserable failure, you need to be doing as much wrong shit as possible in order to truly make the best use out of your worthless excuse for a day. Why not start right now? Grab your phone (if it still works) and prank call your ex! Snatch that bottle of tequila and start drinking! Make a "new window" in your apartment by using a sledgehammer! Royally fucking up every single day is a key attribute of anyone who is trying to become a miserable failure.

Hygiene

How you look often determines how people will treat you. **Since you're a miserable failure, you expect and prefer that people treat you like 100%, complete, dog shit** (NOTE: for life-long miserable failures, these feelings should mirror the feelings of your childhood beatings you received from the various truckers at the mini mart truck stop when your mom was "walking the streets"). A person who is well-groomed with straight, white and clean teeth and clear skin is often overlooked. They blend in with the rest of regular society and are rarely ejected from department stores or hotel lobbies for perceived vagrancy (WINK, WINK: this is NOT you). As a miserable failure, your personal hygiene should inspire both charity (they think you're homeless and give you money) and disgust (BTW: by now in your metamorphosis, you should smell like vomit mixed with a garbage dump, combined with an ass and vinegar combination). This hygiene outlined below will bring donations to your cause (another tribal neck tattoo), and keep anyone from being near you too long (NOTE: you prefer to huff gasoline in private). Your goal associated with hygiene is to achieve an image, odor, and overall presence best described as **"park district public bathroom meets exploding and rotten burrito."** Following the advice listed in this section will assure that you achieve your ultimate horrible hygiene goal, and leave a wake of severely disgusted people behind you (score!). When you enter a room at any social event and when you leave the room, your presence should be KNOWN based solely on your disgustingly grotesque appearance and the horrendous and vomit-inducing smell that is permeating from your scabies-ridden skin. People should be able to smell you from a minimum distance of thirty yards. Your appearance and HORRENDOUS hygiene should scare children, drive people to drink and make folks vomit.

Oral Care

It's a common misconception that miserable failures don't brush their teeth. While the phrase "minty fresh" will never be used to describe the putrid and pungent dragon fire that is your rotten breath, when used correctly, the toothbrush can be a valuable tool for highlighting your horrific hygiene (as well as scratching those hard to reach places). **If you don't brush any of your teeth, they'll all eventually rot, die, and fall out (just like all of your hopes, goals, desires, and dreams have).** Although the pain associated with losing all your teeth would provide significant growth in the miserable department, to passer-byes you'll appear like someone with no oral issues, or at the most, someone without teeth. Yes, the "no teeth look" is appealing to miserable failures, but for the worst oral appearance, there is no substitute for the "checkerboard effect." This oral fashion statement really makes your bad teeth and horrible habits standout! With only one soul haunting smile, you'll let everyone know that "this person has problems that only years of psychiatric treatment and electroshock therapy can fix." This is not true and you have no hope (REMINDER: you're hopeless). The checkerboard effect is achieved by using the "every other tooth brushing technique." Start in the rear right of your upper jaw and simply work your way around to the left, only brushing every other tooth. Repeat this same process in the lower jaw as well, but this time, start from the left and work your way right. To add to the checkboard effect, floss every other space between your teeth with the used floss you "found" from the dumpster behind the local dentist's office.

With your love of smoking and doing chewing tobacco as well as your tendency to eat entire bags of stolen candy as a meal, it won't be long until a stark contrast between the brushed and untouched teeth appears. Flossing every other gap between each tooth will also add to this effect. The pattern that your teeth will begin to develop should resemble a checkerboard (BTW: if the checkerboard was covered in shit and had a decade-long crack addiction). While using the "every other brushing technique", give careful consideration not to accidentally let any of the "miserable failure's toothpaste" seep onto the teeth you wish to not treat. Traditional toothpaste quickly foams up and rapidly spreads throughout the mouth. For this reason, toothpaste is actually not the best option for accomplishing the checkerboard effect. The teeth that are in your mouth should scare small children and haunt the dreams of any dentist who dare examine you. As a cheap alternative to toothpaste, use the miserable failure original concoction known as "Piss-egar." Simply pour out half a bottle of vinegar, replace it with your own urine, and shake (CAUTION: the open sores on your genitals from your recent herpes outbreak will experience a burning sensation if any piss-egar splashes back onto your crotch while filling the bottle). Dip the tip of the brush into the piss-egar and lightly dab it onto the appropriate teeth. DO NOT BRUSH. The brushing motion in combination with the acidic nature of your urine (in reality, your piss is mostly vodka and blood) may actually remove some of the plaque you worked so hard to accumulate. Just use light dabs of the piss-egar on the teeth you wish to treat. In no time, these teeth will begin to get a nice urine colored brown and yellow stain combination on them (NOTE: they'll match your stained and disheveled bedsheets). Again, if you are following the "every other tooth brushing technique," your mouth will take on the "checkerboard from hell look" that miserable failures strive for. This look in combination with your bleeding gums (thank YOU crystal meth) will transform your smile into a bone-chilling, soul-shattering, PTSD-inducing experience for all who fall victim to gaze upon it. Using crystal meth (as always) during long periods of time will also intensify this effect. You might get what is commonly known as "meth mouth" or "mangle mouth" during your piss-egar and meth usages. It is strongly encouraged that during your checkerboard effect program, you visit several trailer parks in search of the glorious crystal meth labs (more on where to hide crystal meth when pulled over by the cops in a later section).

It is also recommended that you remove one of your front teeth if it isn't rotting out at a fast-enough pace. Besides adding to your "unique" oral appearance, **the gap left behind by the missing tooth makes the perfect space for going "hands free" with your crack pipe.** Your empty tooth space should be the perfect fit for the classic aluminum foil pipe, and serve as a stable holder, even when on the move (mobility is key when you smoke crack outdoors). Your new Bluetooth crack pipe is ideal as it allows for uninterrupted enjoyment of your "medicine" while freeing up both hands to prepare more crack to smoke, scratch your crotch without starting a pants fire, and fighting off the gangs of drug-crazed homeless bums who *"just want one hit."* To remove one of your front teeth, simply engage the "crotch punch method." This method of tooth extraction is equally effective for both men and women. Go to a crowded area where couples often frequent for dates (movie theaters, restaurants, methadone clinics, the free health clinic, etc.). Approach the most violent and aggressive-looking couple you can find and begin lightly touching the guy outside of his pants, on his penis (NOTE: your gender does not matter here). When a man does this to a man, or a woman punches a man's penis in front of his wife, violence is sure to occur. Carefully position your head so that the desired tooth receives maximum impact from the onslaught of coming blows that is about to come your way upon your disgusting face. If, after receiving a good ass-kicking, your tooth is not fully extracted, just slap him in the dick again and continue to repeat the process as needed until one of your front teeth gets violently knocked out onto the floor in a disgusting pool of blood by the root. If after receiving the horrible beatdown you still have both front teeth, simply find a pair of plyers and extract out one of your front teeth yourself. Before you pull out your own tooth, simply drink a fifth of whiskey to numb some of the horrendous pain that you're about to experience.

A miserable failure's breath should be considered a lethal weapon in small places (elevator, car, glory hole, etc.). The fog of rancid burning terror that flows from your shit-caked mouth can easily consume a room (FYI: like Indian food baked in the middle of summer in a diaper in Kolkata), and cause anyone who passes by to become immediately violently ill. Small pets and babies are at a much greater risk of instant illness, and seniors have been known to lose control of their bowels upon receiving a full blast of the "shit steam" that originates from the horror cave you call a mouth. It's by design that the miserable failure's breath is so devastatingly putrid. You should have gums that constantly bleed (thanks again, crystal meth), consume a variety of pet food (it was on sale), and use your mouth like it was an ATM (they pay, you play). To protect your investment and achievement, you must always avoid going to the dentist to get your teeth cleaned and stop using mouthwash (properly).

Finally, if you want to give dentists and dental hygienists a scary story that they will tell for the rest of their lives, simply make a dentist appointment, and show up. When you walk into the dental examination room and show the dentist the condition of your mouth, the entire dental team will first vomit. Then after they get done puking, they'll laugh hysterically at you for approximately seven minutes. Finally, they'll ask to take some photos of your mouth so they have proof that they all saw and witnessed firsthand, *"the worst mouth ever."* Also, going to see a dentist for entertainment provides a great opportunity to huff some nitrous oxide when they step out of the room to gag, vomit, or laugh. Whenever the dental staff isn't looking, simply grab the mask and start huffing. When they escort you out of the building, demand that they give you free candy and toys that they give their child patients in the treasure chest. If they don't provide you with your request, simply moon the entire office and throw a rock through their window before you scamper away into the alley like a greasy little rat.

Bathing

In order to be a miserable failure, it goes without saying that you need to smell like a complete and total pile of sea otter shit. In order to accomplish this magnificent feat, you should not bathe regularly in any type of freshwater or use any type of soap to clean yourself. Soap is one of your true enemies. People should always be playing the guessing game, "what's that smell?" So, what **IS** that smell? Is it a sweaty gym sock rolled in expired mayonnaise and covered in dog shit? Is it a hot dumpster filled with dead crabs and rotten grease? Is it an adult diaper filled with onions being heated up in a microwave? Is it a port-o-potty baking in the 100-degree heat in the middle of August at a country western concert? Is it a container of rancid dead fish heads? **No!!!! It's you, a miserable failure!** Your smell alone should be enough to make it clear that you have major PSYCHOTIC issues that only a team of fifty psychiatric professionals from Vienna can properly address (FYI: it's too late to save you). Traditional B.O. (body odor) is easily explained away as someone who forgot to wear deodorant, or who was working really hard and just got stinky (HINT: you **don't work hard**). This low level of repulsive personal fragrance does not meet the standard of a miserable failure (REMEMBER: you **don't have standards**). Of course, wearing deodorant is something you should avoid 100%, but that act alone will not bring you to the personal fragrance level where you can cause immediate dry heaving, temporary blindness, paralysis, and the loss of consciousness when you approach small animals and children. In order to fully develop your putrid and horrid potential for body odor, you'll need to use non-traditional bathing techniques. One would assume that skipping bathing all together would be the best choice when in pursuit of being the "smelliest motherfucker alive," but they'd be wrong. Bathing, when done correctly, can greatly enhance your level of rancidity and repulsiveness. You just need to know **what** to bathe **in**...

Just like a dog who finds something with a strong stench and rolls in it, so should the miserable failure. Most towns have a sewage treatment plant. Go for a midnight swim! You'll definitely be alone so don't be afraid to swim 100% completely and totally nude (NOTE: your staph infection is going to get MUCH worse after said experience...). Swimming in raw sewage is very similar to skinny dipping at a public pool, except everyone pees in this one, and that isn't a candy bar that some prankster dropped in the water, so DO NOT EAT IT. During the HOT and scorching summer months, you should also partake in at least a weekly "port-o-potty plunge." This is very similar to the "polar bear plunge" where people momentarily dive into freezing cold water to raise money for charity. You won't be raising any money for charity and you won't be getting out quickly **(NOTE: you should soak for at least ninety minutes inside of the port-o-potty in order for your scabies-infested skin to absorb all of the wonderful liquids that you're marinating in).** Besides providing a wonderful opportunity to take your personal odor level from *"who shit?"* to *"we're all going to die,"* the "port-o-potty plunge" is a great chance to make new friends too. Here's how you should go about doing the "port-o-potty plunge." Find a port-o-potty in a public place in the middle of the summer in the blistering heat at any well-attended outdoor event (rodeos, carnivals, the circus, the state fair, concerts, monster truck races, a swinger and orgy convention, etc.). Climb into the port-o-potty and jump through the hole (for morbidly obese and fat miserable failures, using the crippled port-o-potty is HIGHLY recommended). During your ninety minutes of "soaking," you are sure to get a few visitors. When they arrive, do not immediately make your presence known to them. The shock of seeing someone wading in waste will cause them to immediately exit the port-o-potty and to lose their lunch. By getting caught swimming in the port-o-potty, you'll be giving strangers a CLASSIC story that they'll be sharing with the psychiatrist on Monday morning. You want them to start "doing their business" before you scream, *"hey, I'm down here, asshole!"* Before your new best friend starts to go to the bathroom, just simply make encouraging comments about how good they're doing or even the size of their evacuations. Some great phrases from you should include:

- *"Come on! You can do it!"*
- *"Just relax and let it happen naturally. That's what my Boy Scout instructor always said to us."*
- *"Hang on a second, let me start filming this first."*
- *"Wow! That was a big one! Good job!"*
- *"Way to be so hydrated!"*
- *"Golden shower time. Goody for me!"*
- *"Need any help?"*
- *"Nice taint."*

These are all great examples of ways to "break the ice" with you and your new BFF. If, after making your presence known, someone continues their use of the port-o-potty and even thanks you for your kind comments, you might have just found your soulmate (NOTE: running away to Vegas to marry and to make miserable failure babies with them is mandatory at this point).

Dry bathing, or "scent rolling," is also another effective form of odor enhancement. You'll want to start collecting various items and substances that have a strong odor (old shoes, used diapers from the garbage dumpster behind the daycare center, abandoned underwear found in a gas station truck stop bathroom, etc.). Store them in your bathtub, or in your personal pile in the alley. When starting your day, just go for a morning "roll in the pile." The larger the pile gets, and the longer it's around, the more potent it becomes and thus the worst you'll stink. Or, when out and about, it's also okay to just, stop, drop, and roll on whatever nasty substance or item you find. This is also a great way of ending a first date once you've determined they have no money (SEE ALSO: "how to scare the shit out of a date" in the romance section of this book). Your new bathing practices in combination with your tendency to become urinary incontinent (thank you, grain alcohol), and your unwillingness to wipe properly (it takes too long) should have you at an acceptable level of stink in no time (NOTE: if you smell too good and you're ever in doubt what to do, we recommend simply hitchhiking to the nearest garbage dump to roll around in all of the waste).

Finally, another great method for bathing is to take a soak in any body of water found near a nuclear power plant (a "DO NOT ENTER" sign translates to, "COME ON IN" for the miserable failure). Once you have found said water, jump in (do a "cannonball" or a "jackknife") and take a swim. Feel free to take in some of the water in your mouth and spit it up through the giant gaping holes in your mangle mouth where your teeth previously resided. The pollution from the nuclear power plant should have already turned the water dark green. Also, don't worry about the abnormally large and slimy swamp creatures that are in there swimming around. The scent of a nuclear power plant's waste and pollution in the water is enough to cripple any able-bodied man alive. You might grow a third eye (SEE ALSO: "the third eye excuse") or an extra pinky toe, but at least you'll smell like disgusting and dangerous, toxic nuclear waste.

Skin Care

If it doesn't itch, you're not doing it right **(HINT: your disgusting crotch should feel like a million fire ants gnawing away at you like a heard of hungry cannibals during a bikini contest).** A miserable failure takes great pride in **not caring** for their skin. Pimples, boils, warts, abscesses, skin tags, scars, blisters, blackheads, moles, ingrown hairs, cysts, freckles, and highly-contagious rashes should be worn in pride like military medals (NOTE: your back and ass are also the perfect locations to grow your zit army and they're going to win the civil war with your genitals this time). Nothing makes a failure more miserable like self-lancing the softball-sized boil in your left armpit in the breadline at the local homeless shelter (NOTE: you should use a plastic spork). A good facial rash with the right smile says to the world, *"I'm contagious, I'm nasty and I'm loving it!"* Both your skin and your life have never been silky smooth. So, a miserable failure's skin should tell the horror story of their life. Each genital scar represents an angry former lover. Each infection is a reminder of the lessons you've learned (yes, urinal cakes are dairy-free, gluten-free, and soy-free, but they won't hold birthday candles). Each itchy irritation shows what's most important to you. Just like your awful personal odor, let your skin speak for you. Your skin should tell the world that you are a miserable failure. Each one of your outbreaks of lice, crabs, scabies, and flea bites should also help whenever you use the "cancer excuse."

Although effective, your terrible diet (NOTE: mostly alcohol, expired ramen noodles, muddy puddle water, and pet food), and horrific bathing practices are not enough alone to produce deep skin infections and numerous ingrown hair follicles. You'll need help from heavily trafficked public places (public restrooms, free health clinics, the county jail, etc.) to score infections that no antibiotic can **HELP**. Before sitting in a public restroom, always observe the cleanliness of the toilet seat first. If the seat looks clean and the bathroom in general looks well-maintained, this is not the right place for you to make a deposit to the toilet goddess. Avoid this environment LIKE THE PLAGUE in the future, and instead focus your energy on finding a bathroom that's more conducive to a good old' fashion, skin infection. The right public bathroom will appear as if a ritualistic slaughter of an animal that bleeds only poop and semen took place over the toilet (HINT: truck stop bathrooms known to frequent hookers, meth heads, heroin addicts, and alcoholic abusive stepfathers are great places to start). The sink should be clogged full of hair, used condoms, and various cigarette butts ("free tobacco"). The water may not work that well, but there'll still be a greenish liquid with the consistency of hand lotion oozing from the floor drain. The mirror will show no reflection thanks to the decade's worth of caked-on smoke film, pimple puss, smeared chicken blood, and chunky projectile vomit (sounds like **YOUR** kind of party!!!). The smell contained within this restroom should immediately cause your eyes to water, induce labored breathing, and make you seriously contemplate suicide (more than your usual ten times a day routine). Old rundown gas stations, strip clubs, nursing homes, porn shops, sex theaters, homeless shelters, and adult book stores are the best places to search for your PERFECT bathroom mecca.

Upon entering your bacteria-infested bathroom, immediately remove your sandals. Walk around the restroom making sure to splash your bare feet in any liquid or semi-liquid puddles that have accumulated on the floor, and use your toenails to scrape up any crusty (or muddy) material you detect on the ground or in between the tiles. Do this until your feet start to burn, tingle, and/or change to a DARK orange color (NOTE: this means **PURE** magic is happening). The best rashes and infections normally start in the feet and always work their way up to the face (**HELL YEAH,** staph infections!). You can speed up this process by giving yourself a relaxing foot rub (apply the lotion like substance oozing from the floor drain), and then follow up with a deep scalp massage (don't worry if you have no hair from your various times you licked the gutters clean at the local nuclear power plant). By doing this activity in the bathroom, you are effectively transferring the goo on your feet to the dandruff-invested hairball you call a scalp (FYI: see the section on the importance of bathing your cat with your own tongue). If you're lucky (HINT: you're not), you picked up a good itchy infection that should start to blanket your entire disgusting body and make you look even more repulsive in only a matter of days (just in time for that "job interview" that your retired grandfather got you at the local toy train shop).

It's also important to specifically focus on your butt for targeted skin infection. Shock and awe should come from all those who gaze upon your pimple-infested, rash-covered, clearly infected, matted hair, fudge machine. Every attempt to sit should be a painful treat and include the unmistakable feeling of puss penetrating your underwear (BTW: let it dry naturally). A dirty toilet seat, nudist resort sauna, hot tub at a swinger's convention, and the bus stop bench are the best places to rub your disgusting bare ass. Grind your naked cheeks on and around these bacteria-laced locations and do it in full view of as many people as possible. If any concerned citizen or police officer interrupts you during this process, just start barking and growling while also attempting to sniff their crotch (see the section on "how to make new friends"). Being that your stink wagon is already irritated due to your continued refusal to wipe, the rubbing action should cause small sores to develop in your anal area **(PLEASE NOTE: miserable failures use both extremes after they have gone "#2" and either don't wipe or use an entire roll of toilet paper for EACH wipe)**. These small tears in your skin create an open door for infection to enter and make itself at home (like the time you noticed your neighbor left their window open during their entire two-week summer vacation). It won't be long until the pressure under the skin starts to build (you'll feel it), and a full-blown puss-filled infection takes hold (NOTE: feel free to use the "infection excuse" during this period in your shitty, miserable life).

Once the bacteria-infested seed has been planted and begins to produce horrible visible results, it's time to bring out your secret weapon. **Black. Leather. Pants**. The power of leather pants cannot be overstated here. Especially during the summer months, leather pants provide the oven-like environment needed to bake in the essence of any good old' fashion skin infection (NOTE: heat + irritation + time = infection). Additionally, any odor that originates from below your waist will become amplified by this leather crotch oven. If you think your dead testicle or yeast infection smells terrible now, try putting it under a heat lamp for a few days (hey, it's science). Sometimes, it's quite challenging to put on and remove leather pants (it's just part of the experience). To avoid this unneeded hassle, plan on each wearing of your leather pants to last from thirteen to fifteen days (**MINIMUM**). This practice creates a "genital time capsule" where your previous day's events, diet, and sexual encounters are cataloged in chronological order through various layers of aroma (HOT TIP: NEVER wash your crotch after sex). Most importantly, leaving your ass bacteria to bake for a fifteen-day period in black leather pants greatly increases its rate of reproduction. As your celebrated skin infection spreads to other parts of your body, you should consider wearing a thick sweat suit (twenty-four hours a day) in hopes of replicating the same benefits your leather pants brought to your genitals and buttocks.

Hair Care and Shaving

With the exception of your record-setting and disgusting mane of pubic hair (#PORNBUSH), the miserable failure does not simply let their hair grow wild and untamed. Your hair will never be considered clean and well-kempt, but there should be a specific order out of chaos that grows from your infected epidermis and your lice-infested scalp. For both men and women, uncut and unmanaged hair will only make you appear as if you're an all-natural hipster, hippie, or at best, homeless (BTW: if you're not yet, you should strive to be homeless). Strangers may even take pity on you and offer to help in some way (FYI: only accept cash for glory hole invites). Outside of a monetary donation, this continuous interference will only slow your pursuit of succeeding at **failing**. A miserable failure's hair should announce to the world: *"I've got serious problems and more angel dust is my only solution."* Just the sight of your matted, greasy, flea-invested, multicolored hair should be enough to keep the well-wishers at bay and provide you the time and space needed to continue to fail miserably with your general hygiene and overall grotesque appearance.

Obviously, you should never rinse your hair in clean water, and/or use any type of cleaning product on it (shampoo = no, no). Your horrific bathing practices will correctly manage your hair's odor and lack of shine. However, it is helpful to apply calamine lotion to your scalp three times daily. This stuff can dry up anything (except your endless tears). In only a matter of days, this process will produce big, chunky, free-falling, dandruff flakes. Your new flaky friends are great for keeping people far away from you (just like your "winning personality" is), and your nasty and flaky particles will deposit themselves on clothing and furniture as you go about your day (NOTE: this is ALSO how a miserable failure decorates during Christmas or for added "parmesan cheese" for pizza night). If you've been inside a friend's house, it should appear as if it had snowed in their living room (besides the fleas nesting on your body, you don't have REAL buddies unless it's your imaginary friends). Briskly scratching your dry scalp in an attempt to release as much dandruff as possible is always a good choice. Be sure to wear a black shirt so that your dandruff really stands out, and shake your head vigorously as you walk. Think of your dandruff as a trail of breadcrumbs that will lead you (and the detectives) back to anywhere you've been that day (FYI: finding that lost bag of horse tranquilizers for self-injection won't be a problem).

A miserable failure does not allow their hair to grow to extreme lengths. Again, this doesn't make you appear screwed up enough as it can easily be mistaken as a fashion choice. **Remember, you're going for a look best described as, "mental hospital escapee" meets "old alcoholic fishing boat captain."** Proper shaving and haircutting practices should also lead to more skin issues (BTW: puss from your various staph infections is the only shaving cream you'll ever need). Be sure that your razor is dull, rusty, and misshapen before shaving. If it looks like it was used in prison as a shank, it's the right razor for a miserable failure. Locating a proper razor (and new underwear) is only a simple dumpster dive away, so go for it!

When it comes to shaving, both men and women should use the "patchy" shaving method. Rather than completely shaving your head, legs, or face, only shave random areas haphazardly and without care. If you're a male miserable failure, shave half your acne-infested face (really dig into those whiteheads, you pimple-popping pervert), and use the other hairy half as a money-saving napkin (you're totally "green" like that). Shave several hairless blocks into your arms and legs (give special consideration to infected areas by adding a few extra razor scrapes), and then play "connect the boils" with a magic marker on your body. Shave baseball-sized bald spots into the side of your head (FORESHADOWING: you'll probably get laid tonight at the nuthouse), and tell your fellow homeless buddies that it's from electroshock therapy (NOTE: you'll definitely get laid tonight from the infamous, "toothless Terry"). Hopefully this chaotic shaving method will give you the appearance of someone with mental illness and intense drug problems (they've got you pegged).

DO NOT SHAVE YOUR PUBIC HAIR EVER! A miserable failure takes great pride in their luscious, full, bush, mane of pubic hair, and seeks to let it live an unbridled existence. It's okay and even fashionable to braid or dye your nasty crotch hair, but do not ever cut it, or trim it. You should draw strength from your pubic hair. Your pube farm should bring you great strength (in regards to odor) and is also an awesome place to hide "valuables" (drugs) from the police officers or S.W.A.T. team. The miserable failure finds awesome pleasure when first unveiling their massive pile of pubic hair to a new lover. Being the showman that you are, you've mastered this act over the years. Rather than strip naked and immediately expose your fiery pond of pubes, like a magician, the miserable failure focuses on perfect timing. The best method for introducing your pubic hair is to slowly coax your lover's mouth toward your nether region (just grab their head and push if needed and neither your gender, nor theirs **MATTER** here). As their hands slide across your still clothed genitals, the curly mound of yet to be exposed pubic hair will feel like you're hiding a wig in your pants (NOTE: you're hiding something and it rhymes with "burpees"). Do not allow the person you're having sex with to remove your pants. This act will create enough physical distance for them to fully take in your abundant mane of pubes. They will then most likely refuse to perform oral sex out of a fear of choking and attempt to escape (again). Instead, wait until your lover's face is directly above your genital area and then quickly expose your hair farm. The putrid smell of your crotch hair and oozing boils would normally cause them to pull away, but at this point they're the perfect distance from your crotch, so that makes them committed (NOTE: this sexual commitment is a state law in Vermont). Since they don't want to hurt your feelings (LOL: you have no feelings), they'll begin their oral descent toward your fun spot. **If all goes well (it never does for you), they'll wade through your pond of pubes and past your barrage of boils, crabs, and bugs eventually making it to your oddly-shaped genitals for some "happy time!"** If you're a male miserable failure, encourage them to go slow due to your propensity toward premature orgasm and the fact that your previous lover did actually die from choking on a pubic hairball (don't hate the player hate the game). If you're a female miserable failure, push his head down on your crotch and scream out loud at the top of your lungs, *"eat it, you wimp!"*

Healthcare

If it burns when you pee, it might be an STD and an infection (SCORE). If you have a compound leg fracture from running from the police and into oncoming traffic, you might need surgery (HELL YEAH!). A miserable failure does not have health insurance. This is precisely why you need to rack up thousands of dollars in medical bills (with the intention of never paying, of course) while receiving minimal care at the doctor's office (or the black magic from the witch doctor). You essentially don't have health insurance because you are a worthless fuck and you like causing trouble, taking up people's valuable time and getting free room and board at a hospital **(NOTE: you need to make sure that you're taking up the valuable time of the doctors and nurses for your cold, fever, head ache, tooth ache, and random muscle pain in your right pinky toe, while the truly injured people needing actual care are temporarily put on the back burner)**. A miserable failure takes PRIDE in causing problems for other people, including health care professionals and the truly sick people in our society (however, you TECHNICALLY qualify as "truly sick" as well, but you're "fucked in the head"). It is these reasons alone why we encourage you to go to the doctor's office, ER or hospital for the most minor injuries. For the major medical problems, you need to tough it out and ENJOY the pain as long as you can, because you deserve severe discomfort. When the pain becomes unbearable, go seek medical help so you can simply get MANY prescriptions for your pain, anxiety, and sleep problems (BTW: getting these prescriptions is a wise move in order for you to sell them on the streets for straight cash, or to take them with your nightly bottles of rum when you're playing "pirate").

Advantages of Visiting the Emergency Room

Sometimes, going to the ER is mandatory and fun. In fact, we must stress again that the miserable failure goes to the ER whenever they can. This is a staple and pillar of the miserable failure's existence. This is also a very important and significant step in your journey. **Can't sleep? Go to the ER. Your left nipple hurts? Call the police and hitchhike to the ER. Stubbed your toe? Call 9-1-1! Hit your funny bone on your "cocaine coffee table?" Make sure you scream in pain when the paramedics put you in the ambulance. Have a toothache from your rotten, inflamed and infected front incisor falling out? It's time to see a doctor!**

The bottom line is this: **GO TO THE HOSPITAL AS MUCH AS POSSIBLE**. Going to the hospital has many advantages. You can get an elderly fight club going and take bets on who is going to break their hip first to make some fast cash. Perhaps you can get some free TV viewing in as you're masturbating in front of your new hospital roommate. Maybe you can steal more "shit" (gloves, band-aids, narcotics) while you're in the hospital. However, the best part of getting yourself admitted into the hospital are "The FDT Perks!"

- Food: Your broke ass won't be eating expired packages of mold-infested ramen noodles for the twenty-ninth day in a row when you go to the ER for an "earache" (feel free to keep your binge and purge eating disorder going VERY strong during your hospital period as well).
- Drugs: Hospitals are a great place to steal prescription pills and sell them on the black market, or use them personally (this includes your hits of morphine from your IV). Find the nurse's cabinet where they keep the pills and STOCK UP.
- Toiletries: Toothbrushes (even though you're not brushing your rotten, mangle mouth teeth), night robes, needles, and medical supplies are great to sell on the black market on skid row for a few crack rocks.

When you get admitted, DEMAND a "suite." When the nurses laugh their asses off at your poor attempt at humor, demand that you get your own room, if possible. However, if you have a roommate, make sure that you completely control the room and show this fucker that YOU'RE in charge. This includes taking control of the remote for the TV and dictating your roommate's bedtime through verbal insults and physical beatings. We must stress that when you get admitted into the hospital, there are some major rules that you must adhere to if you want to be a miserable failure:

1. Never give your name or your address upon entry to the hospital (NOTE: you shouldn't actually have a physical address anyway). No name and no address means, **NO BILL**. If you have to give a name, you're John Doe (or Jane Doe for the female miserable failure) and you live at 123 Main Street (IMPORTANT TO REMEMBER: the only time this rule can be modified is if you TRULY appreciate getting MORE debt and having several bill collectors looking for you. If this is the case, give them your real information).
2. Always complain that you're in massive amounts of pain (this gets you MORE morphine and pain-killing narcotics).
3. The first day you get admitted, ask for your steak-cooked medium rare when ordering dinner for the first time (allow the nurse ample time for proper laughter). When your food is served, ask if you can *"speak to the chef."*
4. Take advantage of having free cable and demand that they give you access to the X-rated movie channels.
5. Find out who the terminally ill people are and buddy up with them on the first day (who knows, you might be written into their will if you're really nice to them during their final days). Also, terminally ill people generally have some damn good pain killers that you can confiscate without their knowledge or consent.

These five rules are essential if you want to be a miserable failure in the hospital. **The miserable failure can also use their time in the hospital to continue writing their death threat notes, suicide letters, and parole board hearing extension applications (all in crayon).** The miserable failure must also never listen to their doctor's advice. When you are in the hospital, they are going to draw your blood and run tests on you. Inevitably, your results will come back and they won't be good. From your STD infections, to your cirrhosis-charred liver, your doctor is going to be telling you that you need to become healthier. Laugh at him in his face when he spouts his *"nonsensical medical bullshit."* Forget the fact that you are in the third stage of syphilis and make an inappropriate sexual hand gesture when he talks about your failing kidneys, infected gall bladder, and your lacerated spleen.

Sexually Transmitted Diseases and Faking Terminal Illnesses

No normal person wants to bang you. You're disgusting, both on the inside (your shallowness, rudeness, bitterness, selfishness, and laziness) as well as on the outside (your club foot, lazy eye, missing teeth, broken nose, infected ear, missing fingernails, and the track marks on your arms). **You couldn't get laid in a morgue (PLEASE NOTE: this DOES NOT apply to female miserable failures due to rigor mortise...).** How do STDs relate to terminal illnesses? The miserable failure must know how to combine these two very different medical "problems" in order to get ahead in life. So why would you have STDs? Well, from the self-prostitution that you have had to do living on the streets, to the shared heroin needles, you should have become a disgusting, disease-catching failure.

If it burns when you pee (and it will), make sure you go into the 24-hour urgent care clinic and complain that your "*terminal illness*" is "*acting up.*" When the doctors ask you what terminal illness you have, make shit up. Create new diseases. Invent new words and phrases. Speak in tongues and gibberish as you mumble if possible. Combine all of your STDs and symptoms to create a fictional terminal illness. The hospital will see through your bullshit, but you should be able to get away with this in an urgent care clinic. You also need to go to the urgent care clinic because the hospital has BANNED you from their premises from your shenanigans (see section above for reminders). Remember, the easiest way to fail a blood and a urine test and get admitted into urgent care is through your sexually transmitted diseases. Use all of your STD symptoms as an excuse to go into urgent care. Faking terminal illnesses and using your STD's to get into urgent care has many advantages.

1. Sympathy - People who have "terminal illnesses" get sympathy and pity. You might score some free food and more painkillers as well. Remember, all of your STDs combined have given you the terminally ill disease of "Miserfailcaucus." If the urgent care doctor questions you, tell him that you were diagnosed with your terminal illness by a voodoo, witch doctor in Papua New Guinea last spring.
2. Money - Urgent care generally has a massive amount of cash on hand. Some people that go to urgent care pay their bill in cash. If you play your cards right, you might be able to steal some Benjamin's when the fat receptionist goes on her hourly smoke break.
3. Rest - Instead of allowing a perverted, rich businessman to insert a zucchini inside of you for a quick $3.00 in nickels as he videotapes it and giggles, you might have an opportunity to get some much-needed rest and relaxation in an urgent care ER bed.

The doctor at the urgent care clinic is going to want to do a full blood panel to see what the fuck is actually wrong with you. **He's going to discover through the blood tests that you have herpes, gonorrhea, chlamydia, syphilis, cirrhosis of the liver, diabetes, hypothyroidism, gout, failing kidneys, coronary heart disease, and hepatitis.** After discovering ALL of your illnesses, your doctor is going to insist that you stay at the urgent care center as they pump you full of prescription medications. Goody for you! The amount of prescription medications they are going to pump into you is going to give you a high like nothing you have ever experienced! Welcome to a miserable failure's health care!

The Diabetes Excuse

Sugar + Carbohydrates + Miserable Failure = Diabetes

Perhaps one of the more infamous excuses utilized by miserable failures worldwide is the outstanding and **classic** "diabetes excuse." If you have eaten poorly and don't drink enough water, you should feel ecstatic when you find out that you have diabetes **(FYI: if you're pissing blood, that's a good sign you're heading in the right direction and you get double, mega, extra, bonus, special points).** Much like the "low blood sugar excuse," the "diabetes excuse" gives you plenty of ammunition to use as a defense on your court cases involving stolen food, as well as your primary excuse for why you CONTINUE to refuse to make any and all child support payments. You should also note that you DO NOT have to be fat or obese to use the "diabetes excuse." Many times, through your binging and purging eating disorder you purposely developed, you will still get diabetes even if you're fifty pounds underweight. However, if you are a fat son of a bitch right now, feel free to run WILD with this excuse!

If you eat extremely poor for many years as you become a miserable failure, **you will develop diabetes** (IMPORTANT REMINDER: your teeth should be rotting out by now due to your meth use, excessive vomiting and lack of any proper dental hygiene practices from your daily consumption of pure white sugar). If you're lucky, you'll need to get a few toes and fingers amputated due to this debilitating disease as well (NOTE: there will be more on how to freak people out with missing body parts in a later section). The "diabetes excuse" should be used to get you out of jams involving, health, wellness, finances, and personal relationships. Some classic examples of conversations that include the "diabetes excuse" might be:

Umpire - *"Are you a coach?"*
Miserable Failure - *"No. I am a miserable failure."*
Umpire - *"Get off the field now!"*
Miserable Failure - *"But I have diabetes."*

Umpire - "*You also have a severed chicken's head under your arm. Now get the fuck off this field.*"

Wife - "*You're cheating on me?*"
Miserable Failure - "*Yes. It's because I have diabetes.*"
Wife - "*I'm still going to shoot you.*"
Miserable Failure - "*Good, I need and welcome the pain associated with multiple gunshot wounds. Fire away, bitch.*"

Receptionist - "*Ma'am, the doctor won't see you to refill your Xanax and Valium prescriptions because you haven't paid for your last twelve visits.*"
Miserable Failure - "*I have diabetes and this is offensive.*"
Receptionist - "*Ma'am, this is a family office. Please put your titty away.*"

Loan Officer - "*It says here that you need to borrow $10,000 to go to Vegas? I'm confused.*"
Miserable Failure - "*Yes. I have a lot of drinking and partying to do there.*"
Loan Officer - "*Sorry, sir. We don't offer those types of loans.*"
Miserable Failure - "*Is it because I have diabetes?*"
Loan Officer - "*No. It's because we don't give low-interest loans to smelly assholes who wander in here off the streets who have a credit rating of 300.*"
Miserable Failure - "*Touché.*"

Police Officer - "*Stop what you're doing, put your hands behind your head, and get on your knees.*"
Miserable Failure - "*I am a diabetic! These are my insulin needles.*"
Police Officer - "*That is heroin. And that is a heroin needle sticking out of your arm. Also, you're sitting in the middle of the kickball diamond during recess at a grade school.*"
Miserable Failure - "*Can I get seconds on chocolate milk from the cafeteria before you arrest me?*"

These are just a few examples of how conversations could go between you and others as you implement the "diabetes excuse" into your daily life. Being a true miserable failure takes time, dedication, persistence, resilience, and hard work. Using excuses such as the "diabetes excuse" is once again, a proven tactic that will allow you to shift your blame on to other things in your life as you focus your deep and desperate journey into the majestic kingdom of "**Miserablefailuredom**."

The Benefits of Losing Appendages from Diabetes

You need to get diabetes. This is essential if you want to be a miserable failure. Not all people with diabetes are miserable failures as some can't control their horrible disease. But you WANT to obtain this! If you don't have diabetes, relax. You will soon enough (IMPORTANT: as always, you CAN still use the "diabetes excuse" even if you don't have diabetes). However, your diet should consist MAINLY of sugar, candy, French fries, chocolate, canned cat food, hamburgers, hotdogs, narcotics, pizza, canned dog food, pasta, rice, cereal, cigarettes, fast food, prescription pills, processed food, and alcohol. **Do not drink a lot of water and try to stay away from those pesky fresh fruits, non-GMO vegetables and clean, organic, grass-fed, free-range meats.** The deadly combination of lethal dosages of sugar and carbohydrates will eventually get you onboard the diabetic train. This is where your fun can begin. Some people with diabetes can lose limbs, fingers, or toes (keep your FINGERS CROSSED). If you do have to get your fingers, toes, hands, feet, arms, or legs removed, make sure you milk your handicap in life as much as possible. Which is why we recommend using the "diabetes excuse" in combination with the "handicapped excuse" (NOTE: the "handicapped excuse" is covered excessively in the section: "Getting Around Faking Being Physically Handicapped or Mentally Challenged").

When you get diabetes, and if you have to have any of your fingers, toes, hands, arms, feet, and legs cut off, you'll want to use your injuries to prank people and to gain sympathy points from them. Also, being disabled with missing appendages will allow you to fake being a homeless veteran in exchange for some sympathetic people giving you money (this is yet another example of why you're going to hell). Whenever you meet someone for the first time and you had your hands amputated due to your diabetes last year, make sure you still extend your nub so people have that awkward "should I shake it or not?" look on their face. This brief moment and personal greeting exchange will make them very uncomfortable around you and it might allow you to get some free money from them later on as well. A simple meet and greet with you and someone might be:

Person: *"Hi. I'm Bob."*
Miserable Failure: *"Nice to meet you, Bobby. Here, let's shake HANDS... Oops, I forgot, I don't have a hand. This must be really awkward and uncomfortable for you."*

Feel free to also openly discuss your handicap and use it to get yourself free shit from people, including car rides to your crack dealers house and the methadone clinic. If you have no legs and are wheelchair-bound due to your horrible diabetes, make sure that you demand to cut ahead in any line you so choose. A long line in the grocery store? Roll your crippled ass up to the front and cut in line. When others start yelling at you, simply shout out, *"I am handicapped and I have diabetes, assholes!"* Diabetes is a horrible and debilitating disease, which is why we encourage you to get it as soon as you can. You're going to WANT the painful and horrible symptoms associated with diabetes. Once you get diabetes, continue to eat the same shitty foods you have before. When in doubt on what to eat, please consume the food choices below:

- Bags of pure sugar (powdered, brown or white)
- Entire loaves of enriched flour white bread
- Industrial Vegetable Oils

- Margarine
- Ice Cream
- Candy Bars
- Processed Meat
- Candy (sweets and sours)
- ALL fast food

Never listen to your doctor and feel free to use the "low blood sugar excuse" any time that you think you might pass out or do something dumb due to your low blood sugar. Using the "low blood sugar excuse" accompanied by the "diabetes excuse" is going to put you on easy street as you continue your journey down the righteous path to become a miserable failure.

Housing Cleanliness

Being a disgusting, unwashed, stinky, grotesque an unclean person are 100% mandatory attributes that you must possess if you want to be a miserable failure. Your house cleanliness needs to match your physical appearance as well as your personality. **Your house should be cold, dark, depressing, and disturbing.** Essentially, you must inhabit an unclean, disgusting, and vomit-inducing domicile. **Having a shit box, unclean and unkempt house, apartment, trailer, or housing project is a pillar attribute that the miserable failure has.** Now, you should probably have one of five following CURRENT living situations:

1. You're currently sleeping on someone's couch (rent-free, of course).
2. You currently own a home (you're behind on your mortgage payments, of course).
3. You're currently "renting" an apartment (eviction paperwork is

currently being processed by the local sheriff's department, of course).

4. You're currently living on the streets (and you're performing various sex acts to support your wood glue huffing addiction, of course).
5. You're currently in prison (and you're everyone's "little bitch", of course).

In the previous sections, we discussed in great detail how you should behave and what your hygiene should consist of if you're squatting on someone's couch. We also briefly discussed life being homeless and what happens WHEN (not IF) you get arrested. We want to focus on your current domicile in this entire section. **Whether you are in a meth lab trailer park or a section 8 housing project, your home needs to be a shit box.** Essentially, you should make sure that your house or apartment is almost uninhabitable.

Your Shit Box

Most normal people clean their house daily or at least once a week. The miserable failure has not cleaned their house in YEARS (REMEMBER: unless you use your children as FREE slave labor). Most normal people vacuum once per week or so. The miserable failure doesn't even own a vacuum (even though you do "SUCK"). Most normal people deep clean their toilets, sinks, tubs, and showers once a month. **The miserable failure's bathroom SHOULD BE covered in black mold, greasy mildew, and SHOULD smell like a raw sewage treatment plant.** Most normal people mop their floors once per week. For the miserable failure, it's difficult for you to mop your floors with all of the cockroaches, ants, mice, and trash that occupy damn near every square inch of flooring in their entire shit box. Again, we want to stress that the miserable failure should never clean their house. Even if you're a hoarder and you have started a collection of various cats, dogs, and miniature pigs, NEVER CLEAN YOUR HOUSE (BTW: we STRONGLY ENCOUR-

AGE becoming a hoarder). We actually encourage the miserable failure to invite people over for a board game night and pizza. Chances are, within five minutes of stepping foot in your flea-infested domicile, the party should be ending soon as head lice, termites, bed bugs, and scabies start to latch themselves to your unsuspecting guests. When you're ever in doubt on how you can royally destroy and permanently fuck up your own house, use each corner as a toilet on a daily basis, never take your trash out, and always make holes in your floors, ceilings, and walls with a sledgehammer.

Bathroom Non-Cleaning

If you still have running water (you probably don't as water companies only provide water to people who actually pay their bill), why waste toilet water? We encourage the miserable failure to only flush once per day. After all, water is expensive! Your shower should also remain dirty. Not because you take showers (which you don't) but because your bathtub is home to the various turtles, lizards, snakes, salamanders, and frogs that you've collected over the past few years. **Your bathroom should basically smell and look like "truck stop restroom where hookers shoot heroin" meets a "slaughterhouse."** The mere sight of your disgusting shit box restroom should send any normal person that unknowingly wanders inside, into a fit of violent vomiting followed by uncontrollable crying. If your toilet gets clogged, just let it overflow. You're going to want used toilet water spilling out all throughout your entire residence as it adds to the horror living situation that we want you to live in.

Being Trashy

The miserable failure also does not own a trashcan, so naturally, there is going to be garbage piled in the corner that mostly consists of empty beer cans, spray paint containers, tubes of glue, liquor bottles, sex magazines and various cigarette butts you've collected. If you have to take out your trash and want to have some fun, just throw it over the fence and into your neighbor's yard. This will piss them off and you might receive a kick to the kidneys for doing so (be still my heart...). You can also take your beer cans and liquor bottles and use them as bargaining chips with your friends living down in the alley. Again, if the trash becomes too much, take a sledgehammer and make a giant hole in your floor. Use your new hole as your permanent trash can and another toilet. You can also start to make various pieces of furniture with your used beer cans, tin foil crack shards, and empty bottles of liquor. Making a recliner out of your daily intake of alcohol containers and drug addiction utensils takes skill and you might be able to sell it to a college Fraternity (HELLLLLLLO $50!!!).

Your Floors

There isn't a strong enough vacuum in the entire world that can clean the carpet of a miserable failure's domicile. The only way your floors are going to get clean is if you have your carpet removed (and burned) and your rotten floor planks permanently replaced. The only use a miserable failure has with a vacuum is using it for sexual gratification purposes (NOTE: this applies to both male and female miserable failures). When your carpet and flooring begin to rot and decay, feel free to steal several pallets behind the local liquor store in the alley to use as walking planks in your disgusting shit box house, as the floor slowly caves in. Using these planks over the gaping holes in your floor also allows you to practice your sobriety check straight line walks that you frequently have for drinking and driving. Furthermore, having disgusting floors with holes in them will allow your new rat "guests" and other "roommates" to begin living with you in no time.

Dusting

Mold, dust, dirt, and grime are commonplace throughout the miserable failure's home. The miserable failure should dust their coffee table

ONLY if they need a clean spot to cut their lines of cocaine. Otherwise, keep the dust on the furniture. This dust also makes it easier for the miserable failure to make homemade chocolate milk (INGREDIENTS: dust, powdered milk, sugar, and puddle water). It should be noted that the amount of dirt and dust on your furniture should increase roughly by 1 inch every year.

Dirty Dishes 101

The miserable failure does not own a fully functional dishwasher. The miserable failure's dishwasher broke with they tried to clean their methamphetamine-cooking supplies by putting them in it. Naturally, when normal people don't have a dishwasher, they clean their plates, cups, and silverware by hand. This is not the case for the miserable failure. **For the miserable failure, keeping dirty plates, dishes, bowls, and silverware stacked up near the sink covered in flies and cockroaches, is paramount.** If you need another plate, just rinse it off with water and use it. The miserable failure does not use soap at all during this process (NOTE: you will get various types of food poisoning illnesses by doing this, so when you get sick, go to the hospital and repeat the steps previously mentioned in the healthcare section). As the dishes pile up, make sure that you steal some paper plates from the grocery store if you need eating utensils. Need to dispose of a used paper plate? Throw it on the dirty dishes stacked in the kitchen. Again, your dishes in your kitchen should be covered in mold, grease, grime, and maggots.

Window Visibility

The miserable failure's windows are so dirty and covered in gunk, that sunlight is barely able to peek its way into your home. If you must clean your windows, there is no need to purchase window cleaner. If you want to see when the delivery man is dropping off various packages on your neighbor's doorsteps so you can steal them, we recommend that the miserable failure hose the windows off (both on the outside and on the inside). If you still can't get your windows clean enough for your theft preparedness, take a crowbar and break out your windows. This will give you plenty of visibility for your neighborhood package theft as well as the ample opportunity for bats and stinging insects to fly into your home.

Laundry Time

The miserable failure does not have a working washing machine or dryer. So, when the miserable failure needs a clean shirt, they simply go down to the homeless shelter and steal a few donated shirts. If you don't have access to a shelter that provides clothing options for the poor, then you'll be wearing the same clothes day in and day out. Eventually, the smell coming from your flea-infested and scabies-ridden body is going to resemble the smell of a decaying corpse stored in a steel port-o-potty during the black plague.

Filth 101

To recap, the miserable failure is a disgusting slob with no manners, self-respect, or dignity. From your unclean body to your horrifying house, the miserable failure must be worthless at cleaning up after themselves. **If your house is not dirty, just leave the door open for five weeks straight.** The amount of leaves, rodents, spiders, animals, and dirt that come in will get you started off on the right foot. If you need to make any "light" redecorating in your home, be sure to use spray paint directly on your walls for an artistic feeling. Feel free to also allow your druggie friends, homeless pals, and prison parolee ex-con buddies crash in your house as often as they want.

Hoarding

You also need to develop a massive collection of various animals, trash, and miscellaneous items to store in your shit box. People that hoard are generally mentally ill and have severe psychological problems. Since you too have horrible problems, you should be "saving" as much shit as you can in your dwelling. Some collections of things you need to be hoarding in your house should include some (if not all) of the following:

- Cats
- Expired Food
- Garbage
- Magazines
- Used Motor Oil
- Mice
- Holiday Decorations
- Cardboard Boxes
- Goats
- Books
- Insects
- Photos
- Newspapers
- Dogs
- Rubber Duckies
- Plastic Bags
- Kitchen Utensils
- Cans
- Sex Toys
- Raccoons
- Snakes
- Human Waste
- Used Paper Plates

The "Rage Room"

Normal people get stressed out in life. This is where **you** can come in and help them! Rage rooms are very popular places in the world. In rage rooms, stressed out people pay money to go into a room or house and literally smash and bash the shit out of it. This is where people can take out their anger, rage and frustration (similarly when you masturbate). So, this is where YOU can come into play! If you're ever in need to make some fast cash, let people know that your house is entirely a giant rage room and you are "*open for business*!" Hitchhike down to your local business or office district and paste flyers advertising your entire house as one, huge rage room. Next, steal a pickax, baseball bat, hatchet, and golf clubs from your neighbor's garage to use for the smashing. Charge people $20 for five minutes in your rage house. After doing this for a few months, your house should be literally crumbling down to the foundation and you could be $20,000 richer (scratch off lottery ticket buying spree, here you come!!!).

Drugs and Alcohol

Like a fine wine paired with aged gourmet cheese, when taken together, drugs and alcohol are paramount and 100% MANDATORY staples in the life of any miserable failure. Why is it that you should drink a gallon of whiskey and wash it down with some oxycodone? **It's because drugs and alcohol are the miserable failure's secret defense against "success"** (FYI: other secret weapons that kill success include your vomit-inducing body odor, your extreme rudeness, and your excessive foul language usage). If you're not careful, you might fall ass backward into something "good" (a well-paying job, a healthy relationship, positive interactions with your children, etc.), and completely derail your pursuit of becoming a complete and total miserable failure. By completely letting go of any faint hint of sobriety, you're essentially guaranteeing that no matter what happens, you'll eventually sabotage anything positive that comes into your life (PERFECT!!!). The day your boss finally promotes you to "head bathroom sanitation engineer," you should purposely get caught stealing toilet paper and hand soap from the storage cabinet. If grandma gives you the rent money to avoid eviction, you better DAMN SURE spend it on a new battery-powered bong with matching carrying case (NOTE: it's sheepskin, so take care of it). When your soon-to-be ex-spouse decides to put the divorce on hold and finally let you see your kids, you'll get shit-faced (AGAIN), sleep with their sibling (AGAIN), steal their credit card to buy more booze (AGAIN), and then projectile vomit in their car on the way to dinner with the family (AGAIN). Remember, sobriety and other healthy choices are not your "thing" (BTW: failing miserably is your #1 "thing"). So, embrace your TRUE nature and drink up, shoot up, snort up, and smoke up, because you're going down, and it's going to be a fucking awesome experience!

Like massive skin infections, your time spent rotting away in county lock up, as well as your "mystery" pregnancies, and your mind-altering substances you consume should be an intricate and inevitable part of any miserable failure's pathetic existence. If you review your horrible and awful life you've had since starting out on your quest to ruin and destroy your own life, you'll easily find that every bad choice you've made was in some way influenced by the unsung heroes known as **drugs** and **alcohol** (thanks again, boys!!). For you, being shit faced, blitzed, stoned, lit, hammered, bombed, wasted, blazed, cranked, zoned, melted, smashed, tweaked, and burned out all at once is a **NORMAL** part of a miserable failure's lifestyle. You've learned to eliminate disease-causing stress, illnesses, and anxiety by completely checking out of sober and mundane reality (NOTE: you never fit-in **there** anyway). The soothing effects of your morning gin and tonic should have significantly lowered your blood pressure (as well as the likelihood of keeping your day job as a grade school bus driver). Choosing meth over food helped you lose twenty pounds (and your kids). Depression is a thing of the past thanks to the ecstasy pills you snort on your lunch break at the fast food restaurant job you have (FYI: your nose is like a booger and blood themed amusement park). An apple a day may keep the doctor away, but an ounce of LSD combined with a fifth of gin will unlock your awesome ability to perform self-surgery (it's face-lift time!). Drugs and alcohol are the miserable failure's ONLY affordable healthcare plan. So, sit back, relax and get ready to be educated on the classic combinations of drugs and alcohol as well as their effect on your mind and body.

Drugs and Alcohol Growing Up

If you had a really fucked up life growing up, you should have a far head start of other people striving to become miserable failures. Drugs and alcohol play a pivotal role in the life of ALL miserable failures. If you grew up with a great family, RELAX, soon they won't be so nice to you anymore and may disown you due to your drinking and drug addiction(s). Some miserable failures grow up in horrible drug and alcohol abuse families (NOTE: if this is you, please start to touch yourself right now). These people have a **MUCH** easier time becoming miserable failures because they're already way ahead of the once normal person with a kind, nurturing, and loving family. If you are from a family of druggies and drunks; drugs and alcohol are the only childhood friends you still play with (except your BFF imaginary friends). Some of your earliest memories might have included helping your abusive, alcoholic and paralyzed stepfather shoplift beer from the local liquor store (he waited in the car patiently), dumpster diving to find Aunt Debbie's lost crack rock, and spending your summers at "Camp Meth Lab" (you still have nightmares about archery class). Other parents would treat their child's skinned knee with a band-aid, but your folks believed in the power of alcohol to heal all wounds (physically, spiritually, and emotionally). There's no feeling quite like the **sting** from a Long Island Iced Tea being poured onto a fresh rug burn, and the thud you feel when your parent cold-cocks you in the forehead and whispers with tequila-coated breath, *"stop being a bitch and go find mommies lighter."* You learned how to pour the perfect tap beer before you could tie your shoes (too much head means grandma locks you in the cage in the attic again). At age nine, your joint rolling skills rivaled those of any of the older kids in juvenile hall (your third-grade teacher who played "find the special spot" taught you well). In junior high, your uncanny ability to spot fake blow made you an invaluable addition to your new "foster family" (NOTE: your REAL father lost you in a poker game with the cartel). By the age of eighteen, you had already drunk yourself into permanent incontinence (thank you moonshine) and the need for an immediate liver transplant (you got moved to the top of the transplant list because of your age, you lucky fuck). You've met some of your best friends in rehab and in prison, but **drugs and alcohol are your only real pals.** They've always stuck by your side and provided both guidance and defense. Drugs and alcohol helped make you what you are today (a failure), and if you stick with them, they'll eventually make you miserable! It's the perfect lose-lose situation, and that means you win! When in doubt, remember this simple equation, D+A:

Drugs + Alcohol = Miserable Failure

Simple Beginning Rules for Using and Boozing

Drugs and alcohol are so ingrained in a miserable failure's existence and DNA that they are an essential requirement for performing all of your daily tasks (NOTE: **especially if you want to have those DAILY and infamous alcohol poisoning vomit sessions**). Below are a few basic rules and traditions that should have accompanied (or will be employed shortly) in your daily usage of drugs and alcohol thus far:

1. Going to see your parole officer requires three ounces of crystal of meth (two for you and one for the cab driver).
2. If you come from a dysfunctional family and you want to visit your "hands-on" and "always willing to wrestle pants-less" Uncle JC, you'll need at least two bottles of scotch (FYI: he gets out of prison soon and will want to be your roommate in your studio shit box you call an apartment).
3. By now in your quest, you should have determined that doing

twelve to fifteen lines of blow in a courthouse bathroom stall, perfectly prepares you to fight any child custody battle (BTW: your kids STILL hate you).

4. After only five shots of whiskey and a handful of uppers, you can easily tackle any task your boss at the adult theater gives you (it's like mopping the inside of a penis).
5. In addition to destroying your kidneys, liver, and frontal cortex, drugs, and alcohol have also hurt your heart. Yes, you've had multiple heart attacks (thanks again, cocaine), but your ticker has truly been touched in an emotional way.
6. If you could legally marry a bottle of coconut rum (while acting like a pirate), you would.
7. If you have a chance to name your firstborn child, be sure to name them, “Narcotic” (it sounds dignified).
8. You should also sob uncontrollably while watching any wholesome beer commercial (NOTE: years of boozing has severely damaged your brain’s ability to regulate any and all proper emotions).
9. It was difficult to contain your excitement when the doctor officially pronounced your nasal cavity has been eroded due to the cocaine usage (persistence pays off).
10. You should contemplate suicide every time you get invited to another drug intervention (it's like going to “fun's” funeral).
11. Back when you could still become sexually aroused without medical intervention, your daily masturbation should have always included visualizations of “sexy” wine bottles, “slutty” burning joints, and “seductive” mounds of crank (BTW: those white powders make you the horniest).
12. It should also be noted that both male and female miserable failures should attempt to sell their bodies, and souls for a simple hit of heroin.

A miserable failure can't live without drugs and alcohol (literally). If you’ve been drinking and using for several years, the abuse inflicted on your central nervous system should have caused your essential body functions to become dependent on a continuous consumption of 100% pure grain alcohol, hallucinogens, narcotics, stimulants, and pharmaceutical sedatives (the miserable failure's "four food groups"). If you are to ever give sobriety another try (LOL!!! yeah right...), seizures, vomiting, blood clots, respiratory failure, more tumor growth, the return of the voices, paralysis, and the sudden urge to bring about the worldwide mass genocide of all kittens would surely follow. Don't go there! Follow your diseased and destroyed heart! Follow your friends (your only **real** friends), **drugs** and **alcohol**!

Loving Combinations

A spoon full of tequila helps the methamphetamine go down! "Drugs" and "alcohol" go together like "you" and "failure." If you're hopelessly addicted to only one substance or the other, you're not doing it right. The miserable magic happens in the combination of using both a drug and an alcohol. There are certain wines that go best with certain cheeses. The same is true with drugs and alcohol. One enhances the other (NOTE: like having herpes AND gonorrhea at the same time, AGAIN). In the following section, you'll learn how to correctly pair the right booze with the correct dope. This method of DUAL consumption will bring you the maximum failure-making benefits from both substances, and move you even closer to being a completely miserable piece of shit.

It must be noted that there is no mention in this section to the most infamous pairing, "The MF'er." "The MF'er" basically occurs when you mix a shot of all of the known alcohols in the entire world (thirty-three to be precise) and chase the bottle all down by consuming all of the illegal narcotics that you have ever done (twenty-one to be precise). We don't recommend this combination because—simply—you will die. We don't want you to die. **We want you to live a long, hard, depressing,**

and miserable existence filled with self-hatred, isolation, sadness, desolation, agony, depression, pain, and defeat.

Beer and Pot ("Bot")

With the exception of Mexican and German brands, beer always goes best with pot. Marijuana is the lazy person's drug, and beer is the sloth-like person's drink of choice. This combination gives miserable failure's pot bellies, love handles, and upper respiratory infections (happy days are here again...). Sometimes it's important to balance out a depressant like beer with a stimulant like crack, but not in this case. With this Bot combination, **your goal is to be as sluggish, fat, stupid, and as sloppy as possible.** Smoking large amounts of weed will cause you to be drowsy, forgetful, and generally unmotivated to do anything constructive (NOTE: in other words, weed will help accentuate your current "winning" personality). Depending on if you're a lover or a fighter, beer may make you passive, calm, and friendly; or angry, psychotic, and self-destructive. Keep your fingers crossed for angry, psychotic, and destructive (NOTE: consuming Bot should cause you to start fistfights with packs of midgets or groups of roaming Arab traders). No matter what effect beer has on you, when combined with copious amounts of cannabis, the outcome almost always involves unemployment, imprisonment, divorce, vomiting, massive weight gain, sleeping in the subway, stealing pizzas from the delivery guy and having random unprotected sex that you fall asleep during (FYI: there goes your wallet and shoes... again).

Mixing Bot with sex is a classic move that could be implemented on a weekly basis. Mexican and German beers are best used for kinky sex while on Bot. Germans pretty much have the "kinky market" cornered due to their particular and popular pornography genres. Furthermore, Mexican beers are good for kinky sex as long as you know WHERE to put the lime... **If you give too much thought as to what sexual infections you might get or what laws you might be breaking during your**

kinky sexual experience while consuming Bot, you'll never get the entire ketchup bottle up your ass (#Goals). For kinky sex, stick with beer and pot because they are also the cheapest combinations of drugs and alcohol for miserable failures. If you're lucky, by now you should be crashing on a buddy's couch and raiding his liquor cabinet for breakfast as you light up a roach. Also remember that Bot is going to give you a giant beer belly, flabby titties ("bitch tits" for men and "flapjack flatties" for women) and horrendous breath (SCORE!!!). So, if you don't feel like doing anything productive for the day, smoke some pot and wash it down with a pony keg of beer.

Whiskey and Meth ("Mesty")

Need the proper and adequate skill to thunder slap the roided-out professional mixed martial arts fighter you just met in the bar? If you answered yes, then you need **WHISKEY**! Do you need the courage to flash your oddly-shaped genitals to that same fighter's girlfriend? Then you need **METH**! Taken separately, these two substances are deadly enough, however, using them together is a beautiful and outstanding, life-altering experience. Need the endurance and pure will to dump "your" tricycle on the east bridge, climb over the suicide prevention fence, strip naked, boldly urinate in front of the gathered crowd of law enforcement officers, and then do a series of cannonball twists before plunging into the icy and frigid water below? If you answered "yes" to that question, make sure you are consuming a large amount of Mesty. It's important to consume these courage-creating substances in the proper proportions. Too much whiskey without enough meth may cause the miserable failure to become overly intoxicated, fatigued, and lazy (more than usual). This level of whiskey intoxication, without the extra stimulation that meth brings, will prevent you from reaching even minor levels of sexual arousal, and in turn, make it difficult to make any honest attempts at collecting new STDs (FYI: STDs are like baseball card collections for miserable failures). Now, too much meth will lead to more psychotic thoughts and **violent** behaviors that gets you locked up in the county jail or psych ward (AGAIN...). While prison and/or mental hospitals are a VERY normal part of the miserable failure's daily existence, it's important to prepare and plan for your stay there. Besides, somebody has to feed that pesky army of wild attack possums you've been training in your serial killer-inspired, creepy apartment. When taken together in equal parts, Mesty provides miserable failures the courage to do nearly any task imaginable. Being chased by the cops? You are going to have a better time if you're on the Mesty experience. Getting involved in another road rage fight alongside the interstate? Again, make sure you hop on board the Mesty train. Whiskey makes you drunk, tired, and sloppy. Meth makes you awake, aware and violent (and aids in your teeth rotting out at a rapid pace). The two are a perfect match for all miserable failures looking for that little, "pick me up."

Rum and Gas Huffing ("Gruming")

The art of drinking rum and huffing gas (A.K.A. "Gruming") is the miserable failure's best method of avoiding time-consuming and failure-preventing "normal" personal hygiene practices (and long-term relationships of any kind). It should be noted that during your Gruming, you are **REQUIRED** to act and talk like a pirate during your entire experience (NOTE: if you have a glass eye or an eye patch from the beat down you received from the MS-13 gang at the pool hall... the better). A good rum addiction alone (one or two bottles daily) is enough to halt any regular showering (this doesn't apply to golden showers). With the exception of coconut rum, which has been linked to nearly all pregnancies south of the Mason-Dixon Line, rum has no magical hygienic or medicinal powers. Pirates didn't become dirty, greasy, smelly, rotten teeth-having, swashbucklers because they drank so much rum that they became absent-minded about bathing, nor did they truly "choose" that lifestyle. But YOU did a long time ago when you decided you wanted to ruin and destroy your own life by becoming a complete and total miserable failure. Rum alters a person's perception of reality. When someone is consuming the recommended daily amount of rum for miserable failures (AGAIN: one or two "borrowed" bottles) their self-image is drastically changed. When the rum-drunk miserable failure looks into the mirror, they don't see their dirty matted hair, dark crusty circles under their eyes, black and rotten teeth, and red bleeding gums (sexy). The rum-altered mind perceives a well-refined, classy-looking PIRATE whose wardrobe is free from tears, bloodstains, and skid marks (IN OTHER WORDS: the fabric "Triple Trifecta" for miserable failures). It's this lack of personal awareness that gives the rum drinking miserable failure the confidence to win at losing.

However, rum alone is not enough to win the personal hygiene war. Rum's high sugar content will give you short-lived energy, and the resulting activity may lead to "accidental hygiene incidents." Maybe it's doing something ridiculous, like leaving your cozy dumpster (home) and getting caught in a rainstorm, or falling asleep inside an automatic car wash (again). You cannot afford even the occasional bath if you wish to become a miserable failure. In order to circumvent the energy-inducing effects of rum while maintaining all its hygiene-restricting qualities, simply add gasoline. This is where the fun Gruming begins...

Like a basket of parmesan and garlic crusted French fries paired with the perfect ketchup, gasoline is the inhalant version of rum and they complement each other PERFECTLY. Huffing gas possesses all the same personal hygiene-ending properties, and is readily available in most parking lots (your third favorite place to sleep). Traditional gas huffing includes using a short hose to siphon gas from the tanks of parked vehicles. The "huffer" would fill up their mason jar or empty beer can and retreat to the safety of their alley for a wonderful inhaled breakfast. This method of huffing greatly restricts the variety of gas available to a miserable failure. Different grades of petrol have different "flavors" and lead to diverse mind-altering effects. Regular unleaded gasoline has a sour smell and produces a full-body buzz with nightmarish visions of the future (relax because you have **no future**). Diesel fuel has a very sweet fragrance that causes an intense cerebral high, deeply depressing thoughts of regret (like, you should've been a rapper or airline pilot), and leads to "surprise" bowel incontinence. The eco-friendly gasoline has a bitter and sweet smell and will cause you to strip nude and roll around in the grass as you pull out your own hair in clumps. Rather than siphoning gas, the miserable failure should open the gas cap of each vehicle, insert their nose into the nozzle hole, and take VERY long deep breaths. **Move from vehicle to vehicle taking large chugs of rum in between each new gas tank. This act of Gruming (drinking rum while huffing gas) should leave you with just enough energy and determination to crawl back to your warm dumpster in time for afternoon trash pickup (hey, it's a free roller coaster ride for failures).** Furthermore, it should be noted that you should be behaving, talking, and acting like a pirate during your Gruming experience. This is precisely why we have provided you with a "Gruming Pirate Slang" cheat sheet. Some of the phrases you should be shouting out loud while drinking rum and huffing gas from parked cars could be:

- *"Abandon ye ship, me matey! Captain Dumb Fuck Beard is here!"*
- *"Ahoy, ye scallywag!"*
- *"Avast, ye drunkenness!"*
- *"Batten down the hatches and secure thy booty!"*
- *"Dead men tell no tales! Especially this heartie."*
- *"I'm hornswoggling two bottles of grog in me Jolly Roger car over there!"*
- *"Plunder the landlubbers!"*
- *"Thar she blows! Time for ye to walk the plank!"*

Vodka and Cocaine ("Vodcaine")

A VERY popular combination and the "creme de la crème" for MANY miserable failures, is drinking vodka while snorting cocaine. When used correctly together, both vodka and cocaine's immense power is undeniable. **The vodka and cocaine combination is one of the most fun combinations of drugs and alcohol a miserable failure can**

partake in. It is essentially the "secret agent" of all of the drug and alcohol combinations a miserable failure consumes. Most alcohols have a distinctive smell that can be easily noticed or detected by any curious daycare worker, water park security guard, or payday loan manager. This fact makes consuming most alcohols prior to dropping your kids off at preschool in the morning, sneaking into "Splash World," or before checking in on getting another 100% interest loan, a chore (REMINDER: a miserable failure doesn't do chores). Vodka, however, is the incognito secret agent of all alcohols. It has virtually no smell, allows for fluent use of all motor functions, and is still an extremely powerful tool when used to help cope with the daily challenges of being a miserable failure (NOTE: it makes your tears taste like candy as well). **Vodka also mixes well with water, giving the miserable failure ample opportunity to walk around all day lit with no one being the wiser (SUCKERS!!!).** Unlike marijuana or meth, cocaine also has no easily detectable odor and allows for easy use of normal bodily functions (CAUTION: if you're a male miserable failure, doing coke will cause you MORE erection problems). As long as you are diligent in keeping your nasal canals free from any signs of recent "snowfall," you'll fly completely under the "coke head radar." The cocaine user may show signs of increased energy and awareness, but their behavior is normally written off as being a personality trait. Vodka and cocaine complement each other perfectly and are the BEST choice for the functional addict "on the go" as they even your personality out.

The best method of consuming these substances is by combining them to create the magical drink known as "Vodcaine." Simply pour your cocaine into a slightly less than full bottle of cheap, broke ass vodka; shake well, and chug (WARNING: do not attempt to snort Vodcaine). You should attempt to consume one or two bottles of Vodcaine before noon each day, and never ever waste this magical elixir by pouring it into a watermelon (NOTE: remember, you don't eat any fruits and vegetables). Vodcaine is the perfect pre-drink for your wedding (trust us...it'll work out this time), criminal court (if it wasn't for your planter fasciitis, you would've never been arrested for streaking), first time colonoscopies (you thought it was kind of romantic), 5K races (it's better for you than water), and dance parties (you perfected your own version of the electric slide called "vomit in the punch bowl"). When consuming Vodcaine, please do not attempt to use any heavy machinery, drive a car, or perform any type of oral sex (NOTE: your tongue won't work properly). After you chug down an entire bottle of Vodcaine, go looking for another fight to get into (to get your ass beat, again). Drinking Vodcaine is also recommended before appearing in traffic court, for any single and dysfunctional stay-at-home (unemployed) moms and for anyone who works for the state or federal government. "Vodka" and "cocaine" go together like "peanut butter" and "jelly," so make sure you get yourself prepared for the horrible life-raping you're going to be getting as you travel down the road to be a miserable failure, by consuming copious amounts of this incredible elixir.

Tequila and Magic Mushrooms ("Mushies")

Tequila and magic mushrooms are a fantastic combination for the more "creative" miserable failures out there (a.k.a. the "delusional lunatics"). Let's say that you just accidentally defecated in your pants when bending over to re-Velcro your shoes. Tequila (and your time in prison) is probably to blame for your abnormally loose bowel problems. After bending over and shitting yourself, you should realize that you were never really wearing shoes to begin with. Magic mushroom-caused psychosis is definitely the culprit... If you've ever walked barefoot in shit-filled pants through the rest of a mall food court, knocking over tables, shoving small children to the ground, and ranting about someone stealing your bus pass, then you've clearly been drinking tequila and taking mushrooms at the same time. **Welcome to the magical world of "Mushies."** Mushies is the tequila and magic mushroom combination for miserable failures that like to get through life stuttering and seeing things that really don't exist (HINT, HINT: that purple baby tiger you've been stalking for two weeks, isn't really there...).

Tequila has a long history of causing projectile vomiting (your aim is impressive), inducing intensely kinky sex (YOUR MOTTO: "the fist ALWAYS fits"), and leading to blackout holes in your memory (you lost your underwear again). Magic mushrooms are also known for producing projectile vomiting, but in this case, your puke should look like a rainbow-colored unicorn horn. Mushrooms do induce kinky sex, but it's mainly the kind of lovemaking where your body gets used as a toilet (just go with it. It's Mexico and it's Spring Break). Mushrooms don't affect your ability to make new memories, but instead change your perception of old shitty ones. In a mushroom memory, a miserable failure may remember achieving something great or being a well-respected member of the community (neighbors that love it when you leave up your Christmas lights and interactive talking Santa display year-round). **In reality, if you are reading this book, you are basically giving up on "traditional" greatness in lieu of pursuing the worst life possible and are legally required to let your community know you live there (skinny dipping in a public fountain at noon on a Saturday should not be a sex offense, but sadly, it is).** The FANTASTIC combination of drinking copious amounts of tequila while taking magic mushrooms makes for an interesting evening, to say the least. Just be sure to steer clear of law enforcement, playgrounds, large holes (geographically, not sexually), pointy things, shiny objects, people wearing fur (no, you can't ride them), and heavy farm equipment (NOTE: it doesn't matter how much you want a cheeseburger, tractor combines should not be used to mass slaughter cattle). So, if you're looking to really give your life a turbo boost into miserable failuredom, we STRONGLY encourage you to consume Mushies on a weekly basis.

Scotch, Opiates, and Gin ("SOG")

When taken together, "SOG" (scotch, opiates, and gin) allow the miserable failure a wonderful opportunity to pass the world's most horrendous farts. SOG is a trifecta of failure that no intervention team, antibiotic, voodoo witch doctor, or deodorant can touch! When you're "all SOG'ed out," life simply slows down. Being a miserable failure means that you don't normally move too fast to do anything (lots of people go to community college for a decade and never graduate), but **when the combination of scotch, opiates, and gin are brought into the mix, everything in life is put on hold.** You were so close to finally completing that toothpick model of Thomas Jefferson's penis (BTW: the kids at the community center will be really disappointed). You fully intended to pay little Billy's tuition this month (learning to read is overrated anyway). You didn't mean to miss your doctor's appointment to check the softball-sized lump growing in your armpit (you named it Sir Larry McArthur III). All your "grand plans" ended when you decided to start substituting breakfast for scotch and gin while snorting opiates like a high-powered vacuum addicted to dirt (IMPORTANT NOTICE: mixing pancake batter into your opiates before snorting does not constitute a healthy breakfast). When you're SOG'ed, everything else comes in second place as your priorities will immediately change. Your new SOG goals will most likely include some of the following:

1. Sifting through the fogginess of your demented mind to remember if that full bottle of Scotch is actually alcohol or your own personal supply of urine (HINT, HINT: either way you're going to drink it).
2. Going on a nighttime needle hunt for injecting opiates (just walk barefoot near the homeless encampment or roll naked through your favorite downtown back alley for said drug utensils).
3. Drawing beautiful landscapes in the vomit that accumulates on your shirt throughout the day (NOTE: you should refer to your puke art as "P.A.R.T.").
4. Yelling obscenities at crippled children outside of various schools.

5. Playing "connect the scabs" (it's like "connect the dots" for miserable failures).
6. Running nude through the cemetery during a LIVE funeral.
7. Toilet-papering and egging the retirement home while shouting, *"be gone you golden devils!"*
8. Walking into the local police station break room to steal **BOTH** doughnuts and handguns from the police officers.

SOGing also causes severe and nose-crippling lethal flatulence. Gin farts are especially clingy odor bombs that attach themselves to furniture, children's toys and any type of clothing for extended and long periods of time. Some farts have been documented to still exist in corduroy and flannel months and even years after release. Furthermore, scotch alone is enough to produce gag-worthy ass gas, but when you down a bottle of gin with three tablets of opiates, your ass becomes a ticking time bomb. These butt clouds initially present themselves to the nose as a slightly unpleasant odor, but grow stronger as they accumulate more oxygen and eventually take over the entire area they were unleashed in (we recommend elevators). Their foul thickness can be tasted on the tongue and this should serve as your first warning to quickly relocate to a well-ventilated area, or risk severe brain damage (FYI: **DO NOT** DRINK SCOTCH IN DUMPSTERS).

The combination of scotch and gin stink torpedoes will cause the poor soul caught in their trail to potentially vomit blood, convulse uncontrollably, and experience temporary loss of all cognitive functions (your typical afternoon). Opiates do not produce gas farts. Their specialty is loose liquid evacuations. One can only imagine the horror that occurs when combining unpredictable liquid ass explosions with the heart-stopping stench of scotch and gin butt bombs. The resulting ass mist can be best described as rotten apples dipped in gym socks, meets expired coconut cream cheese rolled in shit, and covered in the stench of death. Your terrible anal gas on SOG has the ability to make entire apartment complexes uninhabitable for decades, cause blindness in babies from Madagascar, instant evaporation of all insects within a five-foot radius, pacemaker failure, and will trigger the chemical sensors at most airport security checks. **YOU HAVE BEEN WARNED**!

Heroin and Wine ("Heroing")

Some miserable failures try to conceal their "miserableness" as they are drinking wine. We don't recommend trying this as people will see through your bullshit nonsense once you begin to drink the entire bottle without a glass. Like "spaghetti" goes with "meat balls," "heroin" and "wine" are a wonderful and fantastic combination. "Heroing" occurs when you consume multiple bottles (three or more) of wine and flush them down with a quick shot of heroin into your forearm. Drinking wine makes people look refined, distinguished, professional, and wealthy (HINT: you are none of those things). Conversely, shooting heroin makes you look sad, lazy, pathetic, and slow. This is why they are the perfect combination to take together. A miserable failure does not need to refer to themselves a "Wine-O," so simply refer to yourself as a *"cocksucking, motherfucking alcoholic."* Shooting heroin while drinking five or six **BOTTLES** of wine should put you in an alcohol-poisoned hangover coma for precisely three and a half days. During your three and a half day "sleep fest," the miserable failure should be experiencing lucid dreams involving:

- Trolls, fairies, and goblins eating you alive in Pittsburgh.
- A three-way with a crippled monkey and a woman with spina bifida.
- Boxing a coked-up kangaroo in Australia.

The first rule about shooting heroin is simple, **always share needles or use dirty needles.** You shouldn't be able to afford diabetic needles, so stealing them from your buddies on Skid Row is a **fantastic idea**. You can also steal these needles from the hazardous red boxes in any medical clinic if you do decide to go get your methadone treatment (quitter). When you shoot the heroin, you should be AT LEAST three to six bottles of wine deep. Find a comfy place to lay down (a stranger's shopping cart in the grocery store is a fine choice) and sleep! There's nothing more soothing than being completely passed out drunk on wine and high on heroin (so much that people think you're dead and you might end up in the morgue). Drinking massive amounts of wine while shooting heroin is a classic combination that has horrible life-altering effects. So, sit back, shoot up, RELAX, and start guzzling the wine!

Crack, Moonshine and Schnapps ("Howling at the Moon")

Nothing screams, *"I live in the past and I'm an aggressive drunk"* quite like the combination of consuming extremely large amounts of crack, moonshine, and schnapps within the same drunk and drug fest. When taken together, crack, moonshine and schnapps is what we call, "Howling at the Moon." Crack is cocaine's first cousin. Schnapps is Vodka's second cousin. Moonshine is gin's inbred and deformed cousin from central Arkansas. It's with this exact triple threat trio, where a miserable failure gets fired from a job, divorced, arrested and beaten up- all in ONE, SINGLE, SOLITARY, DAY. As a reminder, you are actually legally **REQUIRED** and **MANDATED** to smoke crack while drinking peach schnapps and homemade blackberry moonshine if you're ever in any U.S. state south of Illinois (yes, having sex with your first cousin is a fantastic option as well in some of these prestigious locations).

Smoking crack will turn you into a violent and road-raging, psychotic lunatic (SCORE!!!). Smoking crack while being drunk on schnapps and moonshine basically means that your violent and drunken outburst directed towards the Mall Santa will be the hit "must-see" video on the web and social media for the next fifteen days. Drinking schnapps requires living in the past during the peak of your party years on boats and at the local dive bars. Adding illegal homemade moonshine and a crack rock to the mix is 100% ESSENTIAL if you want to go "Howling at the Moon." You'll be wearing your vintage beer t-shirt while smoking your crack pipe and prank calling your ex-girlfriend (or ex-boyfriend) from the payphone of the local dive bar soon enough. Drink up, you worthless motherfucker. And smoke up, you crack head. It's time that you went, "Howling at the moon."

Champagne and Superglue ("Super Champ")

Champagne is dignified, refined, and fancy. Superglue is used as a strong adhesive to glue two objects together. **However, the combination of drinking five bottles of champagne and huffing copious amounts of superglue from mason jars provides the miserable failure with a high and positive feeling of "euphoria on crack."** You are a worthless, drunk, sack of shit, so it should come as no surprise that we strongly encourage the miserable failure (who is out of options on drugs and alcohol), to resort to stealing bottles of champagne and super glue from supermarkets. Walk into a super market in your black, trench coat duster. Proceed to shove eight packs of superglue down your holey pair of sweatpants you stole from rehab (again). Next, make your way over to the liquor aisle. Along the way, feel free to grab chips and soda's off the shelf and "help yourself to them" as you stumble through the supermarket.

Once you reach the liquor aisle, find the cheapest champagne that you can (miserable failures do not drink expensive and prestigious champagne), next, proceed to stuff eight bottles into your black, trench coat duster jacket. Simply walk out of the store and head straight for the alley. Once you're in the alley, make sure you pop open three bottles of champagne and chug them like the alcoholic that you are. Next, pour all eight packets of superglue into any type of can or bottle and start-a-huffin'! A miserable failure should never get sealed to the jar, so be careful not to splash super glue near the rim. The high you get from huffing super glue combined with your excessive guzzling of cheap champagne will cause you to become overly-confident, aroused, and hallucinate all at once. This is why we call it the "Super Champ." You're going to feel like a million dollars and have tons of confidence when you molest the trash can (you'll think the trash can is a hot model). You're going to feel awesome seeing pink miniature ponies being ridden by cowboy midgets suffering from gout. This combination of alcohol and huffing will cause temporary blindness, partial paralysis, and a horrible and massive hang-over headache (GOOD). All of these symptoms should only last a few hours. Once you're coherent again, chug those last couple of bottles of champagne and breathe in more of that superglue air before passing out (again).

Brandy and Angel Dust ("The Halo")

Brandy is a type of alcohol that is distilled from wine (no, not your "prison wine" you made in the slammer) and is generally around 35-60% pure alcohol. This basically means that drinking LARGE quantities of brandy in one sitting will simply, **fuck**...**you**...**up**...
(NOTE: old people have brandy, so you might have to "borrow it" from your grandfather's liquor cabinet...**again**...). To pair brandy with a fine recreational drug, we recommend using angel dust. Angel dust is commonly known as "PCP" and causes euphoria, paranoia, delusions, hallucinations, and a severe distortion of your perception of reality (SCORE!!!). Essentially, consuming brandy while snorting or ingesting angel dust allows the miserable failure to experience an entire alternate universe and faux reality. We call this, "The Halo."

Want to imagine yourself on a big game hunt in the Serengeti riding a giant dildo with two kittens? Consume the Halo! Want to see yourself as a distinct, refined, upper-class, business tycoon with the head of a dolphin and the body of a goat? Try the Halo! Want to fantasize that you are NOT a miserable failure and are 100% NORMAL? Again, make sure you're consuming huge quantities of the Halo **(BTW: if you don't want to be a miserable failure, stop reading this book and immediately punch yourself in the face thirty-seven times)**. Being a miserable failure can sometimes be draining and exhausting. So, drinking brandy while consuming large amounts of angel dust temporarily allows the miserable failure to experience a non-existent, completely fabricated, made up, invented, and 100% BULLSHIT alternate life story. The Halo has been employed by miserable failures throughout the years to help them deal with the unfortunate reality of their unemployment, terrible credit score, STDs, horrendous living situations, sexual dysfunctions, isolation, and incontinence.

The Long Island Ecstasy

Want to feel amazingly drunk, have orgasms by simply gently rubbing up against furniture as well as freaking out random strangers with your bare hands? Then, we strongly encourage popping a few ecstasy pills and drinking MULTIPLE long island ice teas within the same hour. This is what we call the "Long Island Ecstasy." Ecstasy is a drug that produces great happiness and joyful excitement whenever you pop a pill. For the miserable failure, taking ecstasy while drinking Long Island ice teas provides ample opportunity for you to masturbate on the Abe Lincoln statue in the downtown city park while projectile vomiting the Chinese food buffet dinner you just consumed. For most normal people, Long Island iced tea ingredients consist of 1 shot of rum, gin, vodka, triple sec, tequila, and a splash of sweet and sour mix. **"The Miserable Failure Long Island Iced Tea" should consist of two shots of rum, gin, vodka, triple sec, tequila, whiskey, beer, wine, champagne, and a smidgen of sweet and sour mix.** Consuming this deadly, lethal, and classic combination has been used by many miserable failures over the years to successfully deal with their divorce and their eviction from their house. Got fired again for showing up to work late? Score some ecstasy in the park from a college kid, drink a few "Miserable Failure Long Island Iced Teas," and try to hop on board the hood of a police officer's speeding car. Lost all of your money gambling on sports (again)? Take a few hits of Molly (ecstasy), slam a gallon of a "Miserable Failure Long Island Iced Teas," and show up to your parole hearing in the morning with your hand down your pants touching yourself (the judge will go harder on your sentencing as well). When you consume Miserable Failure, Long Island iced teas and ecstasy at the same time, you will have an uncontrollable urge to touch everything in sight. This is why it is crucial that you never wash your hands or clip your fingernails (see the "hygiene" section for more info). Your hands should be dirty, disgusting, and vomit-inducing. When you're drinking copious amounts of Long Island iced teas and taking ecstasy, you want other people (who you will be randomly touching) to recoil in horror at the sight of your trembling hands and long, black, shit-caked fingernails.

DMT, Peyote, and Wine Coolers ("The Forever Young Experience")

Everyone wants to stay young forever. Especially you, the miserable failure, who ALWAYS lives in the past. We want to help you get drunk while being in a perpetual state of hallucinations and faux realities during your entire trip. If you want to hallucinate that you're much younger than you currently are and you want to play checkers with the devil in a retirement home run by robots, killer whales, and dingleberries, we recommend taking peyote, DMT (Dimethyltryptamine) and drinking wine coolers at the same time. Consuming numerous bottles of wine coolers while being high on DMT and peyote provides the miserable failure with a fun and unique experience that you will never forget. We call this "The Forever Young Experience." This is probably the best combination for the miserable failures out there who like to temporarily live on alternate universes, seeing things that aren't real, and never "aging." Wine coolers are a staple for every person under the age of twenty-one to drink. Most miserable failures have probably stolen a few wine coolers from their parent's garage refrigerator while growing up. Drinking wine coolers underage made you feel like a sophisticated and "cool" adult. However, when you consume thirty-six wine coolers, pop a pill of DMT, and drink some peyote tea; your hallucinations and intoxication will be one, gigantic, terrifying, and epic experience. DMT and peyote are very powerful psychedelic drugs and when you combine them together, you have yourself a recipe for disaster. Adding in a massive amount of wine cooler consumption will allow you to live life to the "worst" while tripping bad on these very powerful drug combinations. Hallucinations that one could experience under the Forever Young Protocol include:

- Living as an eighteen-year-old popsicle in your mythical magical world of "colors and shapes" while being sexually assaulted by a demon wearing a pink tutu.
- Morphing into a twelve-year-old stuttering, colorful cat named, Larry Augustus Thompson III in the magical land of "Fleetius."
- Being eaten alive by a turquoise colored dragon named Carl in the back seat of a kaleidoscope-colored station wagon.

We strongly encourage taking the Forever Young Experience during one of your last days of work in your current office (if you've just now started down your long and painful journey into becoming a miserable failure). **The sight of you standing nude, chasing invisible green letter "H's" while urinating on top of the conference room desk during the weekly Monday morning 8:00 company meeting will be a defining moment for you before you get fired.** The Forever Young Experience is something that is a good fit for all miserable failures. Everyone will have different hallucinogen experiences under this protocol. Sometimes your trip will be fun with wild shapes and vivid colors. Other times, your trip will be bad and you will encounter some really fucked up bad dudes in your haze. Either way asshole, drink up, start taking those pills and begin consuming peyote. You're on board the Forever Young Express!

Diet

Besides the massive amounts of beer, liquor, and random alcohol that a miserable failure consumes, food should play an important role in your newly fucked up lifestyle. Most NORMAL people try to eat a healthy, well-balanced diet. **The miserable failure's diet consists of consuming life-altering amounts of sugars, simple carbohydrates, alcohol, highly processed snacks and expired pet food made in China.** Nutrition is key for most NORMAL people. However, **the miserable failure IS... NOT... NORMAL.** In fact, the miserable failure has a terrible diet that results in a diabetes and scurvy diagnosis from their doctor. Below is a sample food diary for the average day of a miserable failure.

Breakfast

- Expired generic flowered tortillas dipped in chocolate
- A half-gallon bottle of high fructose corn syrup
- Four shots of whiskey
- Smoke three cigarettes
- Five cans of soda
- Huff a can of spray paint
- A slice of cold pizza leftover from seven weeks ago

Lunch

- A can of cat food
- Twelve beers
- Plain white bread toasted and smothered with grape jelly
- Smoke a joint
- Half a pound of deep-fried bologna
- Four cups of straight sugar

Dinner

- A gallon of rocky road ice cream
- Nine shots of tequila
- Three shots of rum

- Two shots of vodka
- Smoke a hit of crystal meth
- One bottle of ketchup
- Ten raw eggs

If the miserable failure eats a combination of this diet, their health is going to deteriorate extremely fast (how exciting!). **You must also continue your binge and purge eating disorder at all times during your quest to fail at life.** Eat a big meal? Time to go use some fingers to make yourself throw up (skip brushing your teeth in toilet water after this as well). In fact, after each meal consumed, the miserable failure should make their way into a bathroom to "take care of business." When people ask you why you binge and purge, simply respond with, *"I want to be a model."* The expression on their face is going to be a combination of utter disgust and extreme confusion. This also applies if your therapist or parole officer takes you out for a nice meal. After you've consumed the meal, announce at the dinner table publicly, that you're going to go make yourself vomit in the bathroom. Also, inform them that the dinner was literally a waste of money for them, and then begin to laugh. Making sure that your eating disorders stay in place is KEY for you during your metamorphosis into becoming a miserable failure.

Carbs

Eat carbs often. Most people avoid carbohydrates because they make you unhealthy, fat, and sick. The miserable failure's diet consists mostly of carbs. Breads, rice, cereals, pastas, and gluten are staples of a miserable failure's diet. Sneak into an all-you-can-eat buffet without paying? Go straight for the macaroni and cheese, doughnuts, and ice cream. Get invited over for a cookout at your life coach's house? Go for the dinner rolls, beer, and dessert. Eat as many carbs as possible. You're eventually going to develop a potbelly and love handles (even with your purging) due to your carbohydrate loading. Eating massive amounts of carbs is also going to give you diabetes (SCORE!!!). For more information on what to do when you get diabetes, check out the previous section on the "diabetes excuse."

Sugars

Even though you have diabetes and you're about to lose toes on your feet, you still need to feed your insatiable sugar cravings. Eat sugars as much as humanly possible. From the sugars in the alcohol to the massive amounts of high fructose corn syrup you consume, the miserable failure eats sugar as often as they can. After all, your diabetes is going to start kicking in and you're going to need to feed the beast with massive amounts of sugar. Soda? Drink up. Candy and chocolate? A staple! Doughnuts? Eat two dozen! Consuming sugar also speeds up rotting of your teeth, which helps your "miserable failure appearance" that you have been ever-so-carefully working on obtaining. Whenever you're in doubt on when you should consume sugar, go to the grocery store, find a five-pound bag of white sugar, sit in the aisle and start eating it like the hungry maniac that you are!

Grains

Similar to carbs, eating grains is a staple part of the miserable failure's diet. Now we must stress that the miserable failure should not eat healthy, organic, and non-GMO whole grains. We demand that the miserable failure eat highly processed and genetically modified, bleached, or synthetic grains. Most of the "grains" you should be consuming can be found in the cereal aisle of any major grocery store. Just like searching for that coveted bag of sugar mentioned earlier, simply stop on by the aisle, grab six to ten boxes of the unhealthiest cereals, and make a run for the exit. If you really want to add to this experience, open a box of cereal and begin to eat it as you run screaming out the grocery store. It's also worth noting that if you eat enough GMO grains found in highly-processed food, you're probably going to develop massive and grotesque tumors on your body (YES!!!). Once you develop these tumors, please refer to the "cancer excuse" or the "tumor excuse" sections in this piece of shit book.

Fats

Avoid eating healthy fats (avocados, organic ghee, grass-fed butter, coconut oil, MCT oil, etc.). Instead, your fat intake SHOULD come in the form of drinking massive and life-altering amounts of disgusting **USED** vegetable oil. We encourage the miserable failure to find used vegetable oil behind the various restaurant dumpsters in your city (BTW: if you can't score any used vegetable oil, you can still go to the store and grab a gallon of it for $.99). However, most of the time, large bins of used vegetable oil and nasty grease are stored behind restaurants in alleys. Go down to your favorite alley and get yourself a few gallons of this used vegetable oil. By the way, no one is going to stop you from taking used vegetable oil. So, stock up buddy. Then, proceed to take a gallon of the used vegetable oil outside of a church on Sunday. As the parishioners are exiting, simply start screaming nonsense gibber and begin consuming the entire bottle. There's a great chance that someone will feel sorry for you and offer you a ride home or a place to stay the night.

Proteins

The only proteins that you should mainly be consuming are raw eggs, cat food, dog food and spoiled chocolate milk. Protein is processed in the kidneys and those organs have stopped functioning properly YEARS ago (WARNING: having poor kidney function is a disadvantage when you attempt to go sell one on the black market). Eating raw eggs and pet food should be enough protein for a miserable failure. Furthermore, your kidneys should be shutting down from the MANY stones that are in them from your lack of water consumption (SEE ALSO: the "kidney stone excuse"). Also, only try to eat proteins high in trans fats. Essentially, eat any protein that is fried or sautéed in large amounts of margarine. Eating trans fats aids in the deterioration of ALL of your internal organs, and plays a key role when you suffer your seventh heart attack (SEE ALSO: the "heart attack excuse").

Using Food Stamps Properly

Most people feel embarrassed or ashamed if they have to rely on food stamps from the federal or state government. This is not the case for the miserable failure. In fact, **the miserable failure brags openly about using food stamps to purchase alcohol, steak, lobsters, superglue, and cigarettes.** When you get your food stamps on the first of the month, go down to the local supermarket. As you walk in the store, have your food stamps out so you can show everyone. Say things like, *"I'm here to spend* ***your*** *tax dollars, bitches."* If you don't want to use them for food, we encourage you to sell them online for some fast cash. The rule of thumb is simple- for every $1 of a food stamp you're selling, you're going to get $.50 cash. You can also use your food stamps as bartering chips down at the local homeless shelter or on Skid Row.

Using food stamps at the store is easy, as long as you follow this guide for what you need to purchase. Keep in mind, that your only goal here is to royally piss off all of the customers and grocery store staff during your food stamp purchase. You need to **attempt** to purchase the following items using your food stamp card:

- Aged Kobe Beef Steaks
- Fresh Caught Maine Lobsters
- Dungeness Fresh Crab Legs
- Imported Beer from Germany
- Blue Label Whiskey
- Spray Paint
- Cigarettes
- Porn Magazines

- Super Glue
- Scratch Off Lottery Tickets
- Whip Cream Canisters (for your temporary whip-it high)

When you go up to the cash register, openly inform both customers in front of you and behind you that their tax dollars are funding your alcohol addiction, cigarette smoking craze, and your "soon-to-be" glue huffing in the parking lot. If you're unable to purchase the alcohol, cigarettes, and nudie magazines with your food stamp card, simply buy a pre-paid gift card with your food stamp money, get out of line, and then go back in line to complete your purchases. Feel free to take a picture of your groceries and post it on social media with a caption that reads: *"I'm living like a king! Thanks for the FREE food stamps, assholes!"*

If you can get away with buying the items listed above, as soon as you walk out of the grocery store, place the bag down in the middle of the parking lot and light it on fire. This wastes all of the good food you just bought and will temporarily cause a distraction, which will allow you ample time to walk back into the store and steal your various horrible, fattening and processed foods by sticking them down your pants and running out the back of the store.

Fitness

You should either be an abnormally obese fat ass, or be a skinny meth-head with a plump little beer belly and love handles. Either way, you should appear that you have never set foot in a gym. You see, **the miserable failure does not exercise on a regular basis, unless you consider "running" from the police as "cardio," or "lifting" kilos of cocaine you stole from the Mexican drug cartel as "weight training."** This lack of exercise has also helped you achieve your NUMEROUS heart attacks, excessive weight gain, horrible diabetes, and staph-infected bedsores due to your long periods of inactivity.

You should never exercise, and you should strive to be an out of shape, loser. Although it is a tempting option, you never REALLY want to become morbidly obese. Obese people who are trapped on their couches, weighing 900 pounds miss out on over 95% of the recommended activities it takes to become a miserable failure. Essentially, you should strive to have a fat gut and love handles, but also appear to be "meth head-skinny" in the other areas of your ugly and grotesque body. Furthermore, being morbidly obese prevents you from actually becoming a certified miserable failure, because you essentially slowly start to die on your couch (RULE OF THUMB: if the emergency personnel have to knock down one of your walls in order to get you out of your house, you've gotten way too fat to be a COMPLETE miserable failure).

We don't want you to become morbidly obese. We just want you to look like complete and total dog shit. **Essentially, we want you to live a long, painful, and horrible life that ends with your tragic death MANY years later.** The miserable failure is a couch potato who can barely muster up enough energy to go to the bathroom to urinate (sometimes, we encourage you to "let her rip" right there as you lay drunk on your couch at 2:00 in the afternoon). That being mentioned, we do recommend that a miserable failure go use their free one-week gym pass just to have some fun and stir some shit up. Most gyms give people a free one-week gym membership if they simply ask. It's time for you to go down to your local gym to get some "workouts" in. This is primarily because you can steal clean towels, rolls of toilet paper, protein bars, and dumbbells from the gym. Before you steal anything, you need to try and blend into your surroundings (this will be difficult as most people that go to the gym don't regularly wear slippers, boxers, and a stained robe to work out in). **We want you to take pride in your disgusting appearance and your lack of a moral compass when you go to the gym.** When you first walk into the gym, yell VERY LOUDLY the following, "*I'm into* *fitness. Fitness dick in yo' mouth!*" This phrase needs to be said by the female miserable failure as well. The expressions on people's faces will be crossed between a puzzled look and an appalling stare. This is the miserable failure's beginning guide to "working out"...

Free Weights

Gyms are full of roid-raging, angry, muscle-bound, hulks (both males and females) who hate people fucking with their gym time. For the miserable failure, making sure that your presence is known in the free weight room to these muscular creatures is key. **If you see a giant man using the bench press and then walk away to temporarily get a drink of water, immediately steal his spot on the bench and try bench pressing the same amount of weight as he did.** As the bar comes crashing down on your chest, breaking your ribs, puncturing a lung, and collapsing your internal cavity, you just won yourself a lawsuit against the gym, my friend! You've also just got your ass BEATEN by Mr. Roid Rage for stealing his bench press when returns from the water fountain (happy days are here again...).

If you want to do bicep curls, stand in front of the dumbbell rack and take up as much room as possible. Start doing bicep curls right in front of the mirror (even if you're only using two and a half pound dumbbells). This prevents people from using many of the dumbbells that you're currently blocking. Feel free to cry out loud as you do your curls. Say things like, "*I wanted a steel dildo for Christmas, Mom!*" We also recommend yelling random curse words out loud as you do your bicep curls. Some of these might make you sound like you have Tourette's Syndrome. The words you should be yelling out at random as your exercise should be, "*disphit, fuckface, cocksucker, motherfucker, asshole, retard, cunt, and fucker.*" Shouting out any of these words will guarantee a swift kick to your windpipe is coming very fast.

For the male miserable failure, if you see a group of muscular men working out together, walk up to them and ask them if you can join in to work out with them. When they ask you why you want to work out with them, tell them that you *"just wanted to know what it was like to work out with the biggest fucking dipshits in this gym."* **As they reign fiery blows of fury with their fists into your face, remember that you are a miserable failure and you deserve the pain, physical scars, and the permanent disfigurement associated with said beating.** If you see a pretty lady at the gym doing squats, stand right behind her and make highly-sexual overt comments about her ass. Make her extremely uncomfortable. We recommend putting your hand down your boxers as you watch her (this also includes for you female miserable failures out there as well). When you see fat people training with a personal trainer, walk up to them in the middle of their exercise session and plead for them to fire their trainer and get a new one. Say to them, *"your fitness and health results aren't quite there yet, are they?"* You can also walk around and offer the fat people at the gym some of your stash of candy bars which you stole from trick or treater's on Halloween as a "peace offering" for your nonstop and constant fat harassment and bullying campaign. If you're a female miserable failure, walk over to any empty weight bench, bend over and scream out loud, *"hey limp dicks, this ass ain't going to eat itself!"* After screaming this out loud and with any luck, you'll have a few men who will be willing to bang you in the dirty and greasy alley out back (#ROMANCE). Furthermore, the female miserable failure should openly mock old women in the gym and pick fights with the angry, CrossFit girls doing burpees in the corner (here comes another "cunt punt" into your crotch).

Yoga

Most people go to a yoga class to relax, stretch out, and become flexible. Not the miserable failure! **The miserable failure attends yoga class to catch up on some sleep and to work on their impromptu comedy routine out loud in front of a captive audience.** The miserable failure also attends a yoga class just after consuming three cans of baked beans, an entire head of cabbage, a pound of cheese, and a gallon of beer. During tough yoga poses, feel free to offer the class the following comments out loud just to spice things up:

- *"I can feel my asshole muscle getting more flexible!"*
- *"I haven't showered in thirty days, bitches. The smell is coming from my body."*
- *"Do we get to keep this yoga mat as a participation trophy?"*
- *"What's with all of these tight yoga pants? Why not wear sweatpants like me?"*
- *"That last fart was from me and it was a hall of famer!"*
- *"Owwww this hurts! I want my mommy!"*
- *"Can we use these poses for sex positions with ALL Taiwanese prostitutes?"*

The combination of your horrendous gas and odor emanating from your butt, as well as your rude, inappropriate, and outlandish comments, will surely get many of the people in the yoga class royally PISSED OFF at you. As you go into Warrior Pose One, feel free to piss yourself. Don't make a comment. Just wait for the gasps and reaction that you get from your fellow yoga classmates. When you do Downward Dog, let out a fart and start barking like a puppy. When the teacher instructs the class to go into Child's Pose, start to snore and even feel free to drool on your mat. When the teacher instructs the class to go into a Head Stand, walk over to the wall and begin to slam your head against it very hard (NOTE: if you find a stud in the wall while you're doing this, you're a winner). Then, turn around and apologize to the entire class before returning to your yoga mat to disrobe completely nude (do this while laughing uncontrollably).

Towards the end of class, make sure to talk during the last pose of Shavasana. Feel free to recite your twelve steps to **YOUR** specific AA program out loud as people are trying to relax in the "Corpse Pose." The miserable failure can also use this time to showcase their hidden talent of singing. Feel free to belt out the Star-Spangled Banner as the class comes to an end. When class is over, don't put your yoga equipment away. Instead, you should take them with you as you exit the room. After all, doesn't the gym give these away free after each class? If not, then they should be, so make sure you steal them. If you follow the step-by-step guide for the miserable failure in yoga class, you're going to be giving these yogi's a story to tell for the rest of their life. You also might get your teeth knocked out in the parking lot afterwards by an angry group of furious, stay-at-home soccer moms (SCORE!!!).

CrossFit

CrossFit is a series of extremely difficult, high-intensity exercises and movements designed to get people into fantastic shape. **For the miserable failure, CrossFit classes are a great way to tear your ACL, bruise your sternum, fracture your tail bone and shatter your wrists.** CrossFit exercises are designed to help people lift their own body weight, shred pounds, and get stronger through extremely intense circuit interval training. When the miserable failure attempts CrossFit, it generally ends in disaster (the police are called, an ambulance is summoned, arrests are made, a severed finger is found, etc.) resulting in a horrible day for everyone at the gym.

When the miserable failure walks into a CrossFit studio, the first thing they need to do is to pick a fight (similar to what you did when you first got into prison or juvenile hall). Figure out who the biggest guy in the room is (or biggest girl for female miserable failures) and tell him (or her), "*your ass is grass, pussy.*" Then, tell him that you "*know karate.*" Let him and his friend's laughter subside a brief moment before attempting a broke-ass, half-ass, roundhouse kick directed at him. Once he grabs your ankle, twists it, breaks it, and you fall to the floor with a compound ankle fracture, laugh at him, and tell him that you're ready to work out.

Working out by doing CrossFit for the miserable failure always ends in a total disaster. If you want even MORE brain damage, then try a handstand. Go up to the side of a wall, plant your hands on the ground and attempt to lift your legs up and above your head. This act will cause your feeble arms to give way and your entire disgusting body will come crashing down on your head. When the miserable failure tries to do a pull-up, it probably isn't going to go over that well either. When you grab the pull-up bar, scream in pain (feel free to shout out, *"Mom, you should have aborted me!"*) as your sad and pathetic attempt at a pull up ends abruptly. When the miserable failure tries to do a push-up, this generally ends with a face-first head plant directly into the concrete on the gym floor (if you bust out your front teeth or shatter your nose, you get ultra, mega, extra, special bonus points). When the miserable failure attempts jump rope, this usually results in a shattered right patella knee cap and a broken left clavicle (along with massive amounts of vomit from the previous night's alcohol poisoning episode).

Sit-ups are going to be tricky for the miserable failure. For the miserable failure, sit-ups are almost not doable due to the gigantic beer belly that you've accumulated over your years of living in "miserable failuredom." When the miserable failure attempts to do sit-ups, they generally get hernia and throw out their back as they TRY to hoist themselves up. We also encourage the miserable failure to shit themselves (at least six times) as they do squat thrusts and burpees during the end of the class. Your goal during your CrossFit workout should be to get seriously injured, steal some steroids from the instructor and to annoy the piss out of everyone else in the gym area.

Spin Classes

For normal people, spin class is a great way to get in shape through rigorous cardiovascular, indoor bicycling in a fun and music-filled intimate environment. **Spin class for the miserable failure involves mo-**

nopolizing the instructor's time, making people uncomfortable, and breaking one of the spin bikes.

Miserable failures should wear road bike-themed tights and a helmet DURING ALL SPIN CLASSES (essentially walk in like you're going on the Tour De France). Pick a bike at the front of the class directly facing the instructor. You're not going in there to work out, you're going in there to cause trouble. When the music starts, we strongly encourage the miserable failure to walk over to the speakers and start unplugging them. Then, announce to the class that you *"prefer to ride in silence."* This act will generally get the stay-at-home moms really pissed off. The miserable failure also needs food and snacks along with alcohol for their spin class cycling bike ride experience. Feel free to bring an entire, fully cooked rotisserie roasted chicken and a side of mashed potatoes and gravy with you. When people stare at you and your feast in disgust, tell them that you *"need your protein"* and offer them a drumstick.

When the class starts, stare directly at the instructor with a creepy smile. In fact, don't take your eyes off the instructor the entire time. There's nothing creepier for a spin instructor than a semi-homeless, stinky, disgusting, smelly, drunk, asshole staring at them in an uncomfortable way during the entire hour-long spin class. Since you're at the front of the class, feel free to let out some farts while openly laying claim to ALL of them. Need a drink to quench your thirst during spin class? Now would be an appropriate time to take a shot of your homemade, illegal moonshine. If you need to vomit from the massive amount of food and alcohol you've consumed both before and during class, get off your bike, make the puking announcement to the entire class, walk over to the trashcan, and heave-ho! **The smell of your vomit, farts, chicken feast, sweat, body odor, and bad breath inside the small, cramped and hot cycle room, will cause the instructor too probably shut down the class, and have security come and escort you out of the building.** The miserable failure should not leave class when it gets canceled. Still ride the spin bike like nothing is wrong. In fact, you should mock everyone as they leave and tell them that you're *"going to win the race"* as they exit the room in a mad panic.

Cardio Equipment

The miserable failure does not work out on a treadmill, Stairmaster, or elliptical trainer. The miserable failure can barely walk up a flight of stairs without labored breathing, crying, or passing out. This is from all of the years of the chain-smoking, excessive drug usage, massive amounts of alcohol drinking, and horrible eating habits. The miserable failure does get some running in on a daily basis. The miserable failure's cardiovascular exercise generally comes from:

- Running from the police.
- Running from the psychiatric orderlies at the mental hospital.
- Running from angry parents at the local playground.
- Running from your parole officer.
- Running from mall security.
- Running from the angry homeless schizophrenics in "drug alley."

It should come of no surprise that a miserable failure does not even know how to use a treadmill, stationary bike, elliptical machine, or stair master. For the miserable failure, the gym's cardio equipment should be foreign to them. The miserable failure wants to become well-known and infamous for being a complete piece of shit. You want to showcase your acting skills so the world can see your total talent for being a complete miserable failure fuck up. When you want the world to notice you, you need to fuck up so bad and get it on video, where it can be posted online for the public to see. You can do this through your cardio at the gym. **When you get to the gym and want to hop on a treadmill, make sure that you crank up the speed to its maximum level before you place your feet on the tread to attempt to run.** When the speed is up to ten miles per hour, jump on to the treadmill. Your feet are not going to be able to run as fast as the treadmill speed. This is going to cause your feet to shoot back at a rapid speed from your horrible body, and you will fall directly on your face getting burn marks from the tread as you get hurled off the treadmill and back against the wall. Generally, this display from the miserable failure will get people to notice them. This is EXACTLY your goal. You want to do this act seven to ten more times, because sooner or later, people are going to be taking videos of you and posting them online. Soon you'll be the star of the hit video entitled, "asshole moron of the gym" that has millions of views and downloads. The miserable failure can also use the treadmill at the gym in their stolen wheelchair. Roll yourself up the treadmill. Put the wheelchair on the treadmill and then sit in the wheelchair. Turn on the treadmill and hold onto the side rails as you roll along. When people look at you in shock, light up a cigarette, and return with a simple, "*this run is a killer.*"

Personal Training

You're an out of shape LAZY FUCK. You need to swindle your way into a gym and get some sessions in with a personal trainer if you want to become a complete and total miserable failure. Your personal trainer ("best friend") is going to HATE you. **Since you have started down your journey into becoming a miserable failure, your diet should have GONE TO COMPLETE SHIT. Your cardiovascular training and your weight lifting should be in the gutter; not because of your six packs per day cigarette smoking habit, the lack of nutritional value in your ramen noodle diet or your fifth of whiskey per day drinking binge, but because you are actively destroying your entire body every day and on purpose with these specific massive amounts of horrible toxins, mixed with no sleep and heavy amounts of stress.** The only workouts that you are getting on a consistent basis, are the times you spend running full speed out of the computer store with a new phone in your hand as the mall cops hunt you down like a pack of rabid wolves. So, win, lose or draw, sooner or later, we STRONGLY encourage the miserable failure to go into their local neighborhood gym and get one of those "free personal training sessions" that most gyms offer people to sucker them into a deal for joining.

The fact that you're walking into the gym smoking a cigarette while wearing a dirty robe, slippers, and soiled underwear should give the people working at the front desk of the gym a reason to gasp in horror at the sight of your disgusting appearance. Once you get in and meet your new personal trainer, we encourage the miserable failure to instantly become friends with them. Refer to your trainer that you just met five minutes ago as *"buddy," "pal,"* or *"friend."* When he gives you the tour of the gym, laugh and mock the 6'6" 250-pound meathead studs that are bench pressing 400 pounds. Feel free to call them *"pussies"* as you cower behind your new BFF personal trainer friend like the pussy that **you** are. As you make your way through the gym for your tour, attempt to hold his hand. When he pulls his hand away, put your arm around him. When he takes you into the locker room, feel free to talk to the nude and semi-nude people getting dressed and undressed in there. The following phrases should be applied to all nude strangers in the locker room:

For the male miserable failure

"Nice cock."

"Greetings everyone. I used to be female, now I am transgendered!"

"How many towels are we allowed to take home at once?"

"Can we shit in the showers?"

For the female miserable failure

"Ew...You need to shave that hairy snatch, girlfriend."

"Are we allowed to leave the toilets un-flushed after usage?"

"I can smell that some of you ladies need to start wearing better deodorant."

As you get to your first workout session with your personal trainer, we encourage the miserable failure to of course show up VERY late. Your new personal trainer friend is going to be thinking that you'll be showing up in workout attire. Little does he know that you don't really wear anything else but your customary robe, slippers, and boxers (FYI: this wardrobe again includes and applies to all female miserable failures). Show up ready to rock. Demand that your personal trainer put on kids' sing-a-long songs over the speaker system to accommodate you through your workout. Also, before you start your workout, let your personal trainer know that you're a closet tickler and that you need to *"get it out of your system"* before you start to work out (and then proceed accordingly).

When you get to the first exercise, ask if you can take a quick cigarette break. When he declines your unusual request, immediately start to cry. As a matter of fact, you should be crying uncontrollably as you start your first set of exercises. Furthermore, always talk about your personal life with your trainer so loud that others in the gym can hear you. Feel free to discuss your open sexual attraction to your red-headed step-brother (BTW: again, gender does not matter on this). As you do some bench press reps, we suggest that a miserable failure piss themselves during the final few reps. As you move onto sit-ups and push-ups, let your trainer know that you expect an ice cream after you're done. Next, complain and demand that you and your trainer leave the gym at once and go get some fast food (that which of course, **he** will be paying for).

When your session comes to an end, your new personal trainer friend is never going to want to see you again. In fact, he might even kick you out of the gym, call the police, or physically assault you for your extreme behavior. This DOES NOT STOP the miserable failure. Make late-night phone calls to him asking if he wants to *"work out with you in the morning."* Feel free to take some selfie pictures of your own ass and ask him if he thinks if your derriere is in tip-top shape. You should also stop by the gym and drop him off some homemade lunch. This generally consists of ramen noodles cooked in muddy puddle water, a can of baked beans that expired twenty years ago that you got from the local food pantry, and a half-eaten banana from your buddy, "Homeless Joe." When your personal trainer responds to your daily advances with a restraining order and a chokehold, it's time for you to find another personal trainer (in the same gym) and repeat all of the steps mentioned above.

Politics

The miserable failure does not read the news, nor are you up to date on current events or even know what day it is half of the time (NOTE: this is due to your severe brain damage from YEARS of alcohol consumption as well as the MANY crowbars you've taken across the face during your numerous road rage fights). The miserable failure knows JACK SHIT about geo-politics, the three branches of the U.S. government, basic laws, or political party stances on issues. However, a miserable failure should know **JUST a little** about each **controversial political subject** in order to fully maximize the mischief that we demand that you get yourself into. Knowing a little amount of information on a controversial topic just to start arguments and stir shit up, is a fantastic play for the miserable failure. In other words, we don't want you to know anything about politics, but you should know **just enough information** in order to confuse people and to piss others off as you make your way to becoming a total and complete miserable failure.

Voting

MOST miserable failures do not vote. However, some miserable failures have been arrested for voting MULTIPLE times in an election (FEDERAL PRISON, HERE WE COME!!!) As a miserable failure, you just simply bitch about all politicians without ever doing anything about it. Sometimes, when engaged in a discussion about politics, you can even cheer the fact that politicians are fucking the general public over. After all, these politicians should be treating **you** like a miserable failure through their voting and the laws they pass. **In fact, the miserable failure is glad politicians suck.** The miserable failure is more than happy to pay higher taxes a.) if you have a job, b.) if your wages haven't already been garnished, or c.) if the IRS hasn't put out a lien on your house.

The only time a miserable failure goes to the polls to vote is when they have a chance to commit voter fraud as well as ruining the days for the poll workers during the election. Remember, it is illegal to talk about candidates near a voting booth. This does not stop the miserable failure at all! Be prepared to YAP and to YAP! For the miserable failure, asking questions as to who people are voting for is paramount. When you're standing in line waiting to vote, feel free to yell out loud, *"who are you folks voting for?! I am voting for the asshole _______."* You can also take out your cell phone and record the entire process (which is ALSO illegal) and upload it online (this also makes it easier for the District Attorney to prosecute you during your future trial). Walk up to a poll worker and ask them if you, *"can have five extra ballots."* When they say no, respond by telling them that you vote at least five times during the election every year. Then, lean in and inform them that you will take cash as a bribe for voting for any candidate(s) of their choosing **(NOTE: sexual exchanges in the alley for bribes is a classic request).** When they don't hand you another ballot and are about to call the police, forcibly take a few of the ballots and run into the voting booth as you push and shove everyone standing in line out of the way in a mad dash. Feel free to turn in the ballots and ask, *"when will I be getting my check for voting?"* As the poll workers begin to back away as the police begin to arrive, sit down in the middle of the line of people waiting to vote and throw a complete temper tantrum/conniption fit/melt down. Scream, cry, curse and piss yourself as you DEMAND $5 for voting five times. After five tasers, a nightstick to the throat and as the cops drag you away in handcuffs, remember that your days of voting just ended...permanently. **IF** you're so lucky to get out of jail, repeat the steps mentioned above every year during voting season.

Talking About Abortion

This is a controversial subject for normal people. Most intelligent people never discuss abortion in social settings because it makes everyone uncomfortable and it's not polite. When normal people walk into a party or social gathering, politics is always an "off the table" and taboo subject (NOTE: most people talk about the weather and sports, but YOU DON'T). For the miserable failure, discussing abortion openly is a trait that they must possess. During a party with strangers, every single person who shakes your hand and says hello should be immediately asked their stance on abortion. The conversation could go something like this:

Example #1
Guy - *"Hi, my name is Bob. What's your name?"*
Miserable Failure - *"What's your stance on abortion, Bob? Are you pro-life or pro-choice?"*
Guy - *"Excuse me?"*
Miserable Failure - *"You're not excused."*

Example #2
Guy - *"Hi, I'm Tracey. What's your name?"*
Miserable Failure - *"I wish my mother had aborted me."*

In fact, bringing up a controversial subject such as abortion is going to guarantee that you'll make people very uncomfortable (GOOD). It's also a great way to get your ass kicked, get thrown screaming out of the front door of someone's house at a party, or even start an all-out brawl. The miserable failure must also know their surroundings. A classic example is during a feminist march. During a feminist march, a miserable failure should walk directly towards the angry feminists with a sign that reads: *"only dumb cunts get abortions."* Chances are, several thousand angry women are going to be chasing you down ready to kick your ass (NOTE: it's your call if you want to let them beat the ever-loving shit out of you, or if you want to run- AND your gender does not matter in this situation).

Discussing the Death Penalty

The death penalty is typically not as controversial of a subject as abortion, but the topic (if used wisely) is a great topic of conversation for the miserable failure **(NOTE: besides talking about the obvious ways in which you have tried to kill yourself but have failed).** Let's say that you've party-crashed an elegant black-tie formal dinner party. When people greet you, the conversation could go something like this:

Example #1
Woman - *"Hi, my name is Mary. What's your name?"*
Miserable Failure - *"If I were going to be put to death and executed, I would want it broadcast on live TV."*

Example #2
Man - *"Hi, my name is Tom. What's your name?"*
Miserable Failure - *"We should kill every last motherfucker who sits in prison."*

The miserable failure never lets a moment go to waste where they can be openly discussing the killing of prisoners (in strategic and often humorous ways). Whatever situation comes up, the miserable failure should be ready to go against whatever the stance of the person they are speaking to has. For example, if someone is pro-death penalty, be anti-death penalty (and vice versa). When an argument ensues, pick a fistfight with them (and then gladly allow that person to beat the devil out of you).

Chitchatting about Euthanasia

Talking about euthanasia is the BEST subject for the miserable failure to discuss in social settings—specifically at formal and elegant dinner parties (NOTE: you're NEVER going to be invited to an elegant party, so you'll need to crash them). Now, we must preface the fact that **the miserable failure has attempted suicide MULTIPLE times** (thirty-seven and a half to be exact). But, just like everything else in life, the miserable failure has **failed** at suicide as well! Remember trying to kill yourself by jumping out of the second story of your home (drunk) during your fifth divorce? The fall didn't kill you, but you did get a compound fracture in your right fibula (hence why you currently limp as you walk). Remember trying to slit your wrists after losing a game of checkers in front of your entire family during game night? Wrists are hard to slice with butter knife (but it did hurt like hell and you have some nice scars). Remember trying to poison yourself in the running car in your parent's garage in hopes that they find your dead, lifeless body? Yes, that works better if the garage isn't open. Remember trying to kill yourself by taking a massive number of prescription pills? Those were antacid tablets that you consumed and all you did was shit blood uncontrollably for the next seventy-two hours in the ER. **We DO NOT encourage suicide for the miserable failure,** primarily because you need the everyday mundane pain (mental, physical and spiritual) that your new life brings you.

How do YOUR suicide attempts relate to euthanasia? The miserable failure is pro euthanasia as long as everyone in the room is against it. Stir shit up. Be controversial. Essentially take it to the limit. You should be advocating for more FORCED euthanasia in the world. In a social setting, ask everyone if they believe in assisted suicide. As the conversations run deep, take a minute or two and wait for the opportune time to yell out, "*everyone over the age of sixty should be killed with cinder blocks!*" As the looks of shock and horror reach people's faces (especially your elderly grandparents and great grandparents who are looking on), make a public declaration that the following people deserve euthanasia due to their constant shenanigans:

- Red-headed stepchildren
- Telethon hosts
- Bums that beg for loose change (a.k.a. some of your "close friends").
- TSA workers (more on your various airport arrests and your "do not fly list" status in a later chapter)
- Guys named Rupert
- Albino midgets (feel free to discuss their sorcery as well as their black voodoo magic as reasons they should be put to death)
- People with a club foot

Watch closely as some people at the party begin to distance themselves from you during your often violent, drunken rage rant. Also talk about the ways in which you feel that the "youths of Asia" should be killed (FYI: the miserable failure often confuses "euthanasia" to "youths in Asia" because you are a stupid, illiterate, dumbass). It will generally take people a minute to realize what a waste of life and a complete moron you are as you discuss this touchy subject with no sensitivity or humanity **WHATSOEVER**. As people continue to listen to your nonsensical rambling bullshit, recommend a few ways that the "youths of Asia" as well as the elderly should be killed. These include:

- Tiger pit wrestling matches
- Rubber dildo beatings
- Volcano surfing
- Swimming race with alligators
- Cheap carnival fair rides

Suicide in general is a touchy subject. Euthanasia or assisted suicide is also controversial. Just remember, that if you're in doubt on what stance to take during dinner and cocktail parties, always discuss your own suicide attempts (in graphic detail and in reenactments if permitted). Make people at the dinner party extremely uncomfortable and become lenient and lackadaisical on what groups of people should be allowed to be put to death. When in doubt on what to do at a dinner party when discussing this subject, scream out loud, *"we're all going to die one day anyway, bitches!"* Then, grab the entire platter of cocktail weenies and run out of the door of the party laughing hysterically.

Vacationing Like a Failure

Miserable failures can't afford to go on vacations (unless it's a "**vacation**" to the county jail, the nuthouse or rehab). Not being able to afford a vacation should be due in large part by your MULTIPLE bankruptcies, your credit cards being maxed out and your lack of any type of savings, prospects or a clear and concise game plan to get you to "Valhalla." Below we have some suggestions on how you can hop on a plane, train, bus or cruise ship and get to the promise land, but it should be noted that **you should not go on vacation to relax** (miserable failures go on vacation to get blasted drunk, shoplift cheap souvenirs from various gift shops and cause trouble for the other tourists). Miserable failures like YOU, should only go on "vacation" if you follow the simple steps we outline below.

The "Stowaway"

Miserable failures should be professionals at sneaking into locations **(sex shops, strip clubs, porn theatres, high school cafeterias, etc.).** You need to put your "sneaky shoes" on for getting on your preferred travel vessel. The first step is to find out where the cargo or the food supplies are being loaded on the cruise ship, plane or train **(NOTE: for vacation-**

ing bus trips, you can simply place yourself into a large suitcase and get checked in curbside with the other luggage in order to ride below deck. So, make sure you have some air holes in that luggage and plenty of DMT "Dimethyltryptamine" to ingest to aid in your road trip). Finding the loading zone in the plane, train, or boat for the cargo and supplies is essential because this is your ticket on board. This is generally located at the back of the boat, train or plane. Locate the surplus that is being loaded in and crawl into any of the containers containing food or supplies (relax, it's going to be a tight and cramped "escapade," but you should **WELCOME** the agonizing pain associated with being trapped in a confined space for a LONG period of travel time). **If you are lucky enough to make it into the crate containing cleaning supplies, hop on in, as this will give you ample opportunity to huff the various chemicals to get you a nice high for your trip.** Once you're on board, and the voyage takes off, feel free to hop out of your container and help yourself to the booze and food containers (NOTE: if you're caught sneaking on a cruise ship, you might get thrown overboard at the next island stop, so be prepared for your departure by being extra drunk and high).

The Sympathy Card

Once you get to paradise, you'll need some cash, food, and booze. If you want to enjoy yourself on vacation, you need to locate a wealthy family and simply beg them for money, food, liquor, and a place to stay (ADVICE: threatening to tear out your own fingernails in front of their children will get those wallets, purses, and pocketbooks opened up **REAL** quick). Next, begin to sob (please feel free to include massive amounts of snot) **and explain to them, in intricate detail, your awful and horrible life story and your journey of becoming a "miserable failure."** Discuss the following aspects about your awful life in very specific detail:

- Your lack of friends (NOTE: please discuss your imaginary friends though).
- Your life savings of $0.00.
- Your family recently disowning you.
- Your detailed history of your drug and alcohol addictions (please tell the unsettling stories of what you've had to do in order to get a "quick hit" on the streets).
- Your homelessness escapades.
- Your entire housing eviction history.
- Your current horrendous hygiene.
- Your MANY failed romantic relationships.
- Your terrible credit score.
- Your MANY bankruptcies.
- Your children hating your existence.
- Your various home foreclosures.
- Your various and elaborate suicide attempts.
- Your hoarding collections.
- Your crack addiction.
- Your deepest fears of what you're actually capable of doing in life as well as your most alienating fantasies.

After three to four hours of you begging, pleading, and sobbing uncontrollably at complete strangers while you tell them your entire disgusting life story on how you became a miserable failure, your new friends are going to have severe, acute and permanent psychological problems. It's also a sure-fire way to get you some cash! Finally, feel free to explain to them how severely depressed you are and also inform them that you're "out of your medication" (twitching and shouting random and offensive obscenities is encouraged to reinforce said point). Once you do this little song and dance with thirty-five (or more) families on vacation, you'll have enough cash to get you around so you can enjoy yourself!

The Bar Tab F.B.I. Experience

Skipping out on a bar tab on vacation is essential for the miserable failure. This is largely due to expensive costs of the alcoholic drinks on vacation **(PROFESSIONAL MISERABLE FAILURE ADVICE: you should stick with consuming fifteen or more Long Island iced teas to maximize your "drunkenness").** Before you decide to get shit-faced at the pool bar at the resort, make sure you get your back up plan ready. Find a small piece of white paper and write in big red letters (using crayon), "F.B.I." on it (NOTE: for legal help involving felonies of impersonating a federal law enforcement officer, please call the Law Firm of **Yor, Fuqed, & Good** at 1-800-JailTime). This "F.B.I. badge" will serve as your momentary "get out of jail free card" if you get busted skipping out on your quadruple-digit check. Once you locate your favorite watering hole on vacation, **plant yourself at the bar, and just start drinking.** When you get hungry as you get lit, the cocktail garnish bar offers many choices for the miserable failure. In the garnish containers, you should be able to find various olives, lemons, limes, cherries, pineapple chunks, and orange slices. If you're still hungry after you steal and eat the entire tray of garnishes, demand a bowl of pretzels, nuts or snack mix from the bartender and chow down. When it's time for you to pay your $1500 bar tab, make sure you leave your last drink full and tell the bartender that you're going to the bathroom to *"drain the main vein."* When you leave, never look back and run like the dickens onto the next bar. If you're caught or busted by security or the bartender, flash you bullshit, highly illegal and fake "F.B.I. badge" and tell him that he's *"interrupting an undercover F.B.I. sting operation."* If they still don't buy your story, do a quick "chicken dance" while pissing yourself and take off running.

How to Get Free Room and Board

When you get to your vacation resort, **try to find a hotel that provides an all-inclusive experience**. When you stay at an all-inclusive hotel, all of your food and drinks are covered by your entire vacation package that you "paid for" (wink, wink... **you** didn't). Once you locate a great spot, immediately search the entire complex looking for the maintenance room, the janitorial closet, or the employee-only lounge to crash in (BTW: channel your memories of squatting on college campuses as a good reference).

These places are going to offer you the greatest potential opportunity to squat at the resort for free! Out of the three places to stay, the janitorial closet is a great place to crash if you want **to huff glue and other dangerous chemicals in order to get high** (while also stealing soap, pens, towels, and toiletries). Staying in the maintenance room is also an option for the miserable failure especially if you want to sleep on a grease-ridden floor with the cockroaches, rats, mice, and poisonous spiders while also stealing expensive and various crescent wrenches (for sale on the streets later on). However, perhaps the safest place to crash is the employee lounge or break room. First, try to steal a shirt from the resort to disguise yourself as an **employee (NOTE: your stained sweatpants and dirty robe won't do the trick for your disguise).** Put on your new shirt and help yourself into the employee lounge. In there, you will find coffee, sodas, tea, and plenty of food in the refrigerator. Load up on your supplies and hide out in a bathroom stall until the twilight hours. Once most of the employees are gone for the day, you'll have the lounge 100% to yourself! This means you get to eat more food, drink more free drinks and even watch some TV!

Finally, at all-inclusive resorts, as long as you wear a specific, customized wristband, you get to drink and eat for free (be still my heart). If you can find a way to steal a wrist band that permits you full access to the unlimited amounts of booze and food, **do it!** Finding this golden goose is something that many miserable failures rarely ever do (NOTE: it did happen to Dale C. Johnson in Cancun twenty years ago, and he is now in the "miserable failure hall of fame"). If you can locate a wrist band, feel free to put on your old clothes (sweat pants, robe, slippers, etc.) and enjoy yourself at the resort! **You're on vacation!**

The "Vacation Excuse"

This one is pretty simple and self-explanatory. Much like the several excuse arsenals available to the miserable failure, the "vacation excuse" is a classic and necessary move as you relax in paradise and when you return home. Get caught stealing towels from the pool? Inform the security guard that you're *"on vacation."* Getting threatened to be thrown out of the swimming pool by the lifeguard for too many cannonballs during the aquarobics hour? Explain to him and that you're on vacation and that you have every right to swim freely in the shallow end, *"near those old, nearly-dead, flappy bags exercising."* Cutting in line at the buffet? You should use the triple threat combination consisting of the "vacation excuse" as well as the "low blood sugar excuse" and the "diabetes excuse" to combat the verbal insults being hurled at you from the other hungry diners and their small children. Didn't appropriately, legally, and authentically request days off from work and just went on vacation with an unapproved absence from work? When you return to work after your unexcused, "no call and no show" fourteen-day absence from your place of employment, explain to your irate boss that you were enjoying yourself on vacation and that he should just *"chill the fuck out"* (FORESHADOWING: it will be your last conversation with your boss in your soon-to-be ex place of employment).

Going "Hollywood"

Pretending to be other people is a hallmark trait of the miserable failure (NOTE: hating your own self-loathing existence will tend to cause this wonderful personal phenomenon). When miserable failures go on vacation, they should pretend to be famous movie stars, musicians, artists and celebrities. To accomplish this extraordinary feat, all you need to have is one thing- **a pair of SUNGLASSES**... Steal yourself a pair of any sunglasses that you can find (price does not matter, but we encourage aviator-style sunglasses). Simply wear the sunglasses around **AT ALL TIMES** and walk confidently (not your usual miserable failure,

Quasimodo-style slouch lumber). When you go into any restaurant, bar, or club on vacation, announce yourself as having arrived. Scream out, *"I'm here, motherfuckers!"* Typically, your conversations for pretending to be a celebrity should go something like this:

Hostess - *"Name on the reservation?"*
Miserable Failure - *"I don't need a reservation. I'm famous."*
Hostess - *"What's your name? I don't recognize you."*
Miserable Failure- *"My name is Darth Franklin and I am famous."*
Hostess - *"Sir, you need to put your penis back into your boxers and leave immediately."*
Miserable Failure - *"Show me those titties. I'm a porn star casting for my next role and you might be a good fit. Now get my table ready, toots."*

SCUBA Instructor - *"Ma'am, I need your permit in order for you to dive."*
Miserable Failure - *"I'm a famous artist. I don't need permission for anything. I do what I want, you commoner."*
SCUBA Instructor - *"Legally, I can't let you in the boat. What's your name?"*
Miserable Failure - *"My name is Josephine Valentine and I am a rich and successful actress."*
SCUBA Instructor - *"Really? You just look like a drunk and disgusting homeless lady trying to pass herself off as a famous person."*
Miserable Failure - *"Can I borrow your wallet for one quick second?"*

Bartender - *"Your tab is $1,205.37. Want to charge that to your room?"*
Miserable Failure - *"My secretary will take care of it for me."*
Bartender - *"But you're alone. Where is your secretary?"*
Miserable Failure - *"Don't you know who I am?"*
Bartender - *"No."*
Miserable Failure - *"I'm famous, motherfucker!"*

Bartender - *"Weird...I don't recognize you."*
Miserable Failure - *"Maybe it's because you're not in the Hollywood circle, jerkoff."*
Bartender- *"SECURITY!"*

Front Desk Check-In Lady - *"Welcome to the Vacation Club, sir. Name on the reservation?"*
Miserable Failure - *"I don't need a reservation. I'm a famous musician."*
Front Desk Check-*In Lady* - "*What's your name?*"
Miserable Failure - *"My name is Rick the Slick McQuick and I am a drummer with the band Pinky Stinky Taco."*
Front Desk Check-In Lady - *"I have never heard of you and you don't have a reservation."*
Miserable Failure - *"Check under my legal name...John Smith."*
Front Desk Check-In Lady - *"Which one are you? I'll need to see some identification."*
Miserable Failure - *"Soo...Are the blowjobs free from the entire staff?"*
(Say this while winking and smiling.)

Since you should hate your own existence, the only recourse is to pretend to be a fictitious famous person. It's a sad, desperate, weird, and lonely tactic, but again, **SO ARE YOU**.

7

CAREER PATH

Lack of a Career

Shhhhhh..... Do you hear that? If you listen closely, you'll be able to decipher it. It's the sound of **nothing**. That is the sound of your nonexistent career. This section is designed to either get you fired from your current job or act as a step-by-step guide for how to miserably fail in your career. It should be noted that **most miserable failures have no money, no job, and no employment prospects.** It should also be noted that most miserable failures fall under one of the following three categories in regards to their job or career:

1. Don't have a job and do not EVER plan to have another one...EVER...
2. Get fired from almost every single job they have ever had...
3. Has a job and is about to get fired from it (more on getting your ass canned later on)...
4. Has quit from almost every single job they ever had...

In this section, we will highlight the various career paths that are going to happen for the miserable failure. We'll discuss ways to get fired, the importance of collecting unemployment, committing welfare fraud as well as ways how to handle past business connections. Even if you've ALWAYS been a miserable failure and you were born into a shitty life, you can still follow a similar path as someone who decides to give everything up to become one. As we previously stated in an earlier section, **ANYONE can be a miserable failure** and you can start at any point in your life. It doesn't matter your wealth, employment situation, or social status. Anyone, at any point in their lives can consciously decide that they want to become a miserable failure and one of the best ways to do that is to fail miserably working at a job.

Choosing the Miserable Failure Career Path

Let's say that you're a big-time lawyer making $500,000 per year with a beautiful wife and have wonderful kids. Guess what, asshole? If you've made the conscious decision to become a miserable failure, it's now time to quit your job, start banging STD-infected hookers, blowing your savings and nest egg on cigarettes, and disowning your own children. Are you a successful neurosurgeon who makes $1.1 million per year, has a great-looking husband, and a sports car? Guess what, bitch? It's time you opened up your house as a homeless and druggie encampment, quit your job, blew your entire savings on scratch-off lottery tickets, and covered your body in tribal tattoos. The point here is that anyone can be a miserable failure at any point in their life. Now, if you come from a long line of horrible miserable failures and you're just carrying the "torch of failuredom" from your parents, you should have a leg up on someone who is just starting to become a miserable failure.

Again, most miserable failures do not have a job. Chances are, you know several fellow miserable failures that can't hold a gig, show up to work on time or actually perform the basic tasks in which they are compensated to do. Some miserable failures are also lazy motherfuckers. Miserable failures generally wake up at noon every day smelling of alcohol, vomit, and body odor. And finally, some miserable failures are prohibited from getting employment due to the house arrest and ankle monitoring bracelet that is currently latched on their leg. Now, a typical structure of a miserable failure's career path goes generally as followed:

1. Gets a job.
2. Gets fired from said job (for MANY reasons we'll discuss later on).
3. Does not look for another job. Instead, drinks, does drugs and watches daytime TV soap operas all day.
4. Cheats on partner (for guys: hookers. for women: the pool guy or gardener...at the same time).
5. "Blows" (steals and spends) the entire family savings.
6. Does not pay bills (instead sends selfies enjoying various and expensive activities to all of their bill collectors, lien holders, and debtors).
7. Gets evicted (forcibly by the Sheriff's Department).
8. Gets divorced or partner leaves them (if you have kids, the kids will hate you and will never want to see you again).
9. Collects unemployment and welfare (uses this money on drugs, alcohol, cigarettes, and psychics).
10. Stalks former boss and co-workers (dressed as a magician or ventriloquist).
11. Gets arrested for public intoxication at their former employer's Christmas party (which you weren't invited to).
12. REPEAT ALL STEPS.

The miserable failure does not have positive relationships or good references from past business connections. In fact, through your various jobs you've held over the years (seventy-three to be exact), you have ongoing **restraining orders**, **active wage garnishments**, **several lawsuits,** and active **violent verbal and physical threats** from some of your former employers. If you want to be a miserable failure, you're going to have to know a few things on losing your job. First, the miserable failure knows **how** to get fired. Second, the miserable failure knows **when** to get fired. And finally, the miserable failure also knows **where** the office supplies are located so they can steal them before security arrives to throw them out on the curb. For the most part, the miserable failure's career navigation mirrors their relationship path, financial status, and their current hygiene. **That is, all of these are in the shit house because of the poor choices that YOU have consciously made.** Whether you're currently a miserable failure (continue doing what you're doing, asshole) or you have your life together and hope to become one, you need to make sure you pay close attention to this section dealing with your soon to be, previous "career path."

Education

We previously touched on how a miserable failure should behave around college students and various acts you should do on college campuses (squatting illegally, crashing parties, and attending classes which you are not enrolled while highly intoxicated). However, in this section, we want to focus solely on your lousy educational path as it relates to your soon-to-be nonexistent career. For most normal people (people that DON'T wake up every day at 2:00 in the afternoon sobbing and immediately start drinking whiskey straight) the career path regarding education goes as follows:

1. Graduate High School.
2. Graduate College or a Trade School.
3. Graduate with an advanced College degree.
4. Starts a career working.

This is DEFINITELY not the case for the miserable failure. Some miserable failures graduate high school, while some do not. Some miserable failures graduate from college, but some do not. Regarding an educational career path, there are two educational routes for the miserable failure: going to college and not attending college.

Not Attending College

It should be noted that, there are many miserable failures who didn't go to college and rack up debt. Their educational path generally goes as follows:

1. Does not graduate high school (due to numerous firearm charges, drinking during French class, fistfights with the all-male cheerleader squad, etc.).
2. Gets denied admission to various junior colleges (your felonies and indecent exposure charges didn't help your college admission applications).
3. Bounces from job to job, getting fired (FYI: no calls and no shows mean your ass is terminated) or quitting your job in a fit of drunken rage.

Your educational path should match your ugly outward appearance (your black eye, missing teeth, etc.) as well as your demented inner appearance (sad, pathetic, anxious, depressed). Essentially, your educational career path should be depressing, slow, pathetic, lazy, worthless and useless. There's no reason to go to college unless you want to party your ass off for at a MINIMUM of at least eight years or to get into a quality career (HINT: you want to do the former, not the latter). The miserable failure goes to college to party, rack up debt, gain STDs, and to actively avoid becoming an upstanding and fully-functioning member of society.

Attending College

If the miserable failure went to college, then their educational path generally goes as follows:

1. Barely passes high school (FUN NOTE: "D's get degrees").
2. Goes to college for over eight years (drinks heavily with severe drug usage and racks up over $1,000,000 in federal student loan debt) and gets a worthless bachelor's degree in "Social Justice." This little graduating miracle is based on the school's limitation policy on years attended, and not because of your "stellar and inspiring" 0.6 GPA.
3. Goes to graduate school for four years (continues to drink, do drugs and racks up another $400,000 in private student loan debt) and gets a worthless master's degree in "Gender Studies." Again, this is also a miraculous moment, not because of your "outstanding and uplifting" 0.7 GPA (NOTE: a corpse could get a higher GPA than you), but because the college feels sorry for you and you've become a liability for MORE lawsuits against the school.
4. Decides to go to a trade school (racks up another $100,000 in private student loan debt) and gets kicked out of school due to you constantly showing up to class smelling of vomit and yelling insults at your teacher.

Going to Class

We do not encourage you to attend class in school or college. However, if you do decide to go to class, always show up late. When you show up, you need to make your presence known. Barge into class like an out of control maniac (this will be no problem for you as you'll be in your daily alcohol-induced binge rage). Take a seat near the front of the class so that the entire student body can smell your B.O. (from never showering or brushing your rotten teeth). Feel free to yell out *"free bird!"* in the middle of class during the lecture. This will startle the teacher and get the entire class laughing at you (not WITH you...AT you). After you get no response from your classmates, laugh out loud and proceed to fire spitballs towards the blackboard and at the professor. If you still haven't been kicked out of class from the teacher yet, raise your hand and ask if you can, *"come up to the front of the class and educate these morons on the hard-knock life."* If you have enough money left on your EBT food stamp card, call and order a pizza in the middle of class. There's nothing more annoying for a class or a teacher than to be interrupted by a pizza delivery man in the middle of a lecture. When your food arrives, proceed to eat the entire pizza while uttering *"yummy"* and moaning uncontrollably after every single, solitary bite.

Tired in class? Take a nap! Thirsty in class? Time to shotgun the three beers that you brought with you. Do whatever you want. After all, without students, the teacher would not have a job. Remind the teacher that you are paying their salary and you demand an A+ on all of your late and absent homework assignments as well as your failed tests. Just for shits and giggles, turn your desk around so that you face the entire class. This is going to make all of your classmates extremely uncomfortable. Simply stare at them as they listen to the lecture. Making inappropriate sexual gestures with your hands is strongly encouraged during this momentous moment.

When class ends, stand up and yell, *"I didn't believe anything that fucker just said!"* Give your teacher the middle finger, smack yourself on your own ass, and storm out of the room as you let out a fart near the door. If campus security isn't waiting for you outside the classroom, chances are, you'll get a chance to repeat these activities in your next class as well. **Being a miserable failure means avoiding basic knowledge altogether, while also hindering others from getting an education.** If you have to attend class, show up nude! If you have to attend class, bring one of your homeless or prison parole buddies with you. (NOTE: both of these sketchy and questionable characters will provide you with endless entertainment for you and your class).

Homework

The miserable failure never does their homework (this is just one major reason as to why you are failing out of school). When given a homework assignment from your teacher, we encourage you to use one of the following responses:

- *"Blow it out your ass."*
- *"My dog ate this homework."*
- *"I'm going to shove your homework up my own ass. Want to video record it?"*
- *"Can I write this assignment in Swahili?"*
- *"I can't do this assignment because I'm getting my nipples pierced in the alley later on."*
- *"I'll do this assignment and then I'll wipe my ass with it, you fuck."*

The miserable failure only does homework, when it's going to make life difficult for their teacher or professor. After you complete the ten-page paper that you're supposed to write on The Civil War (in crayon), feel free to turn in your paper at 4:00 in the morning at your teacher's house. Bang on the door and yell, *"here is my homework!"* If your teacher does not answer, duct tape it to their front door (sealed with a hand-print of your own blood). This action with get you an A+ in the class because it will scare the ever-loving shit out of your petrified teacher.

Studying

The only "studying" a miserable failure should do, is reading and re-reading this horrible and piece of shit book several times... Now, for educational purposes, the library is generally reserved for people that need peace and quiet so they can study, read, write, and become smarter. For the miserable failure, the library provides "free" books, which you can later sell online for a nice profit. The library also gives the miserable failure a chance to showcase their singing skills and to practice their stand-up comedy routine (shouting nothing but curse words repeatedly at the top of your lungs). When you first get to the library, knock the book out of the hands of any poor bastard trying to read it as he walks towards the door. Laugh at him and shout out, *"you're one of those smart people who can actually read"* (FYI: a miserable failure is practically illiterate and is proud of it). Stroll up to the librarian's desk and DEMAND (smacking your hand on the table like a violent drunk) that she shows you where the following book genres are located in the library:

- Unicorns
- BDSM (dominance & submission and sadism & masochism)
- Cannibalism
- Goblins, Fairies, Trolls, Elves, Dragons, and Hobbits
- Nazis
- Fruit Salad Recipes
- Torture
- Hemorrhoids

As her expression turns into a grimaced face, just say to her, *"just joking, where is the porn section in this dump?"* Walk away whistling very loud as you stumble through the library in your customary miserable failure bathrobe with your slippers and boxers. Feel free to unplug computers, knock books off the shelves and bathe in the drinking fountain. Make yourself at home! **If you feel like dancing, do it on a table.** Feel like a snack? Break and snap the plastic barrier on the vending machine open and help yourself! Remember, your tuition and taxes (lol) are paying for the library, so you have every right to do whatever the hell you want in it. If you want to read (if you are literate), read this **very** book out loud (adding some curse words and stuttering adds to the excitement of the other students who are trying to actually become more intelligent). If you want to take a nap, use the janitor's closet (FYI: the plus side to sleeping in the janitor's closet is that there are many chemicals to huff). Finally, if you want the entire library to yourself, pull the fire alarm (this will add another felony to your long police record and get you another night of ass kicking's in the county jail by both the guards and prisoners). Your goal is to completely disrupt all of the other people who are enjoying their relaxing quiet time in the library. So, when it's time to "study," go to the library and wreak havoc.

Skipping Class

Just as important as going to class is NOT GOING to class. We encourage the miserable failure to skip out of class as much as possible. Not going to class means not graduating. Not graduating means no high school diploma or college degree. Instead of skipping class and not informing the teacher, don't show up and email the teacher letting him know that you have *"better shit to do."* Here are the following activities you should be doing when not in class, while informing your teacher of said activities:

1. You're doing charity work (stealing cans from the homeless)
2. You're sick and not feeling well (binging and purging in the parking lot at the all-you-can-eat buffet)
3. You're studying for the test (watching online pornography in your mother's basement).
4. You had an accident (shitting yourself as you fall off a ferry boat drunk and getting rescued by helicopter from the coast guard).
5. You have "jury duty" (your "public defecation in a city park" court trial).

We also encourage you to text various photos of yourself doing the activities mentioned above to your teacher. **Remember, you're not just "skipping class," you're also skipping through life as a miserable failure.** If you are in college, you should be flunking and failing out, without a degree and with HUNDREDS OF THOUSANDS OF DOLLARS in student loan debt (NOTE: the words "debt" and "failure" should be tattooed in your DNA and should permeate through your entire being).

From your failed marriages and relationships to your overdrawn checking account, the miserable failure's educational path needs to mirror the other areas in their life for which they failed (SEE ALSO: section on college and college students).

Past Business Contacts

You've been fired (multiple times). You've quit and stormed out (on many occasions). You've literally left every job in every conceivable way possible. Some miserable failures bounce around from various jobs-to-jobs. Other new miserable failures just got fired from their job (FYI: welcome to the club, asshole). Some of you pathetic morons reading this book right now are about to get fired, but you just don't know it yet. Not all, but MOST miserable failures have bounced around like a drunken kangaroo from job-to-job throughout their entire horrible and unsuccessful "career(s)." How and why does this happen? **The miserable failure has a hard time holding down any job, primarily because showing up late to work at 11:00 a.m. smelling of booze, cheap women, trash dumpsters and motor oil, is a quick ticket out the door, into unemployment and into an alley allowing rich businessmen to circle jerk all over you for a quick $5.** Throughout your long and arduous history of jobs, you've had SEVERAL bosses, MULTIPLE former co-workers, and MANY ex-friends. Now it's time we explained how to handle these past business contacts of yours as it relates to your nonexistent career.

We must stress that the miserable failure does not have ANY good or quality references that you can use when seeking new employment **(FYI: we only want you to look for work as long as you're going to purposely get fired, otherwise stay on unemployment, food stamps and welfare... FOR LIFE).** Several of your past business contacts should currently have pending lawsuits and restraining orders against you. This should **not** stop you from doing what you do best: causing havoc and paying them a few more unexpected special "visits" and "pop-ins."

Former Employers

We encourage the miserable failure to show back up randomly at their **former** employer and act as if nothing has changed and you still work there. Even if you were shit-canned over twenty years ago, show back up to work! Go back to your desk where you previously sat and claim it as your own (NOTE: your former coworkers will be wondering how you got bailed out of county jail, and they'll admire your NEW snake tattoo on your forehead). If you're still banned by security from entering the building, just show up at the company's favorite five o'clock happy hour watering hole, order drinks at the bar, and charge them to your former boss's tab. Which brings us to your former bosses... We STRONGLY encourage the miserable failure to make a phone call to their former boss's house just to *"shoot the shit"* with them (BEST TIME: Sunday mornings at 6:00 a.m.). Your boss has a golf game? Show up on a golf cart asking if you can jump in and play (FYI: the country club has a dress code and your stained and ripped sweat pants and your dirty white t-shirt don't qualify as "acceptable attire" on their golf course). On Christmas morning, feel free to pound on their door asking if he can lend you $20 for a *"small crack rock."* On Thanksgiving, throw a stolen frozen turkey through his front living room window as a "gift." Re-establish yourself in all of your former boss's lives. **After all, they shouldn't have fired you and you still want to be a part of their lives.**

Former Co-Workers

Dealing with ex-coworkers can be a fun experience for the miserable failure. Remember "Fat Sally" who was the receptionist at your former employer who was always looking for ways to lose weight? Simply order ten pizzas and have them delivered to her. Remember "Suicidal Ron" in accounting at your former place of employment who threatened to kill himself a dozen or so times? Send him an email anonymously every hour that simply says: *"do us all a favor and do it already, Ron."* You should be getting back into all of your past business contacts lives as often as possible. Remember, you're a catalyst for failing, so making sure that these people who still; 1.) hate you, 2.) wish you dead, 3.) have a pending lawsuit against you, 4.) have a restraining order against you, and 5.) are scared to death of you, get surprised when you show back up in their lives like the Boogeyman.

Reestablishing yourself in the lives of your previous employers and former co-workers is a great move for the miserable failure. After all, **YOU'RE** doing **THEM** a favor! You're giving them stories that they can tell at cocktail parties (which you'll, of course, crash) for MANY years to come! **Remember the time you were fired from your office job because you dressed up like a mime and went around urinating on people's desks? Guess what? It's time that you resurrected your mime alter ego character and stormed back into your former place of employment for another round of "piss on the table."** Remember the time you stole the entire cake for Joe's retirement party and began a horrible food fight which resulted in you getting canned? Guess what? It's time that you showed up to Ron's house in the middle of the night and pegged it with various brownies, cupcakes, cakes, candy, and pies that you stole from the local bakery. Remember the time that you went around tickling people inappropriately near the water cooler and you were sacked from your gig? Guess what? It's time that you showed back up to your former employer (nude) and began tickling people at random throughout the office! Stir shit up. Get involved in the lives of your former coworkers and bosses. After all, since miserable failures DO live in the past, isn't it paramount that you recreate some of your favorite "firings" over the years?

Unemployment 101

For most normal people with half a brain, unemployment is a temporary, but scary experience. **For the miserable failure, unemployment is a huge part of your life and is 100% necessary.** You not only can't hold down a job, but you're not actively searching for work either- UNTIL NOW... The miserable failure needs money in order to fund their gambling, drinking, drug usage habits, and glue huffing addiction. **You sure as hell aren't going to work and you can only rob so many Girl Scout cookie stands, so the next best thing is to go on full-time unemployment.** In previous sections, we've mentioned how to use food stamps, in this section we'll cover everything from job applications to how to maintain unemployment benefits, government cheese handouts and the rules for being unemployed.

Going on Unemployment

You've lost your job and have no income coming in. That sucks for most people, but for you, this is FANTASTIC news! You need the horrendous pain and horrifying consequences associated with not having any employment whatsoever. Perhaps your spouse will leave you? GREAT!!! Maybe you will be evicted from your home? FABULOUS!!! Whatever your situation is, getting fired and going on unemployment is a great step in the right direction for becoming a miserable failure. Why go on unemployment? It's simple. **You're going to get paid a little amount to NOT WORK.** The first thing you should do when you get fired (for masturbating in front of the entire executive team in the middle of the IPO celebration) is to seek out a lawyer. Now, most good lawyers won't represent you due to your previous frivolous, capricious, unsubstantiated, and arbitrary lawsuits. Public defenders are useless, as they only help you when you're arrested, and most sensible lawyers know that you have no case or any legitimate lawsuit for getting fired. However, there are many slick, slimy and greedy "slip and fall" lawyers out there who will take your case. Generally, they get a percentage of whatever settlement that you get. So, the first thing to do is to hire some piece of shit attorney and claim you were wrongfully terminated. Use your age, race, gender, sexual orientation, religion, height, weight, politics, dress code, health (both mental and physical), and your hairstyle as any of the reasons in which you were fired for "discrimination." Relax, the case will be thrown out of court by an angry judge the first time you expose yourself to the defense and you won't be getting anything, but a huge attorney bill (that you will never pay).

The next thing you need to do is to go down to the unemployment office. When you travel down to the unemployment office, you're going to have to take a public bus (REMEMBER: your car is still impounded due to your DUI, as well as your expired license). When you get to the unemployment office, you need to LOOK LIKE SHIT. This will not be difficult to do as you generally only wear a dirty robe, slippers, and boxers 24/7/365. We also encourage you to show up drunk, hungover, **or both**, while smoking a cigarette inside the building as you stroll your merry ass into the office. You have to then file for unemployment. The only downside to unemployment is that you only get paid a percentage of your previous compensation. So, if you made $1500 every two weeks working, you'll probably only get paid $600 every two weeks on unemployment. This is good because it will speed up the foreclosure process on your home, the repossession on your car, and the collection all of your other property with debt collectors, repo men, and payday loan officers. When you apply for unemployment, you need to let the unemployment office know that you're searching for work (NOTE: selling drugs and shoplifting do not qualify as "work" to the government). You must do this in order to get paid for not working (more on applying for jobs later on).

After you leave the unemployment office, travel on down the hall and get your free medical card, welfare check (which you'll use for scratch-off lottery tickets as well as pornographic magazines), and apply for food stamps **(NOTE: buying booze, cigarettes, and cash advances on your food stamp card is 100% MANDATORY for the miserable failure).** With a small welfare check, free food, and unemployment money coming in every month, you're all set for being a lazy and worthless individual!

The "Unemployment Excuse"

Being unemployed provides the miserable failure a wonderful opportunity to blame all of their mistakes in life on **not working**. The rule for the "unemployment excuse" is simple and similar to your various other bullshit excuses. For every action that you take, you need to have a scapegoat for your shenanigans. No matter what you say, or the actions you take, you need to know when to apply the unemployment excuse. **Got caught stealing a strap on dildo at the porn shop (again)? Blame your actions on unemployment.** Getting busted walking out of a lobster joint without paying AND while stealing five baskets of cheddar biscuits? Put the blame on being unemployed. Rear-ended a person driving a brand-new luxury car by not stopping at the four-way intersection? It's unemployment's fault! **You forgot to pay your child support payment for eight months in a row? Damn unemployment!** Failure to make your house payment (which you're getting evicted for), car payment (the repo man is still looking for your car), student loan payment (which is in default), and medical bills (remember your alcohol poisoning incident on New Year's Eve)? **Blame it all on being unemployed!** This is a key excuse that you must use often. Some classic examples of a conversation you could have when using the "Unemployment Excuse" could be:

Miserable Failure - *"Bless me, Father, for I have sinned."*
Father - *"What are your sins, my son?"*
Miserable Failure - *"I just took a shit in the middle of the coffee table in the rectory, then smoked crack."*
Father - *"Why would you do that, my son?"*
Miserable Failure - *"Because I'm unemployed."*

High School Principal - *"You need to leave the campus."*
Miserable Failure - *"But I'm unemployed."*
High School Principal- *"Yes and you're also siphoning gas from various cars. Now get your broke ass out of here!"*
Miserable Failure - *"But, I'm unemployed."*

Wife - *"You're sleeping with prostitutes again."*
Miserable Failure - *"It's because I'm unemployed, honey. Lighten up. I'm fucking poor."*
Wife - *swings baseball bat at your kneecaps*

Husband- *"You had a gangbang with ten strange men you met at the bar?"*
Miserable Failure - *"I have not been working. I'm unemployed."*
Husband - *"Did you really have to film it and send a copy to my parents?"*
Miserable Failure - *"Yes. I'm unemployed."*

Kid - *"Daddy, can I have $3 for an ice cream?"*
Miserable Failure - *"I'm on unemployment. I don't have any money."*
Kid - *"But you had $50 for scratch-off lottery tickets and super glue?"*
Miserable Failure - *"I'm unemployed. You little shit!"*

Maintaining Your Unemployment

Maintaining getting free money on unemployment for doing absolutely **JACK SHIT** is work in and of itself. **We only encourage you to WORK at NOT WORKING.** For example, if you still want to get your weekly unemployment check from the government (BTW: which you'll spend on gambling, booze, cigarettes, tattoos, pornography and fireworks), you'll need to show the unemployment office that you've actually been "searching" (LOL!!!) for work. Every two weeks or so, you need to go down to the unemployment office and provide them a list of companies and employers which you've actually applied for jobs or had interviews with (NOTE: washing the windows of various cars stopped at red lights does not qualify as a real job search, or seeking gainful employment). You can also fabricate completely phony jobs and 100% bullshit fake companies you've applied to work at (FRAUD + FEDERAL PRISON = SCORE!!!). If you have to list where you've searched for work, be honest with what places you've searched for jobs. Some classic examples of fancy job titles include:

- "Director of Sanitary Operations" (a.k.a. shit and vomit cleaner) at Action Park Adventure.
- "Regional Supervisor of Entertainment" (a.k.a. balloon inflator for Bobo the Clown) at Bobo the Clown LLC.
- "Head Manager of Public Wildlife Safety" (a.k.a. killer of groundhogs) at The Sierra Country Club.
- "Account Reclamation Coordinator" (a.k.a. repo man) at Payday Cash Advance and Loan.
- "Retail Procurement Specialist" (a.k.a. the collector of other people's used shit in order to serve your court-mandated community service hours) at The Indigent Donation Center.

For the miserable failure, being on unemployment is 100% mandatory, if you enjoy getting hired and quickly fired from various jobs. If you don't enjoy actually temporarily working, then by all means, you need to fail the job interviews that you do get. Knowing how to fail an interview is KEY to maintain the miserable failure's elegant and elaborate lifestyle. First of all, anyone who would give you an interview should probably be fired and locked away in a lunatic asylum for having such horrible fucking judgment. When you do get a job interview, here is a list of ten rules and pointers for making sure that you **DON'T** get hired:

1. Show up late and intoxicated (smelling of mothballs, carpet cleaner, and vomit are the recommended stenches).
2. Wear sweat pants, socks, sandals, and a wife beater (bloodstains and cigarette burn holes are welcomed and encouraged).
3. Pronounce the interviewer's name incorrectly on a constant basis ("Bob" should now be pronounced "Boobie").
4. Fart in the middle of the interview (proudly claim it as your own while discussing and describing the grotesque smell in great detail with the interviewer).
5. Don't shake their hand before the interview starts (simply explain that you *"don't shake hands with pricks"*).
6. Text during the job interview (sending old nudes to your ex-partner is the recommended texting experience for this situation).
7. Use profanity when discussing your previous work experience and former bosses (use the words: fuck, shit, cunt, cocksucker, motherfucker, asshole, fuckface, dipshit, son of a bitch, douchebag, and bastard MULTIPLE times).
8. Sit with your back to the interviewer (inform them that you're *"allergic to bullshit"* and how you *"can't stand the sight of their ugly face").*
9. Eat food (use your food stamps to go get some fast food and enjoy it while chewing with your mouth wide open).
10. Be honest (inform the interviewer that you don't want to work and that you're just *"fucking with them."* Also, explain to the interviewer how lazy you are and how much you hate your life)
11. BONUS Tip - Tell the interviewer all of the ways in which you've considered killing yourself (feel free to discuss all of the ways you could "off" yourself in the office if you worked there).

If you follow the steps mentioned above, you'll soon be on your way to getting another paycheck from the unemployment office while you continue to "search and seek" (LOL!!!) for full-time employment. Remember that unemployment DOES in fact run out eventually. This too is positive for the miserable failure, as it means that you'll soon be back selling your body, your hair, and your blood plasma for a quick few bucks on "123 Destitution Lane."

Five Rules for Being Unemployed

Being unemployed is a work of art. For the miserable failure, being unemployed is one of the very few "successful" qualities that you should possess (NOTE: we want you to be "successful" at being "UNSUCCESSFUL"). We will sum up the entire section on Unemployment 101 by discussing the unemployment rules. The five rules for being unemployed are simple, yet they must be mentioned. They are:

1. Always use the "unemployment excuse" (forgot to attend your father's funeral? Oops!!! Blame it on being unemployed).
2. Do not ever get a job, as this will end your free check (fail the job interview and make up phony jobs you've applied for).
3. Get on food stamps, welfare, and all of the government freebies (THEN use this money to fund all of your deviant habits).
4. File frivolous lawsuits against your former employers as well as the places you interviewed who did not hire you (explain that you didn't get hired because the employers were *"uglyists"* who didn't appreciate your facial snake tattoos and your body odor. Relax, as the lawsuits will be tossed out by a judge and you'll have counter lawsuits against you as well as a HUGE attorney bill- SCORE!!!).
5. Continue to "borrow" money from family and friends (use the unemployment excuse as a reason why you need $5000 cash in unmarked, nonconsecutive, brand new, and fresh $100-dollar bills).

Being unemployed is going to accelerate your **GREAT** and **WONDERFUL** journey into miserable failuredom. Again, we must emphasize that sooner or later, the unemployment money is going to run out.

This is great! You'll be even MORE desperate, anxious, and suicidal than you were before! When the unemployment money does run out; the miserable failure resorts to looting during weather-related public disasters or political unrest, stealing the loose change from the bell ringer's red change collection bucket at Christmas while filing multiple unsubstantiated lawsuits. The miserable failure should fail at everything in life. Part of this process is to be unemployed. The sooner you become unemployed, the sooner you're going to become a miserable failure.

Networking Events

Now that you're on the road to poverty, illness, depression, isolation, deprivation, STDs, and self-destruction **(YES!!!!)**, it's time for you to start mingling! Now, most normal people attend networking events in order to find a job, meet potential employees, network with their specific business industries and make new friends. The miserable failure goes to networking events for the free alcohol, complimentary appetizers, and to find new people to stalk and harass. Just think of it this way: you showing up at a networking event by just being yourself (FYI: which is an awful life experience for everyone who has run across you) is going to give **MANY** people **SEVERAL** stories to tell for the rest of their lives about how you acted at the social gathering. You essentially need to become a legend at these events. Here's how to do it...

Networking at Business Parties 101

It's easy to find networking events. These are generally located at various bars, pubs, and restaurants in your nearest city. Find as many as you can, and attend them (NOTE: you'll probably have to hitchhike in order to get to the bar as your AA sponsor will **not** be giving you a free lift **this** time...). If there are dues or a fee to join the networking event, just sneak in by telling the gatekeeper that you're the *"shit cleaner"* for the bathrooms. They will let you in as they think you're just another employee doing janitorial services. **We encourage the miserable failure to dress a little classier than your customary robe outfit. Wear your finest pair of sweatpants (HINT: the ones without the bloodstains), your t-shirt with the fewest amounts of holes (NOTE: your Spring Break in Daytona Beach t-shirt should suffice), and your flip flops that you stole from the rehab clinic you were in for two months.** Don't worry about showering or your physical appearance (if you need a reminder on this, we strongly recommend you to go back and re-read the hygiene section if you're confused).

Knowing where the alcohol and the food are located is KEY. Most networking events have either free alcohol (SCORE!!!), or you can start a tab (which of course, you'll conveniently "forget" to pay). Drink up, buddy! Enjoy yourself! Be the life of the party! Mingle and "make connections." When people ask you what you do, feel free to use some of the following employment and business titles to describe your industry or career you're in:

- "Senior Director of Gaming" at The Golden Acres Retirement Home (you assist with the bingo games for the old timers).
- "Collections Manager" at The Steelyard (you collect aluminum cans to fund your gas huffing addiction).
- "Distribution Manager of Testing" at The Methadone Clinic on 5th Street (you steal methadone from a rehab clinic for sale and distribution on the streets).
- "Vice President of Retail Cashier Sales" at The Naughty Lady Porn Shop (you're a drugged up and drunk porn shop cashier making minimum wage).
- "Regional Supervisor of Collections" at The Dump yard Sewage Treatment Center (you collect "things" that accidentally go down people's toilets).

As you talk, the smell of your putrid breath, your horrible BO, and

your disrespectful manners are going to cause many people at the networking event to avoid being near you altogether. This is great news if you want free food. Find out where the free appetizer bar is located and HELP YOURSELF! If there are chips and dip, make sure that you double and triple dip your chip (NOTE: whoever witnesses you do this act is going to have the overwhelming sensation to gag). If there are mini cocktail weenies, make sure you stand in front of the bowl and bob up and down like a bird drinking water, eating them all using "the toothpick in your teeth extraction method." **If there is a meat and cheese tray, take the entire plate and eat it as you sit over at the bar while making out loud color commentary on people's interactions like a drunk sports announcer as you fill your face.** There's a chocolate fountain? Guess what? It's time you stuck your mouth up to the flowing melted chocolate and opened up wide to drink from the source! Eat as much as you can because you never know when you're going to eat again (FYI: generic frozen pot pies will be served to you in county jail, again and later on in the evening). Also, **drink as much as you want because destroying your liver and temporarily blinding yourself due to alcohol poisoning are both MANDATORY acts for the miserable failure**.

Sexual Harassment at Networking Events

You're so good at sexual harassment, you should teach a course on it (NOTE: part of your court-mandated community service requires you to take 500 hours of sexual harassment training and so far, you've taken ZERO hours). We will cover sexual harassment in great detail later on in this chapter, but we want to focus strictly on sexual harassment during and at networking events. Networking events allow you to really practice your fantastic craft of making people feel very uncomfortable. **The first rule of sexual harassment is to always make inappropriate eye contact with strangers at the networking event.** Simply walk over to the punch bowl, grab a glass, pour yourself a drink (BTW: spike the punch bowl with your home-made gallon of moonshine that you brought with you), and pick out someone to stare at. Inevitably, they'll detect your staring and look back at you. This is when you should look them up and down with a crazed and maniacal look in your eye and lick your lips at them. If you really want to spice up your sexual harassment at networking events, make animated, immature, wild, flagrant, and outlandish sexual gestures with your hands during this exchange.

People could be repulsed by the mere sight of you. You can't get a date, or get laid, so you must amuse yourself at these networking events by being a total creeper. When most normal people want to hit on someone at a networking event, they generally ask for their name and phone number. The miserable failure, asks random strangers for their address **(NOTE: ALSO ask for their social security number, DNA sample, and their blood type if you really want to freak them out).** Feel free to use extreme and excessive sexual profanity and even grab a few random asses "inadvertently" as you mingle around the room.

Asking Favors

Networking events provide the miserable failure an opportunity to get some favors asked and to get some requests checked off of your "to-do list." The miserable failure should ask the following favors from various people who are just trying to enjoy themselves at the networking event:

- *"Can I borrow $20?"* (While holding your hand out.)
- *"Could you pop this for me?"* (Turn around and lift up your shirt to refer to the giant boil on your back.)
- *"Do the drapes match the curtains?"* (Point to their head and crotch areas separately.)
- *"Anyone want to hear me burp the alphabet?"* (After your fifth beer shotgun at the bar or your "attempted" keg stand behind the bar.)

- *"What do you think this rash is?"* (As you pull down your sweatpants for a classic game of "show and tell.")
- *"Can I try your drink?"* (As you aggressively take their drink straight from their hands.)
- *"Would you come home, cuddle me and tuck me into bed?"* (Having a teddy bear and your flea and scabies-infested sleepy blanket under your arm will add to the effect.)

Feel free to also job network at these events by finding who you think is the wealthiest person in the room. Walk up to them and whisper in their ear that you need money and will do anything for $1. Tell the person that you literally hate yourself and have no respect or pride for your eternal existence. **Ask if they and their buddies would like to take turns hurling darts at your chest towards the bulls-eye you drew with the permanent black magic marker for $1 a throw.** You get the drill; if it's shameful, demoralizing, and horrendous, ask people for money if you allow them to do things to you (FYI: basically, anything goes here, so use your imagination).

Topics of Conversation

Topics of conversation vary in many ways for the miserable failure during your network mingling events. Essentially politics, abortion, religion, sex, drugs, and illegal activities are **highly recommended** topics of conversation for the miserable failure. If no one will talk to you (which most people won't), simply walk up to a group of strangers talking and say one of the following sentences just to "break the ice":

- *"Have you guys seen the tits on Granny over there?"*
- *"Five bucks to the first guy to piss in the punch bowl."*
- *"Which one of you fuckers stole my lunch money?"*
- *"I just put a hexed witchcraft, voodoo, black magical spell on you all. Ooga, Booga!"*

- *"Why yes, my asshole is in fact STILL bleeding. Woo hoo!!!"*
- *"Guess what? I'm planning on killing myself tonight."*
- *"Denver sea frogs from the fountain kill many yellow number fours over the rainbow land of majestic fairies."*
- *"Okay, everyone, hand me your wallets and purses. We're going to find which one of you is the tranny."*
- *"I'm on a one-way ticket to hell. Are you?"*
- *"Which one of you pricks has my pickle?"*
- *"Does eating dog shit increase your cancer risk?"*

If you walk up to a group of strangers at a networking event and ask a series of any of the above question combinations, you're going to freak people out. It will be hilarious! In fact, you can walk up to a group of people at a business networking event party and just start rambling incoherent, gibberish, nonsensical bullshit while speaking in tongues. Feel free to make noises and obscene body movements as you do so. Laugh like a maniac and try to give everyone a "purple nurple" on their nipples or an "Indian bear rub burn" on their forearms when you approach the group to start a new topic of conversation. Ask for everyone's contact information because you're actively *"looking for work."* If you really want to have fun with people at a networking event because no groups of people will talk to you, shout out any of the following combination statements:

- *"Stop drinking! You fucking alcoholics!"* (As you stand on top of the bar and down a fifth of whiskey.)
- *"Hey everybody! Guess What? I just shit my pants!"*
- *"Who's taking daddy home tonight?"* (Or for females: *"Who's taking mommy home tonight?"*)
- *"Enough with this networking bullshit. When does the Thailand pussy arrive?"*
- *"My name is ______ and I am a miserable failure"* (Do this while pulling down your pants in shame.)

At this point in the evening, if you're a male miserable failure, you'll probably be getting "escorted" out of the bar (being grabbed and thrown out into the back alley by the two security guards as they take turns kicking you in your abdomen with their steel toe boots). Remember that you can go to these networking events all of the time. It doesn't matter the business group, the topic, or the career. Just show up and be a miserable failure.

Finding the Worst Job Ever

If you have to go back to work because your unemployment and welfare has run out and you need to make money to fund your drinking, smoking, gambling, paint huffing and scratch-off lottery ticket addictions, you need to find the worst job that a person could possibly have. **If the job is shitty and horrible, it's for you!** If it pays terribly, it's right up your miserable alley! If it's dangerous, then make sure you apply! If it is self-degrading, be sure you nail the interview! We must preface the fact that selling narcotics in dark alleys to random junkies does not actually qualify as "work" to the IRS (NOTE: more about getting audited and arrested for tax evasion in a later chapter). **The best way to find horrible work is online in "the back pages" of various suspect websites.** Some of the jobs might be illegal, immoral, and unethical (SCORE!!!). It doesn't matter if you get paid in cash, or it's legal and you get a W-2 at the end of the year; as long as the job sucks donkey balls, do it!

Finding the worst job involves really digging deep into the jobs on the black market. Some obvious examples of horrible legit jobs include:

- Janitorial work cleaning up vomit at Happy Land Amusement Park.
- Waste disposal team at the local nuclear power plant.

- Porn theater mop crew at Trinity Reign Theaters.
- Elephant shit picker-upper for the traveling circus.
- Coroner's clean up staff for the county.
- Port-O-Potty cleaner at the Orange County Fair.
- Cattle semen collector at Farmer Joe's Ranch.
- Suicide clean-up crew at The End is Here Cleaning.

If the job is disgusting, self-deprecating or it will put you in physical danger, then it's the right job for you. When people think of the words: "shit", "semen", "blood" or "vomit", we want them to think about YOU and your job. We want you to find a real shitty job (pun intended) only if you MUST do so in order to stave off your pesky and nagging parole officer. We also expect you to get yourself **fired** when you get hired from said shitty job (how to get fired will be covered in a later section). We also encourage you to continue to do illegal, unethical, and immoral work if you want to get paid cash. Some of these types of jobs are:

- Fluffer on a Porn Set (BOTH male or female miserable failures should apply).
- Discount Generic Prostitute ($25 maximum payment for **ALL** services rendered).
- Drug Mule for the Mexican cartel (you stick drugs up your ass and walk across the border).
- Identity Theft Collection Expert (stealing tourist's wallets).

These jobs are **illegal**, **unethical**, **dangerous,** and **hazardous** (YES!!!). We want you to put yourself in harm's way- physically, socially, and emotionally. When in doubt, walk into a store and steal shit. Don't know how to make some cash? Make a sign that reads: "*I WILL LITERALLY DO ANYTHING THAT YOU WANT FOR $5*" and stand on the street corner (FYI: you'd be surprised at what type of kinky and dangerous shit people will want you to do). We want you to have zero respect and no pride for your body, your family name, or your image. Essentially, be a disgusting miserable fuck and make sure the world knows it.

Stealing, a Last-Ditch Effort

If you can't find a legit job or you are terrible at doing illegal activities, you need to punch yourself in the face as hard as you can... Right now... No, seriously. **RIGHT NOW**. Because you are a fucking moron... When in doubt on what to do in order to make some cash and put yourself in harm's way, simply start breaking into people's homes and steal shit as a last resort. If you are too drunk to steal things from a house, simply go to the local convenient store and start to shoplift (NOTE: most clerks have a sawed-off shotgun behind their counter, so be careful). You can also make some really good money on the streets if you can rob a pharmacy. Robbing a pharmacy is a great play for any miserable failure. First of all, you're going to be getting SEVERAL thousand pills that you can consume and/or sell on the streets. Secondly, stealing from a pharmacy is a felony and you will be looking at, at LEAST twenty years in the can if you're caught. Finally, robbing a pharmacy while sick people are patiently waiting for THEIR legitimate prescriptions to be filled is only something that a total lowlife, cocksucking piece of shit would do (HINT: that's YOU).

How to Get Fired

Miserable failures can't hold down any steady employment. This is due in large part to your constant quitting as well as the various firings you've been involved in over the years since you began your quest. There are NUMEROUS ways in which people get fired. **From banging the secretary across your desk at the company Christmas party, to physically assaulting your boss with a stapler, getting fired is an essential part of life for the miserable failure.** Anyone can just get regularly fired for boring stuff (missing sales goals, etc.). We want you to get fired due to really bad decisions that no normal person would ever make. Essentially, a true miserable failure gets fired from their job for doing really stupid shit! Furthermore, you want your former employee buddies saying, *"now that asshole really got fired!"* All miserable failures get fired and below we'd like to highlight some of our favorite all-time ways in which YOU could get fired.

The "No Call No Show" Firing

This is perhaps the most basic and simple way to get fired. It's super simple and MANY miserable failures over the years have employed this awesome and lazy strategy. **The easiest way to get fired is to not show up at work.... AT ALL.** Just simply stop showing up for work. Have to work on Monday? **Don't** call in sick and **do not** show up. When your boss calls you trying to find out where you're at, simply don't answer the NUMEROUS calls and scathing voicemails. After a few days of this (maybe even a few weeks), you'll stop receiving paychecks and direct deposits when the accounting department receives your internal termination notice. If you are lucky and by some miracle, you're still receiving checks, GREAT! You've just made three weeks of pay without ever getting up out of your sofa (NOTE: except to do the various lines of cocaine on the coffee table). However, sooner or later, you will be fired and the checks will stop rolling in, most likely. Miserable failures do not show up for work and if they do, they're late, drunk, high, abusive, unprofessional assholes. So, get drunk and stay at home.

The "Meltdown" Firing

One of the more dramatic Hollywood-style ways to get fired is the "meltdown" firing. Think of all of your TRUE inner feelings you'd desperately like to say to your boss and coworkers, but can't. Now you can! It is simple. Walk into the company meeting on Monday morning and let it rip!!! Screaming at the top of your lungs as you stand on the conference room table verbally and psychologically tearing apart all of your coworkers as well as your boss, is a FAST way to get fired. It's also a sure way to get dragged out by the neck from the company security guards and thrown screaming out of the front door and onto the street corner.

Here's how to do it... Right in the middle of one of your boss's pathetic PowerPoint presentations at 8:30 Tuesday morning, stand up on the table, take off your shirt (this applies to the female miserable failures as well), and begin to scream how you truly feel about your boss and your peers. Make sure you verbally insult the following people in your office:

- Phil, your "dickhead, fuckface" boss
- Nikki, the "skanky gutter slut" office secretary
- Dave, the "limp dick douchebag" from accounting
- Neil, the "cocksucking motherfucker" from payroll
- Fred, the "smelly piece of shit" that sits next to you in your cubicle
- Sally, the "fat ass wildebeest" from the IT department

When it comes to each person, make sure you're 100% honest with them. Talk about all of the times you've crop-dusted the office. Confess to all of the office supplies that you stole regularly from the supply closet. Inform your coworkers about their re-gifted and stolen Christmas gifts last year. Openly discuss which ones you'd like to assault or have sex with. Scream at the top of your lungs while making verbal threats to all of them. Poke fun at everyone's weaknesses, mock them, and ridicule them. After a few minutes of you going off, you're going to be fired and you'll probably have the police called on you do to your meltdown. The best part of the "meltdown" firing technique is that people are going to be saying for the rest of their lives, *"that was a fucking firing!"* You want to go out with a BANG and give everyone around the office an entertaining show once you get canned.

The "Deadbeat Drunk" Firing

Another fun and exciting way to get fired is the good, old' fashion, "deadbeat drunk" way. Basically, in this method, it's simple: **you show up to work extraordinarily intoxicated and high on any drug you desire**. Showing up to work late and drunk at 11:00 in the morning still wearing the same clothes you had since yesterday, while stinking of vomit and booze is a sure-fire way to get canned. When you show up at the office drunk, you're going to need some water. Walk over to the office water cooler, pick up the five-gallon jug of water and proceed to give yourself a "sip." As the water splashes all over you, rendering you soaking wet, turn around to Cindy in customer service and demand that she partakes in your wet t-shirt contest while proceeding to hurl water at her. Next, make your way over to the break room for a snack...

Some people pack their lunches at work and the drunken miserable failure eats those lunches in a disgusting, force-feeding chow fest. Grab all of the other employees' lunches, take them to your office or cubicle and proceed to eat all of them while continuing your morning drinking routine with mimosas. Make screaming play-by-play color commentary informing your co-workers that you're eating their lunches. When you finish, wipe your mouth with your shirt and proceed to your boss's office.

Your boss is not going to appreciate you showing up to work drunk in the morning after sexually harassing a few people and stealing their food. BARGE into your boss's office, kick your feet up on the desk, and talk about your late-night drug and booze-filled evening. When you need to puke from your severe case of alcohol poisoning, walk over to the file cabinet, open it up, and let it rip! In fact, if you really want to spice up your vomiting experience, you can dance as you projectile vomit in your soon-to-be ex-boss's office. Some of the more classic dance moves you should employ are:

- "The Sprinkler" - Grab a hold of one leg and in circles turn yourself around clockwise as you vomit like a sprinkler.
- "The Robot" - Tuck your arms like a t-rex and vomit all over the room as you walk around dancing like a robot.

Feel free to take all of the candy out of the bowl on the desk, pocket it and proceed to the exit (HINT: at this point, you're probably already fired and security is on the way). When you're about to leave in shame, remind your boss of all of the shit you did over the years. Talk about your hatred of the company, discuss the EXTENSIVE and COMMON happy hour sexual harassment's, and inform your boss of the office chairs and company property that you've stolen over the years. As you leave your boss's office, pull down your pants and urinate and/or defecate just outside their door. Then pretend you're a cat and "cover it up" using various papers, paperclips, pens and file folders (FYI: you should also "meow" like a cat when doing this).

The "Sexual Harassment" Firing

Everyone has been sexually harassed at work. From the infamous "Ass Dan" (the guy from the mail room who always grabs booties) to slutty Sally, the office "blow job in the supply closet" skank, everyone has experienced sexual harassment at some point at work. Now, it's time for the office to experience the miserable failure's sexual harassment. A great way to get fired is to show up completely nude. You must do this while pretending that absolutely nothing strange is going on by acting "normal." Walk through the office completely butt naked making small chat with the fellas at the water cooler. Feel free to do various stretches before you enter your cubicle to work. Showing up nude at work is a great thing to do because it's:

A.) Going to get you fired.
B.) Going to put people in tears at the mere sight of your body.

C.) Going to give the people that eventually come and take you away to the psych ward an unforgettable memory.

If showing cleavage at work is sexual harassment, and if talking about your ball hair at work is considered illicit behavior, then so is showing up to work 100% COMPLETELY nude. You can also get fired for making shallow and offensive wisecracks about people in your office. For example, we suggest you ask the women in your office to line up in order according to their bra sizes. Inform them that you'll be personally inspecting each set of breasts in order to validate or correct their position in line. The female miserable failure can do that same thing for men. A female miserable failure should ask all of the men to line up in order from who has the biggest dick to who has the tiniest one. As the men all jockey for who goes first, pull each of their pants down and ask each of them, *"grow-er or show-er?"*

You can also walk through the office calling out by name who the fatties are, who has the nicest ass, who is the prettiest, who is more than likely to cheat on their spouse with a co-worker, etc. See someone bent over at the copier? Slap them on their ass. Need a cup of coffee from the break room? Tell all of your disgusting and perverted sexual jokes while waiting for the pot of coffee to brew. If you work with someone that you've always wanted to bang, make sure that they know about it as well as your deepest and darkest semi-illegal sexual fantasies involving them. After you do many of these sexual harassment activities, you're going to be fired (SCORE!!!). You are also going to need a lawyer because you're going to have a few lawsuits coming in from your soon-to-be **EX COWORKERS**.

The "Santa Theft" Firing

The next way to get fired very quickly is through theft. In addition to being a cheater, a liar and a pervert, the miserable failure is also a thief. Stealing random shit from people's offices and cubicles as well as equipment belonging to the employer is also a great way to get more charges pressed against you. Walk into your office early before anyone else gets there after an all-nighter of blow and vodka (vodcaine). Make sure that you're dressed in your Santa Claus outfit. Dressing up in your Santa outfit is going to provide you with another funny story that your soon-to-be ex-coworkers will be telling for the rest of their lives. Go around like a cat burglar creeping around stealing random valuables off of people's desks. Feel free to rummage through their desk taking their pens and office supplies (HINT: the messier you make the office, the better). We also encourage you to load up the entire trunk and back seat of your car in various office furniture as well as several company computers. When people start to show up for work, make sure that they not only can see your car, but walk out the door with a trash bag full of their shit hoisted over your shoulder like Santa Claus. This is probably going to result in the police being called and you getting form tackled in the employee parking lot by a cop with a Napoleon complex. As you're being zip tied, your boss is probably going to fire you on the spot. When you get fired, stand up and yell, *"you can't fire me!"* This is probably going to be the point at which you're tasered or subdued in a choke hold as more police officers arrive on the scene (#HappyDaysAreHereAgain).

The "Private Party" Firing

One of the more fun ways to get fired is if you throw a private party in the office after work. **After you've downed a bottle of scotch and fell asleep in the maintenance closet from huffing oil and various lubricants,** make sure that you get all of your "friends" to swing on by for a raucous party. Some of the people you need to invite to an illegal private party in your office are:

- Your homeless buddies.
- Your recently paroled former prison pals.
- Your drug dealer (Joe, the violent one).

- Your former therapist (forget about the "do not contact" restraining order she has on you).
- Your former AA sponsor's immediate family (NOTE: your former AA sponsor killed himself basically because of you).
- Your unemployed and creepy uncle Doug (FYI: keep Doug away from small pets, vacuums, and children).
- Your suicidal friends.

Have a blast! Make sure that you completely trash the entire office. Drink and party hard like it's a Las Vegas bachelor party. **Do drugs in the bathroom**. **Throw chairs through the windows**. Knock over and rob the vending machines. Go to the payroll department and grab and collect as many social security numbers as possible (BTW: for later re-sale on the streets). If people are vomiting and making a mess, remember that in addition to being fired, you might literally get your ass kicked by your boss and you're probably getting arrested (again...).

The "Reply All Email" Firing

In this digital and electronic age, hitting "reply all" on a company wide email chain is a classic way to get fired. When you do this on a company wide email chain outlining your eternal hatred and extreme hostility for the company, as well as your disdain for your fellow coworkers, remember to hold no punches back. When you hit "reply all" instead of the simple, "reply" on an email chain, all of the employees will be receiving your message, so make it COUNT. Most people fuck up and accidentally hit "reply all" thus costing them money, a sale, or even their job. **The miserable failure hits "reply all" on purpose.** Remember that this is perhaps the last email you're going to send, so you want to go out in style. You can use a variety of ways to send your last email. Some people elect to send the entire company pornographic photos (this is a great method by the way). However, the best "reply all" email could go something like this:

Dear Fuckfaces, Dipshits and Douchebags,

In order to fulfill my quest into becoming a miserable failure, I must inform each and every one of you how I truly feel about you. I also must confess my anger and frustration in this worthless place of employment. First, to Danny my boss—FUCK YOU. You're a cocksucking asshole prick who made us work last year on that one Saturday. I don't care if it was for a volunteer toy drive at Christmas. I don't celebrate Christmas. I celebrate Satan. So, you can go to hell and I'll see you in it as well. I also pray that your wife is banging a delivery man right now across your living room table. You deserve this because you're a worthless sack of shit. To Denise the receptionist—you're a big-tit slut. You always wear low cut tops and get mad at me for looking at your massive rack and your gorgeous cleavage. Several times I have stopped working in the middle of the morning, gone into the bathroom and jerked myself off visualizing your immaculate cleavage (a female miserable failure can substitute the phrase, "jerked myself off" and replace it with "diddled my bean"). *If you ever want to bang a miserable failure, I hope you chose me. To Mike in accounting—you're a stupid and slow motherfucker. I have been lying on my expense reports for the past five years. I want to thank you for being such a fuck up. You've given me free money from the company as reimbursements for fake and fraudulent receipts. To all of my fellow cubicle coworkers—eat shit and die. I was the one always farting in the cubicle. I was the employee that put superglue on your keyboards and I was the lowlife scumbag who downloaded and saved pornography on each of your work computers. It was me who never flushed the toilets. It was me who stole and ate our leftover pizza after the party last year. I have also shown up to work with a combination of being drunk and/or high every single day since I decided to become a miserable failure. I want to let you know that it was me who viciously puked in the fish tank last October. I was also the person who ate all of the Halloween candy from the candy dish. I truly hate each and every one of you and I have fantasized about burning this entire building to the ground, with all of you in it. I have also fantasized about bringing an ax to this place in order to get my message of hatred across very clearly by chopping up office furniture and company computers. I hope that you all have shitty lives and miss me around the office. Rot in hell.*

Cordially,
____(INSERT NAME)____, *The Miserable Failure*

P.S. I was the reason why we have restricted website access. I was also the reason why several people who have worked here have gotten divorced.

P.S.S. Good luck without me, fuckers. I'll be stopping by from time to time and you won't know when, so watch your ass.

Sending that email is 100% going to get you fired immediately and on the spot. You also might have to answer a few questions from the IRS in a few weeks as well as attend a cease and desist court-ordered restraining order hearing. Miserable failures get fired from their jobs ALL OF THE TIME. The question is simple: Which method(s) will you chose?

8

FINANCES

Big Spender

You should ROYALLY suck balls at computing basic math. In essence, knowing how to do simple addition and subtraction is not your "forte" (NOTE: you should barely be able to read or write as well). **Not knowing how to add and subtract is a reason as to why you're terrible at handling any money whatsoever.** In order to understand this section, we want you to focus primarily on overspending and not living within your means or your budget (purchase more beer, drugs, fireworks, cigarettes and get pay for more psychics). For example, if you make $1500 per week at your current job, we ask that you spend at LEAST $3000 per week (this can be accomplished via credit card debt, high interest pay day loans and home equity lines of credit with horrible interest rates). Furthermore, if you need to borrow money, try to borrow money from the mob (there's nothing like getting a baseball bat to the kneecaps for failing to make payment for the second straight week that should bring you the intense pain you've ever so patiently waited for). If you want to avoid the mob, borrow money from your immediate family **(NOTE: borrowing money from your sickly, elderly. and dying grand-**

mother without her consent is also going to give you a one stop ticket on a train straight to the fiery pits of hell). Essentially, we want you to spend the money that you don't have, on highly questionable items and services.

A HUGE part of being a miserable failure is failing at finances. If you're in charge of paying your family's bills, then you need to start "forgetting" (wink, wink) to pay them. If you're in charge of purchasing food for your house, then it's time that your refrigerator was filled with only handles of vodka and gallons on homemade moonshine. **We also encourage you to open as many credit cards (and to max out) ALL of them (relax, you won't be paying the bills on these due to a great and GLORIOUS law called "BANKRUPTCY").**

You also have to put your spending priorities in order. The top ways in which you should spend your money should be on the following:

- **Alcohol**
- **Drugs**
- **Lottery Tickets**
- **Fireworks**
- **Pornography**
- **Scratch Off Lottery Tickets**
- **Casino-Related Gambling**
- **Tattoos, Brandings and Piercings**
- **Illegal Gambling**
- **Spray Paint and Super Glue**
- **Cigarettes**
- **Nudie Magazines**
- **Sex Toys**
- **Psychic Visits**
- **1-800 Sex Phone Calls**

Most **normal** people think that paying their rent or mortgage is the number one bill of the month (LOL!!!). For some miserable failures, the number one bill of the month is to go down to the local horse tracks and bet a few dollars on the ponies. Most **normal** people budget and plan meals in advance. For some miserable failures, shopping at random and with extremely high purchases of unnecessary and unusual food items is paramount (five-gallon tubs of mayonnaise, a case of blue label whiskey and a crate of dill pickles). Most normal people pay their bills on time. **The miserable failure does not pay bills, maxes out their credit cards, and resorts to stealing loose change from the fountain at the park in order to fund that new, gargoyle neck tattoo and their frequent visits to see various voodoo witch doctors.**

We also want you to focus on NOT saving money (in fact, your checking account SHOULD BE overdrawn, right now). We also suggest and encourage that you borrow money with high-interest rates with never having the intention of paying them back. **In other words, your credit score should be lower than your IQ when you're done with this section.** You are a miserable failure with all finances and your wallet, bank account and livelihood should be represented by your terrible choices and actions in dealing with money.

Gambling

From the time you were little, gambling has been a big part of your life. It probably started with you and your friends, betting on who can burp the alphabet after stealing a case of your abusive stepfather's expired beer. Since then, you've grown out of those childish games (NOTE: except, you STILL steal your abusive stepfather's expired beer). Now, you're not only addicted to gambling (both online and in bingo parlors), you're also accustomed to having your head kicked in by a pit boss outside of a Las Vegas casino in the alley for counting cards. **A miserable failure is ALWAYS ready to gamble on ANYTHING**. In regards to online gambling, make sure that you tie all of your online gambling habits to your personal credit cards. Maxing out your credit cards is a great start for gambling as you become a degenerate gambler and a colossal fuckup.

Viva Las Failure

You've "gambled" many times in your life for not using protection when having sex (FYI: who knows how you pulled off getting laid as you're a disgusting monster). You've really "gambled" several times in your life when you drank a gallon of vodka, chugged down a case of beer, and took several sleeping pills (just to get you through your ninth divorce). You've also been sneaking into bingo parlors and stealing money from little old ladies for the past five years (yes, "stealing" in bingo parlors does qualify as "gambling"). Now that you've mastered the art of spending money that you barely have on activities, which you're statistically likely to lose, it's time to really get things going in the finance department by implementing gambling into your daily fucked up schedule.

Many casinos have permanently banned your sorry ass for stepping foot on their premises (FUN FACT: your name and your picture are listed under "beat the living shit out of" category in most security offices at all casinos). Gambling is a lot like childbirth. For example, there's a 50/50 chance that a baby is going to be born a boy. The miserable failure LOVES 50/50 chances! When you (the miserable failure fuck) get to a roulette table with your inheritance money from the death of your father, you should bet it all on black. There's around a 50/50 chance you're going to win. If so, great! You get to gamble more and drink copious amounts of alcohol (goody, goody...). There's also a 50/50 chance that you're drug out by casino security for having a nervous breakdown when it lands on red as you try to steal back the chips from the table.

Small Timer

Now, although getting a good ass whooping is always in your cards, we suggest you focus on smaller gambling games. For example, when you walk into a bar, plunk your last $5 on the pool table say something like, *"I'll bet you fuckers that the next person that walks through the door is going to be a midget."* Watch how many people will take your bet (NOTE: you're more than likely going to lose). When the midget fails to show, grab the cash and run like the dickens. After the biker gang gets through slamming your head against a car window in the parking lot, it's time you moved onto the next bar ready to gamble. **The miserable failure can gamble anywhere and at any time.** One of the most lucrative ways to win some money is if you find **another miserable failure** in life. When you find another miserable failure, you need to travel around together making random bets on random, mundane life happenstances. Let's say that you're at your kid's soccer game (FYI: you're also violating the restraining order from your ex, as well as the visitation rights contract you signed during your eleventh divorce). Look at the other parents, pull out a $10 bill and yell, *"my kid is going to be the next kid that scores a goal."* Sometimes, this gambling act causes other miserable failures to expose themselves and come out into the open. If you play your cards right on this type of gambling, there's a good chance that you're going to get banned from the soccer field (NOTE: only miserable failures get banned from watching their kid play soccer).

Two Miserables, Make a Right

Which brings us to the lovable duo... The miserable failure finds even more success in becoming a bigger dipshit when they find another miserable failure to gamble with. When two miserable failures get together, any bet goes. These include the old' finger and knife-stabbing bet **(NOTE: you've lost a few fingers over the years doing this gambling game because of your shaky, trembling, and tremoring hands due to your severe alcoholism).** Essentially, when two miserable failures discover each other out in the open, they can find common ground on gambling on virtually anything while bringing in others to gamble with them. The best occurrence is gambling in bars as we previously mentioned. The following are some more classic examples of gambling in taverns and watering holes:

- Gambling on pool games.
- Gambling on who walks in the door next (HOT TIP: always bet on a "midget" walking in next).
- Gambling on dart games (relax there is a glass eye coming **your** way).
- Gambling on who is the fastest to chug their beer.
- Gambling on the next person to vomit in the bathroom.
- Gambling on how many pool sticks someone can take across their face without getting knocked out cold (HINT: you're wired jaw means that you're a pro at this).
- Gambling on how many motorcycles someone can knock over in the parking lot of a biker bar.
- Gambling on what time the police are going to arrive at the bar.
- Gambling on who can shoot the farthest snot rocket into someone's drink.
- Gambling on how many pickled eggs or pickled pigs' feet someone can eat in a single sitting.
- Gambling on the total number of times you break down into a drunken pool of tears as you discuss your MULTIPLE ex-lovers.
- Gambling on who the next person to take a poop is (determining this act is going to be difficult and cause some major problems and repercussions in both the male and female restrooms...).

Essentially, we want you to team up with other miserable failures in bars and start gambling on ANYTHING and EVERYTHING that you can come up with. Remember, spending your retirement or maxing out your credit cards with cash advances to fund your gambling habits are awesome attributes of a miserable failure. From gambling in casinos to gambling in life, miserable failures put themselves in harm's way with every bet. You must always remember the three rules of gambling:

1. Even when you win, you will eventually lose the money.
2. When you lose, **try** to steal your money back.
3. Keep betting, getting more and more into debt.

If you follow these three simple rules of gambling, you're going to be broke, in massive debt, and will have a few people out there looking for you to "pay up."

Pay Day Loans

For most normal people, using a payday loan service is an embarrassing, temporary, and emergency-only, one-time service. **For the miserable failure, a payday loan is routine as you travel down the road to bankruptcy, terrible credit scores, and future wage garnishments.** Payday loans are recommended for the miserable failure so that you can fund your online gambling, alcohol drinking, cigarette smoking, paint huffing, glue sniffing, firework purchasing, and drug usage habits. Think about it this way, a company is giving you FREE cash (money that they think they're getting back at a VERY high-interest rate, but in reality, they are not getting paid). Paying bills has never been "your thing" (LOL), so paying back a debt is also not recommended for the miserable failure. Drowning in debt with nothing to show for it but multiple STDs and a heroin habit is essentially how the miserable failure "rolls." If you're not in debt yet and you're new to becoming a miserable failure, payday loans are a great way to get started off on the right path!

Payday loans for normal people basically work like this:

1. Normal and regular people get money from a payday loan company.
2. Normal and regular people agree to pay 50-200% interest.
3. Normal and regular people sign over their next paychecks or their car titles as collateral to the payday loan company.
4. Normal and regular people pay off the loan.

For the miserable failure, the payday loan basically works like this:

1. You get money from a payday loan company (again).
2. You agree to pay 50-200% interest (signing the contract while laughing out loud is highly encouraged).
3. You sign over your next paycheck (if you have one), or your car title (if you have one) as collateral to the payday loan company (this also covers the future court-ordered wage garnishment). When you have no job or assets, create a fake paycheck stub or phony and car title.
4. You **don't** pay off the loan, your wages are garnished, or there's a title lien against your car, and you're stalked daily by a big, angry debt collector/homicidal repo man with a drinking problem and anger issues.

If you have a job (relax, you probably won't have one much longer), getting your wages garnished or getting your next check taken from you by an irate payday loan collection company is routine and commonplace (so common is this, the accounting department at your workplace has you listed as a "financial liability fuckup" in their files). To avoid wage garnishment lawsuits and your next paycheck being electronically taken out by a debt collection agency for your overdue payday loan(s), we recommend you go down to the accounting department (again) and demand physical paychecks instead of your direct deposit (the same method applies to your welfare check and future unemployment checks when you get your ass fired). When you get your physical paycheck, you should cash it before any debtor can legally claim it as theirs. Since your bank has kicked you out because of your frequent overdrafts, finding a "check into cash" type place is the recommended location to cash your paycheck. As the various lawsuits from all of your unpaid and overdue payday loans start to pile up, we recommend you file for bankruptcy (which we'll cover in a later section), change your name ("Terry Dick-face" is always a popular new name to choose) or simply skip town. If you borrow money from payday loan companies frequently, you should expect to have random men watching you from parked cars across the street from your house. Expect repo men "popping in" at random times to get a hold of your car. You should also expect an inordinate number of harassing phone calls from bill collectors throughout your days and nights as well. Getting high-interest payday loans, never paying them back, while racking up tons of debt, and with nothing to show for it is something that you need to do if you wish to become a miserable failure.

Playing the Lottery

MANY deadbeats and losers play the lottery, hoping that they will be a lucky winner. Since you're a miserable failure, you should always remember that you are not a winner—**you are a LOSER...** This fact alone, should not stop you from blowing large amounts of money on playing the lottery multiple times each week, however, don't get your hopes up (NOTE: if by some miracle you did in fact win the lottery, you'd need to make sure that you blew it all on hookers, booze, drugs, and MORE riverboat gambling trips). **Your chances of actually winning the lottery are about the same as you getting laid (zero to none).** Your terrible odds at actually winning does not stop the miserable failure from continuing to waste money by purchasing lottery tickets. The miserable failure plays the lottery every week with the hopes to "win it big." The miserable failure also cash advances money off of their credit cards or takes cash out from their welfare card to fund their scratch-off and lottery ticket purchases. Playing the lottery and purchasing scratch-off lottery tickets essentially means that you'll be hanging out in gas station parking lots frequently (more on how to steal gas from unsuspecting motorists in a later section). Even if you win a small amount of money (temporarily) from playing the scratch-off lottery tickets, it's strongly recommended that you either purchase more scratch-off lottery tickets with said winnings, or you take the cash and blow it all on cigarettes, beer, whiskey, pizzas, spray paint, action figures, and donuts.

Big Winner? Fat Chance

Winning the lottery would be awesome for the miserable failure (blowing $41.3 million to continue down the path to becoming a miserable failure would sure feel good). Your odds of winning the lottery are a .0001% chance; if you ever win the lottery, again, blow all of the winnings on random and worthless shit (remember that you suck big balls at handling money). **IF** by some fucking miracle, you win, some of your lottery winning purchases SHOULD include:

- A rare, white, albino miniature pony.
- A weekend of debauchery in Las Vegas.
- An authentic dinosaur skull at auction.
- More neck and facial tattoos consisting of skulls, spiders, dragons, wolves and scorpions.
- Plastic surgery to make you resemble a cat.
- A truckload of cigarettes.
- Seventy-five pallets of blue label whiskey.

If you're ever so fortunate enough to win the lottery, we encourage you to be childish, immature, and rude to all of your family and friends.

Essentially, we want you to rub it in their faces that you're now (temporarily) wealthy. **Start off by hiring a local college band to play "Hail to the Chief" VERY LOUD outside of your parent's house at 6:00 a.m. on a Saturday as you ride in on a white pony dressed in gold chains like a rapper.** We also encourage you to randomly show up at your (ex) friends parties and "make it rain" with $20 bills around a group of crack head street hookers as you walk (trespass) into the pool party uninvited and unwelcomed. Feel free to be drunk (as usual) as you shout expletives and obscenities about how rich you are. We also highly encourage you to ask if you can buy random weird, strange, and inappropriate behaviors and actions from your family and friends. Feel like grabbing your step-sister's breasts? Ask her if you can touch them if you pay her $1,000 cash. **Feel like owning your parents' beloved family cat? Ask if you can purchase Whiskers for a cool $43,000.** Want to see all of your friends down on their knees, dressed like lumberjacks, fairies, magicians, and frogs while praising you like "Allah" and thanking you for being the "coolest person ever?" Tell them that you'll pay them $5,000 cash each for said request. You get the point, whatever you want to happen, or whatever you want to purchase from your alienated family and friends is up for grabs. Be creative!

Funding your Lottery Addictions

Funding your gambling is going to cost you some money (SCORE!!!). First, blow through all of your savings. Next, continue to cash advance copious amounts of money from your already overdrawn checking account (NOTE: it will take the bank 3 business days to catch up to you, so you have a head start!). Next, start to sell your blood plasma and your hair in order to pay for your horrible habits. Finally, sell your sperm (if you're a male miserable failure) or sell your eggs (if you're a female miserable failure) in order to fund your ridiculous hobby of wasting money playing the various forms of the lottery.

If you're ever really desperate for cash, try robbing a liquor store.

If you're really poor, but think that "tonight might be the night" you win, make sure you steal cash from your close family members to purchase some tickets. When you're in absolute dire straits, cash advance all of your money off of your welfare and food stamp cards to fund your ridiculous addictions. You should showcase your degenerate gambler skills very well when you play the lottery. Miserable failures like you, are terrible with money. Part of that is wasting cash on playing the lottery and purchasing MANY ROLLS of scratch-off lottery tickets frequently.

Credit Cards 101

You're a **huge** financial liability and horrendous "risk" ("deadbeat") in the eyes of all credit card companies known to mankind. You know this due to the fact that you're "paying" (LOL!!!) a 45% interest rate on your credit cards **(NOTE: your thirteen bankruptcies as well as your overdue payments on previous credit cards effect this interest rate).** Your credit score also generally remains around 300 or so on average (HINT: it can't get any lower than this, you worthless sack of shit). These combining factors are great indications that you're a miserable failure in dealing with credit cards. The miserable failure is so poor with handling money and overspending on credit cards, that the three main credit-reporting agencies have you listed under the "do not offer credit" list. Some of your more infamous purchases from your questionable past history of spending money YOU DON'T HAVE could include:

- The $15,000 credit card cash advance to wire money to Prince Abubu in Nigeria to free him out of prison in exchange for the "$1.5 million in gold bullion" that is apparently still waiting for you in a small hut at a village in the Congo region of Africa.
- Spring Break when you generously purchased a round of shots

(a $4,000 credit card tab) for the entire club to prove to your date that you were *"loaded with money."*

- The $6,000 you put on your credit card to get your entire back covered in lizard and vulture tattoos.

The miserable failure NEVER turns down a credit card offer. **Whatever you want, buy it!** Want to jump out of a plane drinking a $1,000 bottle of champagne with 10 nude models? Go for it! Want to purchase a mini donkey and baby elephant from the black-market circus in Tijuana Mexico? Put it on the plastic! Whatever you want to purchase, just do it without even thinking about it. **If you see a pallet of toothpaste on sale online, PURCHASE IT!** Make sure to use your credit cards as often as possible for cash advances as well (BTW: the interest rates are even higher on those). You need $3,500 cash to go gamble in Vegas? Cash advance it on your credit card! Need $3,000 in cash to bail yourself out of jail? Find an ATM! You get the point. Using cash advances on your credit card is going to help you max out your credit cards faster. The maxing out of your credit cards is going to do three things:

1. **Lower your credit score.**
2. **Send you to the various collections departments.**
3. **Raise the interest rates of any new credit cards you open.**

Credit cards are a great way to rack up hotel and airline miles as well. The miserable failure does not care about these two factors as the only "hotels" you stay at are fleabag truck stop hooker/serial killer motels; and since you're on the "do not fly list," you probably don't care about airline miles you received from your credit cards, either. The only thing that a miserable failure cares about regarding credit cards is how to spend them and where to max them out before moving onto the next credit card. And remember, there's ABSOLUTELY no need to pay them off because you can always file for bankruptcy (again). Most normal people use credit cards to build their credit and to purchase items that they actually need. **The miserable failure uses their credit cards haphazardly, recklessly, and without any regard to their financial future.** Sooner or later, the gravy train of credit cards is going to run out of steam. You've maxed out all 125 of your credit cards and you owe $850,000 in credit card debt. It's time to file bankruptcy (AGAIN...).

Miserable failures file for bankruptcy many times in their lives; so much that bankruptcy judges have hilariously and mockingly nicknamed you, "Captain Finance." You are also an urban legend in and around the bankruptcy courts. **You file bankruptcy simply due to the fact that you do not care enough about yourself to worry about your future financial well-being** (HINT: the miserable failure lives in the moment and in the past, not the future). Miserable failures hate themselves and one of the best ways you can prove to the world that you hate yourself is to rack up THOUSANDS of dollars in credit card debt with NOTHING to show for it (besides stacked cases of empty whiskey bottles, a staph infection from your vacation in Thailand, and a baby dolphin in your outdoor kiddie pool). For the miserable failure, using a credit card is the only way that you actually can buy anything you want. You have no cash in your checking account. You have no job and you get food stamps and welfare on your government-issued debit card(s). Naturally, you're going to have to resort to using credit cards in all aspects of your life. From time to time you're going to get rejected on your credit cards. Relax. It happens to everyone. When the waiter at the restaurant returns your card and whispers in your ear that it has been denied, simply explain to him that one of the following has occurred:

- Tell him that you've had your identity stolen (even though it is YOU who is stealing identities as a side gig).
- Inform him that it's a new card and they should try it again (when the waiter leaves to run it again, MOVE your ass out the door while stealing the salt and pepper shakers from the table).

- Explain to him that it's your birthday. Ask if they can *"please forget"* about the $1,400 bill.

As a miserable failure, it's your job and your responsibility to go through life completely fucking up your entire financial future. Going into massive amounts of credit card debt is what miserable failures do. We fully expect you to start using those credit cards frequently on worthless and meaningless purchases. Want the gold key chain that says "Cincinnati" on it? Buy it! Want a baby spider monkey from an illegal dealer in South America? Charter an expensive yacht and sail down there to purchase the little fella. Whatever you want, buy it and don't EVER think twice about it.

The Identity Theft Excuse

Getting your identity stolen for most normal people is a horrible, time consuming, pain in the ass experience as you try to rebuild your credit, pay off the debt, and protect your assets. **The miserable failure strongly welcomes having their identity stolen** (FYI: it's even more debt in your name... SCORE!!!). It's not like you're going to pay off the credit cards that someone else racked up in your name anyway. We recommend if you haven't had your identity stolen, that you rent a billboard truck (BTW: charge it to your credit card) and drive around the streets of any major city with your social security number and your full name plastered on the moving truck billboard for the masses to see. Feel free to have a megaphone as you shout from the cab of the truck:

"My name is ______ and I am a miserable failure. Here is my social security number! Someone, please steal my identity!"

If you do this long enough and, in several cities, you're going to have your identity stolen from multiple people (goody for you...). Now, here's how identity theft works... Someone steals your social security number and uses it to open multiple lines of credit and purchase expensive big-ticket items in **your name**. Not only does the miserable failure want to owe back money that was wasted on street tacos, action figures, and modeling glue, you also want others to use your name and social security number to rack up massive amounts of debt that YOU are solely responsible for. You want these other massive amounts of debt so that you'll have yet another excuse for being a complete and total fuck up regarding finances. We'd like to present what we call, the "identity theft excuse."

The "identify theft excuse" is a lot like the "cancer excuse" and the "unemployment excuse." Basically, the same principles apply in all three excuses—**use your excuse to get away with anything and everything in life** (speeding tickets, your angry parole officer, etc.). Some of the more common examples might include:

- Got a dinner bill for $500 at a fancy, five-star steak house? Explain (beg on your hands and knees weeping like a little bitch) to the manager that you can't pay for your multiple entrees because *"your identity was stolen."*
- You owe $75,000 in back taxes for the past several years to the IRS? Call them on the phone and explain to those *"pussies"* that your identity was stolen (more on how to spend your days in a federal prison in a later section).
- Getting a divorce for cheating on your spouse (again)? Tell the divorce court judge that your identity was stolen.
- You set your house on fire due to your unsafe meth lab in your bathroom? Tell the police and the insurance inspectors your identity was stolen.

Whatever situation you get yourself into, it should become second nature to use the "identity theft excuse." **Get pulled over by a cop for speeding down the highway at 100 MPH with an eight ball of coke**

and a loaded and stolen firearm? While the officer is slamming your head against the pavement, handcuffing you, and breaking your left arm, be sure to yell, *"I had my identity stolen!"* The identity theft excuse should be used mostly in financial situations, but it can be applied for all daily events. Can't chip in for your company's Christmas Gift Party? Get wasted at the party (dressed as Santa of course) and explain to your fellow co-workers that you had your *"identity stolen."* **"Forgot" (LOL) to pay the hooker again? Make sure that her very angry pimp is aware of the fact that** your *"identity was stolen."*

Sooner or later, you won't be able to use this excuse as people will quickly detect your bullshit (forgetting your own father's funeral because your *"identity was stolen"* is going to catch you some serious shit with your immediate family). Furthermore, you also can't use the "identity theft excuse" ten years after first using it, as some people will start to catch on to your lies and shenanigans. To combat this, we thus recommend that you mix up the "cancer excuse," the "unemployment excuse," and the "identity theft excuse" interchangeably. These three classic excuses will keep MOST people at bay when they catch you in another lie, scam, fraud, hoax or act of treason. Miserable failures need excuses for their poor hygiene, terrible financial situations, and the various addictions that they have. If you want to be a miserable failure, be sure that you get your identity stolen and be sure to use the "identity theft excuse."

How to Talk to Bill Collectors

Miserable failures do not pay their bills (taxes, credit card bills, court-mandated child support payments, prostitute charges, etc.). Miserable failures are late on their bills or are currently in MULTIPLE lawsuits for failure to pay down their various debts. Some miserable failure's houses are about to be foreclosed on due to missed mortgage payments (SCORE!!!). If you rent, you should be being evicted (by physical force) from the Sheriff's department deputy for failing to pay rent for the past twenty months. Sooner or later, as you continue down your path to becoming a complete and total miserable failure, you're going to have to speak to several bill collectors (that's only "if" they find your new phone number from your burner phone). **In this section, we hope that you gain valuable insight into how to properly use curse words, threats, and jokes in order to kick your can of debt down the road a little longer.** Bill collectors and miserable failures go together like bread and butter. Where there's debt, financial desperation, lawsuits, and repo men, that's where you're going to discover a miserable failure...

Can You Hear Me, Asshole?

If a collection agency or a bill collector has your number, you can expect anywhere from ten to fifty calls from them per day. Now, if your cell phone still works or if your burner phone still has minutes left on it, these collectors are going to track you down (FINANCIAL TIP: failing to pay your cell phone bill is a great way to avoid calls from all angry bill collectors). When a bill collector calls you on the phone, we recommend any of the following to throw off their attempt to get you to pay your debt:

- Mumble incoherent phrases and speak to them in gibberish or tongues (after a handle of whiskey usually works the best for this type of chit chat).
- Shout obscenities and use profanity excessively when yelling (in Swahili) at a bill collector.
- Make jokes about the bill collector's family and mention *"stopping by"* during the night when they are asleep (LEGAL TIP: remember, the calls are recorded, so make sure you put your "comedian hat" on to avoid prosecution).

- Ask the bill collector for their blood type, bank account number, turn-ons, turn-offs, and their social security number.
- Explain to the bill collector that you can't pay your debt because you're still trying to clean the bloodstains up off of your carpet from the *"dead hooker incident"* last night (more on dealing with the local S.W.A.T. team in a later section).
- Be **HONEST**... Tell the bill collector that you can't pay your debt because you spent all of your cash on drugs, alcohol, action figures, cigars, and your black-market baby purchase in the Philippines.
- Tell the bill collector that you are the Easter bunny and you have to get off the phone so you can finish preparing your eggs for Easter (maniacal laughter is strongly encouraged for this recommendation).
- Ask the bill collector if they can personally spot you the money. Tell them that you're *"good for it."* Allow their laughter to subside before hanging up.
- Explain to the bill collector that you just lost your money you *"were going to use"* (wink, wink) to pay off your debt at the horse track (screaming, *"down the stretch they come"* at the top of your lungs during your exchange with the bill collector is encouraged).

Sometimes we encourage you to lie and say that you're *"not home"* or that you *"don't live there"* anymore when a bill collector calls and asks to speak with you. It's also highly recommended that you don't answer your phone at all if they call, but if you really want to have some fun with them, we encourage you to shout out any or all of the following phrases while you speak with them to give the illusion that you're speaking to SOMEONE ELSE IN YOUR HOME. Some of these shout outs can include:

- *"Tie up that cocksucker and grab me that chainsaw!"*

- *"Mary, go breastfeed the dog. I'm sick of the barking."*
- *"Dad, you have to take off your underwear because my straight flush beats your two pair."*
- *"I told you that I only wanted to snort two lines, Junior! Not five!"*
- *"You call this chicken pot pie edible? Here comes the belt!"*

Any combination of those statements will go a long way to keep these bill collectors laughing their asses off at you (FYI: you're going to be a **celebrity** and an infamous star in the eyes of the bill collectors and if you're lucky, one day someone will create a playlist with all of your recorded collection calls on it). **By making those types of statements mentioned above, you'll also be on the collection agencies "most wanted list" after a few weeks of phone interactions.** Be aggressive, be difficult, and laugh at the bill collectors when they try to scare you with legal threats and the high rates of interest that you've accumulated on your unpaid debt. There's no need for you to pay your bills, as miserable failures don't pay their debt. When the collection department is CONSTANTLY calling, you know you're going down the right path to becoming a miserable failure.

Managing Essential Services Like a Failure

Part of the art of being a miserable failure means navigating through life while rarely, if ever, paying for anything financially (NOTE: you will "pay" for all your bad choices eventually anyway). **Whenever possible, you should attempt to use other people's money, utilities, and/or credit to fund your daily life** (FYI: this includes stealing electricity from your neighbor's garage by running an extension cord to your trailer parked outside on the street to power your mobile meth lab). On a side note, if you haven't been stealing from your neighbor's outdoor deep freezer or refrigerator for years, you need to start doing that RIGHT

NOW... So, go over there, grab a few beers out of his refrigerator, and come back to read this section. Go ahead. Hurry up! You essentially need to "borrow" from your unsuspecting neighbors when it comes to services like electricity, cable, and trash pickup. The following sections will guide you on the most effective methods of acquiring free essential services without your neighbors, or the service providers becoming aware. Yes, happy ending massages, psychic visits, and your local neighborhood meth dealer all represent "essential" services to you (your IRS tax write-offs), but the following sections are solely focused on things you can acquire **FREE** of charge from unsuspecting neighbors and companies (you deserve it).

How to Get Free Electrical Service and Still Be Miserable

As a miserable failure, you've been constantly at odds with electricity. Every alarm system you've tripped (BTW: you never thought a dildo factory would have security), and every cell door you've been behind (excluding BDSM cages) have been powered by electricity. **If you've been a miserable failure your entire life, as a small child you probably personally watched it execute both of your grandparents via the electric chair** (NOTE: don't mess with Texas), **and you've had several failed attempts at time travel with the sole intention of killing Ben Franklin** (kite + key = asshole). After extensive therapy (FYI: and years of alcohol and drug abuse), you've finally begun to accept that electricity is not "out to get you" (anymore), and that it's a normal part of everyday life (like spitting on the window of the local pizza shop for not allowing you to wash your crotch in their kitchen sink). However, when it comes to light, you should prefer the more traditional and dangerous method of burning stuff to illuminate the world. Fire should now and will forever be number one in your book on how to get light, but after accidentally burning down several mobile home parks and section-8 housing projects, you should finally be ready to upgrade to a fully electric life (SEE ALSO: section on how to avoid jail time for arson).

Electrical service is a costly commodity that will divert your funds from more important projects **(building a whiskey fountain, remodeling your sex dungeon with a zebra jungle theme, getting your collection of boogers you picked from your nose dipped in liquid gold, etc.)**. Fortunately, electrical outlets are common both inside and outside a home. While it may be possible to splice into a buried electrical line with a razor blade (NOTE: this method is not advisable because it will most likely kill you), you'll be much better off (and much less fried) finding an outdoor electrical outlet on your neighbor's home as your source of power (BTW: you can also find an outlet in their garage if the door is open). Simply wait for your nearest neighbor to leave for work or fall asleep at night. As soon as the house is dark or their car is gone, sneak onto their property and locate an outdoor electrical outlet. If you are detected during this process just act intoxicated and confused (simply act **normal**). Your neighbor will probably just escort you home (WINK, WINK: a chance for sex) and may even attempt to get you into a comfortable chair or bed to help sober you up (HINT, HINT: a chance for sex). This is a wonderful opportunity for your neighbor to see that you don't have working electricity (FYI: at this point, you can use the "cancer excuse" or the "unemployment excuse"), and with any luck, they may offer to let you plug into their outlet (sucker).

If you are not detected, illegally run an extension cord from their home to your domicile. When stealing power from elderly or disabled neighbors, it's not necessary to conceal your extension cord from sight. These old CODGERS have poor eyesight and/or are not physically capable of stopping you (SEE ALSO: your 1996 elderly abuse court case). In some situations, it's not even necessary to use an outdoor outlet. When your neighbor is elderly or disabled, you can simply run the extension cord through an open (or recently "broken", wink, wink) window into a waiting wall outlet, or just crack open their backdoor **(NOTE: "crack open their backdoor" only means "butt sex" in the entire state of Alabama and within the Las Vegas city limits).** For all other types of neighbors, you'll need to utilize your stealth extension cord hiding skills (NOTE: the only other skill you have besides stealing, is your ability to open up a can of beer across the room using only your teeth, a toy army man figure, and a ball of yarn).

You need to first dig a small one-foot deep trench from home to home in which you can lay the extension cord (FYI: "lay" does NOT mean have sex with the extension cord, you sick bastard). Hiding the extension cord underground will conceal it for the most part, but the small portion of the cord that extends from the ground to the outlet will be exposed to plain sight. If your neighbor detects this (or the freshly dug trench), they will immediately move to unplug it, and you'll be back to masturbating from memory again **(NOTE: bye, bye unlimited and free internet porn involving farm animals from New Zealand).** To avoid your neighbor taking this action, you have to make the exposed portion of the extension cord very undesirable to touch. Do this by beginning a midnight ritual of sneaking back onto your neighbor's property and use your talent for laser-accurate shitting to defecate on the extension cord (BTW: your nickname in high school before you dropped out was "The Mad Shitter"). You may also want to use one of your many open and infected sores to add blood and/or puss to the exterior of the extension cord. This method is only necessary if there's not enough blood and/or puss in your feces already **(NOTE: if there isn't enough blood and/or puss in your fecal matter already, you're doing something wrong regarding your diet and alcohol consumption, so you should refer back to the dietary and hygiene sections of this book and re-read them).**

There is also the chance that your neighbor may bypass trying to unplug the extension cord and instead come knocking on your door. If this happens, be sure to answer the door completely nude while singing any Christmas carol. **Just the sight of your naked, overweight, sweaty, cotton candy-covered body will cause them to quickly retreat back to their home, curl into a fetal position, make an appointment with their therapist and never come calling on you again.** Most likely, your neighbor (fucking asshole...) will simply call the power company or police to handle the matter. If this occurs, you're basically screwed because you've been caught red-handed. The authorities will follow your trench, or exposed extension cord back to your home, through the now ripped screen door you "carefully forced" it through, and all the way to the STOLEN laptop computer (your dedicated porn and identity theft machine). When they wake you up from your slumber, try to act surprised! Unfortunately, most of the police force remembers you (BTW: a nude person spray-painted orange running through a supermarket screaming about werewolves and pizza is hard to forget) and thus you no longer have the same ability to talk your way out of things with them. Your best bet is to go with the flow ("go with the flow" is NOT a suggestion to urinate on a cop, **again...**), and let the police do their job, unimpeded. Be sure to tell them about your new job as a prostitute (they already know) and point out the illegal stash of narcotics and drug paraphernalia on display in your dining room (NOTE: they also make great conversation starters with your parole officer). Having the cops find these items will add much needed "study time" to your eventual jail sentence (NOTE: you're going to finish your GED this time... #goals).

Internet Porn Addiction History

Before we discuss how to get free cable, we must inform you about another hidden addiction to the miserable failure: **PORNOGRAPHY**. One of the biggest factors in your decision to switch from various fires to an electric life is your personal discovery of cable and internet and the vast variety of pornography that it provides. **As a miserable failure, masturbation is central in your life.** Not only are most people not willing to sleep with you (thank you, herpes), but nobody knows how to please you like **YOU** do (#BestDateEver).

By now in your miserable failure journey, you should have developed masturbation into an art form that you take very seriously (NOTE:

you've been trying to get a live performance at the local theatre FOREVER). It should be noted that you can also masturbate while visualizing and fantasizing about your own miserable existence. **Getting ANOTHER divorce? Time to masturbate while thinking about your ex with their new lover! Got evicted again? Time to play "diddle the landlord." Got fired from ANOTHER job? On your way out, the door holding your box, feel free to get yourself off in front of the entire office. Got arrested again? Feel free to pleasure yourself in the holding cell. Got another restraining order? Light some candles, start crying, and begin to touch yourself.** Each separate act of "personal love" is a new experience and provides its own distinct sexual pleasure. Sometimes you can make it "romantic" by lighting scented candles, playing soft music, and taking yourself out for a nice meal first (BTW: only fast food drive-thru meals for you). Other times you can make it "Viking" by wearing a horned hat, talking dirty in an Old Norse language, and "conquering and raiding" your genitals **(FYI: DO NOT burn the village scabs afterward).**

For a really depressing moment in your horrible daily life, we recommend that you practice the masturbation technique we call "the miserable failure." This act of self-love is performed in front of a mirror and involves you first spreading old photos of your exes and collection of personal mugshots across the floor. Stand in front of the mirror while nude (it's okay to wear a cowboy hat, nipple tassels, or moccasins) and turn on depressing country-western music. **Stare at the photos of your lost loves and the collection of your own personal mugshots until you remember all the pain and start to weep.** Use your tears as lubricant for intense masturbation while stopping intermittently to look into the mirror and yell, *"nobody loves me anymore," "I fucked it all up,"* and *"they're going to find the body."* Whichever method of masturbation you decide is right in the moment, will never be as satisfying or intense without the use of internet porn videos.

Where you once depended upon print material (nudie magazines,

Suburban Gardening Monthly®, etc.), or mental imagery to masturbate, you now have access to an unlimited and never-ending interactive digital porn selection on the world wide web. After discovering online pornography, you should have quickly lost your job and any friends you still had. Your personal goal should be to masturbate while watching porn from every known fetish all in a twenty-four-hour period. Several miserable failures nearly achieved this momentous goal several times, but due to severe dehydration and lack of conditioning, many have continued to experience terrible hand cramps as well as pain in their genitals. It is our most sincere hope that with increased liquid intake (more booze) and the proper training program (switch hands), you'll stay cramp-free and finally make your way to "zebra porn" (you prefer your pornography in alphabetical order).

Feeding your insatiable appetite for internet porn was no problem when you lived with your former sexual partner. They paid all the bills and purchased the fastest internet package available. You were free to practice your art on an unlimited basis in a judgment-free zone. After things didn't work out with your now ex-partner, and you found that the staff at the public library and local internet cafe weren't as liberal in their understanding of your "self-expression" as you were, you'll have to get creative in finding ways to watch porn online. Now, with multiple public exposure and sex crime charges under your belt (#GOALS), you're finally ready to find an alternative source for your internet porn access: CABLE.

How to Fail at Stealing Cable

Your best source for free cable internet is your neighbors! Thanks to increasing Wi-Fi strength, you may be able to "borrow" your neighbor's internet access without ever leaving your house. You simply need to login to their Wi-Fi network. Some people (the elderly, disabled, and mentally ill) may not have their account password protected. If this is the case, then you're all good! Start by checking your TV or computer (porn machines) to see if there are any unprotected networks within range. If there are no free Wi-Fi accounts, simply grab your laptop or mobile device and walk the neighborhood until you're close enough to the Wi-Fi source to gain access. With any luck (NOTE: you have bad luck) you'll locate an easy access point and be able to start pursuing your passion for free once again. **WARNING:** In this situation, you will not be able to masturbate from the comfort of your homemade coffin or linen closet like normal. For this scenario, you'll need to master the art of "ninja masturbation." This form of stealth masturbation was first introduced by the miserable failures of the "Hu Da Fuk Dynasty" in the late 1600s, and was later perfected 10 years ago by an unpopular, overweight American college student from Columbia, Missouri, named "Casey." **Ninja masturbation involves dressing in all black, sneaking onto your neighbor's property, and finding a cozy hiding place to do your dirty work within Wi-Fi range.** Outdoor trash cans, tall bushes, and empty swimming pools all make excellent places for the practice of stealth and ninja masturbation. Be sure to procure headphones and be mindful of the odd noises you make while climaxing (NOTE: you should groan like a gorilla).

Since your appetite for internet porn is insatiable, it's simply not practical to assume that you're only going to practice your art under the cover of night. Being dressed in a full black ninja costume works in darkness but will stand out in the daytime and may cause overheating during the summer months (FYI: herpes blisters + genitals + heat = **don't mix well**). For your daytime masturbation needs, your best choice is a home-based option. If "borrowing" Wi-Fi access from your neighbor via an unsecured connection is not an option, you will need to splice directly into the cable line and run an extension back to your home (NOTE: be careful not to get third-degree electrical burns... **AGAIN**). In many ways, this process is similar to "borrowing" electricity from your neighbor. If the opportunity presents itself, just loop the cable line around the electric extension cord you've already run from your neighbor's house to your own. In order to connect or splice into your neighbor's cable line, you'll need to gain access to their home and connect directly to the actual cable outlet. **Miserable failures are not good at committing burglary because it requires too much physical effort and skill** (BTW: one of your only other "skills" should be burping and farting the entire alphabet at the same time). Your best bet for gaining semi-legal access to their home is to pose as a cable company employee. This will require a clipboard and a clean polo shirt (FYI: most of your clothing has a combination of blood and semen stains). Although it goes against most recommended hygiene practices for a miserable failure, you may want to consider bathing prior to attempting this scam job. Your neighbor is expecting a representative from the cable company to be presentable, or at least not smell like a burning dumpster, full of armpits, assholes, and Indian food. Simply pick a fake name (NOTE: use your favorite adult film star's name), knock on your neighbor's door, and begin a dialogue as follows:

You - *"Hi there! I'm* (insert fake name) *from the cable company. We've been having trouble with the service in this area and need to check your cable box' "fling, flang thing a ma bob."*

Neighbor - *"Hi. You look and smell a lot like the worthless asshole that lives next door to me."*

You - *"Nope! Your neighbor is pretty awesome, though. I'm just* (insert fake name again) *from the cable company. I need to come inside your house and check the " fling, flang thing a ma bob" now."*

Neighbor - *"Oh good! I'm glad you're not that royal piece of rotten shit that lives over there. That cocksucker steals my newspaper, plays techno music in the backyard until 4:00 a.m., vomited blood on my mailbox last week, and used my woodshed as a toilet for several months. I'm glad you're not that person, or I'd have to shoot you."*

You - *"I need you to move out of the way so I can come inside and service your "fling, flang thing a ma bob." Please remain outside for your own safety."*

Neighbor - *"No problem! I need to wait out here for the police anyway. I found an extension cord running from my back porch to my douche bag neighbor's house. I guess that fucktard is stealing power from me now. When this asshole goes back to jail in a few minutes, I'm going to break into his house and piss on all the furniture."*

At this point just run (or hobble) away. **You're busted**. Your best bet is to attempt to retract the extension cord and hide the evidence of your electrical service theft before the police arrive. If it's already too late to dispose of any evidence, quickly do as many drugs (NOTE: OF COURSE, go straight for the crack) as you can and consume as much alcohol as possible (BTW: it's time to "drain" the bathtub full of your homemade moonshine too). It's going to be one of those days and you'll need your "medicine!"

The Complete Loser's Guide to Free Trash Service

The miserable failure feels a deep kinship with trash (NOTE: and crystal meth). **"Trash" and "miserable failure" go together like "fine wine" and "aged cheese" imported from France.** Just like you, garbage is deemed **useless**, **dirty**, and is thrown aside to **waste away**. For a miserable failure, garbage can also be a source of great comfort (it reminds you of childhood), total sustenance (restaurant dumpsters are buffets without lines), and endless entertainment ("needle hunt" is the best game ever). Throughout your miserable life, relatives and parents have continually disappointed you. You've been let down terribly by entire teams of psychiatrists (they normally just call a priest), and law enforcement doesn't even investigate your claims of alien abduction anymore. However, garbage, your only **true** friend, has always been there for you (just like that pesky rash you've named "Larry" that you have had in your armpit since 2003). Some classic examples of your garbage being "there for you" include:

- When your cold garbage warms you up with a cozy blanket made of newspaper and used diapers.
- When you needed another social security number to sell to Franco "the credit card guy" Jimenez.
- When your stuffed pet possum Thomas got sick, the veterinary clinic's trash bags provided you a variety of free medicine (and introduced you to the fun of horse tranquilizers).
- When you get hungry and go scavenging like a rabid beast through the trash behind a restaurant.

No matter what the circumstance or situation, garbage has always been your strongest and most important pillar of support (it's got your back and you've got its). Your close relationship with trash should begin as soon as you decided to become a miserable failure (just like your fascination with collecting toenails and hamster heads). To you, each dumpster is an exciting adventure that brings about great rewards, powerful life lessons, and brand-new friends (feel free to name that rat "Bloody Beard" simply because he is going to like to nibble on your face).

On Christmas, the only person who got a gift from Santa was your mom (BTW: Santa looked oddly enough like your soccer coach and the "gift" looked a lot like a penis). The only birthday present you ever got was the cigar aunt DeeDee put out on your neck (she was a classy lady). If you've always been a miserable failure, your only hope for a new toy was probably searching through the magical world of garbage. Occasionally, you'd find a slightly broken or barely functioning children's toy that someone had thrown out, but you mainly had to learn to be creative. Someone may have tossed out that pair of barely stained and slightly torn underwear, but to you, they made the perfect superhero mask (you called yourself "Captain Skid"). That discarded fire engine red dildo was designed to provide pleasure, and it truly did as your swashbuckling sword when you played "pirate ship" (#ShiverMeTimbers). It may have come your way after a tragic accident, but the matted hair, dried blood, and the bent front tire never stopped you from enjoying your new bicycle (NOTE: it's your second best find of all time after Eric your pet viper). You never did and still don't understand why anyone would ever let go of such incredible treasures in the trash. Your connection with trash should be a lifelong one, and when you die (most likely in the next six to eight months) you should hope to be buried amongst the broken bottles and torn panties.

It's because of this deep-seated connection with garbage that a miserable failure only begins to discard trash when their current living situation becomes unmanageable due to lack of space (hoarding). Your fountain drink cup mattress and pizza box couch are wonderful, but too much of anything good can be bad. Your dining room table should be made of old liquor bottles and empty beer cans, so it might be time for some change. When your backdoor will no longer close because of the overflow of empty cigarette packs, and your last date disappeared somewhere in the mound of VHS tapes (it's a Bermuda triangle of low definition porn), it's time to send your trashy friends on the fabled "last ride." The "last ride" is when the garbage truck comes to claim its "victims" and take your noble garbage collection on its final passage to the never-ending landfill (your personal paradise). Normally, the sight of the garbage truck turning onto your street should cause you to weep because of the awful sense of **DEEP LOSS** it is going to bring, but today, your feelings should improve. Today, you're going to put your personal preferences aside and finally do what has been needed to be done for months.

The "last ride" normally begins very early in the morning (unless your garbage man is a raging alcoholic, like your dentist). You'll need to prepare the night before to ensure you're ready for the garbage truck's arrival. Begin by sorting through the large piles of trash in your home. It goes without saying that all nudie magazines, sex toys, prescription medications, and alcohol **stays**. Choose the less important items (medical reports, bank information, DNA test results, etc.) to send off first. Since, due to your moral belief and lack of legal income, you don't **LEGALLY** pay for trash removal, you'll have to "borrow" from your neighbors... **again**. Under the cover of night, distribute and spread your outgoing garbage evenly amongst your neighbor's trashcans. During this process, fight the urge to bring your neighbor's trash home. Yes, it's hard to resist, but you're on an important mission to free up space in your home. Be mindful of accidentally leaving a trail of used crack rock aluminum pieces, as well as the happy ending massage parlor receipts on the ground as you transfer the garbage from your house to the cans. A trail of this sort will only lead to your arrest... again. Finally, and perhaps most importantly, you must learn from the miserable failures of the past, and refrain from trying to sneak onto the "last ride." It's extremely tempting to leave enough space in one of your neighbor's trashcans for you to hide, but this will only lead to the same fate that your uncle JC, cousin Lance, and grandpa Paul suffered. Death by garbage truck compaction may seem a suiting outcome for a miserable failure who loves trash, but you can't be **miserable** or a **failure** if you're dead! So, stay out of the garbage truck.

Gas Stealing 101

The miserable failure loves all types of gasses (farts, gasoline fumes for huffing, etc.). Sometimes, a miserable failure's heat or stove will not work. If you're an asshole who lives in terrible winter conditions, this is going to be a "problem" (NOTE: a "problem" just like your defaulted student loans). Simply, sneak over to your neighbor's house with a gas line that you "borrowed" (stole) from the local hardware store. Use a large object, like a rock or a sledgehammer, and break the gas line on the side of your neighbor's house (be careful not to throw any sparks). Then, as the gas escapes (like your dates do when they wake up in your bed after a one-night stand), quickly try to connect your gas hose with the gas coming out of their house. Run over to your house (make sure you get a few huffs in) and connect YOUR new gas line. As the sirens from the fire engine(s) and police car(s) make their way down the street, simply turn on your heat (to heat your shit box, trashy house) or use your stove to cook a gourmet meal (expired macaroni and cheese mixed with barbiturates). When the police and firefighters knock on your door, play stupid when they ask you (at gunpoint) what the hell you are doing.

Water Works

Miserable failures do not use water like normal people (normal people = drinking + bathing). The only time you should ever bathe is in water fountains in the public park as you "help yourself" to loose change (A.K.A. other people's wishes, hopes, desires, and dreams). The only time you actually should consume water (miserable failures are extremely dehydrated from daily hangovers) is when the ice melts in your whiskey and moonshine cocktail and by default, you consume some water. Besides those two times, the only other time you might need running water is to put out the horrendous fire that your meth lab caused in your bathroom. Nevertheless, miserable failures do not purchase water for their home (after you failed to pay for water for more than two months, they will shut you off). If you do need some water in your house, you should follow the below step by step guide into getting free water.

- Step 1 - Locate the fire hydrant nearest to your house on the street.
- Step 2 - "Borrow" (steal) a giant crescent wrench and a hose from your local hardware store.
- Step 3 - Help yourself to some free water by loosening the nut on the side of the fire hydrant (NOTE: gushing water should be coming out as fast as your nose gushes blood after you snort an eight ball of cocaine).
- Step 4 - Attempt to attach the hose to the running water and run it to your home. If this doesn't work, use various buckets and haul in as much water as you need.

When you run into your house with water, be sure to water your marijuana plants and put out any cigarette-caused couch fires that you might have blazing. Don't be surprised if the cops and several fire trucks show up at your residence (they should know where you live by now). As the cops haul your sorry ass into jail hog tied, scream out loud, *"I just wanted a glass of water!"*

Knowing how to properly steal cable, water, gas, electric, trash service, and Wi-Fi are essential parts of a miserable failure's daily putrid existence. **You're a piece of shit.** You don't pay your bills. And, you are a thief. Therefore, stealing everything is something that should be built into your DNA. You can't become a miserable failure until you learn how to steal essential services from your neighbors.

Panhandling 101

As a miserable failure, you are sooner or later going to have to **beg** like a bum, for money from strangers (NOTE: you'll need extra spending money on your various fortune tellers, and continuing your superglue huffing habit). **In this section, we'll discuss various ways and techniques you should scream, plead and beg people to give you their money as you get down on your knees in a total conniption fit, nervous breakdown, meltdown episode.** The idea of panhandling is simple. You create a sign with a cute little slogan, that's made out of cardboard, and then simply beg for money. Another way to panhandle is to just walk up to people on the street and "ask" (demand) that they give you some money (FYI: stealing a frightened man's wallet directly out of his trembling hands does not count as panhandling, and you'll soon have the boot of a sheriff's deputy on your throat after the police chase).

A miserable failure fails and loses at EVERYTHING in life. The only thing that you should be good at is actually BEING a miserable failure.

So, begging for money is something that miserable failures do extraordinarily well! We encourage the miserable failure to beg for money at the following locations:

- Stoplights off the interstate (make a sad face and walk around to each car knocking on their windows asking them to *"ante up"*).
- Outside of church on Sunday (people are generally pretty generous after hearing a sermon for an hour about how they should be more loving and generous people).
- Outside of the bank or an ATM (more on how to press charges on the S.W.A.T. team brutality in a later section).
- Inside of a shopping mall (make sure you have your various shopping bags from your credit card spending spree visible for the people to see).
- Outside of any school (kids get freaked out and will gladly give you their lunch money if you will stop jokingly scaring them with a rusty knife).
- Inside of a bingo parlor (make sure that you're drunk and you haven't cleaned up the vomit stains on your shirt, while you beg in front of the old codgers).

A miserable failure does not hesitate and has no shame in asking complete and total strangers for money. Don't be shy to ask people for money; simply explain to them that you need *"some extra cash to spend"* as you walk around holding out your hand. Making sure that you get the correct slogans written on your cardboard sign is also vital. Some classic slogans you should utilize include:

- "Okay bitches, get your money out." (put your hand down your pants to make believe that you have a gun to maximize your payout.)
- "I need money to fund my scratch-off lottery ticket and my

maple syrup drinking addictions." (exposing your left nipple while you hold this sign does wonders.... just trust us and try it...)

- "Ante up. This isn't a rest home. Get out your wallets, or there is going to be trouble." (while angrily pounding on the windshield of people's cars.)
- "I'll take whatever loose change you have. And I'll do whatever you want." (feel free to bend over and pull down your pants to add to your extreme begging).
- "I'm hungry and need money for a steak and lobster dinner." (make sure you wear a lobster bib for this one.)
- "Who wants to fund my drug and gambling addictions? Please help me with cash."
- "I did have a dog, but he died of starvation and I was forced to eat his carcass. Please give me some money for food." (draw a broke-ass, half-ass sketch picture of a dog.)
- "Just $1 from you will save me from killing myself from running full speed into oncoming traffic." (bring your running sneakers and make sure you record this for your lawsuit later on.)
- "I'll give you the worst and most shitty advice you'll ever receive for $5." (proceed to try to convince them that they should be a miserable failure too.)

Beg, borrow, steal, plead, gravel, and **desecrate your family name** and your "honor" (LOL!!!) by panhandling as much as possible. Remember, you're homeless because you are choosing to not work. You should also remember, being a miserable failure means doing everything in life WRONG, HORRIBLE, ASS BACKWARDS, and PATHETIC. Some people really need money and that's why they beg. For the miserable failure, begging for money should be like riding a bike (NOTE: you should be accustomed to riding a bike because of your eleventh DUI and impounded car). Panhandling also gives you the opportunity to:

- Meet new people (perhaps by forcing yourself into people's cars).
- Get into adventures (running down an alley dressed as a clown chasing children "asking" for a couple of bucks is in fact exciting).
- Get tax free cash (more on your up and coming IRS tax evasion trial in a later section).
- Make new friends (the armed security guards aren't so nice outside of the bank, are they, asshole).
- Get a free ride to the local methadone clinic for "seconds" (find bleeding-heart, hippy liberals for these types of free rides).
- Get your ass beat by the cops (again).
- Get a job (although it might be a job whereby someone pisses on you, giving you a "golden shower" for $8, but HEY, at least it's "work"...).
- Get assaulted from various street gangs (goody for you).

A miserable failure should be begging for money when they are not doing any of their other shenanigans. Panhandling is a great way to continue down the path into becoming a complete and total loser, miserable failure, fuck up.

Dealing with The Repo Man

He's big... He's mean... He's nasty... He's scary... **He's the REPO MAN**. The repo man is the miserable failure's "Boogey Man." The repo man is just one of the MANY antagonists who is against the miserable failure (OTHER ANTAGONISTS INCLUDE: the police, district attorney's, Judges, collections departments and angry drug dealers). Repo men are the re-possessors of cars, jet skis, RV's, boats, motor homes, furniture and other large purchases of which you are late on your payments, or have yet to make a payment on (SEE ALSO: section on how to talk to bill collectors). Repo men are hired by the bank or institution of which you made your large purchase, and their goal is simple—get what you bought, back into the arms of their client, **BY ANY MEANS NESSESARY**. The "by any means necessary" should scare the shit out of the miserable failure. So, you see that brand-new sports car parked in your driveway? Yeah, you only get to keep it if you make payments on it, asshole. Just you wait. The repo man will be coming for that car soon enough and you'll be back to hitchhiking in exchange for oral sex once that automobile is gone...

The miserable failure should rack up massive amounts of debt on extremely fun purchases with the intent on NEVER making one damn payment. Some of these purchases should include:

- Cars (that huge SUV is going bye, bye if you leave it parked outside on the street, so we encourage you to store it in your grandfather's garage).
- Boats (your thirteen DUIs shouldn't count against you driving a boat, should it?).
- Jet Skis (reenacting a classic scene from a 1980s summertime hijinks comedy movie drunk and high on prescription pills while driving a jet ski is fun for you, but not fun for the lake police).
- A Miniature Pony (calling him a "therapy animal" is a stretch when you try to board a plane with him).
- An RV (you're going to lose your makeshift meth lab if the repo man takes this).
- A Motorcycle (the notion of a "road rash" and a "miserable failure" go together like "bread" and "butter").

So, here is how the repo man plays a role in the miserable failure's worthless existence. First, you must purchase many big-ticket items. Second, you will not make payments on said items but you'll continue to enjoy using them (more on siphoning gas from cars to put in your boat for some fun in a later section). Third, the repo man will stalk you and do whatever it takes to get the item back into the possession of the company who sold it to you. **What you must do as a miserable failure is to try and avoid the repo man while protecting your basically illegally purchased items.** There are also five key myths about repo men that we must warn you about.

Myth #1 - Repo men will not take back the item if you beg and plead on your knees like a pathetic little bitch. **FALSE**. Getting down on your knees in front of the repo man is a great way for you to get a boot to the forehead (concussion) and a kick to the gut (a lacerated spleen).

Myth #2 - Repo men will not break into your garage to get the item back. **FALSE**. The repo man is skilled at picking locks and breaking down various doors. They can also hotwire cars, trucks, motorcycles and RVs. Repo men will destroy your shit in order to get the item back.

Myth #3 - Repo men are good guys with good hearts. **FALSE**. Most repo men are parolees, ex-cons, or just big and angry bikers looking to make a quick few bucks as a side gig. They are also immune from bullshit rambling and crying. They don't care about your feelings. They care about getting back the piece of property that doesn't belong to you (anymore).

Myth #4 - Repo men are only called in to repossess transportation vehicles. **FALSE**. The repo man can take back your blood-stained and scabies-infested carpet that you failed to make payments on, they can also take back your jewelry (even if you're still wearing it) and they can even take back couches, chairs, computers and anything else you can buy on credit.

Myth #5 - You can bribe the repo man. **FALSE**. Your broke ass doesn't have enough money to make payments. How in the hell are you going to have enough money to bribe a repo man? Blowjobs don't count as forms of payment, and you can't sell enough of your hair and blood plasma to do a dent in the amount of what he'd need in order for you to bribe him.

Dealing with collection departments, repo workers and bankruptcy judges are just a few of the main "players" that you'll encounter in your life as often as possible as you become a miserable failure. Whatever you do, don't try to stop the repo man from taking back your shit (unless of course you want a severe beat down, then yes, please fuck with him and try and stop him).

Your Bookie

He's sneaky... He's sketchy... He's dirty... He's your bookie! A bookie is a shady as fuck, strange dude who makes highly illegal (and dangerous) bets for you on various horse races, professional sports games, collegiate athletic events and boxing fights in the back of dark alleys and old bars on the east side of town. Your bookie should also have a nickname for you. The nickname your bookie should have given you by now is "Broken Legs McGee." You've PROUDLY earned this nickname because a miserable failure never pays off their gambling debts. Your relationship with your bookie should consist of some of the following situations:

- Late night drunken and sobbing phone calls to your bookie asking for *"a little more time"* time to pay your debt.
- Debiting out your welfare money to bet on the next big heavyweight boxing or MMA fight.
- Getting your ass beat in dark alleys with a baseball bat or crowbar from your bookie for repeat failure to make payment.
- Stealing money from your crippled and wheelchair-bound stepfather to make a few bets on the ponies.

- Wasting all of your earnings (if you win) on even more drugs, cigarettes, firecrackers, hookers, booze and dinners at the all-you-can-eat pizza buffets.
- Getting pistol whipped in a toy store parking lot in front of your illegitimate children during your visitation weekend, by your bookie for failure to make payment.

Your Bets

If you're confused on how a bookie works in the life of a miserable failure, we'll now discuss the ONLY four outcomes of gambling with your bookie. They include:

Example #1 - The Typical Bet

1. A miserable failure makes a bet with a bookie on a professional football game.
2. The bookie takes full payment.
3. You lose the bet.
4. You go back to robbing crack houses and blowing strange men in bathroom glory holes to fund your future gambling habits (you can also re-read the section on "How to Steal from Your Grandparents" if you need to go down that track too).

Example #2 - The Bad Bet

1. A miserable failure makes a bet with a bookie on a professional football game.
2. The bookie allows you to not pay until after the game (with the idea that you'll owe him some interest for letting you slide by just once on the opening bet).
3. You lose the bet.
4. Your bookie comes to you asking for the money.

5. You do not pay your bookie.
6. You then get kneecapped with a golf club in a corn field on the outskirts of town for failure to make payment.
7. You go to the hospital for surgery and to steal opioids and other addictive painkillers.

Example #3 - The Winning Bet

1. A miserable failure makes a bet with a bookie on a professional football game.
2. The bookie takes your money.
3. You win the bet!!!
4. You get paid based on the odds of your bet.
5. You either make another bet, or you squander and waste your winnings on stupid, worthless, and useless shit.

Example #4 - The Unlucky Bet

1. A miserable failure makes a bet with a bookie on a professional football game.
2. The bookie allows you to not pay until after the game (with the idea that you'll owe him some interest for letting you slide by just once if you lose).
3. You win the bet!
4. Instead of paying you, your bookie allows you some GREAT odds on the next professional curling game and you let your winnings ride.
5. You lose the next curling bet.
6. You go back to robbing your nephew's piggy bank in the middle of the night when he sleeps in order to fund your future gambling habits

From getting beaten into complete and absolute submission from the local mob or your bookie, to wasting away the cash you MIGHT win, **the miserable failure should essentially have their bookie on speed dial.** Whenever you get an "itch" to make a bet, make sure you phone in your bet to your bookie. Your bookie is going to operate as your own personal accountant and essentially manage the money that you **PROBABLY WON'T win**. Miserable failures know bookies and make ridiculous and life-threatening bets on professional sporting events in order to bring some spicy intrigue into their pathetic and horrifying lives.

Financial Desperation

Sooner or later, after you've been fired from your various job(s), disowned by your family (again), divorced (for the 8th time) and you're in massive amounts of debt (six million, to be EXACT), you're going to go through what we call, "financial desperation" (SCORE!!!). Miserable failures don't pay their bills. Miserable failures borrow money without the intent of ever paying it back and are constantly trying to avoid repo workers, collection agencies as well as paying legal fees, fines, taxes and penalties. With all of those factors combined, miserable failures are considered by society to be, "broke-ass predators." In this section, we'll cover some of the various ways in which you can earn some quick cash on the side.

Selling Personal Belongings

If you still have any possessions left after the collectors and creditors have taken them, we strongly encourage the miserable failure to sell off their personal belongings. How else are you going to fund your EXTENSIVE drug usage, HORRENDOUS drinking problems, and your LIFE-ALTERING gambling addictions? We recommend that the miserable failure have a yard sale and sell anything and everything that you still have of value. The gold watch your great, great, great, great grandfather gave you on his deathbed and pleaded for you to keep it in the family? Yeah, say bye, bye to it for a quick $20 at a yard sale. **Your elderly grandmother's diamond wedding ring she gave you? It's now going down to the pawnshop so you can get some cash to go purchase a crate of bottle rockets, a baby armadillo and a fifth of whiskey.**

There are several places to sell your Shit. You can have a garage sale, sell it all online, or take it down and pawn it off. Whatever you need to do to sell it, just do it. Bargain and barter with everyone like an Arab trader during the negotiation process. Get the most amount of money you can from strangers, even if you're totally getting ripped off. Selling your personal possessions in order to fund your addictions during your quest to become a miserable failure is a paramount step towards your final end goal. Losers sell all of their shit for cash. And let's face it, **YOU. ARE. A. LOSER...**

Selling Sperm (for male miserable failures)

Donating (A.K.A. "selling") sperm is a great move for the male miserable failure. Making sure you're spawning future miserable failures is a home run bonus feature for donating sperm. Essentially, before you can jerk off, you have to fill out the clinic's intake form to see if you even qualify to donate (FYI: if you were truthful, you'd fail the intake form and be assisted off the premises by security). The first thing you're required to do is to answer a family medical history questionnaire and believe us; it's a bitch. Now, this intake form is going to be difficult to pass, so we recommend that you LIE on it ("lying" and "the miserable failure" go together like "Las Vegas" and "hookers").

- Question #1 - Anyone ever have cancer in your family? Answer "no" (try to avoid bringing attention to the tumorous lump on your neck).
- Question #2 - Are you addicted to any substances? Answer

"no" as your hands tremble when your heroin and alcohol withdrawal starts to kick in.
- Question #3 - Have you ever had a sexually transmitted disease? Answer "no" (after you finish your fifteen minutes of lying on the ground in uncontrollable belly laughter).

After you have lied your way through the questionnaire, it's time for you to go get started! When they take you back to the room, ask if you can watch porn to *"get yourself off."* When they bring you the porn movies, make sure that you ask for specific types. In fact, don't leave the nurse's side without asking for any of the following porn genres:

- Midget Porn
- Nugget Porn
- Lactation Porn
- Granny Porn
- Furry Party Porn

After the nurse stops laughing at your unusual requests, make your way into the room and have a seat on the butcher paper. **After five minutes, stick your head out the door and ask for some assistance.** When the nurse comes over, ask her if she *"could pop a titty out"* really quick to help you. When she walks away in disgust, yell down the hallway at her, *"can you at least give me a candle, some incense and dim the fucking lights in this dump?"* Then, slam the door and let out a terrifying scream for all others to hear. Also, it's also encouraged for you to shout obscenities, profanity, and offensive phrases when you "do your business" in the little room. Make sure everyone in the building can hear you. Some of the following recommendations for phrases you should shout out include:

- *"Damn! That was a hall of famer!"*
- *"Where did it go?!"*
- *"Daddy did it!"*

- *"Ouch!"*
- *"Unleash the hounds!"*
- *"That's an odd color."*
- *"You know, my uncle showed me how to do this!"*
- *"Release the Kraken."*
- *"I'm finished with the dog. Bring me the cat next."*

When you finish donating your sperm, grab your money (usually around $50) and go to the track to gamble on some greyhound races, or use the money to get yourself a useless set of hunting knives at the local swap meet.

Selling Eggs (for female miserable failures)

Donating (A.K.A. "selling") your eggs is a great way for the female miserable failure to make some fast cash. Again, knowing that your spawn will live on and the miserable failure bloodline lineage will continue on is a powerful thing. Female miserable failures should sell their eggs as often as possible. Generally, you can donate (sell) your eggs to a fertility center for $7,000-$14,000! This is great news as that type of cash is going to help you pay your late child support payments (NOT!!!) as well as your crack cocaine and drinking habits. Another perk for donating (selling) your eggs is free room and board and a complimentary hospital bed to crash in during the procedure for a few days. Basically, you're treated like royalty when you sell your eggs (WINK, WINK: yet another opportunity for the miserable failure to raid the prescription closet).

The final aspect that we must preface is your appearance. Most fertility clinics won't take you seriously (nor will your egg donation application be accepted, you dumb bitch) if you walk in off the street being "yourself." **THIS IS THE ONLY TIME we suggest the female miserable failure make themselves look even remotely presentable** (remember, you're getting $7,000-$14,000 to fund your superglue and spray paint huffing habits). Throw on your old hooker dress (no, not the one with the bloodstains), wash your greasy hair (if you haven't shaved it off yet) in the fountain outside the local mall, throw on your old stripper high heels (the 9" clear stilettos), and doll yourself up in enough makeup that would make a clown jealous. You want to look hot, but you have to look "trashy" or "slutty" hot. We don't want you to do any type of makeover as that would imply self-improving. We want you to look just good enough to get accepted for your egg donations.

Most women can only donate eggs from the ages of twenty-one to thirty. However, this should NEVER stop the female miserable failure (at any age) from walking into the nearest fertility clinic. When you walk into this magical location, prop your leg up on the counter and lift your skirt while exclaiming to the receptionist, *"go ahead and take 'em!"* After the receptionist has completed her vomiting, take your paperwork and go fill it out in the waiting area. Remember, this is big money for the miserable failure, so make sure that you do whatever is asked of you during your time at the egg fertility clinic (FYI: feel free to blow the fertility doctor if needed as a last resort to get your application approved). Doing anything so you get approved includes selling your body, mind, and soul to creepy perverted doctors looking to get their dipsticks wet. After you sell your eggs, make sure that you blow all of your money on new neck and facial tattoos, booze, drugs, and ten miniature piglets.

Selling Blood Plasma

If you want to sell your blood plasma, you have to meet some stringent requirements (BTW: if you can't pass the test, congratulations!) Donating (selling) blood plasma can be very lucrative (enough to cover both your ramen noodle and angel dust addictions) but you can only donate twice a week due to FDA regulations. Generally, you can expect to make between $50-$100 per transaction. The process also only takes around two hours (NOTE: plenty of time to take a nap and steal shit from the hospital).

To qualify to donate blood plasma, you need to not have any blood-related sexually transmitted diseases or hepatitis (FYI: informing the hospital about your herpes and your syphilis STD's will get you booted from the donation clinic). However, if you pass their tests and can donate blood plasma, make sure you go in twice a week (if you don't pass the tests, that means you're well ahead of the pack on becoming a miserable failure). We recommend you go on Mondays and Fridays. Mondays are good because you're going to get enough money to fund your new facial tribal tattoo from "Homeless Eddie" in the alley. Friday's are good because the cash you make can be used to gamble it away at the local demolition derby race on the fairgrounds over the weekend. Whatever you do, just make sure you continue to blow and waste your money away with silly, useless shit and dumb activities.

Selling Hair

Most normal and caring people donate their hair. Donated hair is given to wig makers to make wigs for people suffering with cancer or other illnesses (FYI: your illnesses include cirrhosis of the liver, depression, STDs, etc.). **You should not donate your hair. You should SELL your fucking hair.** When you go into a hair selling location, you can generally make anywhere from $100-$4,000! This is good news for the miserable failure who wants to continue their Sunday drinking and sex toy store shopping experience on a weekly basis.

If you want to sell your hair, you're going to have disadvantages that might not allow you to make the top amount of money or even sell it. Some of the main factors that might prevent you from doing this are:

- Your lice-infested scalp.

- Your greasy, nasty hair from never washing it (what's it been, two years?...).
- The bugs, cobwebs, and dirt that occupy the hair on your melon.

To combat said factors, we encourage the miserable failure to make sure that you wash your hair before you enter the hair selling store **(washing your hair with dish washing soap in the mud puddle at the local truck stop does in fact qualify as "washing").** If you need to dry your hair, just hang your head out of the side of the car like a dog as you drive (drunk) down the street to the hair selling office. Also, make sure that you change out of your customary "robe, slippers, and boxers" look and into something much classier (your "wife beater, sweat pants, and sandals look). Remember, being a miserable failure involves selling your body, your blood, your hair, your sperm (or your eggs) for some fast cash. The miserable failure has no guilt or remorse and has no self-respect, integrity, or pride for themselves. Always remember to blow through the money on useless and worthless shit and continue to spend money on your various habits that you've acquired on your quest to be a miserable failure.

How to Deal with the IRS

Welfare cards, social security checks, disability benefits, and food stamps are not "income" to normal people. Normal people might actually need said services because they're in dire straits. For the miserable failure, these might be your only sources of any type of income besides selling your body, blood plasma, hair, sperm, kidney, or eggs. First of all, **the miserable failure NEVER FILES their taxes** (unless you prefer to live in federal prison as a miserable failure instead of on the streets). If you don't file your taxes, you're going to get audited. When you get letters in the mail from the IRS that claim you're delinquent on your taxes or you're getting audited, just use the letters they mailed you to roll up another joint to smoke. However, if you want to file your taxes to try and take advantage of the earned income credit (FREE MONEY!!), the miserable failure DOES file their taxes and writes off multiple illegal deductions in a poor attempt to get even more FREE MONEY back from the federal and state governments.

Sooner or later, the IRS will be knocking at your door. Feel free to let them in for the "audit" that you're about to receive (NOTE: bending over or presenting your wrists for the handcuffs is a nice touch when you meet your new "friends" from the federal government). Start off by making sure you provide the write off receipts that accompany your illegal tax deductions (NOTE: miserable failures file their taxes handwritten in crayon). Some of these "questionable" receipts include, but are not limited to:

- Receipts from "The Happy Ending Massage Parlor" (as a medical expense deduction).
- Handwritten receipts on sticky notes from Eddie your crack dealer (as a "prescription medical expense deduction").
- All of your booze and cigarette receipts (as "client entertainment deductions").
- All of your lottery and scratch off ticket receipts (as "client entertainment deductions").
- Your various porn shop receipts (as "client entertainment deductions").

During the auditing process, feel free to openly discuss any unclaimed income that you "accidentally" (WINK, WINK) failed to report to the IRS. Laugh out loud and discuss the money you made selling your hair, blood plasma and body (for sexual favors of course) to the IRS agent. You can also discuss everything you've stolen throughout the year as well. Also, it is VERY IMPORTANT to make sure you use good manners when the IRS agent is in your domicile. **Offer them a hit of**

cocaine, a glass of homemade moon shine or a slice of moldy pizza (still in the refrigerator from 13 weeks ago). Generally, your audit should take the IRS agent around an hour to do. Once they can't stand the stench from your shit box apartment and they are ready to proceed to legal action, they will leave. On the way out the door, ask the IRS agent if you can borrow $20. When the IRS agent informs you that they will be seeking legal action against you, drop down on your knees as use the "cancer excuse," the "molestation excuse," the "bankruptcy excuse" or the "identity theft excuse" as you wail on the ground in an uncontrollable combination of both laughter and tears.

To Go or Not to Go. That is the Question...

Should the miserable failure show up to their court hearing with the IRS? It totally depends on how and what degree you want to fuck up your life. If you want to go to prison again, simply don't show up to your hearing. This will automatically trigger a warrant for your arrest and when you're caught, you WILL spend the next several years behind bars in a federal prison. HOWEVER, if you want to be ridiculed, humiliated, and given multiple fines, then please show up to your day in court with the IRS. When you're summoned into court, if you decide to show up, make sure that you arrive at least twenty-five minutes late, with no lawyer, and make sure that you're high as hell and drunk as a skunk. As the judge is handing down your jail sentence or fines, laugh at him and leave in the middle of their ruling. Showing up is an option for the miserable failure not only for IRS-related court cases, but for any case. If you decide to NOT show up for your IRS hearing, rest-assured you'll be on a wanted list and you'll soon be going back to federal prison (YAY!!!)

Bankruptcy 101

Well, it's that time of year **again**. It's time for you, the miserable failure to walk (REMEMBER: DUI = impounded car) with your tail between your legs proudly down to the courthouse to file for bankruptcy in order to wipe out that $450,000 of credit card debt, payday loan interest, and your MASSIVE tax bills. The "miserable failure" and "bankruptcy" go together like "surf" and "turf" at a seafood restaurant. **Wherever there is bankruptcy, you'll surely find a miserable failure.** The best part of bankruptcy is that you don't need to return any of the shit you bought with your credit cards (as long as you file Chapter 7 and hide the items in your grandparent's basement or with your stepfather's illegal porn collection in his underground doomsday bunker/sex room). Basically, you won't have to pay any of the debts that you owe when you file for Chapter 7 bankruptcy. How amazing does that sound?! **Everything you've wasted your money on is now yours FOR FREE** (including that baby monkey you purchased on the streets of the Philippines a few years ago on a dare with your parolee prison pal, Tracey). Before we continue, we must pay tribute and note some of your more infamous purchases which probably contributed to your extremely poor financial problems. Some of your hall of famers include:

- A triceratops dinosaur skull (which you purchased drunk at a wealthy estate auction).
- An entire shipping container of nudie magazines (the sticky pages do devalue the collection).
- The truckload of blue label whiskey you purchased for your (eighth) bachelor party trip to Vegas.
- First class flights you purchased for your riverboat gambling trips to Biloxi, Mississippi.

Chapter 13 Bankruptcy

Filing Chapter 13 bankruptcy is NOT ALLOWED for the miserable failure (NOTE: the only advantage of this filing is you might have your assets seized by the county Sheriff's Department in order to repay your creditors). This type of bankruptcy basically means that a judge is going to mandate and order you to pay a certain amount of money each month to your creditors. We really do not recommend this as a first move in the bankruptcy process for the miserable failure, as you're going to need every last dime to fund your video poker addiction. We also don't recommend this type of bankruptcy simply because doing so would allow the banks, and credit card agencies to win (A.K.A. you "pay your bills"). We basically want you to purchase a bunch of shit and then fail to make payments on said shit. Chapter 13 bankruptcy essentially makes the miserable failure pay a certain amount of money each month (normal people call this "a repayment plan"). **The miserable failure does not do this type of bankruptcy. Avoid it, like you've avoided USING CONDOMS or WASHING YOUR HANDS your entire life.**

Chapter 7 Bankruptcy

This is the crème de la crème for the miserable failure. Think about it! You've pissed away all of your money (that you didn't have or earn legally) on shit (useless, worthless, and trivial items), and now you get to keep said possessions without paying the money back! SCORE! This is the "get out of jail free" card for the miserable failure.

When you file bankruptcy (again), you'll need to go down to the local courthouse to fill out the necessary paperwork. Filling out the information on the paper might be difficult for you as your trembling hands will probably be shaking due to your alcohol withdrawal. You must still muscle forward and make sure that the bankruptcy paperwork is turned in to the court. After it's processed, you'll appear in front of a judge (again). The judge is going to wipe away your debt and send your credit back to 350 with one stroke of the pen (NOTE: if there were a debtors prison, we'd recommend that the miserable failure go into it willingly, just for the daily beatings from the other deadbeats). **Filing Chapter 7 bankruptcy is a SOLID and professional move for the miserable failure.** Once you complete your Chapter 7 bankruptcy, you need to treat yourself to a night out on the town! Drink up, have steak and lobster (using your new 55% interest credit card), and party! After all, going into massive amounts of debt and having it expelled from your record is an amazing and FANTASTIC experience... So, enjoy yourself!

The "Bankruptcy Excuse"

In previous sections, we've discussed various types of excuses that a miserable failure makes in their life (the "cancer excuse," the "unemployment excuse," the "molestation excuse"). Now, we want to introduce you to the "bankruptcy excuse." This excuse gets you out of paying for ANYTHING and EVERYTHING in life (NOTE: missed child support payments and overdue mortgages are a hard sell). Whatever situation you find yourself in, just remember to always blame your problems on outside forces (that which of course, you're 100% responsible for). For instance, let's say that your fourth parole officer or your eighteenth therapist invites you to lunch in December (because they feel sorry for FUCKS like you and it's Christmas). We encourage the miserable failure to order SEVERAL expensive entrées on the menu. Blame your ordering habits on the fact that you *"just filed for bankruptcy."* Furthermore, go ahead and ask to borrow $4000 from them because you *"just filed for bankruptcy."* The "bankruptcy excuse" gets you out of paying for dinners, drinks, as well as expensive leather jackets (FYI: mall security begs to differ with your statute).

The "bankruptcy excuse" is a great play for the miserable failure. Whatever your situation is, blame it on bankruptcy. Got caught speeding 110 miles per hour in a school zone drunk on mouthwash? Tell the officer that you just went bankrupt. Can't pay the hooker? Inform her pimp (as he's beating the shit out of you) that you just filed for bankruptcy. Your kid needs new braces? Explain to the orthodontist that you just filed for bankruptcy and you demand that he do the work for free. When you're using this excuse, it's also always a great move to use it on your immediate family around Christmas and Thanksgiving. Generally, those two holidays bring out the "generous spirit" of most normal people. So, when you show up for the family feast, drunk, stoned, with two black eyes, while carrying a feral and stray cat, make sure you ask for money from family members while letting them know about your recent bankruptcy.

Student Loans

This section only applies to the miserable failure that went to college (NOTE: the more college debt a miserable failure has, with NO degree to show for it is very much considered a BIG WIN). Student loans are a form of financial enslavement and indentured servitude (YES!) which most miserable failures with at least some college experience have. Student loans are supposed to "help" students afford getting an education at various overly-priced colleges. Not only is getting a bachelor's degree basically useless, worthless, and pointless (due to the laws of supply and demand), it can cost you hundreds upon hundreds of thousands of dollars in debt. We must note that the ONLY reasons a miserable failure should attend college are:

- To party like a rock star for four or MORE years (your partying in college is going to take ten to fifteen years off your life because your liver is fucked... SCORE!).
- To engage in many unprotected sexual acts with drunken sorority sisters (or fraternity brothers for the female miserable failure).
- To get into MASSIVE debt.
- To temporarily avoid becoming a fully-functional adult living in a civilized society (REMINDER: you're still not a fully functional adult living in civilized society because you're a miserable failure).

Student loans should be taken out excessively during college (BTW: use the excess money for beer, drugs, all-you-can-eat Chinese food buffets, strip clubs on amateur night, and going to expensive music concerts to get high and drunk). Also, we always want you to DEMAND to borrow **more** money from the college financial advisor than the college recommends that you borrow. Borrowing more money is going to give you enough cash to fund your drinking habits as well as your yearly spring break vacations to Panama City Beach, South Padre Island, Daytona Beach, Lake Havasu, and Cancun. The miserable failure should have student loan debts that WELL-EXCEED $600,000 when their "college career" comes to an end (CRYSTAL BALL PREDICTION: you will flunk out of college after 8 years and that is what will end your party run).

"Repaying" (LOL) Your Student Loans

Now that your laughter has subsided due to the subsection title of this part of this shitty book, we want you to realize that **you won't be paying your debts off... EVER** ("repaying debts" and "the miserable failure" go together like "oil" and "water"). Not only should you have hundreds of thousands of dollars in student debt, but you should have no intention of EVER paying off your loans because you're suffering from one of the two following life events:

1. You're unemployed (SCORE!).
2. You have no home address or phone number for the Department of Education to hunt you down like an animal.

If you're unemployed, you won't have to pay off your loans. And, if the government can't find you, (A.K.A. you're "homeless") you won't have to pay off your loans either. However, the government CAN seize your property (or garnish your wages if you have a gig) if you fail to make payments, but **the miserable failure has no assets, does not work and has no real property** (NOTE: unless you count your bag of cans, an eight ball of cocaine and the blow-up doll you purchased at the roadside truck stop to be considered "assets"). We also encourage the miserable failure to defer their student loan payments as long as possible. If your deferment ends, we encourage you to put your loans in what is called, "forbearance" as long as you can. Relax, you WILL be gaining interest over these two postponement periods (#WINNING). This is great news because we want you to rack up as much debt as humanly possible, you worthless sack of shit.

Defaulting on Your Student Loans

After you fail to make any reasonable attempts to make basic payments on your (now defaulted) student loans, you're going to be in trouble (SCORE!). "Defaulting on student loans" and "miserable failure" go together like "the beach" and "Malibu, California." Not only does a miserable failure mock the student loan collection agency when they call demanding payment, you should also verbally express in GREAT DETAIL **where** specifically your money went INSTEAD of paying your student loans. Some classic examples of your personal expenses you've used your money on instead of making your student loan payments include:

- Your extravagant trip to Tahiti with the one-legged prostitute named Stacey.
- Your purchase of a rare, albino alligator during your three-week vacation in the Florida Keys.
- Your excessive drinking and paint huffing habits outside in the parking lot of your local hardware store.
- Your new neck dragon tattoo collection.
- Your addiction for online toy shopping while completely intoxicated on "Cyber Monday."

The miserable failure should explain to the student loan collector how much money you've wasted on said activities instead of paying for your degree. Feel free to mock them and laugh at them over the phone. If you have to let out a fart, put the phone up to your ass and let er' rip. Feel free to inform the student loan collector that you *"can't talk now because you're in the middle of masturbating to midget porn."* That excuse always gets you on the student loan department's "naughty list" (A.K.A. "tax audit list").

The student loan company might tell you that your wages might be garnished. This is FANTASTIC NEWS for the miserable failure that has a job and has not been fired (yet). If you have a job, you'll soon have MUCH LESS take home money (NOTE: working for free is key for the miserable failure). If you CHOOSE to avoid wage garnishment, we recommend that you get fired from your job immediately (SEE SECTION: "How to Get Fired"). The Department of Education might even try to seize your bank accounts. Now that your laughter has subsided again, inform the student loan collector that you're piss-broke and your account is WAY overdrawn by thousands of dollars. Tell them, *"good luck with that"* as you laugh your ass off. If they threaten to take your assets (again, let your laughter subside), inform them that the only assets you have are your excessive herpes outbreaks and your collection of truck stop key chain souvenirs. You also might get a tax bill in the mail after SEVERAL years of not paying one damn cent. Essentially, the Federal Government is going to send you a 1099 form (A.K.A. a "bill") claiming that you earned $500,000 and have not paid taxes on it. This is great news as you can't file bankruptcy on student loans! When you don't pay this tax bill, you'll be soon going into a federal prison (again) for tax evasion. If this happens to you, good! "Jail" and "miserable failure" go together like "meth" and "trailer parks."

Defaulting on your loans is just one more way a miserable failure goes through life completely and utterly fucking up and destroying their entire human existence. You can end up in jail, have your wages garnished, or in a horrible repayment plan where you're basically a slave to the lender of your loans for the rest of your life. All of the said outcomes are awesome news for the miserable failure! Owing excessive amounts of money from your partying college days with high interest rates (with a degree or even without a degree) is something that all miserable failures should at least TRY to do.

9

TRANSPORTATION

Getting Around

You need access to cars, planes, trains, buses, subways, scooters, motorcycles, stolen bicycles and skateboards, in order to get to some of your favorite places (THOSE INCLUDE: your crack dealer's house, your parole officer's office, etc.). In this section, we'll be focusing solely on transportation and how the miserable failure gets around town. We'll discuss how to hitchhike (NOTE: preferably with strange and dangerous truckers alongside the interstate). We'll also cover how to drive a car like a deranged lunatic. We'll even explain to you how to properly fly on an airplane as we delve into deep detail about the "do's" and "don'ts" of the miserable failure's mobility and travels associated with air travel.

As a miserable failure, you should be walking everywhere as much as possible due to your multiple DUIs and because your shitbox car is still impounded (NOTE: if you've had a leg or two amputated due to the diabetes associated with your sugar addiction, and you're wheelchair-bound—FANTASTIC!!!). Even if you're a cripple, you'll still need to know the rules of "miserable failure etiquette" on public transportation, like subways and busses. When we discuss air travel, we'll address and go over in great detail, the entire flying process and how miserable failures should board a plane and act during ALL ASPECTS of air travel. However, perhaps the most daring and controversial section we will discuss is going to focus on how a miserable failure drives a car. We'll answer the timeless, age-old, unanswered, classic questions as to why many people drive like:

- *"Fucking Lunatics"*
- *"Cocksucking Assholes"*
- *"Dangerous Douchebags"*
- *"Idiot Sons of Bitches"*
- *"Motherfucking Morons"*
- *"Fuckface Bastards"*
- *"Motherfucking Cocksuckers"*
- *"Cockbite Cuntfaces"*
- *"Fucking Maniacs"*
- *"Dumb Ass Motherfuckers"*
- *"Pieces of Shit"*

Knowing how to drive like one of the previously mentioned nicknames is going to be of great value for the miserable failure going through life. In the air travel section, we'll be discussing all of the ways a miserable failure can make air travel uncomfortable, unpleasant, and HORRENDOUS for the entire flight crew, pilots, and your fellow passengers. We'll go into extraordinary detail on:

- How to board an airplane intoxicated (the risks and rewards).
- Who to sit next to during air travel (HINT: always pick the fat people).
- Overhead bin etiquette (yes, you can try to sneak up there for an in-flight cat nap).

- Fun phrases to shout out when you're on an airplane.
- Actions you can take on an airplane to make other people's days more "memorable."
- What to steal from the lavatory.
- Reclining seat etiquette.
- How to handle the free peanuts and complimentary drink service.

If you truly want to be a miserable failure, this entire travel section is of vital importance because we will cover in detail how to ruin other people's travels, while giving them stories they will be sharing with their PTSD therapist for many years to come. Whether you're hitchhiking to your crack dealer's house to buy some drugs for the weekend, or you're driving like an asshole on the interstate, knowing how to travel properly as a miserable failure is of vital importance.

How to Drive a Car

You CAN'T become a miserable failure unless you know how to properly drive a car. Not every *"dipshit asshole"* that cuts someone off in traffic is **miserable**. Not every *"moronic cocksucking douche bag"* that goes twenty miles under the speed limit in the fast lane is a **failure**. **It's when that *"worthless son of a bitch"* cuts you off in heavy traffic and then proceeds to travel twenty miles UNDER the speed limit while driving a wood grain station wagon on three doughnut tires, covered in rust spots and shotgun holes, that you may begin to guess that you're in the sad presence of a true miserable failure on the road.** When that same *"motherfucker"* on four wheels is also blaring classic songs of the south on a broke-ass cassette player, huffing on a bottle of aftershave, not wearing pants, currently giving you the middle finger, and has no eyebrows, then you can certainly stop guessing. It's 100%! **You've unfortunately crossed paths with a miserable failure driving behind the wheel!**

Miserable failures come in many forms while driving. Every single person has dealt with a miserable failure at some point while driving down the road. All people have yelled and cursed at those pesky other drivers. From the "*fucker*" who changed lanes without their turn signal, to the "*loser asshole*" who does illegal U-turns and pulls out directly in front of you in a school zone, miserable failures are EASY to spot on the road. And now, YOU.... need to become one. Essentially, miserable failures are the worst drivers... EVER.

As a miserable failure, the roadways of the world are the perfect platform for you to practice your craft and show your true nature to everyone. For a miserable failure, commuting is a joy and something to look forward to (sort of like "pizza day" in the methadone rehab clinic). Yes, the average commute for a miserable failure normally only includes walking (or crawling) to the liquor store, taking the bus to parole check-ins (you're going to fail that drug test **again**), or accidentally going for a free ride in a garbage truck after falling asleep in your favorite dumpster. Occasionally, a miserable failure is fortunate enough, all be it, in an often-short lived experience, to have the use of a vehicle (NOTE: you should not have car insurance, a clean driving record, or a valid driver's license while driving).

Miserable Failures on the Road

Being on wheels brings you ample opportunity to forcefully expose the common person to your shit show you call a "world." Your terrible hygiene, inappropriate sexual comments toward senior citizens, rotten vinegar body odor smell, tendency to vomit blood, and propensity toward stealing underwear from people are easy to avoid on foot. When the common person spots you in an alley dressed like a unicorn, begging for change to buy lottery tickets, and having a yelling match with the table lamp you found in a dumpster (BTW: "Lampy" can really be a jerk sometimes), they can simply choose to walk down a different alley to avoid you altogether. However, when the average commuter is deadlocked in bumper to bumper gridlock traffic on a six-lane interstate highway, there is no escaping your shenanigans and escapades behind the wheel (like when a date "chooses" to take a tour of your mother's basement that you live in). This is why we encourage you to be easily detectable from the other normal members and regular drivers of society.

That daily commute (especially in large urban areas), represents probably the most stressful part of the average person's day. Rush hour and the morning traffic blitz are simply unavoidable for most people (BTW: similar to you having **another** herpes outbreak). **It is YOUR JOB to make everyone else's commutes even more angering and depressing.** The stress these drive times induce has been enough to cause normally peaceful people to become violent and behave irrationally (CAUTION: a miserable failure + meth + cocaine + moonshine = road rage). Add a miserable failure with the use of a vehicle into the mix and it's a perfect recipe for and unavoidable, cataclysmic, huge, life-changing fucking disaster! The following sections will reveal to the unenlightened, not only the correct method of driving like a miserable failure but also the proper way to prepare your vehicle for maximum insult, as well as the perfect attitude to have with fellow non-failure commuters. Remember, when you're on the road, you're not just representing your pathetic, drunk, drug-addicted, greasy, demented, borderline suicidal, miserable self. **You're fighting for all the miserable failures one angry horn honk, obscene gesture, and road rage fistfight at a time!**

Selecting your Ride

Proper vehicle selection is the first and most crucial step in becoming a miserable failure behind the wheel. **The correct vehicle should serve as an annoying accent to your terrible driving skills as well as highlight your entire fucked up existence you call a "life."** The things a miserable failure does behind the wheel are so anger-inducing and rage-inspiring that they can only be made worse by a completely obnoxious vehicle (NOTE: it has been proven scientifically that a vomit green color on a car makes other drivers wish death upon whoever is driving said car). Obtaining a car is tough for some miserable failures. So, how did you get yours? Maybe you stole the neighbor kid's identity again to purchase a car on credit. Or maybe you "borrowed" your currently incarcerated mother's credit card again to illegally rent a car? Or maybe you managed to fool another loan officer into giving you a loan (NOTE: three banker and loan officer suicides have been attributed to your excessive borrowing and nonexistent repayment history). Whatever the case, you've somehow legally purchased, **stolen,** or rented a vehicle to get on the road (BTW: when renting a car, don't take the insurance protection and make sure the car is brought back completely and totally demolished from your demolition derby race you entered it in at the state fair).

The Risky Renter Option

As mentioned above, you should choose to rent your vehicle. Although renting does substantially limit your vehicle selection (NOTE: most rental places don't have buses or dump trucks) it does allow the miserable failure to leave a nearly new car's interior in an "apocalyptic bathroom" meets a "sex crime scene" appearance while taking on zero personal liability or responsibility (FYI: if you chose the insurance on the rental car, be sure to simply NOT RETURN said rental car). The sedan may have cost $199 for the week, but the look on the manager's face when they realize your irritable bowel syndrome acted up after your weekly visit to the "House of Chili Buffet" is priceless. Eventually, thanks to the photos of you posted behind the counter of the rental location, you won't be able to rent a car anymore—PERIOD. It's time to buy!

Getting Started

No matter the make of a vehicle, size matters most to the miserable failure (FYI: this is not a flaccid penis or flapjack titty reference). The idea of a midsize or small vehicle never enters the mind of a miserable failure when selecting their new ride. You should focus on getting the biggest piece of shit vehicle available for you to choose from. Obnoxiously large (like the "large", infected boils on your back) is the only way to go! Your new ride should be wide enough to occupy 1.15 lanes of traffic and be no less than 1.35 times a normal car's size (this will be important when learning "how to parallel park like an asshole" in a later section). Because of always rising oil prices, the larger vehicles have been abandoned for smaller more fuel-efficient models. This has left junkyards and used car lots stocked with large SUVs, full sized windowless panel vans, and ten passenger-cargo busses. Don't worry about how you're going to afford to purchase fuel for one of these gas-guzzling beasts (HINT: gas siphoning). If you don't huff gas, you'll simply use the credit card you "borrowed" from your grandfather, or go back to begging for change next to the bus stop. Most people are so willing to get rid of their gas-sucking houseboats on wheels, they can be bought for a fraction of their original price. Additionally, if you chose something with over 200k miles and that is over fifteen years old, a significant discount can be expected as well. Don't worry about an older high mileage vehicle being in poor mechanical shape. Near poisonous exhaust and frequent breakdowns only aid the miserable failure in accomplishing their goal of building the shittiest life possible while offending everyone they encounter on the road. If you can essentially find an old, big, junky, piece of shit to drive, you're well on your way to become a miserable failure on the road. You should easily be able to procure a vehicle that meets all of the aforementioned criteria for around $250 (or two sex acts, three lines of blow, and a bottle of rum to "Car Dealer Dan").

It's extremely annoying being in heavy traffic, but **nothing will piss someone off more than being stuck behind your slow-moving, mammoth vehicle.** The massive size of your ride will make it impossible for them to see the road ahead and safely pass you. Wherever they're going, they better not be in a rush because they're on "miserable failure time" now (NOTE: with the exception of sex and maxing out credit cards, you do nothing fast). Their annoyance will quickly turn to anger and pure **RAGE** when they are subjected to the large clouds of black exhaust smoke coming from your piece of shit vehicle's tailpipe. As they slowly become light-headed and the color of their vehicle's paint changes thanks to your black exhaust, be sure to constantly lock up your breaks only to suddenly speed forward before once again locking up your breaks (this discourages tailgating and if you get hit, it's **THEIR FAULT**... #helllllooooolawsuit). This will teach the commuter following you a valuable lesson about staying alert and not getting behind a vehicle with a bumper sticker that reads: "my other car is a meth lab" (BTW: it was either that bumper sticker or "honk for polio"). Speeding up like a lunatic to dangerous speeds, and then randomly slamming on your breaks (break checking) while no one is in front of you in the fast lane or carpool lane is just one of the simpler moves for the miserable failure on the road.

Prepping your Shit Mobile

After choosing the correctly-sized humongous vehicle, it is also important to prep your vehicle for maximum attention and annoyance for all other drivers that happen to have the unfortunate experience to be near you on the road. The terms *"shitbox," "shit wagon," "garbage cruiser," "bullshit buggy," "piece of shit," "rust bucket"*, or *"roller turd"* should apply to your new ride perfectly as other drivers encounter it. Begin by picking the perfect color. **Bright or exotic colors typically bring a lower sale price, and can significantly add to your vehicle's ability to piss fellow commuters off.** If you can't find a brightly colored vehicle, simply find one with giant rusty and gaping holes in it.

Being sideswiped on the way to work by an asshole driving a wheelchair van, wearing a leather beret, covered in vomit, smoking a three-foot Native American peace pipe, and blaring techno music **may** cause the average commuter to extend their middle finger in frustration or angrily honk their horn. To add to their anger and frustration, simply make that same wheelchair van bright orange accompanied with a large mural of two pink dolphins having sex in a tuna net painted on the side **(FYI: you can also simply spray paint, "FREE CANDY" on the side of the van as a secondary option)**. If you are unable to obtain a vehicle with an atrocious factory paint color, you'll have to take matters into your own hands (NOTE: this is NOT a masturbation reference). Simply "purchase" (steal) a few gallons of paint from your local hardware store and splash them onto your vehicle at random. The paint will splatter and run in different directions leaving your shit box vehicle looking trendy and extremely "artistic" (extremely shitty). None of the standard colors will do, so you'll need to have them mix several colors together. This is a wonderful opportunity to be creative and express your inner miserable failure (as well as your psychosis). You could mix neon green, tree bark brown, and corn yellow to produce an original "diarrhea" shade that'll keep everyone on the road guessing: *"did someone shit on that station wagon?"* Or, you could mix Panama red, midnight black, and convict orange to make your camper van appear like it's either on fire or the scene of a horrific sex cult attack crime (NOTE: both COULD BE true, you sick bastard). Other colors you could use on your car are:

- "Violent Blood Red"
- "Stomach Bile Yellow"
- "Noose Suicide Blue"
- "Meth Teeth Tan"
- "Puke Green"
- "Shit Stained Brown"
- "Infection Puss Cream"

Having a uniquely colored vehicle alone is not enough to reach maximum "shit wagon" status. Adding words, phrases, and/or depictions of various sex acts is a simple way to expand your ride's vulgar offensiveness (NOTE: DO NOT PAINT HUMANS HAVING SEX ON YOUR

VEHICLE!) This act is illegal in most states, and will only get your thirty-year-old hot pink tour bus with seventeen broken windows and a painting of an astronaut riding a unicorn on both sides, prematurely impounded (again...). **Large vehicles provide ample canvass for painting a multitude of politically incorrect murals and/or messages on your vehicle.** Don't waste this critical artistic space as its impact on the public is immeasurable (BTW: just like your heartbeat most Friday nights after the eight ball of blow). If ever you had a chance to teach society in the ways of sucking at everything and show the world a new way of delusional thinking, that time is now (AS WELL AS: the time when police raided your tax-exempt environmental preserve/pot farm on live TV)! Due to your trembling and shaking hands from alcohol withdrawal, most of your attempts to draw or paint real people often turn out looking like oddly shaped beasts with large genitals, so you should just go with an "animal sex" theme on your ride. **The sight of a bright yellow cargo van painted with a full-sized mural of a screaming giraffe taking a bong hit while mounting a Saint Bernard wearing neon green yoga pants, in the downward facing dog yoga pose is a powerful tool to teach society about the many benefits of your "miserable failure addictions"** (AGAIN: thank you, LSD and DHT). The kids on the daycare playground you repeatedly drive by (FYI: parole violation #146.2b) will both love and learn from the large painting on your oversized SUV of a gorilla wearing a purple cowboy hat while choking himself with a violin bow and shitting on a dictionary (NOTE: it would be easy to say that image is a hidden message about the dangers of learning, but it's just LSD and DMT... **again**).

If you have absolutely zero artistic ability, just stick to writing offensive, obnoxious, and cringe-worthy statements on your shit box ride. Small politically incorrect bumper stickers are an effective way of offending commuters traveling directly behind you, but to ensure that everyone on the road reads your rage-inducing messages, paint them on the front and sides, as well as the rear of your vehicle. To ensure maximum exposure, use large letters painted in bold colors. Due to your total lack of an education, and the fact that you started huffing gas after your fifth divorce, your vehicle will most likely be whittled with basic misspellings and punctuation errors. These **welcomed mistakes** should be celebrated as they are another perfect tool for projecting your desired image (**alcoholism** meets **retardation** meets **psychosis** meets an **adult diaper**). The following is a list of suggested messages and thought-provoking questions to paint on your shit mobile. They have all been proven by MANY miserable failures over the years to cause shock, disgust, anger, and a complete loss of bowel control. Choose wisely and don't be afraid to create a new original phrase of your own. Remember, nobody likes you already, so why try to make friends now? Either find the following bumper stickers and plaster them all over your ride or spray paint these phrases on your unsafe vehicle. Some classics include but are not limited to

- "The voices in my head say you're next."
- "There is a dead hooker in my trunk."
- "My crotch has itched for the last eleven years."
- "Hit me. I dare you."
- "Come ride in my love burrito."
- "XXX Nude XXX."
- "Do you like ice cream, too?"
- "Go fuck your mother."
- "I dress like a clown and I collect knives."
- "It was the only way to stop the screaming."
- "Any sexual favors - $5."
- "The demons made me do it."
- "Keep watching. The fun is just about to begin!"
- "If you can read this, watch the fuck out."
- "I hope you're recording what I'm about to do."
- "Adult swim lessons in kiddie pools filled with vodka is in the back."
- "No Pants? No Problem!"

- "I'm trying to drive fast enough to outrun my problems."
- "I drive slow because you suck balls."
- "How's my driving? Call 1-800-GO-FUCK-YOURSELF to report me."
- "Live Tonight Only... YOUR DETH!" (HOT TIP: keep this misspelling of "death" to attract new sex partners)
- "Car and health insurance are for pussies and wimps."
- "Honk if you're horny...and are willing to be ball gagged, duct taped and urinated on."
- "It smells like an outhouse in Kolkata in here."
- "It still burns. These antibiotics are bullshit."
- "CALL 1-800-WILL-BUY-DRUGS... No, just honk. I'll pull over and buy everything you have."
- "The asshole behind this wheel has been drinking."
- "Blind person driving... Just kidding, I'm only 'blind' drunk."
- "Just Paroled" (write this in soap on your rear window).
- "Want to go to heaven? Follow too close and you'll find out if you made the cut, motherfucker..."
- "I'm drunk. Pull me over."
- "I found Satan."
- "Horrible car accident straight ahead."
- "If you can read this, stay tuned, because it's going to get interesting on the road."
- "If you're a biker gang... FUCK YOU."
- "I like to piss and shit myself as I drive."

In addition to prepping the outside of your vehicle, it is equally as important to stock the inside of your shit mobile with the proper items. **It goes without saying that your ride will, at the very least, contain a full day's supply of drugs, alcohol, and pornography** (ALSO KNOWN AS: "the three amigos for the miserable failure"). There's no reason to let traveling stop you from developing stronger addictions and lose the endurance you established with your ten times per day masturbation habit (NOTE: to be the champ, you must train like a champ). Additionally, having to drive home your mobile meth lab quickly to get more crack before the hooker wakes up AGAIN is a sure way to miss a memorable moment at your kid's (DNA not confirmed, unfortunately) cowboy-themed tenth birthday party.

You'll be surprised how often a warm blanket (newspapers or cardboard boxes count) and a comfortable pillow (newspaper stuffed inside a plastic trash bag) will come in handy in your shit mobile. Additionally, thanks to your "rock and roll lifestyle" (large amounts of late-night techno music and loneliness), you're always behind on sleep (just like your child support payments). Deadlocked traffic jams provide a great opportunity to kick your feet up, grab your bedding, and take a quick cat nap. No need to set an alarm because car honks and the inevitable police presence will eventually wake you up. When the other cars begin to drive, put the car in park and take a snooze (NOTE: this scenario will cause obese truckers, out of work stockbrokers and angry soccer moms to exit their vehicles to come give you a "little chat" with various baseball bats and crowbars).

Be sure to also have a healthy collection of empty plastic bottles and/or plastic containers within arm's reach of the driver's seat at all times. Years of alcohol abuse and the resulting head injuries from drunken falls from balconies in Tijuana Mexico have made it nearly impossible for you to control your bodily functions (or formulate complex sentences). Being caught in heavy traffic is no excuse to soil your "new" sweat pants (unless you really want to), and potentially ruin the upholstery of your neon yellow fifteen passenger cargo van. If you experience a toilet emergency while on the road, having plastic bottles and various containers around is the perfect "life hack" to save the day (FYI: you should also have SEVERAL random fast food wrappers and bags, as well as a few angry feral cats and woodland critters littered throughout your car). **The toilet using method while driving works great for both sexes and is a real time saver**. Just direct your bodily excretions toward the plastic, close your eyes and hope for the best (NOTE: it won't be "the best"... it will be "messy and disgusting"). If performed in a traffic jam, this should be fairly simple, but defecating in an empty coffee can at seventy-five miles per hour while drinking a beer and texting your ex-spouse vulgar and insulting remarks is an extremely dangerous art form (NOTE: which we do not recommend). It's best to practice first before hitting the roadways. Don't worry about the smell associated with using your vehicle as a portable toilet because **your ride should essentially smell like a homeless encampment meets a Vietnamese sweatshop.** This new odor will be a great improvement over the horrendous smell of old sneakers and Indian food that's been coming from your eleven-year-old checkerboard cargo van since you purchased it.

Your "Supplies"

Far too many times has a potential new sex target slipped through your fingers because the drive between the party (the dumpster in the alley behind "The Big Burger Shack") and your house (dumpster in the alley behind the liquor store) has given them too much time to ponder their miserable life and reconsider the terrible choice they're about to make (having sex with a person they just met in an alley who also lives in an alley). It's for this reason, that every miserable failure's vehicle should be equipped with a portable "love box" for use in their many sexual adventures (FYI: mostly your tearful masturbation). Be sure your "love box" contains all the following items:

- Zip ties (in case of a full moon, or you happen to be in Tampa Bay, Florida).
- Duct tape (also in case of a full moon, or if you meet a woman named Tiffani or Nikki).
- A vintage camcorder and tripod (you'll finally get to use all those blank VHS tapes you bought at that garage sale).
- Adult toy collection (you inherited most of them when your great grandmother died, and yes, they are dishwasher safe).

- Action figure collection (your ungrateful little children won't miss their toys).
- Blindfold (because sometimes it's easier that way).
- A paper bag for your own head (because sometimes, it's less scary for your sex partner).
- Dog leash (use your imagination).
- Leather belt (to be worn when nude for attaching your flashlight and cell phone on).
- Condoms (LOL!!!! **just kidding**).
- Fake I.D. (because it's always easier that way).
- Childhood photo (to help you remember how far you've fallen in life).
- A candy cane (don't ask, just have one handy).
- Hairdryer (for pubic hair only).
- Various animal masks (for playing your favorite sex and role-play game, "zoo keeper").
- Your library of lubricants (it's extremely impressive).
- Mop and plastic sheets (for quick and easy clean-up/evidence disposal).
- Garbage bags (to stand in while taking your "golden shower" from Alex the Escort).
- Plastic wrap (definitely do not ask).
- Chocolate syrup (for your diabetes and sugar cravings).
- Prop gun and knife (to help get your point across to other motorists).
- Puke bucket (you always end up needing it from your hangover, alcohol poisoning, or eating disorder).

Having these products in your car is mandatory for the miserable failure. You should keep these in your back seat for easy access or in your trunk for security purposes.

Being a "Bad" Driver

You found the right vehicle that's at least ten years old, has over 200k miles on it, is large enough to block out the sun, ugly enough to cause seizures, and gets 4.5 miles to the gallon. In a "normal" person's hands, an automobile like this vehicle would never be utilized properly and could end up being only a minor annoyance to the average commuter. **However, in your miserable hands, the oddly-colored ancient shit mobile you purchased for $30 and a can of chewing tobacco becomes the perfect tool for wreaking havoc on the highway**! While it's important to have the correct tool, it's equally important to know how to use that tool the right way. In the simplest terms, you're going to be "that person." That "person" **who is always driving twenty miles under the speed limit** in the fast lane during morning rush hour (a heroic and CLASSIC move for miserable failures worldwide). You need to be that "person" who sees lane divider lines, posted speed limits, school zones, and one-way roads as only being mere **"suggestions"** (BE SURE to have your sixth public defender on speed dial on your burner phone). You should also be that "person" who manages to lose every "drag race" they start despite being the only driver who knows they're actually racing. You need to be that "person" who plays their radio at ten times the normal volume with all the windows down while "singing" (screaming) incorrect song lyrics laced with EXTREME racial and sexual vulgarities and profanities.

Remember, a miserable failure can make one of their biggest impacts on society while on the road. Do not take this opportunity lightly. Hone your craft, practice your horrible driving skills, and treat driving while wearing an over-sized orange foam cowboy hat and drinking rubbing alcohol mixed with mouthwash like the art form it truly is! Continually review the following miserable driving techniques and don't be afraid to create your own. For safety purposes, it is suggested that you practice all of these **shit maneuvers** in a "less than crowded" parking lot, or neighbor's front lawn before hitting the roadways. Happy driving and enjoy the hemorrhoids!

"The Mysterious Blinker"

Are you going to turn? Switch lanes? Nobody knows!!! Keep these sons of a bitches guessing! Driving behind someone who's unknowingly left their turn signal on can be really annoying for everyone on the road. Traveling behind a miserable failure who, especially during times of heavy traffic, intentionally turns on their blinker and leaves it on for several miles at a time is **rage-inducing**! Here's how the "mysterious blinker" move works for miserable failures. When on a multiple lane interstate highway, position your vehicle in the center lane. At random times, turn on your turn signal making fellow commuters aware of your "intention" to travel into the left or right lanes. You can either leave it on **without turning** or turn the **OPPOSITE** direction that you have indicated you'd like to turn (NOTE: this really keeps these other drivers guessing and scared shitless). Additionally, tap your breaks whenever you pass a side street or exit. This will aid in convincing your fellow commuters that you're about to turn. **Of course, you have no intention of ever turning**, but if you do, make sure you turn the opposite direction that you've indicated you're turning. You can also randomly slam on your brakes as you take the next right turn at fifty miles per hour WITHOUT using your blinker. The choice is yours! Here are the three basic RULES for the miserable failure when using a blinker.

- Option #1 - When using your turn signal, turn the opposite direction than you've indicated.
- Option #2 - Keep your turn signal on the entire time you're driving and DO NOT EVER TURN.
- Option #3 - Randomly turn like a maniac when your turn comes WITHOUT using a turn signal.

Utilizing one or all of the above techniques is strongly encouraged for the miserable failure. After all, you are the "king (or queen) of the road." These other drivers should be happy to witness your elegant grace and presence on the several highways and interstates that you drive on.

So, make sure that you leave a "miserable failure memorable road experience" with other drivers by adhering to the blinker rules listed above!

"Getting Horny"

You probably failed miserably at both guitar and piano lessons (NOTE: you were required to **wear** pants and **not** smoke cigarettes). You were probably banned for life from your local music store (you vomited in their entranceway and tried to steal a cello). Despite those setbacks, a musical genius still lives **DEEP** inside you (just like your horrendous staph infections). Finally, you realized that the instrument that suits you best is the one you've been playing all along, your CAR HORN! "Rock and Roll Hall of Shame" here we come! Here's how to properly use your car horn... Put on your headphones and crank up the techno! Like drums and triangles, the car horn is best used as an accompanying base instrument to accent and highlight great beats of the horrendous music. Since you'll be hearing the lead music though headphones, to others, all of your jamming will sound like long, chaotic, non-rhythmic, shit-filled, random, and psychotic car horn honks. **Add some random, high speed, non-signaled lane changes into the mix and you're sure to have a morning commute for all to remember!** Honking does not just apply to jamming techno while wearing your headphones. Randomly honk your horn while driving past cop cars, ambulances speeding down the highway and especially through school zones. See a pretty girl (or guy)? Honk! Running a red light? Honk like a lunatic while avoiding getting t-boned by the speeding semi-truck with the green light. It is suggested that you honk your horn a minimum of 400 times each day you drive. Finally, always make sure you LAY on your car horn when you drive home high on cocaine at 3:00 in the morning (shouting, *"woohoo!"* with your head hanging out the window is a great move to accompany this).

"Slow Turn Terror"

Stopping at random or slowing to a nearly immeasurable speed in moving traffic is a dangerous maneuver and will likely cause an accident (#GOALS). Despite this obvious truth, no traffic laws exist to prevent or punish this awful driving behavior. In fact, if you were to rear-end someone who chose to stop at random or slow to a snail in moving traffic, **you would be at fault**. Even if someone is fortunate enough not to have a collision, they'll still have the joy of having to come to a complete stop while some pot-bellied asshole (wink wink... **you**) turns into the "Taco Barn" for the third time today (NOTE: the vegetarian burrito is surprisingly good as long as you add the jalapeno sauce). Here's how "slow turn terror" works... Your exit may be three miles away, but you better slow down... **NOW**. Whenever you finally do make it to your turn off, be sure to come nearly to a complete stop before turning (it'd be a shame to spill another margarita). The poor tortured soul who's following directly behind you, and all those following them will be forced to stop and smell the roses before they continue on down the road in pure blind rage anger (NOTE: those are not roses they're smelling, it's the mixture of oil and methane coming from your engine). The annoyance level of this behavior will only grow when you don't actually turn, and instead speed ahead to attempt the same shit maneuver at the next exit. "Flipping the bird" and/or "raising the roof" are both great hand gestures to add insult to injury when performing this infuriating move on other drivers. Sometimes, simply stopping your car in the middle of horrible rush hour traffic, putting it in park, shutting off the engine and taking a quick nap is also a great move.

"Rush Hour Horror"

Every Halloween people dress up in spooky costumes and try to scare their friends. For the miserable failure, behind the wheel, every single day is Halloween! This particular move works great on unsuspecting cross fitters, vegans, Satanists, and feminists. You'll need to borrow the fake blood; a prop gun and fake knifes from your "love box" as well as have a piece of raw chicken for this one (FUN FACT: you

SHOULD by now have a collection of rotten meat in your linen closet). Here's how "rush hour horror" works... It's best to attempt this when in a horrible traffic jam or waiting for a stoplight to change. With your driver's window down, begin screaming loudly at your crotch area. Do this so loudly and in such an animated way that you quickly attract the attention of the drivers positioned next to you in the other lanes. Yell things at your crotch like:

- *"You're not getting away this time!"*
- *"This one deserves to live."*
- *"It's all your fault again."*
- *"Chew with your mouth closed."*
- *"I'm better off without you."*
- *"Stop itching or you die."*
- *"You forced me to do this."*

Consider that your fellow commuters will not be able to see your crotch, but will be able to see the prop knife or gun in your hands. If you're using your prop knife, begin to hack forcefully at your lap while squeezing some concealed fake blood onto your fists. If you're using your prop gun, simply fire off a few caps in the direction of your lap. With each hack or shot, do not yell out in pain or discomfort to better "sell" the theatrics of your behavior. Instead, with each seemingly painful action, moan in ecstasy and say things like:

- *"Yes!"*
- *"It's over!"*
- *"I'm free again!"*
- *"It's so warm."*
- *"Bye, bye old friend."*

Finally, with all eyes on you, raise your fake blood-soaked hands and toss the piece of raw chicken out of the window before speeding away with a psychotic-looking grin on your face. **The commuters who wit-**

nessed your outburst are going to think that you lost a kidney or cut off your creepy conjoined twin brother, Timmy. You're also giving these fuckers a story that they can tell for the rest of their lives as well as providing them nightmares that they will be discussing with their therapists next week.

"The Breakdown"

Much like your conniption fits, psychological meltdowns, and nervous "breakdowns," your automobile should also "break down." Your vehicle could be leaking transmission fluid, burning a quart of oil every thirty miles, and have severely bald, illegal, and DANGEROUS tires on it when you bought it. That was six months ago, and now your shit wagon should be even **worse**. Another breakdown is coming (NOT a reference to your mental breakdowns in which you strip naked and pretended to be a time traveler from the planet Pluto), and this time it's not going to waste! Here's how "the breakdown" works. The best location for a breakdown is always a busy parking lot. There's a better than average chance of this happening since you routinely take slow late-night rides through the poorly lit parking lots near porn shops, weight loss clinics, and halfway houses (because it's easier than online dating). Additionally, you won't have to worry about being hit by fast-moving traffic, and there's a high probability that you'll get the opportunity to expose large numbers of the general public to the awesome ways of the miserable failure.

Begin by ensuring that your vehicle stops moving and halts in the middle of everything. Do your best to block as much drivable space as possible. If you're able to position your broken-down shit wagon correctly, you should be able to prevent several other drivers from moving their vehicles out of their parking spots (FYI: blocking people from backing out of their parking spots is a MANDATORY behavior that we fully and completely expect and demand that you employ on a daily basis). When your hot pink conversion van finally comes to rest, make no attempt to assess the reason for the breakdown (also, do not put out the fire coming from the hood). Simply get out of your vehicle while finishing your fifth of tequila and walk away. Go sneak into another movie (the adult theater), take a nap at the park (NOTE: no one will recognize you with your clothes on), or grab a bite to eat (rummage through a dumpster looking for half-eaten doughnuts). Just don't be anywhere near your no longer functioning shit box on wheels. This is sure to at least inconvenience, and hopefully piss off someone royally (if **you** have to suffer with **you** then so do **they**...). With any luck, a tow truck will eventually be sent to take away your four-wheeled problem, and all the evidence contained within. If the tow truck does not come, simply take your keys, grab your case of beer, collect the illegal pharmaceutical pills you bought on the street and hitchhike home (NOTE: when you return, your car will be missing in action).

"The Pirate Ship"

Thanks to your odd passion for maritime law, eye patches, rum, prostitutes, stealing, poor hygiene, hook hands, and swashbuckling, **the pirate life should be an intricate part of YOUR life!** Now, when performing this maneuver, it's best to get fully into character by wearing the sexy pirate costume from your love box. Be sure to say *"argh," "shiver me timbers," "avast ye matey,"* and *"ahoy"* as often as possible, and appear to have out of control scabies (pirates and antibiotics don't mix). Here's how "the pirate ship" works. When stopped in traffic, attempt to position your shit wagon door to door with the vehicle next to you. Before traffic begins to move again, quickly put on your sexy pirate costume, and take several more shots of rum (it'll count as your lunch). Retrieve the 6ft wooden plank you normally travel with or the extension ladder in the back that came free with the van (FYI: best deal EVER). Slide your plank or ladder out the window of your vehicle and into the **unsuspecting person's car** next to you. It's best to find a vehicle stopped in traffic with the window down. If the day's forecast is causing everyone to drive with their windows up, just use the end of your plank or ladder to break their glass (have your plastic sword and fake hook hand ready because breaking someone's window really gets their attention fast). As long as traffic still isn't moving, climb across your plank or ladder toward the person's vehicle who's next to you. Then, like all the pirates that came before you, board their vessel and begin to loot and plunder your way throughout their entire car. **Loose change, random documents in their glove compartment, and items in the back seat are great grabs.** Make sure you hold onto YOUR new possessions as you climb the plank again to your vehicle (NOTE: at this point, you might be bleeding from the knife wound you sustained from the single soccer mom, or even treating the gunshot wound from the asshole father who has a conceal and carry gun permit). Any type of injuries only add to your pirate legendary maneuver. When you get back to your car, pull in the plank or the ladder, scream to the driver, *"Davy Jones' locker!"* and speed away down the road.

"Bass Ackwards"

This move is very simple and is just like your life. In this driving maneuver, you need to go backwards. Here is how "bass ackwards" works... This is a really fun move! Instead of driving normal, simply drive in REVERSE as much as humanly possible when you're out and about in your extremely unsafe vehicle. After you back out of the methadone clinic, keep that piece of shit in reverse and drive to your next stop (probably the crack house or homeless encampment). The looks you're going to get from the other drivers are going to be PRICELESS. Feel free to wave at people and attempt to make small chat about the weather and other mundane topics when stopped at red lights.

Another way of doing something backwards is by driving in reverse, the **wrong direction**, down one-way streets and interstate ramps. **The expression on the other drivers' faces are going to be epic as you come speeding down a wrong way, one-way alley doing sixty miles per hour backwards in your shitbox** (NOTE: do not hit the other cars and try to avoid them). Also remember that you're "perfecting" your reverse driving skills. When the cops come and take you away in handcuffs, try to walk backwards when being escorted to their patrol car.

"Merger Maniac"

Poor merging causes even the nicest drivers on the roads to become mouth-foaming and homicidal maniacs at others who do not merge with the speed of everyone else. When merging onto a street, the law states that you must be going around the same speed as the other drivers. We do not want you to adhere to this rule. Here is how "merger maniac" works... When entering an interstate where the cars are driving seventy miles per hour, make sure **YOU** merge at forty miles per hour. As people scream past you, unroll your window and yell out, *"you fucking crazy lunatics, slow down!"* The same can be true for merging onto roads when all other drivers are going twenty miles per hour. In this case, you should go at least sixty miles per hour as you merge. If there is traffic, drive on the shoulder like a complete asshole while screaming profanities at the other drivers. Merging like a complete and total asshole is a great step in perfecting the art of driving for miserable failures. You're going to cause havoc on the road and be the reason for many traffic jams (EXCELLENT!).

"The Swivel"

This particular move can only be used in multiple lanes on interstates and freeways-mostly. This move allows you to be the "cop" and slow down the other drivers in traffic. Here is how "the swivel" works... Start in the far-right lane and swerve over slightly all the way over to the carpool lane or the farthest left lane. As you do this, put your hazard lights on. Cars should be honking and slamming on their brakes by now. Simply give them the middle finger salute and gingerly drive your car back over to the far-right lane. During this move, DO NOT use your turn signal, and when the cops light you up, DO NOT PULL OVER

(SEE ALSO: section on high-speed police chases). The swivel will cause severe traffic for others and you're more than likely going to get arrested... again (#happydaysarehereagain).

"The Sloth"

Sloths are animals that move VERY slow. This classic driving move is very simple. Simply get into the carpool lane or the fast lane and drive twenty miles an hour **under** the speed limit. This maneuver causes uncontrollable road rage for other drivers and will turn even the most mild-mannered, God-fearing granny into a psychotic, screaming, raving mad lunatic towards you.

"Litter Critter"

Miserable failures litter uncontrollably. Your car should look like a dumpster (and smell like one too). Your car should contain various empty beer and liquor bottles, used heroin needles, fast food restaurant wrappers, empty soda bottles, and full bags of trash you stole from your wealthy neighbor. Simply find the nicest neighborhood in town (gated communities work the best) and proceed to do a few laps tossing out all of your trash and litter throughout the road and their fancy neighborhood. When you get pulled over during this and get a $1000 ticket from a cop, simply laugh at him when he hands it to you, rip it up and litter it again out of the window near his feet.

"The Unicorn U-Turn"

This classic move was first invented and used in Las Vegas by a miserable failure known as "Fred, the Fuck Up." This move is effective in any traffic situation for the miserable failure and causes the various motorists around you massive amounts of road rage, inappropriate hand gesture usage, and profanity-riddled insults hurled at you from their cars. When you're driving on a road, if there is a turn lane, get into the left turn lane (don't use your blinker of course). Without giving a care in the world (by now you should be smoking a cigarette or finishing a line of cocaine on your dashboard) proceed to pull a U-turn so fast that you miss the lane of traffic that you're trying to turn in and drive along the side of the road on the shoulder. This *"cocksucking, motherfucking, asshole move"* will no doubt cause the other driver's around you to call the police and report you (here we come DUI #13!). While you're pulling your illegal or dangerous U-turn, unroll your window and shout out at the top of your lungs, *"I'm a unicorn! I'm a unicorn! I'm a unicorn!"* The nearby drivers and other pedestrians will all start to take videos of you and you'll have another online viral video "hit." The dangerous U-turn combined with your, *"I'm a unicorn"* phrase will also, no doubt give commuters a hilarious story to tell for the rest of their lives.

"Fast Eddie"

This is a simple one. Drive as fast as possible speeding like a crazy person as you out drive and speed past the other "slow ass" drivers. If you're stuck in traffic, take the shoulder and let those tires burn! Feel free to drive on the side of the road or simply pass dangerously cutting off other cars during your reckless driving shenanigans.

"Manual Maniac"

Miserable failures should not know how to drive a manual stick shift in a car. It is for this reason that we encourage the miserable failure to "borrow" (A.K.A. "joy ride") a friend's (or stranger's) stick shift, manual car to use. When you get into the car, you will see three pedals. The clutch should be on your far left, followed by the brakes, followed by the gas on the far right. Most normal people who know how to drive a stick shift car, know to shift only while pressing the clutch and shifting at the appropriate speeds for the particular gear. Normal people also know to shift from one, to two, to three, and so forth. A miserable failure does not drive like this in a manual stick shift car. **A mis-**

erable failure completely ignores the clutch while driving and shifting at random, haphazard times. In fact, feel free to make laser and explosive noises as you violently "shift" the car (HINT: those grinding noises means the transmission is fucked) while fantasizing that you're the commander on a space force ranger ship. Rev the engine as much as possible by putting the pedal to the metal. This non-shifting and non-clutch usage will cause the engine to begin to smoke, as well as the car to violently shake. Feel free to randomly move the shifter into any gear you want forcibly while driving. At this point, your car will begin to make squealing noises and if you're lucky, it might catch on fire (hellllooooooo recall and lawsuit!).

"Jousting Joker"

For this driving technique, you're going to need a really long stick. Break off a tree branch at the local conservation park and make it into a jousting stick. Remove all of the smaller branches so that it is one, straight and long stick. To add to your set up, you might want to put a small, metal trash can on your head (be sure to cut out eye holes so you look like a medieval knight in shining armor). Next, find a busy shopping parking lot in the middle of a Saturday or Sunday afternoon. Drive around the parking lot very slow and stick your jousting stick out of the window. When you see a car driving towards you, speed up a little and drive towards the vehicle coming at you. Stick your head out the window and aim your jousting stick at the car. As you get closer, shout out, *"en garde!"* This will cause the other driver to swerve to avoid you. If they **don't** swerve out of the way, you can thank them later for your new hook for a hand (SEE ALSO: the "hook for a hand excuse"). When, not "if," but **WHEN** the other car comes back in the parking lot to hunt you down, get out of the car, and begin to urinate on yourself before the beating that you're going to take can begin.

"The Alligator"

When you follow people driving down the road, make sure that you **RIDE THEIR ASS** in your shit mobile. This can be accomplished by keeping a **maximum** distance of one foot between the front bumper of your car and the rear bumper of their car. Sometimes people will take notice and give you the famous, "brake check." When this happens, do not slow down. Also, when you get into a fender bender, do not pull over (BTW: you'll need the excitement of a police chase later on in the evening to help sober you up). The alligator should be used in dangerous rush hour interstate drives as well as old country road Sunday trips. Doing the alligator will eventually end up very badly for the miserable failure. You generally will end up with a "following too closely" ticket and a totaled piece of shit car (SEE ALSO: section on hitchhiking and hotwiring your grandmother's car).

"Breaking Bad"

This technique is the opposite of the alligator. In this technique, you should randomly brake check the cars that are driving behind you (FYI: it should also be tough for them to see your car through the plumes of smoke and smog emitting from your shit box ride). This technique REALLY pisses the people off and if you're lucky, you'll end up getting your nose broken during a one-sided fistfight beat down session along the side of the road.

While you're driving down the road, make sure that you randomly brake check all unsuspecting motorists that you can (your brakes should squeak and squeal due to your lackadaisical car maintenance as well). Remember that **THEY** will be getting the ticket and it's **THEIR** responsibility when they total your shit hole ride (NOTE: if you play your cards right, their insurance will pay for a rental car for you). Upon being rear-ended, a miserable failure should immediately start to complain and scream about neck pain (hellllooooooo **LAWSUIT** and free massages #insurancefraud). You should also wait to exit the car unless a "slip and fall," ambulance-chasing, dirty lawyer shows up.

Fun Things to do While Driving

The following is an incomplete list of things you could be doing as you drive. This is not a complete list, they're just some of the most classic things miserable failures have employed over the years.

- Drive in the carpool lane with a blow-up sex doll (when the cops ask you why you're driving alone, simply respond with *"my imaginary friend, Tom, is riding shotgun."* You can also tell the officer that you self-identify as two people and tell him to *"back the fuck off..."*).
- Hang your left foot and arm out the window while driving (NOTE: the sign of your horrible, disgusting, foot fungus and toe jam will cause other drivers near you the uncontrollable urge to vomit).
- Pick your nose and flick your boogers on the person's car next to you at the stoplight while yelling, *"gooooooaaaaaaalllllll!!!"*
- At a red light, ask the person next to you to roll down their window. Then proceed to ask if you can borrow some French mustard.
- Leave your headlights completely off while driving at night.
- Stick your left arm out the window and flip off everyone and every car during your third consecutive trip to the liquor store.
- Flicking your cigarette butts and marijuana joints out the window as you aim for the back of the guy's pick-up truck next to you.
- As you drive down the road, toss out each beer bottle up in the air in the middle of the road (other drivers will think it's raining beer and liquor bottles).
- As these road bike-riding assholes approach you to try to drive in YOUR lane, open up your door and keep it open and

propped up with your leg (NOTE: you get five points for each bicyclist asshole that runs into your car door).

- Lay your seat back and steer the car with your feet as you take selfies for social media purposes.
- "Pulling a Vegas." Put your car on cruise control and stand up through your moon roof (if your car doesn't have a moon roof, we suggest that you start to learn how to weld and use a blowtorch).

You can do a variety of things while driving. You want to have fun! Enjoy yourself! After all, life is way too short to obey the rules of the road. So, use your imagination, you miserable failure piece of shit!

Asshole Parking

Miserable failures **CANNOT** park a car worth a shit. When pulling into a parking space, make sure you take up TWO parking spaces by parking your vehicle right in the middle of the white line that separates them. You can also park diagonally taking up two parking spots. People will call you an asshole and spit on your car when they see it parked like this. These people should secretly be thanking you because miserable failures ALWAYS give other cars door dents (FYI: swinging your door open without any regard for the car next to you is MANDATORY for all miserable failures).

A miserable failure should also park their car illegally in red zones, in front of fire hydrants, in handicapped spots, in reserved places, and in tow away locations. In fact, we encourage miserable failures to parallel park their cars on top of the curb wherever they go. Drive like a maniac through a busy grocery store parking lot. Then, proceed to launch your car up on the curb. Once there, keep it there. When you come out of the store with your booze and cigarettes, you might have a parking ticket (which you WILL NOT EVER pay), or your car might be towed ("being towed" and "miserable failure" go together like "sneakers" and "running").

A miserable failure should also double park and park perpendicular behind other cars, thus blocking people in. A miserable failure is also encouraged to park in the middle of a busy interstate during rush hour **(since you don't wake up before noon, it will have to be the 5:00 rush hour).** A miserable failure can also keep others on their toes by parking their piece of shit car without putting it in park, and instead putting it in neutral (HINT: your public defender will be getting a call after you park like this, #outcomes). Feel free to also have SEVERAL hand-written notes (in crayon) with you at all times to leave on the other cars. When you park your car, grab these notes and place them on the windshields of the other cars as you make your way into the store. Some suggestions for what to write on the notes include but are not limited to:

- "Don't start your car, there is a ticking sound coming from it."
- "Nice car, motherfucker." (with the optional key scratch)
- "I have a midget tied up in your trunk."
- "Let's see those titties."
- "Guess what? My car is a piece of shit."
- "Can I please make love to your car?"
- "Don't back up, there are several nails behind your tires."
- "Good luck with those breaks."

Hitchhiking 101

Hitchhiking has, unfortunately, had a very **"negative stigma"** associated with it (NOTE: sort of like your career, hygiene, marriage, friendships, and family relations). Hitchhiking is a taboo, dangerous activity to engage in. It is for that main reason, why we **STRONGLY encourage the miserable failure to partake in said activity** (FYI: if you get kidnapped and pistol-whipped at gunpoint by an obese lunatic serial killer while you're hitchhiking.... SCORE!!!!).

First of all, you must remember that all people who would stop alongside of the road to pick you up for a ride are completely and totally fucked up as well. This is good as it presents itself with a "match made in heaven" event for the miserable failure. When a nut job picks up a miserable failure hitchhiking, sooner or later the police are sure to be involved in some way. When a miserable failure hitchhikes wearing a robe, slippers, and boxers, there is a good chance that one of the following people will pick you up. They include:

- Truck-driving serial killers
- Escaped mental patients in stolen cars
- Angry, road-raging lunatics who just want to use the carpool lane
- A young gang looking for their next "initiation activity"
- Drunk drivers (people on narcotics also qualify in this category)
- Off duty pimps
- Human traffickers
- Transvestite vampires (don't ask, but they're out there...)

Slogans for Signs

When you start out hitchhiking, you can either just give a universal thumb's up sign, signifying your complete and total willingness to let a stranger pick you up alongside the road. Or, you can get creative with some custom signs written in black marker on cardboard. Some of the sayings on your hand-written sign might include:

- "I'm a closet tickler. Pick me up for a good laugh."

- "I promise that I won't kill you or steal your car. I just need a lift."
- "I will go down on you for a ride."
- "I'll let you use my body like a billiard table if you pick me up."
- "I am mentally handicapped. Please give me a ride in your vroom, vroom thing."
- "You can throw me in the trunk. Just give me a lift."
- "I am unarmed and intoxicated. Please pick me up."

When you do get picked up hitchhiking, make sure that the driver knows how desperate you are. Discuss your unemployment, depression, drug and alcohol addiction, and your current "financial situation." Feel free to let out a few farts while proudly proclaiming them as your property (describing the awful smell permeating from your ass, in great detail is also a fantastic way to start off the free ride that you just received). **As a miserable failure, you should discuss any subject that either makes the stranger uncomfortable, or that makes you look like the total and complete fuck up that you are.** Some of the topics of conversation for hitchhiking roads trips include (but are not limited to):

- Discuss the ways you've thought about killing yourself.
- Discuss your successful history of burping the entire alphabet in one breath after chugging a six-pack of beer.
- Discuss your cough syrup addiction.
- Discuss in gruesome and great detail the various ways that people can die in traffic accidents on the highway.
- Discuss your intimate knowledge of the history of roadside serial killers (if you don't know any, just make shit up).

Fight Crazy with Crazy

As you "wear down your welcome" in the stranger's car, you're either going to be asked to leave the car, or you'll creep them out so much, they might even just hand you over their wallet! These first outcomes are only for non-violent people who pick you up. The flip side of this coin is that the driver might be even CRAZIER and deranged than you are (goody, goody). We must strongly caution the miserable failure to watch out for the crazies (not because you don't enjoy being physically assaulted) but because the last thing a miserable failure wants is to end up in a body bag, dead along the side of a road. **We want you to live a long, painful, and not so prosperous life being a miserable failure.** Messing around with crazy, lunatic, psychopaths is a sure way to get you killed. Therefore, we must encourage the miserable failure to always act crazier than the nut job behind the wheel. If the driver pulls out a gun, laugh at him and explain your DEEP and internal desire to die (BTW: you'll be safe after this, don't you worry). **If the driver tries to punch you or hit you in some way, start punching yourself in the head instead as you shout out inappropriate obscenities and vulgarities.** If the driver pulls out a knife to strike you, rip open your dirty robe and tell him, *"stab me in the heart, so I can go live with Satan in the eternal depths of hell"* (NOTE: again, doing so, WILL in fact keep you alive). The basic point is simple. If you cross paths with a crazy person while hitchhiking, make sure you act crazier than they are. This will keep your ass alive so that you can continue hurting yourself emotionally, spiritually, and physically over the next several decades.

Ride Sharing and Cabs

Due to your **several DUIs** as well as your car being impounded (PRAISE the good Lord), you'll be walking (like a bum), riding a bike (like a drunk) and hitchhiking (like a sociopath) your way through the various dangerous parts of the city to complete your weekly dice game with your bookie and your coke dealer(s). However, you're probably going to need other forms of transportation to get you around town to visit your tarot card reader and personal exorcist (NOTE: buses, subways, and hot-wiring cars will be discussed in another section). Now let's get your broke ass to wherever you need to be, shall we?

Ride Sharing

Let's start at the beginning concerning your relationship with all of the ride share services available. First of all, your passenger rating should be less than one star when using any ride sharing service **(BTW: your excessive projectile vomiting in the back of each car while you're blacked out drunk, as well as your consistent racist jokes are probably going to be the main causes of your poor rating).** It should also be noted that a miserable failure's credit cards FREQUENTLY get rejected, thus preventing you from engaging in said transportation. Furthermore, due to your VERY LATE and overdue cell phone bill, you might no t have access to your phone for using ride sharing services anyway. However, if you are somehow able to still have an active ride share account (by some miracle), you need to follow the following steps as close to them as possible.

- **Step 1 - "The Arrival."** When your driver shows up, be as drunk and high on illegal drugs (or prescription drugs) as possible. **The more completely and totally FUCKED UP you are, the better stories you'll be providing your driver for MANY years to come.** Next, ask if YOU can drive the car. After your request is denied, walk around their car and critique (in detail, like an insane food critic berating a rookie chef) all of the subtle abnormalities of the driver's car. Essentially, you should point out all of the scratches, dings, nicks, dents, and dirty parts of their car. Make sure to mock them and openly laugh at them as you walk around the automobile pointing out all of these blemishes on their ride (NOTE: feel free to kick the bumper to "check for sturdiness" or spit on the windshield to "clean it"). You should also never sit in the back seat. Sitting in the back seat makes you feel like royalty. You, as a miserable failure are not royalty, you're a peasant and a commoner. Make sure to sit in the front seat (BTW: this position also gives you the opportunity to offer sexual favors in exchange for cash from the driver). Next, cross your arms and make play-by-play color commentary on your driver's driving abilities. No matter how small of an infraction, make sure that you point it out and inform them about their shitty driving. Do this by screaming out random noises at the top of your lungs. As the ride begins, feel free to try and grab the wheel like a lunatic as they drive your sorry ass to your final destination. Doing the latter will no doubt cause your rating to go down even further and the police will probably be involved at some point during your ride.

- **Step 2 - "The Ride."** As you roll along with your driver, feel free to enjoy a few cans of beer (NOTE: shotgunning them will ruin the car and leave you and the driver smelling like a dirty bar). We also recommend lighting up a cigarette, a joint, or your crack pipe as you stroll down the road. Make sure you make small talk with the driver. Some of the topics of conversation should include porn, lactation, torture, and bestiality. Going into great and gruesome detail on those topics will no doubt scare the living shit out of your driver.
- **Step 3 - "The Delivery."** Before you leave the car, try to steal the driver's car charger, air freshener, or anything from their glove compartment. Also, shout obscenities out loud like a lunatic as you leave the car. Remark on how bad of a driver they were and even make a few threats as "jokes." By now, your case of beer should be almost empty. Make sure you use the driver's car as your own personal garbage truck. Leave those empty beer cans and cigarette butts on the floorboard of their car. Rate the driver with a one-star rating, flip them off and shout out incoherent, mumbling curse words as you stumble drunk away.

Taking a Cab

"Cab rides" and a "miserable failure" go together like cocaine and vodka (SEE ALSO: drugs and alcohol section on "vodcaine"). This basically means that miserable failures LOVE cab rides because of their suspended driver's license as well as their MANY drinking problems (DUIs, towed car, totaled ride, impounded automobile, etc.).

To begin with, when the cab arrives to pick you up from the methadone clinic, ask the cabbie if you can ride in the trunk. When they deny your unusual request, jump on top of their cab and start screaming bullshit nonsensical phrases. Finally, sit in the back seat and make outrageous comments on how bad the cab smells. Openly burp and fart in the back seat as you finish your fifth of gin. While you're polishing off your latest bottle of booze, feel free to practice your racist, offensive, disgusting, repulsive, and insensitive "stand-up comedy routine" with the driver. Start off with any racist jokes and move on from there. **Once you start your comedy skit, the cabbie is probably going to be pulling over to 1.) kick you out of the cab and 2.). to beat your sorry ass.** Cab rides can ALSO offer the miserable failure a chance to practice the art of vomiting out of the backseat window during your hangover ride home from your buddy, "Crack Head Larry's" shack. Simply hang your head out of the back of the right window (don't use the left window, because you can't live as a miserable failure in a horrible and painful way if you don't have a head). Put three fingers down your throat (channel your eating disorder) and let it rip! If you have a cell phone, take it out and snap a selfie of you the moment you start to vomit. After your racism and vomiting, your cab ride will more than likely be coming to an end. As you're getting kicked out of the cab, take off all of your clothes and start yelling *"rape"* at the cab driver. Once you're out of the vehicle, smack your own ass and run away without paying.

Freebies

Using cabs is a good move because a miserable failure can get MANY free rides. Below, we'll explain how to accomplish this FANTASTIC move. The cab won't charge you until you've reached your destination. When you arrive at your destination, you'll have around five seconds to MOVE YOUR ASS. Five seconds is a perfect amount of time for the miserable failure to run away from the car to avoid payment **(NOTE: running in slippers is going to slow you down, so we encourage you to wear your Velcro shoes that you were given during your time in the mental institution).** Sooner or later, the more cab rides you don't pay for eventually, you will get caught by either the police or a quick-footed cab driver with an anger problem and a tire iron. Getting caught means another weekend in the county jail with all of your old pals (SCORE!!!). Getting FREE cab rides is an essential part of being a miserable failure, so take advantage of your cab rides and never pay for the trip.

How to Ride a Bike

If you've been following our step-by-step guide to becoming a complete and total miserable failure, by now you should not be driving a car. This could be because the police for impounded your car (or put a boot on your car) for probably one of the following reasons:

- Your 300 unpaid parking tickets.
- Having no insurance on the car.
- Having an expired driver's license.
- Your multiple DUIs.
- Your 150 unpaid speeding tickets.

Although you might not be able to drive a car legally, a miserable failure can still hitchhike, hot wire a car, take public transportation, call a cab, or book a ride share service. However, another way to get to where you need to go (the welfare office or your ex's house) is through the use of bicycles. Riding a bike is a great option for the miserable failure (NOTE: if you still have the use of your legs due to your diabetes and POOR general health). Nothing screams **"BROKE ASS" like a grown adult riding a bike (high and drunk) in their bathrobe, slippers, and boxers down the street at 1:30 in the afternoon on any given Tuesday.**

Obtaining a Bike

Getting a bike is easy. If you have around $100, you can purchase a bike. If you don't have $100 (because you've used the money to purchase crack, superglue, and spray paint), just confiscate a bike from a nearby school parking lot. The type of bike DOES NOT MATTER. In fact, riding a tricycle, mountain, road, hybrid, unicycle, BMX, tandem or cruiser bike is perfectly acceptable. Go for the bikes that do not have a lock attached to the bike rack. Those are SUPER EASY to get. However, we must inform you to avoid the bikes with the "D" shaped bike lock. Those are tough to pry off of a bike rack, even with a file.

If you can't get a bike from a school, feel free to go into any large store that sells them and roll out on one. Most security guards won't be able to catch you either. Just peddle fast as you can as you ride through the store while trying not to get the belt from your robe caught in the spokes. Another way to get a bike is around your neighborhood. Walk around the neighborhood and any open garage, **help yourself**. After all, isn't life all about "finders keepers, losers weepers?" Steal a bike; because let's face it, miserable failures steal bikes in life.

Bike Riding Etiquette

First and foremost, when you ride your bike around town, **make sure you're HEAVILY intoxicated**. Feel free to ride while consuming an entire pizza, or even while chugging a fifth of rum straight from the bottle. Riding a bike is going to be super fun! The golden rule for riding bikes as a miserable failure is simple: **"ALWAYS RIDE YOUR BIKE IN THE MIDDLE OF THE ROAD, THUS CAUSING TRAFFIC AND MORE ROAD RAGE."** Every miserable failure riding a bike should "own" the road. After all, roads are for bikes and NOT CARS. We strongly encourage the miserable failure to ride their bike against traffic in the middle of the left lane and into oncoming automobiles (NOTE: a head-on collision for you means a lawsuit or permanent disfigurement, and both are highly acceptable outcomes for the miserable failure while riding a stolen bike). We also encourage the miserable failure to ride a bike with traffic, but do so in the middle of the right lane. Go slow. Make those gas-guzzling clunks of iron WAIT in line for **you**. Riding a bike like this will result in a good beating from a large group of angry motorists or you might end up getting smashed over in a hit and run scenario. Remember that YOU own the road. Flip off drivers as you light up a cigarette, crack pipe, or marijuana joint. Feel free to chug a six-pack of beer as you ride causing traffic during rush hour. When cars pass you and honk at you, feel free to let them have it! Some of the following are acceptable sayings for the miserable failure to yell at other drivers:

- *"Bikes own the road, not cars!"*
- *"Move! Get out the way, motherfucker!"* (Use your middle finger for this one.)
- *"I am drunk. I can't drive a car!"* (FREE LEGAL ADVICE: yes, you can still get a DUI from riding a bike.)
- *"Fuck you all! If you don't like it, pass me!"* (Shout this while grabbing your crotch.)
- *"I dare you to hit me or run me over!"* (If you're finished with your fifth of tequila, toss it at the car behind you whose horn keeps honking.)

- *"Get out of your car! I want to see how well you can break my windpipe."*

Being drunk, high, aggressive, abusive, abrasive, dangerous, incoherent, and combative as a bike rider are strong attributes and are very much encouraged for the miserable failure. When in doubt, always own the road by proclaiming it as yours and cause as much traffic as humanly possible (NOTE: mostly during rush hour). The outcomes are all good for the miserable failure when riding a bike and causing a ruckus. You're either going to get your teeth kicked in by a roid-raging truck driver, arrested and maced with pepper spray by a cop, or ran over by a texting soccer mom. Riding a bike for the miserable failure should feel like a joyous occasion. Take advantage of the fresh air (car exhausts) and the freedom of riding a bike semi-nude, drunk, and high.

Public Transportation

Most people that take public transportation are either 1.) poor, 2.) mentally challenged, or 3.) prohibited to operate a motor vehicle by a court order from an angry judge. A miserable failure can and should cross all of those attributes off the checklist simply because **you are ALL THREE OF THOSE**. Poor people take public transportation because they can get free rides from state and local government programs. **As a miserable failure, you damn well better be POOR and on WELFARE (by choice), so you should automatically qualify to receive these free ride vouchers on public transportation.** Mentally challenged or handicapped people also take public transportation because they're too dangerous behind the wheel of a car due to their illness or injuries. Fortunately for everyone driving on the road, the miserable failure is psychologically fucked up in many ways, thus preventing them from legally driving a car (NOTE: this is clearly outlined in MANY psychological disorder textbooks). Due to your lack of car insurance, your expired driver's license, your car being impounded, and your ankle monitoring bracelet you can't legally operate a vehicle anyway (FYI: if you're caught, you get to go back to your favorite state prison where there are five daily beatings). Below, we'll cover the two most commonly used transportation services utilized by miserable failures over the decades—buses and subway cars or trains.

Buses

Have you ever actually ridden on a public bus? A public transportation bus smells similar to the combination of a vomit-riddled car seat and the pungent body odor of a schizophrenic homeless man in an elevator. **In other words, public transportation buses SMELL LIKE SHIT.** This is ironic, as a miserable failure should not have a hard time fitting in on a bus, as that's exactly what you smell like on a daily basis (BTW: except for the days you steal loose change from the water fountain in the park, thus washing off SOME of your terrible aromas).

When you FIRST get on a bus, ask the driver if you can borrow $5. After his laughter subsides and he tells you to *"go sit your drunk ass down,"* make sure you find and sit next to the most frightened person on the bus. As you roll in drunk and high on the bus, feel free to let out a burp and a fart from underneath your dirty robe. Sit next to a person and begin to make "small talk." Feel free to talk about not-so-normal things with the person sitting next to you **(TOPICS INCLUDE: how you enjoy projectile vomiting, why you're banned from all school playgrounds and your fascination with midget pornography).** Riding a bus also gives the miserable failure more time to drink the ENTIRE bottle of vodka you brought with you while you drunk text your ex-spouse. It also allows you more time to light up your crack pipe or your black-market cigarette.

As the bus strolls down the road, make a play-by-play comments on the bus driver's driving ability. **Feel free to even walk up to the front of**

the bus (beyond the yellow line) and inform the driver on ways he can be a better bus driver. Asking if you can drive the bus is mandatory. However, it is optional if you want to try to grab the wheel of the bus (be careful as many bus drivers have police-issued nightsticks they use for self-defense). Feel free to use your time standing at the front of the bus to practice your infamous drunk dance routine. After you're threatened by the angry bus driver, walk back to another seat, asking everyone on the bus if you can borrow $5 (HINT: the more frightened and nervous a person is, the more likely you're going to get some cash from them).

Whenever the bus makes stops, while letting people off or picking up others, make sure that you bitch and complain using vulgarity and curse words on *"all of this fucking stopping."* Also, make sure you run to the front of the bus and demand that everyone who enters the bus give you the magic password. If you've been following the rules by now, the bus driver, as well as the other riders, are going to be wishing a slow and painful death upon you (good karma). If you play your cards right, you might get the opportunity of an entire angry bus mob beating the shit out of you for your poor behavior, harassment and general manners.

When (not if, but **when**) you; 1.) do get kicked off the bus by the bus driver, 2.) you make it to your stop, or 3.) the police drag your SORRY ass out of the bus as you're kicking and screaming, you need to make sure that you grab a few souvenirs along the way to your exit. The cash box containing the bus driver's money is an easy grab. Newspapers, magazines, briefcases, suitcases, purses, wallets, and handbags are also VERY smart choices. Make sure you don't leave the bus empty-handed. Remember that you're giving the other passengers a horror story that they can tell **forever**. Think about it, a person wearing a dirty white robe, filthy slippers, and nasty boxers running down the road as random people or police chase you is a great visual for everybody. Riding on a bus should be a pleasurable experience for you. Take advantage of it daily.

Subways and Trains

Whether you plan on riding the subway, the elevated train, or the light rail, the miserable failure needs to really make the most out of the trip. You, in essence, need to make the trip as memorable for everyone as possible. Before the subway car comes strolling into the tracks, make sure you stay away from the ledge to avoid falling in **(NOTE: it's tempting to commit suicide, but don't do it, as you need the pain and misery of your new "miserable failure existence").** Avoiding falling onto the tracks as a train is approaching will be difficult for you because traveling on the subway intoxicated on 100% PURE grain alcohol and on a heavy dose of oxycodone will cause you to be a little sloppier than normal as you walk around the train platform.

When you enter the subway car, the first thing you should do is to grab a hold of one of the poles and give the other passengers a striptease/lap dance show (NOTE: your pole dancing classes that you took at the local gym should kick in). Spin around the pole like an exotic dancer (this includes either the male or female miserable failure), **in fact, even feel free to give some unsuspecting people a few unrequested and unsolicited lap dances.** As the train continues on, make sure that you occupy as many seats and spread out as much as possible. Whether you're a man or a woman, make sure you do plenty of "manspreading" (taking up a lot of room in your seat) to discourage others from sitting near you (FYI: your foul odor, terrible hygiene, and dirty clothes should also help you riding solo). If there are three empty seats in a row, we encourage you to lay down, occupying all of them, and take a nap (pass out). If there are two seats in a row available, sit in the middle of them and relax. As you spread your legs, we encourage you to use some of the following expressions to the other passengers as you sprawl out.

For Males

- *"My cock and balls need some room to breathe folks."* (While gesturing towards your crotch.)
- *"Does anyone else have the uncontrollable urge to storm the driver's car and hold him at gunpoint? Or is it just me?"* (Screaming this while you pull your own hair out will add to the experience for the witnesses.)
- *"I just shit myself. I need to air out my boxers and I need a boobie in my mouth before naptime."*
- *"Anyone want to sit on daddy's lap?"* (Do this while eying single women riding the train as you lick your ashy lips while exposing your discolored, brown, crackpipe teeth.)
- *"I know it's crowded in here, but I need some room to itch my crotch due to my infestation."* (Feel free to show the man sitting next to you the crabs on your crotch as well.)

For Females

- *"I know I smell down there. I don't need any of you people reminding me of it!"* (While scratching the track marks on your forearms.)
- *"I'll show you some dirty titties if you hand over $10."* (Grab ahold of your robe top ready for the show.)
- *"Quife or a fart, it wasn't me... Or was it?"* (While smiling.)
- *"Is it time for the subway gangbang yet?"* (While getting on all fours in front of two businessmen reading their newspapers.)

Sooner or later, the passengers on the train are going to get fed up with your fucking bullshit. Some of the more dangerous people might threaten you, or (if you're lucky) they'll just beat the ever-loving shit out of you as the other passengers cheer them on and videotape it on their cell phones. Have a great time on the subway! Feel free to pleasure yourself if needed. **Also, feel free to recite Hitler's book, *Mein Kampf* verbatim and openly discuss the holocaust in great detail in the form of an award ceremony acceptance speech for your crowd.** It is also strongly encouraged that the miserable failure tries to earn some cash on the subway ride as well. You can ask each person for money, or you can try to pickpocket people (CAUTION: the latter will land you pepper-sprayed with mace by single women or the police). Sooner or later, your ride will come to an end. It is at this time that we recommend the miserable failure strip nude and do various yoga poses as you exit the train. When you leave, you're going to hear loud cheers and celebrations from everyone on the train. If you hear the applause and the excitement from your ex-fellow passengers because you're gone from the train, you have done your job as a miserable failure.

Getting Around Faking Being Physically Handicapped or Mentally Challenged

A miserable failure is such a worthless sack of shit, that pretending to be handicapped or mentally challenged (or both TOGETHER) are great ways to get you a one-way ticket down the fiery path to the gates of hell to burn for all eternity (NOTE: this is only after you've been beaten to death in a Mexican jail soccer prison riot). Only a real lowlife, scumbag, fuckface, cocksucker would fake being handicapped or fake being mentally challenged to get through life. Since the miserable failure is such a pathetic cocksucker, faking these two horrible life circumstances are highly recommended for you. Remember, you are a miserable fucking failure, so act accordingly, asshole...

The "Mentally Challenged Excuse"

Let's face it, since you are a miserable failure, you're pretty much mentally handicapped and psychologically ill already (years of self-inflicted mental and physical abuse will do that to someone). However, we want to focus on PRETENDING to be mentally challenged in order to get what you want in life for free. The first rule of pretending to be mentally handicapped is knowing how and when to properly use the "mentally challenged excuse." You need to use this excuse for any legal situation you get yourself into, as it provides a great way "out" of your current predicament. Got caught stealing bras and panties at the sex shop on a motorized scooter? During your court hearing, make sure you drool and mumble incoherent phrases as you twitch. Sometimes, you won't need to fake shaking, as we encourage the miserable failure to drink as much booze and consume as many narcotics as you can before your court proceedings commence **(FYI: if you're on the right combination of alcohol and drugs, this should also help you fake being mentally challenged, so see the "alcohol and drugs" section(s) for some good concoctions.)** Also, your excuse and legal defense should be centered around the fact that you're "mentally challenged" and that you didn't know what you were doing. Want to expose and piss yourself on the elevator ride up to the second floor of the mall? Let 'er rip! Want to strip nude in the middle of the park and fly a kite? When the police arrest you, tell them that you're "mentally handicapped." However, you must be careful to not **overuse** the "mentally challenged excuse" or you'll find yourself locked away in a nuthouse for the rest of your life (CLAUSE: if you choose to really fake being crazy and get sent away to a nuthouse, this is the equivalent to being sent to a dangerous prison, and both are AWESOME paths for you to take).

Got pulled over in a stolen police cruiser drunk on grain alcohol and high on meth? Make sure to tell the arresting officer that, "*the green juju zebra bean God of Zoron will strike you down with the mighty banana man of the city of Torgamonti!*" Scream this nonsensical, crazy, bullshit, psychotic and incoherent phrase as you dance around while flailing your arms like a helicopter and pissing yourself simultaneously **(shitting in your own hand and making some fine impromptu "artwork" on the police car is also a classic move to aid and to escalate this situation)**. In essence, we want the cop to think that you're some crazy fuck (which you clearly are anyway), so pretending to be absolutely NUTS is a great way to get around being beaten by the police. Whatever form of transportation that you take, faking being mentally challenged and then using the "mentally challenged excuse" is a **must use** for the miserable failure. You didn't pay for a taxi and instead ran away down a dark and dangerous alley to go buy some more drugs? Use the "mentally challenged excuse" with the cabbie and when you're in front of the court as the judge listens to your "impeccable defense." Want to board a plane with a rat, scorpion, spider, and python (all in open containers by the way) to qualify them as your "service animals?" Use the "mentally challenged excuse" and threaten to sue the airline as you scream profanities and touch yourself in the middle of the boarding process (BTW: finding some piece of shit "slip and fall lawyer" to take this case is going to be easy as they too are mostly all miserable failures as well). Essentially, any time that you need to get out of something, we want you to use the "mentally challenged excuse" to get yourself out of some of the jams that you'll no doubt be getting into.

The "Handicapped Excuse"

If you are not already in a wheelchair due to your legs being amputated because of your horrible bout of SELF-INFLICTED diabetes, you will need to fake being physically handicapped so you can get through life using it as an excuse for EVERYTHING. Also, unless you're in a wheelchair due to your DUI car crash, or the nasty (back-breaking) bar fight you got into during the Super Bowl party, you will need to fake being handicapped in order to get through life being a worthless sack of shit, miserable failure. This is why we encourage a miserable failure to "borrow" (steal) a hover round, wheelchair, walker, crutches, and cane whenever you need to travel somewhere.

The "handicapped excuse" is the next tool in the arsenal of excuses of which the miserable failure makes. Accidentally run over a man's foot while cutting line waiting or your cab ride after your AA meeting? As the man screams on the ground in pain (due to his compound foot fracture), make sure that you inform him that you should be forgiven because you're *"handicapped."* Let's say that you "forget to pay" (LOL!!!!) to get on the subway. Simply inform the teller and the security guard that you're *"handicapped."* You can also use the "handicapped excuse" for cutting in lines at the local soup kitchen, stealing charity money from the Santa bell ringer as you stroll by on your walker, or even as you try to occupy a first-class seat while boarding an airplane. Whatever ways you fuck up, the "handicapped excuse" is a great tool to have in your excuse belt.

You also need to have a sense of humor when using the "handicapped excuse." You can use this excuse if you're lucky enough to be missing any hands, fingers, toes, or feet from the numerous "firework accidents" you have gotten yourself into every summer. For example, if you're lucky enough to have a missing right hand, and in its place is nothing but a nub, whenever you meet someone, stick out your hand-less arm and demand that people "shake your nub." If they hesitate for a single second, scream out to them, *"you're a handicapphobe!"* As they recoil away in horror and shame, laugh at them and then ask them if they'd like to see what "holes" you can fit your nub into. Missing hands, finger, toes, or feet can provide you with endless amounts of opportunity to mock your disability while making others feel extremely uncomfortable. Feel free to use any of the follow lines if your handicapped:

Wheelchair-Bound

- *"I want to give you a STANDING ovation, but I can't dickhead."*
- *"Anyone want to play soccer with me?"*
- *"I'm going to KICK this cigarette habit when I'm dead."*

Missing a Hand, Arm, or Fingers

- *"Could you, HAND me that?"*
- *"Who wants to play charades?"*
- *"Clearly, I can't pick my nose. Who wants to help me pick a boogie?"*

- *"All HANDS on deck!"*
- *"You caught me red-HANDED!"*
- *"Give me a HAND."*
- *"You have the upper HAND."*
- *"Do you need a helping HAND?"*

Missing a Foot, Leg, or Toes

- *"This little piggy went to the market."*
- *"I'll KICK your ass."*
- *"You have a LEG up on me."*

How to Fly on a Plane

Most people have experienced horrible plane delays, flight cancellations, and random rage-inducing air travel experiences. From the smelly, morbidly obese son of a bitch and his stomach hanging over the armrest occupying your side of the seat, to the elderly and nearly dead cripples who move slower than molasses up and down the aisles—all normal people have experienced these types of annoying fuckers when they've flown on an airplane. **As bad as those people are, they pale in comparison to experiencing the miserable failure during air travel**. The coup de gras for flying on a plane is to make sure that all of the pilots, aircrew, and fellow passengers take part in (and experience) the complete and total **"miserable failure air travel experience."** The "miserable failure air travel experience" involves YOU, and all of your shenanigans during the flight and afterwards in the baggage claim area. You need to know what to do from the moment you get to the airport, to the point at which you're getting your teeth knocked in by a pissed off police officer on the tarmac or jet bridge.

The "miserable failure air travel experience" allows you an opportunity to ruin everyone's air travel, delay the flight (NOTE: canceled flights are ultra, mega, bonus, extra points) and to give all of the passengers and flight crew several stories that will end up in the **"travel hell hall of fame."** If you have the **opportunity** to fly on a plane (FYI: being on the "do not fly list" is a HUGE win for you by the way), make sure that you make the flight(s) as memorable as possible (EXAMPLE: urinating in the middle of the aisle during the beverage service). Flying is a privilege, and you'll soon have it revoked once you adhere to these STRICT guidelines outlined in this section.

Pre-Flight Prep

For the miserable failure traveling via air, making sure you plan and pack accordingly beforehand is a solid and professional move (FYI: this includes not bathing for several weeks before your scheduled flight). **In the weeks prior to your air travel, make sure you consume LARGE AND EXCESSIVE AMOUNTS of cheese, cabbage, beans, hotdogs and beer as your primary diet.** This deadly and hazardous combination is going to be a good enough reason to ban you from flying for life due to the smell of the farts you will be emitting in midair (NOTE: your farts on this diet should smell like someone crawled inside of you, and died). Since you're going to smell like a rat's asshole, you are allowed to pour an entire bottle of perfume or cologne over yourself from head to toe the morning of your air travel. The horrendous odor combination of your farts, body odor, halitosis, and copious amounts of cheap perfume is going to be enough to fumigate and decommission the plane after your flight.

We also want to make sure that you're packed and ready to roll for the hell flight that you're about to embark on. A miserable failure does not own a suitcase (unless you stole it from a department store and it still has the ink tags on it). The only way you "pack" your shit to travel, should be in large, black trash bags (NOTE: when you think of the words "**trash**" or "**garbage,**" people should think of "**YOU**"). If there is a hole in your suitcase (trash bag), simply use duct tape to repair it. The sight of you wearing a dirty bathrobe and slippers with a black trash bag draped over your shoulder during the check-in for your flight is going to provide the ticket counter lady a story that she will be telling for MANY YEARS TO COME. Now, as you pack, you should consider what to bring that might be entertaining for you and for the other passengers on the flight. The miserable failure NEVER leaves home to board an airplane without a combination of the following items:

- A brand-new, unopened package of razor blades (feel free to use some of your infamous suicide jokes if and **when** you're caught with them).
- Michael, your pet king viper snake (HEY, it's **your** "emotional support animal").
- A lighter and matches.
- Various sewing and knitting needles.
- A hatchet or ax.
- Spike, your pet lab rat (again, he is another one of your "emotional support animals").
- A rusty pair of scissors.
- A crème brulee mini blow torch.
- Jim, your pet black scorpion (yet **ANOTHER** "emotional support animal").
- Your ice pick.
- A carton of cigarettes.
- A camping knife.
- A water gun.
- A can of baked beans.
- Nail polish.
- Your great grandmother's dildo and vibrator collection.
- Nail polish remover.
- Hand sanitizer.

- A fake, plastic toy gun.
- Cologne/Perfume.
- A water pistol
- A fake rubber knife.
- Your entire vintage pornography collection.

CAUTION: We must inform you that SOME of the following items mentioned above will more than likely prevent you from boarding a plane, or significantly delay your travel as you're questioned in an iron box by an out of shape CIA agent named Carl.

To add a little more "excitement" for the other travelers, we also HIGHLY recommend you wear a turban and a fake long beard. This terrorist-inspired outfit will scare the living shit out of the other passengers as you speak in Arabic (NOTE: you don't know Arabic, but you should mumble incoherent and nonsensical words and phrases to fool people). Also, make sure that you do a few shots of vodka (drink the entire damn bottle) and smoke your pot and/or meth **BEFORE** you leave your shit box house (BTW: if you take them with you, they will be confiscated and your travel day "will be abruptly cut short"). Being drunk or high is MANDATORY behavior for the miserable failure on all domestic and international flights. Pop those pills, drink that liquor, and get ready to **party** during your air travel. The more shit-faced and fucked up you are, the greater number of people who will have a more "memorable" time on the plane with you. Remember, you're flying to give all of the passengers, crew and airport personnel stories they can tell forever, so make them ALL count, motherfucker.

The Ticket Counter Experience

As you stroll your sorry drunk ass up to the ticket counter to check in and to drop your trash bag full of shit off, do a few cartwheels, just to entertain the other passengers (NOTE: you should check your bags except for your "comfort animals"). Doing a few cartwheels as you cut in line ahead of everyone else while THEY wait patiently in an orderly fashion is a hallmark trait of a true miserable failure. If your suitcase, (trash bag) is over fifty pounds, walk over to a trashcan, dump out the contents and proceed to put your mini liquor bottles, your grandmother's dildo and vibrator collection and your extensive VHS vintage pornography collection in it as your carry on. Then, check your original trash bag with the ticket counter lady.

Make sure that you have your ID on you. **Since your driver's license will most likely be expired or still confiscated by the cops due to your multiple DUIs, you might need to use your welfare card or your food stamp ID to check in.** If you don't have an ID, show the ticket counter lady your ankle monitoring bracelet (NOTE: the light on it should be flashing wildly since you've left your house away from the court-mandated two-mile radius area) and ask if it will work for identification. If that STILL does not work, disrobe and show the ticket counter lady your tattoos, brandings, piercings, and scars over your entire disgusting and grotesque body and ask if those work as identification for you.

We also encourage the miserable failure to ask for a pre-boarding ticket due to your *"fear of flying."* If that excuse doesn't work, tell the ticket agent that you self-identify as a cripple and fall down on the floor as you scream profanities in pain. Getting in a wheelchair and boarding a plane early by faking being handicapped is something that only a miserable failure would do, so go for it! You can also tell the ticket counter lady that you're *"technically mentally handicapped"* and you need *"special assistance."* Miserable failure studies have repeatedly shown that this will work around 44.3% of the time.

If you don't get a pre-boarding ticket, cuss out the ticket counter lady, expose yourself to her, and stroll your merry ass up to TSA security checkpoint for the next part of the "miserable failure air travel experience." However, if you DO get a pre-boarding ticket, ask for a wheelchair or a ride on an electronic people mover. These are designed for the elderly, invalids, and the cripples. Again, since you're "technically mentally handicapped," you should have no problem hitching a FREE ride or getting a pre-boarding ticket.

It should also be noted that if a stranger whom you don't know asks you to take their bag on board the plane and give it to a particular person whom you've never met, once you land, make sure that you take it! Who knows what is in it (HINT: it's probably not something good or legal). It could be poisonous spiders you're illegally carrying into another state or its contents could land you face-first with the heel of a pissed off airport cop as you stroll through the TSA line with your mystery bag. It could also be a glitter bomb, two kilos of cocaine, or parts of various dead bodies. Whether you make it through, or you don't make it, it's fine! Because either way, you win! Either, A.) you're going to make it through with said bag and its contents contained within, or B.) you're going to be stopped, arrested and given a full body cavity search by the airport police and the Department of Homeland Security (FYI: when you're getting a full-body cavity search, ask the person giving it to you to rub your back slowly and to whisper sweet nothings in your ear as you get defiled. Then, once it's done, ask for a cigarette.)

Going Through the TSA Security Checkpoint

No one likes going through TSA at the airport (HINT: **the miserable failure LOVES it**). In fact, most people DESPISE the entire TSA screening process. This is for good reason as many TSA workers look like incompetent, ineffective, compromised, unintelligent, high school dropout, mouth-breathing, dipshit, buffoons (HEY, just like you!). **This is why the miserable failure would fit in PERFECTLY working with all of these delusional dickless lunatics that work for the TSA**. When you reach the security line, and you are not given a pre-board ticket with a wheelchair (thus allowing you to bypass the "commoners" and get into the front of the line), make sure you scream out loud and complain excessively how long the line is (NOTE: do this while using curse words and sexual hand gestures to animate your frustrations). Bitching and moaning is going to cause the other people around you to start to become annoyed and grossed out by you (FYI: this combined with your stench of alcohol, vomit and body odor are going to be some of the other reasons). Feel free to try and cut in the security line, but after several people fall down due to your excessive and unnecessary shoving and elbowing, the TSA agent is more than likely either going to call the airport police or ask you to return to the back of the line (NOTE: if the airport police get called, PRAY that one of them stomps on your abdomen when you **refuse** to follow their commands—HELLO LAWSUIT!!!).

Since you'll probably be all fucked up on prescription medications and pure grain alcohol, standing in the TSA checkpoint line might be a potential problem for the miserable failure. This is why we suggest you sit down on the floor and scoot yourself along on your ass or army crawling (being low also helps your dry heaving as well) as you move along in the line. You can even walk backwards if you want while asking the person behind you in line if they would mind *"switching bags"* with you. When they deny your unusual request, simply call them a *"pussy."*

When you approach the first TSA agent who will be checking your ID and your boarding pass, ask if you can have their *"bullshit badge"* as a souvenir (BTW: do this while laughing out loud, two inches from their face as you attempt to grab their security pin on their shirt). Feel free to inform them that you're an out of work miserable failure and that you would fit in working with them perfectly at the TSA. Then, proceed to ask for a job application (**HINT: you won't get one**). When you reach the conveyer belt to put your trash bag on it (CONTENTS INVENTORY CHECK: your pet viper "comfort pet," mini bottles of whiskey and your VHS vintage porn collection) please feel free once again to work on your racist, insensitive and unfunny stand-up comedy routine material out loud. Some of the topics you should be making jokes on as you go through TSA include:

- Vagina jokes.
- Suicide jokes.
- Titty jokes.
- Gun jokes.
- Missing persons jokes.
- Hijacking jokes.
- Death jokes.
- Knife jokes.
- Dick jokes.
- Bomb jokes.
- Terrorist jokes.
- Famous airplane crashes jokes.

If you want to really step up your game as you go through TSA, throw **yourself** on the conveyor belt, lay straight, and ask if you can be screened that way. If by some miracle, you're not thrown out of the line yet, then prepare yourself for the screening process.

Opting In

If you decide to avoid the TSA groping and rape process, you're going to need to go through the cancer-causing radiation machines (**SCORE!!!**). Before you do this, you'll need to disrobe, put your slippers on the conveyor belt (**or strip nude**) as you proceed to the next part of the security line. As you walk through the metal detector or body scanner machine, make sure you discuss with the TSA agents (in great detail) all of the potential ways in which an average person **"could be killed by a maniac on an airplane."** (NOTE: doing this is going to cause the airport police to be called again and your trip might end abruptly). After an hour-long mental evaluation and a full body cavity search (double SCORE!!!!) by a member of the Department of Homeland Security, you'll be cleared for departure. **Just make sure to inform the police and the DHS Agent that you're on a "miserable failure quest."** If they don't believe you, feel free to lie and proclaim that you are acting like a fuck face because of your Asperger's and your OCD (REMEMBER: when in doubt, lie and fake various illnesses).

Before they allow you to leave, they will confiscate your pet viper snake, but continue to insist that he is your "comfort-flying animal" and inform the TSA that you'll be *"calling your lawyer"* on them for them taking away your comfort animal **(NOTE: miserable failures do not have "lawyers," they have court-ordered and suicidal "public defenders").** The TSA also might take your thirty-four mini bottles of vodka as well. The only thing you might have left in your carry-on trash bag is your entire vintage porn collection. However, if by some miracle, you were able to keep your pet snake in your carry on, remember to conceal him before you actually board the airplane. When you leave the security checkpoint, just to have fun and spice up everyone else's day, point out beyond the crowd still in line and yell, *"he has a gun!"* as you run screaming towards your gate.

Opting Out

If you decide that you want to get felt up and sexually caressed in your private parts by a creepy pervert in a royal blue shirt at the airport, be sure that you "opt out" of the cancer-causing radiation machines (NOTE: this physical touching experience is the only time, you might get any sexual "action" this year, so enjoy it!). When you opt out, shout out loud at the TSA agent, *"I prefer to have my crotch and genitals grabbed, and I don't want to go through that unconstitutional piece of shit machine!"* Once you proclaim that, a TSA employee who matches your gender will come over and search your entire body and pat you down (FYI: it is totally and completely acceptable to ask for the full body cavity search and a cigarette for afterwards). The TSA agent will ask you if you want to be searched (groped) in a private area, or in front of everyone. **ALWAYS decide that you want to be sexually assaulted in front of everyone because it reminds you of an "orgy" that you've never experienced, but have fantasized about.** (NOTE: if you're a male miserable failure, make sure that you scream out loud, *"I want one of those fat, bull-dyke, lesbian TSA sluts to come and search my junk."* If you're a female miserable failure, make sure that you shout out, *"I want one of those creepy, perverted male TSA agents to come over here, grab my titties, and search my snatch"*). During the pat-down (groping) process, giggle like a schoolgirl and inform the TSA agent that they're tickling you. Ask if you can tickle them in return. As the TSA agent has their hands near your pants around your private parts, look down, lick your lips and begin to sway your hips back and forth thrusting towards them, then proceed to sing any song out loud (while saluting) as the groping and body-searching process continues.

If you've cleared security by a miracle, make sure to inform the TSA agents that they'll all *"suckers."* Stick your tongue out at them to mock them. Grab your carry-on trash bag, swing it above your head like a monkey, and yell out to the others waiting in the TSA security line that they can, *"all suck balls!"* Remember, that you're going to be giving all of the people you encounter at the airport and on the plane, stories that they can tell for the rest of their lives- SO MAKE THEM COUNT! And also remember... **You're** doing **them** a favor! So, be sure to make their travel experience memorable. Part of that is being a rude, inconsiderate, creepy, annoying, perverted, lunatic, degenerate, stupid, and silly son of a bitch during all phases of air travel.

The Gate Waiting Experience

Waiting at the gate before your flight is a lot like someone unfortunately having sex with you, it's slow, boring, uneventful, and sad. Most travelers are waiting at the gate holding their phones in their hand trying to avoid eye contact with others (knocking their phones out of their hands when you enter the gate area is also one of our solid recommendations as well as a classic move used by miserable failures throughout the history of air travel). Also, there is usually one seat between each person in the waiting area. When the miserable failure reaches the gate area, make sure that you announce your presence. Shout out, *"I have arrived, bitches!"* Then proceed to step up (cut in line) at the ticket counter and **DEMAND** to be upgraded to First Class for FREE. After the ticket agent's laughter subsides, inform them that you have irritable bowel syndrome and that you'll be *"shitting all over the plane"* like a *"mad shitter"* unless you get upgraded. If that excuse doesn't work, relax; it doesn't mean that you can't occupy a first-class seat during the flight (wink, wink).

The next thing to do is to find some poor bastard to sit next to while you wait at the gate. We encourage you to sit next to anyone who looks like they're well put together or are wealthy. Feel free to inform the person you're sitting next to of your cost for the sexual proclivities that you're willing to engage in, *"in the bathroom before the flight"* (FYI: the gender of the person does not matter). **Who knows? You might make a quick $10 going down on an old, wealthy, business lady in the private family bathroom!** Next, feel free to do a show and tell with your VHS vintage pornography collection for everyone in the gate area. Talk about your favorite scenes in great detail as you laugh like an asshole during your extremely detailed "show and tell session." This might also be a good time to inform all of the fellow passengers that you have a pet viper snake, a scorpion, a tarantula, and a rat in your trash bag acting as your "comfort animals." By announcing this, you're going to start pissing off many of your fellow passengers. Next, stand in your seat, throw your trash bag carry-on over your shoulder and discuss your demands with everyone. Make sure that they are aware of your "requests" for the entire duration of your air travel. Those requests (demands) for your air travel include:

- Everyone is required to do "the wave" during takeoff.
- You are allowed to give the safety information lecture on the PA system.
- You are the only one allowed to fart (warn the people and dis-

cuss in GREAT detail how bad your gas is going to be to prepare them for the "odor chamber").

- You demand free alcohol because yours were confiscated earlier.
- You get first dibs in *"the shitter."*
- The pilots must let you fly the plane for thirty seconds (more on how to avoid being accused of hijacking in a later section.)
- You get five pairs of the toy airplane wings upon arrival in the cabin.
- You finally get your name on "The Mile-High Club" with **ANYONE** (or any object) that is desperate, dumb, and drunk enough to meet you in the lavatory.
- The stewardesses must provide you with an entire case of the mini peanuts.

You can even stand up on the chair and shout out a simple speech after your demands are announced. A sample speech, after you have shouted your demands previously mentioned should be something similar to this:

"Those are my demands, motherfuckers. But, my name is (INSERT YOUR NAME), *and I am a miserable failure. I am unemployed and I am addicted to drinking, drugs, smoking cigarettes, and pornography. Some of my traits, you might all get to experience when we're on the aircraft together in close confines. In preparation for this trip, I have not bathed in several months. My clothes only get washed when I pass out drunk outside in the rain, or when I'm stealing loose change from the water fountains. I have terrible body odor, foul breath, and repugnant farts. I basically smell like a decaying person dipped in vinegar, cooking inside of an outhouse near the all you can eat hamburger and tuna casserole buffet.*

I can't wait until you all hear my new stand-up comedy routine about airplanes getting hijacked and crashing into the ocean. Speaking of that, I also am eager to share with you my expertise in the history of infamous horrible and grisly airplane crashes. By the way, I think that thing on the wing (while pointing out the window at the plane) *is broken too. If we're all lucky, maybe a gremlin will show up on the wing of our airplane as well. I hope all of your life insurance policies are paid up and you've said goodbye to loved ones in case the plane goes down, crashes and bursts into flames. I will be flying with all of you commoners because the FAA and the airlines won't let me fly in the luggage or cargo holes. Sit, back and relax because this is going to be one hell of a flight!"*

After you've informed the entire flight crew, pilots, and passengers of your demands and have fully introduced yourself, find one of the nearest bars and proceed to drink **many** shots of gin, rum, vodka, whiskey, tequila and scotch (NOTE: in that order too). If you see pilots eating in the nearby bar prior to takeoff, ask them if you can buy them a drink. If they refuse, call them *"pussies"* **and tell them,** *"the flight will be much more fun for all of us on board the airplane if you're shit faced."* Continue to pound the shots down and of course you should conveniently "FORGET" (wink, wink) to pay your bar tab by the time they have announced the boarding process has commenced.

The Boarding Process

Before your boarding section is even called, the miserable failure should push others out of the way as you make a mad and panicked rush to board the plane first (throwing elbows and stepping on toes is HIGHLY encouraged during this moment). **And after all, you are technically and potentially legally mentally handicapped, so you should board FIRST, anyway**. If you didn't get a pre-boarding ticket, steal a wheelchair (or kindly ask an old man to depart his if you can't locate a vacant one) and roll your merry ass down to the front of the line as you wait for the gate agent to roll you down the jet bridge.

Once you reach the jet bridge and you're forced to stand in line, make sure that you bitch out loud and complain once again as you pass your horrendous gas (HINT: by now the other passengers are going to be tired of your shenanigans and their anger might start to become physical). **When you make it in the plane, immediately ask to visit the cockpit so you can do a "*meet and greet*" with the pilots**. When the stewardess refuses, simply shove her out of the way and forcibly make your way into the cockpit to introduce yourself. Once you enter the cockpit, now would be an opportune time to use some of your hijacking stand-up comedy routine material during your brief and momentary discussion with the pilots. As you are informed to vacate the cockpit, make sure to ask the pilots before you leave if you can fly the plane after takeoff. When you walk down the aisle to your seat, make sure that you try to sit in an empty first-class seat (NOTE: if no one sits in one of the first-class seats, you get free drinks and get to fly like royalty!). However, **if and when** someone shows up demanding that you leave their seat, make sure to steal all of the flight material from the pouch in front of the seat, rip it up and shout curse words at them. **As you make your way past the first-class folks, crouch down like a humpback lab assistant and shout out, "*yes, me master*" as you lurch down the aisle. (BTW: using the phrase, "*don't beat me, sir*" in a British accent is also suggested)**. As you walk down the aisle to your seat, make sure that your trash bag smacks each person in the aisle seats in the head, arm, or shoulder. As you make your way down the aisle, make unnecessary comments about various persons that you stroll past. Some typical examples of rude comments you should say are:

- Parents with Kids and Babies - *"Your little demon baby better shut the fuck up during the flight or there will be BIG trouble. Are we clear?"*
- The Fat Passenger - *"Your fat ass is going to be stuck in the seat when the plane goes down because no one is going to help you out, tubby."*
- The Elderly - *"You cripples should have boarded last. Do you have a couple of painkillers I can snag from you?"*

- The Wealthy Businessman in the Suit - *"Can I borrow $20?"*
- The Military Veteran - *"May I sit in your lap? You may pet me."*
- The Typical Busty Blonde - *"Got milk?"*

When you get to your assigned seat (if you have avoided being beaten by the other passengers), feel free to use the little white barf bag. Stick a few fingers down your throat (**channel your time in the clinic for your various eating disorders**) and let 'er rip! You're going to want the people sitting to the right and left of you what they're in for, the entire flight (BTW: miserable failures only get middle seats). Also, when you sit down, ring your stewardess call button. When she comes over to ask what you need, DEMAND five free mini bottles of whiskey and ask her if you can use the intercom to buy some anti-anxiety medication off of anyone on the flight (SEE ALSO: section on "drugs and alcohol"). We also strongly encourage the miserable failure to press the oxygen release button just to scare the ever-loving shit out of the people seated next to you as the four oxygen masks drop down rapidly.

After you're buckled in (or zip tied) and you've vomited (at least three times), **make sure that you claim both of those armrests as YOUR PERSONAL PROPERTY.** If they are occupied by either one of your fellow passengers, simply use your elbows and forcibly shove the other passenger's arms out of the way. By now, both of your fellow comrades should be secretly wishing for you to have a slow and painful death consisting of gruesome and severe physical torture. Before the flight takes off, now would be an ideal time to do another "show and tell" of each one of your VHS vintage pornography tapes. Take out each VHS videotape and describe in GREAT DETAIL your favorite scene from each movie. Finally, make sure that you turn each of the three air vents on full blast and aim them at yourself. Turn on all three of the lights and open the window shade if it is closed. As the air from the vents hits your body, along with the light from the window, the odor you emit will be enough for the two people seated next to you to use their vomit bags as well (good... welcome to the club, assholes). Finally, after you have boarded and the stewardess informs everyone to put their seat belts on, ring your call button. When the stewardess arrives, explain to her that you don't know how to fasten your seat belt. When she assists you, look directly at her as she buckles it for you, then look at your crotch and then back to her. Then, get close to her and whisper, *"It's not going to get itself off, honey..."*

The Takeoff

Immediately before takeoff, unbuckle your seat belt and get your grandmother's dildo and vibrator collection ready. Taking off your seat belt is key because you should be praying for strong turbulence in the middle of the takeoff so that you get thrown screaming out of your seat as the plane makes a 700-foot sudden drop (HELLLOOOOO **another** AIRLINE LAWSUIT!!!). As the plane starts to take off, ring your call button. When the stewardess doesn't arrive, scream out loud, *"we're all going to die!"* This phrase will scare the daylights out of all of the passengers on the airplane. Feel free to snuggle, cuddle and attempt to hold hands with the people sitting next to you. Ask them to hold you as you weep like a baby. You should basically turn into a panicking, paranoid, schizophrenic, psychopath during the takeoff. **If you're ever unclear what to do during takeoff, just make everyone uncomfortable and scream obscenities**.

As the plane begins to climb, **start to talk to your row partners (again) about infamous fiery and gruesome plane crashes.** Specifically, start to discuss ways the three of you should all ally together and plan your escape as a group "**WHEN**" the plane crashes. Talk about the people you're going to need to take down so you can exit the plane quickly after it crashes. Look around and find tiny children, the frail, and the elderly. Point out to your "new best friends" sitting next to you that you intend to, *"knock those fuckers out of the way first."* As the plane is still climbing, you should exit your seat, kneel in the aisle and begin to shout, *"Allah Akbar!"* very loudly. This act will again begin to scare the crap out of the other passengers around you. As the plane levels off and the captain turns off the fasten seatbelt sign, make sure you make your way to the front of the plane and "help yourself" (steal) to the mini liquor bottles in the stewardess' cabin. Feel free to grab some peanuts as well. If you're asked to take your seat, stick out your tongue and thumb your nose at the stewardess. Then proceed to go back to your seat with your new treasures.

When you get back to your seat, grab your sex toys from your trash bag. Feel free to then hand them out to various women on the plane as a "donation." Explain in great detail that you have not washed them and that they're "previously used" from your grandmother. If someone doesn't take one when they are offered, simply grab one of your suction dildos and stick it on their tray. After you hand out 15-20 dildos and vibrators, feel free to make your way back to your seat and sit your merry ass down. Before you get comfortable, recline your seat back AS FAR as possible. Feel free to really give that asshole sitting behind you **EVEN LESS LEGROOM**...

The Flight from Hell

All of the horrible experiences that people have had on an airplane are going to pale in comparison to what a miserable failure has in store for the other passengers (INSERT: wicked smile). To begin with, your foul body odor, rotten breath, and farts should be stinking up the entire cabin by now. **The various odors your body is producing should make horse manure smell fantastic in comparison to your personal stench and aroma**. If the people sitting next to you have not vomited yet, you smell way too good. Speaking of vomiting, you should also be utilizing and puking in the small, white trash bag behind the seat as often as you can (NOTE: remember your eating disorder training on making yourself puke). We also encourage you to keep ringing your call button to summon over the stewardess—OFTEN. **When the stewardess arrives, ask if you can see the "*wine list*" and demand the lobster thermidor as**

your meal. We also need to list some of the actions that are mandatory for miserable failures to do while flying. They include:

- Light up a cigarette or a cigar (or several) while announcing to the entire cabin, *"you fuckers want calm people on the airplane, don't ya?!"*
- Destroy and tamper with the smoke detectors in the lavatory (an FAA violation and 100% conviction rate).
- Tickle all the people around you.
- Paint both your fingernails and toenails with nail polish. Then, use nail polish remover and repeat this entire process… **fifteen times**.
- Try to crawl in the overhead bin so you *"can take a quick nap and to huff some superglue."*
- Run full steam down the aisle screaming nonsensical phrases with your arms flailing about.
- Fall asleep on the lap of the person sitting next to you (snoring and drooling is recommended).
- Drink as much alcohol as possible (if you still have a credit card, use it, and continue your quest to max it out ASAP).
- Rip out pages from the magazine and make several paper airplanes to fly around the cabin.
- Ask the entire plane (via the intercom) if you can "*perform mammograms on all of the women*" (FYI: for confusion purposes only, explain that you're a licensed "dermatologist").
- Spray cologne or use hand sanitizer every five minutes.
- Ask the entire plane (via the intercom, AGAIN) if you can *"check the prostates of all of the men"* (FYI: for confusion purposes only, explain that you're a board-certified "podiatrist").
- Pull out, put on, and inflate your life preserver from underneath the seat.
- Cough, sneeze, yawn, burp, fart, and hiccup as much as you can

(FYI: if you do all of these at once, you win ultra, mega bonus points).

- Chew your peanuts with your mouth open. This is a classic move and will further cement your name in the "travel hell hall of fame" as the peanut pieces slowly fall out of your disgusting mangle mouth.
- Ask the people around you, if they'd like to play duck, duck goose. When they say *"no,"* still play the game anyway.
- Stand at the front of the airplane (using the intercom once again) to practice your comedy bit about a 747-plane crashing into a cornfield.

By now, if you've been following our directions on how to fly on an airplane, several of the other passengers are going to start to ally together to discuss the ways in which they'd prefer to brutally torture and kill you. This is good news! **Just remember that a miserable failure needs to be that "one person who always does _______" on an airplane.** You should be the person who occupies the bathroom for an hour. You should be the person who is slow to board the plane. Monopolize the stewardesses' time by being that typical, needy lunatic. Bang on the cockpit door a few DOZEN times. Be obnoxious, sloppy, sad, and inconsiderate. Feel free to recline your seat as far back as you can to stretch out (do this especially if there is a tall or fat person behind you). **Make yourself at home!** If you want to air out, take off your slippers. If you get too hot, disrobe. Do what makes you happy and do everything in your power to make this a memorable flight for all of the passengers.

Since you're really desperate and are continuing to make a fool out of yourself, it's a great idea for you to start asking people on the airplane if they want to join you in the bathroom to get to the *"mile-high club."* **First of all, NO ONE will want to bang your stank ass.** Secondly, no one would ever voluntarily join you in any bathroom, let alone a small lavatory on an airplane. Finally, it's illegal and dangerous to bang on the plane. It is for these reasons why we encourage the miserable failure to say anything in order to get laid on an airplane. Some of the classic phrases miserable failures have shouted out over the years have included:

- *"Who wants to fuck in the plane?"*
- *"Who is willing to bang me in the bathroom right now?"*
- *"I will give someone my entire vintage porn collection right now if they allow me to make sweet love to them in the airplane lavatory."*
- *"I'm already high. I now need to join the mile-high club. Who's coming with me?"*
- *"Relax people, I'm only going to have sex with one of you. Eenie, Meanie, Minie, Moe..."*

After a few hours of all of your horrible shenanigans, you are going to be **lucky** if you're not zip tied to your chair and have duct tape placed over your mouth. Finally, if the pilots have to make an emergency landing just to get you off the plane, you've done your job during air travel.

The Landing

When the pilots have informed everyone that the plane will be landing soon, we recommend that the miserable failure use this time to get up out of the seat and run down the aisle screaming, *"get down!"* It's also an adequate time to find the stewardesses and complain that you never received your *"complimentary blue label whiskey bottle or your lobster thermidor dinner"* that you "were convinced" you'd be receiving. When the stewardess tells you to go back, sit down and buckle your seat belt, ask her a very important question... Ask the stewardess why they get the extra shoulder strap seat belt support in their chairs while everyone else has the *"white trash seat belt single straps?"* Before the stewardesses begin to taser you or you get zip tied like a sheep by federal officer, we encourage you to stand at attention while singing any offensive rap song to the entire plane as the landing continues.

Feel free to randomly grab bags out of the overhead bins and switch them around as you stroll your merry ass back to your seat. By this time, you should be praying for heavy turbulence (again) so you get tossed into the air and onto the lap of an attractive person to "accidentally" (wink, wink) cop a feel. When you get back to the seat, ask the person sitting in the aisle seat to *"get the fuck up."* Remember, give the other passengers stories they can tell for a lifetime...

The Deplaning Process

The first rule of deplaning is "the miserable failure gets off first" (NOTE: just like you always do during sex...). As soon as the plane comes to a complete stop, hop out of your seat, and charge the aisle, pushing and shoving everyone else out of the way so that you can deplane first. Feel free to shout obscenities and speak in gibberish, nonsensical bullshit as you badger the other passengers and whirl your trash bag carry on above your head like a helpless lunatic (FYI: **we must caution you that you are MORE THAN LIKELY going to be greeted at the gate by the TSA, airport police, the Department of Homeland Security, and a representative from the local mental institution upon your arrival**). However, if you can't get up in time fast enough to be the first person off the plane, make sure **you take a MINIMUM of ten minutes** to get your trash bag out of the overhead bin, so take your time, **nice** and **slow**. As you deplane, you might have a great opportunity to steal yourself a few small bags as well. Feel free to grab whatever you can in the overhead bins as you make a mad, panicked dash towards the exit door.

As you run full steam up the jet bridge towards the airport, make sure that you give everyone waiting to board the plane an entertaining show. Some of the things you should be doing as you enter the airport might include:

- Crawling on all fours like a dog (marking your territory is bonus points).
- Doing jumping jacks as you enter the airport from the jet bridge.
- Doing an army crawl while yelling random shit about Vietnam.
- Run out screaming, *"those pilots are drunken maniacs!"*
- Walk out backwards with your ass out and in the air as you demand a wheelchair.
- Inform all of the people waiting to board that *"the plane is probably broken."* Feel free to tap them on the shoulder and wish them good luck.

Scaring and berating the shit out of the (now frightened and terrified) passengers waiting to board the plane you just got off of is a classic move employed by many miserable failures over the last few decades of air travel.

The Baggage Claim Experience

This is the last step in the entire flying process for the miserable failure. Below are a few great ideas on how to end your travel nightmare with a **bang**. We suggest that you re-read this section several times to grasp the importance of what we call, "the baggage claim experience." The baggage claim experience should include all of the other people on your flight as well as airport police. **When you reach the baggage carousel, feel free to hop on and go for a ride**! There is nothing funnier and more disturbing than watching a dirty, disgusting person in a stained white bathrobe, slippers and boxers "bag surfing" on the baggage claim carousel (NOTE: this scene may result in you starring in a streaming online viral video later on). Feel free to high five the other passengers waiting on their bags to arrive as you pass them by. Then, hop off and look for your OTHER trash bag that you checked in. As it comes tearing ass down the conveyor belt ripped and taped up, yell out, *"there it is, you cocksuckers!"* or *"everybody, back the fuck off!"* Then make a beeline, full sprint, to collect your trash bag, tackling it on the metal conveyor belt (BTW: knocking others out of the way is optional here). Proudly proclaim victory and mock everyone who is still waiting for their bags. Swing your trash bags over your head (again) like a deranged and mentally ill asshole and begin dance around (HINT: at this point, airport police will probably be dispatched... **again**).

Next, we want you to grab a few more bags that aren't yours. Go around asking everyone, *"are these are your bags?"* If you give someone their bag, demand restitution from them for your services rendered. In fact, we encourage the miserable failure to pull every piece of luggage off the carousel (if you want), take them a few feet away from the conveyor belt, make a fort out of them and hide in it. As people come by to grab their luggage or to kick your ass for stealing their bags, make sure that you've hidden in your new fort and jump out to scare them as they collect their possessions. You can even open people's bags and go through their possessions while narrating out loud every single one of their items as you take their stuff out of the suitcases. Pick through some stranger's luggage making sure that you discuss in detail:

- Their underwear (while sniffing).
- Their souvenirs they purchased (explain their horrible taste in souvenirs).
- Their toiletry selections.
- Their clothing outfit choices

Speaking of souvenirs, make sure that you grab (steal) yourself a few "souvenirs" out of their bag. These might include their dirty laundry bag or any food that they have stashed in the side zipper compartments. At this point in your air travel experience, the airport police are probably going to be arriving shortly. When they arrive, ask them, *"can I go shoot one of your guns out in the parking lot?"* When they ask you to leave the premises, ask them if you *"can do a selfie together?"* When they refuse, take off on a full sprint with both of your trash bags and head for the exit.

The Airport "Tuck and Roll"

Since you're going to be needing a free ride home from the airport, we encourage you to do the CLASSIC "tuck and roll" technique. The "tuck and roll" is a move whereby the miserable failure allows a car to hit them (NOTE: **a miserable failure walks out into oncoming traffic on purpose**). The miserable failure should tuck their feet and roll onto a nice and expensive car as it speeds by. You can especially do this at the airport too! Once outside the airport, we encourage the miserable failure to walk out in front of any expensive car that is driving by (CHA CHING!). This is your free hotel room for the night. Once a car hits you, demand that the driver put you up in a hotel for the evening or you'll *"sue their ass off."* Also, demand a ride to the hotel and $50 for dinner and drinks. Your travel day nightmare is over. So, we encourage you to make sure that the trip to the local hotel is one that mimics your entire air travel experience.

Places to Be Yourself

Miserable failures like being around other miserable failures for the most part. However, there are some places that you can go that offer a miserable failure a chance to "be YOU." Some of these places might be the inpatient or outpatient rehab center, the psych ward in a mental hospital, the dirty porn theater, a crack house, or behind bars in the local county jail.

If you want to be around other miserable failures, you have a few different options. **You can find some miserable failures "being themselves" outside of a liquor store, drunk at 10:00 a.m. on a Sunday morning.** You also might encounter a miserable failure shoplifting cigarettes from behind the bar at a strip club (NOTE: more on getting your windpipe kicked in by a stripper in 9-inch stiletto's will be addressed later on in the book). Even with all of the places we mentioned, there are a few staples for you. You should go to these places as often as you can so you can truly be free to be YOU. If you want to be a miserable failure, we strongly recommend you attend the following locations as often as possible in order to maximize your miserable failure title.

Porn Shops

Most really deprived and fucked up people visit porn shops. So naturally, you, the miserable failure, should frequently visit them (a minimum of eleven times per week). The fact that someone still goes into a porn shop is amazing, yet disgusting and disturbing. A miserable failure is HIGHLY addicted to pornography. One of the ways in which you can really fit in and be yourself is to always be near and in porn shops. Porn shops are generally located on "the bad side of town" or in sketchy and shady neighborhoods (good, there is a better chance you'll get knifed when you're leaving). The miserable failure finds comfort and solitude in porn shops. In fact, the porn shop is the miserable failure's church and place of worship (NOTE: besides worshiping Satan, miserable failures worship porn). You might encounter some of your BFF's in the porn shop. Some of your more infamous buddies that frequently visit the porn shop include:

- Larry "the meth head" trucker.
- Carl "the perverted and kinky" businessman.
- Sally "the cheating slut" housewife.
- Floyd "the homeless and paralyzed" mute.
- Rhonda "the black albino transvestite" hooker.

When you go into a porn shop, walk up to the counter to the fine young gentleman openly masturbating to an adult video and ask where the most *"vile and sickening pornos are located."* Once you get where the section is from the perverted cashier, make your way over to said aisle.

When you get to the aisle where the really strange and bizarre kinky videos are located, lay down, grab a few DVDs and read the back covers (out loud) before taking a nap (NOTE: pleasuring yourself is optional at this point). After your three-hour drunken, passed-out nap, make sure you put a few of those disgusting DVDs under your robe and make a run for the door. Stealing is bad. Stealing pornography is even worse. Even worse than stealing pornography, is getting a baseball bat taken to both of your kneecaps in the parking lot of the porn shop by a coked-out and horny cashier.

The State Fair

Most state fairs have an extraordinarily high amount of **trashy**, **disgusting**, and **fucked up** people. State fairs also bring out the **crazy** and **psychotic** thrill-seeking, fat ass **drunks**. This is exactly why a miserable failure will fit in PERFECTLY attending any and all state fairs. **State fairs always allow the fatties, the criminally insane, the housing project junkies, the perverts, the drunks, and the trailer park people to crawl out from their shit box, meth houses, and get into violent, drunken fistfights in the beer tent.** This is also precisely why the first thing you should do when you arrive at the state fair is to locate the beer tent ASAP (NOTE: you SHOULD be getting the withdrawal alcohol shakes by now). When you go into the beer tent, announce yourself. Shout out to all of the partiers, "*I came here to drink beer and kick ass, and I'm all out of beer*" (FYI: you should be praying that "white trash assholes" or the "ghetto-ass gangstas" are ready to do the latter). Then proceed over to the bartender, plunk down your welfare or your food stamp card and demand a beer. Once the bartender laughs at your payment request, simply hop over to one of the kegs and ask, "*who wants to hold my feet up as I do a keg stand?*"

Once the state police have escorted you out of the beer tent, it's time for you to go get some food. Find an ATM machine that charges $5 for every cash withdrawal and proceed to use your food stamp card to get out a quick $50. We then expect you to proceed to eat ALL OF THE FOLLOWING FOODS at the state fair in this exact order; we like to call this the "tremendous twenty."

1. A hotdog (apply and add every condiment to it).
2. A big greasy plate of chili cheese fries (make sure you ask for extra cheese).
3. A lemonade shakeup (the amount of sugar in this is really going to fire your diabetes up).
4. A BBQ pork chop sandwich.
5. An ice cream sundae.
6. A hamburger (apply and add every condiment to it).
7. Fried avocados (dip them in ranch dressing).
8. A giant turkey leg.
9. A doughnut.
10. Fried cheese curds (also lick the grease and oil off the bottom of the plate).
11. A basket of chicken strips.
12. A corn dog (apply and add every condiment to it).
13. A chocolate ice cream cone.
14. A funnel cake.
15. A lollipop (lick it while creepily staring at others).
16. A slice of pepperoni pizza.
17. Fried dill pickles.
18. A cotton candy roll.
19. A big plate of French fries covered in ketchup.
20. Three large sodas.

Once you've consumed all of this food, it's time that you went back to the beer tent to start pounding down a few cold ones. Feel free to challenge people to a fight in the beer tent. Also, feel free to dance like a drunken maniac in the very front part of the crowd near the stage as the cover band plays their shitty music. Light up a cigarette (BTW: your meth pipe or your cigar both work) and dance around. Feel free to try to start a "mosh pit" during the next song. When you become conscious after irate roadies beat the shit out of you outside the tent, make your way over to the rides and games area.

By now, the miserable failure should be full of food and drunk on beer. You should be so full that you should probably go to the hospital or the port-o-potty. **However, we mandate that the miserable failure go on the fastest and most deadly spinning ride possible.** Once you get going on the ride and it begins to spin, this is when the miserable failure either accidentally vomits, or you make yourself vomit (NOTE: see section on eating disorders and total number of fingers required to go down your throat). All of the above-mentioned food you consumed is going to come shooting out of your pie hole in a horribly and life-altering way for all that witness this momentous occasion in the life of a miserable failure. Once you vomit, the ride is going to be shut down. You'll be covered in vomit and so might some of the other people (which is why getting another good ass beating is probably coming your way from a group of incensed and sober soccer moms). As you're getting escorted away by the creepy carnival perverts, make sure to inform them that you, *"plan on suing their asses off."* Next, proceed to the game area in your vomit-covered white robe. Stop by the various games and just start playing them. See that classic knockdown clown game? Grab a ball and start throwing it at the clowns without paying. When the carnival workers tell you that you need to stop, try and snag one of their money fanny packs and run like hell.

The final stop for the miserable failure should be the barnyard where all of the sheep, pigs, cows, goats, and horses are stabled. Go into one of the animal cages, bundle up some hay, and take a nap (this including spooning with the animal). As little kids, farmers, and state fair patrons walk by, if you're lucky, you might hear a father say to their children, *"look kids, it's one of the most disgusting animals around; it's a miserable failure!"*

Crack Houses

If you ever want to run into a bunch of other miserable failures, look no further than stopping by and visiting your local crack house (NOTE: you should have several of your drug dealers on speed dial on your burner, broke ass, pre-paid phone). A crack house offers miserable failures a place to truly be themselves (BTW: we must also recommend that you read the section on "drugs and alcohol" as it pertains to how to maximize crack cocaine usage in your life). When you go to a crack house, you're going to encounter some (if not all) of the stereotypical people that you'd expect to be there, so you must be prepared. In a crack house, you're going to encounter:

- Crack heads (your old prison buddies).
- Crack whores.
- Strung out hippies.
- Speed freaks.
- Bikers high on crank.
- Various shady and sketchy homeless people.
- Pot smoking jazz musicians.
- Coke head werewolves.

Crack houses offer the miserable failure several opportunities to smoke crack or get into dangerous broken bottle glass fights with delusional, cracked-out psychopaths (NOTE: getting hepatitis C during your fight is a bonus). When you show up at a crack house, ask to see "*the main man.*" This is a code term for, "CRACK DEALER." When you get to the crack dealer, make sure that you have some of your grandmother's stolen jewelry with you so you can exchange it for some crack (TRUE FACT: crack dealers do not take the food stamp card or the welfare card, but they do accept stolen jewelry). Feel free to smoke crack in front of the various homeless and other mentally ill strangers as this gives you the perfect opportunity to get some "chit chat" in. If you play your cards right, you might have (another) opportunity to sell your body out sexually in order to obtain even more crack (or any other drugs for that matter). Make sure that you snap a few selfies with the other druggies as you make your way through the crack house, then send said pictures to your parole officer, ex-spouse, therapist, life coach, children, and AA sponsor.

Finally, crack houses offer the miserable failure an opportunity to make some "fast cash" by stealing the little metal cash box filled with blood-ridden Benjamin's, and running for the door. If you're able to escape the crack house, unscathed with the money, make sure that you blow the stolen money on cheap women (your gender does not matter), booze, gambling, and MORE drugs. However, you're probably going to get caught running out of the crack house by one of the huge and intimidating angry crack head security guards. When this happens, **feel free to piss and/or shit yourself during the altercation.** Doing so will give you a temporary break in the bloody beat down which you'll definitely be getting by the crack dealer. As the crack dealer and his thugs throw vicious blows down upon you, make sure that you pray for a lacerated spleen or a broken jaw (for sympathy points alone). If you can make it out of the crack house alive, make sure that you visit your local hospital to, 1.) get treated for your injuries and 2.) to steal some more painkillers.

The Swap Meet

One can buy everything from pet rattlesnakes to newborn babies for cash at swap meets. Swap meets offer a variety of low-quality goods (and some back alley sexual services), as well as odd gifts and junk that vendors are selling. **Essentially, swap meets are one big garage sale.** The odor that comes out a swap meet matches the odor that a miserable failure has (vomit, mold, mildew, feces, vinegar, and coffee breath), so getting around without people getting physically sick due to your smell, won't be an issue. The first thing you can do at a swap meet is to barter or trade. This is why we strongly encourage a miserable failure to bring the following items with you:

- Your vintage VHS porn collection.
- Your black, cowboy duster jacket.
- Your used knife collection.
- Your grandfather's gold watch from the war.
- Your grandmother's sex toy collection.
- Your mother's diamond wedding ring (you stole during your third intervention).

These items should give you ample opportunity to get a bunch of other useless and worthless shit that you don't need, nor can afford. Feel free to trade down. Most people trade up. The miserable failure trades down. For example, trade your mother's two-karat diamond wedding ring for a box of little green army men. You can also trade your entire vintage porn collection for a hot ham and cheese sandwich in the cafeteria of the swap meet. Whatever you do, don't trade your shit up, always trade down because you should be negotiating in "opposite land." You can also do other activities at swap meets. You can look for a date (REMEMBER: the more obese the better) and you can even steal shit off of people's tables.

Perhaps the best part of going to a swap meet is the fact that you're going to run across several other miserable failures. These folks might be doing the exact same things that you're doing. Try to hang out with them and compare notes as to who is the biggest miserable failure between you all. There is an old expression of "birds of the same feather flock together." This statement has never been truer than when a miserable failure makes new friends at a swap meet. When you're at a swap meet, the miserable failure needs to find other miserable failures so you can swap jail stories and compare your scars, your STD history, and your current credit scores.

Swinger's Parties

Swinger's parties are a lot like pot lucks at Christmas parties. If you want to eat, you're going to have to bring a dish to share. If a miserable failure wants to participate, you're going to have to show up with a partner of the opposite sex. Now, since each sex role is uniquely different at swinger's parties, we will break this down between how male and female miserable failures should act and behave at these glorious events. We mention that swinger's parties are a great place to be yourself because they provide many opportunities to let everyone down, especially sexually.

For Male Miserable Failures

Getting into a swinger's party as a male miserable failure is going to be VERY difficult. This is going to be due in large part to your grotesque and poor physical appearance, terrible hygiene, ugly face, and your out of shape body. Basically, no normal or willing person of sound mind and body would ever want to bang your stank ass. To combat not being able to get into a swinger's party, just as you are, we encourage the male miserable failure to find and bring the hottest hooker, prostitute, or drugged-out gutter slut that you can find. Take your last $200 that you cash advanced off of your welfare card and use it to purchase a street walker's time for a couple of hours.

When you show up at the swinger's party uninvited and unwelcomed, the ONLY reason you'd get in is due to the hot piece of ass that's with you. Stroll in like you own the place and throw your car keys in the empty punch bowl. Check out which women you want to bang (NOTE: being on coke and drunk as a skunk is going to make getting an erection VERY difficult). Next, scope out the buffet (BTW: all swinger's parties have buffets) and help yourself to a giant plate of food. As you mingle around getting to know everyone, lie and tell every woman at the swinger's party that you're a former porn star. Feel free to get the party started by taking off your robe, laying down in the middle of the living room, and shouting out to all of the women, *"It's not going to suck itself, ladies."* Doing this act is going to cause one of two things to happen: 1.) a large and angry husband is going to "escort" (throw you) outside, or 2.) you're going to have the most sickly and desperate housewife take you up on your offer.

When it comes time for the punch bowl game, you and your hooker date should be very high and drunk by now. The way the punch bowl game works is like this... The men throw their car keys in an empty punch bowl. Men then go around picking out another man's set of keys. Whoever's keys you get, that's the wife you get. If you get the hottest housewife at the party, make sure to trade her in for one of the fattest housewives of the party (REMEMBER: you are a lowlife, so your standards must be low too; thus, you don't get to bang any hotties). As everyone starts to "swing" (A.K.A. bang), the miserable failure should walk around the room making play-by-play color commentary at each sexual act by describing it in great detail like "Captain Obvious." Feel free to reach in there and get your hands on whatever part of the body you can in a poor effort to join in. As you get pushed away, move onto the next couple. Feel free to ask to give some women a golden shower. If you're able to get it up, make sure that you don't use a condom if you have sex. Remember, miserable failures do not use condoms. Feel free to break the cardinal sin of swinger's parties and take out your cell phone to live stream everyone on social media and to take various compromising photographs of the entire orgy. After doing this, you will get thrown out of the party-permanently. Your slutty hooker friend will still be allowed to participate because she'll be known as a "unicorn" (NOTE: a unicorn for swinger's parties is a woman that goes single with no man). As you lay outside on the curb crying, you might still be able to hear the faint moans and screaming orgasms coming from inside the house. **This is the opportune time to pleasure yourself in the middle of the dirty sidewalk.** After you "finish your business," run back to the house and pound on the door screaming nonsensical gibberish bullshit. At this point, one of the VERY pissed off husbands is going to pull a handgun on you demanding that you leave his property (BTW: getting a bullet in the kneecap is bonus points). Hobble away and make your way down the street looking for open garages to steal shit in.

For Female Miserable Failures

If you're a female miserable failure and want to "be yourself" at a swinger's party, go out and find the nastiest, trashiest most disgusting and mentally ill man that you know (NOTE: incestual cousins, creepy step-brothers and alcoholic fathers are all great choices too!). Remember, if you want to really have some fun, you'll need to add a male. However, there is one caveat that we touched on earlier. A single woman going to a swinger's party alone is called a "unicorn." So basically, if you can't find a disgusting and disturbing homeless man to go with you uninvited and unwelcomed at a swinger's party, then don't fret and go by yourself! You'll be known as the "unicorn."

Most men are pigs and the female miserable failure knows this fact and exploits this situation. When you show up at a swinger's party, your appearance might give men the heebie-jeebies (BTW: this might be due to your foul odor, greasy hair, and your lack of using razors). However, **a female miserable failure will almost always find that creepy "one dude" at a swinger's party who will stick it in anything that is warm and has a pulse.** The female miserable failure stakes out the room in the corner (while eating the entire bowl of guacamole using only her fingers) looking for the perfect pervert to bang. If you can't find him, before the buffet dinner line starts, take off your robe and get on all fours in the living room. This is breaking the rules of the party, but so what? Feel free to shout out, *"someone put something inside of me, now... anything."* This response will inevitably trigger another male miserable failure at the party to come out of hibernation and over to you to do nasty things with your foul body. If no one will touch you, or you're asked to leave due to your disgusting physical appearance, crawl over to the tv stand, lift your leg and mark your territory like a wild animal.

As the other women gang up on you, tackle you to the ground and drag your sorry ass outside for a "bitch slap fest", make sure that you inform the women that you'll *"be banging their husbands while they are at work."* As the swinger women rip your hair, punch and slap you, you'll start to get dizzy and see stars. This is a good sign and there is a real chance that you'll be getting your tenth concussion from their "curb-stomping head games" which might ensue outside. After the women go back inside, feel free to strip completely nude and try and get back into the swinger's party. Walk straight back in the door and ask for a *"quick gangbang."* Or, simply walk back in like nothing has happened and help yourself to some food in the buffet and then leave again. If any single girl should be getting kicked out of a swinger's party, or not being able to get laid at it, it should be the female miserable failure.

Interstate Gas Stations and Roadside Truck Stops

Wherever there is a giant and sketchy interstate gas station or a dangerous roadside truck stop, you'll find tons of other miserable failures to hang around with. These locations also give the miserable failure plenty of things to do in order to "be themselves." From meth head bikers and obese drunk truckers, to roadside serial killers and lot lizards (prostitutes), the miserable failure can find comfort in being around all of these "outstanding and stellar" individuals. To start with, **interstate gas stations and roadside truck stops are dangerous places to hang around and to hitchhike.** The miserable failure should be camping outside of these locations so you can get your next ride. Sometimes a miserable failure might have to give sexual favors for a ride—DO IT! Sometimes the miserable failure is risking their life by getting into a large, white cargo van with black tinted windows on it. DO IT! Sometimes the miserable failure can find prostitutes, pimps, and drug dealers in these dangerous locations. FIND THEM! There is also a good chance that you will get an opportunity to steal someone's car and take it for a small "joy ride" as you drive away inebriated and high on drugs.

When you get to the interstate gas station or roadside truck stop, the first thing you should do is go into the bathroom. Some of the bathrooms require a key **(if you have a prostitute or a date with you, simply explain to them that banging each other in the bathroom with a lock and key is the equivalent of a five-star hotel experience and just as romantic).** When you go into the restroom, feel free to waste a few dollars of quarters in the adult novelty machine (French ticklers are the #1 score). You also might have an opportunity to find a strung-out tweaker, a drug dealer, or one of your escaped prison buddies in the bathrooms at these locations as well. So please act accordingly. Next, after you take a shit without washing your hands, you should leave and survey the parking lot and try to make some fast cash. Walk up to the various people pumping gas, grab the window cleaner, and start to clean their windows WITHOUT THEIR CONSENT. When you finish, tell them that they owe you $5. If they refuse to pay, strip nude and start screaming until they hand you $5 from their trembling and terrified shaking hands. If you can make a few bucks off of washing people's windshields, feel free to offer your body up sexually for cash as well. If you're having a hard time making money, go behind the gas station and look for the drug dealers. If you have some cash, you can find basically any drug that you want at roadside truck stops. Get your drugs and move inside for your next act.

Next, when you walk into the truck stop, the man behind the counter will probably have a sawed off twenty-gauge pump action shotgun, so be careful. Feel free to make your way over to the beer cooler and grab a twenty-four pack (NOTE: the cheaper and more generic the beer, the better). Grab a few snacks (get all four food groups: "sweet," "salty," "savory," and "rich") as well. As you're walking up to the register, immediately take off running through the door. As you run screaming through the parking lot, hop in the first car that you see and tell the driver to, *"step on it!"* This will inevitably leave you temporarily blinded by the pepper spray mace that they shoot in your face. As you fall out of the car writhing in pain, unable to see, the big, hefty cashier will probably be outside already "taking care of your kneecaps." However, if by some miracle, you have somehow managed to convince some random stranger to give you a ride, remember that they might in fact be a serial killer (FYI: you don't want to die because you need the painful experiences that life brings, so be careful). If you're unable to steal a car, hitchhike or convince a nut job psychopath to let you ride in their car for free, you need to make sure that you find the nearest eighteen-wheeler, climb aboard and hop on the top of it. This will get you a few miles down the road to avoid being beaten or shot by the cashier.

Discount Department Stores

There are various disturbing and disgusting photos on websites showing how bizarre and creepy people dress (and behave) in various discount department stores. In fact, some of those people might be miserable failures! From the 400-pound obese man in drag, to the skinny meth head skanks shoplifting, these stores offer you ample opportunities for you to find other miserable failures; as well as many freak shows, nut jobs, psychopaths, creepers, thieves, drug dealers and disgusting people with foul body odor. When a miserable failure strolls into any discount department store, make sure that you stop at the elderly door greeter and say hi to them with a few tickles. As the old codger lays on the ground laughing, feel free to give him a few belly raspberries as you blow on his stomach (FYI: thus making a farting sound). After you've tickled the retiree door greeter into a mild cardiac arrest, make sure that you leave before the out of shape security guard form tackles you on aisle six with a "purple nurple." If you're hungry, these establishments offer you the perfect place for you to eat for free!

Miserable failures LOVE the chip and snack aisle at these large department stores. When you get to the aisle, grab whatever chips you want, open the bag and proceed to eat them at random. If chips fall from your open mouth as you chew, don't worry about it and make your way over to the women's changing room, leaving a trail of disgusting, half-eaten chip crumbs behind you. **When you finish the bag of chips, simply toss the bag on the ground, or stash it on a random shelf.** This is an important act because you're providing job security for someone at this business. If it were not for pieces of shit like you, stealing food and leaving the wrappers in various locations, the person cleaning up after you wouldn't have a job, would they? If you are thirsty, grab a two-liter bottle of soda, shake it up, open it, and have a few gulps (NOTE: be careful not to blind yourself from the pressurized soda that will be spraying you in your eyes). Don't worry about the soda mess you've just created. Again, some asshole with a mop will be by soon enough to clean up **your messiness**. Along your way, make sure you swing by the liquor aisle for your much-needed fifth of whiskey.

The next place you should go is over to the clothing section to get yourself a quick cat nap in the women's changing room. When you get over to the women's changing room, finish your fifth of whiskey and walk around asking various women if you can give them free mammograms for breast cancer awareness month. When they decline, inform them that you're a doctor and offer to give them an *"OBGYN appointment free of charge"* in the dressing room as well. As the women run away in terror, try to make your way to the pharmacy. The pharmacy is a FREE FOR ALL. Anything goes. When you walk up to the pharmacist's counter, rip open your robe and flash everyone, thus exposing yourself. Next, find the condom section, and stash a few boxes under your robe (you can sell these later for cash in various high school parking lots later). You can also see if you can make your way into the prescription section of the pharmacy to grab some of your favorite pills without being caught. Some of your classic addiction pills might include:

- Xanax
- Valium
- Oxycodone
- Darvocet

- Codeine
- Adderall
- Ritalin
- Percocet

If you had the opportunity to grab a few illegally obtained prescription drugs without getting busted, you should feel very happy. **Pop a few and make your way over to the hunting section.** The hunting section offers the miserable failure a chance to purchase (if you have enough of your grandmother's stolen cash left) a shotgun or a rifle. Even if you're legally not allowed to own a gun due to your many felonies, still try and buy one if you can. If you don't have enough money to buy one on the spot, you can still ask to "hold one." If the manager of the hunting section is dumb enough, he'll hand you a gun to "check out." As you hold the gun, feel free to roll on the ground with the gun while screaming, *"get down, enemy approaching!"* Then proceed to cause a diversion that gives you enough time to sneak away with the weapon. With your shotgun draped over your shoulder, make your way over to the electronics department next (FYI: the sight of a miserable failure strolling through a store carrying a shotgun is going to alert the local S.W.A.T. Team).

Before the cops arrive (again), feel free to pick fights with various people in the electronic section (after all, who do these fuckers think they are?). If you see someone reaching for a DVD that YOU want, grab it before they can and shove them to the ground (NOTE: channel your "Black Friday" Christmas shopping fighting experience RAGES for reference). As the two of you scrap and fight, feel free to make sure you knock over as many shelves as possible while maximizing the damage of as many goods as possible.

After you've gotten your ass kicked in the electronics section by the pissed off and over-worked school bus driver, head over to the beer section, grab a case and start pounding those suckers down. Ask a few employees if they'd like to challenge you to shotgun a beer (BTW: if you ask enough employees, you will have a few takers). After you have finished your boozing while eating frozen and raw pizzas from the freezer section, make a full-blown sprint through the store while shouting at the top of your lungs, *"I'm a blood-thirsty vampire!"* End your sprint by running full-speed into the center aisle display of popcorn. After you've destroyed the popcorn display, walk down any aisle of the grocery section and stick out each arm. As you stroll along, make sure that you knock as many items as possible off of the shelves **(AGAIN: think of the job security you're going to be providing the janitorial staff- who subsequently might be waiting for you in the parking lot as you leave so they can shove a mop stick up your ass).**

By now, you're going to be asked to leave the store by an angry manager. When they ask you to leave (remember that the cops are probably on their way), ask them if they'd like to dance with you to the soothing sounds of the elevator music being played over the intercom. When they turn down your request, give the manager an "Indian rub burn" on their forearm and take off running as fast as you can towards the exit while pissing yourself. As you run through the store, grab as much shit as you can hold to take with you. When you reach the exit, you're going to be greeted by a close line from a police officer just arriving on scene (HELLOOOOOOO police brutality lawsuit!!!!). As you're taken away in cuffs via the ambulance, be sure to sing various Christmas carols to the employees of the store who are actively videotaping your shenanigans and broadcasting it live on social media. The point about these stores is simple..... Be yourself.

Strip Clubs and Whorehouses

Whether you're a male miserable failure or a female miserable failure, going into strip clubs and whore houses in order to "be yourself" is mandatory. When you walk into a strip bar and you're a female miserable failure, ask the manager when *"amateur night"* is. Stripping and taking your clothes off for a group of perverted, creepy, little Japanese businessmen in from out of town is a great way to make a few extra bucks for Christmas. Now, due to your rather grotesque and non-sexy appearance, the strip club might not let you on stage to perform. If this is the case, run up there anyway and give the strip pole a few grinds as you toss your dirty robe into the crowd. When no one tips you because your physical appearance is so repulsive, physically walk out to the crowd and try grabbing as many wads of cash or wallets as possible. When an angry group of real strippers beat the shit out of you in the parking lot, remember that you deserve the pain you're getting.

For the male miserable failure, going to a strip club is a great place to find other guy miserable failures and to have some fun by being yourself. When you walk into the strip club, sit at the front table closest to the stage. Even though you don't have any cash, just relax. Simply use your welfare card at the ATM for some tip money. When the strippers dance in front of you, if you'd like to play with yourself- GO FOR IT! Feel like making it rain? Hop up on the stage and make it rain with your five $1 bills on Stacey the stripper. If you don't get kicked out, make sure that you try to get a private table dance (they say that strippers like money enough to dance for anyone and this does not apply to you as you're a special exception to the rule). When you're taken into the VIP private lounge, ask the stripper for any sex act that you want and inform her that you can pay her in drugs or stolen merchandise. If they refuse, ask them, *"can you at least show me a nipple?"* The final rule we will discuss is a rule we like to call, "The Midget Rule." Upon entering a strip club or a whore house, you must request *"The Midget"* (NOTE: how to deal with an overdosed small person will be covered in another section). Every strip club has little people secretly working there as backup strippers. Most of the time they keep these little bastards locked away in treasure chests in the back and only bring them out for special requests. This is why you need to request one. When the little person stripper comes out to dance for you, ask them if you can rub their little head for "good luck." This is going to cause your little person striptease dance to end abruptly. Remember that all strip clubs and whorehouses have a token midget, so please use accordingly

Whorehouses are a special place where you can find all sorts of broken miserable failure fuckfaces. It is also another place that gives you a chance to truly be yourself. Most whorehouses are illegal, so finding one might be difficult. If you can't find a whorehouse, remember that crack heads will do anything for more drugs, so you can use your narcotics to lure the crack heads to do whatever you want sexually from them (ADVICE: male crack heads have a difficult time getting erections and female crack heads are often unclean). If you're fortunate enough to find a whorehouse, walk in and ask the pimp or the madam, *"I want your nastiest hooker that you have."* If you're lucky, you'll get a hooker with just as many STDs as you do, so don't worry about wearing any protection (AGAIN, miserable failures don't use condoms). When they ask you to pre-pay for their services, simply distract them by pulling out your little bag of illegal drugs and offering a "peace treaty." As you cut out the four long lines of cocaine on the table in the waiting room, ask if they will trade drugs for sex (sometimes this is a good exchange). Feel free to share your drugs with the hookers regardless of their "exchange policy." Whorehouses are also a great place to drink for free. As long as you're still negotiating a price, they're going to be serving you up FREE alcohol, so drink up buddy! Now, sooner or later, your whorehouse visit will end abruptly and you'll more than likely be asked to leave at gunpoint immediately from the pimp or madam (FYI: if you have to take a gunshot anywhere, choose the kneecaps or the foot so you can hobble around and use the "cripple excuse").

Dog and Cockfighting Matches

Only real lowlife, scumbag degenerate losers attend illegal dogfights or cockfights. This is precisely why miserable failure' should attend them! Generally, cockfights happen at 3:00 in the morning in an abandoned warehouse downtown. Dogfights take place usually on someone's property, so finding one of those might be more difficult.

When you attend a dogfight, remember that there is a good chance that you'll be getting your unconscious body badly assaulted by angry gamblers in the back yard of an illegal dogfighting house (be still, my heart). Dogfighting matches are dangerous and deadly places to go. Failure to pay your debt s, or your attempts to rob the mobsters and gangstas that attend them can and will result in a broken jaw, smashed face, and a lacerated liver. When you first get to a dogfight, remember to always bet on the bigger dog. The bigger dog generally wins the fight. If the big dog loses the fight, try to grab your money back off of the bet table and run like hell. Whenever you do win the dogfight bet, brag and strut about like a douchebag while fanning the other losers' faces with your dirty cash that you just won. If your dog is about to lose a fight, jump into the middle of the ring (more on how to deal with rabies in another section) and protect your dog from the other dog. As you're drug out screaming by your hair, remember that dogfighting matches are illegal and you might get arrested when the cops are called.

Cockfighting matches are very dangerous and sad. Most of the people involved in cockfighting matches are Mexican drug cartels, strung out speed freaks, guys named Kyle who live in the trailer park, Colombian drug lords and angry Cuban mobsters. The same rule applies for gambling on cockfights as it does to dogfights; always bet on the "bigger cock." If your cock (LOL) is losing the fight, hop in the ring to protect him (more on how to get chicken feathers out of your punctured skull in a later chapter). When you lose a bet at a cockfight, cry like a schoolgirl as you lay down in the middle of the ring protesting (HINT: you will not be getting your money back, so don't even try). As the sun comes up, the cockfight will end and you'll be in a great possession to wander the streets downtown looking for more drugs. Remember that miserable failures attend cockfights and dogfights, so making your presence known is essential (more on the various and numerous uses for dead roosters and dogs in another section).

County Jail

When you're arrested again, you're going to end up in your local county slammer. When you enter the jail again, you should be getting a standing ovation from some of your former prison pals and even by some of the guards. Do a little dance! Get into it! After all, miserable failures set records for the total number of times they've been arrested. In fact, miserable failures have been in jail and arrested so many times, you might even have your own entrance theme music, just like a professional wrestler. When you make your way into the jail for the intake process, make sure you make small chat with the other guards and officers you've come to know over the years. **Give them fist bumps and watch as they exchange money with each other betting on when your ass would show back up in the slammer.** The first stop you're going to be making is in the fingerprinting room. When you walk into the fingerprint room, make sure that you grab the ink pad immediately and playfully joke around with the officer that you're going to "tattoo" him with the ink. After you regain consciousness due to the thunder punch to the throat you've probably just received from the officer, make sure you comply with him and allow him to take your fingerprints (NOTE: even if your fingers are broken and smashed do to the bar fight you just got into).

The next stop in the county jail arrest process is the classic mugshot photograph experience. Miserable failures get arrested frequently. This is why you should have an elaborate series of eclectic, infamous, and memorable mugshots you've accumulated over the years in your extensive rap sheet. **In fact, your mug shots should be so funny, unique, and interesting that they should show up in "funniest mugshots" during a simple internet search.** When the police tell you to stare at the camera for your picture, quickly turn around and laugh at the officers. When they spin you around to forcibly hold you while attempting to take the next photo, make some silly faces and shake your head like a wild, heavy metal headbanger rock star. Next, the police will give you your one and only, single and solitary phone call. Most normal people would call their parents (you can't because you've been disowned), or their spouse (you can't because you're divorced), or their children (you can't because you're forbidden to contact them unless it's a supervised phone call), or their lawyer (you don't have a lawyer; in fact, you have gone through MANY public defenders that openly refuse to defend you). The miserable failure instead should use their one and only solo call on one of the following:

- A local radio station (to try to win those two free tickets to "Princesses on Ice").
- Your fifth ex-spouse (while sobbing and asking for bail money).
- Your life coach (to fire them).
- Your drug dealer (to ask to purchase another ounce).
- A pizza joint (ordering a pizza for yourself to be delivered to the local county jail is a classic move).

After you've made your call, they are going to issue you your familiar and customary orange jumpsuit (relax, there will be bloodstains on them momentarily) and escort you through the jail as various prisoners make commentary on what they "intend to do to you" in the mess hall, in the showers or out in "the yard." Taunt your fellow prisoners! Flip them off and make obscene sexual gestures with your hands (FYI: this will come back to bite you in the ass). When you get to your jail cell, make sure you physically proclaim to your new cellmate which bed you intend on taking over. After the first beating takes place, you should ask your new cellmate if you can call them, *"master."* Going back into the county jail for the twelfth time is par for the course for the miserable failure. In fact, the miserable failure might find comfort in being behind bars as opposed to being free out in public. You can find miserable failures in just about any county jail cell in the country, and they are great places to be yourself.

Rehab

You're a boozer. You're a druggie. You're a pill popper. Yes, you are a miserable failure. Going in and out of rehab on a consistent basis is something that you should be doing monthly. If you want to make some side cash, loot your grandparent's bathroom cabinet and grab their prescriptions so you can sell them in the detox wing at the rehab clinic before you get admitted again. Sometimes, you need to go into rehab because you have no place to go after your apartment eviction. Sometimes, you are court-ordered to go into rehab (again) after your ninth DUI. Whatever the case is, when you go into rehab, you should treat it like a luxury resort. When you walk into the detox room drunk for the intake process, they are going to give you a brand spanking new sweatpants outfit (SCORE). They're also going to feed you and they are going to give you a warm, cozy bed to sleep in (NOTE: when you're detoxing, you're going to be sick, so vomiting is probably coming).

After you've detoxed, make sure that you make your status known in the smoking yard with the others in rehab. The first day you go into rehab, you need to find the biggest dude possible (for ladies, find the scariest bitch around) and attempt to pick a fight with them. Getting two black eyes, a broken nose, a busted lip, and a hairline fracture to your jaw is a great way to show the entire rehab clinic that YOU'RE THE MISERABLE FAILURE AROUND THESE HERE PARTS! When you are in rehab you must do any following of the suggestions below:

- Gamble and play strip poker in the lounge area with the other recovering addicts.

- Attempt to trade prescription pills for cigarettes (or sexual favors).
- In a group class, laugh at the others as they share their sob stories (HINT: no one has more sob stories than you do).
- Take in unsupervised late-night snacking sessions in the cafeteria.

The workers and counselors in the rehab clinic should know you very well. In fact, they should have an entire cabinet saved for you which is filled with a giant large folder file listing your EXTENSIVE treatment history. You might even have some nicknames from the staff at the rehab clinic. Your nicknames might be some of the following:

- Shitface (or Mrs. Shitface).
- Kleptomaniac Kerri (or Kleptomaniac Karl).
- Pill popper McGee.
- Meth Head Marty (or Meth Head Mary).

The only reason you will ever be kicked out of rehab is if you break their rules (doing drugs, drinking alcohol, stealing, etc.). And you do not want to leave rehab too soon because you actually have a place to stay and hot meals served to you daily. Rehab is actually a great place to live in "luxury" for a while. So, sit back, relax, and enjoy some much-needed R&R on the back of the taxpayer.

10

THE FRUITS OF YOUR LABOR

Crying 101

If you follow the methods outlined in this book, crying (mainly thanks to your self-inflicted depression, current bank account balance and painful anal fissures) will eventually become an everyday occurrence. **USE THIS TO YOUR ADVANTAGE!** Like sex and blackmail, tears are powerful tools in the "miserable failure manipulation arsenal" (PRO TIP: combining sex with blackmail is a great way to get laid). Free food and booze, extensions on overdue rent, and even forgiveness (to only name a few perks) can all be yours by tapping into the awesome power of "crying like a little bitch." It's also important to remember that no one wants to associate with a "downer" who is always tearful and constantly upset about everything. This negative energy repels people, and thus is a perfect pathway for you to achieve isolation and loneliness (two of a miserable failure's favorite things). Taking advantage of your daily tears is an essential skill for any miserable failure to master. Not only is it an incredibly important part of being a manipulative, lonely, bastard, but it's also awesomely easy! Study the simple principals listed below in this section, and it won't be long until you're sipping a hard apple cider in a tarot card reader's shop with a heroin needle sticking out of your arm.

Something To Cry About

As someone with terrible hygiene, multiple addictions, and a preference for unprotected sex with strangers; you're going to have LOTS of physical pain to cry about. Bad hygiene will most certainly lead to deep cavities (in the few remaining teeth you have), constant painful infections (puss = you're doing it right), and severe rashes. Your multiple drug and alcohol addictions (if managed correctly) are also an easy way to increase your physical pain. Hard drugs and booze can cause significant injuries via "face plant" type falls, but also when you're not using them (due to the intense flu-like withdrawal symptoms). Years of unprotected sex have left you the PROUD owner of multiple STDs (and infertility). With "classics" like herpes and gonorrhea "under your belt" (literally), you're also no stranger to miserable making benefits of painful urination, infections, and genital bleeding. So, don't hold back when the burning and/or stinging starts, cry about it (A LOT)!

Crying is especially effective in alienating people when you're sobbing because "things didn't go your way." This *"life isn't fair"* victim mentality is an essential attitude for ALL miserable failures to employ and should be adopted by you immediately. You should NEVER accept responsibility for your own behavior and ALWAYS seek to blame others for your misfortune. Remember, self-reflection (unless used to deepen your depression) is the miserable failure's enemy. Nothing is ever **your fault**, and make sure everyone around you knows it by crying like a little bitch. If you're caught masturbating in the produce aisle again, call all your "friends" to bail you out of jail while you're sobbing hysterically, and tell them you blame the grocery store for "rating you out." If you're financially broke (and you definitely are) visit everyone you know, and beg for money while letting your river of tears flow (yes, they know you're a lazy bum who refuses to work and wastes your welfare checks on "full-service" massage packages). However, despite their annoyance, they will still "fork over" the cash to you because you're so "upset" (#SUCKERS!!!!!). They'll then do their best to avoid you after that, and that's a "win-win" situation for a miserable failure. When in doubt, "squirt" a few tears out, and no one will want to associate with you, EVER!

How To Make Yourself Cry

Just in case the physical pain, and mental anguish of just being you isn't enough to produce nearly nonstop tears, you should also learn the skill of making yourself cry on demand (C.O.D.). The ability to C.O.D., or produce tears whenever needed is less of an art form and more of an endurance test. Much like a great actor who can make themselves cry on demand, a miserable failure needs to be able to shed tears whenever it will benefit their life. You'll need to improvise your form of self-punishment based on each particular situation, but the concept always remains the same. Inflict intense physical, or psychological pain on yourself, severe enough to produce tears, but in an undetectable way as to not appear phony. Again, you'll need to improvise in most situations, but the list below conveys the core methodology of making yourself C.O.D.

- **"The Prick"** - Carry a tack, small nail, or dirty syringe in your pants pocket at all times. When you need to cry, just stick your hands in the appropriate pants pocket, and begin POKING the shit out of your leg. Stab yourself enough times with a rusty nail (being sure to twist with each prick), and you'll be watery-eyed for sure. (PRO TIP: refrain from following your natural instincts, and DO NOT carry a razor blade or knife in your pocket, as these stabbing items go too deep, and thus produce too much easily detectable blood).

- **"The Pull"** - The miserable failure is quite proud of their "flowing bush" of pubic hair. Besides being a wonderful way to hide genital warts, your pubes are a great tool to make you cry. Just pre-cut a hole in one of your pants pockets. Then, when the time is right, reach in and pull out a handful of hair (FOR MALE MISERABLE FAILURES: this is the only time you should participate in "pulling out").
- **"The Flick"** - Continue utilizing your pre-cut pocket hole with this method. Simply reach down to your genital area, and rapidly flick your pee pee or wee wee until the tears of pain begin to flow. If this fails, be sure to attempt the emergency "grab and twist" method before retreating from your "naughty zone."
- **"The Blast From the Past"** - This psychological method is always most effective when combined with one of the above listed physical C.O.D. methods. Simply hyper-focus your thoughts on all the emotionally painful events that have occurred in your life. Think about the untimely death of pets, the time you tried to trade your elderly mother in for cocaine, your spouse cheating on you with the entire local school board, being made "fun of" in school for "wetting yourself" (your complete lack of bladder control continues to this day, thanks to alcohol abuse), and all your life destroying divorces. These horrendous thoughts, especially when coupled with physical pain, will turn on the "tear fountain" quickly, and easily.
- **"The Drop"** - This method is the easiest way to produce tears, but BE AWARE that when using it, you also run the greatest risk of detection. All you need is an empty eyedropper and any kind of citrus liquid. Fill the eyedropper with your chosen citrus or hot pepper liquid (lemon juice, orange juice, ghost pepper oil, etc.), and simply release a few drops into your ocular cavity. This will burn terribly bad, and will produce instant

tears. Just be sure to only use this method when you are not being watched.

Using Tears To Your Advantage

Be it for getting sympathy, more free stuff, pity sex, or even after being pepper sprayed by the local church pastor; miserable failures always cry as an act of manipulation. The miserable failure will most often use crying to their advantage when attempting to get out of a "jam," or to seek temporary relief from the consequences of their own awful and deliberate behavior. Since you truly possess ZERO empathy and NEVER feel remorse, your phony tears are the best way to "convince" others that you're "sorry" and/or have "learned your lesson" (this is obviously total bullshit). It's not that you don't want to face the consequences of your transgressions (you certainly do), but you'd rather face the intensified vengeance of someone who "gave you a break" the first time (because you cried like a little bitch) only to later realize you were completely full of shit, and never had any intentions of discontinuing being a total dick. The following are examples of when the miserable failure should definitely cry to take advantage of other's kindness:

- You're in court facing charges of public nudity/intoxication (you got drunk and forgot to wear pants to the supermarket). Sob uncontrollably and blame one of your other "personalities" until the judge lets you go home, or gives you another eleven-month "psych ward vacation."
- After a drug-fueled night full of unprotected sex and Russian Roulette, you stumble into your pathetic excuse for an apartment early one morning. To your surprise, your court appointed AA sponsor, life coach, and entire family (A.K.A. the source of 91% of your "leaching" of free stuff) are waiting in the living room to perform another "intervention." This time,

they're threatening to "cut you off" financially if you don't go to rehab AGAIN. You know this won't work because "Reggie" (your longtime drug dealer) told you that tomorrow he expects a shipment of the best Colombian "Bam Bam" on the planet Earth. You can't miss that! Just start crying, and ask to leave next week after you've had time to get your "affairs" in order.

- Thanks to some great PCP, you get pulled over for reckless driving on the way back from your kid's school in the morning. As the police officer (his name is Jerry and he's arrested you fourteen times) asks you to "step out of the car slowly" you begin to squirt tears. While being handcuffed for driving through the unoccupied playground, really turn on the "tear fountain," and ask him to "cut you a break" because you didn't run anyone over this time.
- It's court-supervised visitation day with your "pain in the ass" kids. You head off to the mall (your predetermined public meeting place), but decide to stop for a quick game of "bully the homeless" on the way. Time gets away from you (because it now takes you over an hour to chase down, harass and threaten the homeless), and you miss your meeting. Just call your children crying loudly about getting your car stolen, and how "sad" you are about *"standing them up."* To back up your story, be sure to drive your, or whoever's vehicle your kids see you drive, into the nearest lake so you're not seen driving it again.
- Everyone at church knows you're financially broke because of your gambling addiction, expensive sexual fetishes, and your refusal to do any legal work. Don't let this stop you from letting tears stream down your face as you stand in front of the exit door holding a sign that reads: "I need money, you fuckers."
- So, your ex-partner caught you in an orgy at your neighbor's house, your obsessive calls got them fired from their job, and you've wrecked both of your credit scores. That doesn't mean

you shouldn't try to get them back, or at least "creep them out." Call your ex sobbing uncontrollably and ask them to *"take you back."* Whenever possible, leave them long voicemails where, thanks to your nonstop crying, the only words that can be clearly understood are *"suicide"* and *"dead."*
- You have a disease (NOTE: you have multiple diseases), and you NEED your medicine to "stay cool." When you run out of booze, just stand on your neighbor's doorstep crying as you plead for "a quick sip" from their vintage liquor cabinet. If they refuse, just cry harder, and remind them what happens when you don't "stay cool."
- Cry loudly, and publicly at the car dealership when they refuse to let you test drive another vehicle (because you have no money, no driver's license, horrific body odor, and you still haven't returned the last car you "took for a test drive"). Let the tears fall like rain, throw in a temper tantrum in front of the other customers, and you'll be driving away in no time.

It's important to remember that the aforementioned situations to cry in, are only those commonly occurring in the life of most miserable failures. You may encounter them, or similar circumstances on your journey to failing miserably. No matter what situation presents itself, ALWAYS default to crying like a little bitch. The power of your tears just might be enough to get you anything you want (like the crack dealer to stop punching you in the throat for not paying), and also everything you need (like MORE free crack cocaine).

Crying Like A Little Bitch: The Dos and Don'ts

When the miserable failure cries to manipulate others, it must look natural. If you need to pause and think about becoming tearful before you start crying, people will see straight through your manipulative bullshit, and you won't get what you want. The tears need to flow on demand and without any hesitation. Study the list below of do's and don'ts carefully and repeatedly so that when the appropriate situation to cry arises, you'll immediately default to crying like a little bitch. Again, we are not referring to the "all-natural" tears that come automatically as a result of you getting into another bloody bar fight (you always lose), or looking at pictures of your ex as you drink copious amounts of gin alone in your shitty apartment (your typical Friday night). This is all about being a manipulative fuck face that uses crying as a defense mechanism.

- **DO**: Talk about your ex and cry about the breakup in an attempt to get "pity sex" on every first date.
- **DON'T**: Stop crying during pity sex because it's making them uncomfortable.
- **DO**: Cry uncontrollably and beg for forgiveness as your boss fires you for downloading porn on your work computer.
- **DON'T**: Let them delete the files before you make copies and cry even harder when they do.
- **DO**: Cry while masturbating because of the intolerable pain from missing your ex.
- **DON'T**: Allow your orgasm to stop your "sob fest," and don't allow the bleeding to stop your masturbating.
- **DO**: Cry when you're knocked over, and trampled by a crowd of Black Friday shoppers trying to get a cheap big-screen TV.
- **DON'T**: Cry because of the physical pain, but rather because of your lack of a new TV to pawn for drug money.
- **DO**: Let the tears flow while you stand outside the veterinarian's office waiting for your dog to be "put down."
- **DON'T**: Tell the vet that you made a mistake, and that wasn't really your dog.
- **DO**: Cry while an entire lesbian biker gang beats you mercilessly for your "nice bikes, buttheads" comment.
- **DON'T**: Stop crying just because your tear ducts have been smashed-in with a crowbar.

- **DO**: Cry when you get banned from all social media sites for posting photos of your bloodstained morning bowel movements.
- **DON'T**: See a doctor despite everyone who sees the photos urging you to.

Depression 101

If.... "Depression" is an "Illness."
And... a "Miserable Failure" is always "Depressed."
Then... a "Miserable Failure" is an "Illness."

A miserable failure is not happy... At all. Period. It doesn't matter if you win the lottery, have a threesome with two hot models, or become wealthy and famous, it's never going to be enough to make you happy. The only thing that truly makes you "happy" is being depressed. That's the reason you're called a "MISERABLE failure." If you follow the methods outlined in this horribly-written book, depression will come naturally, and will usually require no extra effort on your part. The combination of painful breakups, frequent job loss, and multiple infections, is normally enough to "get the job done." However, even the most experienced miserable failures (often called "fuck faces") can still find themselves trapped inside a "positivity streak." This is just a series of random events that the "average" person would consider positive (getting promoted rather than fired, not having an STD, etc.). If this happens to you, it is of the utmost importance that you remain negative, and focus solely on cultivating your deep dark depression. DO NOT be "sucked in" by the lure of the "good life." It's only the "shit life" for you! In order to ensure your continued lack of success, it's crucial that you develop a practical understanding of the two pillars of depression: **loneliness**, and **desolation** (A.K.A. "the twins.")

Loneliness

You destroy everything you "touch," especially your personal relationships. Friends, family and exes; they all hate you! Maybe it's the money you still owe your spouse for paying off all nineteen of your over the limit and maxed out credit cards. Maybe it's the sex brothel you started in your grandparent's basement when they went on vacation last summer (it also doubles as a doomsday bunker). Maybe it's the fact that you constantly try to stab your friends in the back (FYI: plastic forks can hurt others). Maybe it's the fact that most of your days are spent watching soap operas, drinking scotch, prank calling your ex, and pissing yourself on the couch (this is considered "phase one" on your journey to failing miserably). Whatever the reason, they definitely don't want anything to do with a chump like you! In fact, if you don't count your drug dealer, the fun folks down at the local crack house, or your recently paroled prison buddies; the miserable failure has nobody in their life they can "lean on" for support. This is PERFECT... Being totally isolated is exactly what you want, and should be considered a milestone on your journey to failing miserably. This way, you'll be all alone when the proverbial "shit hits the fan" and you'll have no one to ask for help when that proverbial shit ends up all over you (stop smiling, you fecal freak).

Miserable failures should not be referred to as "lone wolves." A wolf is far too powerful of an animal to be associated with a pathetic loser like you (NOTE: however, you should have a wolf tattooed somewhere on your face, neck, scalp, or cheek to complement your scorpion, spider, bat, and dragon ink). Instead, think of yourself as a "lone jellyfish" that just floats along as a useless blob of existence, stinging the hell out of everyone around it (especially friends and family). Your goal is not to hurt anyone (except yourself), but to end up totally alone, and thus free from the potential failure blocking influence of the "normal" people around you (welcome to isolation....). Remember, on your race to the bottom, you will encounter plenty of assholes who "only want to help." Screw those people! It's your choice to be miserable, and no one has the right to stop you. If they really wanted to help, they'd buy you a gift box filled with illegal drugs, pure grain alcohol, random unlabeled painkillers, a copy of this book, and some brand-new shiny razor blades.

With the exception of interacting with the occasional liquor store clerk (that you rob at gunpoint), or the pizza delivery person (who you also robbed at gunpoint), the miserable failure doesn't have many people in their life, outside of their court-ordered support group (the COSG). The "COSG" consists of a long list of buttheads who some "jerk off" judge thinks can "help you turn things around." These are the only long term "friends" you may not be able to avoid having in your life. However, with focus and use of the proper "leverage" (calling in suicidal threats, texting photos of your bowel movements, etc.) the miserable failure can effectively cause several members of their COSG to pull themselves out of your "situation" voluntarily.

The Miserable Failure Court Ordered Support Group

- Therapist (you are currently on therapist #14 due to the suicides from the others having to deal with you).
- Backup Therapist (just in case ANOTHER one commits suicide after your session).
- Addiction Specialist (this is the person tasked with getting you off drugs... LOL).
- AA Sponsor ("you" and "alcohol" go together like "coffee" and "creamer").
- Sex Addicts Sponsor (you attend these meetings solely in hopes of hooking up).
- Life Coach (just describing your weekend activities has made this person puke).
- Backup Life Coach (just in case ANOTHER one tries to murder you after your session and failure to make a payment).

- Anger Management Coach (thanks to them, you no longer hit anyone except for yourself).
- Parole Officer (you call him the "Drug Test Nazi").
- Personal Psychic (it may seem a little unorthodox, but the judge was out of ideas).
- Volunteer Coach (volunteering at the local soup kitchen and breadline that you ransacked last Thanksgiving is going to make for awkward times during your "giving back" times).

Since all of the above-mentioned members of your COSG are technically required to give reports to the judge, you need to make sure that you're at least "going through the motions" of trying to "clean up" your life. For example, show up for all of your court-ordered AA meetings, but do so high as a kite. You won't be drunk, and you won't smell like booze (this will keep your "ball sucking" AA sponsor off your back). However, you will have a great time thanks to the six blunts, three fat lines, and a quarter ounce of shrooms you consumed in the parking lot. Be sure to attend all of your therapy sessions, but also be sure to "go above and beyond" by attending a few "extra" sessions. Just show up at your therapist's home randomly, crying, on Christmas morning (7:13 to be exact), extremely high, and extremely "suicidal." There go their holiday plans that day! The point is to only do the bare minimum, be as annoying as possible, and to do it heavily intoxicated whenever possible. In other words, just be yourself.

Outside of meeting with the "dumb fucks" in your COSP, you should remain completely isolated, eating giant cinnamon buns for every meal, and drinking handles of vodka to wash them down. The combination of carbs and lots of hard liquor is the perfect "depression diet" for a miserable failure (miserable failure = "fat mess"). If your near-total isolation has got you super bored, entertain yourself by making a few prank phone calls to any of the judges preceding over one of your many active cases (give a fake name and claim to be their unknown love child). If you're stilled bored, just take the "easy way out", and simply increase your drug use to "coma levels" (at least you won't be conscious). Remember, your ultimate goal is to have your loneliness lead to deeper and darker depression, but you should still have fun doing it!

Desolation

Desolation is an absolutely horrible place to be in for a human. **This is exactly why we want you to be in it.**

des·o·la·tion
ˌdesəˈlāSH(ə)n/
noun
noun: **desolation**

1. A state of complete emptiness or destruction.
2. Anguished misery or loneliness.

You have heard professional athletes refer to magical moments when they are "in the zone." Being in the zone is a rare occasion when everything works out easily, and effortlessly in their favor. The basketball player seems to make all the shots, the pitcher just keeps throwing strikes, and the quarterback can't help but complete every pass for a first down. For the miserable failure, achieving a constant state of desolation is considered "being in the zone." When your spouse asks for a divorce, your car gets repossessed, you have a gnarly herpes outbreak, AND another family member attempts to murder you (all in the same day), YOU ARE IN THE ZONE!

Being in a constant state of desolation (A.K.A. "the zone"), sets the tone for your life perfectly, and is a fantastic way to achieve even deeper darker depression. It causes you to hyper-focus on feelings of frustration, hopelessness, and being alone. Engaging in these types of thoughts and feelings consistently over time will mentally "beat you down" and will hopefully lead to things getting even worse (fingers crossed). The goal is to stack failure on top of failure, infection on top of infection, and break up on top of break up, until you've created an existence of total dark desolation. Then, after you've built and now permanently reside in the desolation "zone", depression will become automatic. You'll no longer have to think or do something to trigger your depression. While you're in the zone, it'll just happen as a function of you breathing.

As a miserable failure, you are keenly aware of how big of a piece of shit you really are, so finding yourself living a life of total desolation should come as no surprise (and should be celebrated!). However, when and how you finally reach "the zone" of desolation is anyone's guess. You just have to believe 100% that the "shit storm" is coming, and then it will come. Just trust in this program, and your ability to be a complete "dip shit." Remember, you've purposely caused self-destruction on a level beyond comprehension, and a life of ultra-depressive desolation is your just reward. You've striven to become broke, drink too much, be hated, have bad hygiene, be a social retard, and not be employed. Years of drug abuse have eliminated your ability to become sexually aroused, you know the repo guy by name, and your credit score just hit 350 (again). You're genuinely excited to file bankruptcy a personal record, nineteenth time (congratulations!), and your friend's car just got impounded because of your parking tickets (you'll be down one more friend in no time!). This terrible behavior has set the stage perfectly for a life of complete desolation, and inevitable deep dark depression. One day you too can wake up naked, still intoxicated, and bleeding from the anus in an abandoned dumpster with no idea how you got there. Dreams do come true! Don't ever give up!

The Law of Depression

If, despite your continued efforts to destroy your life, you still have not achieved maximum depression, it's probably because you're not following the law. The "Law of Attraction" is a universal law of life, just like the law of gravity. The law of gravity says that "what goes up must come down," and the law of attraction says that "like attracts like." Gravity is working all the time, with or without your permission, and so is attraction. Basically, the law of attraction works like this... If you think positive thoughts and try to feel good, happiness and prosperity will come your way with no further effort on your part. This combination of laziness and wishful thinking is the perfect recipe for failure! These same principals can and should be liberally applied to your depression.

One of the most effective methods of invoking the law of attraction is through visualization. It's a very simple process (which is perfect for a moron like you). If you want a new house, all you need to do is visualize yourself living there, and soon you will be. If you want a million dollars in your bank account, just visualize yourself cashing a big check, and soon you'll be rich. In order to deepen your depression, the miserable failure should ALWAYS and ONLY visualize **negative circumstances** and **outcomes**. Below you will find a list of suggested visualizations that are geared toward attracting the worst possible things into your life. Use them daily, especially prior to falling asleep, as this is a time when your mind is most open to suggestion. With continued practice of this method, you should quickly begin to see the manifestation of desolation in your life and become even more depressed as a result.

Negative Visualization Ideas

Visualizations for your Overall Health

- Visualize yourself standing in front of a team of doctors, and hear them say things like, *"we've never seen this many infections before," "we're going to have to amputate,"* or *"you have worms growing in there."*
- Visualize yourself lying in a hospital bed getting your semi-blood-filled colostomy bag changed.

Visualizations for your Finances

- Visualize yourself running down the street chasing your repossessed vehicle, and screaming, *"I left my pot in there, asshole!"*
- Visualize bill collectors waiting outside your home with baseball bats and samurai swords.
- Visualize a zero-dollar balance on your next bank statement with a personal note from the bank manager that reads: "Do us all, and yourself, a favor and drink bleach."

Visualizations for your Love Life

- Visualize yourself walking into your bedroom to find your spouse in the middle of a "five-way" with a few truckers and cocktail waitresses from the local roadside bar and grill.
- Visualize your love interest laughing uncontrollably (while vomiting) when they see you naked for the first time.
- Visualize the courtroom during your next divorce proceeding, and your soon-to-be ex-spouse jumping up and down while screaming "FREEDOM!"

Visualizations for your Job and Career

- Visualize yourself getting fired by your boss... On your birthday... Just as the police are arresting you.
- Visualize getting sued for sexual harassment by Tracey from accounting when you suggested that all employees should line up in order of *"genital size."*

Do these visualizations daily, and soon, you'll be on a road of isolation, desolation, and depression. **Remember, asshole, there is no hope for you because you're a miserable failure.**

Suicide 101

Before reading this awful, life-altering, and horrific section, please memorize this disclaimer...

DISCLAIMER: DO NOT HURT YOURSELF, HURT OTHERS, OR ATTEMPT TO COMMIT SUICIDE... IT'S HARD TO BE A MISERABLE FAILURE WHEN YOU'RE DEAD.

Don't Do it, You Need the Pain

Suicide is for quitters. It's the ultimate "easy way out." When things get tough, some individuals choose to end it all, forever. Often, a severe mental health issue, terminal illness, or traumatizing event is to blame for someone taking their own life. Well, as a miserable failure, you certainly have no shortage of mental health issues, your lifestyle is DEFINITELY leading to multiple terminal illnesses, and your entire life could be considered one long traumatizing event. However, suicide is NOT for the miserable failure. For the "average" depressed individual who gets fired from their job, and then comes home to find their spouse banging a group of circus midgets (and the mailman), suicide might be the logical choice for them. For the miserable, losing another job, and catching their spouse banging the door-to-door salesman (and the mailman) is considered a great day! With the exception of threatening it to gain attention, suicide has no place in the miserable failure's manipulation arsenal. You need pain to be miserable, and you can't feel pain if you're dead. You need to live a long, arduous, and shitty life full of pain, suffering, depression, alcoholism, isolation and desolation.

It's impossible to be a miserable failure if you commit suicide, and end up burning in the fiery pits of hell for all eternity. Yes, chances are good that you'll end up in Satan's hell hole no matter what, but at least you can delay your arrival by not killing yourself. You need to stay alive (at least for now) so that life has a chance to kick you in the crotch with a pair of steel-toed work boots for the next thirty-plus years. Just consider that you going to hell is something to look forward to (at least you'll be around people just like you...and please make sure you say hi to Dan). Miserable Failures don't run away from pain, they sprint toward it (NOTE: if we're being honest, thanks to your lust for pure grain alcohol, you can barely walk most days, nonetheless sprint). It's the pain of living a completely shitty life that will make you truly miserable, and bring you the freedom that only comes with failure. Remember, if your life SUCKS BIG HAIRY GOAT BALLS, you're doing it right!

A miserable failure takes pride in having a horrible credit score, loves getting their car repossessed, and can't wait to receive their next eviction notice. Getting arrested for public nudity, served with a **new** restraining order, and breaking out in a terrible staph infection is considered REALLY COOL! This world has so many awful things to offer, and it would be a shame for you to miss out. So, DO NOT take any shortcuts like committing suicide, or inflicting any other form of physical self-harm (NOTE: inflicting mental self-harm is VERY MUCH SO encouraged). If you follow the methods outlined in this book, things are going to steadily get worse over time (we promise), but it won't happen immediately. Just be patient and enjoy the process of personal self-destruction.

Volunteering at the Suicide Hotline

With the exception of "providing" others with a variety of STDs (you pretty much have them all), and over-contributing to the world's growing antibiotic resistance (you get A LOT of infections), the miserable failure rarely has the opportunity to "give back" to the community. Most of your areas of expertise (destroying marriages, wrecking careers, getting evicted, etc.) are of little value to "normal" people. However, your long list of past failures and current shitty circumstances can act as inspiration for the average person in order to get them back on track or talk them down off the ledge. Basically, if someone thinks their life is bad, they'll start to feel a whole lot better about themselves after talking to a "fuck up" like you. This realization alone could prevent someone from committing suicide, or at the very least slow the process down. Thus, the suicide hotline is the perfect volunteering job for the miserable failure (and yes, just like any job, you can and will eventually be fired). Let's be clear, volunteering at the suicide hotline is the ONLY time you are encouraged to actively help others (unless "actively helping others" means "getting friends addicted to crack"). Miserable Failures do not work on breadlines, participate in community clean-ups, or donate to charities.

Volunteering at the suicide hotline should be an easy process, especially since you've been a regular caller for years. However, your outward appearance turns off most folks (it's probably all the shit stains on your clothing and the face tattoo), so you may need to present your "suicide resume" to the hotline supervisor in order to get hired. Thanks to your propensity for total failure, you've become an expert at NOT successfully committing suicide. Yes, you've tried many times, and yes, you've failed many times. Here is a sample **suicide resume** to use as a guide for creating your own:

NAME: Bob (Insert Your Nickname) *Richards*

PURPOSE: Helping People Not Commit Suicide / Fulfilling My Court-Appointed Community Service Hours... EAT SHIT, Judge Sullivan!

EDUCATION: The School of Hard Knocks (Bitch)

EXPERIENCE: I've attempted to kill myself multiple times, and have failed miserably. Please see the list of my most previous efforts below.

- The Rusty Razor Blade Incident: Tried to cut my wrists, but instead ended up with tetanus. So, not a total loss.

- The Bungee Cord Attempt: Wanted to hang myself, but a bungee cord was all I could find. More embarrassing than anything else, and I still need to see a chiropractor weekly due to this.

-The Overdose Fiasco: Thanks to years of prescription drug abuse, I've built up quite the tolerance to all medications, and am no longer able to over-

dose effectively. It took four bottles of aspirin and half a pound of cough medicine to figure that out.

-The Alcohol Poisoning Pursuit: Attempted to drink myself to death, but ran out of alcohol. I tried to shoplift more, but was caught, jailed, and later sobered up in my holding cell. Not the first time this happened.

-The Wrong Track Tragedy: After laying on the railroad tracks for multiple days, and not seeing a train, it became clear that they were no longer in service. I became bored and just went home to drink. And it's worth noting that the buzzards and vultures flying in circles over me were mighty disappointed when I got up and left.

CONTACT INFO: This really depends on the day. During the week you can find me in, or around the dumpsters behind "Bag of Burgers," and the free health clinic on Walnut Street. Most weekends you can get a hold of me at the county jail.

Saving The Day!

When a truly depressed person calls the suicide hotline, they are reaching out for help in their most vulnerable state. They expect to have their call answered by a compassionate, and understanding professional who has been trained to help someone in a crisis situation. While their expectation to speak with a compassionate, trained "professional" will certainly leave them disappointed (the joint you smoked in the parking lot made you "zone out" for most of your training), their call with you will not leave them dead. When someone calls, DO NOT tell them to not commit suicide. They're expecting this, and will likely be resistant. Instead, simply ask them why they want to kill themselves. You'll hear all about how their lover left them, or how they lost their job, etc. Allow them to speak for a minute or two about their misfortune, and then interrupt them with the phrase, *"shut the fuck up."* This obscene, shocking, and graphic language will momentarily interrupt their depressed thinking, and give you the opportunity to interject. Say to them, *"If you think you've got it bad, wait until you hear about my shit storm of a life."* Then, go into EXTREME, mind-blowing detail about how terrible your completely screwed up excuse for a life actually is. Some topics of conversation for "talking the person down" include, but are not limited to:

- Your DUI history (how many drinks you had, what pain killers you were on, how long you ran from the police before being beaten, tasered and arrested, etc.).
- Your long list of sexually transmitted diseases, and the daily pains they cause (NOTE: be very graphic when describing the burning, itching, oozing, and bleeding).
- Your current bank account balance (HINT: it should be in the negative).
- Your terrible credit score and the bill collectors currently trying to assassinate you.
- Your extensive arrest record (BTW: this may take hours, so just stick to the times you got "pinched" for drugs and public nudity).
- Your awful failed investments (PLEASE: include the story about the $5000 you gave to the African Prince to help "get him out of jail" a few years ago).
- Being chronically unemployed (mention the bias you face because of the scorpion tattoos covering your entire body).
- Your multiple bankruptcies, and daily repossessions (DO NOT mention that you became so close to the repo guy that he invited you to his birthday party... Happy 40th Todd!).
- The multiple active warrants out for your arrest (they're not taking you alive this time... well at least not sober).
- Your student loans currently in default (getting a degree in "Ethnic Studies of Albanian Elves" seemed like a safe bet at the time).
- ALL of your failed romantic relationships (again, this may take hours, so stick to your 44 failed marriages only).
- Your wage garnishments (back when you had a paying job).
- Your long history of drug abuse and how it's affected your

body (just text them a photo of your mangled and useless genitalia...they'll get the point).

- Your current wardrobe (NOTE: be sure to mention the tear stains).
- Your current lack of any basic hygiene (start with your lice-infested head and work down to your gangrene toes.
- The fact that the majority of your family hates you, and actively seeks your destruction (thanks for the mail bomb, Uncle Steven).
- Your lack of friends (this does not include paid sex workers, and/or drug dealers).
- The various things you've had to do in order to "survive" on the streets (blowjobs, hand jobs, rim jobs, foot jobs, etc.).
- Your many fistfights with bounty hunters, angry bikers, pimps, and bail bondsmen (SPOILER ALERT: you never have won a fight).
- Your various rare eating orders (having "Chewer and Spewer Syndrome." This is where you chew your food, and then spew it towards random subway passenger's).
- Your children hating your guts (at least the ones that you've met).
- Your current disgusting physical appearance (140lbs overweight, devastating body odor, multiple infections, rotten teeth, scars, acne, hair cleanliness, etc.).
- The drugs you did in the parking lot prior to showing up for volunteering today (it's okay to take a break and go do more, just put them on hold).

After listening to you ramble on and on about how shitty your existence is, you're going to essentially give the caller a new perspective on their own life. Their spouse may have left them, but at least they didn't leave them AND fuck their neighbor(s), drain their bank accounts and get them evicted. They may have lost their job, but at least they didn't lose their job AND find out they have a new STD, got arrested for public nudity on a playground, have a hooker steal their rent money, and get their pinky toe caught in a bear trap. No matter what any caller has to say, your life will always be legitimately worse, and thus you'll always have the ammo you need to stop their suicide. This is a win-win for everybody! You get to be the hero, by being a zero! Once you talk to multiple suicidal people calling in about how awful your life is, they will be scared straight and will 100% change their lives around. So, talk about all of the ways in which you've purposely become a miserable failure and start saving lives!

Playing The Suicide Card

As a miserable failure, you're going to play the "suicide card" as often as you use the cancer, identity theft, or diarrhea excuses. It's always believable (your life REALLY sucks), fits every situation (go ahead and think about it...we're right), and when utilized properly, can get you out of anything (except herpes). The catch is that it can only be used once with any one person, and then it loses all its power forever. Telling the landlord, you're suicidal will buy you a month without paying rent, but come next month (slit wrists or not) it'll be time for ANOTHER eviction notice (HALLELUJAH!). Be aware that when you play the suicide card with an authority figure or a friend, that they are legally required to report it. This is a really awesome way of getting attention, free stuff, and lots of behavior-forgiving sympathy points. So, one of your primary goals should be to convince your AA sponsor, therapist, life coach, parole officer, and all your friends that you "might" kill yourself. Of course, you're NOT going to follow through, but if you're lucky (NOTE: you are not lucky) they'll put you on a "suicide watch."

Suicide Watch is basically a set period of time when people believed to be suicidal are closely supervised to prevent them from visiting the "Prince of Darkness." While you're being "watched," a team of professionals will be responsible for supporting you, and assisting in your daily care because you *"just don't have the strength to go on."* Play this angle up BIG TIME! While you're on suicide watch, you will be much too "fragile" (wink, wink) to prepare your own meals, bath yourself, and even wipe yourself after using the toilet (NOTE: if you're in the county jail again, yell at the guards, point your butt in the air and scream that it's time for "*wipe wipe*"). You should also make it clear to your supervisory team that not having access to your extensive action figure collection and vintage pornography stash makes you want to die even more. So, it'll be their responsibility to ensure that your needs are met in those areas as well.

Basically, no matter the situation, playing the suicide card is always effective in getting you out of the bullshit you created, and getting you lots of free stuff. Nobody wants to be responsible for "pushing you over the edge," or being the catalyst that finally causes you to act. So, in any situation that you're not getting your way, just say, "*no worries, I'll just go kill myself now.*" Like magic, all of your previously refused/ignored requests will now become everyone's new top priority. Call up a friend at 2:00 in the morning and ask for cash. When they say, "*no and don't ever call here again,*" just say, "*no worries, I'll just go kill myself.*" After they spend the next 3 hours getting you to put the knife down (NOTE: the butter knife), you'll end up getting paid! When you're caught shoplifting porn magazines, and bacon again, just tell the security guard you're going to kill yourself. You'll be walking out the front door with your porn, and bacon (handcuff free) in no time! If you're a female miserable failure and your husband catches you having an affair and threatens divorce, just tell him that if he leaves, you'll "*kill yourself.*" At the very minimum, this will afford you a few extra days of marriage, and thus the opportunity to drain your joint bank accounts. Just remember, that when it's a bad day, "let the suicide card play." It's way better than everyone knowing the real truth; your life sucks MASSIVE DICK, but that's the way you like it!

Your Purposely Failed Suicide Attempts

Finally, you should also discuss all of your failed suicide attempts in order to acquire money, get sympathy, and get yourself out of jams in great detail. Some of your infamous PURPOSELY FAILED suicide attempts could be:

- The time you tried to shoot yourself in the head at your grandfather's funeral using an airsoft pellet gun (the tiny scar and glass eye is still there).
- The time you tried to hang yourself with dental floss on the day of your wedding (this almost worked, and you became known as "the dental death guy" by the entire field of dentists and orthodontists).
- The time you tried drowning yourself in the kiddie pool at the local water park (this was doomed to fail once you pooped in the pool and the manager started to drain it).
- The time you tried cutting your wrists in the bathtub using a butter knife (the scars are still there and the staph infection is also very much present).
- The time you tried to walk out into oncoming traffic on Christmas morning (being drunk while wearing the bright red Santa outfit caused the drivers to notice you and only "clip" you.)
- The time you tried jumping off the rooftop (it was only two stories high and you suffered horrible double compound fractures to both of your legs).
- The time you took a bunch of pills to overdose and spent the next three weeks strapped to a toilet in the nuthouse (taking 100 laxatives and washing it down with a bottle of gin isn't going to cut it).

Affirmations

Affirmations are powerful tools that are used to tap into the subconscious mind in order to bring about positive change in the life of the person. Basically, they're a form of self-hypnosis where an individual makes **positive** statements, and through the repetition of this process, is actually able to see what they've been affirming, manifested in their real-world experience. Sounds like a load of bullshit, right? Well, affirmations actually do work! Some of the greatest minds and most successful people in history credit them as being an integral part of their "amazing" achievements. Although you DO NOT have a great mind (your love of dropping acid, sniffing rubber cement, and taking PCP has left you nearly brain dead), and you have no desire to ever achieve anything (anything "good" that is); you too can benefit from the use of affirmations. It's the same way that a "normal" person can attract "positive" situations and circumstances through affirmations, a miserable failure can more rapidly bring about their own personal self-destruction by repeatedly affirming the proper self-defeating and extremely negative statements.

Below are a few sample affirmations we strongly encourage you to utilize while on your journey to becoming a HUGE sack of shit. Don't just say them, **you need to scream these** at home in front of the mirror (preferable while crying and masturbating), during your next therapy session (while crying and masturbating), and in any crowded public area (definitely while crying and masturbating). Use these affirmations until they are firmly ingrained in your tiny, worthless, useless brain, or until you're no longer able to cry AND masturbate due to severe dehydration (NOTE: you consider drinking anything but alcohol a waste of valuable bladder space). You should also write each of these affirmations at least twenty-five times daily (PRO TIP: write them in your blood, and/or feces for SUPER MEGA "DUMB-SHIT" BONUS POINTS). The act of writing them down, in conjunction with screaming these affirmations out loud, becomes very powerful very quickly. If you really want to make sure you get the "most" out of these, simply record yourself saying them enthusiastically with your phone, and then play them out loud on repeat as you sleep. If you've been "teetering on the brink" of fully becoming a miserable failure (NOTE: somewhere between an "asshole" and an "idiot"), this may be the final catalyst to push you off the proverbial "fuck face balcony" (just like your former spouse tried to do to you on your wedding night).

The Miserable Failure Affirmation - *"I am a miserable failure. I suck at life. I am a terrible person. I make awful life choices and create the most horrendous personal circumstances possible. I smell like shit. I look like shit. I am shit."*

The Bad Luck Affirmation - *"I have horrible luck. Bad shit is always happening to me, and it will continue to happen to me because I am a fuck up. I will forever be a victim."*

The Nickname Affirmation - *"My legal name should literally be Fuck-face, or Shit-Bag. I don't deserve to be called anything else, ever."*

The Baby Daddy Affirmation (for female miserable failures) - *"I am pregnant again, and don't know who the dad is. SWEET!"*

The Cheating Affirmation - *"My romantic partner is definitely cheating on me because I am a miserable failure. I hope it's with a family member or one of my close friends."*

The Prison Affirmation - *"I am definitely going back to prison where I will get my ass kicked every day. I can't wait!"*

The Bad News Affirmation - *"Bad news is the only news I get! I love hearing that I have no hope. I deserve a shitty life. I look forward to all the hemorrhoids and hepatitis to come."*

The Financial Affirmation - *"I am dead broke. I will never get ahead financially because of my drug addictions. My credit score is laughable at best. I will continue to borrow money and never pay it back."*

The Sex Affirmation - *"I am horrible in bed. I have never brought anyone but myself to climax. Premature ejaculation and the inability to become aroused are commonplace for me. I also fuck like a dead fish."*

The No Friends Affirmation - *"I have no friends because most people don't like me. Liquor, drugs, and sex toys fill the void in my life where friends should go. I deserve to be severely assaulted over and over again. Please stab me in the back."*

The Family Values Affirmation - *"My family hates my guts. I have been disowned and cut out of the family will. I am a horrible excuse for a* _________ (insert your legal last name)."

My Ex-Spouse Affirmation - *"All of my ex-spouses despise me. I cheated on all of them and broke their hearts. I am a miserable failure, worthless sack of shit. Maybe one day, they will all gang up on me, tie me down, and exact torturous revenge upon me. I can only hope and dream of that beautiful day."*

My Children Affirmation - *"My children detest and loathe me. They are not proud of me being their biological parent. They are ashamed and I soon hope they will beat me with lead pipes while I sleep."*

The Situational Affirmation - *"I make the worst out of any and every situation."*

The Non-Confidence Affirmation - *"I do not believe in, or have any trust or confidence within myself. I am truly and completely a royal fuck up and a colossal loser."*

The Intake Affirmation - *"I eat like shit, drink a lot of alcohol, smoke* *many packs of cigarettes, eat thousands of grams of sugar each day in my diet, and I curse like a sailor in front of women and small children outside of churches."*

The Life Mistake Affirmation - *"I do not learn from my horrible, life-altering mistakes. In fact, I enjoy making even more mistakes."*

The Loser Affirmation - *"I can't accomplish anything that I set my mind to... With the exception of becoming and being a miserable failure."*

The Anti-Forgiveness Affirmation - *"I do not forgive myself from any of my past actions. I am a horrible and terrible human being. May I die of a severe herpes infection and rot in the fiery pits of hell."*

The Live Your Life Affirmation - *"I do not live life to the fullest. I live life one lie and one swindle at a time."*

The Golden Rule Affirmation - *"I treat others like I treat myself... like complete and total HORSE SHIT."*

The Self Loathing Affirmation - *"I hate myself."*

The Dictionary Affirmation - *"When someone looks up the definition of failure in a dictionary, they're going to see a picture of my ugly, monster face."*

The Flunk Affirmation - *"I am so happy and grateful now that I flunked out of* ___________(insert college/ high school/etc.)."

The Divorce Affirmation - *"I am so happy and grateful now that got another divorce. Woo hoo!"*

The Job Affirmation - *"I am so happy and grateful now that I was fired from yet another job. Woo hoo!"*

The Family Affirmation - *"I am so happy and grateful now that my family has disowned me."*

The Ungrateful Children Affirmation - *"I am so happy and grateful now that my children are secretly plotting my death."*

The Credit Score Affirmation - *"I am so happy and grateful now that I have filed for yet, another bankruptcy."*

The Police Brutality Affirmation - *"I am so happy and grateful now that I am getting arrested and going to jail again."*

The Eviction Affirmation - *"I am so happy and grateful now that I am getting evicted from my house for MULTIPLE unpaid mortgage payments."*

The Disappearing Friends Affirmation - *"I am so happy and grateful now that I have zero friends."*

The Sexual Satisfaction Affirmation - *"My* (insert spouse's name) *has never had a real orgasm."*

The Disgusting Affirmation - *"No one wants to sit next to me on a plane, subway car or the bus because I look and smell like human feces and vomit married, and had a child."***The Hospital ER Affirmation** - *"I am eagerly awaiting and anticipating the next bar fight I get into, so that I can get my jaw wired shut again."*

The Bill Collector Affirmation - *"I am going to max out all of my high-interest credit cards without the intention of ever paying them back. I am proud of myself for this."*

The IRS Affirmation - *"I am happy that the IRS is auditing me again and I might go to federal prison for life."*

The Daily Affirmation - *"I am a lonely, pathetic sack of shit. Bad news follows me. I deserve horrible life circumstances due to my extremely poor life choices."*

The Deadbeat Affirmation - *"I gamble, drink a lot of alcohol, do massive amounts of drugs and deserve the staph infection on my genitalia."*

The Early Morning Affirmation - *"Every day, in a variety of ways, horrible things come into my shitty life and I love it."*

The Hate Affirmation - *"I hate myself."*

The Money Affirmation - *"I am so happy and grateful now that I am a broke-ass predator."*

The Art of Excuses

As the old saying goes, "Excuses are like assholes. Everyone has one, and they all stink." Well, as a miserable failure you are definitely an asshole, you definitely stink (refusing to wipe and/or bath will do that), and you are FULL of excuses! On a regular basis, your terrible behavior is going to get you into BIG trouble. Rather than "owning up" to what you've done, and facing the consequences like an adult, you should ALWAYS seek to blame others and make excuses for your constant misfortune. Being that you are involved in a plethora of nefarious activities, you will require an extensive repertoire of readily available excuses.

In this section, you will find a variety of easily usable excuses as well as suggestions on how and when to best deploy them. Don't be afraid to combine some of these together for any situation that calls for a REALLY creative excuse (you're caught shoplifting pork loin AND masturbating in the freezer section of a local grocery store while wearing a cape and top hat). Keep in mind that the excuses outlined in the following sections are only mere suggestions, and will not cover all your bases. You'll need to be able to create new ones to adequately manage whatever psychotic situation you find yourself in.

The "Race Excuse"

Being a miserable failure has NOTHING to do with being racist. As a miserable failure, or someone hoping to become one, you should only hate yourself. Not being a racist-miserable-failure has little to do with morals, but rather with the fact that there is only so much hate to go around. Thanks to your constant use of pharmaceutical downers, and hard liquor, you barely have enough energy to keep your heart beating. Hating takes time and effort. So, only use what little energy, and conscious thought you have each day to direct your vengeance toward yourself.

The "race excuse" can and should be used by **all races** at all times. No matter what situation you get yourself into, just remember that anything can be blamed on racism, or because you happen to be of a particular race. Additionally, if your actual race doesn't quite fit the scenario in which you find yourself requiring a good excuse, you can also self-identify as another race entirely (and on the spot). For example, if you're Caucasian, but find yourself in a situation where being Asian would come in handy (you're applying for a job as a sushi chef to gain unfettered access to the "sake" supply), just claim to be "Asian," and call anyone that questions your chosen nationality a "hater." A few examples of the "race excuse" in a real conversation could go as follows:

Police Officer - *"Do you know why I stopped you?"*
Miserable Failure- *"It's because I'm white. Right?"*
Police Officer- *"No. It's because you were doing 110 in a 35, and if you haven't noticed, your car is on fire."*

TSA Agent - *"I need to search your front right pocket for drugs."*
Miserable Failure - *"It's because I'm Black. Isn't it?"*
TSA Agent - *"No. It's because you have a crack pipe hanging out of your sweatpants, you smell like marijuana, and you're wearing a t-shirt that says, "I Love Meth."*

Husband - *"Why don't we stop fighting?"*
Miserable Failure - *"It's because we're Native Americans."*
Husband - *"For the fifth time tonight, we are not Native Americans, sweetheart. Please stop drinking, and put the handgun down. You're scaring the kids."*

Repo Man - *"I'm here to take back your car."*
Miserable Failure - *"It's because I'm Indian right?"*
Repo Man - *"No. It's because you're a lowlife motherfucker who never made one, single, solitary payment. It's been two years fuck-tard."*

Child - *"Why can't we go get ice cream?"*
Miserable Failure - *"It's because we're white and I am high on PCP, kid."*
Child - *"I'm only half white, mom. Can daddy take me then?"*
Miserable Failure - *"Your daddy is in prison, you ungrateful little bastard."*

You get the gist of it. Just remember that it's never your fault and that anyone who has a problem with you is just a "racist." You didn't get arrested for "arson" because the meth lab you built in your unknowing neighbor's garage exploded; you got arrested because you're "white." You didn't get evicted because you "failed to pay rent for eleven consecutive months"; you got evicted because you're "Mexican." The race excuse can go on, and on, and on. Also, thanks to current societal pressures, it is very unlikely that anyone will challenge your race excuse due to their fear of being labeled a racist. So effectively, you've got a free pass! The excuse-making possibilities are endless!

The "Gender Excuse"

Similar to the "race excuse," the "gender excuse" can be used by anyone, at any time, and for **ANYTHING**. There are only two ways you can use the "gender excuse." The first way is to blame all of your horrible life decisions (getting your body covered in cartoon anime art), and all of your obvious shortcomings (bad breath, extreme temper, drug addictions, etc.) on your actual, God-given birth gender. The second way is to randomly self-identify your gender. Basically, this means you get to pick whatever gender you want to be at any particular time during any particular day. You can also "choose" to be a completely inanimate object, or select a favorite animal to live as. So, like the race excuse, the gender excuse is essentially an unlimited free pass for your bullshit (WONDERFUL!).

Your Real Gender

The "gender excuse" is most commonly used in its purest form. The straight forward "I can't do this because I'm a man/women" version. We call this the "real" gender excuse because it refers to only acknowledging your actual birth gender as the reason you suck at life. This method is most effective for people who never self-identify as the opposite sex, as a donkey, or as a trashcan. Using the real gender excuse is quite simple (so, it's perfect for you). If you're a man, blame everything on your penis. If you're a woman, blame all of your screw-ups on your vagina. It may seem simplistic, but don't worry, it works! Some example conversations are listed below:

Parole Officer - *"You didn't pass your court-ordered drug test."*
Miserable Failure - *"It's because I'm a female! I'm tired of this sexist crap!"*
Parole Officer - *"No. It's because your urine is 80% heroin, and 20% staph infection. By the way, you're pregnant."*

Therapist - *"If you come by my house at 3:30 in the morning again, I'm calling the cops."*
Miserable Failure - *"It's the fact that I'm a dude, isn't it? You're a terrible therapist!"*
Therapist - *"No. It's the fact that you drove your car through my front lawn, preceded to urinated in the mailbox, and then tried to physically assault my dog."*

Personal Trainer - *"You seem to be making no progress. In fact, you've gained weight and look like complete shit."*
Miserable Failure - *"I can't lose the weight because I'm a woman."*
Personal Trainer - *"No. You can't lose the weight because you're a lazy cheapskate who only pays for one session a month, and washes down every carb-filled meal with a two-liter bottle of root beer. Enjoy your diabetes, douchebag."*

Life Coach - *"You're not even taking any of my advice anymore. I'm dropping you as a client."*
Miserable Failure - *"It's because I'm a man, right?"*
Life Coach - *"No. It's because you got arrested for heroin trafficking AGAIN, and because you called me from a Mexican prison demanding that I wire you five grand for bail money, jackass."*

AA Sponsor - *"Robert, we're all worried about you. You are obviously off the wagon, and need to go to a meeting."*
Miserable Failure - *"It's because I'm a man, right, asshole?"*
AA Sponsor - *"No. It's that you drank brandy out of two homeless midget's ass cracks this morning, and then let them bang you for a crack rock. You must not remember sending me the video. By the way, who was filming"?*
Miserable Failure - *"Your wife."*

Your Self-Identifying Gender

Stop reading (or attempting to read) immediately, and look down between your legs. If you see a disgusting, misshapen, tattooed, heavily scarred, and herpes-covered penis, **you're a male miserable failure**. If you look between your legs and see a vomit-inducing, overgrown bush covered in crabs, **you're a female miserable failure**. Now, to effectively use the "self-identifying gender excuse" simply pretend that your infected, rarely used genitalia is actually the opposite of what you currently possess. It's that easy! Just be sure to tell everyone you see about the "new you", and publicly shame anyone that challenges your "instantaneous sex change" as an "indentiphobe."

This subsection of the "gender excuse" is most **commonly** used by male miserable failures who only want to gain easy access to the women's restroom in order to finish off their eight ball of blow. Using your self-identifying gender to sneak into the lady's room when you're a male miserable failure is accomplished simply by walking in. There's no need to dress up like a woman or make any attempt to appear feminine. When you're confronted by an angry security guard, or a frightened mother holding her daughter, simply exclaim, *"I'm a lady too, you identiphobe!"* We also highly encourage male miserable failures to book an appointment with an OBGYN for a "routine" gynecological examination. The look on the doctor's and nurse's faces is worth the trouble. If they refuse to treat you because of a small technicality like *"you don't have a vagina,"* just continue to angrily demand a pap smear until the police are called. When the officer arrives, shout out, *"there they are, arrest them for being sexist identiphobes."*

If you're a female miserable failure, and you want to play on the men's basketball team (no, last night's gangbang with the starting five doesn't count), show up to the first practice and explain to the coach that you self-identity as a male and will be joining the team. The coach will most likely chuckle because they'll think you're joking. This is the perfect opportunity to call the coach an identiphobe, and angrily tell him to *"suck your dick."* As you are escorted off the court, yell out, *"I have a set of cock and balls. Want to see?"* (BTW: do this while flashing them your vagina). You may not make the team, but at the very least you'll end up in another free-for-all gang bang that night (talk about a slam dunk!).

The "Age Excuse"

The age excuse is another great way miserable failures can explain away their awful behavior (especially shitting your pants). The "age excuse" basically argues that anything bad you did (shoplifting, breaking and entering, drunk driving, etc.) can be attributed 100% to your age. **You can even self-identify as another age altogether!** For example, if you're a forty-five-year-old, illiterate, drug-addicted, parolee (#congratulations) you can self-identify as a twenty-one-year-old buxom, blonde female stripper! (PRO TIP: giving random people sitting on park benches lap dances is a great way to get a black eye and cash tips). You've got two choices with this excuse; your real age, or your self-identifying "fake" age. Even you can't screw this one up! Well, you can screw anything up, and even if you do, you still win! Have fun, you miserable failure!

Your Self-Identifying Age

Whenever you find yourself in another jam (just wait, it won't be long) simply deploy the "self-identifying age excuse," even if it doesn't make any practical sense to do so. It may be difficult for your significant other to see the correlation between getting caught having an affair with the pizza delivery person and being a "pretend" ninety-four-year-old, but this actually gives you an easy out by blaming your betrayal on senility. You can basically identify as whatever age you want whenever it suits your purpose, or when you just feel like being a douchebag (this is easy because you are a douchebag). Remember, to label anyone who questions your chosen age an "ageist," and be sure to publicly shame him or her to ensure they never give you any shit again. Some examples of conversations involving the self-identifying age excuse are listed below:

Store Manager - "*We're going to have to ask you to leave. You're not allowed to sit in the middle of the toy aisle playing with action figures, and we require clothing.*"

Miserable Failure - "*Excuse me. I am only six-years-old. So back off, pedophile!*"

Store Manager- "*No you're not. You're a balding, middle-aged, fat man not wearing pants. We can't sell anything you've touched, and you're scaring the customers. Please stop sitting on the pile of stuffed animals, and get the fuck out.*"

Cop - "*You seem a little too young to be drinking.*"

Miserable Failure - "*Oh, I'm really twenty-one.*"

Cop - "*Can I see your driver's license?*"

Miserable Failure - "*I actually just had it suspended again. Thanks for asking, you fat pig.*"

Cop - "*Step out of the car nice a slow, you drunk little bastard.*"

IRS Agent - "*Your taxes do not seem to be adding up here.*"

Miserable Failure - "*It's because I'm only eleven-years-old, jerkoff and I don't need to file taxes!*"

IRS Agent - "*You're actually a fifty-year-old man doing cocaine off the table in the middle of the afternoon, on a Tuesday, in front of an IRS agent, during an audit.*"

Whatever age you want to self-identify as is completely and totally up to you! If you get caught selling bootlegged pornography on the street corner, explain to the cop (and the judge at your trial) that you self-identify as an eight-year-old Iraqi immigrant named Abdula, so you can attempt to be charged as a minor and seek asylum (free housing and free food). The self-identifying age excuse is timeless and **MANY** miserable failures use this often.

Your Actual Age

If you want to use the "age excuse" classically, just blame all of your problems on your current age. No matter what your current age is, the "age excuse" provides the miserable failure another cop-out excuse for all of your royal mishaps and disappointments in life. Some examples of this during conversations might be:

Employer - *"I think we are going to hire someone else."*
Miserable Failure - *"It's because I'm forty-years-old, right?"*
Employer - *"No. It's because you showed up to this job interview late, drunk, stinking of marijuana, and wearing your pajamas."*

Judge - *"You're losing all visitation rights to your children."*
Miserable Failure - *"It's because I'm thirty-years-old, right?"*
Judge- *"No. It's because you're a miserable failure piece of shit who comes into my courtroom late, with a hooker, while drinking a fifth of whiskey with a lit cigarette hanging out of your mouth."*

If you're thirty, blame your age as an excuse for the reason you were **shoplifting dildos at the porn shop**. If you're eighty-years-old, blame your "old age" on your "unintentional grabby hands" while the stewardess bends over in the aisle on the plane during the snack service. **If you're a forty-year-old mean, fat and disgusting bitch, blame your age as an excuse why you "can't get a good man" to marry you.** Miserable failures have been using the "age excuse" since the beginning of time (pun intended). It's now time for **YOU** to start using it haphazardly.

The "Depressed Excuse"

Most miserable failures are extremely sad, lonely, desperate, self-loathing, dangerous, isolated, angry, bitter, nervous, clingy, crazy, lunatics who are extremely **DEPRESSED**. If you want to become a miserable failure, you're going to become VERY depressed, or at least need to use another classic excuse for "getting ahead at being behind" in life. One of the most frequently used excuses in the life of a miserable failure is the "depressed excuse." The "depressed excuse" is for all miserable failures to use at random in any situation that comes up in order to explain away to the world **your terrible life decisions** and to gain some sympathy points (SEE ALSO: the "fake suicide excuse" for more empathy, pity and sympathy from others). Some examples of conversations you might have when you use the "depression excuse" might be:

Wife - *"You cheated on me... On my birthday... With my sister!"*
Miserable Failure - *"It's because I'm depressed, honey."*
Wife - *"No. It's because you're a creepy, perverted, sick son of a bitch who just wasted his entire inheritance on cheap women, drugs, and booze."*
Miserable Failure - *"So, what's your point?"*

Child - *"Mommy, why did the house catch on fire?"*
Miserable Failure - *"It's because I'm sad and depressed, you little shit."*
Child - *"No, Mom. I think it had something to do with the fire in the bathroom from your homemade meth lab."*
Miserable Failure - *"Oh, you just reminded me. You need to go clean that asbestos off of the ceiling in your room before the Child Protection Agency swings by."*

Boss - *"You're always at least three hours late to work each day? Why?"*
Miserable Failure - *"It's because I'm depressed."*
Boss - *"I don't give a fuck. You're a lazy, self-entitled, ignorant, drunken asshole and you're fired!"*

AA Sponsor - *"Are you off the wagon?"*
Miserable Failure - *"No. I'm depressed."*
AA Sponsor - *"You seem to be shooting heroin right in front of my eyes. Am I wrong or hallucinating?"*

Therapist - *"You are not getting any better. In fact, you're getting worse. I am giving you a referral because I'm in fear for my safety around you."*
Miserable Failure - *"You can't do this to me! I'm depressed!"*
Therapist - *"I can do this and I am doing this. Now get the hell out of my office and please pull your pants up and stop urinating on my couch."*

The "depressed excuse" is used primarily to gain sympathy points and pity from others. If you're lucky, no one will pity you and you'll continue down a path of severe self-destruction until you become a full-blown miserable failure.

The "Size Excuse"

The "size excuse" is similar to the "weight excuse," however, the size excuse is a little different altogether. The "size excuse" is for miserable failures who have an abnormal sized body (you should be either too skinny or too fat in your metamorphosis thus far). You can be excessively tall, skinny, short, or a fat fucker and still use this excuse.

If you're a midget miserable failure, we **ENCOURAGE** you to use this excuse as often as humanly possible (you dopey little bastard...). If you don't get the job offer, call the EEOC (the equal employment opportunity commission) and file a complaint against the "regular-sized" man interviewing you is a "**sizeist**." If you're a tall, lanky and skinny meth head looking weirdo creeper (and look like you have full-blown AIDS), you can use the "size excuse" as the reason why you always need to ride shotgun in police cars (FYI: cops generally don't allow people they are arresting to sit up front, so you might have a legitimate discrimination lawsuit against the department coming again...SCORE!). If you're a fatty (400 plus pounds) and are still hungry after eating your dinner in a restaurant, simply walk over to any table and say, *"My name is ______ and I am fat, so I am going to eat your food because I'm still a hungry hippo"* (do this while grabbing food off of their plates-mid dinner and mid-bites). When the manager comes over to kick you out, **explain to her that you need extra food because of your weight and your "low blood sugar"** (FYI: the "size excuse" can accompany the "low blood sugar excuse" interchangeably). Even if you're muscular (due to your many years of pumping iron in the prison yard and shooting Mexican steroids), you can use the "size excuse" (CAVEAT: we do not encourage any miserable failure to work out, which would cause your muscles to grow... unless of course, you're lifting weights in a prison yard while shooting steroids).

The "Weight Excuse"

No matter what your weight is currently (crackhead and meth head miserable failures should be weighing NO less than 100 pounds; and pothead miserable failures should be at least 350 pounds), you can use the "weight excuse" to get things that you want in life. The "weight excuse" is a **FANTASTIC** excuse that works perfect, especially for fat miserable failures. If you've been following along, your hygiene should be in the shitter right about now. If you truly want to be a miserable failure, you should either be gaining massive amounts of weight (beer + pizza + pot + ice cream + stealing food from the soup kitchens and bread lines = **fat miserable failure**) or losing massive amounts of weight (cocaine + meth + homeless shelter = **skinny miserable failure**). Below we'll elaborate on the extreme traits of each species of the miserable failures as they pertain to the "weight excuse."

The Fat Miserable Failure

The fat miserable failure does not work out and eats nothing by carbohydrates, sugar, alcohol, genetically-modified, artificial, processed **foods**. It is for this reason why a fat sack of shit would want to use their weight as an excuse for their poor life choices (BTW: after reading this section, you should eat two large pizzas and wash them down with a gallon of beer mixed with soda). The fat miserable failure uses the "weight excuse" to convince the manager at a $5 all-you-can-eat Chinese food buffet why you are demanding that you take home food in several "to-go" containers (NOTE: a miserable failure's "to-go container" are trash bags and buckets). The fat miserable failure uses the "weight excuse" during their trial as to the **main reason** and primary defense why the pizza delivery guy was beaten and robbed of his ten pies. The fat miserable failure blames their weight on why their husband left them (actually, becoming a huge behemoth, fat cow might be just ONE of the **MANY** reasons why your husband left your fat ass). The fat miserable failure uses the "weight excuse" as the reason why they were fired (REMEMBER: fat people are lazy and so is a miserable failure). If you do not work out and you eat like shit, you're going to gain weight and become a worthless tub of lard. Some common "weight excuse" conversations you have could be:

Wife - *"I'm leaving you."*

Miserable Failure - *"It's because I'm fat, right?"*

Wife - *"Yes, Partially. And it's because you smell, lost your job, drink alcohol all day, and to top it off, you have been cheating on me with the hole in the back-yard fence again."*

Miserable Failure - *"Splinters hurt."*

High School Principal - *"We're kicking your children out of school."*

Miserable Failure - *"It's because of my weight, right?*

High School Principal - *"No. It's because we witnessed them selling pot and handguns to the middle school students."*

Miserable Failure - *"I couldn't be prouder than I am right now as a parent."*

Airline Pilot - *"You can't come up here in the cockpit. It's against all FAA regulations."*

Miserable Failure - *"It's because I'm fat, right?"*

Airline Pilot - *"Actually, yes. Your disgusting, fat ass would not fit in here anyway, tubby."*

The Skinny Miserable Failure

The skinny miserable failure loves drugs and **rarely eats food**. Skinny miserable failures should also have a horrible binge and purge eating disorder. A skinny miserable failure should look like a crackhead dying of full-blown AIDS. If you're a skinny miserable failure, you should use the "weight excuse" as a way to explain to the bankruptcy judge that your $400,000 in credit card debt is the result of you being a *"skinny piece of shit."* Skinny miserable failures blame their boney asses as to the reason why they fail the drug test at work. Skinny miserable failures use the "weight excuse" to explain why they tried robbing a convenience store at 3:00 a.m. on Sunday morning. Some common interactions on a daily basis for the skinny miserable failure using the weight excuse could be:

Restaurant Manager - *"I'm afraid I'm going to have to ask you to leave."*

Miserable Failure - *"It's because I'm too skinny, right?"*

Restaurant Manager - *"No. It's because you can't do cocaine off the table in the middle of dinner rush with a children's birthday party seated next to you."*

Child Protective Services Representative - *"I'm here to take your children away from you so they are not in danger or in harm's way anymore."*

Miserable Failure - *"It's because I'm a skinny bitch, right?"*

Child Protective Services Representative - *"No. It's because you're a hoarder, you don't have running water, and you have a PCP pipe hanging out of your mangle mouth."*

The "Drunk Excuse"

Perhaps one of the all-time classic and most-widely used excuses for miserable failures worldwide is the **infamous** "drunk excuse." The "drunk excuse" is a fairly common and universal excuse that most miserable failures are proud to utilize and employ. To maximize the potential of this type of blame-placing and to get you really thinking about the various ways you can use this excuse, you should be drunk while reading this section (NOTE: the "drunk excuse" should never be confused with the "blackout excuse." With the "blackout excuse," you actually have no recollection of why you did what you did the night before, because you were **blacked out drunk**). The "drunk excuse" has been used by miserable failures for many years to explain:

- Why you got your thirteenth and fourteenth DUI arrests.
- Your gambling habits and debts as well as your various Las Vegas casino bans.
- Why your house burnt down (HINT, HINT: alcohol + lit cigarette = fire).
- Why you got divorced for the ninth time.
- Your extra-marital affair during your trip to Thailand last summer.
- Why you were expelled from college (HINT, HINT: your 0.0 GPA *might* have had "something" to do with it too).
- Your cigarette smoking and chewing tobacco addictions.
- Why you were issued several public defecation tickets.
- Why your children were taken away from you from child-protective services.
- Why your mortgage was "late" (LOL) for over thirty-three months causing your eviction.

- Why you've been fired from several places of employment.
- Your entire neck tattoo artwork (NOTE: consisting mostly of armadillos and platypuses).
- Your dishonorable discharge from the military.
- Your banishment from life from Bourbon Street in New Orleans.

The "drunk excuse" should be employed anytime you make some very bad decisions in life **while drinking excessively**. Got into a fist-fight? Blame it on the booze. Get caught giving black market and illegal ear piercings to middle school girl scouts? Again, **it's alcohol's fault**. Vomited in the aisle of the porn theatre (again)? Explain to the other creepy perverts that you're just *"drunk."* Cheated on your spouse? It's not your fault, it's the liquor! Got caught being a potty mouth in front of small children? Remember, it's *"just the booze talking."* Remember, if you've been drinking since 10:00 a.m., chances are you will be able to use the drunk excuse to explain away anything you did during your extraordinarily unproductive day on the couch.

Drunks vs. Miserable Failures

There is a common misconception that we must briefly address and discuss. **Miserable failures** are **drunks**, however, not all drunks are miserable failures. Some drunks can actually function in society intoxicated 24/7/365. These people are known as "functional alcoholics." Miserable failures do not function well **IN ANY SITUATION** after a few drinks go down (NOTE: you should be waking up at noon every day by starting your morning off with a shot from any open bottle of liquor).

There are many differences between a miserable failure and a drunk. A drunk regrets drinking as much as they did during a funeral service and then goes to an AA meeting to get back on the wagon. A miserable failure openly brags about how "shitfaced" they got at their mother's funeral during their next AA meeting speech (while simultaneously drinking). A drunk might try to correct their life and fix it by helping others through the twelve-step program. A miserable failure is only out for **numero uno** and steals booze from their grandparent's liquor cabinet. A drunk will go on and off the wagon several times. A miserable failure is never on any wagon (unless you're drunk and you decide to physically steal a small child's little red wagon so you can joust with your imaginary friend, "Bobby the Bubble Boy McGee" on the playground). Use the "drunk excuse" in life whenever you completely and royally fuck up while consuming massive amounts of alcohol. People hate excuses, so make sure that you use them as often as you can, because this excuse holds merit and credibility.

The "Sexuality Excuse"

Whether you're straight, gay, bisexual, asexual, transgendered, trans-species, or transabled, the miserable failure uses the "sexuality excuse" for many of life's shortcomings and pitfalls. This excuse generally explains away your cheating habits with a spouse or partner. And when employed correctly, the "sexuality excuse" can provide a long enough momentary pause in the screaming, for you to run away before your spouse takes a baseball bat to your legs (again). Some common "sexuality excuses" exchanged in daily life could be:

Wife - *"Are you cheating on me?"*
Miserable Failure - *"What? Is it because I am straight?"*
Wife - *"No. It's because I saw a homemade pornographic video of you that was texted to me by a dominatrix calling herself Shirley Sucky."*

Grandfather - *"You're stealing my liquor, my cash from my wallet, and the keys to my Cadillac."*
Miserable Failure - *"What? Is it because I am bisexual?"*

Grandfather - *"No. It's because you're an elder abuser, miserable failure piece of shit and a disgrace to this family."*
Miserable Failure - *"Do you want the belt again, old man?"*
Grandfather - *"Please don't beat me.:*
Miserable Failure - *"Then zip it, old man river, or I'll break your hip."*

Cashier - *"The total comes to $187.45. All you gave me was a roll of Canadian dollars."*
Miserable Failure - *"You won't allow me to buy this because I am transgender?"*
Cashier - *"No. You don't have enough money. Now please put your penis back into your pants and leave."*

Getting your car repossessed by a large, angry, and menacing-looking man covered in tattoos? Use your sexual preference as an excuse as to why you haven't made a payment in two years. Getting tossed out of your own wedding for being verbally abusive and sexually aggressive towards others? Blame it on the combination of your alcohol intake and the fact that you enjoy dancing with the bridesmaid in that particular way because you're "straight."

The "Low Blood Sugar Excuse"

We must briefly mention this excuse because we touched on it earlier (NOTE: the "low blood sugar excuse" should never be confused with the "diabetes excuse"). The "low blood sugar excuse" is an infamous excuse that can be used for:

- The reason for your frequent violent verbal outbursts towards women and small children in shopping mall parking lots.
- The reason why you stole non-perishables by piling them up in a wheelbarrow from the local food bank.

- The reason and explanation for your excessive cigarette smoking on the airplane in the middle of a six-hour flight from Boston to San Diego to finally formally meet your drug mule.
- The reason why you maxed out your husband's credit cards on male strippers, lottery tickets, giant black dildos, and psychics.

Whatever situation you get into that requires you to get angry or cry, make sure you explain to others that you have *"low blood sugar."*

The "Random Identity Excuse"

The coup de gras excuse for the miserable failure is the "random identity excuse." The "random identity excuse" is simple: **YOU CAN SELF-IDENTIFY WITH ANYTHING INCLUDING INANIMATE OBJECTS AND FICTITIOUS CHARACTERS**. This is the "ace in the hole" for the miserable failure. Using the "random identity excuse" has helped miserable failures win court battles, get out of parking tickets, get "discharged" (escape) from the nuthouse, win divorce settlements, and not pay taxes. You should only take responsibility for one thing: **ACTUALLY**, being a miserable failure. Outside of that ownership and title, you need to blame others and have many excuses for all of your "mishaps" in life. **Essentially, your entire life should be a lie**. Your entire existence should be a fraud, because YOU. ARE. A. Miserable. Failure...

Miserable failures have been known to self-identify with the following objects and fictitious people (NOTE: this is not an aggregate list for you and the potential possibilities are LITERALLY endless). Some of the more infamous ones used by various miserable failures over the years have included:

- Self-identifying not as John "The Body Odor" Smith, but as "**beautiful ornate building in downtown Seattle**" instead.
- Self-identifying not as Tim "Motherfucker" Jones, but as a "**gi-**

ant, red rubber band" instead (REMEMBER: ask the IRS agent to show you in the U.S. tax code where it says that a giant rubber band MUST pay taxes... #WageGarnishment).

- Self-identifying not as Mary "Blowjob" Jane, but as a "**golden dragon**" instead.
- Self-identifying not as Tom "The Nipple Pincher" Anderson, but as "**Stinky Fuzznut**"
- Self-identifying not as Angela "Meth Head" Thomas, but as "**Daisy the Purple Cat**"
- Self-identifying not as Dave "The Lowlife Scam Artist" Miller, but as "**the roman numeral number thirty-three**" instead (NOTE: it's XXX).
- Self-identifying not as Lisa "Skid Mark" Thompson, but as "**an old oak tree**"
- Self-identifying not as Tammy "Armpit and Crotch Hair" Reynolds, but as "**the letter Q**"
- Self-identifying not as Mark "Needle Dick" Franklin, but as "**a tattoo of a wolf-bat (wat) hybrid**" instead (NOTE: you can point to the current tattoo of this mythical beast on your cheek in order to explain it to someone).
- Self-identifying not as Doug "Heroin Needle" Williams, but as "**a small flaccid penis**"

You get the idea. The possibilities are endless! Whatever you need to self-identify as, is 100% up for grabs. **There ARE NO RULES. Go beyond the boundaries!** If you want to self-identify as a former US President, go for it! If you want to self-identify as a cherry popsicle, let people know! If you want to self-identify as a 1993 white Chevy Lumina, do it! A typical conversation between a miserable failure self-identifying as something completely random could potentially go something like this:

Miserable Failure - *"I am not Stan! I am Wazuro the Great and ruler of Toppasland!"*

Therapist - *"Your name is Stan Johnson and you have been court-ordered to see me once a week since your parole. Now put down that flashlight, put down the steel dildo, get up from underneath the blanket, and sit down in that chair."*

Miserable Failure - *"Yes, me lord."* (try to use an old English accent on this line).

Police Officer - *"License and registration please."*

Miserable Failure - *"I don't have them, you pig."*

Police Officer - *"Why not?"*

Miserable Failure - *"Because I am Yolanda the Leopard. Rarrr... And leopards don't need licenses."*

Police Officer - *"Alright, step out of the car nice and slow, you crazy bitch"* (with his gun drawn).

Miserable Failure - *"Leopards can't open car doors."*

Life Coach - *"You haven't paid me for our monthly session yet."*

Miserable Failure - *"I don't have to."*

Life Coach - *"Of course you do. I have been counseling you and mentoring you."*

Miserable Failure - *"No. Because I self-identify as nothing. And nothing does not have to make payments on* ***anything****."*

Life Coach - *"Could you at least put the knife down and hand me my wallet back?"*

If you truly desire to continue down your path to becoming a complete and total miserable failure, using the "random identity excuse" is a classic and professional power play for you.

The "Height Excuse"

It does not matter if you're a tall person (suffering from acromegaly), or short person (a midget), you can use this excuse for **anything**. The height excuse is fairly simple; when you get into trouble or royally fuck up (which is constant for the miserable failure), explain to others (the police officer, your soon to be ex-spouse, or the judge in your criminal sentencing) that the cause of the problem is 100% due to your height. Let's say that your wife catches you in bed with another woman. As your wife is throwing your shit out on the front lawn in a fit of violent, drunken, anger and rage, simply explain to her that you were *"banging that dumb hooker"* (please use those exact words) because you are too tall. She'll look confused and angry and she might even assault you (SCORE! Miserable failures **LOVE** having the police called on them for another "domestic disturbance" incident). Let's say that you stiff a waiter at a restaurant for not bringing you your tenth shot of whiskey in a timely manner (NOTE: miserable failures should always ask the waiter to *"keep them coming"* as you get shit faced). Write on the receipt, *"I am not leaving you a tip because I am too short. Go get a real job, you fucking loser! Actually, I am the loser. I am stiffing you on a tip because I have no more stolen money."*

The "height excuse" is great to use especially when boarding an airplane to get a first-class seat. When boarding an airplane, immediately sit down in any open seat in the first-class section (REMEMBER: you should be hitting your stewardess call button immediately while asking for *"more booze"* upon sitting down in then now stolen seat). When the person who actually paid for the seat or the stewardess comes by to ask you to leave, simply reply with, *"I am too tall to sit in coach"* (say this even if you're a 4'5" little person). Another great reason to use this excuse is if you're about to be fired again from another job. When you arrive late to work (five hours late to be precise) for the twelfth day in a row and your boss confronts you, explain to him that you're always late because you're "too short" (even if you're a giant, monster looking motherfucker). Miserable failures can even self-identify as a different height altogether. If you're 6'0", but always wanted to be taller, **force the DMV** to put your height as 6'9" on your (soon to be suspended for yet another DUI) driver's license! Tall, average, or short, use the "height excuse" haphazardly as you further down the road of miserable failuredom.

11

THE MISERABLE FAILURE

The Grand Finale

Well, is the end, or is it the beginning? **IF** you've made it this far, and followed the methods outlined in this book exactly, YOU ARE INCREDIBLY STUPID (congratulations, asshole!) and have earned the coveted title of "Miserable Failure." If you skipped directly to the final chapter, and are currently standing in a bookstore reading this masterpiece with ZERO intent of ever purchasing, YOU ARE ALREADY A MISERABLE FAILURE (but don't be a dick, use your grandmother's stolen credit card to buy this book anyway). You've come very far going nowhere, and got really good at being bad. Only this book, your psychotic childhood, and the amazing power of pure, uncut, cocaine are to thank for the "new you" (hard liquor you've consumed, cleaning products you huffed, and sex that you have paid for definitely deserve an Honorable Mention). Make no mistake about it; the "gift" you've been given by reading and following the teachings contained within these life-altering pages is the uncommon ability to truly live a life of REAL

FREEDOM. While others live in the self-imposed prison of needing to "keep up with the Joneses," you choose to have a "five-some" with the entire Jones family and get them to "loan" you the rest of the cash you need to complete your new nipple piercings, finish your branded skull tribal art and to finalize that facial tattoo of a zebra fucking a block of cheese. Now that's a real miserable failure!

Remember, you started out as a "regular" person fighting to get ahead in life. You cared what other people thought, and tried to maintain "healthy" relationships. Being employed full-time, and NOT abusing drugs, was your status-quo. You actually tried to "do well", NOT get arrested, and regularly practiced safe sex. Despite all your continuous effort, and relentless positive attitude, "it" was not enough, was it? You have never been able to become the "winner" you hoped you'd be and regularly serve as a constant source of disappointment for your family. Rather than once AGAIN following all the "good" advice you've gotten, and deciding to "pick yourself up by the bootstraps," "dust yourself off," and give it another try, you FINALLY mustered up the courage to say, *"fuck this, I quit!"* You FINALLY gave up on life, because life gave up on you (a long time ago)! You now freely accept, celebrate, and strive to "fuck up," "not make the grade," and "fall short" in every, single, solitary aspect of your shit-filled life. **You have become the best at being the worst**, and that's FUCKING AWESOME, in a really shitty way.

No longer do you have to strive to conform or be "successful" in the normal sense. No longer do you have to embellish your menial accomplishments (or the lack thereof), and feel bad about not achieving. No longer do you need to "try" to be a good parent. No longer do you need to "keep a job." Doing it wrong, is doing it right! You can now bask in the victory of your defeat! You can now love the high of your low! Broken relationships, bad credit scores, and severe drug addiction are your new "benchmarks" for success. Your only real friends are your imaginary buddies and your pals from prison, rehab, and the nuthouse. Your credit score is below 350. Your hygiene is in the shit box and your love life is nonexistent (except when you "make sweet love" to your robot sex doll in the dumpster behind "Chuck's Chicken Shack"). You didn't "buck the system" or "go against the grain." You "fucked the system" (without using protection. You became a miserable failure! This is a terrible accomplishment, and you should be both ashamed and proud of yourself at the same time.

Your Nicknames

You obviously don't, and should never give a shit what anyone thinks about you (especially those "dick heads" like county judges, district attorneys, and AA sponsors), but it's the reaction you invoke in others that will serve as the best gauge of your "miserable failuredom." Ultimately, it's the words that others use to describe you, and your terrible behavior, that will bring the greatest insight into how high on "Asshole Mountain" you truly are. The following are only some of the nicknames you should've already been called by those "close" to you. **If you have NOT been called at least five of the following nicknames in the last twenty-four hours, YOU ARE NOT A MISERABLE FAILURE AND NEED TO START OVER:**

- "Drunk impotent loser" - This is what your family priest calls you during confession (after trying to strangle you for stealing wine and crackers from the rectory).
- "Lazy fat slob son of a bitch" - You should have first heard this one from your dad on your birthday (after you drunkenly urinated on your presents in the corner of the living room).
- "Disgusting, smelly crackhead" - Other crackheads call you this.
- "Piece of shit" - The folks on death row gave you this nickname last time you were in prison.
- "Cocksucker" - Your kids can say the damnedest things (NOTE: all of them hate you).

- "Unproductive abject failure" – Thanks, Grandma!
- "Motherfucker" – Thanks, Mom!
- "Brainless idiot waste of space" - Your fourth ex-spouse listed this as your name on the divorce papers.
- "Worthless sack of monkey shit" - Your ex-spouse says not to take this figuratively. A sack full of fresh monkey feces literally has more value than you.
- "Deadbeat alcoholic cheapskate" - The folks down at the state child support office gave you this one (plus a summons and wage garnishment).
- "Unfaithful, delusional, motherfucker" - Your ex-fiancé says hello (and wants their missing underwear back).
- "Kleptomaniac fuck-face" - Your former employer called you this after discovering you were stealing office supplies (and getting high huffing rubber cement under your desk).
- "Lunatic stalking creeper" - You may have only gone on one date with your sex target, but that doesn't mean they EVER get to be with someone else.
- "Crazy, homeless dickhead" - When other crazy homeless people call you this, you're doing something right.
- "Degenerate gambler asshole" - Back when you could still legally have a bank account, this is the name that appeared on your statements (the folks down at the credit union have an amazing sense of humor).
- "Bankrupt, depressed loser" - This is what your third therapist previously called you (before he committed suicide because of you).
- "Slutty broke ass whore" - Thanks again, Mom!
- "Druggie shithead douchebag" - This is what you say to yourself while staring into the mirror every morning.
- "Fucker who stole my identity" - This is also what you say to yourself while staring into the mirror every morning.

- "Depraved vile pervert" - Yes, you took nude photos of your grandfather, but never meant for them to go viral.
- "Miscreant pile of garbage" - This is the "pet name" your third parole office gave you.

You may have been called worse names than those listed above. If so, **GOOD JOB**! Again, if you are yet to be referred to as, "that shit pants-wearing slime ball" by your personal psychic, or *"Fuckie McFuck Head"* by your toddler; YOU ARE FAILING AT FAILING! Punch yourself in the head fifteen times, start re-reading this book again, and consider using harder drugs this time around.

The Final Asshole Checklist

Before you can be officially certified as a Miserable Failure, you must first review the checklist below, and ensure that 100% of it applies to you. If you are only able to answer yes to a portion of the list, you're probably a dumbass, shit bag, or moron, but NOT a miserable failure. Again, if you followed the methods outlined in this book exactly, your life should be a MASSIVE train wreck, and thus successfully completing this checklist should be no problem. In a sense, this is your final exam, and the only way to pass is by failing. So, good luck being bad! Enjoy the victory of defeat! Here's to winning at losing! Most importantly, THANKS FOR BUYING THIS POORLY-WRITTEN AND GRAMMATICALLY-INCORRECT BOOK...

- **At least one of your multiple parole officers has decided to retire early, and live in total seclusion because of your "bullshit." YES ____ NO ____**

- **The only thing longer than your personal arrest record is the list of sexually transmitted diseases you've "earned". YES ____ NO ____**

- Your credit score once made a loan officer vomit. YES ____ NO ____

- You have been divorced multiple times. YES ____ NO ____

- Your children (if you have any) openly proclaim their intense desire to watch you suffer in a North Korean prison torture camp. YES ____ NO ____

- It's easier to list the drugs you're NOT hopelessly addicted to. YES ____ NO ____

- You are an alcoholic. YES ____ NO ____

- You have less than four teeth remaining, body odor that is beyond description, and at least two areas on your lower torso are currently leaking some sort of discharge. YES ____ NO ____

- You've had a "previous" therapist who attempted suicide, and/or tried to murder you, no longer than twelve hours after your first session. YES ____ NO ____

- You have a drug dealer on speed dial. YES ____ NO ____

- You ALWAYS have at least one active restraining order against you at all times. YES ____ NO ____

- You've gotten into a fistfight with a bill collector in front of your kids. YES ____ NO ____

- If you don't have kids, you have still got into a fistfight with a bill collector, and can't wait to do it again. YES ____ NO ____

- You ALWAYS have at least one pending lawsuits against you. YES ____ NO ____

- You're currently being evicted from somewhere. YES ____ NO ____

- You've been fired from at least one job for stealing copy paper, or flashing a coworker in the break room. YES ____ NO ____

- The only thing darker than your urine is your soul. YES ____ NO ____

- You have self-inflicted diabetes and an active staph infection from not eating right or showering properly. YES ____ NO ____

- You got into a fistfight with a repo man, and your kids helped. YES ____ NO ____

- You ALWAYS have at least one active arrest warrant at all times, and are chased by a bail bondsmen at least once every ten days. YES ____ NO ____

- You were divorced by your spouse, and/or dumped by your dating partner for banging a hooker at their birthday party. YES ____ NO ____

- You were divorced by your spouse, and/or dumped by your dating partner for banging thirteen illegal immigrants from the Congo at their birthday party. YES ____ NO ____

- SEVERAL members of your family have tried to kill you. YES ____ NO ____

- You refer to video poker as your "retirement plan." YES ____ NO ____
- All of your friends (including the homeless bums and street hookers) testified AGAINST you in your child custody case. YES ____ NO ____
- You've stolen money from a child's piggy bank to pay for sex, action figures, fire crackers, and/or drugs. YES ____ NO ____
- You've been kicked out of a drug rehab center for being "beyond their capabilities" and "better off dead." YES ____ NO ____
- Your body fat percentage is at least 10% more than your age. YES ____ NO ____
- Your personal psychic and spray tan addictions make up more than 11% of your personal budget. YES ____ NO ____
- Your doctor CONSTANTLY talks to you about "the benefits" of assisted suicide. YES ____ NO ____
- You are currently saving money that you have stolen from various charities to "finish" that swordfish tattoo above your collarbone. YES ____ NO ____
- You are banned from being within 500 feet of a school or grocery store. YES ____ NO ____
- You have meth lab and ping pong table in your basement. YES ____ NO ____
- You declared bankruptcy after your new "just buy scratch-off lottery tickets" business idea failed. YES ____ NO ____

- You have no visitation rights to your children because you attempted to sell them for cash and have never made one of your court-ordered child support payments. YES ____ NO ____

- You are currently wearing an ankle-monitoring bracelet. YES ____ NO ____

- You currently have MULTIPLE sexually transmitted diseases. YES ____ NO ____

- Your car has been repossessed. YES ____ NO ____

- You have been banned from being within 500 feet of any animal shelter. YES ____ NO ____

- You've been arrested and sent to prison. YES ____ NO ____

- You are on the "do not fly list." YES ____ NO ____

- Your driver's license has been suspended." YES ____ NO ____

One Last Thing

Almost as difficult, and certainly as important as becoming a miserable failure, is remaining a miserable failure. You must be prepared to defend your right to be wrong. Old friends may show up unexpectedly with the willingness to forgive your past discretion's, and help you "put your life back together." It's easy to let yourself be seduced by the lure of free food, potential cash, and not sleeping in a dumpster anymore. However, you must resist the urge to, "only do for a few days" because this is often the first step on the path out of misery and darkness. Yes, there is value for the miserable failure to gain, take advantage of, and then lose friends. However, once you've hit "rock bottom" (and if you've made it this far in your readings you're definitely there) it's best to avoid all friendly social interactions. So, always do your best to avoid these "blasts from the past," and if you do encounter someone trying to "assist" you, simply act "crazy as fuck." Begin by smacking yourself in the face, removing your clothing, and screaming about the "demons" that live in your genitals. By the time you get your pants off (if you're wearing any) they'll be long gone.

Making the "Least" Out of Your Day

If you're ever in doubt of what to do, remember that you can always resort back to the basics. Just open this book, and begin reading at chapter one. If, in-between skull-branding appointments and parole hearings, you can't find the time to study this material, just refer to the miserable failure's "daily standards" listed below:

- Drink MASSIVE amounts of alcohol.
- Steal shit (lots of shit).
- Stop bathing, stop brushing your teeth, and stop doing laundry.
- Cheat on your partner (without protection).
- Do drugs (lots of them).
- Feed your extreme pornography addiction (via the free internet at the public library).
- Get fired from your job (if you still have one).
- Get into bar fights (you will lose badly).
- Use EVERYTHING in your house as toilet paper.
- Break into your neighbor's garage only to take a nap.
- Get arrested (again).
- Max out your credit cards (or the one you "borrowed" from your roommate).
- Stop making all payments on EVERYTHING.
- Call you ex in the middle of the night, and reminisce about the

times you had sex (of course you should do this while masturbating AND crying).

- Gamble your rent money at various bingo parlors.
- Huff spray paint and modeling glue before going for a long drive on the interstate during rush hour.
- Make yourself vomit on your outfit, and then go on a date without changing clothes.

The Miserable Failure Hall of Fame

This book cannot be completed without acknowledging some of the most infamous dirty, scum ball, bastards across the globe. All of the following "worthless pioneers" have been awarded the very un-prestigious and dishonorable "Validation of Failure" certificate from "The University of Miserable." You should strive to reach the level of "shitty" that these worthless fuckers have achieved:

- **George "The Dick" Henderson from Columbus, Ohio** - George was the first person ever to avoid arrest by hiding (bathing) in the "shit tank" of a port-o-potty at the Ohio State Fair for sixteen hours. He's also the first person to legally attempt to marry his pet rattlesnake "Ginger." Today, you can find George living on the steps of the Flint Michigan public library. He enjoys shouting at empty office buildings on Sundays, and hurling excrement at the librarians who are trying to "steal his brain."

- **"Cheatin'" Sally Losko from Miami Beach, Florida** - Sally is in the miserable failure hall of fame for impressively EXCESSIVE cheating. Sally has successfully cheated on all eight of her husbands (four of which involved making sweet love to a family member). She has also cheated on her taxes every year and continues to cheat in games of dominos at the Federal Detention Center in Miami. Sally credits all of her success to reading this book and her meth addiction.

- **Carl "Tall Tales" McGee from Springfield, Illinois** - Carl is a pillar of the miserable failure community. He currently has over 310 illegitimate children and has not made a child support payment in 18 years. Carl is nicknamed "tall tales" because of the elaborate lies he constantly tells the judge at each child custody hearing. From being hijacked on an airplane to getting his right ear caught in a car door of the US President's limo, this guy is completely full of shit. Today, Carl is living in his grandmother's basement addicted to "the triple P" (**P**orn, **P**izza and **P**op).

- **Penny "Plier Hands" Thompson from Seattle, Washington** – Years ago, Penny suddenly decided (after a bad acid trip) that she hated her hands, and needed to have them surgically replaced with pliers. Penny's conducted the surgery in her bathroom using instructions she found online. Since that time, she developed a terrible staph infection causing her to go blind. Rumor has it that she now "dwells" under the overpass next to Pike Place Market in Seattle Washington. Go looking for her if you dare... or need pliers for something.

- **Duke "Die Hard" Kloker from Vancouver, Canada** - Duke is the first person EVER (over the age of seventy) to "successfully" steal an entire cart of casino chips (while high on the deadly combination of superglue, pot, and crystal meth) from an armed security guard in Las Vegas, Nevada. Duke is also the first person EVER to be shot in the ass eleven times and survive. Today, you can find Duke living in a wheelchair, drooling, and shitting virtually pain-free at The Golden Arches Retirement Home in Vancouver Canada.

- **"Let It Ride Eddy" Sir. Edward Wellington Esquire III from London, England** - Sir Edward Wellington Esq. III is in the miserable failure hall of fame for successfully squandering his entire family fortune (roughly $200 Million) in under sixty days on the following items:
- Various real dinosaur skulls from auctions (in which he outbid several wealthy celebrities).
- Three shipping containers full of cotton candy.
- Fourteen babies from various poor women begging for money on the streets in the Philippines.
- MULTIPLE cash loans to His Majesty, Prince Abubu of Nigeria's legal defense fund in an attempt to get him out of an unjust prison sentence.
- 150 gallons of homemade prison wine (SPECIAL THANKS TO: Lenny from cell block four in San Quentin for arranging the sale and distribution of this "near-deadly" beverage).
- MULTIPLE drug addictions (this include narcotics as well as his prescription drug abuse).
- 20,000 gallons of human breast milk (in which he bathed in) from various Argentinean immigrants.
- Nasty, skank, stank-ass, street-walking hookers (lots of them).

- One game of roulette for $199 million. He actually won, but then "let it ride" on black and lost everything.
- Purchased an entire cigarette factory that, despite being extremely profitable, he immediately closed, and then smoked the remaining product (in the same year).

Sir Edward Wellington Esq. III sadly passed away from a combination of scabies, hepatitis C, and a scorpion sting. He will never be forgotten and is a pillar in the miserable failure hall of fame.

- **Ned "Credit Score" Ryan from Phoenix, Arizona** - Ned "Credit Score" Ryan is the first person to have a NEGATIVE credit score in the history of "credit scores." He's also the first person ever to successfully pick, and then flick a booger into the mouth of the judge presiding over his divorce trial (from 25.8 feet away). Ned also deserves an honorable mention for successfully losing all of his teeth during the infamous "Jacksonville Biker Brawl" (which **he** started and twenty-five **bikers** finished...). Today, Ned lives in solitude off the grid with his deaf, blind, and mute mail-order Russian bride. They reside in a teepee on the outskirts of Phoenix, Arizona and make a modest wage selling armadillo shells to tourists alongside I-17. Ned also hasn't had an erection in eleven years.

- **Betty "Mile High" Smith from New York City, New York** - Betty is a legend in the miserable failure community (crack houses, psych wards, cell blocks, etc.). She was the ONLY woman, who you may remember hearing about on the news, who was "involved" in the infamous "Twenty-four-Person Airline Gangbang" flash mob. She set several records for time and distance that day in addition to fucking a bunch of dudes. As expected, her personal life is fraught with sexual misbehavior. She is currently being divorced by her husband of two days for having sex with all five groomsmen (and the ushers) **DURING** their "hunting/disco-themed" wedding reception. Betty is also a pioneer in the **"art of successfully washing your crotch in a truck stop water puddle."** Recently, Betty was diagnosed with chlamydia, gonorrhea, HPV, scabies, and syphilis. Today, she lives in New York City, and vows never to go to the doctor again.

- **Wendell "Blackbeard" Stinson from Baltimore, Maryland** - The miserable failure hall of fame could not be complete without this total loser. Wendell is the very first person to perfect the art of "skipping out before the check arrives" at a restaurant. After finishing his meal (including coffee and dessert), Wendell excuses himself to the bathroom where he uses a black magic marker to give himself a temporary beard disguise (thus giving him the name "Black Beard"). Wendell would simply walk out of the restaurant completely undetected without ever paying. He is credited with consuming over $1 million worth of food before his felony arrest. Upon being released from jail, he was quickly jailed AGAIN on St. Patrick's Day for tackling eight fat people and nineteen senior citizens at a charity basketball game.

(NOTE: In Wendell's defense, he was under the influence of some really good LSD, and thought they were all leprechauns carrying pots of gold and more really good LSD).

Despite all these great accomplishments, Wendell is perhaps best known for his twenty-five failed suicide attempts that have left him without an upper lip, a left ear, and a right pinky toe. Today, he calls the "Mendelson Home for the Criminally Insane" in Baltimore, Maryland home. Rumor has it that he still uses a marker to disguise himself after every meal.

- **Don "The Frog" Shelton from Salt Lake City, Utah** - Don "The Frog" Shelton is best known for tattooing all of his skin green, and claiming to self-identify as a frog in order to not pay taxes. This did not work, and he spent eleven months in a federal prison where he demanded a pond to swim in, and large quantities of flies to eat. Today, Donny continues to live the life of a frog/psychotic moron inside his broken Winnebago parked in the hills outside of Salt Lake City, Utah.

- **Tammy "Garden Hose" McAllister from Chicago, Illinois** - Tammy is one of the first miserable failures to enter into the hall of fame. She is the ONLY woman to EVER successfully "suck a golf ball through a garden hose" in order to get a crack rock. She still to this day performs her ENTIRE "golf ball routine" in various Chicago alleys. Many onlookers agree that while the garden hose portion of her performance is "not to be missed," the crotch projectile portion is the most impressive overall.

- **Stuart "Armless" Rifkin from Trenton, New Jersey** – Years ago, Stuart woke to the stinging pain of two fully-formed whitehead pimples on the tip of each elbow. After several "normal" attempts to pop the zits resulted in his complete loss of consciousness, he decided to take things to the extreme. Stuart carefully positioned his arms on a train track and began to wait. As the roaring locomotive crossed his path, he hoped that only his large protruding pimples would be popped, and his arms would remain unscathed. His plan may have been successful if it wasn't for the full bottle of whiskey he drank for breakfast. The blurred vision and inability to stand up straight caused by the alcohol did NOT work in his, or his arm's favor (and the rest is history). Today, Stuart volunteers at the local library where he teaches blind children about the dangers of elbow acne. He still cannot masturbate.

- **Tim "The Hoarder" Thompson from St. Paul, Minnesota** - Tim "The Hoarder" Thompson has never thrown anything away, EVER! Paint cans, dollhouses, old newspapers, VHS porn; you name it! Tim's hellhole of a house (A.K.A. "the shit shack") is full of useless crap, and lots of decomposing garbage. Rumor has it; that the smell emanating from Tim's house is enough to kill small animals, and induce vomiting in older adults. In fact, according to the miserable failure archival records, Tim currently has four birds, five cats, seven hamsters, three dogs, two bunnies, one goat, five tarantulas, and two scorpions that are currently "unaccounted for" and are believed to be dead within his 400 square foot house of horrors. Tim is also well known in the miserable failure community for paying off his mortgage in hand jobs. Three years ago, Tim had surgery to repair cirrhosis of the liver but still manages to pound down a fifth of rum each day (like a true champion).

- **Helen "Greasy" Williamson from Los Angeles, California** - Helen is best known for getting banned from every porn theatre in the tri state area of Nevada, Arizona, and California. She was "patient zero" for the "Gloryhole Herpes Outbreak" in which 474 people were infected with genital warts. It's said that even to this day, porn theater gloryholes have never fully recovered in popularity thanks to Helen's "cold sore." Helen was given the nickname of "greasy" due to the fact that she has not washed her hair since 1977. Today, you can find her in downtown Los Angeles publicly defecating on the streets of Skid Row.

- **Allen "The Driver" Smith from St. Louis, Missouri** - Allen is a pioneer in the art of driving like a miserable failure. He's truly perfected the "slow turn," "break slam," "ultra-slow fast lane driving," "terrible tailgating," and the "exit ramp breakdown." To date, Allen has had ninety-four shots fired at him while driving and has been responsible for well over 200 multiple vehicle accidents. Today, despite losing his license years ago, you can still find him terrorizing the streets of America, and smiling while he does it.

- **Claire "Fight Club" Donaldson from Bridgeport, Maine** - Claire has won "Miserable Failure Mother of the Year" every year. She accomplished this great feat by building a steel cage fighting arena in her backyard and instructing her small children to "fight for dinner" (with only the winner getting to eat that day). Claire's genius was in her decision to live stream the fights on the internet, and allow other miserable failures to place bets on the winner(s). Unfortunately, the "Children's Backyard Fighting Association" (the CBFA) has been disbanded due to multiple steroid doping scandals. Today, you can find Claire's grave being urinated on daily by any one of her surviving children at the Fortville Cemetery in Bridgeport Maine.

- **Monty "The Nugget" Stevens from Boise, Idaho** - The miserable failure hall of fame could not be complete without mentioning this total loser. Monty "The Nugget" Stevens is the first person to ever have their arms and legs surgically removed so that he could be "trans-abled" (SEE ALSO: the "trans-abled excuse"). Today, Monty lives in a basket strapped to the back of his "Perv Daddy" in the Pacific Northwest.

Miserable Failure World Records

In addition to the "Hall of Fame," they are a number of important "Miserable Failure World Records" that you should be aware of and strive to beat.

- **Most Consecutive Days Absent from School** - Thomas G. Anderson (1499 days... and counting).
- **Largest Amount of Liquor Drank During a Wedding Reception** - Frank K. Wright (two handles of vodka, nineteen shots of tequila, and eighty-four beers... May he rest in peace.).
- **Most Marriages/Divorces** - Raquel D. Delson (sixty-five legal marriages, mostly ended because of infidelity on her part... #COCKHERO).

- **Longest Streak of Getting Fired from a Job On The First Day** - Jake F. Tucker (84 jobs, mainly fired for not wearing pants and stealing office supplies).
- **Most Blisters on a Single Testicle** - Stanley B. Renfield (twenty-one blisters on the left one).
- **Most Bar Fights** - Scooter F. Barger (973 fights, of which he won ZERO).
- **Most Times Being Forcibly Removed From an Airplane** - Danny O. Beddington (seventy-eight, although this record is currently under dispute by the TSA).
- **Most Unpaid Parking Tickets** - Oscar De La Santo Sr. (1,288... and counting).
- **Most Years Attending College WITHOUT Earning a Degree** - Pat P. Gigliano (thirty-three years... and counting).
- **Most Arrests for Public Urination** - Tommy T. Tillery (329... and counting).
- **Longest Stretch Stealing Cable from a Neighbor** - Victor J. Hood (two years, nine months, two days, nineteen hours, and thirty-six seconds before the arrest was made).
- **Most Death Threats Received from Family Members in 24 Hours** - Zed L. Broomfield (twenty-one, or twenty-five if you count second cousins).
- **Most Portable Toilets Tipped Over While Inside Taking a Dump** - Stan W. Pleasanton (thirty-three "shit showers").
- **Most Shoplifted Items On Your Person When Arrested** - Harry Neil Friddleman (298 items, it was mostly energy drinks and decks of nude playing cards).
- **Most Midgets tossed out of a moving horse trailer while under the influence of LSD** - Georgia T. Bessi (fifty-nine, she thought "those little fuckers" were gremlins).
- **Total Number of Teeth Lost with one Hit to the Face from a Cop's Nightstick** - Rhonda K. Smith (thirty-two teeth).

- **Most Active Restraining Orders** - Benny L. Hellson (forty-five restraining orders... and counting).
- **Most Days Spent in County Jail for Public Exposure** - Adam L. Lopper (9,552 days... and counting).
- **Most Illegitimate Children Attempted to be Claimed on Taxes** - Rodney P. Fotty (thirty-nine kids... of which ZERO child support payments have been paid).
- **Most Number of Times Kicked Out of a Fast Food Restaurant for stealing condiments** - Shelby R. Fieldhouse (364 times. Eighteen fast food restaurants in eleven different cities).
- **Total Amount of Money Raised for a fake charity**- Rebecca M. Looker ($35,665 for the "Buying Breasts Implants Foundation").
- **Total Number of Days WITHOUT Wiping** - Jack S. Kellington (1239 days... and counting).
- **Most Consecutive Curse Words Used in a Sentence with a Pastor... On a Sunday... During Church Service** - Thomas R. Harbor (341 consecutive curse words hurled... Enjoy your time in hell, Tom.).
- **Most Number of Packs of Cigarettes Smoked in a Day** - Janice A. Earl (124 packs... May her soul rest in peace).
- **Most Spring Breaks Attended After Graduating College** - Scott A. Brinson (thirty-nine spring breaks attended and forty-six coeds impregnated).
- **Most Times Kicked Out of a Strip Club for Stealing Hand Soap** - Rene Y. Toten (694 times, or 91 gallons).

REFERENCES

The following books, articles, websites, and journals will serve as wonderful guides on your personal journey to failing miserably.

Asshole, P. (2019) *How to fuck up your life in 5 days*. Chicago, IL: Dingleberry Press.

Blankosarus, B. (2018) *Wet dreams, sobbing and gangbangs: A sexual history for the lonely*. Partytown, GA: Twisted Testicle Publishing.

Bookface, Z. (2005). *Lowering Your Neighbor's Property Value In 3-Simple Steps*. The Dumherst Journal, 555(5), 900-999.

Burns, S.T.D. (2009). *Secondhand toilet paper: A hygiene guide for disgusting jerks*. Chicago, IL. Niel Anblowme Publishing.

Cali, H. (1988). Driving like an asshole driver for beginners. *The American Publication of Drinking and Driving*, 387(107), 370-387.

Clements, CJ. & Clements, E. (2020). *How to lose a fist fight with an angry biker*. Los Angeles: CA. Life Destroying Publishing.

Clements, D. & Clements, V. (2018). *Driving techniques for morons*. Salt Lake City: UT. Flipperbush Publishing.

Cockbite, W. L. (2018). Cheating on your spouse and your taxes. *American Journal of Fucking Up your Life*, 33(2), 111-201.

Comfort, L. (2007) *Ruining your spouse's life in one easy step*. Orlando: FL. ELHA Cockswab Publishing.

Cumagain, Q. (2013). *How to win fist fights with the elderly and cripples*. New York: NY. Diabetes Publishing.

Cunt, M.S. (2008) *Who would want to fuck you? A practical guide to swinging and divorce*. San Diego: CA: B. Rednut Publishing.

Dickless, D. (2000) *The complete history of torture and porn in films*. Honolulu, HI: Tornado Blower Press.

Dong, D. (2001) *101 things to say to your parole officer*. San Diego: CA: Kathy and JC Press Inc.

Dragon, H. (1999). *Pissing While Driving Fast 101*. New York, NY: Railroad University Press.

Easy, R. (2000). Destroying your career with one email. *The Recreational Journal of Canadian Workplace Violence*, 12(3), 888-889.

Failed, M. (2001) *Gambling, alcohol and lottery addictions for beginners*. Meredosia: IL Titty Press.

Felatio, Z. (2006). "Do you have an onion for lunch? A practical guide to bad breath" *Wyoming Journal Review*, February 20, pp. 15-18.

Frankenipple, F. (1999) *How to get your children to hate you*. Boston, MA: Palm Plant Publishers.

Fucked, U.R. (2000). *The complete guide to alcohol poisoning*. Wilmington, DE. Watson Herbusch Publishing.

Fukfase, T. (2004). *Destroying Everything You Touch*. New York, NY: University of Colorado Press Inc. LLC.

Fukinga, Q. (2015) *Being worthless: How to completely suck big, hairy donkey balls at life*. Los Angeles, CA: Cocks Publishing.

Fuzznut, S. (1994) *The STD Alphabet*. Toronto, CA: Seal Club Bashing Press.

Giggles, M.R. (2005) *Bankruptcy and you: A love story*. New York: NY: Hallowcat Press.

Goodwin, V.M. (2016). Stealing from the blind and wheelchair-bound. *The Western Journal of Pickpocketing*, 311(1), 33-777.

Goosey, L. (1997). *How to handle the bomb squad at your house*. New York, NY: Mamma Snow Blower Press Inc.

Hardon, E.W. (2012) *Falling Asleep at Bus Stops*. Fort Collins, CO: Beach Bay LLC Inc.

Hardwood, H. (2014). Exploiting your children for financial gain: The Hollywood Addition. *The Poor Parenting Journal*, 555(5), 900-999.

Howie Dicter, O. (2012). *The complete guide to being a fuck-face*. Anchorage, AK: Twisted Nipple Publishing.

Jardon, Hugh. (2018, January 2). Bestiality Jokes & 100 Other Topics to Discuss At Dinner Parties. *The Wrinkled Titty. RSS*. Retrieved from http://www.brokenhopesdreamsandgoals.org

Kathy, J.C. (2010, October 14). Faking Aids for Beginners. *Excuses Galore.* http://www.scapegoatliesandexcusesvolume33.com

Kloker, D.L. (2017, November 1). Celebrating Air Travel Horror Stories. http://www.howtoruineveryonesfuckingflight.net

Kloker, D. & Kloker, DD. (2017). *How to get on the "do not fly list."*. Tulsa: OK. Owasso Publishing.

Kloker, L. & Kloker, J. (2019). *Drugs and you: A love story*. Little Rock: AR. Drunk Pilot Publishing.

Kunt, P. (2011). *Gambling addictions and broken limbs*. City of Industry, CA: Hoodwinkle Press.

Licket, Will. E. (2013). *Body hair for disgusting human beings*. San Francisco, CA: J.S. Publishing.

Masturbater, H. (1984) *How To Shave Your Nipples*. Youngstown, OH: Critter Creek Shit Hole Publishing.

McBasketball, F. (2007). Dances With Mescaline. *Bad Break Quarterly*, *213*(13), 207-245.

McGee, S. (20014) *Hygiene for lonely losers*. Syracuse, NY: Betty Kitty Publishing.

Muncher, A.S.S. (1993). *Arguing with a cop: A lose, lose battle*. Springfield, IL: Vector Victor House.

Nellsex, A. (2011). The Art of Poor Timing. *The New England Journal of Family Studies*, *444*(2), 711-777.

Nisenvi, P. (2016). *Santa Meets The Swat Team: A Christmas To Remember*. Phoenix, AZ: Snyder University Press.

Nipple, F. (2006). The complete guide to rest stop prostitution & hitchhiking: Dangerous roads ahead. *Eastern Journal of Integrated Tire Slashing*, 20(1), 120-133.

Nonuts, D. (2018) *The complete guide to losing your job over body odor*. Miami, FL: Curious the Cat Press.

Nuts, E.A.T. (2003) *Face Tattoos and You: A practical guide for never getting hired.* Salt Lake City: UT. Glue Huffing Addiction Press.

Palmer, R. (2015) *Cheating at your wedding 101: Who, how, where, when and why.* Jacksonville, FL: Fruity Nipple Publishers House.

Pesky, P.P. (1996). The everyday benefits of drug and alcohol abuse. *Journal on Bad Parenting, 99*(9), 99-111.

Snyder, B. (2004, September 10). How To Sleep with Your Therapist. *Eat an Ass. RSS.* Retrieved from http://www.thesmellyfuckface1.com

Snyder, T. (2020). *Fired: How to do it the right way.* New York, NY: Manager Publishing.

Stumpy, D. (2014). *Road rage and you: A complete guide to voluntary manslaughter.* Denver, CO: Dinosaur Publishing.

Sukbals, I. (2013) *Streaking At Major Sporting Events 101.* Los Angeles: CA. Streaking Press.

Swallows, S. (1979). *Faking A Pregnancy for Vacation Time.* Boston, MA: Franklin Times Publishing.

Taint, B. (2017) *So your parole officer committed suicide: A Book of Poetry.* Houston: TX. Burning While Pissing Publishing.

Taint, T. (2010). *The complete guide to video gaming and wasting your life doing other useless shit.* Chicago, IL: Busty Blonde Free Press.

Throat, D.P. (2018). Leather Bound: My Life As a "Gimper". *The Tickle Monster Journal of medicine, 67*(3), 999-1011. Boston, MA: Handsome Hand University Publishing Press.

Wieners, I.C. (2001). *Cocaine and you: A guide for beginners.* Los Angeles, CA: Hope Golden Publishing LLC.

Yankit, I. (2007, July 7). Your New Career In Prostitution. *Social Services* http://www.varioushookersnamedmandy11.com

Zomby, I. (2019). *Getting Laid with Bad Hygiene: An Introduction To Roofies.* Pittsburgh, PA: Pot Smoker Press.